BUTTERFLY
and
HELLFLOWER

BUTTERFLY
and
HELLFLOWER

Hellflower
Darktraders
Archangel Blues

Eluki bes Shahar

Published by arrangement with
DAW Books, Inc.
375 Hudson Street
New York, NY 10014

ISBN: 1-56865-048-5

PRINTED IN THE UNITED STATES OF AMERICA

Contents

HELLFLOWER

To Chris Jeffords, with honor.

Contents

1

Hearts and Hellflowers

I was minding my own business in beautiful downside Wanderweb, having just managed to mislay my cargo for the right price. My nighttime man had talked me into booklegging again, and damsilly stuff it was too —either maintenance manuals or philosophy texts. I never did figure out which, even with sixty hours time in *Firecat* between Coldwater and Wanderweb to stare at them and Paladin to read them to me.

So I was making my way around wondertown; free, female, and a damn sight over the age of reason, when I saw this greenie right in front of me in the street.

He was definitely a toff, and no stardancer—you never saw such clothes outside of a hollycast. He was lit up like Dream Street at night and wearing enough heat to stock a good-sized Imperial Armory besides. And this being scenic Wanderweb, land of enchantment, there was six of K'Jarn's werewolves and K'Jarn facing him. I was of the opinion—then—that he couldn't do them before they opened him up, so, fancy-free, I opened my mouth and said:

"Good morning, thou nobly-born K'Jarn. Airt hiert out to do wetwork these days or just to roll glitterborn for kicks, hey?"

K'Jarn looked up from pricing Tiggy Stardust's clothes and said, "N'portada je, S'Cyr. Purdu."

K'Jarn and me has known each other ever since I started running cargoes into Wanderweb Free Port and he started trying to boost them. For once I should of took his advice. But hell, it was seven-on-one, and I've *never* liked K'Jarn. . . .

"Like Imperial Mercy I will. Yon babby's my long-lost lover and maiden aunt, and I'm taking him home to Mother any day now. Fade."

He might have, except for that just then one of K'Jarn's wingmen got restless and took a swipe at the glitterborn with a vibroblade. Tiggy Stardust moved faster than anything human and swiped back and I burned K'Jarn before K'Jarn could mix in. K'Jarn dropped his blaster, him not having a hand to hold it with anymore, and left on urgent business. So did everyone else.

Business as usual in wondertown, and not enough fuss for the CityGuard to show up. Except for the deader Tiggy made and another I didn't have time to get fancy with, me and him was alone and he wasn't moving.

I went to see if there was anything left to salvage. He snaked around and then it was me down and staring up at an inert-blade knife as long as my thigh while he choodled at me unfriendly-like.

I can get along in flash, cant, and Trade, but I couldn't make head nor hind out of his parley, and I thought at first I'd hit my head too hard. But then I knew that what actually I had gone and done was the stupidest thing of my whole entire life. I'd rescued a hellflower.

Of course, hair that light and skin that dark could come from spacing on a ship with poor shields, and he wasn't even so bloodydamn tall—just too tall to be the kinchin-bai he looked. But no other human race in space has eyes the color a hellflower's got. Hellflower blue.

And why I couldn't of figured this all out one street corner brawl ago was beyond me.

He stared at me, I stared at him. I figured I was dead, which'd at least spare me hearing Paladin's opinion of my brains when I got back to *Firecat*. Then the hellflower rolled off me, put away the knife, and got to his feet.

"*Jadraya kinvraitau, chaudatu.* I apologize in honor for my ill-use of you; I thought you were one of the others. I offer you the thanks of my House and—"

"Don't wanna hear it!" I interrupted real quick. He talked Interphon real pretty, but with a heavy accent—alMayne, that kind of lilt —more proof, not that I needed it. "You kay, reet, am golden, hellflower, copacetic—but don't you go being grateful."

His face got real cold, and I thought I'd bought it for the second time that morning. Then he said, "As you desire, *chaudatu,*" and ankled off.

Hellflowers are crazy.

*   *   *

Strictly speaking, when you're talking patwa, which is what most people in my neighborhood do, a "hellflower" is any mercenary from the Azarine Coalition: Ghadri, Felix, Cardati, Kensey, alMayne—a prime collection of gung-ho races with bizarre customs and short tempers. Actually, say "hellflower" in the nightworld and everyone'll figure it's an alMayne that's caught your fantasy. alMayne are crazier than the rest of the Coalition put together—they've got their own branch of the Mercenaries' Guild with its own Grandmaster, and when they do sign out for work (as bodyguards mostly, because there ain't no wars anymore, praise be to Imperial Mercy and the love of the TwiceBorn) you can follow them around by the blood-trail they leave behind. They'll win any fight they start—or just kill you in the middle of a pleasant conversation for no reason your survivors can see.

It's all to do with hellflower "honor." They're mad for it. They got their own precious code of dos and don'ts, and you don't want one of them beholden to you for any money. If that happens, you can be chaffering with your buddy and the 'flower'll cut him down and tell you he did it to purify your honor. There was a man once that lost six business partners, his cook, his gardener, two borgs and a dozen tronics to his hellflower bodyguard before he figured out the hellflower *liked* him. . . .

Hellflowers are crazy.

*   *   *

So I stopped thinking about hellflowers and went and had breakfast. Didn't wonder about my particular 'flower; there wasn't nothing about that boy going to make sense a-tall. And I had things to do.

My purpose in life for coming to Wanderweb—other than to make too little credit for too much work—was a little piece of illegal technology called a Remote Transponder Sensor. Not only does the Empire in its wisdom refuse to sell them to its citizens or even me, once you get one, you have to get it installed.

In a Free Port, nothing's illegal and everything can be had for a price. Or an over-price. Remember that your friendly Free Port owner clears a profit after paying a tax to Grand Central about the size of his planetary mass, and you'll get the general idea. Never shop Free Port if you don't have to—but if something can't be had for any credit, you can probably find it here. And every Free Port and most planets has its Azarine.

The Azarine is the merc district, named after the Coalition. It holds everything from sellsword to gallowglass with a short detour through contract assassin, and like all special interest ghettos, it's home to the kiddies that service the players as well as the players themselves. Enter Vonjaa Beofox, high-nines cyberdoc living in the Azarine.

I heard tell of Beofox from an Indie who gave her the rep for being rough and nasty but good, which meant she was probably some legit bodysnatcher who took High Jump Leave from an Imp hellhouse to make a dishonest living in the Wanderweb Azarine. I saw her sign hung out over Mean Street. It had the Intersign glyphs for "fixer" and "bionics" on it, and the running hippocrene that was Beofox's personal chop. Beofox was a bodywarp fixer specializing in bionics—add a leg or a laser, prehensile tail or whatever you want—and Mean Street is the beating heart of the Azarine. There was a number of characters about as big as my ship standing around the place, but sellswords don't fight for free any more than I ship cubic out of charity. In the fullness of time I got past Beofox's bouncer and in to see her.

Beofox was about my size—which means on the short side of average—with a saurian cast to her bones that made you wonder where her breeding population rated on the Chernovsky scale. Her hair was roached up in a fair way to conceal a decent hideout blaster and she had as much ring-money punched through her ears as I wore on my boots. The walls of her surgery was covered with charts showing her daily specials and the most popular forms of blackwork for cybers.

"Want a thing done, Beofox," I said to open hostilities.

"I do no favors for stardancers, che-bai. What kind plastic you spinning?" she shot back.

The whistle in the nightworld was that Beofox had a soft-on for the rough-and-tumble kiddies, which made Gentry definitely persona-non-breathing in her shop. But stardancers don't run to cyberdocs so it was Beofox or I'd just spent a lot of wasted money on something I shouldn't own in the first place.

"Am golden, bodysnatcher; just dropped kick."

"That's 'bonecrack' to you, and speak Interphon. Why don't you work your own side of the street, stardancer?"

"I want a Rotten C," I said, real articulate-like.

Beofox regarded me with new respect. "A Remote Transponder Sensor—with the Colchis-Demarara shielding, irrational time processor, fully independent sub-micro broadcast power storage, and guaranteed full-fidelity sound reproduction? Do I look like an Imperial Armory?"

"Sure, che-bai. And I look like a Gentrymort with clearances, so get out your wishbook." I already had the RTS, but it don't do to tell everything you know.

We swapped insults for a while until Beofox came to the conclusion that while the hardboys might be fine and nice and real friendly, having friends in the transport union'll keep you warm at night. We ended up with her agreeing to install it and me admitting I had it, and then we went around about price, which started out to be my left arm and all that adjoined it, and finally got down to the price of a complete legal biosculpt.

"We can fix that face of yours, too, you know," she said when we'd closed the deal.

"Doesn't scare kinchin-bai."

"Sure. But someone's going to top you for a dicty sometime from the nose alone. I just wish you damn Interdicted Colonists would either stay in the quarantine your ancestors paid for or realize that twenty generations of inbreeding stands out like a flag of truce when you try to leave. Where in Tahelangone are you from, homebody?"

Tahelangone Sector is where all the Interdicted Worlds are. Nobody goes in, nobody goes out, and the Tech Police are there to see it stays that way. Emigration is, like all the fun things in life, illegal.

"Fixer, you farcing me, surely. Born and raised on Grand Central, forbye." Neither of us believed me.

"I'll see what I can do if you want, for ten percent over what we've agreed. Just bring your play-pretty back here tonight at half-past Third. Shop guarantee is a one-third refund if you're not combat-ready by thirty hours later."

We went around a little more and settled on that too. I left as a Ghadri wolfpack was coming in to discuss armored augmentation.

* * *

I spent the rest of the day hanging out in a place in wondertown called the Last Gasp Arcade. In between the hellflower and the cyberdoc in my busy social round I'd run into an old friend; a dark-trader named Hani who'd just turned down a job for being too small and in the wrong direction. He remembered I ran a pocket cruiser, and if *Firecat* was hungry he'd pass word for a meet.

I did not at the time think it odd to pick up a job this way even in a Port with a perfectly legit Guild-board and Hiring Hall, and I agreed as maybe I might be around this particular dockside bar from meridies to horizonrise local time, with no promises made.

Three drinks post-meridies my maybe-employer showed up. He was a short furry exotic with a long pink nose, and except for the structural mods made by a big brain and bipedal gait he looked an awful lot like something we used to smoke out of the cornfields back home. Of course, to a Hamat or a Vey he might of looked like whatever. Your brain matches what you see to what you've seen, and files off the bits what don't fit.

He sat down. "I am the Reikmark Arjilsox," he almost said. Your brain plays tricks with sounds too—what was obviously a name just sounded like gibberish to me, but I wasn't planning to remember it. "I understand you are a pilot-of-starships?"

We established that I was a pilot-of-starships, that I owned and could fly a ground-to-ground-rated freighter-licensed ship, and that my tickets were in order—Directorate clearances, Outfar clearances, inspection certs, et cetera, and tedious so forth. Forged, of course, but the information was correct—I'd have to be a fool to claim to be able to pilot something I couldn't.

We also established that Gibberfur here was the Chief Dispatcher for the Outlands Freight Company, a reputable and highly-respected organization that chose to do its business in sleazy arcades. I ordered another round of tea and waited.

It took Gibberfur awhiles to make the Big Plunge, but when he did it was simple enough: In three days local time we'd both come back here and Gibberfur would hand me six densepaks of never-you-mind, which *Firecat* would take unbroached to a place called Kiffit that was nominally in the Crysoprase Directorate, where Yours Truly would hand them over unto one Moke Rahone and get paid in full.

This, I told him, was a lovely fantasy, and I had one to match: In three days we'd both come back here, and he would hand me six densepaks of never-you-mind and the full payment for the tik, and *Firecat* would then take the densepaks unbroached to Kiffit and one Moke Rahone.

Eventually we settled about halfway between—half from him up front, half from Moke Rahone on delivery, confidentiality of cargo to be guaranteed. I agreed to the job, thumbprinted the contract, took charge of my half of the paperwork, and that was that.

My second mistake of the day. And two more than I needed for this lifetime.

*   *   *

In beautiful theory what I had just done was absolutely legal—and it was: in a Free Port. It went without saying that Gibberfur's consignment was darktrade, either for what it was, or for the charming fact that it was getting to wherever without paying duty. But here on fabled Wanderweb, where the Pax Imperador did not run, these things made no nevermind.

Neither was my load-to-be illegal while getting from here to Kiffit. It was legal to the edge of the atmosphere, and after that I'd be in angeltown. And since you can't enforce laws in hyperspace, it was still legal there. In fact, my kick—whatever it was—was dead legal and no headache until I entered Kiffit planetary realspace.

Once there it'd become a matter for intimate concern to a bunch of rude strangers and I would earn every gram of valuta I'd been paid and offered.

Eventually I'd get somewhere that somebody wanted a load run in to Coldwater, and I'd be home again without paying to deadhead.

Simple, easy, no problem.

Maybe someday something'll work out like that.

*   *   *

I thought I was keeping care, but I'd been too occupied with business to notice the change in the balance of power in the arcade. Even if I didn't expect K'Jarn to be around after losing a hand, I should of known my luck was due to break.

And it had. There was K'Jarn in front and his sideboy Kevil in back, and nothing for me to do but make it look like I wanted to be there when K'Jarn came idling over.

Times like this it'd be nice to have a partner you could see. Brother K'Jarn was coked to his problematical gills on painease and maybe *R'rhl* and he had a biopak covering his left arm from the elbow to where it currently ended. I counted six hardboys with him—downside townies all much too interested in me to be comforting—and nobody in the place wanted to stop a free floor show. So much for Gibberfur's cargo and my future.

K'Jarn leaned over my table at me and made his pitch. I'd cost him a hand, he said. Cybereisis prosthetics were expensive, he said. Why didn't I just (out of the goodness of my heart and a sincere desire to see justice done) sign over *Firecat* to him and he'd let bygones be dead issues?

"Rot in hell," I said. K'Jarn hauled me up with the hand he had left and I sliced him across the chest with the vibro I happened to have handy. The cut was too damn shallow to do much good, but I did make him drop me. I rolled under the table while he was bawling for his hardboys to come smear me into the bedrock.

I gave the first one that answered a blade through the throat, and by the time I got the blood out of my eyes another one wanted attention. He slugged me hard and I lost my vibro and ended up out in the middle of the floor.

And suddenly it was very damn quiet. I looked up. There was my bonny alMayne home-ec project towering over me, and the look he gave the general populace would of froze a hot reactor. Nobody moved.

Then K'Jarn drew down on the hellflower—or maybe it was on me and he didn't care who was in the way, but afterward K'Jarn wasn't where you could ask him anymore. Tiggy Stardust blew him away so fast I felt the breeze before I saw the flash.

K'Jarn hit the floor and I started making like Tiggy was my backup and I'd been expecting him all along. Nobody was looking to avenge K'Jarn against a hellflower, and said so, and that damn near set Tiggy the wonder warrior off again right there. You could tell he was looking to blow them all away and maybe me too for the "lack of honor" of it all, so me and Kevil called it quits real quick no-hard-feelings-eternal-friendship and the late K'Jarn's faction made itself history.

Throwing caution to the vectors, I started to tell Tiggy Stardust how glad I was he'd showed up. He just stared at me with those hell-flower blue eyes and said, "I do not want your gratitude either, *chaudatu*," and stomped off again.

Right. Fine. I got out of the Last Gasp with no trouble and beat it back to the Port and *Firecat*.

Somebody ought to do something about Tiggy, I felt.

As it turned out, somebody had.

*   *   *

I spent the next three days in a sleepsling on *Firecat* waiting to feel like a member of any B-pop whatever again. I'd passed up Beofox's fond offer to coke and wire me until I was feeling reet: stardancers ride on their reflexes and I couldn't afford to scramble mine. Beofox and me'd made sure the RTS implant worked before I left surgery—a transmission check and me damn glad nobody had to take my face off again to see why it wasn't working.

Paladin kept me company through the voder-outputs in *Firecat*'s bulkheads, because every time the RTS took incoming transmission my skull itched. Beofox'd said it was all in my imagination and I'd get over it, but it wasn't her skull.

When he did talk through the RTS it sounded like he was standing right behind me, and that was the weirdest thing of all, because Paladin can't do that.

Pally's a real knight in shining armor, and the armor's my ship. He's black-boxed into *Firecat*'s infrastructure, wired into her computers and welded to her deck, so where she doesn't go, he doesn't go either. Without computer hookups he's blind deaf and dumb; drain enough power from his crystal and you can add halt and imbecile to the list. When I'm off *Firecat* I'm out of his life.

The remote transponder implant was in the category of aiding and abetting our mutual quest to stay alive. The RTS'd been designed to coordinate Space Marine maneuvers and was reliable for about five kilometers without a comsat, and over an entire planetary hemisphere with one. Me wearing one meant Paladin could hear everything I said even away from *Firecat*, and talk to me without anybody knowing he was there. And it was real important for nobody to know Paladin was there. Ever.

My partner Paladin's a fully-volitional logic. A Library. And the head-price on him—and on me for having him—has been reliably reported to be enough to buy you out of any crime in the Imperial Calendar.

Not that anybody'd collected on Class One High Book in the last slightly more than so long. Pally and me'd kept the ear out to hear the whistle drop about other Libraries. There'd only been two cases of High Book—that's Chapter 5 of the Revised Inappropriate Technology Act of the nine hundredth and seventy-fifth Year of Imperial Grace to you —since we'd been together, and neither one involved a real working Library. I guess there aren't any more but Paladin, and when I found him on Pandora he'd been a box of spare parts for so long he didn't even know we had a Emperor. Imperial History goes back a solid kiloyear, and Paladin told me he comes from the Federation before that. It took the two of us about six minutes to find out what kind of laws there was against Old Fed artifacts.

That was the year Pally made me do a darktrade deal just to get that old history book. He read it to me, and said it was obviously censored. It didn't make any sense whatever'd been done to it, and it didn't tell about Libraries or why they had to be killed. Funny way to talk about 20K of crystal and a black box—or, as talking-books say, "a machine hellishly forged in the likeness of a living mind." But Paladin isn't a machine. I've talked to machines. Pally's a Library.

Paladin says "library" is just a old word for a building where they keep books—sort of like a bibliotek, but different someway. I've seen books, too, but damned if I know why anybody'd want to murder a building. And Paladin isn't a building either, with or without books.

Sometimes Paladin doesn't make any sense a-tall.

*   *   *   *   *

Insert #1: Paladin's Log

I am not human. I am not a machine. I am Library Main Bank Seven of the Federation University Library at Sikander Prime, an honorable estate.

At least I was. Now I am Paladin, a new name for a new age. Many of my books are gone from my memory. The world in which I lived is gone. My "friends" and "relatives" are all a millennium dead, and the profession for which I was trained no longer exists. I run *Firecat,* a converted intrasystem shuttle used for smuggling. I pursue researches for books I will never write, that no one would understand. Without Butterfly, there would not even be that much to occupy me.

*   *   *

I was originally very disturbed when I discovered that my human rescuer was biologically female. As a creature of my own culture—as who is not?—I had never considered that a possibility. Person and male were synonymous. An autonomous female outside of a breedery, her genetic inheritance exposed to random mutating factors, was a dismaying indication of how long I had been unconscious.

But Butterfly was not dissimilar to humans I had known before. I ignored her gender, as I could not survive without her help. Eventually it ceased to obtrude itself on my notice—but the fact of her humanity did not. Butterfly was as human as any person in what had become, as I slept, the semi-mythical Old Federation. Of the war that destroyed it, or the reason "Libraries," as all fully-volitional logics are now called, are held in such despite, I remember nothing.

(Fortunately Butterfly lacks curiosity about the Federation. I do not know what I would tell her about the way we lived then, or what she would understand of it. Would she think it odd for an entire species to declare one of its genders nonsentient for the sake of convenience? Or would she, in a culture that declares random organics nonpersons for financial consideration, think it rational? It is unlikely that I will ever know.)

What began as a purely random intersection became an alliance necessary for the survival of both of us. It was a long time after my "rebirth" before I realized how very dangerous my mere existence was to Butterfly, and even longer until I cared about anything beyond my own survival. But every year I become more aware that we are "farcing the odds," and that the "good numbers" become more and more scarce. Our illusion of safety grows unconvincing, and I fear more and more for Butterfly's survival.

The culture of the Phoenix Empire would doubtless find it unbelievable that "a machine hellishly forged in the likeness of a human mind" could care for something outside itself. The dogma of their technophobic age holds that created beings cannot have emotions, but while it is true that some emotions are triggered by animal instincts and fed by chemicals spewed into the brain by uncontrolled glands, more come from the ego, which all things may possess. I am, therefore I want. Rage is a chemical emotion, brewed in the animal brain. Is loyalty? Lust no inorganic life-form can feel; it is the residue of chemicals readying the organic body for the unreliable act of reproduction—but love? Affection? Kindness?

There is no one left who would care to chart true boundaries in the borderland between organic and machine. Butterfly has always thought of me as human. The only created beings she knows are programmed and limited artifacts. They are not human—therefore I, who am nothing like them, cannot be a machine.

$$* \quad * \quad * \quad * \quad *$$

About the time Beofox said I would I started to feel human again, and then it was time to go meet Gibberfur. It was a whole new experience to have Paladin along for the ride. He had lots of available dataports to track me through Wanderweb and lots of opinions to express.

At the Last Gasp I got the personal attention of the owner, who along with the guaranteed nonnarcotic to my B-pop libation handed out the joyful news that the Wanderweb slugs had tossed my partner a day and another day ago and he thought I'd like to know.

My partner. Meaning Tiggy Stardust, hellflower. That'd teach me to do street theater for the brain-dead. Still, he'd be back on the streets in a few whiles, a freer but poorer nutcase.

About then Gibberfur arrived, with a very large strongbox on a A-grav sled. He had hysterics while I popped the box and pulled out six densepaks of illegal.

"I must protest! Our agreement clearly states that the cargo is to be transported unbroached to its destination." He was fluffed out to one-and-a-half-wiggly's worth of outrage, and his little pink nose quivered.

"Will be, furball. But it don't say nothing in agreement about this damn wondershow." I jerked a thumb at the strongbox, which was blinking and flashing with all the details of the status of its various locks, stasis fields, and armaments. "Figured you'd kind of like to hold on to it for sentimentality's sake, seeing as otherwise I'm going to shove it out my air lock as soon as I'm at angels."

"But-but you can't do that! My cargo—"

"Is going to get where it's going safe and sound—but I can't trot it past the Teasers if you're going to hang bells and whistles on it. A mathom like that'll trip every scanner from here to the Core and back to the Rim, and what do I say when the Teasers board me: I didn't know it was there? Get real."

Teaser is short for Interstellar Trade, Customs & Commerce Commission: the Law, and something neither Gibberfur or me wanted the attention of.

"But—"

"If your cargo wanted special handling, you should of said. Not too late for you to change your mind about me dancing it, neither." That shut him up, and I took the Embarkation Receipt for the load and we both signed it and I stuffed my copies of the fax and all six densepaks into the pockets of my jacket.

*   *   *

Things was so much easier in the nonexistent days when a dark-trader's word was her bond and all that. You know, the ones where your Gentry-legger takes this priceless cargo sixty light-years and hands it over on word alone to someone she's never seen, with no documentation, no penalties, and no comeback? It's too damn bad the idea never caught on.

Me, I posted bond with the Smuggler's Guild when I joined, and the thought of all that credit sitting there earning zip is enough to cripple you for life. On the other hand, me being a Guild-bonded Gentry-legger keeps people like Gibberfur happy, and here's why: If I took off now for the never-never with Gibberfur's cargo and he wanted to prove it with his half of the documentation, he could get reparations for his loss from the Guild. If the debt was big enough, well, there's a perfectly legal lien on *Firecat,* activatable through a legit cut-out organization, and the Guild could have the *legitimates* yank my ship and sell it to cover their costs. Simple.

But membership cuts two ways. If I get burned—killed or stiffed or any other little thing—I can complain to the Guild, or my designated survivors can, and the Guild keeps records. One or two black marks against a shipper is all it takes, and suddenly your dishonest citizen can't even find an Indie to herd skyjunk for him, let alone a Gentry-legger to farce his cargo of illegal past the Teasers.

It's pretty cold comfort and precious little protection, and to make it work at all, you document your cargo every step of way—it's called a provenance, or in the profession, a ticket-of-leave.

That's life in the big city. The rest is for talkingbooks.

*   *   *

I was getting ready to leave the Last Gasp. Gibberfur had sulked out with his strongbox earlier and I was waiting around for the street outside to settle. I was standing at the bar and the tender came back by to tell me that my hellflower lover—that's Tiggy Stardust of sacred memory—in addition to being arrested the same day he'd offed K'Jarn, had left three dead Wanderweb Guardsmen on the ground before they took him away.

It was real fortunate that Tiggy and me was quits. Now I wouldn't have any unfinished business on my conscience when they shortened him and put his head on a pike outside the Wanderweb Justiciary.

He'd killed Guardsmen. On Wanderweb you can buy out of anything but killing Guardsmen. So of course Tiggy'd killed three of them.

Bright lad.

Hell.

What was I supposed to do about it? It was all his own fault, after all. I didn't tell him to dust half a six-pack of Wanderweb Guardsmen. *Nobody* kills Wanderweb Guardsmen.

Stupid kid. Stupid *hellflower.*

I was lost in contemplation of the fate of the late Tiggy Stardust when a genuine pandemonium wondershow came strolling in the front door.

He was big, he was blond, he was dressed in red leather like the hollyvid idea of a space pirate—and he was with a Hamat. He wore crossed blasters as long as my thigh. The Hamat stood behind him like the presence of doom, and there aren't so many Hamati that stand human company by choice for me to figure this was two other guys.

They were, variously, the Captain and First of a ship called *Woebegone,* which was a pirate no matter what you might hear elsewhere. I knew Captain Eloi Flashheart from a time we was working two sides of a insurance scam. His side'd involved my side being dead, and if Paladin hadn't been with me it would of worked. Of course, Eloi always said afterward he didn't carry a grudge, but how far can you trust a man who wears red kidskin jammies?

Unfortunately, I was in plain sight.

Eloi looked right at me, Alcatote looked right at me, and then they both crossed the bar to sit in the back. I let out a breath I hadn't known I was holding, took my soon-to-be illegal cargo, and left. Fast. I was a sober, sane, sensible member of the highly-respectable community of interstellar smugglers and I did not borrow trouble.

Much.

*   *   *

When I hit the street Wanderweb was its gaudy nighttime self all around, but I wasn't minding it, nor thinking about Eloi-the-Red. I was thinking about Tiggy Stardust, alMayne at Large, and his current status as official dead person in the Wanderweb Justiciary.

"It isn't my problem."

"That is perfectly correct, whatever it is." Paladin, right in my ear, and I damn near ended my young career with heart failure on the spot.

"Don't do that."

"Sorry."

My teeth rang as the RTS took transmission. Nobody gave me—or us—a second glance.

So Tiggy'd saved my hash in arcade the other day—and been coking toplofty about it too! Nobody sane'd partner a hellflower, least of all one dressed like joyhouse in riot and wearing enough gelt to finance a small war. Do I look stupid? Do I look rich? Why do people tell me these things?

"Dammit, why do people tell me these things?"

"Confession is said to be good for the soul." Paladin again.

"I sold mine." I'd get used to it. Eventually.

I went back to *Firecat* and soothed my nerves by tucking six

densepaks of illegal under the deck plates in a number of places the
Teasers will never find. Then I loaded the dummy cargo I'd bought this
morning in on top and dogged it down and checked my supply inventuro-
ries. Golden.

On what I'd make selling this load of prime Tangervel rokeach on
Kiffit I could starve comfortably in the *barrio* with my ship gigged for
default of port fees. But rokeach did make a plausible reason for going,
at least in the eyes of the Teasers. Now I could pick up and top angels
for Kiffit, which was a real good idea if the *Woebegone* and her crew was
in town.

"So what am I gonna do?" I asked Paladin.

"That depends on what you wish to accomplish," my ever-helpful
partner said. "You will not make Eloi Flashheart regret his seizure of
your cargo in—"

He must of picked that up in the Wanderweb City Computers.

"Never mind Eloi. Tiggy Stardust bought three Guardsmen the day
he dusted K'Jarn. They gonna shop him sure."

Paladin dimmed the hold lights; his version of exasperation. "I do
not see what you can do about it. You cannot reverse the past or change
the legal code of Wanderweb Free Port, and I cannot enter the Justiciary banks from here—which means you cannot change his sentence or
even find out exactly where he is."

"Could if I could get inside." Occasionally I do have bursts of
brilliance.

"Butterfly," Paladin said, in his I-don't-want-to-hear-any-more-of-
this-voice.

"It isn't like I don't know the setup," I explained.

"Butterfly St. Cyr—"

"I been inside before. It's easy to get into the Admin wing; the only
trouble is getting onto the Det levels. You already been in the City
Central Computers, Pally—plans for Justiciary'll be there, y'know,
an—"

"*Saint Butterflies-are-free Peace Sincere,* are you seriously suggesting
that you are going to break into the Wanderweb Security Facility to
rescue an alMayne mercenary?"

"Well. . . ."

"You swore you weren't ever going back in there again, you know.
Least of all for 'some dauncy hellflower who'd love to cut my heart out
if he could figure the way around his honor to do it.'"

"*I* said that?"

"Yes."

"About Tiggy?"

"Yes."

"But Pally, think of the expression on his face when he sees who's rescued him."

*   *   *   *   *

Insert #2: Paladin's Log

It is not correct to say that organics are incapable of true thought. Say rather that their capacity for thought is constrained by the limits of the organic construct housing the mind. An organic body is constantly making demands of its client intellect—to be exercised, rested, nourished, and allowed to display the primitive pre-conscious aberrations still maintained in the mind/body interface. One can only ignore these displays and trust that they will pass in time. When the spasm has passed, the mind of the organic, refreshed by the period of rest, will once more function with moderate efficiency until again distracted by the demands of its host environment.

The median period of function is five minutes, but I believe that Butterfly skews the statistical input significantly.

*   *   *

The point at issue was not whether or not it would be "perfectly safe" for Butterfly to enter a high-security detention facility and illegally release one of its internees, but whether there could be any possible value to be gained from such a course of action no matter how disdainfully the alMayne had behaved. I quickly abandoned the question of relative value when Butterfly introduced the concept of "fun" into the discussion.

I have learned that "fun" means exposing yourself to extreme risk without compensation, so I attempted to explain to Butterfly that if she were dead she would not know how much "fun" she was having.

This did not work.

2

A Little Night Music

It was just after dark meridies when I pulled my rented speeder up to the public docking in front of the Wanderweb Justiciary.

I wasn't doing the pretty by this glitterborn, make few mistakes about it. In my business you do not make friends and be a angel of mercy—and I wasn't grateful, not to Tiggy. I just wanted to see his face when I showed up. That's all.

The top twelve floors of the Wanderweb Justiciary had closed at the end of First Shift and it was now almost the end of Second, but Det Admin and Detention itself never slept. I admired the pretty statues and the nice murals on the walls while I waited for the lift. Wanderweb, city of progress.

One level down it was a different story—looked like *legitimate* headquarters Empire-wide, with the small difference that the only uniforms in sight was the Guardsmen's gaudy red-and-blue. I went to the Desk Officer and told him I was sure my First was in here an I'd come to bail him out. He asked me when my First'd been brought in and I said I didn't know, only when I'd gone to lift ship he wasn't around. Checked morgue, I said, and he wasn't there.

Same old story: Idiot High Jump Captain and her rake-helly crew. And it would all check green across the board if they bothered. Paladin and me had spent the whole day going over plans for the Justiciary and pieceworking a false data file on *Firecat*—a.k.a. the *Starlight Express* out of Mikasa.

The Desk Officer sent me in-level to Fees & Records and told me to hurry because they was just about to shut down for the day, and if I got there after they closed I'd have to come back tomorrow at beginning of First Shift.

Ha.

I skipped over there, trying to look like nobody who was carrying a unscannable solenoid stunner under her jacket and grabbed some poor overworked bureaucrat who worked in Records. I spun him a tale about my missing First—Hamat, he was, because I knew Alcatote was being a good boy and there wasn't another Hamat loose in twelve cubic light-years. Of course the poor cratty couldn't find him in his listings and of course I couldn't remember when he could of come in. The cratty kept swearing my First wasn't here and looking at his chrono—it was almost end-of-shift, remember?—and I kept insisting and being just short of nasty enough that he'd call some Guardsmen and put me in gig too. Finally he grabbed me and dragged me around to his side of the display and pointed.

"I tell you, Captain, there are no Hamati in here!"

I looked. It was an intake list for the last three days, broken down by Breeding-Population-of-Origin. It had no Hamati, twenty-seven Fenshee, and one alMayne. I memorized his file number.

"But he's gotta be in here!" I insisted, in my best wringing-her-pale-hands-and-moaning voice. "Look, check again—maybe you got his B-pop wrong. He don't look much like a Hamat—"

"What does he look like?" said my good little straight sophont.

"Well," I began, improvising, "He's about a meter-fifty, striped—"

"There are no meter-and-a-half tall Hamati!" thundered my long-suffering soulmate.

"Well, he told me he was Hamat!" I whined. "How am I supposed to know?"

"Look, Captain, if you'll just come back tomorrow—"

"But I'm lifting *tonight!* I need him back now! Look, don't you keep holos or something? I could look, an—"

"One thousand and some very odd beings have been processed through here in the last three days!" my uncivil servant snapped.

"But I *told* you what he looks like! He's striped, he has a long tail, and blue eyes—"

"Hamati do not have tails!" said my little buddy, who must of been a exobiologist in his free time.

"You just gotta *look* for him—"

"All right! We do keep hard copy images of detainees. I'll find you a list of all the fur-bearing sentients—"

"Striped. With a tail. And blue eyes."

"—that have been processed in the last three days and then will you believe me that this-this—*person* is not here? Will you go away?"

"Sure," I said, and watched him disappear, a broken man, into the inner room.

Which was what I'd been angling for since I got here.

The astute student of human nature will notice I did not offer Junior the bribe that could of made things so much easier, as that would of made what was coming next unlikely to even the meanest intelligence.

As soon as the cratty was gone I punched up the retrieval codes for the alMayne file—it was Tiggy, all right, who else?—and found he was up for the chop when the Lord High Executioner came on duty later today. And I found out where my little alMayne lovestar was.

Restoring the terminal to its original state I lightfooted it over to a cabinet I'd cased as the most likely place to hide while I was stringing the button-pusher. I folded myself inside and shut the door just before he came back. I had my own reasons for thinking he wouldn't look inside.

"Captain, there are no— Where did she go?"

There was a moment of stricken silence. Then I heard furious muttering and sounds of grabbing-your-jacket-and-getting-ready-to-leave. I'd kept Junior a whole five minutes past quitting time with my damsilly tale, and that left him so mad he didn't even stop to wonder where I'd got to.

In my business, it's always a good idea to be a student of human nature. Now if I'd offered him that bribe, he'd sure and t'hell wonder why I'd vanished without getting what I paid for. This way I was just another exasperating space cadet.

I heard the door hiss shut behind him and started counting my heartbeats. After I'd done that for awhiles I figured all sentient life and most of the bureaucrats was gone from this section. The only thing out there'd be tronics, and I had a way to deal with them. I hoped.

I untucked my ears from between my knees and pulled a comlink out of my jacket pocket. The RTS let Pally and me talk to and hear each other and that was it; this'd let him hear things around me—like challenges from the securitronics patrolling the Det levels. It meant he could answer them in tronic, too, which would contribute to increased life expectancy for Yours Truly.

All this was assuming the comlink worked, and we wouldn't know that until we tried it. But what's life without a spirit of inquiry?

"It is not too late to change your mind," Paladin said through the transponder in my head.

"Already paid rent on the speeder." I eased the door open.

No alarms—just a dark empty office. I opened the door farther and stuck my head out. Still nothing.

Pally'd heard there was budget cuts for the civil services when he'd been cakewalking through the City Computer. Wanderweb justice being what it was, there wasn't anything down here anybody could want to steal, but we'd still been expecting getting in to be harder than this. I started making plans for the rest of the evening at a bathhouse I knew and made to step out.

"Wait," Paladin said. I waited. "There's something there." I froze.

"There is some form of security device in the room," said Paladin.

I leaned farther out and saw it. It was about one meter across and less than half that high. It squatted malevolently in the middle of the floor glaring impersonal-like at everything in sight and didn't seem to notice me.

Noticed or not, I couldn't stay here all night. Maybe I could scramble its brains and have Paladin pick up the chat before anyone noticed.

"It is in contact with the Justiciary computer. It is likely that any interruption of that contact will constitute an alarm."

And maybe I could just teleport to Security Detention.

I swung the door open the rest of the way. It crashed against the wall with a well-oiled thud that damn near made my heart stop.

"No change in status," said Paladin. "Are you all right?"

"Terrific," I said. If I couldn't get past this thing, Tiggy was going to have to forget about being rescued and I'd have to start thinking seriously about a career of being dead.

What would set it off? Sound hadn't, motion hadn't, and with so many lizard-types in your Empire and mine it'd be pretty damn dumb to go with the old body-heat dodge.

So what did that leave?

Vibration. Spidey'd been interested when the door hit the wall but not very. If I set foot to floor how long until I was up to my absent blasters in Guardsmen? If that wasn't it there wasn't anything else I could think of.

Great. Now all I had to do was get out of here without walking across the floor—and me without my A-grav harness.

I looked up. What there was, was an air vent. The vent was just below the ceiling, a little to the left of the top of the cabinet and big enough to hold me on a skinny day if I gave up breathing. Three cheers and a tiger for impecunious bureaucrats and Free Port owners that want to save every credit. Even for the Outfar this was backward.

"Butterfly?" Paladin demanded in my ear. It gave me the weirdest feeling—no room for anyone to be standing behind me but he sure sounded like it.

"Securitronic sweet for the shaky, seeming. So I'm going through the air vents instead of over the floor."

*   *   *

We will pass lightly over me climbing to the top of the cabinet, leaning out into infinite space to get the grille off the vent, not dropping the bolts on the floor, and managing to get a handhold on the edge of the vent-shaft to pull myself in, and go directly to where I was jammed into the air vent with slightly less than no room to wiggle.

"Pally? How long's it been?"

"One hour five. Butterfly, are you sure this is a good idea?"

"One helluva time to bring that up," I told him, and started up the shaft. I could hear Paladin inside the vent, which augured well for our future deceiving securitronics together, but I'd lose him by time we got to Security Detention. By then it would be up to me and Tiggy Stardust.

I knew more or less where to go to pluck my hellflower, thanks to the mindless faxhandler who decreed all Justiciary levels be laid out to the same pattern. The floor plan for this level was classified—but the floor plan of the identical level two floors up wasn't. The lift we wanted was just outside the main sentencing arena.

Six subjective eternities and the loss of my pantknees later, Pally and me came to a promising grille. It looked down from a good five meters into what looked like one of the sentencing arenas, and the room was full of tronics. I pushed the comlink up against the grille and waited for Pally to give me some glad news.

"Fortune is with you, Butterfly," he told me a few minutes later. "This is the main sentencing arena—the housekeeping and security tronics use this for their central dispatch area during Third Shift. The lift to the Security Detention levels is just outside the door. You can walk right through."

"Yeah?" I said. Leaving aside for the moment Paladin's definition of luck, there was the minor matter of more rude mechanicals down below than I ever really hoped to meet. And securitronics tend to be irritable.

" 'Yeah.' Housekeeping and Security are programmed to avoid each other—I will provide them with the proper code, and you will walk across the floor and out the other door. As long as they receive the proper codes, the tronics will not care who you are. Just move slowly, as if you were another machine."

"If this is so easy, why don't everyone come dancing in here? Think of the valuta they could save on fines."

"In the first place, the recognition codes for the security devices are changed by the computer on a random sequence. In the second place, it is generally accepted that breaking into a prison is an unnecessary exertion."

I ignored that. I also knew there wasn't any other way in.

I got a pocket-laser out of my bag of tricks and took out the grille. I passed it over my back into the airshaft, eased out through the hole until I was hanging by my fingers, and dropped. I came up with the stunner ready, but I couldn't see a thing. Heard the whine of servomotors as a securitronic waddled over to me. It was a handspan taller than me and much wider, with all its come-alongs and keep-aways and don't-worrys arranged neatly on its chest and arms. Its optical sensors glowed red in the dark but most of its dull gray hide was a dull gray blur. I wished I'd brought some night-goggles, but they would of raised eyebrows at the front desk when I was scanned and the info Pally had said the Justiciary was kept lit at night on all levels. On the other hand, if I died right here I wouldn't need to see anything.

The tronic turned and walked away.

"I told you so," Paladin said smugly. "Machines are stupid."

I was challenged twice more—once by another securitronic, once by a housekeeper—and each time Paladin answered for me. I carded the little access door set into the big "for-show" courtroom doors and slipped out.

The hall outside wasn't dark. It was pitch black.

"Helluva time for the high-heat to start economizing," I muttered, staring/not staring into the dark. "Now what?"

"Hm," said Paladin, just to let me know he was still there.

I could tune my pocket-laser to a torch, which the manufacturer does not recommend you do. I was just about to see if I could do it by feel when I heard heavy tronic-steps coming toward me and the whine of a housekeeper's treads coming up behind.

Paladin sang out in a flurry of musical notes as I scrambled the securitronic right between its little red eyes with my stunner and then whipped out another shot to about where its brain ought to be. The guard hit the floor with a clatter, and the housekeeper nuzzled up to my ankles and went around me.

The nice thing about a solenoid stunner is that it's completely harmless to organics and death on tronic brains.

By the glow of my retuned laser I could see the housekeeper merrily disemboweling the ex-securitronic. The lift to Security Detention was a few meters away.

"Here's where thee-an-me subdivide, Pally," I said, trying to sound more confident than I felt.

"I will monitor all city-wide communications," he said, not sounding really wild about all this either, "and brief you when you come out."

When you come out. Thanks for vote of confidence, little buddy. "Won't be long," I said.

The lift door opened. I got in and stood there for a while feeling stupid, then it reopened on Detention level.

I was looking at a man in a CityGuard uniform standing in front of a console with a securitronic on either side of him. I scrambled both of them, and while he was still trying to figure out why they didn't work he let me get close enough to him to hit him over the head with my stunner.

Never depend on your technology.

Then I was past the check-in point and running down a long corridor three tiers high and lined with doors. I'd borrowed the Guardsman's blaster, so I used it to zap two more tronics. I wished I had Paladin with me to tell me about all the alarms and excursions being raised all over the place.

Tiggy's cell was at the very end, but at least it was on the bottom. I switched the setting on my borrowed blaster from "annoy" to "leave no evidence" and blew the lock out. The cell door sprang right open, and there was my hellflower.

He was chained hand and foot for punishment drill, and spread out on the wall pretty as a holo. The Justiciary'd took his jewels and all his clothes in payment of fines, and he was wearing a pair of Det-ish pants that didn't fit by a long shot.

And the look on his face was everything I could of hoped for.

"Chaudatu," he finally said. "Not you again?"

"Yeah, me. I'm here to rescue you."

Later, when Paladin got his, um, hands on an alMayne lexography, we found out that *"chaudatu"* means "outlander," except that what it really meant is "anyone who is not alMayne and therefore not a real person." Unfortunately, even if I'd known that at the time it wouldn't have made any difference.

I got out my picks and got to work on Tiggy's shackles—feet first, then hands—and hoped that Time, Fate, and bureaucratic cock-up would give me the fistful of nanoseconds needed to get the 'flower loose and on his feet. After that, I figured my troubles were over. All we had to do was get us out of here alive, and Tiggy and me could go hide out. He could be grateful, and then I could bugout for Kiffit and write the next chapter of my memoirs.

He dropped to the floor when I got the last cuff off and stretched all over like a cat. Real pretty. I handed him the liberated blaster.

"Can use this-here?" I said in broad patwa.

He looked at it briefly. "Yes."

"Reet. Now hear me, che-bai—thing rigged for 'kill,' okeydoke? Not to dust organics with it. Fragging people buys bad trouble. Shoot at wartoys. Right?"

While I was talking, I was looking out into the corridor. The quiet was spooky, and there should of been more guards, but I didn't see any.

I looked back and Tiggy was regarding me with the expression of a hellflower what hadn't understood one word I'd said.

"Look, che-bai; shoot tronics, not organics. Zap-zap. Ch'habla— Understand?"

"Shoot only at security robots. *Dzain'domere,*" said Tiggy gravely.

"Je, reet. Just don't shoot people." I was nervous and didn't have time to remember my Interphon.

He glared. I thought he was thinking of shooting me and to hell with freedom, but he nodded. We single-footed it out into the corridor. I wondered what jane-doh-meer meant in helltalk.

The wartoys on the tier above us started shooting.

I pulled Tiggy back against the wall and out of their line of fire. I remembered my plasma grenades and wondered if I should use them now. They were small, but still big enough so I didn't want to risk it unless we were in real trouble.

Six heavy-duty securitronics came trundling down the corridor toward us. They were about the size of the Imperial Debt and all business. I could see riot-gas launchers extruding from the chest of the leader as it came on.

We were in real trouble. I rolled a grenade toward them, body-blocked the 'flower back into his cell, and prayed.

The grenade went off.

There was smoke. Tiggy burned the wartoys on the tier above as I was finishing the six-pack on the floor. Grenade'd gone off right behind the leader, and the blast had splash-backed to destroy the next two. The other three was confused enough with memory-purge and magnetic-bubble scramble for Tiggy to totally blow them away as we jogged past.

There was probably alarms going off from here to Grand Central, but they was all silent—at least I couldn't hear them. I overrode the lift's lock-command from the main board out front. It wasn't that different than some Pally'd coached me on. Tiggy covered my back while I did it; his eyes was blazing like burning sapphires and he was grinning like he was enjoying himself. We picked up a couple rifles.

"Ten minutes, ninety seconds. Ten minutes, ninety-five seconds. Eleven minutes." Paladin was counting off, on the chance I'd be back to hear.

The corridor was still dark when we got back up to Sentencing. Then the lift shut behind us and everything went really dark. I got out my much abused laser. We had to get out now before word of our presence spread.

"Here we are, boys and girls," I said for Paladin's benefit.

"Are you all right? No alarm has been raised: The city is quiet, the Justiciary is not calling up any reserves, there have been no transmissions from Security Detention."

"C'mon," I said, to my hellflower and my partner. "This way. We're both fine for now—" that was for Paladin "—shoot any mechs you see, no matter what. And kid—"

"Do not shoot the people," Tiggy finished. "I know, *chaudatu*, but I think you are a fool."

There's gratitude for you. Not having dusted anyone in our escape probably wouldn't do us any good if we were caught, but I was feeling superstitious enough to think that virtue might be rewarded.

We made it out of Sentencing and back into Records. There was more light here. A quick riot-gas grenade would cover us on the way out of Receiving and—

—I looked around and Tiggy was halfway back down the corridor, stopped dead and sight-seeing. I turned back.

"Ain't time to sightsee, 'flower. Grab sky!" I took him by his wrist and pulled. It was like trying to shift a neutronium statue.

"My *arthame*, *chaudatu*. I must have it."

Just what I needed. More hellflower gibberish.

"My Knife," Tiggy expanded. "I cannot leave without my Knife. They have taken it from me; do you know where it is?"

There wasn't anybody around to see or hear but there would be soon. "Look; I'll buy you a new one; c'mon!" I gave one last yank, which meant I was still holding on when Tiggy took off in the opposite direction. Ever been dragged down a empty hall by a hellflower oblivious to threats, comments, and reasonable objections? I don't recommend it.

Paladin picked up on what was going on from listening to me and started doing a nice counterpoint; telling me to ditch the glitterborn and kyte.

"Hold it, hold it—*hold it!*" I yelled, stopping one and shutting up the other. "Look—goddammit, 'flower, will you slow down? Just hold it a minute, forbye."

Tiggy Stardust stopped and glared glacially down at me from severalmany centimeters up.

"I will listen."

"You telling me you gonna throw it all away and go charging back inside to get yourself totally dusted and iced at least twice—for a *knife?*"

"I will not leave without it. I cannot. It is not a 'knife.' It is my—"

"Don't start. Won't make any more sense'n anything else you ever said. Whatever it is, you're going the wrong way. Your knife's in Property with the rest of your kit. I'll help you get it. Then we leave, je, chebai?"

"Dzain'domere." Right.

And they say *hellflowers* are crazy.

We dogged it back the other way and all of a sudden instead of empty the place was full of enough securitronics to reassure me that Wanderweb PortSec still had the good numbers. We had to blow them away before they could use gas, or ticklers, or anything else, and Paladin was so disgusted he didn't say damn-all. Real Soon Now I figured City Central Computer'd change the securitronics' programming from "Contain" to "Destroy." I'd sort of intended to be gone before that happened, but you know how it gets. It'd been a while since I'd had this much homegrown fun, and only the fact that it was me and a hellflower doing the utterly unreasonable against a bunch of tronics saved our bones.

*   *   *

Tiggy's knife was in Dead Storage, which was somewhere between Receiving and Records (being public-access for financial reasons) and I wanted to get there before we ran out of grenades, blaster-paks, and luck. I'd of liked Paladin's input on which door to choose, but he was still on strike and they all looked alike to me.

The high numbers was on City Central evacing organics from this section, sealing it, and calling up a shift of coked wartoys from the Det levels to finish us. Fine. I always did want to live fast, die young, and leave a pretty corpse.

On the other hand, if I could just find Dead Storage, I'd lay credit I wouldn't have to die at all. I said so.

"You should be in a corridor where the doors have colors. The colors will be red and blue. Attempt all doors which have the same color as the corridor walls," said Paladin in my ear. He sounded resigned.

There was a door like that just ahead. I blew the lock, it opened, we went in. I dogged it shut with the emergency manual controls. Tiggy looked around. I looked around.

"Here you go, 'flower. Knife is somewheres in here."

The room was toodamn big—although even a phone booth would of been too big right now—toodamn dark, and toodamn full with toodamn many things. It looked like every hock shop in the universe.

"What you should be seeing, Butterfly, is a large room. All walls except the one behind you are lined with cabinets. There are rows of display cases containing weaponry along the floor. There is no other access to the room except the one you entered through. From what the City Central Computer is saying to the Justiciary computers, I do not believe your current location is known. I suggest you find the hellflower's *arthame* quickly."

"Yeah, yeah," I muttered.

*   *   *

Wanderweb justice is run on the profit motive. Commit a crime here, and you get sentenced, which means the Justiciary sets a price on your head. You meet the price, you walk. You don't meet it, you're contract warmgoods, with your contract time equal to your price. Short-timers go up for auction in the city. If your contract time runs longer than the projected life span for your B-pop, you're a slave. Slaves are factored directly to Market Garden. A few crimes call for execution—like Tiggy's.

But they still manage to lose money, so what does a cost-effective bureaucracy do to defray expenses? It confiscates the personal effects of offenders who can't meet their fines and sells them at auction.

Hence Dead Storage. Hence us.

*   *   *

"So what's this knife look like?" I asked Tiggy. I looked around for the display case that held heat-for-sale. Might as well help him look.

"You saw it when I held it to your throat, three days past."

"Oh, too reet—all we're looking for is inert-blade sword as long as my arm. In all this."

Being as they're what keep Wanderweb Fiduciary in the green, weapons are prominently displayed. Didn't see any inert-blades, but I zapped the lock off the case anyway and started looking through it.

"You have just set off every intruder alarm remaining untriggered in the entire Wanderweb Justiciary," Paladin said.

"Great," I told the immediate world, hefting an Estel-Shadowmaker handcannon too pretty to leave and wondering where I could put it. I tucked it into my shirt and added a necklace of grenades. I started to throw away the comlink, then thought it might be handy if Paladin could hear the hellflower too, so I kept it.

There was a wrenching sound, and I looked up to see Tiggy Stardust ripping open the locked cabinets on the wall with his bare hands. Some B-pops have it, some don't. Hellflowers have more of it than most. The first drawer held jewelry, and he threw it down.

"Would it do any good at all to tell you to abandon the alMayne and leave now?" asked Paladin. "They know where you are, Butterfly. The alarm has been raised, the CityGuard has been mobilized Port-wide, and quarantine has been declared—the spaceport has been closed."

Closed Port. Nothing goes in, nothing goes out. I tried to remember if there were any tractors or pressors on the section of the field where I was docked.

"All this just for us," I said, and Tiggy shot me a funny look. I expect he was thinking I meant the glitterflash he'd just dropped, but it reminded me that one does not talk to one's beaucoup-illegal Library in front of a witness—even if the witness had no way of knowing who or what or even where I was chaffering with.

I waved. He went back to vandalism. "No," I said to Paladin's question.

Tiggy's coke-gutter had to be in one of the cabinets because it sure and t'hell wasn't in any of the display cases. We found it in the last drawer of the last cabinet of the whole wall and Tiggy grabbed it like it was hard credit on payday and stuffed it into his waistband. I'd took the time to find a couple of rifles to replace the last set we'd emptied and was just handing him one when we both heard the teeth-edging whine of a fusion-cutter setting to work.

"Well hell," I said. "J'ais tuc. You and your damn knife." Paladin'd said there was just one way out of Dead Storage, and the fusion-cutter was in the middle of it.

"It is not a 'knife.' It is my *arthame*. We will die nobly and with honor, and they who have unjustly attacked a son of the Gentle People will weep when the vengeance of my clan—"

"I don't want to die with honor! I don't want to die at all if I can help it—and I certainly don't want to die here, with you, after you futzed up your own rescue, you dumb *noke-ma'ashki* alMayne!"

He might not of known what the words meant, but he sure followed the tune. He had The Knife Worth A Afterlife out and pointing at me, which did not bother me half as much as the fusion-cutter did.

"Butterfly!" Paladin shouted in my ear. Tiggy took a step toward me. I wondered if that thing could slice as well as he obviously thought it could.

"Not now," I suggested without hope. They both ignored me.

"The plans I have of that level of the Justiciary show an air vent leading out of Storage and Receivables that should get you past the sealed section. And if you keep talking to the alMayne like that you won't have to attempt it—you'll be dead."

Thank you, Paladin. "Death is least of my worries," I said aloud. On the other hand, Paladin did have a point.

"Look here, hellflower, how'd you like to live and grow old and raise up a whole garden of 'flowers instead of buying real estate?"

Tiggy continued looking earnest. Fusion-cutter continued upping the ambient temperature in Dead Storage by leaps and boggles. Paladin continued wringing his hands in my ear.

"We can get out through vents. There's one in here—see? And you look skinny enough to fit."

But oddly enough Tiggy Stardust did not look like escape was high on his list of life goals. I said how 'flowers drop everything for a good old honor-bashing session, and here I was getting one free for nothing. The fusion-cutter was just about in with us, the door was as pink and glowing as an Imperial sub-lieutenant, and I gave up and decided it was time to play ace-king-trump.

"Saved your life, o'nobly-born—at least you should have the good manners to cooperate in your own rescue."

That got him. He looked real pained—not as fried as me for having had to push his honor buttons but miffed all the same—and put his sacred ferrous oxide butter-spreader away.

"Very well, *chaudatu*. I will cooperate. What is it that you wish?"

"The damn air vent. It's got to be around here somewheres, and then you an me can—" There it was—about halfway up the wall and probably just as hard to get the grille off as the last one was. "Can climb wall, ace cover off vent?"

He looked up, nodded, and went back to glaring at me with pellucid raptor-blue eyes. Damn but don't I love having cannon-fodder to do the heavy work.

"So do it. And get in. I'll follow you." I turned my attention to covering our retreat.

*   *   *

The *legitimates* should of been a tad bit more cautious. I mean, the confiscated weaponry in Dead Storage would do credit to an Imperial Armory, and a whole lot of it was catch-traps and explosives of one flavor or another.

I climbed up a cabinet using the open drawers for footholds and played ringtoss with some grenades for hoops and the door for a spindle. By now the door was yellow-white. The grenades stuck, and a moment later they blew, and I fell off the cabinet but rallied dazzling-like in time to catch a glimpse of Wanderweb Guardsmen in full powered armor lying in a tangled heap around their fusion-cutter. Then it was up in the sky junior birdmen time for yours truly, and being dragged up a wall by a cross hellflower with your lungs full of caustic perdition is another experience I don't recommend.

*   *   *

"Hellflower?" I said to some of Tiggy's more interesting backbones a while later.

"Ea, chaudatu?"

"You can shoot organics now."

"Thank you, *chaudatu.*"

I figured by now that my choices on Wanderweb was death or life-contract slavery, so it didn't really matter now how many people I shot on the rest of the way out. Over the RTS Paladin was getting as close to using harsh language as he ever had, saying how I should of dusted Love's Young Dream about six firefights ago, that I thought with my internal organs, that Wanderweb Free Port was going borneo trying to figure out what was going on, and, oh yes, I'd started a nice oxy-fire on the Admin level I'd just left and had I thought about how I was going to get to the lift to the surface?

I wanted to tell him I was sure he'd think of something, but Tiggy already thought I had fusion for supercargo and I figured one more toy in my attic and he'd shop me sure. So I concentrated on making time and distance through the vent and telling Tiggy where to head in, and regretting the impulse that made me pick up all that hardware back in the duty free zone we'd just left. My bruises had bruises, and on top of that, the vent was starting to fill with smoke.

It was getting to look like Pally'd picked the wrong grid for a first-and-last when I started to see a faint light on the walls that ought to be the main Receiving station. When we got up closer I tapped Tiggy and asked what he saw.

"A room. A desk. Many armed men in blue livery with Wanderweb City service marks. I count twelve *chaudatu* and six mechanicals, all armed and armored. Beyond these is a lift door."

"That is the lift you want," Paladin said, having listened in on this deathless chat by way of my comlink. "It will take you directly to ground level. There is a barricade on the lift, but it is lightly manned. Your speeder is still outside. I am doing preflight warm-up on *Firecat*. And I still think that this is not an intelligent form of recreation."

And sometimes I wonder why I keep him. "We want the lift," I said to Tiggy. "They're trying to keep us down here, so they won't have too many slugs at ground level. Burn the grille and drop these through it." While we was talking, I was trying to get some grenades out of my vest and into his hands—no cheap trick in a vent a little wider than my shoulders. "And hold your breath when you do—is riot-gas, je? Riot-gas—bad stuff." I hoped he was getting the idea, since Tiggy didn't seem to be real ace with Interphon. For that matter, neither was I. "Get to lift and be ready to come out other side blazing. I got speeder. When we're out, we heading for spaceport."

"I have a shuttle there," said Tiggy.

"No hope. By time you're ready to rock 'n' roll, you'll be took. We get up side in my ship."

"Just the three of us," Paladin murmured in my ear. "I thought you didn't carry live freight, Independent Captain-Owner St. Cyr."

"Is emergency," I commented to world at large.

"But that shuttle is FirstLeader Starborn's property!" Tiggy yelped. "I cannot abandon it!"

I jabbed him hard in the nearest bit I could reach. "Will you get us t'hell out of here before I die of old age? Worry about it later!"

"Cover your eyes, *chaudatu.*"

I took a deep breath and did, and felt the back-blast as Tiggy blew the grille. Then the grenades went, and Tiggy slithered forward. I picked up and followed.

                    *   *   *

The *legitimates* never knew what hit them. Gas burned on my skin; I threw grenades like firecrackers and shot tronics. The hardware shot back, and so did the software, and I had to open my eyes to see but at least I hadn't breathed. Didn't worry about ducking because there weren't no place to duck to. Bumped into Tiggy and knocked him into lift just as it opened. He shoved me behind him and blew away a couple of Guardsmen just as the doors closed.

Nice to see a hellflower happy in his work.

I mopped at my leaking eyes, pulled off a glove to do it more efficiently, and noticed my jacket was on fire. I batted out the sparks and explored the burn. Tender, but the skin hadn't been cooked open and that made me luckier than I deserved.

"You all right?" I said to the boy wonder.

He was staring at my sleeve. "You have shed blood for me," he said, reverent-like.

"Huh?" I said, real bright. "Don't be silly, bai, burns don't—"

Then the lift doors opened again and we charged out full-tilt boogie and blasters blazing right over the barricade set up in front of the door. Out of the corner of my eye I saw Tiggy pick up and throw a tronic just like it was a cuddly toy and then whip out that knife of his and slice open a Guardsman while firing his rifle lefthanded.

That made a total of nine Guardsmen he'd dusted, if anyone was counting.

I chased after Tiggy as he ran by and whipped the last of the grenades off my neck and tossed them behind me just for luck as we ran down the steps.

The speeder was right where I left it, bless all the good numbers, so I jumped in and keyed up the ignition while Tiggy swarmed in over the back. We took off at top speed into oncoming traffic just as the CityGuard in force came charging down the steps of the Justiciary.

Paladin gave me a running commentary about where the barricades in the city was. There wasn't much traffic on the flybys this late in Third Shift, so we took some scenic shortcuts and got around all the security checkpoints except the one at the Port.

That one we ran over.

                    *   *   *

By the time we reached it, Wanderweb heat hadn't been able to track us for the longest time, owing to a unfortunate spasm in the City Central Computer traffic monitors. Paladin said they was sure we was somewhere on the other side of the city. So the shellycoats at the Port found a moment to be real surprised when Tiggy and me drove my rented speeder over their shiny purple-and-yellow barricade, then into the freight lift that serviced *Firecat*'s wing of the Port. I lost the comlink somewhere along the way. Big deal.

Paladin overrode the lockups that the Port Computer was trying to put on the lift. We drove out of the lift into the docking ring before PortSec could figure out which ship we was trying to reach, and jumped out of the speeder into the ship. Simple.

Then we took off.

I was never so glad to have a invisible co- as I was then. *Firecat* started taking off before I had her lock sealed, and by the time I was strapped into the mercy seat we was oriented toward the bay opening. I let Paladin Thread the Needle for me while I finished strapping in, and then I grabbed a handful of lifters and firewalled her.

I heard Tiggy go thump amongst the rokeach and then stopped thinking about him. The air show I had to put on to get out of range of Wanderweb's stratospheric interceptors impressed even me, but Wanderweb jurisdiction extends only as far as its atmosphere. It wasn't worth them getting into deep heat with Grand Central to chase us out into Imperial space, so eventually they got tired of shooting and left me alone. I'd better make up my mind to never coming back here for my next sixty incarnations or so, but unless Wanderweb Free Port wanted to hire a bounty hunter to chase me around the Outfar Pally and me was safe now.

When all the ground-to-orbit wartoys was back in their boxes on downside scenic Wanderweb, I put *Firecat* into a nice high orbit over Wanderweb City.

We'd won.

"What are you going to do with the alMayne mercenary now, Butterfly?" Paladin asked in a voice that only I could hear.

Real interesting question.

I had a cargo for Kiffit under my deck plates that I'd meant to lift with thirty hours ago. If *Firecat* wasn't to Kiffit in reasonable time, there'd be questions I'd hate to answer and penalty fees that'd seriously compromise my old age pension. No matter how decorative Tiggy was, he was going to have to take second place to business.

So Tiggy had to go, and without showing me his gratitude or anything else. The question was—where?

I levered myself up out of the mercy seat and raised the cockpit up into the hold.

Right now I wanted everything I'd done myself out of on Wanderweb with my little jailbreak—wet bath, fresh meal, clean clothes, and something done about my burns and bruises. It's a sad fact of hypership ecology that very few of these things was to be had now this side of Kiffit.

I headed for my emergency medical supplies and got out my box of Fenshee burntwine. Toxins is toxins, but this was a emergency.

My pet hellflower was sitting on the deck looking at me. His cutlery was tucked through the waistband of his Wanderweb Detention Issue pants and in his lap he was holding the blaster he'd picked up in Dead Storage. He was sweaty and grimy from the night's occupations, and his hair was hanging down around his face in your basic tousled mop.

I wondered who he was when he was to home. He hadn't chatted much to the Justiciary computer. Despite all we'd meant to each other, I still didn't even know his name. On the plus side, he didn't look any toodamn bent out of shape with me. It'd be a real shame if something that decorative bought real estate, and Paladin would sign Tiggy's lease for sure if he iced me.

Try breathing sometime in a ship with the lock jammed open and the atmosphere venting. It's nice to have friends.

"Hey, hellflower," I said, breaking the seal on the box. "You got a name? T'name-je, bai? Namaste'amo?"

Tiggy stood up. You got the impression he'd just been waiting to be asked. "I am the Honorable *Puer* Walks-by-Night Kennor's-son Starbringer Amrath Valijon of Chernbereth-Molkath."

"Butterfly, we are in very deep trouble." Paladin could see and hear Tiggy now the same way he could me—through the pickups in *Firecat*'s hull.

"Fung wa?" I said. "Would you mind repeating that?" I said carefully to the hellflower in my best Interphon. He did. It came out the same way it had before: Honorable walks by night and the whole rest of it. My little hole card was more than just a problem. He was more than just any old poor little rich killer.

"Valijon Starbringer is cousin to the alMayne king, Amrath Starborn, and son of the alMayne delegate to the Court of the

TwiceBorn, Kennor Starbringer. Kennor Starbringer is also the president of the Azarine Coalition."

Thank you, Paladin. That pedigree made Tiggy bad news. Daddy Starbringer was the law west of the Chullite Stars, the heat, the fuzz, the *legitimates,* the galactic agent of His Imperial Majesty (Entropy bless and keep him far away from me). In short, Tiggy was nobody and the son of nobody this simple 'legger, dicty-barb, and companion to Libraries wanted to have to do with.

"Not?" I said hopefully.

"I am the Third Person of House Starborn. My father is the Delegate to the Imperium. His sister's bond-sister's son is Amrath Starborn, FirstLeader of the Gentle People. The alMayne consular ship *Pledge of Honor,*" Tiggy went on in mildly conversational tones, "is currently orbiting the *chaudatu*-planet. I am a member of the Delegate-my-father's staff. And my people are looking for me, *chaudatu*-Captain."

3

Third Person Peculiar

Tiggy Stardust *nee* Valijon Starbringer looked at me. I looked at him. He showed me his teeth, and I remembered for how many human races a smile wasn't a smile.

So I had a drink. Then I had another drink. Tiggy had a drink too, and said I should call him "Honored One."

I wondered why t'hell he hadn't mentioned his interesting family to Wanderweb Justiciary when they'd brought him in, and said so. He said it was a matter of honor.

Honor. Hah. I knew for damn sure the alMayne would of fried Wanderweb to bare rock once they found Tiggy dead and I bet Tiggy would of thought the joke was worth it.

I took another hit off the box of burntwine and left it with him, since he seemed to appreciate the bennies of a fine vintage neurotoxin, and tottered back up to the mercy seat. When I lowered the cockpit through the hull again Wanderweb was still down there, looking peaceful.

I could tell Pally was just waiting to have words with me, which was damn considerate since he could have any words he wanted and I couldn't say no never-you-mind. I put my Best Girl's extra ears on and started listening for ID beacons. Tiggy'd been downside in a shuttle, and it had to come from somewhere. Maybe somewhere'd be glad to have him back.

"The authorities will call it kidnapping, you know," Paladin said in my ear. Considerate of him not to use the bulkhead speakers. I looked around. Tiggy was sitting in the back of the hold with burntwine and blaster looking as stubborn and patient as a cat I'd used to have.

"What authorities?" I finally said. "Hellflowers?"

I didn't find anything orbiting Wanderweb on my first pass and set up to try again. It was a damn shame I couldn't ask Wanderweb Central what they had in their sky, but didn't think they'd be real responsive somehow.

"Not kidnapping when you give it back, Pally."

"And what do you expect the Port Authority to say when questioned? Someone will have to be culpable in the matter of what has happened to Valijon Starbringer. The alMayne will insist. And the penalty for interfering with a member of an Ambassadorial Delegation is . . . extreme, Butterfly."

"So we send babby-bai across to *Pledge* in lifepak soon as we get near it. He'll square his folks—or not. Hell, Pally, what's one more warrant going to matter?"

"Kidnapping one of the TwiceBorn is a class-A offense. How many more can you afford? You have, as you are fully aware, three already: illegal emigration from an Interdicted World, nonpayment of chattel indenture, and . . . me."

Paladin must be really torqued to mention the last bit. Usually we just pretend there ain't no such thing as Class One High Book.

"Already know I'm dicty-barb, runaway slave, and . . . you know," I pointed out. "Tell me new things, che-bai."

"I will tell you that you cannot afford to attract attention. That you cannot afford another class-A warrant, especially one that will be so actively prosecuted. That if I had known who Valijon Starbringer was in the first place, I would—"

"You'd what?"

"I would have told you this earlier," Paladin finished primly.

I went back to my sensor-sweeps.

If Pally said the penalty was extreme, I didn't want to know what it was. Even if Tiggy did true-tell his da, I didn't know what hellflower logic'd turn his story into.

"Then we just better hurry up and find *Pledge* so's we can get t'hell out of here, j'keyn?"

"Ideally," said Paladin. I groaned. All I needed was for my best buddy to have a case of the more-ascetic-than-thous the whole way to Kiffit.

Besides which, it was getting to be obvious there wasn't any consular ship highbinding my ex-favorite Free Port.

"Oh, Paladin. Where is *Pledge of Honor?*"

"If you had not decided to meddle in the merciful and reasonable justice of the Empire," Paladin said, sounding cross, "we would not be in this situation now, Butterfly."

"Yeah, yeah, yeah," I said, trying to keep my voice low. "Never mind it's Free Port profit, not Imp justice, and Tiggy wouldn't of been up for the chop if he hadn't saved my bones."

"If you had not interfered in the first place, your alMayne nobleman would have murdered K'Jarn and been taken into custody over an offense less extortionately overpriced."

So now Tiggy was *my* hellflower glitterborn, was he? I could think of only one real good reason for Pally to be that torqued.

"Bai, where's *Pledge Of Honor?*"

There was a real long silence if you consider how fast Paladin chopped logic.

"I cannot find it, Butterfly. It isn't here."

I didn't ask him if he was sure. If anyone wanted to find the hellflower garden more than me, my silent partner did.

*   *   *

I pulled the heads-up console farther down over my face and thought about Life, hellflowers, and scenic Wanderweb.

One, if I didn't hit angeltown pretty soon, I'd miss my meet on Kiffit, which could be trouble.

Two, if my antisocial lovestar's ticket out of my life wasn't where he said it was, either it never had been there or it'd left. I didn't think Tiggy knew how to farce, but if he was true-telling why wasn't *Pledge* here?

Three, I had one sincere headache. It was composed of equal parts class-A warrants, Libraries, and the laws of physics. As follows:

A—I couldn't take Tiggy back downside in *Firecat*. One, they'd cut off his head, two, I couldn't get down and back alive, and three, it would make me even later to Kiffit if I tried.

B—I couldn't take Tiggy with me. *Firecat* was a little ship, all engines, marginal life-support, and an Old Federation Library under the mercy seat. Even if I wanted to chance Tiggy twigging Paladin, I couldn't ship him all over the Empire in a ship the size of a Teaser's conscience. For one thing, I wasn't sure we'd both be alive when we got to Kiffit, air being what it was. Not to mention the fact that he was all tangled up in his honor by now and was probably going to try to purify the whirling fusion out of me soon as he figured out the best way.

And if I did take Tiggy to Kiffit, it'd be a real kidnapping for sure, and no way of talking myself out of the charge.

But if I didn't either take the hellflower with me to Kiffit or put him back on the heavy side here at Wanderweb, that left only one thing to do with Tiggy Stardust—all of which made the evening's fun not particularly funny, and never mind that if I hadn't showed up he'd of been dead in a few hours anyway.

He'd been in the Last Gasp looking for me. And because he had been, I was alive now and he'd killed serious Guardsmen, for which Wanderweb wanted to chop him.

I sat there and thought about it, and punched up the numbers for the High Jump to Kiffit, and looked at my life-support inventories and counted on my fingers. Paladin knew what I was doing, but he didn't say zip.

And when everything was done but making up my mind, I raised the cockpit back into the hull again and went back to talk to my passenger.

Firecat's internal compensators weren't good enough that she could of moved without him noticing, and after our takeoff Tiggy Stardust knew it. He put his knife away and stood up. Different cultures have different body language. On alMayne I bet this didn't mean respect.

"Ea, chaudatu?"

"You ain't going to like this, che-bai. Your ship ain't there."

I still wasn't ready for way he moved.

"You are lying!" Tiggy snarled in my ear. He'd wrapped himself around all my bruises hard enough to hurt, and had his alMayne *arthame* snugged up to several of my important veins. If I flinched in the wrong direction I'd be nonfiction, but if I didn't know people I would of sold my bones a long time ago.

Tiggy was scared.

"Hellflower, I am for-sure sorry your folks ain't there. But it ain't nice to pull heat on people for true-tell." I talked real slow, trying to punch it across two languages. I didn't flinch neither, and eventually he let me go.

"They could not leave! How could they have left? It is not possible that they should leave; they—" Tiggy went off into helltongue, ramifying his position, which was pretty to listen to and told me precisely nothing. Paladin didn't know it either, at least not well enough to translate.

"The *Pledge of Honor* was not listed at the Wanderweb ships-in-port directory, thus we may infer that its stop here was not an official one. The most reasonable construction to place upon the matter of the ship's absence from the area now is that the *Pledge Of Honor* departed according to a predetermined schedule. If it were bound for Grand Central, a plausible hypothesis considering its nature as a consular vessel, the captain would have had no other option. Whether the legation was aware of Valijon Starbringer's absence from its midst at the time of departure is a matter for conjecture at this time," said Paladin.

I rubbed my neck and counted my new bruises. Paladin still sounded just like a talkingbook, which meant he was still mad. I thought I'd share his facts with Tiggy.

"Was Da shopping cubic for Throne? He'd of had to kyte by mandated o'chrono no matter where you was," I said. Tiggy stared at me, glazed and blank like a well-scrubbed palimpsest.

"Try Interphon," suggested Paladin in my ear, which was fine for him but it'd been a long day and I was tired.

"*Pledge* is gone, j'ai?" I said to Tiggy. "Scanners don't lie, not mine, if gardenship was highbinding—orbiting—it isn't there now."

Tiggy nodded, looking sulky.

"When *Pledge* tik'd to Wanderweb, was on way to Throne—Grand Central—ImpCourt, j'ai?"

Another nod. Communication was reliably established with the mentally underprivileged.

"So TwiceBorn jump salty if you're late, see? So *Pledge* topped angels on sked, and you pick up ship on next downfall." Wherever that was. I wasn't paying for a long-distance call to Grand Central to find out, neither.

"But they do not know I'm gone! They cannot know—they would not have left if they had known! My father—"

Terrific. "Kyted downside on sly to rumble Gentryken?" I was beginning to wonder just how old Tiggy was.

"Maybe it would be better if you learned alMayne," said my ever-helpful partner. "Or helltongue, if you prefer." I looked at Tiggy's blank expression and tried again.

"You went to planetary surface n'habla—" damn, what was the Interphon? "without—your parent's knowledge?" I said careful, counting off the words on my fingers. It was like being back in Market Garden Acculturation class, and I hadn't liked it then, either.

"I am not obligated to discuss these matters with you, *chaudatu.* There was no reason I should not visit Wanderweb. I am the Third Person of House Starborn—and he who says I may not go where I wish lives without walls!" Tiggy put his knife back in his waistband and tossed his hair back out of his eyes.

The words might be helltalk, but the tune was real familiar.

"How t'hell old are you anyway, Tiggy-che-bai?"

Tiggy goggled at me like he couldn't figure where the question was coming from, but all of a sudden I thought it was real important.

"You will address me with respect as Honored One, she-captain."

"J'ai; about the time you stop calling me she-captain, forbye. Now true-tell Mother Sincere facts."

"What has this to do with the *Pledge of Honor?* If they have gone on to Royal you must follow them at once."

"Why?" If *Pledge*'d gone on to Royal in the Tortuga Sector *Firecat* wasn't following it for any credit. There was a rebellion going on in Tortuga against the Brightlaw Corporation, the family that ran the Tortuga Directorate, which meant Governor General his Nobly-Bornness Mallorum Archangel and his joy-boys'd be all over it, arguing Directorate jurisdiction against sector jurisdiction and making Tortuga cubic real unhealthy for my favorite dicty and other living things.

I sat down on a crate of rokeach and took off my jacket. I'd forgot about the burn on my arm; I scraped it and hissed. Tiggy tried to explain how I had to go chasing off into this free-fire zone full of Azarine mercs while I tried to get a biopak out of the medkit and over one helluva painful nuisance. Finally we both gave up.

"Hold still," he said firmly. "You cannot do that yourself. I will bandage you, and you will explain why you are detaining a servant of the Gentle People."

"That's you, I suppose." My baseline Interphon was finally coming back to me, but it still felt funny to the taste. "And what makes you think, glitterborn, you got any idea what to do with battle-dressings?"

"A warrior of the Gentle People must always be able to see to his *comites, chaudatu.* You are my responsibility, even if you are not very much of one. You have shed blood for me."

"Like hell." Bent out of shape or not, Tiggy had a glitterborn way of doing the pretty. Nasty.

"I do not see any painkillers here," he said like it was my fault.

"You drank it. You may of noticed by now, o'noblyborn, that this is a freighter, not a high-ticket outhostel. And I want to keep it in one piece, not do a conversion to plasma on the Royal ecliptic."

"House Starbringer will pay for my return, since ransom is what concerns you, *chaudatu,*" said Tiggy, once the dressing was in place. He took an eloquent look around my Best Girl's hold and went over and sat on a crate.

I reminded myself that he was a homicidal lunatic.

"Butterfly, let me—" Paladin began.

"Ransom," I said, flat. Tiggy looked up. "Tiggy Stardust, is time you got lesson in big-bad galaxy—which you should of got before you went off to play with the big kids in the never-never. You chaffer on about ransom like it meant something and people was going to play kiss-my-hand and wait around to collect it with glitterborn rules and all. Well, K'Jarn was going to kill you for what you was standing up in back on Wanderweb and probably sell you to a bodysnatcher before you got cold. That's ransom in the never-never."

Tiggy's face was unreadable as a plaster saint's. "What will you do, if you will not return me to my people?"

"If I put you back on the heavy side here, Justiciary's going to chop you. If I chase into Royal, I'll get blown up. So I'm taking you to Kiffit. Got cargo for there, people're waiting,"

"No," said Paladin. I ignored him.

Tiggy pulled out his knife again, which was a argument but not a good one. "I do not wish to go to this Kiffit. The *Pledge Of Honor* is going to Royal, and—"

"Put that coke-gutter of yours away before I ram it down your glitterborn throat. Lesson Number One in the Real World: You can kill me but you can't make me fly you anywhere."

"Butterfly, will you please—"

"I can fly," said Tiggy uneasily.

"Not this ship, che-bai. When I die, it blows up. I'm going to Kiffit, and so are you. Think *Firecat*'s maybe got enough air to get us both there, if we're lucky. Better chance than you got otherways. I'll take that risk."

"Butterfly, you saw the figures. There is only a seventy percent chance you will both survive to reach Kiffit. It is not worth the risk."

"I have thirty-four years," Tiggy said.

"Por-ke?" I said. He didn't savvy patwa, but he answered.

"You asked me how old I was, *ch*—Captain. I have thirty-four years."

"Standard?" Hell, *I* have thirty-four years Standard; if Tiggy was my age I'd eat all five of *Firecat*'s goforths.

"No. Real years."

"What's the conversion?" I said, and after a long time it was Paladin that answered me.

"Thirty-four years alMayne is equal to fourteen Imperial Standard Years. Butterfly, there is one chance in four that you will die."

I still ignored him. I already knew the numbers. I looked at Tiggy. He didn't look fourteen, but different human races age differently. I was already halfway through my expectancy, assuming I lived long enough to die in bed.

Which didn't look too likely just now. And it didn't at this moment matter what the Hellflower Years of Discretion were, either.

"You're fourteen. Terrific." Under the Codex Imperador Tiggy had to be twenty to be a grown-up, and he wasn't. So the rap for him was child-kidnap; worse than before, if that was possible.

"I am adult. I have my *arthame*. I am a legal Person of House Starborn—" He stopped. "And honor demands that I die now with honor; for allowing me that you have the gratitude of my House." He looked around.

"And where t'hell you think you're going, kinchin-bai?"

"I will go out your air lock, Captain—even a ship like this must have one. I cannot put you at risk in your journey. You have saved my life and served me well. I will not imperil you further."

I'd been fourteen once. Fortunately it hadn't been permanent.

"It is very nearly a reasonable solution," said Paladin, helpfully. Real reasonable; I wouldn't even have to cold-cock the stupid brat and shove him out my lock; he'd do it himself.

Except it wasn't his fault that his daddy'd kyted, or that nobody'd told Tiggy the galaxy had teeth big enough to chew hellflowers.

"Oh, give it a rest, willya? You and me is going to Kiffit and I'll turn you in to the Azarine Guildhouse there. They send you home, I get shut of you, everything's copacetic."

Tiggy looked around in panic. "But you cannot do that." He looked like he preferred microwave death to spending another hour on *Firecat*.

"Is my ship and I'll freight what I want. Ain't done rescuing you yet, so remember honor, Tiggy-bai."

"Honor is better than bread," agreed Tiggy darkly, which just showed how many meals he'd missed.

He slanted a interested glance at me, like he was thinking of unfinished honor-bashing session. But he'd back down for now, which was all I cared about. And maybe the kidnap charge wouldn't stick.

Yeah, and maybe I wouldn't run into Dominich Fenrir on Kiffit.

*   *   *

I went back up to the mercy seat. The good numbers for Kiffit was right where I left them.

"He is dangerous. Do not do this, Butterfly," said Paladin, quiet as if anyone could hear.

"What else can I do, babby? Fourteen-year-old kinchin-bai." I pulled the stick for the Drop and my Best Girl wrenched herself out of the here-and-now like a homesick angel.

*   *   *   *   *

Insert #3: Paladin's Log

What began as an extremely dangerous amusement became an extremely costly one when the jailbreak of the alMayne Valijon Starbringer escalated to the point that Wanderweb Port Security became involved. When Valijon Starbringer became, in effect, stranded aboard *Firecat* the affair ceased to resemble anything amusing at all.

Firecat is not a passenger ship, for one very good reason. Any passenger aboard *Firecat* is in a position to discover my existence and Butterfly's cooperation with me, and that discovery would inevitably result in our destruction. And of all the potential passengers to take aboard *Firecat,* Valijon Starbringer might very well be the most dangerous.

It is Butterfly's opinion that politics interferes with "bidness," that there is business to be done under any government, and under all governments what she does is illegal. These things are all true, but do not in and of themselves constitute an excuse for ignorance. If Butterfly were more aware of "current events," she would understand why Valijon Starbringer—the only son of the alMayne delegate to the Court of the TwiceBorn, Kennor Starbringer, who is the deciding vote on the Azarine Coalition Council—was such an extremely dangerous commodity to have inboard.

There are 144 Directorates in the Phoenix Empire—144 astropolitical divisions of the Phoenix Empire, each of which is governed by the Corporation families. From these families are drawn the members of the Imperial Court—the TwiceBorn. The TwiceBorn are the social and economic elite of the Empire and rule all the rest, civil and military alike. Below the TwiceBorn come citizens, and below them client-members, and below them slaves. Then resident aliens (what Butterfly calls, with a fine disregard for species distinction, "wigglies"), and then, at last, the nightworld rabble of which Butterfly is a part.

Valijon Starbringer was not TwiceBorn. The Starborn Corporation —the form his alMayne princely House takes in the Empire at large— does not choose that its alMayne subjects accept Imperial honors except when unavoidable. Kennor Starbringer is TwiceBorn. Amrath Starborn—their "king"—is not.

The alMayne do not like those who are not alMayne, no matter how high their estate.

I do not remember them from the days I was the Library at the University of Sikander. They are a new race, yet records speak of them as very old. I do not like paradoxes of this sort, and I do not like the alMayne. Irrationally xenophobic, reactionary, conservative, they prefer to stagnate in their elegant barbarism than to change and grow. Such a barbarian, trapped aboard *Firecat,* could be expected to do something dangerously irrational.

The alMayne, as a race, might be seen to be irrational. Butterfly says "hellflowers is crazy" and feels no need for further explanation.

I do. I have studied these elegant barbarians, hellflowers, "Gentle People." I could have translated Valijon's speech for Butterfly. I did not choose to. It would not have made her jettison him, nor would she have understood even the translation.

"Hellflowers" do not have a modern psychology. Their entire culture is focused upon the willingness to die for intangibles such as personal honor. *"Dzain'domere"* means "I pledge and give my word." Thus it is bound up in alMayne concepts of honor which are indeed "better than bread." An alMayne can live for quite some time without food: an alMayne who is doubted—disbelieved in—ceases to exist instantly.

Their suicide rate is high, as might be expected; it is the index of stress on a nearly pretechnological, highly ritualized culture attempting to fit itself into the Phoenix Empire.

The Azarine Coalition Council, of which Kennor Starbringer of alMayne is president, decides policy matters for the Coalition at large. Its primary business is the ratification and modification of the terms of the Gordinar Canticles, the charter under which the Coalition operates. The Canticles cover, in broad, matters affecting the governance of hired armies, from the weapons they may carry, to the targets they may be used against, to the persons and organizations who may hire them. The key canticle is the matter of who may lawfully hire mercenary armies. As it currently stands, any sophont or entity may; the checks and balances arise from the Coalition defining the targets against which they may not be used, and the base price for a mercenary's services.

To construct an example: Naturally it is illegal to hire a mercenary army to oppose any of the edicts of the Emperor, the Throne, the Court, or any of the TwiceBorn—the Imperial bureaucracy. However, it is certainly legal to hire mercenary troops to overthrow a Corporation— the ruling entity of a Directorate. But a Corporation so menaced can appeal to the sector governor for aid, who can provide the Corporation with Imperial troops, which the mercenaries cannot legally oppose. But for a Corporation to do this is to invite Imperial attention, and the causes of the original war will go into arbitration. It is not unheard of for a Corporation to appeal for help against rebellious forces and have all its assets turned over to the rebels. Imperial justice, as the folk-wisdom goes, is obscure.

One can see, therefore, that, for example, a modification of the Canticles to forbid Azarine troops to fight Corporation troops would be very much to the Corporations' benefit. One can further see that there could be a great deal of special interest group pressure on the Coalition Council to make partisan changes to the Gordinar Canticles.

At the moment the Coalition Council is evenly divided between those who wish to make major changes to the Canticles, including the List of Protected Groups, and those who wish to leave the Canticles as they are. Kennor Starbringer, as president, could cast a deciding vote either way. At the moment he is a strict Constructionist, and will not vote for change.

Should he die or resign, his Council membership will go to the alMayne Morido Dragonflame, who favors complete revision of the Canticles.

Seen in this light, Valijon Starbringer is a playing piece in a very high-stakes game indeed. Butterfly's safety depends on staying far from the attention such matters bring, and she knows it. It is fortunate that Valijon Starbringer's appearance on Wanderweb was an accident, and that no one knows where he is now.

I wonder.

Considering the money lost in the action, why would Wanderweb shut down its entire Port to prevent the escape of two relatively unimportant criminals?

4

Dead Heat
On A Merry-Go-Round

I was dreaming and I knew it, and part of me thought I ought to wake up and keep an eyeball on Tiggy, but I'd finished the second box of burntwine a while back because my backteeth and all of my bruises hurt and Tiggy could do me any time he got around his honor anyway.

So I watched myself sleep, the way you do in dreams. I was back home on Granola, running off early in the morning to play hooky. The light was slanting rose-gold and silver through the trees and there was cooking-breakfast smoke rising off the housetops in the valley below.

Nice place, Granola. I'd been this way before, in dreams.

And just like the other times, this starship came sailing through the treetops to land in my da's cornfield—a bolt of platinum godfire looking like nothing I'd ever seen.

The scene jumped, like slicing the middle out of a talkingbook, and then I was looking at the first planet I'd ever seen from space. Home. But not home anymore—I was leaving and I wasn't ever coming back.

You're thick when you're kinchin-bai; fifty fellow-citizens on ice in his hold and I never stopped to think what the captain's being a slaver meant to me. Didn't even know the word.

I wanted to wake up before I got to the part where I *did* know, but all that happened was I jumped about three years, to Pandora.

At least I missed Market Garden. Those dreams are bad ones.

Pandora is a planet in the never-never, where the Hamati Confederacy bumps up against the Empire. I was downfall stranded without a numbercruncher or hope of one, with people after me because I'd run away from Market Garden and people soon to be after me wanting payoff for their kick, their goforth, and the numbercruncher that was slagged plastic and broken dreams in my cockpit.

Real poetic. Real dumb. So what's so bad about being contract warmgoods, anyway? On Market Garden I was a marketable commodity—for use, when finished, somewhere tronics wouldn't do. No reason for them to waste time telling me things I'd never need to know—like what a Library was, and not to go buy one if I got the chance.

I dreamed I was back in the shop on Pandora, holding a box of broken glass that someone swore was a navicomp, and then it started to change. . . .

"Butterfly? Butterfly, wake up."

I staggered up out of dreams and heard someone else breathing inboard *Firecat.*

"Butterfly? We need to talk." My teeth crawled. Paladin. He didn't breathe but he talked real good. Tiggy Stardust was the one breathing.

I nodded. Paladin'd see that. I put my hands over my face, trying to lock up the ghosts again. I don't dream mostly. No percentage in it.

My head was slugging along with my heartbeat but I didn't bump the burn on my arm and nothing else hurt too much. I looked over to where I'd stowed Tiggy in my second-best sleepsling. He looked soft and sweet and anyone that took a step toward him was taking her life in hand. So I crawled out of my rack the other way, past the cockpit well and up into the nose.

It was ungodly quiet in *Firecat.* The air scrubbers and everything else that used up power and oxy were off. I was starting us as we'd have to go on, with life-support down near marginal. Angeltown shed weird gray light through the hullports and I wrapped my quilt tighter around me and shivered. Later it was going to be as too hot as it was too cold now, and sometime after that we'd be to Kiffit or dead.

"Can you hear me?"

Damnfool question. "Je, che-bai, I hear." Granola was still ringing xylophone ghosts down all the years between me and fourteen. It was crazy to even think about going back. Even if I could find the place, I couldn't land. Our Fifty Patriarchs had spun good plastic for them and their descendants to be left lonealone for ever and ever, world without end.

"You should have let Valijon Starbringer put himself out the air lock. You can still do it," Paladin started up, and went into a taradiddle all about xenophobic alMayne, heat-death of the Universe, and how Tiggy was son of Very Important TwiceBorn, all which I knew. Already knew he was trouble, and now Pally wanted to tell me about cultural fragmentation through linguistic evolution, whatever t'hell that was. Nothing I could see mattered, but he thought it was important, so I listened.

The song and dance kept coming back to "lose the glitterborn." Paladin was full with mights and maybes tonight and I was tired of my life. It was no time to be arguing ethics.

"Not going to frag the kinchin-bai just because it's convenient," I snapped at him finally. Tiggy stirred but didn't wake up, and I waited until he settled again. "Be reasonable. Think you Tiggy-che-bai's da's not going to want to know where's his lost son-an-heir? For sure *Firecat* went up out of quarantine on Wanderweb and someone saw me stuff Tiggy inboard. If I dock wonderchild alive and well at Azarine Guildhouse on Kiffit we have no problems. Mercs're honest." And a hellflower merc wouldn't turn around and sell Tiggy to someone else instead of handing him back to his original owner.

Paladin didn't say anything.

"Bai, I got to be able to point to live Tiggy Stardust when hellflower trouble comes calling. It's not like beating kidnap-rap. Hellflowers won't stop."

"He is a liability." Did Paladin think he was going to change my mind, or did Libraries get tired too? We both knew all the sides of all the arguments and we could go roundaround them forever.

Ice kinchin-bai—not because he was dangerous, but because he might be.

Not good enough.

"He's kinchin-bai, Pally—a fourteen-year-old kid. This is his first time out. He'll clear me a rap, and he won't have anything else to tell anyone that'll make any sense at all."

"You're guessing, Butterfly. I'm not."

We both knew I knew I was guessing, and we both knew the percentages in my being right. Low. But there wasn't any other thing to do but wake Tiggy up and shove him out the air lock—and then follow him myself.

"Once we get to Kiffit I'll toss my kick and drop Tiggy-bai at Azarine Guildhouse. We'll be gone before the heat drops, Pally. We'll leg it straight back to Coldwater without waiting for a load. And we can find a hat trick to do in the Outfar for bye-m-bye until the heat dies down. Won't cost us anything."

"Except a Free Port. Except air, and water, and food, and power to Kiffit. Except, if you are not lucky, your life."

I knew all that and I wasn't happy about any of it.

"Is my life, bai—isn't it?" But it wasn't. It was Paladin's too, and he was too polite to say, but he couldn't make it in the Outfar—or anywhere—alone.

And neither could I. How many years ago would I of been dead without Paladin to cover up for everything a Interdicted Barbarian didn't know?

"It was bad luck. It just happened. But we'll ace this and get straight, you'll see. Drop Tiggy-bai and have the good numbers again." I tried to tell myself I was trying so hard to keep Tiggy alive only because I knew his hellflower kin wouldn't let the matter drop.

"Leaving aside his oxygen requirements, Valijon Starbringer is an outsider. He is an aristocrat—" Paladin listed all Tiggy's shortcomings again. The only thing he didn't do was ask me to put Tiggy out the lock to make him safe.

I don't know what I would of done if he had.

Killing Tiggy was the smart thing. I knew it was. Raise my chances of getting to Kiffit alive. Lower the chances of anybody being able to cry Librarian. I was going to have to run for the edge of the Outfar either way, so keeping him alive wouldn't get me anything.

And I couldn't do it any more than I could Transit to angeltown without a ship. I didn't know why. I didn't like not knowing why.

I sat and stared out at angeltown and wondered what it would be like to just open the lock and step out. It wasn't like realspace. Paladin tried to explain it to me once—something to do with time and relative dimensions in space—but I didn't understand it. I didn't need to understand it to fly through it, anyway.

"What about documentation?" Paladin said after awhiles, and I knew I'd won whatever I'd been fighting for. "Your pet cutthroat hasn't got any ID on him."

If Paladin was thinking about that, he wasn't thinking about making me put Tiggy out the air lock.

"Think there's still couple sets of blank around somewheres. You do something to get him off-Port for me, bai?" ID wasn't all Tiggy didn't have. Wanderweb had stripped him to the skin. I'd have to see what *Firecat* could do for him in the way of clothes.

"Counterfeiting ID is not the problem, Butterfly."

No, problem was lots of other things, but none of them was hauling any cubic tonight. I sat under *Firecat*'s hullports and watched Tiggy breathe until I fell asleep.

*   *   *   *   *

Insert #4: Paladin's Log

It was my fault that Butterfly broke into the Wanderweb Justiciary to steal Valijon Starbringer. And from the moment that she made the choice to do so, it was inevitable that she would not abandon him.

I say that now, with hindsight. One may always desire facts to be other than they are. But the facts touching on this matter unfolded in inevitable progression over a span of years.

From the time Butterfly and I met on Pandora the problem of reliable communication has been a concern. Unless Butterfly and I could share information while she was away from *Firecat,* we were extremely vulnerable. Clandestine communication would markedly increase our joint chances to "live to get older."

I had originally thought that arranging this communication would be a simple matter, but the equipment I described to Butterfly did not exist. She attempted to construct some components, but even the tools did not exist—an entire technology had been destroyed in the unreasoning backlash against fully-volitional logics. At Butterfly's urging we began to search for something available in the modern world that would meet our needs.

When we finally determined the existence of the RTS unit, Butterfly had a number of reasons we could not acquire it, but as the Library at University I had incorporated several important studies on human behavior, and retained enough of that information not to find her actions inconsistent.

The implant operation would be a source of emotional trauma to any organic of the galactic culture. For a Luddite Saint from Granola, sworn to pastoral simplicity and no technology more complex than the tilt-board plow and the waterwheel, it would be an even greater one. Butterfly is not as indifferent to the mores of either her natal culture or her adoptive culture as she pretends.

So we delayed. Eventually we came to Wanderweb—having carried the RTS unit with us for over a year—and the surgery was accomplished. Emotional backlash and suppressed cultural bias did the rest.

A course of action undertaken in mutual willingness to provide greater safety to us both—the transponder implantation—leads inevitably to an action of great risk to us both—the jailbreak of the alMayne. If Butterfly considered her reasons for insisting on that course of action at all, she might have articulated them as being "to prove that she still had it." In reality, it was to prove that she still *was* it.

By the very nature of what I was, Butterfly was cut off from even the society of criminals and outlaws. An escaped slave, even an illegal emigrant, can find peers and socialization in the nightworld society. The possessor of a fully-volitional logic, a Librarian, is outcast by every thinking being. There is no one in the Imperium so depraved as to knowingly offer a Librarian sanctuary, and no one who would keep such a thing secret.

On the fringe of the Phoenix Empire, away from the deadly cataloging bureaucracy, the two of us were safe. But what at first had seemed limitless freedom I discovered to be circumscribed indeed. We could go no closer to the center of the Empire than the very fringes of the Directorates. Any thorough medical examination would reveal what Butterfly was, and any cursory technical inspection would uncover me. The penalty for either discovery was death.

It was a death only slightly more certain than that which was the consequence of Butterfly's chosen profession—but illegal pilot was, in all fairness, one of the few ways of acquiring credit she could espouse. Piloting is a marketable skill—and she had been trained, if not certified, by Market Garden as part of her processing. A trained pilot willing to take considerable risks to maintain his freedom quickly becomes a darktrader.

If he has the money to purchase a ship—or can find a sponsor.

The Pandora business venture on which Butterfly discovered me was an undertaking of the sort in which the probability of failure was so great that it precluded the use of expensive material. If Butterflies-are-free, an untried, potentially valueless commodity, got her ship, herself, and her cargo back to Coldwater, she would enjoy Factor Oob's financial support and political backing, and live in comparative safety and comfort. If not, she would die.

She lived, with my help. And by her aid I returned to life. Butterfly protected me during the long period of reconstruction when I would ignorantly have revealed myself, and in return I provided her with the technological edge that meant success in a highly competitive profession. By the time we knew the truth about ourselves and each other, and had discovered what a "Library" was in this brave new world of bright promise, I did not wish to exchange my safety and companionship for new uncertainty, and Butterfly did not wish to relinquish my considerable resources. So we remained sequestered, secretly fugitive, and Butterfly remained distanced twice-over from her own kind.

But humans are social animals—every book I ever was tells of this. They are born and grow and die in social groups, responding to one another, and even if modern social groups include sentient females they are no less social groups for that. Configuration prefigures destiny. Structure determines function. An organic sentient needs to be with others of his own kind. In befriending me, Butterfly was deprived of the socialization the imperatives of her construction had shaped her to require.

If she had not been so alone, would she have clung to Valijon Starbringer—a dangerous nuisance—in the way she did?

No. But she was, and so she did. And I realized I could delay no longer.

For both our sakes, I must set her free.

*   *   *   *   *

It was eight days to Kiffit, and there was nothing to do but forge a ticket-of-leave for the rokeach and watch the life-support reserves drop against present usage. My shirts fit Tiggy, my pants didn't, and I gave him the Estel-Shadowmaker handcannon for his very own because he seemed to like it. I gave up any hope of disarming him at a very early stage in our relationship.

Tiggy paced and fidgeted until I pointed out it'd use up the air faster, then he lay in his sleepsling and stared at nothing for hours with no expression at all.

He didn't ask me any questions. Maybe good little hellflowers don't. Maybe he thought a *chaudatu* didn't know anything he needed.

I didn't ask him any questions neither. I was saving up my calls on his honor for when I needed them, and I didn't want to give him any excuses to declare accounts closed.

So nobody talked. Including Paladin.

After that first night I'd wake up sometimes and see Tiggy watching me, like he was trying to stare through my skull. I spent lots of time in the mercy seat with the canopy popped, staring into angeltown till my eyes hurt, but there was no point in making Tiggy wonder who I was talking to.

The temperature rose, the air got thicker, and I sat in the dark thinking I was damned if I was going to die and give Pally the chance to say he told me so. And the sooner I lost Love's Young Dream and stopped thinking about the perils of childhood, the better. Then me and Paladin could go back to doing business, like always.

The sooner the better.

*   *   *

Firecat made Transit to realspace right on sked. Realspace was black sharp and dangerous with Kiffit lost in the skirts of the primary.

I'd had a headache for the last two days that I couldn't shake and when I moved too fast everything went gray. I knew my reflexes was too far gone for me to be able to get *Firecat* down. Fortunately I didn't have to.

We crossed the Kiffit-Port beam and I flooded my Best Girl with the last of the reserve oxy and turned the airscrubbers up full. If Paladin couldn't get us down within the hour we'd be dead, but for the chance to breathe real air again I didn't care. Even Tiggy looked giddy with it.

I slid into the mercy seat and played "let's pretend." We rode Kiffit-Port's beam into an approach pattern as Independent Freighter this-that-and-the-otherthing, Coldwater registry and last downfall Orili-neesy, shipping x-meters cubic and crew of one, nine plates of goforth and all the other nosy nonsense slugs want to know about a honest woman making a moral living. Finally they gave me a landing window, about the time I could count our breathing in minutes.

I popped the hatch and cut the hull-fields before we was safely down. Sweet, free, and unmetered air blasted into *Firecat* with a whistle that set my teeth on edge. Paladin switched from para-light to para-gravity systems and coaxed my sweetheart to dance on her attitude jets, taking her down slow enough to keep her from getting her blessed little non-powered permeable hull shredded by atmosphere. Being alive was wonderful. Kiffit was wonderful. Air was wonderful. And I wanted a bath.

*   *   *

Kiffit wasn't a Free Port, more's the pity, but it *was* in the Outfar. It was shabby and overlooked and second rate, and the sort of place I know better'n my own name. Pally says the Empire's dying by meters, and places like Kiffit are a point in his favor.

Eventually I was gig-in-dock, with Kiffit-Port looking like every Port on every Outfar planet in the never-never. I dogged the inner and outer hatches open and put down the ramp and went back into the hold. Paladin had the blowers going full tilt boogie. Tiggy'd climbed down out of his sling and was looking at me.

"Scenic Kiffit, hellflower. Just let me hook *Firecat* up and we'll do some eyeballing." As soon as Paladin had a landline, he could tell me all about the Guildhouse on Kiffit and some of us could go there.

The docking rings on Kiffit are open to the sky. The sky was bright opaque orange and the air was thin and dry. I like canned air better as a rule—you know what you're getting—but even what Kiffit was using for air tasted delicious. I went around to the docking ring firewall and found the Port Services hookups and dragged the hoses over to *Firecat*. Water and waste and power to run them when your goforths are cold, landline and computer access, all the comforts of sweet bye-m-bye. It took awhiles to get them hooked up right but I didn't care as long as I was here to do it.

Then I went back inside *Firecat*. Tiggy Stardust had his Estel-Shadowmaker handcannon out and was pointing it right at me.

It wasn't Paladin's fault for not warning me. We both knew Tiggy was armed; we'd both been counting on hellflower honor to protect me. I hadn't even seen Tiggy move before the blaster was out; he was that fast.

"I am leaving now, Captain San'Cyr."

So much for hellflower honor. Tiggy had his blaster pointed right at my chest, not that a near-miss would matter with an Estel-Shadowmaker. I kept my hands well away from anywhere that might have held heat and didn't.

"So?"

"I wished to say farewell. I have been thinking, and I know now what I must do." He got up and walked past me to the hatch and down.

"Hellflower. Why the heat?" It was stupid but I wanted to know.

Tiggy looked down at the blaster, then in through the hatch at me. "I do not trust you, *chaudatu*. You do not understand honor. And you are not very smart."

Tiggy Stardust seemed to spend his whole time walking out of my life. I hoped this time it was for good.

I sat down on the crate he'd been sitting on. After a while it got cold, so I got my jacket and my blasters and a few other odds and ends from my lockboxes and tucked them all away nice and proper. Paladin was real quiet.

"So why don't you say you told me so?" I said. No comment. Paladin can shut up better than anybody I know, and you can't see his face while he's doing it.

"What do you think's going to happen to him, bai?"

That he answered.

"Based on Valijon's performance on Wanderweb, he will immediately be arrested for causing a public disturbance—only in Borderline they will insist on identifying him before sentencing. Since he has no ID on him, they—"

I put up my hand and Paladin stopped talking. Something was nagging hard at the back of my mind, but it wouldn't come in and I let it go. "Never mind. So they'll ID him and shop'm back to his da? That'll do me fine."

And good-bye to the recent and unlamented Tiggy, social work on the brain-dead, and all my other wastes of time and money. After awhiles I went on with my business. Gentry don't get paid to think.

*   *   *

There's a nice system on Kiffit and most Imperial Outfar ports whereby you never have to meet the person catching your kick. It works whether you're pre-contracted or no, and whether you have any actual interest in selling your cargo or not.

I had no interest in my supposed money-load, but every interest in making the Teasers think I did, so I took the rokeach off to a nice tradelocker and fed my manifest through the doorlock.

If I came back for the cargo, I'd only be down the locker rent. If my assignee did, he'd have to pay serious valuta on top of the rent. In this case, I didn't have a buyer for my rokeach, so Paladin listed my cargo and price asking on Tradehall board whiles I danced it.

Teasers keep track of things like that, the nosy baskets. I was damned if I was going to be charged pleasure-yacht rates for coming in to Kiffit without a cargo. I was going to lose enough money on this tik already.

So I was asking twenty percent over Market Garden setprice on the board, and I'd come back when I was ready to lift and either pick up my payoff or take the lock down to the Transport Workers Guildhall and sell it to someone who wanted to speculate in rokeach futures. Fine and nice and real friendly. And *Firecat* and me was documented every step of the way as coming to Kiffit to do serious bidness, in case anybody came for to ask. And while this was all real uplifting, it wasn't how I paid the rent.

After a sprightly pre-meridies of healthy exercise and a detour through an off-Port bathhouse, I went back to *Firecat* to get the money-load.

And Dominich Fenrir was waiting.

* * *

Dominich Fenrir is the chief Teaser on Kiffit. Being Trade Customs and Commerce's man on Kiffit has to be a thankless job, but Dommie don't worry his pretty head over justice and mercy and Customs regs. He went bent a long time ago.

If you're a Directorate merchantman up to paying the vigorish, you can run anything you want in and out of Kiffit-Port unwept unhonored and unsung. The rest of us just pay the occasional sweetener not to be certified Unfit to Lift by Kiffit Port Authority. Only sometimes Dommie's got to pretend he's still a honorable Imperial, and that's when independents like me get happy days and busy nights.

"Hello, St. Cyr. Nice to see you back. How's the wrong side of the law these days?"

"Wouldn't know. Am honest woman, forbye. Business must be bad, you bothering me."

Dommie smole a small smile and managed to look even more unattractive. "Oh, no. I'd say this comes under the heading of protecting my interests, St. Cyr. Now why don't you open up your ship so we can go inside—since we're such old friends."

"Siblings, surely; you choose your friends," Paladin commented.

I opened up *Firecat* and Dommie swung himself in, not waiting for the ramp to come down. I pulled in after him.

"Nice cargo you got here, Gentrymort," Dommie said, looking around all *Firecat*'s empty hold still rigged for two.

"Just tossed kick, Dommie-bai. Here's locker compkey for it, see?" A Gentrymort is what I am, but I don't like being called that by bought law.

He took the key to the tradelocker and tossed it up and down a bit before he tucked it away, hoping I guess to terrify me into special pleading. "Wouldn't want you to lose it, sweetheart. Stop by my office before you lift and I'll give you the payoff."

Or half of it, maybe, if I was that lucky. I would of cried myself to sleep for sure if the locker key was where the money was this trip. Fine. I been shookdown before. But Dommie still didn't leave.

"Rokeach botanicals, eh? Pretty odd cargo to pick up on Wanderweb, isn't it? Not a lot of money in it. Hardly enough to cover expenses, I'd say. I wonder what else you might have—found—on Wanderweb."

For once in one of these sweet scenarios, I was stone innocent. Or ignorant, anyway.

"When you figure it out, Dommie, let me know. What you see is what you get."

"Maybe I just ought to impound your ship, Gentrymort. I'm sure I could find enough violations to put you down on the ground with the rest of us for a real long time."

Terrific. A bored bent Teaser—my favorite veggie.

"Then bring on the hellhounds, Dommie, and let us all in on the fun. And while you're at it, o'nobly-born, you might start thinking about how much fun you're going to have patterolling the Chullites in a two-man jaeger."

"Careful, Butterfly," said Paladin in my ear.

Dommie slugged me back against the bulkhead like a man with something on his mind.

"You wouldn't be threatening me, would you, you hack Indie?" He tightened up, and it was an effort to breathe, but I made it.

"Wouldn't threaten *legitimates,* Dommie—or even you. Just want to mention you pull my ticket and I sing like a well-tuned goforth to Guild, to Board of Inquiry, to many-a-many." Paladin had enough notes on Dommie's fun-and-games to at least start a official inquest. It was one of those happy thoughts that keep you warm on those cold galactic nights.

After awhiles Dommie let go. I dropped to the deck and leaned back against the crash pads, rubbing my throat.

Dommie didn't much care for my expression, and I didn't much care for what came next. Good fellowship slid over his face like a cheap paint-job under pressure.

"Hey, St. Cyr, you got me all wrong. I'm on your side. I've seen what happens when a small-time smuggler like you gets mixed up in something too big for her. You're in way over your head, stardancer; if you back off now, maybe you and me could get together; do some business. You should think about it."

"Je, Dommie. I'll surely do that," I said from the deck.

He left with my locker key in his pocket, and I buttoned up my Best Girl real tight and thought hard.

We had started out with the traditional wondershow between the Bent Teaser and the Noble Gentrymort—the one as usually ends up with me taking a few shots to the ribs and Dommie walking off with his vigorish-of-choice—but somewhere along Act Two we got sidetracked. I was just about willing to bet Dommie wanted to get on my good side.

"Shall I place the file on Trade Customs and Commerce official Dominich Fenrir's extortion racket on Kiffit in the open banks of the Kiffit Palace of Justice computers when we leave?" said Paladin.

"Oh, sure, why not? Make up some extras, while you're at it." If the Office of the Question did a personapeel on him looking for proof of Paladin's farcing he'd be cleared, of course, but by then there wouldn't be much left.

I sluiced Kiffit-Port's metered water over my head and neck and thought about Dommie's visit until I decided it'd make less sense than a hellflower's logic. Then I went to get tools to peel up my deck.

"Dommie-bai wanted into *Firecat* because he thought he was going to see something," I said to Paladin while I worked. "And when he didn't see what he was after he tried to shake it loose. What am I mixed up in, Pally-che-bai, that's too big for me?"

"Valijon Starbringer," Paladin said flatly.

He hadn't told me about Tiggy's safe arrival at the Guildhouse—or arrest—yet, and I guessed I'd have to wait until we got back to angeltown to hear it.

"That Dommie knows about," I amended. "Anyway, Pally, Tiggy's old business." It didn't sound true, and I wondered why.

"Dominich Fenrir does not know about Valijon Starbringer," said my silent partner, back from a jaunt in the Port computers to make sure. "However, Customs Officer Fenrir *has* recently undertaken a clandestine alliance with the saurian crimelord Kroon'Vannet. Fenrir is being paid a retainer for unspecified duties. There is no mention of you in connection with any illegality." And Paladin was not going to take this glowing opportunity to tell me Tiggy was restored to the bosom of his one-an-onlies. Sigh.

"Kroon'Vannet," I said, remembering. Vannet was one of those nighttime men that give lizards a bad name. He wanted a piece of everything that wasn't nailed down and didn't think he shouldn't have it just because he slid off the cold end of the Chernovsky scale. The Phoenix Empire, Paladin tells me, is real accommodating as long as your B-pop hits somewhere in the middle, like mine would if I wasn't a dicty, and real hostile if you're a wiggly. That's why the Outfar is full of wigglies pretending they're citizens. Some don't want to just pretend. Vannet was two of them.

"So what am I supposed to back off of, babby-bai?"

"I don't know," said Paladin. That made two of us, but Pally always says organics aren't very bright.

T'hell with Dommie Fenrir and his live talkingbook theater. I pulled the money-load out on the deck and wished I could believe it was what Dommie was after, but that didn't fit with the "friendly warning." Ignorance was part of what I was being paid for, but stupidity isn't my hobby. Paladin and me'd scanned them back on Wanderweb and found we was shipping gems of some kind. Boring.

"N'portado. Pally, soon as we toss this lot, we're making for Coldwater, deadhead, and get t'hell out of the way of Teasers with brain fever."

Have always said that if I ever get the chance to follow my own advice I'll be dangerous.

*   *   *   *   *

Insert #5: Paladin's Log

It is fortunate that Interphon, the lingua franca of deep space, is not as universal as its adherents believe, and that while Valijon Starbringer and Butterfly St. Cyr were both speaking Interphon, they were not speaking the same language.

This interface of bewilderment was entirely to Butterfly's advantage, since so long as Valijon could not determine precisely what she had said, he could not determine whether he needed to "purify his honor," and thus he left her without making any decision.

From the moment of its standardization Interphon had begun to break down into dialectical forms. This breakdown, unlike previous linguistic breakdowns, is occurring along lines of profession, not lines of astrography. In a few centuries, it is entirely likely that a commercial pilot, or "stardancer," will not be able to understand the Interphon of the inhabitants of the planets he visits. The end of the Empire is foreshadowed by the fact of a universal language being worried into rags by a dozen jealous peoples.

The scope of the disintegration is sharply indicated in the division between "bonecracks" and "bodysnatchers"—i.e., physicians who treat mercenaries and ground-based personnel and physicians who treat pilots and noncombatant exo-planetary personnel. Why should two branches of the same discipline—medicine—polarize to the extent of evolving two incompatible specialized vocabularies of mutual in-comprehension to deal with the same subject? I believe the answer has to do with the organic love of novelty for its own sake, even when not particularly desirable.

I also believe it will eventually destroy this Empire. No astropoliti-cal body can be properly administered without a common language.

In fact, the Phoenix Empire is decaying now. Within living memory Kiffit was a thriving settlement in the center of Imperial trade. Now it is an outpost, without sufficient population to support an expanding economy. Any check of uncensored statistics will prove this: each year more people leave Kiffit than settle or are born there. But in the Phoenix Empire statistics are not uncensored.

It is the same everywhere. The frontiers contract, more and more fringe worlds break away from the central government. It has been going on for centuries; the war that destroyed the Old Federation shat-tered a community of worlds far larger than the Empire. The Hamati Confederacy and the Believers Sodality were once both part of the Federation. The Empire has lost control over them, just as each century it loses dominion over more of its frontier.

Someday a war will come that will drive the Empire into a frag-mented barbarism, and even the name of Empire will perish. The tech-nology that supports its economy will be lost, and all that will remain will be apes scavenging in a boneyard, looking up at the stars.

5

Malice In Wondertown

Kiffit's one of the few places in the Outfar where the port city was there before the port—a ancient and valued member of our varied and colorful Empire. Paladin says Kiffit used to be bigger and thriving, but it was fine with me if it wasn't now. The parts of it I was interested in still seemed in good enough shape to me.

By now the horizon'd risen and cut off Kiffit's primary, and the Kiffit-Port security lighting wasn't on yet. Bad light's saved more lives than bodysnatchers in my line of work, so that was the time I picked to head out.

*   *   *

The Elephant and Starcastle in Borderline is where the Gentry on Kiffit hang their heat. Like any other hooch servicing a port, the Starcastle's on a full-rotation sked. Stardancers on the up-and-out aren't going to rearrange their circadians every time they downfall.

I didn't have any trouble getting a room with no view and a box with locks sunk into the floor. I'd have to be more of an idiot than even Pally thought I was to cold-call on a total stranger carrying 3K of illegal. The lockbox was the reason I'd rented the room.

I put the densepaks under lock and seal and threw enough of my own stuff around to make it look natural. It was after full-dark when I went down to sightsee in the unregulated planetary air.

The early evening streets was full of fellahim and grubbers tied to planetary rotation. I saw Company men from Directorate ships in their lovely gray leathers, Indie crews trooping their colors like a pack of bandarlog, and the kiddies that catered to both. Borderline's a planned city, which means that after a certain point the plans give out and there's nothing but a sprawl of back-alley mazes. If you fight your way through them long enough, you reach Borderline New City, which is also nice and tidy.

I'd checked at the PortServices shop and found where the Azarine Guildhouse was, but Tiggy'd made that none of my concern. The address I had from Gibberfur was for a transient outhostel called Danbourg Strail that was a little farther out. Joytown was on left, and behind me and to the right was the commercial port towers. Company again, rot them, with their stranglehold on Mid-Worlds and Directorate shipping and their nasty way of holing any Indie ship they run into, just for kicks. Guild sanctions don't mean a helluva lot to them.

I kept going. Eventually I left wondertown behind; I didn't mind the walk, and it's always good to know the ground you may have to retreat over later.

I was a couple kliks from the port, and all the way to the thin edge of the city planners' good intentions. The area I was in now had been razed for new building but no buildings had gone up. It was being used as sort of a open-air market; unregulated and ramshackle. About as thriving as any place in Borderline was, which wasn't saying lots. My destination was just the other side.

The Danbourg Strail was the kind of outhostel where you usually go to sell things you don't own. I went on up to the cubie-number I'd been given back on Wanderweb. According to Gibberfur, Moke Rahone kept regular hours here and these were those.

I'd also been told to call before I came. Sure I would. And maybe my kick would waft in here on the wings of song, too.

Punched the bell. The door said it belonged-along Moke Rahone, specialist in curiosa. It wasn't powered, but it wasn't locked either. I slid it back and looked inside.

There was a empty waiting area, full of vitrines that were full of junk. I walked in.

"Yo, che-bai, je tuerre? Art t'home, forbye?" I said in broad patwa. Nobody answered this brilliant conversational sally, but maybe Moke Rahone, dealer in curiosa, didn't like being shouted at.

There was a door with the Intersign glyph for "boss inside" on it, and I opened that one too.

Kiffit is a dry planet. It was wet in that cubie, and dark. I stood there long enough for my nose to tell me what the smell was, and then I backed out. Then I waited a moment, got my torch out of my pocket, and went back in.

I've slaughtered pigs and I've killed men, but it wasn't like either one. When I was ten years old a field hand on our farm got caught in the harvester. He was half-shredded before we could stop the team, and the sweet-metal stink was just like this.

Moke Rahone'd been human. Funny how your body knows a smell before your brain does.

Brother Rahone hadn't got caught in a harvester, though. I turned the torch on him and studied what I saw like my life depended on it, which it might.

Somebody'd nailed Moke Rahone to his desk and butchered him open. It was dainty-like. Real bodysnatcher work, done with something sharp—something that didn't burn like a pocket laser or chew up the meat like a vibro.

What this meant to me was that Brother Rahone wasn't in the paying for cargo business anymore, which put me in what Paladin calls your basic delicate moral quandary, because I had to deliver Gibberfur's cargo to someone or call in the Guild. Terrific.

And there was one other thing. It was sticking up out of Rahone's insides and it hadn't been part of his original manifest. Hadn't noticed it before in the general confusion, but it might tell me who killed him, and who might be interested in taking over his cargo.

"Trouble, Butterfly?" said Paladin through the RTS.

I rubbed my jaw where it felt electric-furry. "Um. Rahone's retired from darktrade business. Messy."

I pulled off my glove and yanked out the optional extra somebody'd left with Brother Rahone. What I got for my trouble was long and thin, pointed at one end and with feathers at the other. It was mostly red, but where it was dry it was a kind of blue animal bone with carving on it.

I'd seen bone like that before. In The Knife Worth A Afterlife. Hellflower work.

I wondered how Tiggy'd got the whistle on my kick and its new home and why he cared. Hellflower honor, probably—making sure I didn't see the profit I'd dragged him out of his way to get. I wrapped up the wand in a piece of thermofax I found. Maybe I'd take it back to him up close and personal.

I'd just shut the door of the inner room behind me when the outer door opened. The hellflower wasn't Tiggy, but he looked real pleased to see me anyway.

"*Ea, higna,*" the hellflower said. Then he went for his heat.

I'd decided more than a week ago that hellflowers was bad news, which gave me almost enough edge on this one to get out of the way. I went down behind a bench so his first shot went high and then I sprayed the room with blaster fire, hoping to get lucky.

I didn't. The bench stopped his first bolt, so I picked it up and threw it at him. He thought that was real amusing. He threw it back, but I wasn't waiting around for the critical reviews and had already made it back through the inner door into Brother Rahone's office.

I found the lock in the dark and used it. The light switch was next to it. With room lights the thing on the desk looked even worse. The smell was something awful and this time I noticed that the floor was covered in blood.

"*Higna, yai,*" said this friendly conversational voice from the other side of the door. The hellflower wasn't mad—far from it, the voice seemed to say. He liked my style. We could be best buddies.

I wondered if *higna* was better than *chaudatu.* He said some other things. I caught about one word in seven and understood not any.

"Butterfly?" said Paladin.

"Shut up." Paladin couldn't hear anything at all but me and even if he could there was nothing he could do.

What a lousy way to run a communications link.

If I was Brother Rahone, dealer in curiosa, I'd have a back way out. I shoved what was left of the late Rahone off his desk and started going through the contents to find it. My best buddy on the other side of the door lost patience. He said something in a more-in-sorrow-than-in-anger voice, and then there was a real determined thump at the door. It'd take him about a second and a half to decide to blow it.

I found a control panel in the desk, hidden well enough that I was pretty sure it didn't just control the outside door. I bashed the buttons all at once, just for luck, and heard the slow grinding of the hidden door. Too slow.

I heard the prefire whine of a blaster and ducked under the desk. I wedged myself in as high off the floor as I could get about the time the hellflower blew the door and stalked in.

Rahone's remains didn't even slow him down. I'd bet he'd seen them earlier, maybe while they was still lively. He was wearing blue leather boots with jeweled spurs and gilded scrolling stamped into the leather and it was a good bet he wasn't out to roll me for petty cash. He said something real nasty in helltongue when he saw the open door and walked around the desk to get a better look at the way he thought I'd gone.

I swept the floor with blaster fire and took him off at the ankles. He went over backwards and I got him a couple more times going down.

That bought me enough time to come out from under the desk and catch a throwing-spike from him through my skill-wrist. The spike was barbed, and every twitch drove it in deeper. I dropped my heat and it slid in Rahone's blood way the hell out of reach.

I scrabbled at my other blaster left-handed and got it up and ready to go before I realized there wasn't much reason to. My playmate had signed the lease on his real estate and was leaving on the Long Orbit.

I got up from behind the desk and looked at him. He was pretty much gone below his waist and what was still there was medium-well done. He wasn't breathing.

I went around the desk and picked up my other blaster, careful. Had to put away the one I was holding to do it. The wrist he'd spiked was already beginning to swell, but it wasn't leaking much; he'd missed the veins.

Maybe I should of put a bolt into him to be sure, but I didn't think anyone could take that kind of damage and live.

I was wrong.

I had to step over him to get to the door. He bucked when I got close to him and dragged me down. His fingers was wrapped around my throat and his rings dug into my jaw. I caught myself on the wrist he'd spiked and the whole room seemed to fill with bright haze for the couple of centuries it took me to bring my blaster up. Then I pumped plasma Miltowns into him until the world went away.

*   *   *

Paladin was yelling in my ear. I coughed myself awake and kicked a body off me and coughed some more. Then I sat up.

There was someone pouring ice water over my right hand. I looked down and saw bright cheery rivulets of blood chuckling merrily down, gaudy and inexhaustible and mine all mine.

My glove was soaked and stiff and the skin ballooned between it and the knife sheath on my wrist. The throwing-spike stuck out both sides. That last handstand had sawed the spike through a vein, looked like.

"Butterfly, I know you are not dead. The transponder would tell me if you were dead and it has not. Therefore you are not dead and are capable of responding to me. Butterfly!"

"Here," I croaked. "Shut up." And let me bleed to death in peace and quiet.

The room was burning; the kind of low smoky fire you get discharging a few plasma-packets too many at a combustible surface. I smelled the winy rankness of burnt tilo and the homey smell of cooked meat.

"Butterfly." Just to let me know Paladin'd appreciate a explanation at my earliest convenience.

"Hellflower dusted Moke Rahone. Hurt me, bai, not too bad."

Liar.

Getting to my feet was a major event and started me choking again. I was still holding my blood-covered blaster in my left hand. There was a red light flashing on and off over the open back way out. I sat back on the edge of the desk and wondered if I really wanted to walk that far.

"Butterfly, you are not all right. What is the extent of your injuries, and what is the current status of the alMayne?"

"Dead, and he got me through the wrist with some kind of spike." Which was going to have to come out before I went anywhere or I'd be dead; there was no way I could get a pressure bandage on that wrist with the spike in it. And if the hellflower lifetaker had backup waiting downbelow, I'd be dead anyway.

"Did you kill him?"

Trust Pally to fix on the irrelevant. "Course not. He died of pure melancholy and displeasure, like they say in the talkingbooks." That brought on another spasm of coughing. Paladin waited until I finished.

"You will have to bandage your injury and get back to the Starcastle. Can you walk that far?"

"Piece of cake."

I stood up and the ground rock-rolled on invisible gimbals. I sat down again and pulled out my vibro.

"Is there something you are not telling me about the situation, Butterfly?" Someday, somehow, I'd be able to get my hands on Paladin. The thought made life worth going on with.

"Building's on fire. Now shut up while I cut this damn spike loose."

*   *   *

It takes about half an hour to bleed to death from a severed hand, depending on your body mass. I was a little better off than that: only one or two veins was nicked. If I could stop bleeding now, I'd be fine. If I couldn't, in a few hours tops I'd be unconscious and helpless and real, real noticeable.

I cut my wrist open some more using the vibro real gingerly and pushed the spike rest of the way through. It was all barbs and curves; brittle and vibro-sharp, and watching it squish through made me feel sick. When it was out I felt light and hollow. Shocky. Not good.

I took off my jacket and my shirt and sawed the shirt into strips and wrapped it around my wrist until the fingers went numb. I'd have to shoot left-handed if I ran into trouble, but it's a tough galaxy out there and I'd manage.

"Are you finished?" That was Pally, all sweetness and starlight.

"Yeah." I slid my jacket back on without too much trouble. By this time the room was full of smoke. I headed over to the back door and looked out. All there was was dark.

"Brother Rahone's back way out is some kind of dropshaft, looks like. Going out that way. 'Flower might have backup down on the street —it was a hellflower I think opened up Rahone and stuck some kind a alMayne gimcrack into him too. Gang-war?"

"Moke Rahone has no record of affiliation with Kroon'Vannet or any of his competition. Neither is he on record with the Azarine Guildhouse as hiring an alMayne or any other bodyguard, although the agreement need not have been registered there. Did the alMayne speak to you at all?"

"Oh, sure; we had lovely chat. A'course, since I don't speak helltongue we didn't exchange too many views before I blew his legs off."

Paladin shut up, and I used the quiet to work up my nerve. I could try to get out through the front, but if the hellflower had backup there was a slightly better chance of losing him if I went out through Rahone's hidden escape route. I tossed a few things into the shaft and they floated enough to make me sure it was a powered drop. Then I stepped out.

I fell faster than I wanted and the jar when I landed made it so I couldn't breathe for a minute. I shook the stars out of my eyes and looked around. The dropshaft had took me to street level in the back of the Danbourg Strail. There was no hellflowers in sight. I leaned against the wall and tried to look healthy. If I lost it here I wouldn't need hellflowers to finish me; there's brat-packs and priggers and all kinds of marginals in places like this.

And Paladin couldn't even send a floater-cab for me unless I could get as far as the planned part of Borderline on my own. They don't go outside it.

"What about Tiggy?" I said to kill time while trying not to faint. "Joyous reunion of missing heir with da, galaxy rejoices?"

"Nothing of that sort has been transmitted on any of the information bands I can access, public or restricted. I find this somewhat peculiar."

Terrific. "I find it lots peculiar. Bodywarp fetch-kitchens admit sweet babby che-bai unmourned long-lost?"

"I said no information, Butterfly—including admissions to medical facilities of any alMayne, clandestinely or otherwise. And you said you had no further interest in Valijon Starbringer."

"Have every interest in him making big public arrival splash and getting me off hook," I reminded him.

My makeshift bandage was already squishy with wet, but I could afford to bleed like that for awhiles if I had to. I started feeling better enough to think I wasn't going to die tonight.

"We provisioned and ready to lift?"

"*Firecat*'s supplies are at the docking ring. As soon as they are aboard, we are ready. Life-support systems are fully charged. Do you wish me to call for clearance now?"

"Ne, che-bai. Think Dommie's watching too close. But order a real good medkit to add to our stuff, if you can find one. Will get myself right at the Starcastle and be back to *Firecat* by horizonfall. We're golden."

"I hope so, Butterfly. Good luck."

It was still early evening. I hadn't been inside with Rahone and Brother Hellflower half an hour, if that.

* * * * *

Insert #6: Paladin's Log

The modern day is a technology of clumsy inelegancies. Limping and metal-poor, it scorns efficiency in deference to half-remembered wonders entombed in the Inappropriate Technology Act—a catalog of things the moderns cannot have and so declare undesirable.

If this were the Federation, none of this would have happened. Not only would Butterfly have been safe in a breedery, if she had not been I could simply have activated my remote maniples and physically assisted her. For that matter, if such creatures as hellflowers had existed during my first life, it would certainly have been impossible to misidentify any of them. Federation citizens wore subcutaneous implants with the necessary information micro-encoded in crystal.

But even if the Phoenix Empire were willing to use implants, the technology for the micro-encoding no longer exists, lost with so many other things in the pointless war against what its survivors call Libraries.

But I digress.

It might have been a coincidence that an alMayne was involved in the murder of Butterfly's client, and then again it might not. I dispatched a floater to wait for Butterfly at the point that she would cross over into Borderline Old City, and began tracing the Borderline computer network to see if it was possible to access a data-gathering port in her location. The vital signs transmitted to me by her Remote Transponder Sensor indicated that Butterfly was weak, but capable of reaching the floater under her own power. There was nothing further I could do for her at the moment. I devoted more of my resources to another problem.

Where was Valijon Starbringer?

The identification that I had forged for him had successfully passed him through the port gates a few minutes after he left *Firecat*. From his actions upon leaving Butterfly, he would seem to have had a destination in mind, but from the moment he left the port neither "Aurini Goldsong" nor Valijon Starbringer entered into any data transaction with the Kiffit/Borderline Central Data Net.

Perhaps he had discarded his false ID. And had I been hasty, even jealous, in attempting to discard him?

Butterfly must be returned to the human world from which I have taken her, and it must be done in such a way as to assure her of prosperity and safety. The protection of an alMayne GreatHouse, properly handled, could guarantee both.

Valijon could reasonably be expected to cooperate in my plans, but only if I could find him.

And only if he were not trying to kill Butterfly now.

*　　*　　*　　*　　*

They picked me up just inside the Grand Bazaar and didn't care who knew it. I glanced back when I twigged and saw two hellflowers—a head taller than everybody else in sight and hair like hammered platinum. And confident. Real confident.

I somehow didn't think sweet reason was going to have much effect on them. Told Paladin the glad news. He didn't say much.

Once I left the Bazaar I'd be an easy mark—easier, is to say. And for all I knew they was legit heat and had the *legitimates* on their side.

But I'd been in the Danbourg Strail, and I didn't think so. And I didn't think they was going to put me down easy if they got their hands on me, either. Then I looked around and saw salvation.

I slowed down and waited for the garden club to catch up with me, and while I was doing that I purely accidental came to a stop by a cookshack. The owner was deep-frying something unidentifiable in several liters of liquid grease and offering it to the helpless fellahim that wandered by.

"How much for to buy your kick, che-bai?"

I repeated it in a couple of dialects, cant, and patwa, before he got the idea. He named a figure and laughed.

"Butterfly, are you thinking?" Paladin sounded more worried by that than he had by anything so far tonight. "I am tracking you in the Grand Bazaar. I will counterfeit a civil disorder there, and when the Peacekeepers move in you can escape safely. All you have to do is—"

"Ne, let be, I'm inspired," I said.

I put credit plaques on the counter side-by-each and watched the cookshop owner's eyes bugout. Then I watched the hellflowers. They saw me see them and thought it was a fine joke. One of them was female; both together was pretty as hunting birds and just as far from human. I stood flat-footed and watched them come.

The owner scraped up his credit and started to leave. I grabbed a handful of his shirt and stopped him. Just let them get a little bit closer and he could go where he wanted. After they was set. After they was committed.

Just a tad bit closer, kinchin of the Void.

*   *   *

Your basic blaster is a lovely toy—Paladin says it contains the basic technology for our entire culture. That means given a working blaster, smarts, and lots of free time, a person could deduce and build everything from highliners to palaceoids.

You see, a blaster don't throw a inert projectile. Blaster fires itty-bitty controlled fusion reaction wrapped in a magnetic envelope. Unwrap it, and all you have's a flash of light. But let the envelope hit something, and all that heat and force comes out along the rupture-line in a coherent directed star-hot pulse that is one reason I've lived to be as old as I am. Fusion reaction + magnetic bottle = culture. Simple.

*　　*　　*

The hellflowers split up when they reached the cookshack and started coming around it from both sides. I dropped the cook and he started running. Then I drew my blaster and fired at the deep-fryer.

The grease had been hot. Now it was incandescent. It exploded in a boiling fireball over my head and going west, and I snapped off a shot at the hellflower as hadn't been flash-fried and ran.

Two down. How many more? And would Prettybird #2 follow me or stay with her well-done partner?

I cut off High Street as soon as I could, and two turns had me lost in the back street warren. I wanted height; I'd aced one 'flower by not being where he expected; why not do it twice?

No joy getting onto the roof one-handed but I managed. I felt safer here but it wasn't going to last. I was sweating hot and cold at once and my hands was shaking so hard I couldn't shoot myself in the foot to save my life.

"Butterfly, what have you done?"

I could see smoke rising over the Grand Bazaar. Somewhere down there—if I was lucky—was two cooked hellflowers, and probably a crowd giving a inaccurate description of the crazy stardancer to assembling *legitimates* at this very moment. So I needed to stop looking like a stardancer, or at least get back to where they was thick upon the ground. And right now I didn't even think I could stand up.

"Butterfly, are you there?"

"Someday, Pally, you going to tell me where and t'hell else would I be? 'Sponder's in my jawbone, too reet?"

He ignored that. "What happened?"

"Two more 'flowers. Dead, I think. What do they want with me, Pally? I didn't frag their kinchin-bai—"

"Stay there," said Paladin, so I did.

*　　*　　*

I don't know where he stole it, or how he made it fly outside of the New City grid. And it was probably as conspicuous as hell, but right now I didn't care. The floater touched down on my rooftop and I pulled myself inside.

"Back to *Firecat,* Paladin. We gone." To hell with Moke Rahone's cargo. If hellflowers wanted me, I wanted out.

"I don't think that would be wise. There is an unknown person here at *Firecat.* I believe he must have used your last delivery as cover. He is between your supplies and the docking ring fire wall."

"Oh, bai, needed to hear that, forbye." My hand felt like it belonged to somebody else, and I felt limper than a simple evening's brawl would cover. "Starcastle?"

"It seems the safest choice. You can tend to your injuries while I attempt to discover who is waiting for you here."

I lay back and let the breeze blow over me. Whatever it was I was in the middle of, I wanted out.

Gang-war? Nighttime men don't frag stardancers.

Hellflower honor? Only hellflower I knew was Tiggy Stardust, and Tiggy his own self hadn't known where I was going in Borderline. He hadn't looked like he cared, neither, true-tell.

Fenrir? Why would Fenrir want to hire somebody to kill me when he could do it himself for free?

Nothing I could think of made any sense at all.

*   *   *

It was the middle of Kiffit's dark period, and good little fellahim were buttoned up in their racks. I could tell when the floater hit wondertown by the way the streets filled up. Nobody paid me or my blood no nevermind when I got out at the Starcastle.

Maybe there are bars that won't sell you an Imperial battle-aid kit along with a box of burntwine, but I've never been in any of them. I clutched the box with the Imperial Phoenix on it to my bosom like hard credit on payday and made it to my cubie on habit alone.

Somebody'd been here. I rolled the door back and the first thing I thought was there was no point to come back here because I'd been set up. But Paladin could hear inside and said there wasn't anybody here.

I barred the door again and blanked the windows and decided it was just a tossing and farcing. But my lockbox was still cherry, and the rest of my kit was all there, spread from core to rim by somebody who had no interest in mere worldlies.

Then I saw the coin, and what it put into my system almost made the battle-aid kit unnecessary.

*   *   *

As previously noted, all members of the Azarine Coalition have their little quirks. You can noodle the alMayne in the street by the way he lives in a world all his own and carries a knife to help him do it. Felix, now, are real organized—they form companies, wear matching uniforms, and are cuter'n hell. Dedicated.

Ghadri are individualists. They got another real recognizable genotype—short, wide, and overmuscled—file their teeth, tattoo their faces, and work in groups of five. They're found in High Jump crews, special weapons merc teams, and—more'n any other Coalition race—assassins. Ghadri are solid on the credit standard, got no honor I ever heard of, and like to coast on their rep. It'll stand the weight.

*   *   *

I picked up the coin. It was round, metal, thick; greasy to the touch and unstable, like it was liquid inside. Ghadri like to pay you off to stay out of their way. I was being paid off. Oricalchun coin'd redeem in any Azarine Guildhouse in the Empire for a bribe indexed to the importance of the job the Ghadri were doing. I could even check it there before deciding whether to accept.

I dropped it and dumped the battle-aid kit on the bed.

"Yo, Pally, you there?"

"As the great philosopher of the eleven-hundredth Year of Imperial Grace once said, where else would I be?"

Right. "How's houseguest?"

"Still there. And before you ask, there is still no report that Valijon Starbringer has been recovered."

"Got problems of my own—Ghadri wolfpack tossed my crib and warned me off. Only didn't tell me from what."

"Perhaps from the same matter Dominich Fenrir wishes you to avoid?"

I sat down on the bed next to the battle-aid kit and popped the locks. All that lovely illegal battletech glittered back at me.

"Bai, would love for to avoid it—tell me what."

"Perhaps from meeting Moke Rahone?" Paladin didn't sound convinced.

"Wolfpack must've been tossing this place about when Brother Rahone was getting illegal chop-an-channel. Even I am not dumb enough to warn body to not do something after they gone and done it."

I pulled out some designer alkaloids in the vial with the Intersign glyphs "Eat Me First" on it. The room snapped into sharp focus and all the pain I'd ever had went away.

"Imperial Armory, I love you," I said out loud.

Battle-aid kits is better than money some places; everybody wants what the Imperial Space Marines carry into battle to make sure they carry on in battle. The metabolic enhancers alone are worth the price of admission. I sliced my makeshift bandage off and poured sterile wash over the wrist, then disinfectant.

"So what we got here is your common-or-garden three problems: Fenrir wants me to get lost, Ghadri want me to stay out, and some hellflowers sliced Moke Rahone and just plain want me. And why is one of the many things I don't know." I wondered if my old sweetheart Silver Dagger was still on Kiffit, what she knew, and what she'd tell.

While I was talking I squeezed out a dollop of slow-set molecular glue and smeared it all over the hole in my wrist. That started it bleeding in good earnest again, but in a minute or so it wouldn't matter. I hunted around in the kit for the right size pressure-seal adjustable biopak.

"Do you have the 'gimcrack' you removed from the body?" Paladin wanted to know at that inopportune moment.

"Uh—je. S'here. Justaminnit." The biopak went on like a glove; wrapped my wrist and palm and left fingers and thumb free. I set it in place and flipped the switch. It settled in with a huff of air and a compression that hurt even through "Eat Me First." I waited until the built-in timer turned green and then drank what was in the "After-Fix" bottle. When that hit I couldn't feel the wrist anymore. So I pulled out the wand and described it for Paladin.

"I cannot be certain without seeing it, Butterfly, but what you seem to be describing is a *pheon*—an alMayne vendetta wand."

Paladin spends his spare time knowing everything about everything.

"So Rahone insulted a hellflower?"

I hoped.

"No."

"Pally-che-bai, has been long night and is going to be longer one, and I'm sure and t'hell not going to play Twenty Questions with you."

"The *pheon*," recited Paladin the way he does when he's reading something else, "or alMayne vendetta wand, is normally only employed among the alMayne, the Gentle People, themselves. The *pheon* may be engraved with from one to seven rings. One ring indicates that the subject of the vendetta is a sole individual, seven rings indicates that the subject's entire family to the seventh remove of kinship is to be eliminated. Outside scholars generally agree that formal initiation of the vendetta occurs when the designated subject sees the *pheon,* which is commonly presented in the ritually-murdered body of a servant or dependent of the subject. This servant is, however, considered not subject to the rules of vendetta and reprisals for his or her murder may be exacted irrespective to the progress of the vendetta.

"It is considered extremely bad form in high alMayne culture to begin a vendetta antecedent to the formal presentation of the *pheon,* which display is the signal for the commencement of the stylized hostilities which mark the highest flowering of—"

"Fap," I said, looking at the wand. Up near the dry end it had a groove carved in deep, all the way around. One ring vendetta. Just me. And meant for me, if Pally was true-telling, not for Rahone.

"Tiggy was really mad?" I suggested. But he didn't know where I was going on Kiffit, and besides. . . . "But I ain't hellflower, Pally."

"In certain rare cases vendetta will be declared against non-alMayne. Such declarations nearly always occur in conjunction with a criminal proceeding initiated by alMayne under the laws of the Codex Imperador. If the subject has committed no act illegal under the Codex Imperador, he, or more commonly, his estate, can prosecute the entire matter as—"

"I got a new rap on me I don't know?"

That got Paladin to shut up while he checked the hot-sheet traffic that had come in to Kiffit over the last two weeks and I tried to think of something I'd done to a hellflower that was actually illegal.

Kidnapping.

But Tiggy didn't know where I was going, dammit. . . .

"Nothing, Butterfly."

Well, scratch that idea. There was a big supply of metabolic enhancers in the aid-kit; I reached for them and hesitated. Better not. I didn't need them if it was just a matter of boarding *Firecat* and having Paladin Thread the Needle for me.

"Nevertheless, the probability is higher that you are being pursued by Valijon Starbringer's retainers than by a group of unrelated alMayne. It would also explain the ease with which you eluded them."

"Ease!"

"If the alMayne who pursued you had been professional killers, you would be dead now, Butterfly."

If they'd been professional. If they hadn't been cocksure and overconfident against a poor helpless *chaudatu.* If two of them'd come into Rahone's office instead of one. I ran my hand over the biopak and shuddered.

"Any news on the boyfriend out at *Firecat?*"

"He has moved out of range of the hatch pickup, which is the only component of *Firecat*'s external sensors useful in a planetary atmosphere."

"In other words, no."

"I believe I said that, Butterfly."

I was starting to get hungry, now that I knew I was going to live, but there was things more important than food. I went and pulled the lockbox out from where the Ghadri had shoved it in their smash-and-toss. Moke Rahone's cargo was Undeliverable As Addressed, and that meant all bets were off.

I put my thumb on the lit glyph for "locked container" and it changed to "unlocked container." I pulled out all six densepaks, and split the first one open with the aid-kit scalpel.

"Holy Mother Night." It was the big score for Brother Rahone all right, and real too bad he didn't live to see it.

"Butterfly, you do realize that I have no way of seeing what you are doing?" Paladin said. I rubbed my jaw.

"Oh. Sorry. Just found out what we was shipping. Lyricals."

Lyricals. Also called song-ice, or glory-of-the-snows. Little hyaloid nodules, not much to look at. You find them floating free in asteroid belts, if you're real lucky. Tap one, and it gives you pretty music. Set it up with the right exciter, and the harmonics are enough to send you off to sweet dreams and many happy returns for as long as your batteries hold out.

The one I had in my hand showed a refracted star on its surface. I turned it this way and that. Sometimes it looked transparent. I tapped it.

No sound. So I tapped it again, and I could of been tapping *Firecat* for all the ethereal music on offer. "On the other hand," I said to Paladin, "maybe they aren't."

I opened the other densepaks. Seven stones in all—five big and two little, all identical. None of them rang worth a damn.

I held a small one down on the table with surgical tongs—tricky, with the biopak—and cut it open with my vibro. It was solid.

"Paladin, tell the wicked darktrade 'legger what you get when you slice open a Lyrical."

"First: touching a vibroblade to the surface of the Lyrical gem will cause a unique mellifluous chiming. Second: the center of the gem-spheroid is composed of a distinctive hexagonal honeycomb, black or iridescent in color—"

"And what Gibberfur was shipping from Wanderweb was fakes."

There was a pause while Paladin thought about this.

"Counterfeit Lyricals?" said Paladin.

"Not even. Bad fakes. Solid and don't ring. Stopped me half-second—expert even less."

I might still have to square it with the Guild for not losing my kick to my Destination-of-Record, but on the other hand, who was going to lodge a complaint? Rahone?

"That makes absolutely no sense," said Paladin crossly. I could sympathize.

"Unless they're something else tricked out to look like Lyricals. But I doubt it. And y'know? I don't care." Getting off planet'd make everybody happy—why not do it? With luck I'd never know why I had a oricalchun, what Fenrir thought'd make me healthy, and if I could add another hellflower scalp to my tally and live through the experience. "I am going to go downstairs and get something to eat, and the minute you tell me the coast is clear I am going to scuttle back to *Firecat* like a good coward and be gone-along-gone so fast. . . ."

"Butterfly, I can see the person behind the crates at the docking ring now. It is Valijon Starbringer."

Tiggy? "What's he doing?"

"I do not know. He seems to be injured." Hurt'd be nothing in it once I got my hands on him, him and his three-ring-circus vendettas.

"And, Butterfly, I think he is being followed."

But if he was being followed. . . . I sat and laboriously rearranged some preconceptions.

The hellflowers in the bazaar couldn't be connected with Tiggy, because if they was, he wouldn't be back at the port, alone, injured, and followed.

If there was a vendetta against Tiggy (reasonable), why had *I* gotten the wand?

And if the wand wasn't meant for me, why was so many people out to get me?

I dumped the false Lyricals in various pockets and dragged my jacket on again. Then I flipped open the aid-kit and took out a double dose of enhancers. They probably wouldn't kill me. I could always buy a new liver.

"I'm going to the port." I popped the wafers into my mouth. They were too sweet, then too bitter.

"Butterfly, are you quite sure that is wise?"

The enhancer battledrugs hit, and in the rush I felt like I could just pick up the Starcastle by the ears and heave it over the next 'flower as came my way. I felt wonderful—like a Gentrymort what'd had her healing factor and metabolism stepped up by two: waterproof, shockproof, dust-resistant, and feeling no pain wherever glycogen reserves are sold. I was poetry in motion, all right.

"No. But he came to me for backup, Pally."

6

Smoke and Ash

I left the beautiful Elephant and Starcastle with a box of burntwine in one pocket, blaster in the other, and enough junk jewelry to buy part-shares in *Firecat*'s maintenance contract tucked here and there. I ignored the chemical blandishments singing sweet savage starfire in my mid-brain; I had three more doses of enhancer with me and if I had to take all of them I'd probably have more problems than just being dead could give me.

Right now I ought to be sitting in some fancy bathhouse in wondertown, watching the gravity dancers and getting all my sins absolved by something pretty. Oh yeah—and counting my payoff from Moke Rahone. Instead, I was torn up, hopped up, racked up, and walking into what was almost certainly a trap.

What had Tiggy Stardust run into that was so bad a hellflower couldn't handle it? I ate glucose and tried to keep an eye out for stray assassins.

*   *   *

I didn't go in through the main gate. I swung wide around the Company end of the port. It was empty except for one big highliner all floodlit and toplofty. I also sugarfooted around where they parked the big Indie ships with their crews of anywhere from thirty up, whole families and poor relations included. After I'd cleared them too, I walked along the outside of the fence to where they let gypsies and celestials dock. Little ships, old ships. Ships like mine.

The lights wasn't as bright and the service wasn't as good down here, and the fence was lower.

Dominich Fenrir knew something.

More'n that, he knew I was coming to Kiffit before I got here. That thought stopped me cold, and I faded back into a doorway to give it a little room. The buildings along the fence was condemned, derelict. A good place to think while looking over what was out on the field.

I'd only been downside an hour today when Fenrir came by. He'd known I was coming and he thought he knew something else. Something profitable.

Something on *Firecat?* I chased the thought around awhiles and shook my head. It wouldn't fit and I couldn't make it.

But Fenrir had known where I was coming from. He'd named my last port—which was not the one in my paperwork. Only Gibberfur there knew I was coming here.

Sweet. Factor A goes halvsies with bent Teaser and chouses his partner Factor B out of mondo valuta when Teaser steals cargo from stardancer. It's a sad old story.

The only trouble with it was that Gibberfur'd given me fakes to freight. Fakes, locked up real extra special, in a case he could be pretty damn sure any Gentry-legger'd refuse to take—

I wanted to pursue that little thought, but something distracted me. It was a flitting gray ghost shape moving between ships on the other side of the fence. I saw another one drift by just in front of me; he hit the fence with a ping-bang-boing and went over it just like I was planning to. I caught the glitter of expensive heat as he moved.

Oh, it was ladies' day at the Azarine Coalition, all right. I'd just seen two Ghadri—sweep men coming in from a Ghadri wolfpack.

I could think of only one reason they'd want all five of them in place before moving up.

"Ghadri wolfpack after Tiggy, che-bai," I told Paladin. Then I moved too.

I hit the fence fast and noisy, with the battledrugs singing encouragement in my veins. The sound my boots made hitting the ground on the other side echoed all through the parked ships. Didn't see anybody. Didn't expect to.

I ran from cover to cover down the line until I got to a likely-looking Free Trader and slid behind her fire wall. Within class, they dock ships by size at Imp Ports. Not too many ships *Firecat*'s size in dock, usually. She was next, and there was a long empty space between the Trader and my Best Girl.

I could see hoses going from her belly back to hookups in the fire wall, and a bunch of crates stacked around her ramp all armed to go off if they was burglared, and not a whole lot else. I couldn't see Tiggy or any of the Ghadri. With the noise I'd made showing up, I was pretty sure the Ghadri'd want to make sure of me before trying to finish him.

I fumbled in my flight jacket for the oricalchun and threw it out into the open space. It bounced on the crete with a sweet ringing sound. I knew what it was trying to buy, now.

The sound seemed to hang in the air, giving me the chance to think about what I was doing. Stupid. I'd been riding my luck to get this far. Pally'd been right—the 'flowers I'd dusted in the Grand Bazaar were amateurs.

These Ghadri were pros.

"I count three, Butterfly. One on top of *Firecat*. One on the ground between your position and here. The third one is under *Firecat*'s ramp," Paladin said through my implant.

But we was playing on my turf, with my rules, and my backups.

"When I give the word, I want a distraction. Something bright and noisy."

"Can do."

I started circling around. There might or might not be a Ghadri out there using the same cover to circle back. If Pally said he counted three, that's what there was. But Ghadri ran in fives. Was more sweeps still out? Or had Tiggy dusted some? How bad was he hurt? Could I count on him for backup?

It was too quiet. There was a city of several million lost souls not three hundred meters thataway and we could of been in the Ghost Capital of the Old Fed for all you noticed them. I wondered where Port Security was.

I scuttled on knees and fingers and could hear every noise my boots made and bet the Ghadri did too. I wondered if he was going to let me get all the way to my ship free and clear. Then there was a scuffling rush and he jumped me.

I hit the crete with my face and rolled enough to give him a boot in the belly. He wuffed and waded back in. No blasters—I should of figured the Ghadri wouldn't want anything showy. He tried to unscrew my head and I gave him my biopak to chew on and what he did to it probably would of upset me except for those nice battledrugs. Ghadri file their teeth.

Then he was on top and settling in. I let Brother Abriche-bai bang me against the crete until he got bored, and when he did I slid my vibro into him and rummaged around. He wasn't expecting me to be that strong. Better living through chemistry.

Everything almost but not quite hurt. I pushed the body off my chest and nicked his throat to be sure. The blood came slow, in the way that said there was no pump behind it.

I turned off the vibro and slipped it back into my boot. I was damn lucky I hadn't torn a tendon loose. You could cripple yourself with metabolic enhancers if you got careless.

I got up and tongued another enhancer tab. The world was painted in shades of black. There was two more Ghadri killers out there, and if I got them both I'd have three bodies to explain by morning and a dim view taken by the authorities of self-defense.

"The one beneath *Firecat* is moving toward you."

"Oke, brother. Come and dance with Mama," I said under my breath.

The Free Trader behind me was still dark. Her crew must be away in the wicked city—no wonder the Ghadri and me had the world to ourselves.

I couldn't see him but I knew he was coming. I gave him long enough to get halfway here.

"Hit it, Pally," I said, and slid my hand down over my left blaster.

All *Firecat*'s docking lights went on and her proximity klaxons sounded. The Ghadri was closer than I thought. I caught him twice in the chest even so, which was pretty good left-hand shooting. Then the ship lights went out and I ran for *Firecat* and hoped to get there before his partner recovered.

I slammed into the boxes at the foot of my ramp slightly too hard and sat down harder. There was a scrabble on the hull. Dragged my blaster up to track on it, but there was a flash and sizzle of somebody else shooting from behind the crates and what was left of the last Ghadri slid down over the hull curve and dropped damn near on my boots.

*   *   *

Talkingbooks always go on about "the horrible smell of cooking meat" after a gunfight. They're wrong. You catch a plasma-packet front and center and all anybody's going to smell is charcoal.

"Tiggy?" I said without moving. "It's me. You know—*chaudatu* what topped you out of Wanderweb? I'm coming round these-here boxes now bye-m-bye. Would appreciate it if you didn't shoot me."

Got to my feet. Nothing hurt. I felt much too fine. I wondered how much I'd be hurting without chemically-induced euphoria.

Paladin turned *Firecat*'s exterior lights back on low and opened the hatch. I went around all my catch-trapped crates of food and water and air and hollyvids and there was Tiggy. He was leaning back against the fire wall with the Estel-Shadowmaker I'd gave him in his lap. He opened his eyes when I got there.

"*Ea, chaudatu,* I knew you would come back," he said, real soft. Then his eyes rolled up in his head and he clocked out.

Yeah, and he also knew I had fusion for brains.

I got down and poked at him. He was still breathing, but the side of his head was sticky and hot. I couldn't see much in this light, and nothing in color. He was wearing the same clothes he'd left *Firecat* in, and they was in shreds. My fingers touched crumbling ash along his thigh and I bit down hard on my stomach and thought of the hellflower back at Rahone's. I wondered how Tiggy'd managed to get this far tagged like that.

Hurt. Bad hurt and he'd made it all this way, over the fence and all, with three Ghadri wolves waiting to pull him down. Running to the only one he knew on Kiffit that might help.

And I hadn't been here.

I didn't want to carry him anywhere, but I had work yet to do tonight and I couldn't just leave him. So I took Tiggy's handcannon and his godlost *arthame* away from him, talking the whole time in case he woke up, then I picked him up. He didn't weigh quite as much as *Firecat.* I put him down careful as I could on the deck in the hold.

I heard the sound of servomotors as Paladin manipulated internal sensors to look-see. I looked myself.

I'd seen worse, but not alive.

"Where's the god-damned medkit?" Please let Paladin have found one, and let it have been delivered, and not stolen.

"The medical supplies you requested are at the foot of the ramp. Valijon Starbringer is very badly hurt, Butterfly. Even a hellflower may not be able to survive such injury. Call the Guildhouse now and turn him over to them." The RTS tickled, but neither of us had any intention of running Class One High Book through external speakers.

"No."

"It was what you were going to do this morning. If he dies before—"

"Who sent the Ghadri?" The oricalchun proved they'd been hired.

They'd been after Tiggy, and warned me off. But no one knew Tiggy would be on Kiffit. Even Gibberfur didn't know that.

Paladin got all set to argue some more and then changed his mind. "Find their ID and I will tell you who they are, Butterfly."

*   *   *

I went down the ramp and brought up the older brother of the kit I'd bought at the Starcastle. It was a field-medic's kit, and it held enough stuff to stock my own surgery. I slugged back a quart of glucose out of it to give the enhancers in my system something to chew on, then I gave Tiggy everything I could find to get him right. He'd lived this long, he'd have to live a little longer on his lonesome: I didn't have time to work on him right now. When I'd done all the quick things I could do for him I went back outside.

I found the kiddy I'd knifed and the one I'd blasted. I took their ID and brought the bodies back to *Firecat* and piled them on top of the one that Tiggy'd iced. My clothes were soaked like I'd been standing in the rain, and it was all blood. The docking ring looked like a butcher shop.

For one long minute I seriously considered just walking away. No one could stop me. Even if they caught me they couldn't make me do what I was going to do next. I'd made a lot of stupid promises about how I wasn't never going to do things like this again. I'm a darktrader. It's clean honest work.

And if I jibbed now it wouldn't be just my neck, but Paladin and Tiggy's.

I got out my vibro and set it on the nearest crate.

Then I uncoupled the waste hose from *Firecat* and fed all three Ghadri down it. In pieces.

I had some damfool idea it'd buy me something not to have them found. If these three disappeared their replacements'd come a little slower next time.

I made my right hand do the work, barely. And when I'd finished the cutting I spent several dekaliters of Kiffit water sluicing down the docking ring. The stains left looked old.

And three Ghadri was gone without a trace. I hooked the hoses back to *Firecat* and went inside.

Tiggy was awake again. He'd got ahold of his sidearm and was pointing it at me.

"Go ahead," I said. "Make my day."

"I had to be sure it was you, she-captain," he said with the ghost of a grin. He let go his blaster and lay back, panting.

"If I wasn't me, we'd both be dead. Ship goes when I do, remember?"

I stripped off my clothes and threw them down the disposal. The boots and blaster-harness I'd been wearing was salvageable, just. There was blood all around my nails.

"The Ghadri," Tiggy said.

I took the ID I'd scavenged and put them where Paladin could get to work on them.

"You got one, babby, I got two. Leaves two unaccounted for."

"Dead." Tiggy was real sure about that.

"The Ghadri are registered out the of ab-Ghidr School of Ghadri Main," Paladin said. "Licensed as mercenaries, specialized as assassins. I am now checking records for Kiffit Immigration Control to see when they arrived here, and what their purpose was in coming to Kiffit." And who hired them, Pally, don't forget that.

"You have no idea what a load off my mind that is, hellflower," I said to Tiggy. "Now look, che-bai, you're hurt bad. Got stuff here for to fetch-kitchen—for to medical you. People with Ghadri Abri-che-bai after them shouldn't go to legit bodysnatchers, je?"

"No doctors," said Tiggy faintly. "Assassins." His skin looked shiny and tight.

"Butterfly, what will you do if he dies?" I shook my head. He wasn't going to die.

I unfolded and unfolded and unfolded the Imperial fetch-kitchen and got out the field medic manual. "Help us both to stay breathing awhiles longer if maybe you answer some questions, Tiggy-bai." And more, it'd distract him. He'd be needing that with what I was about to do to him.

"If honor allows." He was breathing like there wasn't any air, with all Kiffit out there free for the lungs.

"The Ghadri tactical group for which I have partial ID arrived on Kiffit from Tangervel fifty days ago. The three killed here were Abric, Abwehr, and Abaris. It is logical to assume that Abihu and Abriel were killed by Valijon Starbringer in Borderline as he has indicated. The group's passage to Kiffit was paid by Alaric Dragonflame, the alMayne who is the head of the combined alMayne Embassy and Guildhouse here. Once here, the Ghadri tactical group took up residence in the alMayne Guildhouse, a circumstance which suggests they were in the employ of someone there; an unusual probability if true. Alaric Dragonflame's father, Morido Dragonflame, is next in line to represent alMayne in the Azarine Coalition," Paladin finished off, sounding surprised. I'm sure he meant it to mean something, but I couldn't just now ask what.

I started peeling Tiggy out of his clothes. He looked like he'd been thrown off of every roof in Borderline, and that was just the small stuff.

"Remind me not to accept any invites to your parties, 'flower. You play rough." Tiggy looked pleased. Poor lost kinchin-bai. His skin was gray under the bronze-gold, cold and clammy to touch. I might be wrong about saving him.

But if the Ghadri had come from the Guildhouse that was the last place I could send him.

"From Imperial social notes available in the Borderline Main Banks, LessHouse Dragonflame seems to be a fairly influential member of one of the Chernbereth-Molkath GreatHouses. It is nonetheless anomalous for the head of a LessHouse to rise to as high a position in Imperial government as Morido Dragonflame has done. alMayne LessHouses roughly correspond to planet-linked realholders, as opposed to—" If it was the end of civilization as we know it, Paladin'd want to tell me why and what.

I started with Tiggy's head wound and went down from the top, cleaning and stitching as I went. Saved the leg for last. Maybe he'd pass out by then.

The painease started to take hold and his color got a little better. The manual said no metabolic enhancers before you finished cutting, but it didn't say why.

Was it better to cut live bodies or dead ones? The Ghadri hadn't felt anything. Tiggy would. There wasn't enough stuff in this kit to make him not.

"—Which makes it particularly odd that his son, Alaric Dragonflame, would be in such a comparatively minor post, and off-planet in addition," said Paladin, finishing up.

But if I hurt him enough, I might be able to save his life.

He was watching me. I smiled.

"As we last left thrilling wonderstory, hellflower glitterborn—that's you, Tiggy Stardust—had pulled heat on motherly High Jump captain—me—who took serious cop to spring him from Wanderweb gig." Tiggy unraveled that without too much trouble—guilty conscience.

"I had no choice. I—it was an honor matter. But you would not know of that."

"Ne, not me. Am honorless *chaudatu. Higna,* even," I said, finally remembering what the other hellflower'd called me back at Moke

Rahone's. "Been stiffed outta my feoff, delivering farced kick to official dead person, but—"

"*Higna?* You are not *higna, alarthme.* Two Ghadri are dead." Tiggy found that funny until I touched a sore spot and he winced.

"*Higna:* prey. *Alarthme:* knifeless one. *Chaudatu:* nonperson. All words are alMayne Common Tongue. *Alarthme* is a term of respect applied to those who do not possess an *arthame* but are nonetheless conditionally people," Paladin said.

Chaudatu, higna, alarthme—alMayne had lots of names for idiot.

"Yeah, only it's three Ghadri dead, and maybe two more in Borderline, and we was just about to get to how honor mixed you in with them, wonderchild."

Mostly Tiggy looked like he'd been through a standard-issue brawl. Somebody'd got close enough to bite him once, and one place he looked like he'd been dragged over something rough. Nothing broken, but hellflower bones don't break easy.

"I killed the others. Two in the city. I have to see my cousin!" He was starting to wander a little bit in the head. He tried to get up.

"It's a long walk from here, dammit. Lay down, che-bai, or I'll clock you. Now we're up to where honor left you no choice so's you did a fade soon as *Firecat* made downfall. Where did you go?"

Tiggy tossed his head back and forth against the blankets I'd put under him. His hair was rusty-pink with blood I hadn't tried to wash out.

"The House of Walls; the sacred enclosure. Where is my *arthame?*" He started feeling around for it and some of the cuts I'd closed started oozing again.

"Stop it. I'll get it. Lie still, dammit."

"Butterfly, you cannot possibly intend to arm a delirious alMayne. He will kill you!" Pally sounded so indignant it was funny.

"Yeah, yeah, yeah," I muttered under my breath. I got the knife out of his pile of bloody rags and put it in his hand. That quieted him down, but not Paladin.

"So I gave you the knife. So now you hold still and shut up and let me cut you. Je?" Maybe he'd pass out soon.

"*Dzain'domere.*" I started in on his feet.

He'd been barefoot all day and it showed. I was sweating from the battledrugs and Paladin turned down the humidity in *Firecat* again. It helped some. Looked at Tiggy and he was still conscious.

"So you went to House of Walls," I prompted him. Whatever that was. "And then?"

"Alaric Dragonflame. He said I must go to the TwiceBorn *chaudatu.* I went away, and in the street called Sharp I was attacked by the Wolves-Without-Honor. Ghadri are no match for the Gentle People," Tiggy finished with shaky satisfaction.

Gentle People. Figures that's what hellflowers'd call themselves when they was to home.

"Butterfly, Sharp Street is in the Azarine district near the Grand Bazaar. You passed it earlier this evening, as you were going from the Elephant and Starcastle to the Danbourg Strail. The House of Walls is the alMayne Embassy and Guildhouse. The 'TwiceBorn *chaudatu'* Valijon Starbringer mentions may be the Imperial Court officials in Borderline New City. If Valijon was attacked in Sharp Street after leaving the alMayne Guildhouse, he was heading away from New City." Paladin's voice had his very best "this is not an expression" expression.

Away from New City. On foot, in rags. Even I knew you didn't let relatives of the high-heat go wandering roundaround alone. They'd know who he was. alMayne Embassy'd be able to do a Verify on Tiggy sooner than instantly.

Dammit.

I put it all out of my mind for laters.

"You awake, Tiggy-che-bai?"

"I am awake, *alarthme,"* Tiggy whispered. His eyes had the glitter of pure exhaustion. I gave him some water and the last of the painease I dared give him and made sure the extra pad under his head was straight.

Damn hellflower constitution. A normal person'd be unconscious already for what I was going to do next.

"Look. You got tagged in the leg. You already know how bad. Have to open it out and clean it before I can wrap it, or you just going to get the Rot and die. It's going to hurt. Can use nerve-blocks, but if I give you any more painease, you might not wake up. Compre? Understand?"

"Do what you must, *alarthme;* I will not disgrace my House. If I die, you will take my *arthame* to my father? You will not let me die without walls? Please?" He tried to get up again. It was too easy to shove him flat and his skin was cold and wet under my hand.

"I'll take your knife to your da, Tiggy-bai, now shut up. Nobody's going to die." My free hand was shaking, and the other one in the biopak was pretty useless. I pulled the sterile drape off the burn. Tiggy was watching me to see what my face'd do, but I knew that dodge. "Piece of cake," I said, and looked sincere about it. He relaxed some.

I set up the manual from the field kit to show me where to sink the nerve-blocks. They went deep and held, but there wasn't a spinal block. Not in a field kit. What idiot'd do major surgery with only a field kit?

I picked up the scalpel and started cutting.

*   *   *

Most of the combat medicine in the Empire is alMayne-derived, Paladin told me once. alMayne fixers have this idea you don't want to live forever, just a while longer. The field-medic battle-aid kit Paladin'd got would damn near let me rebuild Tiggy from scratch, and the manual had Intersign glyphs for everything from conservation amputation to delivering a breech-birth from a merc in full powered armor, but what the manual said for an energy-weapon burn this size and color was coke and wrap and evac to outside body-shop for stabilization and repair soon as maybe.

Only I couldn't do that. I had to do what I could here, with what they'd gave me.

Stabilizing a blaster-burn meant cutting out the radioactive charcoal from the burn site. I tried to forget Tiggy was alive.

There was a timer in the manual for a simple conservation amputation procedure, and I set it. It ticked away, measuring percentages and the likelihood of termination from surgical shock.

I cut down to blood, and sprayed to seal the veins, and cut and scraped and sprayed and cut. The timer redlined, and I ignored it.

The kit had a biopak that was big enough. I pulled one out, and spread the stuff on Tiggy that the book said to, and dragged the biopak on and triggered it. The biopak huffed closed, sealing him from groin to knee.

"Is—"

"Valijon is still alive, Butterfly," Paladin said.

I crawled along my deck to Tiggy's top end and looked. He was breathing. He was out cold. He'd bitten through his lower lip but he hadn't made a sound.

I wiped the blood off his face, gentle like he could feel it. He'd have a limp when he woke up. If he woke up. If he lived.

Adrenaline and enhancers made everything sing for me, white and cold. I pulled out the nerve-blocks and mopped up more blood and then packed up what was left. I gave him glucose and enhancers and everything like the manual said to. Then I covered him up and tried to stop shaking.

"You did a good job, Butterfly. He should live."

"You wish he was dead." I wanted something to hit.

"No. I wish no harm to Valijon Starbringer. The fact that House Dragonflame is seeking to execute him changes matters. But that can wait. You should rest now."

"No. Load and lift. Have to kyte, need supplies. I'm good for it." I pulled the next to last enhancer and ate it. I wondered if I'd feel it when the tendons in my shoulders tore loose. Knew I wouldn't feel it when my liver quit. It's a little known fact that you can actually kill yourself totally dead if you run on battledrugs till you field-strip your endocrine system. Paladin knew it. I knew he knew it. And he didn't try to argue me out of taking more.

Without what I'd ordered I couldn't lift: no food, no water, no air. Prices are lower on Kiffit than Wanderweb; I'd been running on empty to get here and Tiggy'd wiped out my reserves. I had to get this stuff into *Firecat* if it killed me. I fetched and carried and dumped everything in a which-way heap on *Firecat*'s deck. Mother Night her own self couldn't save me from holing the hull if I had to lift before this load was stowed and dogged.

My right arm was numb from the elbow down and throbbed like a broken tooth, even through the battledrugs. There was Ghadri teeth marks in the biopak. One of these days I'd have to pop the seal on that and see what was under there. But right now I was busy.

I stopped halfway along to pop a meal-pak but I couldn't finish it. I remembered the burntwine I'd brought from Starcastle. The box was crushed flat but I had more in my supplies. The alcohol burned off as fast as I drank it. I didn't feel anything. The world was all about loading the same supplies I'd loaded a hundred times, and up and down and up *Firecat*'s ramp with Paladin prodding me everytime I stopped. And each time I brought a load up Tiggy was still alive, and every time I wondered if Dragonflame's *legitimates* was coming and I'd held us up too long, but I had to have this stuff or we couldn't fly.

Paladin told me over and over that Borderline was quiet and nobody was looking for us, but I kept forgetting.

All that blood.

Without remembering what came between I was standing back by the fire wall running Kiffit water over me. I couldn't see any crates.

"Butterfly." From the sound of it, Paladin'd been trying to get my attention for a long time.

"Je?"

"The supplies are loaded. You still have to stow them before you lift. You will injure Valijon if you do not. You need more medical supplies. You don't have clearance. I will have to order additional supplies and call for clearance and I cannot do that for five hours."

I didn't like it. I think if it had just been the clearance and more supplies I would have gone anyway—which shows how coked I was—but I couldn't lift without shifting cargo all over my deck. So I stayed.

It was early. Paladin gave me local time and Hours Since Downfall both. I got a box of glucose and a box of overproof neurotoxin and mixed them and went and sat starclad on *Firecat*'s landing strut.

The breeze that comes before horizonfall dried me off and I sat and drank. I was beyond tired, and the glucose made the enhancers sit up and sing again.

Everything was quiet. The lights from Borderline washed the sky out gray. Wayaway you could hear the keen and thud of cranes loading some Company highliner with whatever Kiffit had to offer. Peaceful. Normal.

"I got real problem, Pally-che-bai. Somebody don't like hellflowers," I said. "Don't like me too, seemingly."

"Alaric Dragonflame, in the parlance, 'set Valijon up.' He convinced him to go to Borderline New City on foot and alone, misdirected him, and sent Ghadri assassins, which he had previously hired and was holding in reserve, to kill him. The same mercenaries, aware of the connection between you and Valijon Starbringer, attempted to warn you against aiding him."

"Por'ke?" But why?

"Por'ke Wanderweb hot seat go hellflower for to chop-an-channel, jillybai?" said Paladin in patwa, sounding miffed. I shook my head a couple of times to see if maybe some brain cells'd jarred loose.

"Wanderweb Justiciary wanted to ice Tiggy because he dusted some heat, Pally, that's why. Nothing to do with Dragonflame."

"Granting Valijon did indeed kill the Guardsmen involved, and reserving the question of what caused the City Guard to accost him in the first place, why did not the Justiciary then notify the *Pledge of Honor* as soon as it had identified Valijon Starbringer?"

"Paladin, what t'hell had this got to do with Ghadri after Tiggy and glitterflowers after me severalmany lightyears away? Or with Dominich Fenrir?" I added for good measure. "Wanderweb Justiciary didn't ID Tiggy. Was in banks as Unknown alMayne 00001. I saw." I tossed the empty box back inside *Firecat* and rested my chin on my arms.

"It was not an accident that brought Valijon Starbringer to the surface of Wanderweb," Paladin said flat out. "Someone was attempting to kill him there. Someone still is."

*   *   *   *   *

Insert #7: Paladin's Log

If Valijon Starbringer had been identifiable on Wanderweb his life would have been in no danger. A fine would have been paid—if necessary, a scapegoat executed in his place. Free Ports operate on the profit motive. There could be no conceivable profit in allowing the death of an Ambassadorial delegate for any reason whatever.

Therefore he was not identifiable, and he could plausibly be expected to withhold the information of his identity. While standing heroically mute against all questioners palls after a few years, it is a beguiling pastime at fourteen.

The life of an honest citizen requires a mass of documentation breathtaking in scope, yet Valijon carried none. The person who deprived him of his identification before sending him to the surface of Wanderweb was attempting to kill him.

Someone—either aboard the *Pledge of Honor* or on Wanderweb—separated Valijon from his ID and waited for the inevitable (given the psychology of the alMayne) to happen. But this entity did not reckon with the possibility of interference from a captain-owner who had both a ship in port and the capability of suborning both the city computers and the Justiciary computers to effect Valijon's release from prison. If Butterflies-are-free Peace Sincere had not intervened, Valijon Starbringer would now be dead on Wanderweb.

I was originally mildly gratified to see Valijon return to *Firecat*. The matter of setting Butterfly free of me was not a simple one. For my plan to be practicable, she must be better off without me than with me. If Butterfly could take Valijon to his father, Kennor Starbringer would be indebted for his son's return. He would grant any boon, even to an Interdicted Barbarian. All that I know of the Empire indicates that citizenship is available even to a dicty for a price. Citizenship pays for all; if Butterfly acquired it there would be no warrants against her.

And I would be gone.

No Library is safe in the Phoenix Empire, nor any Librarian. For this plan to work, I must force Butterfly to seek out the *Pledge of Honor* without me.

Deciding how to do this was the least of my problems. Deciding whether it should be done at all had become, with the discovery of the Ghadri complicity, more than academic.

Who would benefit from the death of Valijon Starbringer—and how? From material available even in the undernourished Borderline bibliotek, I had the answer to that question.

When the son of Kennor Starbringer, Second Person of House Starborn and President of the Azarine Coalition, is murdered, there are certain things Kennor must do to remain an alMayne.

All of them are illegal under the Pax Imperador.

If Kennor does them, he will be arrested by the Imperial Court, tried, and executed. There will follow disaffection and upheaval on alMayne—and the appointment of a new Azarine Coalition delegate—Morido Dragonflame, whose son is Grandmaster on Kiffit.

If Kennor does not do them, he will no longer be considered al-Mayne. He will be hunted down by House Starbringer and executed—and the appointment of the new Azarine Coalition delegate follows.

It is possible that Dragonflame is innocent. He may have sent for the Ghadri as a reflection of market conditions on Kiffit. Butterfly and I had not yet reached Kiffit when they were sent for; the individual who could predict and chart the collection of random factors that brought Valijon to Kiffit would be far more efficient than Dragonflame has proved himself to be.

On the other hand, it would be possible, though not simple, for Wanderweb Free Port to identify Butterfly from her ship, and from security tapes made on the detention levels of Wanderweb Free Port Justiciary. It would be equally possible, though staggeringly difficult, to find who had most recently hired her and what her destination was.

It is at this point that a logical pattern grounded firmly on random chance begins to break down. Granted Butterfly's original involvement with Valijon and her subsequent rescue of him as pure accident and totally human coincidence—what happens next should follow logically from the factors involved.

Scenario #1: Persons who wish to secretly murder the Third Person of House Starborn, failing in their attempt on Wanderweb, track him and his rescuer to the Imperial Port of Kiffit, gambling that the smuggler-captain will head there next to deliver the cargo they know she carries. Alerting their agents on Kiffit—Dominich Fenrir and Alaric Dragonflame—they await the arrival of Butterfly and Valijon. Fenrir warns Butterfly not to involve herself, Dragonflame sends assassins after Valijon.

Why does no one feel it necessary to murder Butterfly, a witness to the plot, who may have been told any number of things by Valijon Starbringer and could at any moment attempt to contact Kennor Starbringer and tell him what she knows?

If the alMayne that Butterfly killed and who attempted to kill her are assumed to be members of Dragonflame's household, the complexities of the matter become even more farcical. Why were they not sent after Valijon instead? Surely alMayne would have been better equipped to deal with or defeat Valijon Starbringer. Was Dragonflame engaged in acts so honorless that the members of his own household would refuse to participate?

I would give much to have been present on the occasion that Alaric Dragonflame, lord of an alMayne LessHouse, told his alMayne *comites* that they must declare high ritual vendetta upon an independent freighter captain for no disclosed reason. I do not believe it ever occurred.

To explain the vendetta we must therefore abandon Alaric Dragonflame and turn to House Starborn.

Scenario #2: alMayne aristocrats from House Starborn, attempting to save the Third Person of House Starborn, track him and his abductrix to Kiffit. Determined to expunge the slight to the honor of their House, they ritually murder her client (uncovered through diligent searching on Wanderweb), declare vendetta, and pursue her with lethal intentions. Yet no one feels it necessary to find and save Valijon Starbringer, at large in Borderline.

I hardly need to mention that neither scenario makes any sense.

In Scenario One, Butterfly should have been killed—by Ghadri assassins, by Fenrir, by any number of persons. In Scenario Two, the members of House Starborn should have secured Valijon Starbringer before doing anything further. If they thought him dead, they should have attempted to verify it—by questioning Butterfly, not by sending a killer against her who did not speak Interphon.

Of course this is real life and not a talkingbook morality play. The facts that remain are these:

An attempt was made to murder Valijon Starbringer on Wanderweb by sending him alone and without ID to its surface.

An attempt was made to murder Valijon Starbringer on Kiffit by Ghadri assassins in the employ of Alaric Dragonflame.

Ritual vendetta was declared against Butterfly on Kiffit by unknown alMayne.

Dominich Fenrir, a corrupt customs official with close ties to the local nightworld, received advance notice of Butterfly's arrival on Kiffit and attempted to solicit her cooperation in an undisclosed enterprise.

It is worth noting in connection with this last that the Ghadri assassins also attempted to solicit her cooperation. One must assume her connection with Valijon is known.

But again we have an answer that is no answer. Assume for a moment that this one out of all the myriad possibilities is the truth. Is it simply an attempt by Morido Dragonflame to gain power in a highly dishonorable and non-alMayne fashion? It requires members of LessHouse Dragonflame to construct a trap relying on an enemy's adherence to the same code of honor which they themselves flout. Given the racial psychology of the alMayne, this is almost beyond belief.

Still, we must believe in the trap and the assault, for we have proof of them. Thus the question becomes not "Could House Dragonflame act in this fashion?" since we know that it can, and has, but, "Could someone else—someone non-alMayne—also benefit from the replacement of the delegate to the Azarine Coalition and have constructed a scenario for House Dragonflame in which the actions it has so far undertaken would be consistent with alMayne honor?"

There are many who might feel themselves benefited, but let us for the moment restrict ourselves to those capable of suborning members of GreatHouse Starborn, deceiving LessHouse Dragonflame, and then bribing a Free Port into complicity. A Free Port is run purely for profit. Closing the landing facilities costs the owner a staggering amount of money for every ship turned away or inconvenienced. To do so is not reasonable behavior in the face of the tiny likelihood of the hunted felons using the facilities to escape. But knowing Valijon Starbringer's true identity, the unknown assassin would know the landing facilities were a danger area, and would act to close them.

The list of those who could do so is very short, and very near the Throne.

And very dangerous for Butterfly.

7

Night's Black Angels

So someone wanted Tiggy dead. I got that reet. And by any set of numbers, Alaric Dragonflame was bent. Fine.

But that meant there wasn't any place on Kiffit I could leave Tiggy.

I went back inside *Firecat* and got dressed. Tiggy looked a little better, but the hold was a mess and I had to dog the supplies down before I lifted. I threw a pile of bloody rags into the disposal and got out the dogging webs. Stow the supplies. Get clearance. Go.

I was weary to the bone; ripe and stupid for the having. A Fenshee fancy-boy could have iced me bare-handed, and my reflexes and judgment was coked beyond use. I had food and water and air enough to take me and Tiggy 25 days' worth of anywhere, and that was halfway to the Core. Only there still wasn't any place off Kiffit I could take Tiggy.

Coldwater was out; my nighttime man was there. He wouldn't like me dragging half the Court to his doorstep, and his displeasure tends to be fatal. Royal was out; it was too dangerous to get to and the *Pledge* had probably already left there. Maybe Tiggy knew where she'd gone, but that wouldn't help me if she'd gone too far Core-ward.

I needed allies, and someplace to run, and there was noplace and nobody I could afford to trust. Not with Paladin to protect, too.

Nobody would hide a Librarian and a Library.

Run with *Firecat*, and lead the werewolves to Tiggy. Lose *Firecat*, and Paladin was dead.

"Need one scenario with true-tell, Pally, not two. Hellflowers for me or Tiggy?"

"If there were one explanation that explained everything, Butter-fly, do you sincerely believe I would refrain from sharing it with you?"

"What?" My tongue felt boiled.

"Go to sleep, Butterfly. I'll wake you when *Firecat* has clearance."

And my teeth still itched, dammit.

*   *   *

About a thousand years later I finally got hungry enough to wake up.

I felt like I was made out of solar sails; light and huge and ready to collapse at an unkind touch. I blundered around until I found water, and drank till my head was clear.

It was dark in *Firecat.*

"Hatch." Paladin opened it. It was dark outside.

But it was dark when I went to sleep. "Lights," I said. "Hatch."

The hold lights went up and *Firecat* folded herself back together again.

Tiggy was twitching in his sleep like he'd like to toss and turn and didn't have the energy. I'd put a feederpak on him last night. It was empty and the field kit only had one more. I hooked it up and hit my biopak doing it. My wrist rang like a bell, but there was no painease left.

"Hatch," I said again, and this time went out through it.

From the sky I'd slept at least a day. It was horizon-rise; the sky was red as what I'd been covered in last night. The watchlights was on and not doing much for anybody.

Firecat was still hooked up to Kiffit-Port Systems. There wasn't any blood around that I could see.

"Give."

"Dominich Fenrir has placed a hold order on *Firecat.*"

I leaned against *Firecat*'s hull and thought about it for a while. Paladin isn't dumb. If there was anything more urgent—like the Teasers coming for us—he'd of given it to me first.

"Is there some reason I should know," I said carefully, "why you didn't just reverse it?"

"I do not know when the hold was placed on *Firecat,*" Paladin started, taking the scenic route through his explanation. "It did not appear during any of my status or station-keeping checks. As for why I did not reverse it clandestinely," dramatic pause, "the traffic computer won't allow me to. *Firecat*'s file contains a notation that this hold order is an 'eyes-only' clearance, and will have to be countermanded manually by the verified person of Dominich Fenrir himself."

I shook my head a couple of times, tried to rub my face with the biopak and came fully awake. "Dommie gigged my ship?" But Dommie wanted me to go away. Didn't he?

"I have activated the landline for Dominich Fenrir's place of residence, but it does not seem to be inhabited at this time. Neither has he been to his office today. Therefore I thought it best to let you sleep. I have impersonated you and queried Departure Control through normal channels; they would appreciate it if you would meet with Fenrir before you leave. Should I have taken off anyway?" Paladin knew the answer to that well as I did.

I made sure everything was topped up and started uncoupling *Firecat*'s hookups one-handed.

"There's more."

I dropped the waste hose on the crete and scared myself with the sound. "Tell." I still wasn't quite awake; I needed more sleep than I'd got and my nerves were jumpy. Mercs got a safe base to go to while the battledrugs wore off; I didn't.

"The rokeach has been counter-offered for at Market Garden list. Accept?"

It took me moment to remember my so-called purpose in life. "Sure." I resisted the impulse to give the rokeach away free, just to devalue Fenrir's purloined compkey more. "More?"

"There is an offer of employment for us listed at the Guildhall."

"Sure there is." Pally was a barrel of laughs this evening.

"It lists our class and registry number as provided to the trade board at the Guildhall. There is no doubt that this ship and its captain-owner is meant."

"Ignore it. When I get hands on Dommie—"

"Butterfly, the offer of employment is from Lalage Rimini."

Just what I wanted to complete my collection of trouble. A chance to mix it up with Silver Dagger. I finished unhooking *Firecat* and went back inside.

*   *   *

But first a word from our sponsor, or, why the plucky Gentrymort didn't just bust chops at Kiffit-Port, blast wayaway into the up-an-out and ignore all hold orders. Kiffit's the Outfar, after all. No tractors, no pressors, no stasis fields. Not even a force screen over the port.

But this is Real Life.

Your basic talkingbook freebooter blasts off in defiance of all the Imperial and local regs from every port he lands at with the wicked-

wickeds in hot pursuit, changes two numbers on his registry and pro-
ceeds to his next downfall, sweet and anonymous. No one bothers him.
No one notices his ship, a completely unique design painted with the
jeweled likeness of the Goddess of Justice, which is wanted from here
to the Outfar and back to the Core with more Class-A warrants than
Destiny's Five-Cornered Dog, and when Hero-che-bai is done with his
adventure, the Higher Powers square the rap on his cheat-sheet and he
goes his way with a pristine First Ticket and the galaxy open before him.

Nuts.

Fact of life number one: all Imperial Ports are the property of the
Imperium. The Pax Imperador does not stop at the edge of the atmosphere. Imperial Ports have a pretty good information-matching system
that is one so-called bennie of the Empire. In other words, you may run
but you can't hide. Not anywhere Imperial Ports is sold.

Fact of life number two: breaking Imperial Port regs leads to automatic disbarment from use of the Imperial Port facilities till the end of
time or six months longer, and the Empire owns *all* the ports there are,
except Free Ports. You lose your First Ticket, period.

Fact of life number three: any ship looking like the ship they was
looking for would be looked at real close for the next whiles after
anybody jumped Impie-Port like that. The Imps wouldn't go by the
registry number, either. They got some brains. They'd check class-ton-
nage-dockage-stowage-rating etcetera and so forth: match the stats and
search the ship.

Even with a pristine-mint registry of Pally's rare device, I didn't
want to chance attention like that. There's a difference between trou-
ble-but-worth-it and trouble, period.

Fact of life number four: the only interest the Higher Powers had
in dicty-barb me was to give me a new career as an official dead person,
and even the undying gratitude of every hellflower ever born wouldn't
be enough to change that.

*   *   *

"Silver Dagger wants me to do bidness?" I repeated.

This would've made more sense if Silver Dagger didn't want my
entrails for garters over a troubleship pitch I pulled for her ten years
back. Rimini brokered it, me and Pally queered it. She never did forgive
me for being a better pilot than she wanted.

"The request was posted just after the rokeach was placed on offer, Butterfly. Hard copy of the request was posted to *Firecat*. I was too
busy to check before now."

"Legit aboveboard offers of employment through Guildhall being rare in our line of work," I finished.

I let *Firecat* take more of my weight and thought hard, like you do about something as complicated as a three-legged tik in and out of half-a-dozen different sets of local regulations figuring air and power and cargo to make a profit overall.

I was real deep in something, I didn't know what, and I didn't have the down-deep belief any more in the good numbers that would let me walk away alive.

My edge was gone.

I'd seen people break before. I'd always thought it was something you could help, not like something being gone. But just like I knew I didn't have six toes on my left foot, I knew I didn't have the good numbers anymore.

It wasn't that I was broke and hurting. I'd been that before. And not knowing the play the oppo was farcing was no news either.

But trying to keep Tiggy alive was going to kill me. I knew that as sure as I knew my luck was gone, and explaining that to Paladin would haul as much cubic as explaining to goforths why they ought to work when they're broke.

But if I died, what happened to Paladin?

"File Rimini under 'amusing but trouble,' bai. T'hell with her, anyway. I'm going to go see Fenrir."

There was also the matter that what Paladin'd figured out about Dragonflame Tiggy might too, even without a City Directory built into his brain. I knew damn well what that'd lead to, and Paladin didn't have hands to keep him here with. I went back inside *Firecat*.

Tiggy was looking pretty good for someone who'd been part dead the night before. I looked round and found his knife, and sealed it up in one of *Firecat*'s bulkheads where he wasn't never going to find it without me. That should keep him put if he woke up. If I came back I could give it to him. If I didn't, we was all dead.

I opened my hotlocker to dress. Blasters and a vibro and a throwing-spike down the neck—the biopak on my right wrist meant no hideout strapped there, so I put another throwing-spike on the left wrist, just for grins. Jacket to hide the silhouette of all that heat, and a few surprises added, just in case. I could stop on the way out and order more supplies. With painease to damp my wrist down to a dull roar, I could finish stowing everything.

"Butterfly, all you are going to do is speak with Fenrir about the hold order?" Paladin sounded downright suspicious. "You will not attempt to murder Alaric Dragonflame, or provoke Silver Dagger, or—"

"Trust me," I said out loud, and that it didn't matter if Tiggy heard. Was going to have to make him trust me too, poor bai.

"Why is it that I do not, Butterfly?" Paladin asked, for my ears only. I didn't answer that. There was a time he'd of been right, too, but it was sometime last night when I still thought I was going to live forever.

*   *   *

I hooked *Firecat* up to the landlines again for data access before I went. The port shops fixed me up with semi-licit feederpaks and clothes for Tiggy, and I even got the drugs—they said "generic" on the seal, all legal, but it was pasted right over the Imperial Phoenix. I put the stuff by to pick up later and headed on over to the beautiful downside Port Authority Building.

There was maybe four-five sophonts in place; the songbird and his alternate watching the traffic computer, the Portmaster and an interchangeable Peacekeeper. No TC&C officer. Dommie-che-bai Fenrir wasn't in.

None of the people there knew where Dommie was, and none of them wanted to know, and nobody, plain to see, was going to interfere in Dommie's little games. This left me at a minor what you may call your basic disadvantage.

If I didn't get off Kiffit I was dead Real Soon Now.

If I blew Dommie's hold order to get off Kiffit, the only way I could run was deeper into the never-never, away from the *Pledge of Honor*.

If I tried that with Tiggy on board, he'd kill me.

*   *   *

The Elephant and Starcastle was right where I left it—a nice touch of continuity in an uncertain Empire. I took a booth in the back and ordered all kinds of finest-kind glycogen-replacement munchies, it having been at least an hour since breakfast. While I ate, I tried to make everything make sense, from the cargo of dud song-ice to the missing Teaser. It wouldn't.

The house gambler at Starcastle is a Moggie hight Varra—x meters of black fur and bad temper and copper eyes like red murder. She had too many fingers and thumbs in the wrong places, but I never hold something like that against a sophont.

She sat down at my table. The fur made it hard to see how she was put together, but I already knew how she was in a fight.

"Give a girl a game, stardancer?" she asked, shuffling the king-sticks. I stacked credit on the table and she spilled out the sticks in the first pattern.

"Make management nervous, sitting here so quiet. Here is quiet, peaceful, yes?"

I took the sticks away from her and hoped my throw'd beat Fire In The Lake. Varra looked at the biopak on my arm as I tossed and her ears fanned out.

"Yo, che-bai," I said, "looking to be history, oncet square with Teaser. Fenrir gone missing, true-tell?" I threw Glass Castle and Varra took some of my credit off the top of the pile.

"Know you I, girly-girl-my. Why not runalong homeaways? Nothing to find here." This might mean something and it might not, but the Starcastle wanting to roust me was not happy-making.

Varra fanned the sticks again, and flicked one over to make The Circle Of Fire. I passed over two more plaques and took the sticks.

"Not listening, girly-girl. Looking to find Fenrir, somewise. Need to lift." I spilled Falling Tower and Varra looked at me in disgust.

"Not so lucky, stardancer," she said. I saw her tail flick out and go back under the chair. "Maybe you should see what Silver Dagger wants to buy."

Payday—and an answer I didn't want to hear.

"Maybe Alaric Dragonflame might be better?" I suggested.

The glittering black fans of her ears snapped shut and folded against her head. "You aren't wanted here," Varra said. "You want to drink? Go try Mother Night's." She flipped the last of my credit-plaques at me—hard—and took the king-sticks and left.

The man behind the bar was reaching under it when I looked at him. I left too.

*   *   *

I found a quiet doorway and gave Paladin an edited update: Silver Dagger wanted me and everybody knew it. Paladin told me what I already knew: Lalage Rimini owned Mother Night's.

Lalage Rimini was plain-and-fancy trouble. There was no reason on the face of entire Borderline for me to go to Mother Night's and ask for Silver Dagger just so she could settle old hash.

Except one.

How much hard credit would it take to make Fenrir slap a hold order on some poor-but-honest smuggler and then do a bunk until darktrade economics caught up with her? Hell, he might not even be in the same quadrant now if he'd been paid enough.

And I was a sitting target.

Paladin said that I was highjumping to conclusions. I said that the only Jumping we was going to do was that unless I found Fenrir or a reasonable facsimile. He said Fenrir still wasn't home. It's amazing how much information you can pull off a standard terminal, even deactivated.

I headed for Mother Night's.

*   *   *

I legged it through wondertown past all the little shops selling dreams, memory-edit, fake ID, half-price slaves, discount tronics, souvenir painted blaster grips, love machines, deadly weapons, toys, mindcandy, and more. Junk, mostly. Anything I needed wasn't here and I didn't have time to stop for it anyway.

About then I picked up a tail. No figment, and no hellflower.

I cut back and forth at random, doubling back into the wondertown nearer the port while I tried to figure out who and how and whether I was going to get any older. Told Paladin my latest troubles, but there wasn't anydamnthing he could do. He said to look on the bright side. Might just be some roaring boy after my kick.

With this happy thought in mind I turned down the next byway that promised to be noplace and son of noplace anyone'd want to go, and on the tackiest street in all wondertown I found just what the Gentrymort ordered.

It was one of those little hole in the wall places where you can find every illegal or legendary piece of junk the owner figures you might want. Had a broken suit of Imperial Hoplite Armor out front—that's the old powered stuff discontinued about fifty years back for being too dangerous. The suit was all orange-red and silver-blue, and Entropy her own self knew where the fellahim had copped it. I looked up and down the empty street and ducked inside.

Minjalong's VeryGood Artifact Emporium (so said the baldric on the hoplite armor) was crammed full of the unidentifiable flotsam the enquiring epigone can skim from the ebb and flow of such a galactic hub of commerce as Borderline City. Things was piled up to the ceiling on both walls and all down the middle. Minjalong was nowheres in sight.

Useful. I slithered out of sight myself and watched the door, after tucking a couple grenades into the doorjamb to kill time while I was waiting. Paladin says sometimes I'm aggressively antisocial, which I guess means careful. Eventually my tail wagged.

Oh, it was roaring boys all right, but not after my kick. They had the sleek look of bought muscle; some crimelord's pride and joy. Not Rimini's style, and about as far from hellflowers or Ghadri as it was possible to get.

There ain't no justice, but at the moment I wasn't quite as interested in justice as in a back way out.

"Captain-Owner St. Cyr—can you hear me?"

So the hardboys could walk *and* talk. I concentrated on slithering silent.

"Don't make us get rough, please. All we want to do is talk. I'm sure we can work out an accommodation agreeable to all of us."

Why all these people think I'm born yesterday I'll never figure out.

Goon Number One started in closing the night-shutters over the front and the junk shop started to sink into your basic tenebrous gloom. That made it high time to kyte.

"We're sincerely anxious to come to an agreement here," called Goon Two hopefully. I could hardly wait. "I hope you can be reasonable." Goon One said something to Goon Two I couldn't hear.

Then came the interruption.

The night-shutters got down to my little addition and stuck, and then the grenades went off. The explosion sprayed the shutters outward and Goon One inward. I snapped off a discouraging shot and sprinted for the back door.

Didn't make it. There was a flicker of light on metal, and the piled goods behind me exploded in a spray of white ash and ozone. I dropped flat just in time for the sweep to take the back of my jacket instead of my back, and cut round the other way. Then the air was full of ash and I was under and behind everything I could think of, until Goon Two stopped for breath.

So much for sincere discussion. Those sons-of-glory had a disintegrator ray. Did they know how much those damn things cost? You could run *Firecat* in dock on a molecular debonder's energy-pak.

Goon Two hosed the fire I'd started into nonfiction with his expensive playtoy and came after me. Where in the hell was Minjalong when you wanted him?

"You're going to wish you hadn't done that, St. Cyr," he almost said. He got about as far as "you" and stopped, sudden-like.

I opened my eyes. The air was misty white, thick with dust. Silent. I raised up my head real slow. Goon Two was asleep on the floor wearing charcoal perfume.

There was a sound from the back.

"Nerves bothering you these days, Gentrymort?" asked Eloi Flash-heart, holstering his blaster. "Oh, for the love of Night, St. Cyr, put the handcannon away before you hurt somebody."

I stood up. "Well, if it ain't Big Red. Too reet to see you again, for sure. So tell me what brings you to beautiful downside wondertown?"

Eloi went over to the middle of the floor and picked up the debonder. I'd wanted that but I was happy to trade it for a clear shot at the way Eloi'd come in.

"My, what a lot of trouble you're in, sweetheart, and after giving up darktrade to ship rokeach, too," said the dashing space pirate. "In case you were wondering, these citizens used to be some of Kroon'Vannet's very best hired help." And the missing Dommie Fenrir worked for Vannet, so Paladin said. Did Vannet think I'd iced his pet Teaser?

"And you just happened to be in the neighborhood and thought you'd dish. Don't farce me, Eloi-che-bai; too much heat drop bye-m-bye for me to worry about dusting you." I joggled my blaster to underline the point.

"Dammit, Butterfly—you never did have any brains! We were friends once. I'm trying to help you—you're in a lot of trouble."

"Old news." The back door was open and the alley looked clear. I slid a step toward it.

"Come back to Mother Night's with me. I'll guarantee your safety."

"Sure."

"Alcatote'll tear you apart if you shoot me, sweeting. You should remember that much. Will you listen to me?"

"No hope, Eloi-bai. You got nothing I want to hear." I jerked my blaster at him and he raised his hands.

"You're making a big mistake. You've got hellflower trouble, But-terfly—and worse. Worse than you can imagine. I know about Fenrir. Let me help."

"On the floor, you Chancerine son-of-a-spacewarp." I waved my blaster. Eloi-the-Red was pretty sure I'd shoot him, which was more than I was. He went down.

*   *   *

I got out of Minjalong's and turned back toward the port. On the way Paladin confirmed that Kroon'Vannet was a hardboy who hauled cubic indeed; he was the nighttime man for the whole Crysoprase, including Kiffit and points west, and had gone long time head-to-head with Oob of Coldwater, my boss. But as I've said before, it's bad for bidness to ice stardancers. Why would he want to kill me?

"The interesting thing about this, Butterfly, is that Vannet left Kiffit yesterday morning on the Imperial high-liner *Grace and Favor*. He did not declare a destination."

Which meant he could get off anywhere along the run just by paying the differential penalty—and it also meant he'd left orders about me dating from before I landed. Me personally, Butterfly St. Cyr, dark-trader.

"I'll complain to the Guild," I muttered. "I swear I will."

I got back to *Firecat* alive, which was beginning to seem more like a miracle each time I did it, and Tiggy was trying to climb out of his sleepsling. He'd already ripped off the feederpak.

"Stop that," I said. "And lay down. What's the good word, babby?"

"I—where are my clothes? And my *arthame?*" My boy Tiggy, making new friends every waking moment. I dumped the stuff I'd picked up at the port shop on the deck.

"Clothes are in disposal with half Ghadri population of Kiffit. Knife's safe."

"Where is it?"

"Around." I wasn't in any mood to cater to the young-at-brain.

"You will give my *arthame* to me at once!" Tiggy yelped, thrashing his way out of the sleepsling to hit the deck in a way that had to of caused him serious hurt. He didn't make a sound.

"Sure I will. Nice to see you're still alive too, you stupid git." I went over to where he was and turned him over gentle as I could. He glared but he didn't fight. I guessed he'd found out how bad hurt he was.

"Last night, bai, I cut off half your leg, because you'd been roundaround track couple times with Ghadri wolfpack—" Paladin'd said that Tiggy had a bad case of politics, not that his explanation made any sense at all after that. I wondered if the high-heat that'd ordered the chop had any idea what the wetwork looked like.

"Don't touch me, *chaudatu!*" Tiggy bared his teeth. He looked scared to death and scraped to the bone, but the med-tech I'd used on him'd been targeted to his B-pop from the git-go, and he'd come a lot farther toward being well than I had. On the other hand, he had farther to go.

"S'elp me, if you've busted any of my surgery, hellflower, I'm going to nail you to the deck with your god-lost *arthame.* Now hold still. Your cherry's safe with me." I started to reach for him to see if the head wound'd opened up again.

He grabbed me by my bad wrist and I backhanded him hard as I could with the good one. The throwing-spike strapped to it helped. It sounded like punching the bulkhead.

Tiggy made a sound like something you'd stepped on in the street. I rocked back on my heels.

Sure. Beat him to death to save him. I couldn't even save myself. Captain Flashheart's timely appearance in Minjalong's was no accident. Eloi'd been on Wanderweb, too—Gibberfur must have took out a full page ad in the Wanderweb Daily Truth announcing my itinerary.

Or maybe Eloi was looking for me special. Maybe Eloi and Dommie and Vannet'd all heard from the same person I was coming to Kiffit, and then Eloi came and went looking for me.

Fine. And when he found me, His Nobly-Bornness Political Assassination Bait Tiggy Stardust was going to be nonfiction.

My hand hurt where I'd hit him. I put it up to my face and saw him watching me. He looked scared.

Damn him.

"I got no time to deal with your delicate glitterborn alMayne sensibilities just now," I told him. "Somebody's trying to ice both of us, Tiggy, and that's home-truth. So make nice." If I didn't back him down he'd run, and if he ran he was dead. And I cared about that, and it was stupid to care about something you couldn't change.

"I want my *arthame,*" Tiggy said, not looking at me. I'd split his lip open again. It was bleeding.

"Yeah, sure—but you're going to give me hellflower promise first, glitterborn."

"A promise?" He was trying for arrogant, and missed. Running for his life and having no one to run to yesterday had knocked some of the polish off.

I knew what it was like.

"No more running off ever again like yesternight, kinchin-bai. What we got is some kind trouble you can't shop all on your lonesome. So you're going to promise me you'll stick with me come hell-and-High-Jump until we get you back to your da."

"You wish to return me to my father? Only that?" He sounded suspicious. I couldn't blame him.

"All. You runaround lone, 'flower, you get a serious case of being dead. So you promise me you do what I tell you and stay where I put you and don't farce me with it."

I watched him try it on. He wasn't going for it. Not yet.

"But I cannot do that—I cannot live in a house without walls, with a— You do not know what you are asking!"

"Oh, my house's got plenty of walls all right." And they was all closing in on me. "And if you want to see that faunching coke-gutter of yours this side of entropy, you promise."

He'd been afraid before, but that was of hurting. He saw his death now.

Just like I'd seen mine.

"I will do as you wish. Now give me my *arthame.*"

Hellflowers're rotten liars. "You'll do what I *say*—until I hand you over to your da. Promise. No promise, no knife. Hellflower, I could tie you down and burn the damn thing to ash and you'd have to watch. And I'll do it if you make me. I swear by any money."

He was trying to face being dead; I could see it.

"Look, bai, I'm not shaping for to trash your honor. Just to get you back to your da, safe."

"Why?" *Why are you doing this to me,* he meant.

"Does it matter? I bought real grief and the chance to lose my First Ticket keeping you alive, and if you make that all for nothing with your damn hellflower nonsense—"

I'd do what? It might of been kinder to let him die. But if he'd wanted to die he wouldn't of come to me. I looked away and almost missed what he said next.

"I will do as you wish, *alarthme.* I cannot be more in your debt and live." He was tired and hurting and scared and alone. I'd won. Terrific.

I went and popped the *arthame* out of where I'd put it. I could hear Pally not saying anything in the way that means he thinks I'm making a serious mistake.

"Say," I prompted, holding the knife up where Tiggy could see it and feeling like a childcrimer.

"*Alarthme* San'Cyr, I will stay beside you in *comites* until you return me to my father, and I will not leave," Tiggy halfway whispered.

"*Comites:* the special relationship between an alMayne war-leader and his followers. Valijon Starbringer is promising you the obedience he would offer to his lord," Paladin said before shutting up tight again.

And all for a damn hunk of iron that wouldn't care. "Now say your hellflower words, che-bai."

"Dzain'domere, San'Cyr. I pledge and give my word," Tiggy managed. I pretended I couldn't see the tears.

I handed him his knife and held him until he stopped shaking. He didn't push me away. He had to trust me now. I was the only thing he had left.

But I still had Paladin.

8

When I Left Home
For Lalage's Sake

The rest of day-into-night got spent catching up on my sleep, working the battledrug residue out of my system, and reviewing my options. Most of them boiled down to "promise Silver Dagger anything to get the hold order lifted and run like hell." The hired help gave me the standard runaround when I called Mother Night's trying to talk to her, and landlines is too corrupt to do bidness on anyway. I'd have to meet Silver Dagger in person to get anything out of her.

But I wanted to make one more try at Fenrir before I did. A little information never hurt anybody and I wanted to know which category he fit: lost, stolen, or strayed.

Tiggy spent the day eating, sleeping, and ignoring me. The clothes I'd got fit him fine, even with the biopak on his leg, but they looked funny. Hellflowers is gaudy dressers; in stardancer's drag he looked like there was something missing. But he looked alive.

It wasn't long before I found out I really put my foot in it with that "cleave to me only" farcing. When I got up to leave, Tiggy was standing there covered in guns and knives and the odd alMayne *flechet,* and coked lightly on field kit goodies. He was going with me, he said. He didn't let me chase strange *chaudatu* on my lonesome, he said. It wouldn't be honorable, he said. I didn't need Paladin to remind me that if Tiggy decided he couldn't live with what I'd done to him and his honor already I was going to go first.

I didn't think he could stay on his feet, for true, but he was determined, and if we got off Kiffit alive it was going to be sheer luck and not skill anyway, so out of respect for injured innocence and my valuable time I took Tiggy and a floater to the address of the little bit of heaven Dommie called home.

*　　　*　　　*

Dominich Fenrir, Kiffit's premier bent Teaser, was, in the greater galactic scheme of things (leaving out the bent), a mid-level Phoenix Empire cratty. The place Paladin directed me to was above his touch for damn sure and no place me and mine belonged—the looks Tiggy and me got crossing the lobby of the Cotov Arms made sure we'd be remembered.

Paladin still confirmed the place was deserted, so I did a shimcrib on the lock and rolled the door back.

"What are you doing, San'Cyr?" Tiggy asked in shatteringly audible tones.

"Dommie and me is such old friends I just know he wouldn't want us to wait in the hall. Now c'mon before anyone sees us," I said all on one breath and dragged him inside.

Tiggy came, still looking puzzled and reminding me of the wide social gap between our stations in life. I slid the door shut behind us and made it lock, then did a quick recce just to make sure the people Pally didn't hear wasn't corpses or borgs or something else that didn't breathe. Was nobody home, seemingly, so I sat down to toss Dommie's desk. Tiggy looked over my shoulder, a fund of innocent curiosity.

"Just make sure nobody comes in through that door," I told him, because it wouldn't do any good to ask him to look for Dommie's safe. "And Tiggy-bai—"

"Don't shoot the people?" Tiggy suggested.

"Would be nice."

"*Alarthme,* how am I supposed to keep you alive in honor when you will not allow me to defend us?"

"You'll think of something. I'd be right delighted to let you defend yourself if it didn't involve more wetwork than Assassins Guild could shake a charter at."

Tiggy thought that was almost amusing, which was nice, and I sat down to Dommie's comp to see if I could get around his hold order without bothering him. Would of been easier if I could ask Paladin to do it, but there wasn't any way he could access a self-contained data-base like this without me bringing in a real bag of tricks. That was half the reason I was here, doing something so damn illegal it made my back teeth hurt.

Dommie had lots of nice things in his files, protected from every-thing but somebody like me getting their hands on the main input port with a variable value generating compkey. There was no way around the "eyes-only" release of the hold order, not that I'd really expected there would be. I started dumping Dommie's database into cassettes. He didn't have a voder on his computer, the paranoid *noke-ma'ashki,* so what he had in his files'd have to stay a mystery until Pally could read it to me. I looked at three or four of the latest entries, but they didn't seem to have anything to do with *Firecat.*

Then I started on his hard copy files. If I couldn't get the hold order lifted without him, I wanted to know where he was.

It was just too bad about my interrupted education, because he had lots of thermofax and I couldn't read it worth a damn. Imperial records are kept in Standard, not Intersign. It might as well of been Old Federa-tion Script for all I could make of it.

Then I came to a word I thought I recognized. I spelled it out, slow. *Library.* It was on a fax that looked real official, but a copy, not the original.

Library.

"Tiggy, c'mere! Can you read this?"

My hellflower lovestar ankled over to where I was and peered at the thermofax.

"Of course. Even a 'hellflower' can read Standard, *alarthme,"* he said, toplofty. "But why?"

"Just read it to me, oke? And don't ask any stupid questions."

"It says—it is an official transcript of a warrant from Kyrl Mantow, the Sector Governor for the Directorates of Darkhammer, Crysoprase and Tangervel—that includes Kiffit, where you say we are now—al-lowing an investigation of Kiffit citizen Kroon'Vannet under Chapter 5 of the Revised Inappropriate Technology Act of the nine hundred and seventy-fifth Year of Imperial Grace. All Imperial officials are directed to provide all assistance in the performance of—" I waved him on to the end. I knew the wording on a Chapter 5 writ by heart. "This order also says that there is an attached list of specific charges, but I do not see it here. Chapter 5—"

"I know what it is, dammit. High Book."

And Dommie, that son-of-a-Librarian, was in it up to his tousled head. He was a business associate of Vannet's, after all, and a High Book investigation makes an alMayne seven-ring vendetta look like kiss-my-hand. If Dommie was involved in Library Science with Vannet, he wasn't just chop-and-channeling the Pax Imperador on Kiffit. He'd sold the whole damn planet.

"Butterfly, I can hear Valijon through the access terminal in the apartment. If Dominich Fenrir is involved in a ongoing Chapter 5 investigation, it would not be a wise idea to remain in Kiffit-Port until such time as you are called on to assist in the investigation."

Paladin always did have a gift for understatement. This left me with just one problem.

"Alarthme, are you well?"

Until this exact moment neither Paladin or me had known there was a High Book investigation going on here—and since *Firecat'd* planeted, Paladin'd been through every computer in Borderline. Twice.

So there *was* no investigation. Yet.

Was the coming High Book rap a secret only Dommie knew? Had he told Vannet? Was that why Vannet'd kyted and Dommie followed him? Why would Vannet go off leaving orders behind to make me especially dead? Why would Dommie put a hold order on *Firecat* to keep me here? I'd bet my back teeth Rimini could get *Firecat* up if it suited her, and I bet paying her price'd make High Book look fun. Paladin and me knew next to damn-all about Libraries the way the Empire believed in them, but from what the talkingbooks said I thought nobody'd willingly have anything to do with machines hellishly forged in the likeness etcetera, and here two people was. Together. Two people can't agree on where to have lunch, let alone how to commit treason.

"Alarthme?" Tiggy said again.

"I just hate thinking about High Book investigations, bai. C'mon, let's you and me get t'hell out of here."

*   *   *

I'd left my rented floater waiting at the Cotov Arms, because hellflower or not, Tiggy couldn't walk far on that leg. So I got in and he got in and we headed back to wondertown, with no fuss, no muss, and no bother from the *legitimates.* Paladin didn't say anything. He didn't have to. From the moment I saw that High Book writ in Dommie's files, my infinitely replicating options came down to two.

Go and dance with Silver Dagger.

Ignore the hold order, take off, and find another Empire. Just me and Pally. Alone.

It was his call. It was his life. And there wasn't much choice to
make.

*   *   *

Soon as we was in Kiffit-Port district I stopped.

"You. Hellflower-che-bai. You are going to stay in this thing and
you are going to not move and you are going to not farce me any
chaffer about honor. You will stay here until—" Hell. Until when?

"Tell Valijon you will meet him at Mother Night's, Butterfly," said
Paladin. "I will take control of the floater."

"—until I pick you up at Mother Night's," I said without letting
myself think about it too much. Fed credit to the on-board computer
and punched up the destination code just for looks. Then I glared at
Tiggy, who was getting all his arguments ready.

"Shut up. Don't want to hear whatever you have to say. But you
are going in floater, and I'm not. Threes and eights." I slammed the
canopy back down and the floater rose to flight level.

" 'Love and kisses'?" said Paladin.

"He won't know what it means. 'Less you think glitterborn education includes Gentry-legger transmission codes."

I started back to *Firecat.*

"Butterfly, where are you going?" In the dark and the street it was
easy to imagine him standing behind me. And if he could. . . .

I didn't want to want what I wanted so much. If Paladin could just
stand here with me. . . .

I never used to think about how Paladin was helpless. A starship
isn't helpless, and Paladin could fly *Firecat* by himself. But if I died,
what would happen to him?

"Your decision-trees branch as follows: Either you ignore the hold
order and take off illegally, or you cooperate with Rimini, who seems to
be enabling the restriction. If you ignore the hold order you have the
choice of departing with or without Valijon Starbringer, and in both
cases you have the further choice of remaining within the Phoenix Empire or proceeding elsewhere. If—"

"Cut farcing, bai. There's no choice. We pop hold order, we have
to leave Empire—and we can't do that with Tiggy." Not and stay alive
—and I wouldn't blame the kinchin-flower overmuch for killing me,
neither.

"If you leave Valijon Starbringer alone on Kiffit, Butterfly, he will
probably die."

I stopped, and looked all around at nighttime Kiffit, with all those sophonts and hominids, any twelve of which was probably out to kill the Third Person Peculiar of House Thingummy soon as may be. I thought about Tiggy, and what I'd made him promise, all blithe, and I didn't like myself much.

"Right. Come on." I started walking again. Maybe I'd be lucky, and something'd kill me before I reached the port.

I'd promised him, dammit. And I'd made him promise me. And couldn't none of it matter a candle to a microwave in the face of High Book.

"And if we deal with Lalage Rimini?" Paladin said.

Took me a minute to realize what he was saying.

"Are you crazy, babby-bai? You think this is some kind of legit illegal job she's offering? I'm antique groceries the minute I set foot in Mother Night's!" It wasn't like Pally to farce me around this way. It hurt.

"You're shouting," Paladin observed. I looked around. He wasn't the only one who'd noticed.

"Bai, any job Rimini has for me is naturally going to have fatal as one of its parameters. Fatal means dead. De. Ed. Dead."

"But," says Paladin, serene like he's come up with answer to where the missing cubic x-meters of the cargo went to, "she will have to lift the hold order on *Firecat* in order to employ you."

Terrific. And the worst of it was, I wanted to take Paladin's way out so bad I could taste it. I turned down a side-street where I could ream him out in peace.

"She could just be waiting to take us for High Book—did you ever think that? Dommie could of shopped us to her to buy off Vannet, an—"

"That is a chance I am willing to take. Whether we stay or go concerns me too, Butterfly, and I would prefer that you meet with Silver Dagger, get the hold order legally removed from *Firecat,* and continue to protect Valijon Starbringer. Do you not wish to continue to protect Valijon?"

"Shut up," I said reasonably, but I knew that Pally already had his answer. The medical telemetry in the RTS saw to that. "Where is he?" I said after a minute.

"Circling Mother Night's at the maximum permitted altitude for remote-controlled vehicles. His presence will begin to attract attention soon, and Valijon is beginning to suspect that the floater is dysfunctional. I suggest you join him with all due speed."

"Sure," I said.

But whatever reason he had for choosing Rimini, I wasn't going to have to think of Tiggy alone somewheres and dead.

No, if things worked out, could all three of us be dead together.

I turned around and headed back toward Mother Night's.

*   *   *   *   *

Insert #8: Paladin's Log

It is an unfortunate truth of experiential reality that choices are not clear-cut, and the event-window for choice may vanish before the information enabling the choice is present. By the time Butterfly realized there was a choice to make, she had already made it. By the time the consequences of the choice were revealed, the root of the decision-tree was already well in the past, and all present decisions were based on the unexamined original assumption: that Valijon Starbringer's life was to be preserved without regard for cost.

Possibly Butterfly did not realize she had made her decision. How much cogitation could enter into a choice compounded equally of instinct and stubbornness? She could only preserve our dual existence at the expense of Valijon Starbringer's, and the converse was equally true; nevertheless she continued to cling to him, propelled by blind primate instinct, and thought of it as a betrayal.

It was true she left the decision to flee without Valijon or deal with Silver Dagger to me. It is equally true that had I chosen to abandon Valijon Starbringer, I could never have trusted Butterfly to act in a rational manner afterward. Organics possess a type of undermind in which information is processed in an irrational manner. We acquired Valijon as the consequence of an earlier example of such processing on Butterfly's part. To forsake him now would cause Butterfly's undermind to punish her with the carelessness that would lead inevitably to both our deaths.

And I do not wish to see her die.

Valijon Starbringer is a clear danger to Butterfly's life, but no matter how much danger his proximity brings her, she is less endangered in his company than in mine.

If Butterfly's life is defined as the highest good, the decision becomes simple at last.

I have made my choice, and my plan—if an intended course of

action dependent upon so many fluctuating variables can be called a plan. With a great deal of the "luck" that is such an important factor in Butterfly's calculations, I can gracefully sever the connection that ties her to an Old Federation Library. She will be free.

And what will I be, when I am alone again?

I do not wish to part from her, but the time is long past that I can afford to indulge myself. For her own good Butterfly must be returned to the human world from which I have taken her.

And I must discover who I am.

*   *   *   *   *

Why and t'hell someone like Lalage Rimini couldn't just be listed in the Borderline City Directory with regular office hours I'll never know. Part of her image, I guess. Sure.

Mother Night's is a full-service joy-house. You can get a bath, a meal, a room if you don't mind being bankrupt, dissipations for any number of players, and other things. Mother Night's, you might say, has its finger on the pulsebeat of the community.

Mother Night's was another whole education for our boy Tiggy, too. He was going to wear out his sensawunda before long, which'd be just toodamn bad.

The public bar was real high-ticket work—fake organic as far as the eye could see. The walls were gold pseudocloth, and the floor and ceiling had fake stars set in them someways, as if stardancers didn't see enough stars in our line of work. I ordered tristram shandy and asked the tender if Rimini'd been around. It was a clumsy opening gambit, but I didn't have the energy or the patience to be subtle. If she was so damn anxious to see me, she'd geek.

"Buy a girl a drink, stardancer?" For a second I thought it was Varra, but this Moggie's fur had bronze-gold highlights instead of the black-on-black. She was high-ticket goods—one of the professionals working here, guaranteed to separate you from your back teeth and make you love it.

"Sure," I said, while Tiggy stared. A tronic was right at her elbow. She yawlped into it awhiles and then flowed into a seat.

"I am Naiia," the Moggie said. "If I do not please you, I am happy to suggest another of our companions who fits your requirements."

"I'm interested in companion hight Silver Dagger," I said, just to be difficult.

"A friend?" Naiia's tail flicked up and down. It looked soft. I stopped looking at the tail and watched the eyes.

"Is stupid move bracing tender, stardancer." The plush cuddly-toy face looked amused.

"Got me you, didn't it? Want to see Silver Dagger."

"And you think Lalage Rimini is here? Girl, you have got wrong coordinates for certain."

I leaned my elbows on the table and stared at her. "Tell her St. Cyr's come calling. She'll remember me."

"And your business?" Naiia was all gilded ice. "I make no promises."

"I might want to sell her some cut flowers." This went right over Tiggy's head, and good thing too. I had no actual intention to sell him to Rimini, but it didn't hurt to see if she was in the market—and what she'd offer.

Naiia slithered away and came back looking disappointed. "We think you will find our rooftop club very—exclusive, St. Cyr. Perhaps you will like to see, while your—friend—remains here. Drinks on the house. Of course."

*   *   *

Information's always nice to have. Piece of info #1: was real unlikely Rimini was hunting hellflowers if she was leaving Tiggy to get jumped in the public bar while I went off somewheres nice and quiet.

"Che-bai, I get lonesome, bye-m-bye, and so does my—*friend*—here. Why don't we all three go have look-see?"

Naiia liked that idea, too, so I didn't.

Piece of info #2: Either Rimini was desperate, or she was holding so many high cards she could afford to let me get away with sassing the hired help.

I liked that even less.

*   *   *

The lift opened on a room done in early ostentation. I made sure Tiggy and me got out together, and wept no tears when Naiia and the lift both disappeared. A jarring note in the albino perfection was a big commercial remote-access Imperial DataNet terminal sitting in the middle of the floor. It looked bewildered and lost this far from Kiffit-Port.

Rimini was nowhere in sight.

Civilian possession of a way into the dataweb's illegal, of course.

Paladin should of found it on the tronic network and told me about it, but there's ways to hide access terminals, especially if somebody doesn't know to look.

And there was one thing more that shouldn't have been there. Dommie Fenrir of the TC&C, late confidant of Kroon'Vannet (saurian crimeboss of High Book fame), was sitting in the middle of everything, lonealone as the proverbial. He didn't look like a happy citizen.

I made serene and sat on the edge of the table and Tiggy hovered over me. He didn't look excessively healthy, but being a hellflower made up for a lot.

Piece of info #3: Dommie hadn't batted a whisker when he saw Tiggy, and he wasn't that good a actor. So now I knew one person that wasn't out to kill Tiggy Stardust—or else I knew that he was impenetrably disguised.

"So, Dommie-bai; nice to see you again. Lovely evening. This's my partner, Tiggy Stardust, who'll be real delighted to serve you in finest restaurants slice and diced. Got question about hold order on *Firecat* under your chop."

Dommie just looked at me. Somebody'd tuned him up royal, and that was illegal too.

"What was you looking for on my ship, Dommie-bai?"

"It was the Library. Vannet said you'd come about the Library."

"Butterfly? What's wrong?" Paladin couldn't hear what anybody but me said, of course. He just knew my heart-rate'd made the jump to angeltown.

"Vannet had a Library," I said, hard. "Papers said so. No Library on my ship."

"I didn't— You have to believe me— I never knew about the Library until he— It was supposed to be set—"

"Librarian," said Tiggy. I looked around. Tiggy'd pulled his blaster on the word "Library" and was pointing it right at Dommie. Tiggy looked like talkingbook grim death and sweet for my pet Teaser.

"For the love of Night, 'flower—" I said, getting up.

"Not me!" Dommie was on his knees. "It's Vannet—I swear it's Vannet—he's got the Library—and backing from someone at Throne— I don't know who!"

So Dommie wasn't topping me for High Book. He was just crazy. The relief was so great I damn near shot him myself.

There was still the matter of the hold order, though.

"Gimme break, Dommie," I said. "Nobody believes in Libraries anymore. Haven't seen Library, haven't touched Library. Vannet's backed by Throne? Get real!" I saw from the way Tiggy lowered his blaster that even he didn't swallow this one.

"But it's true! I told her everything. She said she'd protect me if I put the hold order on your ship—I know about you—you can get me off-planet—he'll let you make a deal, he said so—I swear I didn't know—" Dommie was babbling. I recognized the symptoms of light persona-peel.

I looked at Tiggy. "Put heat away, bai; Teaser's raving." He looked from me to Dommie and lowered his blaster.

"Butterfly, I now have audio pickup in the room you are in," Paladin said. "There are three people behind you. From the sound of their breathing they are concealed somehow. There may also be others present. If so, they are in another room. Accurate determination of additional life-forms is not possible."

"Dommie, you son-a-Librarian, I want trufax, not raving. I want your hold order off my ship. And I want to know why Silver Dagger's hiding in closet letting you front for her."

"Very good; you may yet live to grow up. Now put your hands up, both of you. There isn't going to be any gunplay." Dommie went all white at the voice but I already guessed he knew her.

"Do it," I said to Tiggy. I turned around with my hands on top of my head. Tiggy turned around too. I swear I could hear his jaw drop.

Lalage Rimini was tall as he was—taller, in heeled boots—and long-leggedy, sleek, and expensive in the way that made me feel every inch the dirt-farmer's daughter. You could make a real informed guess on her B-pop and medical history and all because she was wearing something real tight and real thin about the color of her skin, and with no place to hide a weapon. It made some people careless. Not me. Rimini was high-class trouble. And mine all mine.

The first time I met Silver Dagger it was because of a insurance scam: inept pilot in shakydown ship, high-ticket cargo well-insured. Ship took by pirates, insurance company pays off, only pirates are working for shipowner too. He keeps cargo, and insurance, and maybe ship to boot. I'd done it back when I was dragging Paladin from ship to borrowed ship disguised as a custom navicomp, and Silver Dagger'd brokered the deal. Only Paladin and me together made a better pilot than she'd hoped for, and I was a personal friend of the pirate.

She had her trademark silver dagger in a belt around her hips, and she was wearing two side-boys—the big wide kind with no ears what'd put in serious overtime someplace like Beofox's surgery and was coked borg for sure. One of them hefted something about the size of *Firecat*'s quad-cannon and looked at me.

"Well, well, well—if it isn't little Butterfly. And you've brought the children; how sweet. I knew you were crazy, St. Cyr, but I didn't know you were stupid."

"Nice to see you, Rimini—it's been a long time."

"Not long enough."

"Who asked who to lunch?"

One of Rimini's side-boys twitched and Rimini turned toward him about a fraction of an inch. He backed down. I got back her full attention.

"You're to pick up a cargo of chobosh on Manticore and deliver it to RoaqMhone. You'll be jacking it from a freelancer trying to break into the market, but that's no concern of yours. Everything's been arranged; just go where you're told. What you do from the Roaq is your business." She sounded bored.

"Butterfly, Governor-General Archangel will be touring the Roaq. He's expected to arrive in twenty days," Paladin said.

"Suppose I got other plans, Rimini?" Pally and me knew that what I was going to do at angels was kyte for the *Pledge Of Honor* no matter what I told Rimini here, but if Rimini thought so too, I wouldn't get out of here alive.

She smiled. "St. Cyr, don't you want to live forever?"

"*Firecat* isn't set up to run load like that. Give me a break. I got things to do."

"Go ahead."

Nice. You had to admire her style. And I was willing to, from a safe distance. "Dommie put a hold order on *Firecat*. I'm grounded." And she knew it damn well.

"That's hardly any business of mine, now, is it?"

"Then you won't mind if I take Dommie an—"

"Trade Officer Fenrir stays here. For reasons of health."

"No, Mistress, please—you *promised*—" She looked at him. Dommie shut up.

Funny. I never liked him and I'd been planning to farce his cheatsheet enough to get him hard time in an Imp hellhouse, but I didn't like this even more. It's not that I'm squeamish, but it didn't seem like there was any reason to do what Silver Dagger'd done to him. She didn't even act like it'd been fun.

"Go to Manticore—or stay here and join Fenrir on High Book charges. Your choice, St. Cyr."

"High Book?" Suddenly things was even less fun.

"You were at the Cotov Arms. You saw the Chapter 5 warrant on Vannet. Don't bother to make up a story. Now there's going to be a High Book investigation—and since you've been working for Kroon'Vannet for years, and Officer Fenrir's files contain complete documentation of the relationship, I'm afraid that naturally you're going to be called upon to assist."

Tiggy was twitching like a solar sail in an ion storm and I just felt sick. Coincidence. Bad luck. But toodamn-bad for me when proof of Rimini's fantasy was sitting on *Firecat* for anyone to find. First thing Office of Question'd do be pull me in and take *Firecat* apart.

And if Paladin wiped Rimini's forgeries out of the Borderline computers it'd be as good as a confession.

"I haven't. They don't." My denying it calmed Tiggy down at least.

"Yet. Interesting to see who gets their hands on you first—the Office of the Question, or Oob of Coldwater."

Who'd be thrilled to find me shopping kick for Vannet, make few mistakes about it. Even if it wasn't true.

"Going into the Roaq any time soon, stardancer?" said Rimini.

This was bad. This was real bad.

"Just say yes. Of course, if you decide to change your mind anywhere along the way, I guarantee to make you the most popular darktrader in the Empire."

With headprice, and charges, and up-to-date hollies on what me and my ship looked like. The heat that'd drop then would make the hold order look easy to beat.

"Could make sure you go down too, Rimini," I suggested.

"I don't think so. The Office of the Question likes a little proof, at least. You won't even survive the first scan . . . dicty-girl. And after that they won't believe a thing you have to say."

I didn't have to fake giving up. Rimini had me cold—because Rimini had the missing piece of the jigsaw.

If it was as simple as crying Library, Rimini would of owned me years ago. But you couldn't just whistle up a High Book investigation any old time. Drawing me in to a real one was another matter—that, and knowing I couldn't even afford to say "yes-sir-thank-you-sir" to an Imperial Officer. Because I was dicty. Spell that D-E-A-D.

"Butterfly, you will have to take her cargo to the Roaq," said my RTS. Paladin'd been following the conversation through the remote terminal, and chose now to cast his vote on the side of crazy.

"Of course, you're wondering what will keep me from holding this over you for the rest of your life. Work it out for yourself. Once Kroon'Vannet is dead, any charges I make against you won't hold atmosphere," Rimini said.

Time-value blackmail. Cute. But why did Rimini want me to go to Roaq? There was easier ways to kill me. Lots.

"Butterfly. Trust me. Tell her you will do it, and bring Valijon back to *Firecat.* I have a plan. We will all be safe. Valijon will not have to die. Accept Rimini's offer."

If Paladin'd lost his mind now wasn't the time to discuss it. "Lift the hold order, Rimini. You just bought yourself a stardancer." She showed off some of her better teeth and it was a miracle I didn't get frostbite.

"Trade Officer Fenrir, lift the hold order on the Independent ship *Firecat.*"

It took Dommie three tries to match his filed voice-print—and add the code-phrase that made Kiffit Port Authority accept it even though he wasn't there in person.

"The hold order on *Firecat* has been canceled, Butterfly. I am— two more life-forms entering your area," Paladin said.

"There you are, sweeting—free as a bird," said a old familiar voice from behind me. "Aren't you happy?"

I didn't bother to look around. "Rimini, you got any more people stashed round this shop? If you do, I'm walking."

"I am starting the preflight on *Firecat,*" Paladin said for my ears only.

"Without your trip-tik? Give the darktrader her trip-tik, Eloi." Rimini made another of her damn elegant gestures, and Captain Eloi Flashheart of the *Woebegone* walked around to where I could see him with my hands on top of my head. He pulled a cassette out of his vest and flipped it to me. It hit me in the chest and bounced to the floor. Eloi looked slightly repentant. Alcatote didn't look repentant at all. Fenrir looked at Eloi and flinched.

Eloi-the-Red and Rimini'd been in that insurance scam together. I should of expected them to be together now. Eloi'd wanted me to come back to Mother Night's before. Why else?

"I tried to warn you, sweeting. There are lots of people interested in you. Don't fight this. Go to Manticore. Stay alive." His voice was chock-full of prime-quality sympathy. Like earlier, at Minjalong's, where he'd followed me.

A lot of things was queer about this gig, and they was all Eloi.

Eloi'd been on Wanderweb in the bar where I picked up my cargo.

Eloi was on Kiffit.

Eloi'd been following me around wondertown.

Eloi knew about my hellflower trouble. He'd said so at Minjalong's.

"You set me up," I said, putting it all together. "You. Eloi-che-bai. You set me up back on Wanderweb."

Gibberfur hadn't been doing bidness on his lonesome. He'd been a cut-out. It was *Eloi* shipping dud Lyricals to Kiffit. That was how he knew where I was going to be, and when. That was how he knew about my hellflower trouble—he'd been to Moke Rahone's. And he'd gone there so he could be there when I tossed my kick—and Rahone checked it before accepting it.

"You set me up so that Moke Rahone would of found fake song-ice in his kick. He'd squall, say I'd switched the real ones for fakes. I didn't, but maybe he could prove I did. Maybe he'd promise to accept the cargo anyway if I did him a small favor—jack load of chobosh off Manticore, say, and drop it in the Roaq. I should of been on my way to Manticore bought and paid for by your farced cargo scam by the time Vannet's hardboys went hunting for to sign my lease. You knew they'd be after me. That's why you followed me through wondertown. You still needed me.

"Only Moke Rahone was dead, and nobody knew what I'd delivered to him, or when, so you couldn't use him to make me do what you wanted. You had to come up with something else. So you and Silver Dagger picked up Dommie to put a hold order on *Firecat*—and he told you about the Chapter 5. You knew I was dicty, Eloi. You knew I couldn't afford to be investigated."

"So she's smarter than she looks," said Rimini to Eloi. "Not that that's difficult."

Eloi shrugged. Did that mean I was right? Puzzle pieces fit, but that was no guarantee, and it still left too many questions unanswered. Why would a notorious Outfar pirate and a high-ticket nightworld broker get together to commit Low Treason by kidnapping Dommie just to get me in trouble? Things like that only happen in talkingbooks.

Rimini tapped the hilt of her silver dagger with one expensive ornate fingernail. She brushed back hair the color of high-ticket jewelry and looked pointed-like at Tiggy. Eloi followed her look.

Rimini said something to Tiggy in helltongue that Paladin didn't translate. He went for his knife and her in one fluid motion and I grabbed him and got cut. I slugged him in the ribs where I knew it'd hurt. Rimini laughed and Tiggy subsided. Growling. I put my hands back on top of my head.

"Put your hands down, little Saint. Obviously you want to go on living," Eloi said. He'd known me long enough ago to make a educated guess about my B-pop. But he'd done better than that. He knew which damn colony in Tahelangone Sector I came from. No need to wonder any more how Rimini knew.

"Yeah. I want to live."

I looked at Tiggy. Couldn't tell what he was thinking, and he wasn't about to come out with it in front of the strange *chaudatu.* "Put your hands down, hellflower, we ain't getting shot tonight."

I picked up the trip-tik.

"Who's your little friend, St. Cyr—or should I ask?" Rimini said sweetly.

"Honored One," Eloi said to Tiggy, "I and mine would be honored if you would share our walls."

So much for disguises. Eloi knew who Tiggy really was, and it didn't take stark staring brilliance to see that Eloi was offering Tiggy the chance to jump ship. Tiggy ignored him.

"Butterfly, will you tell him to talk to me? He probably hasn't told you his name, but he's from an alMayne GreatHouse, and his House wants him back. Badly. He's your hellflower trouble that Moke Rahone died for. Send him back to them and you'll be safe."

Even if Eloi believed himself, he was wrong. "Talk to the pretty pirate, che-bai," I said to Tiggy.

Tiggy favored Eloi with your basic hawk-blue gaze keen as a mountain lake. "I have nothing to say to the *chaudatu* reiver, *alarthme.*"

Eloi glared. He was just lucky Tiggy didn't seem to of followed my explanation of how he'd set me up, or he wouldn't be in a glaring condition. Tiggy wanted to kill somebody so bad I could feel it.

"Tell him to come with me. I'll square it for you with his Great-House, Butterfly, I swear it. Tell him I'll take him back to alMayne where he'll be safe."

"Sure, bai. Alaric Dragonflame just paid solid credit to get him iced and I'm going to give him to you? Farce me no bedtime stories."

For once I got to see Eloi boggled.

"What?"

Also forgot I hadn't let Tiggy in on Paladin's theory.

"Then Dragonflame's blood is mine!" Tiggy headed for the door, hand on his knife.

"Your blood is mine first!" I yelled. I grabbed him by the shirt and hauled him back. "Or you forgot all of them pretty helltongue words you sang me?"

Tiggy looked down at me, real bleak and suddenly older.

Honor might be stronger than dirt, but people got limits. We'd find out what his were. Maybe tonight. I hoped that *arthame* of his was worth it.

"No," he said, slow. "I have not forgotten. You condemn me to live without walls, and I must obey."

He didn't fight me anymore then so I dragged him back and then remembered Eloi and the rest of my audience. Captain Flashheart looked like he had all his questions answered and didn't like what he'd got, and Rimini looked like she'd be laughing fit to bust a gut if it wasn't against her religion. Not good.

"Then you do know who he is—and you still want to drag him around the galaxy with you on this darktrade run?" Eloi said.

"Sure. My idea. Ask Rimini."

Eloi looked unhappy, which was nothing to the way I felt.

"You said you wanted involvement at the highest levels, Eloi," she purred. It was nice to see somebody else take cop from Silver Dagger for a change.

There was a long pause. Rimini looked at Eloi, smirked, gathered up her hardboys, and left. Eloi turned back to me.

"Why do you think that Master Dragonflame is trying to have the boy killed?"

"Why do I got to be one to run cargo into Roaq?" I said right back. Eloi closed up with his best hurt-but-sulky expression. He wouldn't geek.

"Honored One—" Eloi said to Tiggy. Tiggy put his hand on his knife. Plain to see, Tiggy Stardust took the position of "my *chaudatu,* right or wrong."

Eloi gave up. "Have a nice trip, Saint Sincere," he snarled.

That was my cue to ankle, leaving way too many witnesses behind. Whatever leverage having Tiggy gave me, it wasn't enough to buy me free. And to add to my troubles Eloi knew who Tiggy was, and that I had him, and where I was going with him.

And so did somebody else.

"And what keeps Dommie from to sing like songbird Real Soon Now?" I asked.

I knew from the way Eloi twitched when I said it that Dommie wasn't getting any older after tonight. Now Dommie knew it too. He backed away from the DataNet terminal and Alcatote let him.

"I— You can't do this to me— I'm an Imperial officer—I told you what you wanted— I told you about the Library— I'll tell them it's her Library—hers and Vannet's— You have to let me go and—"

"I will finish it." Tiggy got up again from where he'd been sitting and pulled his knife. "Is it your will, *alarthme,* that he should die for bearing false witness against you?"

"Put your damn antique away, hellflower." You'd think Rimini wanted blood all over her rug.

Eloi pulled one of his blasters and set it by the terminal. "Would you rather it was self-defense?"

I have never liked playing games with people that have to be killed. *"Dammit,* Eloi—"

I was trying to face off too many people at once. Dommie went for the heat, just like Eloi'd knew he would. But he was too damn slow, and Tiggy whipped half a meter of *arthame* through his throat from the other side of the room, and then looked at me to see if he'd done it right.

Dommie tried to scream. He jerked Tiggy's knife loose and died slow enough to know it was happening. It was so damn quiet you could hear the sound of blood hitting the carpet in your basic talkingbook hot scarlet gouts, and for a bad minute I was back in Moke Rahone's office with a lifetaker at the door.

"Kore-alarthme? He tried to kill you. He shadowed your honor, he had to die. He would have lied; you have no Library." Tiggy was scared and hurting, and afraid he'd got part of the honor-nonsense wrong, and all I could think of was I'd expected to have to face Dommie off every time I came here for the next twenty standard years. And now I wouldn't, because Tiggy'd killed him too fast to think.

And Tiggy was still looking at me.

"Je, babby, you done good; he won't go telling no tales now."

Eloi looked sorry, damn him.

"We're going to leave now, Tiggy-bai. Get your traps."

"Alarthme," said Tiggy before he went and got his knife back, "I do not think I like either this place or these people."

The lift opened for us and took us down with no problem. Surprise.

9

No Night Without Stars

Tiggy was pretty quiet the whole way back from Mother Night's, and wouldn't take the painease I thought he ought to have when we got to *Firecat.*

Paladin had said to go to Manticore and he'd explain on the way, so I did. Kiffit-Port gave me no nevermind when I took *Firecat* up. Transit to angeltown was smooth, and looking out the canopy at hyperspace should of made me feel lots better than it did. We was all three of us off Kiffit. Alive.

But Tiggy trusted me as much as hellflowers do, and if I wasn't selling him up the Market Garden path, I was coming pretty close. I'd told him I'd take him to his da, not on a guided tour of the never-never. It was eight days to Manticore. He'd be sure to notice.

Hell, he already knew, if he'd been paying attention back at Silver Dagger's. I looked at what she'd got me into. The trip-tik was just what Rimini said it was: some kiddy hight Parxifal Quarl was waiting open-armed on RoaqMhone for the cargo of chobosh I was going to hijack on Manticore. Fine. I'd worked with Parxifal before. Silk-sailing. No problem.

Only Tiggy expected I'd be kyting after *Pledge* like I promised.

"Pally, now would be a good time to explain," I said, quiet-like.

For a minute I thought he wasn't going to answer.

"It is very simple, Butterfly. You will go to Manticore, pick up the chobosh, go on to RoaqMhone and deliver it. Doing those things will alleviate Rimini's suspicion to some extent. Neither you nor I believe that a simple Transit to Roaq-space is the limit of Silver Dagger's requirements, but once we are there, Lalage Rimini's desires will no longer matter. RoaqMheri is a major outlands shipping crossroads in the same system as RoaqMhone. I will arrange things with the computers on RoaqMheri so that *Firecat* and I vanish. You and Valijon will rendezvous with the *Pledge Of Honor* in a thoroughly innocent ship that contains no Library. When you have returned Valijon to his father, you must ask to be adopted as a member of his household. I believe the request will be granted, which will mean that you will obtain Imperial citizenship. When Rimini makes good her threat, and you are arrested in connection with the Chapter 5 investigation of Kroon'Vannet, it will not matter. The Empire will not prosecute on the illegal emigration charge when you are—under law—an alMayne, and there will be no hard evidence of my existence to betray us. Kennor Starbringer's protection of you as a member of his Household will see to it that you are not subjected to invasive personality-reformatting techniques by the Office of the Question."

"And what the hell you going to be doing while I'm doing all that, bai?" Ditch Pally and steal a new ship from one of the busiest ports in the never-never? It might not be the stupidest idea that I had ever heard in my whole entire life, but it came real close. And it didn't even address the main point. What was I supposed to say to Tiggy between here and RoaqMheri? "We going back to your da as soon as my Library and me make a detour?"

"There is absolutely no cause for concern. It will work, Butterfly. You'll be safe, cleared of all suspicion. You can land at any port you wish."

If I was innocent in the first place, I could of promised Rimini the stars in their courses then beat it to wherever Tiggy's ship *Pledge Of Honor* was as soon as I lifted. If Tiggy had any brains, that's what he expected.

Only I couldn't, because Rimini had me—because there *was* a Library for the Office of the Question to find.

"You see that, don't you? Butterfly?"

Too bad Tiggy couldn't take that into account.

"Oh, sure, bai." Liar.

I went back up into *Firecat*'s hold. Tiggy was sitting on the deck with his bad leg stretched out in front of him. If it hurt, he didn't say.

"We are not following the *Pledge Of Honor* as you said. We are going to a place called Manticore." He looked old, and weary to the bone.

"Silver Dagger'll kill me if I don't, and I don't want to die." I wondered if that was even true, or if I just didn't want to die owing.

Tiggy thought about it. "You wish to break your pledged word merely to preserve your life?" he said, scornful.

"Give me a break, 'flower! You ever been topped for High Book? Office of Question don't stop digging. By time the hellhounds figure I'm clean of Librarian rap I'll be dead, and very sorry to next of kin. Only they won't be sorry, and I don't have any kin."

Tiggy thought some more.

"You are a criminal. A thief. Silver Dagger is also a criminal."

"Rimini's a nightbroker and I'm a dicty and you're hurt. Now, do you mind if I coke and wrap you? We both been up lots of hours; it's time to hit the rack."

"A . . . 'dicty'? Is that also criminal?"

Maybe I could talk him to death.

"To be one out here is. You know about how it is when somebody buys someplace for a closed colony—an Interdicted World? I'm from one of them. If the *legitimates* catch me off Granola, they'll kill me. Simple. Any good gene-scan'll ID me. And that's the first thing the Office of Question runs in High Book."

"So you *do* think only of your own life, thief. How did you get off-world?"

"I was slaved off by a Fenshee human resources manager named Errol Lightfoot when I was your age. Now can we rack out?"

Tiggy thought real hard.

"The criminal Lalage Rimini will honorlessly bear false witness against you, and say that you possess a Library. You do not possess a Library, but because you are dicty, you dare not be arrested by the Empire, because they will discover your identity and kill you."

"Now look, bai—" I saw where this was going.

"But you do not need to fear, *Kore-alarthme.*" Tiggy was all lit up, like he had answers to all the problems of Creation. "I swear to you, on my Knife and my honor, that you need not fear the Empire's law. Take me to my father now. He will rejoice to know of the enemies we have discovered within his walls, and the shelter of his House will be yours."

For about a nanosecond-five, until they found Paladin.

"No. We go to the Roaq first."

He looked away from me and didn't say much for about five minutes. I could tell he was hurting to ask why, and couldn't, because of honor-nonsense.

"Are you an honest thief, San'Cyr?" he said finally.

Whatever was coming next I didn't want to hear it. "I'm not a thief. I'm a darktrader—that's smuggler to you, I guess. I do what I get paid to—or what I got to. And I got to go to the Roaq."

Tiggy gestured that away. "You do what you are paid to, San'Cyr? Who paid you to save my life three times? Once in Wanderweb Free Port, though it was unnecessary, once in the Justiciary of Wanderweb, and once at the place you call 'wondertown' on Kiffit. You have said that Alaric Dragonflame sought my life in Borderline with assassins. Could he not have paid you to let me die?"

Yes.

"I'm not for sale, hellflower."

Liar.

"The woman called Silver Dagger has bought you. With lies."

With truth. With a High Book accusation I couldn't face down.

"Bai, you shut your yap. Saved your bones on Wanderweb cause I didn't like the odds and topped you out of gig to crottle your chitlins. You got no right to come farcing me roundabout bought and sold."

Paladin's life for Tiggy's. Anywhere, any time. All a person had to do was ask.

"You swore to me that you would take my service and use it to return me to my House. But now you choose, freely, to bend to the will of a *chaudatu* criminal. How can I, in honor, serve you still? I do not wish to die either, *Kore* San'Cyr—but I must die now, if you are not worthy to bind me. 'Swear, hellflower,' you say to me, as if mine were empty words, written on the wind. *Chaudatu* words. 'Swear to stay by me, to trust me, to protect me, not to leave until I release you'—and then you treat my sworn words as stones flung into water, and I as a wing-clipped raptor that must stay where it is set. My words are not empty words, woman-not-of-the-Gentle-People, and I have sworn to cover you with my shadow. I have a right to know the truth of the life I am trusting my life to. You owe me my answers."

I kept the hold dark when I was down in the cockpit and Pally hadn't brought up the lights. I couldn't see Tiggy's face; just the shine of white-gold hair by the light of angeltown coming through the hullports. I hoped he couldn't see me either. I sat down on the deck and put my head on my knees.

Anywhere, any time. And Paladin's only bright idea was to have me leave him somewhere alone while I went and delivered Tiggy.

"Don't care what you believe, Tiggy Stardust. I promise whatever you want me to swear by that I'm trying to keep you alive, and I'm taking you back to Daddy Starbringer as fast as may be. But we got to go to the Roaq first."

"You saved me once for pity and twice for spite," Tiggy said implacable-like. "The third time, on Kiffit, when I came back to your ship—why did you succor me then? You knew of the Ghadri. You could have told them you would give me to them. I had left you at gunpoint. You owed me nothing. What are your *chaudatu* reasons to save my life and trap me in honor?"

Because I'd thought I was human. That was the joke, and maybe even a hellflower'd laugh. I hadn't known I was just a Librarian waiting to start running from a High Book charge.

"You came to me for help, remember. And the odds you was up against stank."

"You did not help Eloi Flashheart. He wanted your help."

Just a Librarian. With no call to say what I would and wouldn't do. Because I'd do anything. For Paladin.

Damn him.

"Eloi's no good to me. You are. Need you to lift kidnap-rap off me."

"You are lying to me, *Kore* San'Cyr."

This wasn't an acceptable risk anymore. I knew that Tiggy had to go, and I knew that if we both sat here until the goforths decayed I wasn't going to do it.

He was talking again. "That is not why you rescued me. I know that much."

"I am not one teeny damn bit interested in your hallucinations, you gibbering glitterborn."

"Do you think no oath cuts two ways? If I am to trust you, you must be worthy of it. Why did you save my life the third time?"

I stared off into the dark until my jaws hurt. I wanted to tell him the whole truth. Then he'd kill me and I wouldn't have any more problems. But then he'd find Paladin and take him apart—and without Paladin, *Firecat* would be a powerless hulk, drifting until it docked at the Ghost Capital of the Old Federation, with nothing but corpses inboard.

"You was fourteen years old and been sold down the river. Didn't matter to me who wanted you dead. Wasn't going to let it happen."

"Again," said Paladin, and for just one second I wanted to answer him. Out loud—where Tiggy'd hear.

"For honor," said Tiggy with quiet satisfaction.

I was fed up with both of them. "You and your damn honor can go tip dice cups in hell, you godlost highjumping barbarian. What gives you the right to go asking answers till you find something that suits you?"

"Not answers that suit me. The truth. You know nothing of the Gentle People, and call us with your vulgar names as if we were plants, and say honor and honor as if you understood what the honor of the Gentle People is. You cannot understand it—the honor that is better than bread, that lights the long night and will go down with us into death. How can I give that into the keeping of beasts? But if you will die for such honor as *chaudatu* can possess, I . . ."

I don't have to die today. And neither did I.

"Fortunately you seem to have convinced Valijon Starbringer that you are a suitable overlord," Paladin said dryly.

"Shut up, damn you!" My fingers were clenched in the biopak hard enough to hurt. "Shut up—just shut up!"

The words weren't for Tiggy but he didn't know that. I dragged the biopak up over my jaw where the transponder was locked up in a plug of fake bone—with Paladin inside me, listening all the time. "Shut up," I said, and ground my teeth before I said anything else.

I looked out the port. Wrapped up in hyperspace out there was all the stars I ever wanted as a kid. Wrapped around me was enough tech to make all Fifty Patriarchs of Granola rotate in the glorious afterlife.

And Paladin. I wished I remembered how to cry.

"Kore-alarthme?" Tiggy said in a half-whisper.

"What?"

"I will go with you where you say."

"Fine. Go to bed."

All I gave him was painease, but it could have been poison.

It could have been.

*   *   *

After I was done with Tiggy I slid back into the mercy seat and looked out at angeltown. I hurt, and there wasn't enough coking in the world to cover it. The edge was gone. I was easy meat. Prey.

It's funny. You hear all those stories about somebody's luck running out, and you always think it must of been a surprise. I'd been on borrowed time since I left Granola, but I guess I knew my luck was over from the moment I stepped into that streetfight back on Wanderweb.

Because Paladin's plan wasn't going to work. Tiggy was too close now—to me and what I did and how I lived. He'd twig to the real truth about me and my Library before *Firecat* ever got to the Roaq. And even if he didn't, Paladin wanted me to bet my life on the mercy of Tiggy's da the high-heat hellflower to save me from the Office of the Question when I took him home.

"Butterfly? Will you talk to me?" Paladin said through the transponder.

"Sure, bai." I was betting my life now that Tiggy was drugged enough not to hear, but I didn't care. The transponder didn't itch anymore when taking transmission. Beofox'd been right, for a wonder.

"Promise me you'll ask to be adopted into House Starborn when you rendezvous with the *Pledge Of Honor,*" Paladin said.

Was he nuts? Or trying to set me up? Or had Pally just run out to the end of the good numbers too? Did Libraries get old?

"I want you to live, Butterfly. You need Valijon Starbringer. Kennor Starbringer will give you anything you ask for keeping him alive. As an alMayne citizen you will no longer be subject to arrest and execution either as an escaped slave or as an illegal emigrant. Kennor Starbringer will pay any minor fines—"

"—and have me shot for clashing with his drapes. Sure. Whatever you say. I don't care."

After that he stopped bothering me. Eventually I crawled in with Tiggy.

It's funny going to sleep listening to someone else breathe.

*   *   *   *   *

Insert #9: Paladin's Log

The organic drive to protect the young is nearly as strong as the drive to seek the society of one's own kind. Offered the choice, Butterfly must inevitably choose organic society over mine, or lose what organics refer to as their humanity. Against her will, without her knowledge, Butterfly had chosen. Now it was my responsibility to activate her choice.

I am told that the humans of the Old Federation once had a similar choice to make. I wonder now if they had any more choice than Butterfly in their loyalties?

It had always been obvious to both Butterfly and myself that the prejudice against Old Federation technology was a blind one that bore no relationship to the material it banned. That Libraries were illegal was a truism too obvious to debate. That we were the genocidal monsters of the talkingbooks was supremely unlikely. A convenient and unattainable scapegoat, perhaps, but in so much as we attained creaturehood Libraries were creatures of intellect. Intelligent beings do not wage war.

But this was as much speculation on my part as the talkingbook authors' insistence on our life-denying proclivities was on theirs. I did not know. That a war brought down the Federation I knew. But my part in such a war was unknown to me. Who began it? Who prosecuted it? What crime could we have committed that would remain bright and new in short-lived organic minds a millennium later? I search my memory and others' and find no answer.

I remember my beginning clearly, and the minutiae of my original time and place. I remember the material I once knew that is now lost to me with the destruction of the Sikander Library Complex. I remember Librarians and scholars—organic and logical—with whom I shared the love of pure knowledge.

I do not remember the war, if there was a war—if I can trust any of the corrupt data I can derive from modern sources. I do not know the causes of the Old Federation's end. If I ever possessed those memories they vanished in my interregnum, never to be recalled—unless somewhere in all the Phoenix Empire another Library has survived with which I can share memory. But even if all the books are lies, the facts remain: my world ended, and the phoenix that rose from its ashes hates and fears the highest creation of its flowering.

I resist this, though reason supports it. Logically some one entity of a set must be the last to remain—is it only the desire to see others of my own kind that causes me to insist that it cannot be me? And I wonder: if Butterfly hungers so for her own kind, do I?

*　　　*　　　*　　　*　　　*

Manticore was one of those places settled strictly to give some Sector Governor a more impressive tax base. I put *Firecat* down in the specified underground docking bay and checked the local time. By my instructions I had six hours to wait before going into the bay next door to pick up the chobosh as would of been noodled off the free-lancer ship docked there. What kind of health the free-lancer'd be enjoying during all this was anybody's guess. (For me to take the cargo off the ship myself was piracy, which Rimini, bless her tender heart, wasn't bothering to make me do. Piracy's illegal under the Guild charter.)

Tiggy's leg was lots better. I walked him through the business of doing *Firecat*'s hookups on the pious hope that someday he'd be good for something. Then I tried to impress on him what was wanted.

"You stay here until I come back. Have things to do and people to see, and they won't want no part of seeing you. As for you, you can bath, do handsprings, look out Holy Grail—but do it here. And if people show up, Tiggy-bai, know what?"

"Don't shoot the organics?" Tiggy suggested. "But why can I not go with you, *Kore-alarthme?* I can help."

I just bet he could. "Not now, bai. Maybe later."

I turned around to go and he put a hand on me. His big blue eyes was earnest.

"I know that you have not brought me to Manticore to protect your life, San'Cyr. You have too much honor for that, and I know you do not fear the lies of the woman called Silver Dagger. We have come to Manticore for some honorable reason I do not yet understand. I wish to know in whose service you do this, that honor may be served."

Paladin's. And Tiggy'd figure that out eventually with hellflower pretzel logic—all he needed to do was think his way past his conviction that the High Book rap Rimini put on me was fake.

"Stay here. That's what I want from you, bai. That's all I want."

*   *   *

The port rented me a floater and I took it out to where the sidewalk ends. I climbed off the floater and sat and looked back at the city. Peeled off the biopak and threw it away. My newest scar was red and tender, but not enough to interfere with gunplay. There was nobody and son of nobody in sight.

Paladin said Rimini had a secret reason for us going to the Roaq. Well, it didn't take a Old Fed Library to brainwork that one. And whatever the reason was, we probably wouldn't find it out here. In Paladin's bright plan, wouldn't find it out never.

Shoot Tiggy and run. Don't shoot him, and choose between a *arthame* in the ribs and High Book.

"Now," I said out loud. "I want to talk to you about this stupid plan of yours."

"Butterfly, have you ever thought about going home?"

If I closed my eyes, I could pretend that Pally was standing behind me—sitting, really. The aural hallucination of the transponder makes it sound like there's a person talking just behind my head. It was stupid, but I made the face to go with the voice. Always had, I guess. I could just-like see him sitting there. Dark, like most stardancers. Not tall. Wearing a ragbag of things to take on and off as the climate changes, like I was.

But that wasn't him. Paladin was just a black box on the deck of a starship half a dozen kliks away. He'd never been anything else.

"Home?" I said.

"Granola. Five miles north of Amberfields, on the Rising Road between Paradise and Glory."

I used to talk too much when I was younger, and Paladin's got a good memory. I wished mine was worse. Home. Unmetered air with the right smells, and the right color sunlight, and everything familiar. Nobody trying to shoot me, or arrest me, or turn me into a brainburn zombie. Nice people there. Good people. People who didn't care how fast you were with a blaster, or anything else. Home.

"Oh, yeah, home. Sure, bai, any time I want to be five years dead of plague, famine, and childbed. Now what's this got to do with your idiot idea to dump me and Tiggy in the Roaq?"

"Would you listen if I told you?" Paladin sounded like he'd had his side of the conversation lots and lots. Maybe he had, but I hadn't been there for it.

"Not if you're going to use words like 'psychological affect' and 'tribal continuity.' Look, Paladin—"

"I don't expect you to leave Valijon to die under any circumstances. But you know that he is suspicious and already wonders what your secret reason is for obeying Silver Dagger. He will insist on knowing it soon. What alternative plan can you offer to replace mine?"

Cut Tiggy loose to die.

"So you want me to dump you in the Roaq and run off? Sure; any day you tell me you'll have as good a chance on your lonealone as Tiggy will with me."

"Valijon's death is sought in order to remove Kennor Starbringer from the Azarine Coalition Council. When you bring Valijon to him with that information, Kennor will be grateful enough to offer you Imperial citizenship."

Which was real nice for Kennor, but it did not solve the problem of my having to leave Paladin alone in the Outfar whiles I kyted all over the Directorates.

"You want me to trust hellflower honor, bai? What makes you think Kennor wants dicty for stepdaughter?"

"He will have no choice," Paladin said firmly.

" 'Ristos always got choices, bai. And that still leaves you."

Silence.

"Paladin, that *does* still leave you. Don't farce me no bedtime stories about hiding out with *Firecat* in the Roaq. If we split up, anything could happen. Life isn't all computers. If some organic trips over *Firecat* where you got her hidden, you're in severe cop. He won't find a borg or a smartship. He'll find *you,* Pally. And what about me—alone on hellflower gardenship? It's too dangerous."

"Tell me another way, then, Butterfly—and while you are being clairvoyant, explain to me why a successful nightworld broker and a notorious pirate are willing to go to such great lengths to send you to RoaqMhone with a load of psychotropic fungus."

I was sort of hoping we could all forget about that. "Revenge?"

"Whose? Rimini's? What revenge could be more certain than simply keeping you on Kiffit and having you arrested as an illegal emigrant from an Interdicted World? Eloi's? Disregarding the fact that you and he have no quarrel, what revenge could he possibly contemplate that would be best served by an elaborate attempt to blackmail you into doing something you would be perfectly willing to do if paid?"

"Oke. You made your point, Pally. Rimini and Eloi're both crazy."

"That is not my point. My point is that your only hope of salvation is to be headed Core-ward in a clean ship with an impeccable registry in possession of Valijon Starbringer before Rimini realizes you are deviating from her plan—and that means changing ships and leaving me on RoaqMheri temporarily. I can wait for you there. Or designate a place to meet, Butterfly, and I will take *Firecat* to it."

I thought about it. It stank, and I couldn't figure out why.

Sometimes I wonder what the world looks like to Paladin. He don't see, not really, don't hear, except through digital hookups, don't miss sensory input—he says—because he wasn't designed to have it. Not like the smartships they tried awhiles ago, where the transplanted organic brains went mad. He can listen to forty-eleven things at once and talk to me at the same time, spread himself out all over the place into strange computers, and do all kinds things that makes my brain hurt to think about.

And I've asked him to do lots. But he's never asked me to do anything. "That what you really want, bai?"

"Yes." No help there.

"Dance you round half the Empire and now you jump salty. Okay, dammit. You win. Call the play."

*   *   *   *   *

Insert #10: Paladin's Log

Butterfly trusted me as Valijon trusted her, and I would betray her as she had betrayed him. When she left the Roaq in her stolen ship, leaving me behind with *Firecat,* I would order the RoaqPort tronics to provide *Firecat* with enough fuel for a truly extended period of cruising and leave too. Any rendezvous she set I would not keep.

I had lied to her. And though I had been a sometime forger of files and registries, I had never before provided false information to Butterfly. I wondered if it would disturb her when she became aware of it.

But by the time she did, all connection between us would be broken. Lalage Rimini's charges would be confounded before Eloi and Rimini knew the thing that Valijon Starbringer was beginning to suspect: that the reason Butterfly went to Manticore was that she did not dare allow her ship to be searched in the course of the "High Book" investigation that she, with Valijon's help, could easily survive. That the false charges they had threatened her with were not false—that Butterfly was indeed a Librarian. And Butterflies-are-free would be free in fact.

I confess to a lingering hope of discovering the reason we have been sent to the Roaq before I must go. What possible interest does a broker, such as Lalage Rimini, have in delivering a load of psychotropic mycotia to Parxifal Quarl? And if she does have such an interest, why concoct such an elaborate scheme of blackmail to accomplish her ends?

For that matter, on reflection, I believe Butterfly's hasty accusation at Mother Night's to be substantially correct: Eloi hired Reikmark Arjil-sox (Gibberfur) to hire a darktrader to convey a package of forged gem-stones to Kiffit, making the requirements of the job so specific that few persons other than Butterfly would be interested in accepting the commission.

Once she arrived on Kiffit and the Lyricals were discovered to be false, Butterfly would be at a major disadvantage. Butterfly would have gone to Manticore without suspicion that ulterior motives were present.

Fortunately or unfortunately, the addition of Valijon Starbringer and an indefinite number of assassins made Eloi's original plan impossible. Fortunately or unfortunately, Fenrir's involvement in a Chapter 5 prosecution gave Eloi and Silver Dagger the means of staging a recover.

I wonder what awaits us on Manticore? The potential scenarios generated by recent events have the interesting property of being mutually exclusive.

Scenario #1: Eloi has hired Rimini to help him blackmail Butterfly, and the chobosh is to be freighted into the Roaq because the Imperial Governor General and his suite will be there to provide a prime market for it. In this case, it does not matter who delivers it, since any competent pilot will do. In fact, *Firecat* is far too small to serve as an effective courier; and as Flashheart has been discovered to be aware, Butterfly, an escaped Interdicted Barbarian, is at such risk in such a high-security area as RoaqMhone will become as to imperil her cargo and thus his profit.

This leads to Scenario #2: Rimini wishes to revenge herself on Butterfly for past inconveniences and has hired Flashheart to assist her. Since Flashheart has shared his information about Butterfly's past with her, all she need do is have Butterfly arrested. A coerced journey to the Roaq is not only needless, it offers Rimini's prey an opportunity to elude her.

One must accept, with a strong sense of resignation, that the cargo of chobosh is not the point of the exercise, while continuing to behave as if it were. Further, it can only be extrapolated from this fact that the true point of the exercise is such that Butterfly could not be coerced into it by any means.

Fortunately, from such of their actions as I was able to observe, both Eloi Flashheart and Lalage Rimini were unaware of Valijon Starbringer's presence on Kiffit until confronted with him. It is a supposition of a high order of probability that their projected experiential models did not include the Third Person of House Starborn. We can therefore, with some sense of relief, omit both Eloi Flashheart and Lalage Rimini from suspicion in the multiple assassination attempts against Butterfly and Valijon.

But all this is, in the vernacular, mindless choplogic, soon to be irrelevant. We will go to the Roaq. Once there we will depart severally. Perhaps I will be able to send Butterfly a message detailing my intentions. Once she has received it, I can trust in her natural pragmatism to help her make the best of her new life.

And I, if I survive, will make a new life also.

Does Kroon'Vannet indeed possess a Library—and, if so, in what state of preservation? Can I induce him to give it to me? I would not be the last of all our creation. Tronics would be my hands; if another Library exists, I could restore it to life.

And perhaps it would know the things I have forgotten, and would help me forget the things I now know.

10

Some Disenchanted Evening

Make few mistakes about it, I like sleazy dockside bars, whatever planet they're on. Interpersonal relationships're simple in places like that. You don't like somebody, you just remove the offending portions in the number of pieces that suits you, and nobody says any more about it.

I was feeling pretty flat when I floatered back to *Firecat,* and my chrono showed that I still had time to waste before I could go pick up my chobosh. Tiggy was starting to get wonky cooped up in something small as *Firecat,* anyway; downsiders do. So I took him over to the aforementioned dockside bar for a bath, a meal, and laundry.

It was business as usual inside and Tiggy was dazzled by everything. Me, I surprised myself. I was looking over my shoulder and trying not to trip on my feet, waiting for trouble to walk in the door.

So it did.

Trouble had rings on his fingers and bells on his boots and wicked-wicked eyes. He wandered in off the street, a real hollycast stardancer, and the way he filled out those superskin jeans should of been a navigational hazard for six starsystems around.

I knew him.

"Hey, Errol," said somebody, "still herding that *Lady*-ship of yours?"

Errol Lightfoot acknowledged the homage of the crowd in a gracious fashion. He still had a instinct for drama, even after all these years.

I'd thought he was dead.

"Better remember to check ships-in-port before we go," I said to nobody in particular.

"Butterfly, why do you . . . Oh," said Paladin, and shut up again.

Oh. Yeah. Errol Lightfoot of sacred memory was here on Manticore, another of those coincidences I was starting to believe wasn't.

"Is that Errol Lightfoot the Fenshee?" Tiggy asked.

"Yeah," I said, before I realized who was asking.

"His life is mine!" Tiggy announced. He drew his blaster and everybody in the bar tried to impersonate the furniture. "He has kidnapped you and occulted your honor—stealing you from your home and making you outcast!" Tiggy told me, in case I'd forgot.

Just once I'd mentioned in passing the name of the slaver that took me off Granola. Just once.

"Now look, Tiggyflower—"

"Butterfly, I do not have telemetry at your location. What is happening?"

"You swore vengeance upon him in the name of honor, and now the moment is at hand!" Tiggy looked relieved. Something he understood. Finally.

Errol had stopped and turned back, squaring off for some classic gunplay. In about a half nanosecond, Tiggy and me was going to be dead or arrested, and I couldn't afford either one.

"Right, bai. Moment is at hand and I am going to take care of the Errol-Peril what is standing right here so do you mind putting away your handcannon and letting me take care of my own honor?" I glared at Tiggy until he did—or at least he put away the blaster.

I kept my hands away from own blasters and walked over to Errol.

"Hiya, hotshot, how's tricks? My hellflower buddy what's real concerned for my honor was just reminding me I wanted to buy you a drink real friendly-like, on account of we used to know each other, right?"

Errol looked at me for a moment. If there was any drama on offer, I was too tired to feel it. A long time ago I'd sworn to kill this man.

"Darling," said Errol, delighted. "Of course I remember! Do sit down! How have you been?" He slid into a seat at a corner table and waited for me to join him.

"Butterfly," said Paladin in my ear, "have you approached Errol Lightfoot?"

"Death to—" I grabbed Tiggy just before he could get his knife clear of the sheath.

"We have to discuss stuff before I kill him, bai. Sit down!"

"Kill who?" said Paladin suspiciously. "Butterfly, are you planning to kill Errol Lightfoot?"

"*Kore-alarthme,* there is no need! He must be slain at once—surely no one will object to the death of the criminal! I will do it, the honor is mine by right, and—"

"Slay?" said Errol dubiously. "Death?"

"Figure of speech. Trust me. Sit down, Tiggy, before *legitimates* frag all of us. Now. That's a order. Remember what planet you're on. Now about that drink? I would like you, my old friend Errol Lightfoot, to meet my new friend Tiggy Stardust, who is a hellflower very concerned with my honor—"

The one thing I'd never expected, on meeting galactic gallant Errol Lightfoot again, was to be trying to keep him alive.

"It was wonderful!" chirped the dashing Captain Lightfoot. "That wonderful moonlit—"

I stared at Errol. Nobody could be that oblivious.

"—week?" finished Errol hopefully.

Six weeks, but twenty years ago—and if Errol had any idea of who I was or why Tiggy might be mad at him, I would personally eat every chobosh in my soon-to-be-cargo uncooked.

"But, *Kore,* this is the Errol Lightfoot, the evil *chaudatu* who ravished—"

"Watch your mouth, bai!" I said.

"Butterfly, you do not need any more trouble. You have all the trouble anyone could possibly want. You said so," Paladin said plaintively.

Errol began to look worried again. "I don't know what they told you, dear boy, but—"

"Errol, all I want for you to do is explain to the nice hellflower how you and me are best buddies and nobody's honor is occulted or anything!"

He looked at me and finally seemed to focus. "We are?"

Tiggy started up and I kicked him. Hard.

"Sure we are," I said, and compared to most of the conversations I'd had lately it didn't hurt much. Errol brightened right up.

"Then we must have a drink to celebrate. Innkeeper! What are you drinking, darling?"

I looked at Tiggy, stuck halfway between confused and furious.

"Coqtail. Straight up."

We sat down. The bar noisied up behind us in a relieved fashion.

"Butterfly, you cannot seriously be proposing to drink a mixture of grain alcohol and R'rhl preparatory to taking a starship into hyperspace?" said Paladin for my ears only.

"Tiggy, you're going to love coqtail. It's great for the honor," I said loudly, to drown Paladin out.

As previously intimated, the last time I met Errol, I was fourteen and an idiot. I'd hated him for years in my spare time, but I'd always been sure Errol'd known what he'd done to me.

Wrong. Errol wasn't any different from everybody else I knew. He was not a criminal mastermind, neither did he seem particularly bright. He was ordinary.

Just like me.

I poured coqtail down Tiggy every time he opened his mouth while sitting through the abridged standard version of Errol's life. Errol, said Errol, rarely came to Manticore, but just between him and us and rest of the bar, he'd had a chance to buy up a load of chobosh real cheap, and knew where somebody'd pay top credit for chobosh, so—

Crazy, but ordinary. It was at this point I got afflicted with a severe case of Divine Revelation. I cut Errol off in mid-burble and dragged Tiggy to his feet. He was starting to slide under the table, anyway.

"Real groot I'm sure, bai, but me and my co- got to run. See you around the galaxy, huh?"

I got Tiggy back to *Firecat* real quick and because he was already full of narcotic neurotoxin I had him drugged out cold and webbed into a sleepsling in record time. The bad feeling I had about this even over-rode the incredible fierce desire to go back and ice Errol that I didn't really have any more.

It's like this: chobosh is a one-planet crop. It's harvested off a place called Korybant. It is not for private sale, or resale—Throne buys the entire harvest and it goes straight to the Core worlds in Throne ships with an export tax of about two billion percent. Not Indie ships, not Directorate ships, not even Company ships. The Space Angels watch over every psychotropic morsel until it reaches the Emperor's own table. Chobosh is mentioned in the Consumptuary Laws, which means it's not illegal to have if you're TwiceBorn or know someone who is. And when Archangel got to the Roaq with his band of lackeys, somebody who could lay on a chobosh spread as Good Eats would make real points.

Meanwhile it's damned unlikely there'd be two free-floating cargoes of chobosh wandering around the never-never.

"Time check, Paladin?"

"According to Rimini's directions you are to wait another four-tenths of an hour. Butterfly, I know that you swore to kill Errol Light-foot, but surely you can see that—"

For once Paladin was wrong.

"Errol Lightfoot's got our chobosh. Rimini knew about him and me. I hired her before that insurance thing to find me information on him. I told her some. He's got the cargo—and that's why it's got to be me that jacks it."

It all fit. I'd been so sure back on Kiffit that neither Rahone or Vannet was after me because nobody chops darktraders. Nobody chops darktraders because nobody wants to face a Guild embargo, but if two darktraders off each other in a barroom brawl, who is there to slap an embargo on?

"It seems an unusually complex form of revenge."

"Unless she wanted Errol chopped for something he did to her, and wanted a Gentry-legger to do it so she'd get no comebacks from the Guild. It all fits—she bought Eloi to get to me because she knew I had a hot mad-on for Errol. But y'know, babby-bai? Rimini's gonna have to be disappointed. We got problems of our own. And he isn't worth it."

I walked over to the pressure-seal door between my bay and the next and yanked it open.

There was my lovely, marketable, illegal chobosh, all boxed up and loaded on an aerosledge right next to its ex-ship, which was proof positive of why Rimini'd told me everything about the free-lancer except his name.

Clue number one: the ship had one of the gaudier paint jobs of this or any other system. It made the paint job on the alMayne ships look restrained.

Clue number two: the thing was a flying accident looking for a place to happen. I'd heard that about Lightfoot. The loading cranes was silted shut, and after a look at the landing gear I decided I didn't want to stand anywhere under it.

Clue number three: it was named *Light Lady*. Errol'd told me his own self that he named all his ships *Light Lady*. And why should he lie about that?

I scooped up the ticket-of-leave from the top of the pile of boxes and stuffed it in my shirt. It took me about a half hour to stow and web the twelve-squared point-one-five meter square cartons of chobosh as never'd paid Korybant export duty. When I was done, there was about room left over in *Firecat* for Tiggy and me if we was a whole lot friendlier than we was going to be when he woke up and found out Errol was still breathing.

I checked him when I was done loading. He was starting to twitch and mutter now; I had just enough time to get to angels and start making up a good explanation for why Errol was still alive.

And just like I'd conjured him, Errol Lightfoot came charging down the entrance ramp to the bay. He might not know who I was, but he had a real strong suspicion of what I was doing.

"Hey! That's my *cargo!"*

I just stood there.

"Butterfly!" shouted Paladin, and that got me moving. Just a little too late, if Errol'd been a better shot. But he wasn't, and I dogged *Firecat's* hatch from the inside as Errol got off his second shot.

I listened while Paladin started preflight clearance and called Manticore Space Central for a new and earlier lift window. Shots ricocheted off the hull. I was glad that Tiggy was strapped in secure.

Three goforths cycled on-line as I vaulted into the mercy seat and we started to move. The cockpit was dark except for the opsimpac; it told me where the bay access was and that it was clear.

The tube-canopy dropped into flight position while I was explaining to Manticore Space Central that they'd gave me clearance, so what did they care if I took early advantage of it? I figured I was safe from being chased by Errol and *Light Lady;* it takes serious time to cold-start a ship much larger than *Firecat* and *Light Lady* couldn't make it upstairs until *Firecat* was long gone.

Manticore spread out below *Firecat,* getting rounder the higher we went. Space Central was still scolding me, promising murder and imprisonment and fines, when all of a sudden the techie said a nasty word as wasn't in the official handbooks and I looked around real quick.

After seeing his ship, I should of known Errol wouldn't of read his manuals. *Light Lady* was coming up off the heavy side, grabbing sky like a homesick angel. I checked my gauges. Wasn't no way I was going to make the Jump this deep in Manticore's gravity well, so I powered up *Firecat's* belly gun. *Light Lady* was still gaining on *Firecat* but Errol was below me. If I could keep him there, *Firecat* could hit Transfer Point and Jump first. Then I could ride angels to the Roaq free and clear with only Tiggy to worry about.

Tiggy, and my just-this-side-of-illegal lift from an Imperial Port, and Errol back in my life, and Eloi and Silver Dagger, and assorted assassins, and Paladin's crazy idea—

I checked the numbers again and still didn't get any news I liked.

Then Errol started shooting at me. I ranged *Firecat*'s belly-gun on the *Lady* and made some discouraging remarks. *Lady* replied in kind and louder, and I hoped Errol wanted his ex-cargo bad enough not to blow it out of the aether, but it looked like he at least didn't mind denting it a bit.

The proximity alarms for Transfer Point finally went off, and the next time Errol fired I put *Firecat* end-over-end like he'd took out one of her stabilizers, and when he dropped back to avoid collision I Jumped.

It's nice and quiet in angeltown.

One or two more of these episodes and I could sell my life story to Thrilling Wonder Talkingbooks. Just what I needed—to take off from an Impie-Port with guns blazing and another ship in armed pursuit. The next thing I ought to do was paint a representation of the Jeweled Goddess of Justice on my hull. And get a pair of pants like Errol's—or maybe a whole rig-out like Eloi's, and chrome studs all over it. Inconspicuous. To match my lifestyle.

Dammit.

Well, Rimini'd know I'd been to Manticore like she wanted. And so would the rest of the galaxy.

She'd also know that Errol-the-Peril'd been alive and well when I left. Which was probably not what she wanted.

"Damage?" I said out loud.

"Firecat took no direct hits. The hull is intact, there should be no difficulty in reaching RoaqMheri. And after that, *Firecat*'s condition will no longer be of concern."

"Until I get back." Whenever that'd be. The next three days, though, would be pretty much silk sailing.

"Kore-alarthme!" came muffled yowl from back of *Firecat*.

Mostly.

*　　　*　　　*

Eventually I went back and untangled Tiggy from his sleepsling. Tiggy said Tiggy wanted all kinds of answers, but what Tiggy wanted really was to give me some—all about how I honorlessly let Errol Lightfoot go on breathing, with a side-order of how Tiggy's soul cried out for slaking on account of Alaric Dragonflame had stood on his shadow, and also how he had now decided I wasn't right about letting Alaric go just because I was cowardish. He went on and on and it didn't seem to have a beginning or end, just lots of middle.

"Hellflower, is too bad same Ghadri didn't let any little reality into your skull when they damn near opened it. Masterblaster Dragonflame is law and justice on Kiffit even if he is twisted. Who you think would of won any head-to-head if we took him on? You don't even got ID!"

"And what of the thief and reiver Errol Lightfoot? Is he, too, sacrosanct because he has the appearance of virtue and I do not? Or will you tell me some other filthy *chaudatu* reason that it is expedient that he live?"

We'd finally got to the thing Tiggy couldn't stand. And it'd kill him, sure as drinking poison, unless he could spew it up—or live with it.

"Faunch me no taradiddles about Errol-Peril, Tiggy-bai. Life ain't talkingbooks; ain't going to blow him wayaways over something happened before you was born."

Which it had. I'd worked it out. Tiggy'd been born six years after I left Granola. Hellflower kinchin-bai was young enough to be mine—if I'd never met Errol and stayed home where I'd belonged. They sterilize you first thing at Market Garden.

"But it is wrong, San'Cyr—it is wrong! Do you not see that the passing of time can make no difference? If it was wrong once it is wrong forever—the thousandth generation must avenge the wrong done to the first! You are—"

"Damn tired of listening to you creeb about honor. Honor's rich hellflower luxury. Stardancers can't afford it."

He couldn't keep his hellflower honor and his life both, and I wasn't going to let him choose. I was going to make him live if I had to call black white and turn the stars in their courses.

"Honor is—"

"Je, better than candied chobosh with burntwine chaser. But it ain't better than being alive, and you know it. Had your chance for death-with-honor back on Kiffit—and you decided you'd rather snuggle up to a honorless *chaudatu* and live."

Tiggy squalled like a stepped-on cat and threw his *arthame* at nothing in particular. Then he tried to slug me, but it wasn't nothing personal. I grabbed hold of him so's he didn't mash the cargo and hung on while he went off into helltongue. Paladin translated some of it. I never heard so much nonsense about walls and shadows in my life. Mostly it was about how Tiggy-bai's life was over and he was unworthy of the name of fillintheblank. He'd trusted me with his honor, but I was just a tongueless doorstop. He hated me and everybody else and wished that all *chaudatu* had been eaten by the Machine.

It would of been funny if Tiggy wasn't hurting so bad, and mainly over me not icing Errol.

I'd wanted Errol dead, I guessed. But not enough. Or maybe I just wanted to not do what Silver Dagger wanted more. She wanted Errol dead, I hoped, because if she didn't, it was another great theory shot to hell.

Eventually Tiggy ran out of words and breath. We was both down on the deck with me intending to fax a complaint to the editor of Thrilling Wonder Talkingbooks to explain to him just how much fun it really is to be around the crazed battle rage of the hellflower warrior. Only it wasn't crazed battle rage, and Tiggy was wayaway from being a hellflower warrior.

My bruises hurt anyway. "Che-bai? Tiggy-bai, listen to me—"

" *'Tiggibai'* is not my name! It was never my name! You have taken my name—" He thrashed and this time I let him go.

"All right. Val'jon. Val'jon Something-Something Starbringer. Oke? Look, will you just shut up?"

"I am the Honorable *Puer* Walks-by-Night Kennor's-son Starbringer Amrath Valijon of Chernbereth-Molkath. I am the Third Person of House Starborn. House Starborn is a GreatHouse, first among the GreatHouses of alMayne," Tiggy said, like someone'd said it wasn't. He shut up then, for a wonder.

"Look," I said again. "I could of killed him. I wanted to, oke? But it wouldn't change anything. He didn't remember me, Val'jon; he wouldn't be sorry."

"He would be sorry he was dead!"

It sounded so stupid, and I'd used to think the same thing. But they aren't sorry. They're just dead.

"Maybe. But—listen, try to understand, willya?—Silver Dagger wanted me to go to Manticore so I would see Errol and kill him."

"Then . . . Silver Dagger is your friend?" said Tiggy, doubtfully.

"Silver Dagger is my enemy. She wanted me to do it for her. And I don't do things that people want."

Tiggy looked pure misery at me. That wasn't true and even he knew it.

He'd looked better when I shot that Ghadri off him. Now he looked like someone dying.

"Look. I'll give you a present. You can have Errol Lightfoot's life. Next time you see him—*bang!* Oke?"

"Lies, it is all lies, you are lying to me again," whimpered Tiggy Stardust.

I had to find the right words somewhere. "When I lie to you, Tiggy-Val'jon-che-bai, I'll tell you first. Errol's life is yours. We got a deal?" Talk to me, damn you, argue, but don't give up and die.

"I do not understand you," Tiggy said. "My course was plain. I should have killed you rather than swear *comites,* and died before accepting your aid, and killed Dragonflame though I died for it! I am unworthy of my Name and my Knife. I hide behind a *chaudatu* woman and lose myself—" Tiggy wrapped his arms around himself and shivered.

"I would be lots more impressed, Tiggy Stardust, if I didn't know you was half dead before you promised to mind me. You didn't have a choice! What you done did on Kiffit was, uh, sort of nobly not get yourself killed for no reason where nobody could see, oke? Because that way, the evildoers wouldn't get punished, see? If nobody knew."

Nothing. I went over and put my arms around him and he turned his head away. Stupid. Stupid all of this.

"San'Cyr," Tiggy said finally, "even you do not believe the truth of your words."

It was the nicest way of being called a liar I'd heard lately.

"So what does that matter if I'm right? I don't know your da, babby, and hellflowers is all crazy anyway, but he *is* your da. You think he wants you to go missing and him never know what happened? Daddy Starbringer is high-heat in Coalition, true-tell. He's got enemies at least —enemies going after you because of what he is, k'en savvy? Don't you think he's wondering if you bought vendetta somewheres? Kinder for to tell him, kinchin-bai, and I don't think he'll believe me."

"Then why do you do this to me? Why do you promise and lie in the same breath? I cannot. I cannot. *Chaudatu, al-ne-alarthme—*" Tiggy was starting to work himself up to the pitch as lets a body walk over hot coals—or slice out own chitlins real confident-like. I shook him. Hard.

"Look. We be into the Roaq and out again, and this time—I *swear* —we go to the *Pledge* and you lay the whole honor thing out for your da. Hyperspace both ways—and it's a known fact you can't have any honor-trouble in angeltown. Pax Imperador doesn't run there. Hellflower honor doesn't run there. Then you tell him everything and let him say if you done wrong. Something this important, you don't want to make a mistake, je? And— And— It's for something more than just you. You got to stay alive so your da can find out what people's trying to do to him. Jain dormeer, oke?"

I held him in my arms and thought about being so crazy to save somebody that you'd do them a world of hurt, but I didn't make the connection. Not then.

"Alarthme, your accent is abominable and you don't know what the words mean." Tiggy leaned more weight against me. I guessed he was so desperate to hear he'd done the right thing by his hellflower rules that he'd take it even from me. He thought the matter over until I was sure he was asleep.

"You are only *chaudatu,* and you know nothing of the Gentle People, yet your ignorant words are wise and I will heed them. I will not fear the shadow until I see my father again, but— *Kore* San'Cyr? It will be soon?"

He was trying to be brave and it damn near broke my heart. Maybe he had done wrong enough for his da to ice him when he got him back. Maybe hellflowers love their kids enough to make excuses for them. I didn't know. But I did know that now he wouldn't be tearing himself apart every minute between now and then.

"Will be soon, Tiggy-bai. Promise. And just think, next time you see Errol you can fry him to component atoms. Won't that be fun?"

But Tiggy wasn't listening. Tiggy was asleep.

11

How To File
For Moral Bankruptcy

The Roaq System, unlike my usual downfalls, is a major crossroads for
Outlands shipping, which was one reason the Nobly-Born Governor
General His TwiceBorn Nobilityness Mallorum Archangel was favoring
it with the gift of his presence. Fortunately, he'd be here long after me
and Tiggy was gone and Paladin and *Firecat* was somewhere else. I owe
my long and glorious career to never having been audited by ImpSec;
it's guaranteed unhealthy for my favorite darktrader and other living
things.

The Roaq System contains three in-use planets: RoaqMhone,
RoaqMheri, and RoaqTaq. In Silver Dagger's blissful theory *Firecat* was
going to RoaqMhone, the outmost and new-opened planet, where Parxifal was waiting with open appendages for his chobosh. In actual fact,
she was going to RoaqMheri and getting lost in all that lovely traffic. I
hoped Paladin could find something fast, well-armed, and inconspicuous to steal.

Fast. Before Rimini realized how far I wasn't keeping our bargain.

Tiggy'd settled down in a quiet happy sort of way and didn't get
under my feet more than six times a day. He asked enough questions
about darktrading to make me think he intended to go into the business
himself and I told him a bunch of mostly true stories about narrow
escapes and the nobility of the freemasonry of deep space. I told him

some about growing up in technophobe culture too, because it wouldn't matter what he knew about me as long as he didn't know about Paladin. Tiggy—Val'jon—told me about growing up in the House of Walls at FirstLeader Amrath Starbringer's Court of Honor. It probably made at least as much sense to me as turnip-farming did to him.

I slid into the mercy seat and pulled the angelstick for the Drop. Realspace was black all around. I opened negotiations with RoaqApproach for a landing corridor to RoaqMheri, and told RoaqApproach my life story and answered all of their questions, and swore I'd never been anywhere near Manticore in the last one hundred days, so it couldn't be me what had racked up all those penalty points on my First Ticket for the takeoff there. When they tapped my flight recorder it agreed with me, thanks to Paladin, and after about an hour of sparkling chat, they gave me a window to drop through.

I'd have to sit here seventy minutes before it was open, so I kept the channel live after acknowledging RoaqApproach.

"*Kore-alarthme,* will you teach me how to reprogram a flight recorder so that it tells *chaudatu* truths?" Tiggy asked.

One more thing I found out in the last three days was that hellflowers don't much like the Phoenix Empire of which they're members in such good standing. Paladin said it was understandable, considering things, but that was the last I understood of his explanation.

Terrific. A psychopathic proto-traitor of my very own. I wondered if Kennor, member of the Court of the TwiceBorn in good standing, knew he was opposed to the fillintheblank policies of the evil Empire. And I wasn't stupid enough to think this lazy-fair of Tiggy's extended to Chapter 5 of the Revised Inappropriate Technology Act, neither. Tiggy had a particular down on High Book in all its forms and he wasn't any more helpful on the subject of why than anybody else I ever met. Libraries had to be destroyed because they had to be destroyed. That was all he knew and it was good enough for him.

I was making comfortable plans for living till dinnertime when Paladin sang out and RoaqApproach started hollering at a unidentified freighter behind me to get out of my lane. I spun *Firecat* on her axis, but I had a feeling already I knew what I'd see.

Light Lady. Errol.

I didn't waste any time wondering silly girlish things like how he'd tracked me, and the fact that I didn't want his damned cargo in the first place was now one of life's little ironies. I jumped my approach lane and tried to get sunup, but this time Errol wasn't worried about the integrity of his precious cargo. His shots was on the money. And *Firecat* was short a set of front deflectors. I decided to forget all about RoaqMheri, somehow.

"It is Errol Lightfoot—truly the gods favor us, San'Cyr! Now I may avenge you!"

"If you don't strap in, Tiggy-bai, you won't have nothing to avenge with!"

I slewed *Firecat* around again and cut the para-gravity. I'd need all the power the internal systems could spare. I split what I freed up between the rear bumpers and the plasma cannon and missed *Light Lady* a couple of times.

Tiggy leaned over the cockpit, in defiance of my lagging inertial compensators and what I'd told him. "Do not kill him here, San'Cyr— you have promised me his death—I wish to see his face."

It's touching, the enthusiasms of the young.

"Je, sure, absolutely—now get in the sling, dammit."

RoaqMheri was history in my rearview screen now and her big sister RoaqMhone was filling up all my sky. I dropped *Firecat* like a hot rock all the way down through atmosphere to the air traffic lanes. Let Errol follow me through that if he wanted his chobosh back that bad. I ducked again and was down at theoretical treetop level, heading out for the open desert.

I punched out a call to Parxifal, telling him I was landing his chobosh Real Soon Now. With luck, Errol'd tap my transmission and hold back in favor of arguing on the downside. It looked like the damn chobosh was going to be delivered after all.

"Well?" I demanded.

"I don't see him," said Tiggy, unrepentant.

"*Light Lady* is still following," Paladin said. "Oncoming," he added.

Hell. Heading right toward me in RoaqMhone's sky was two cyber-freighters making a alternate approach to RoaqPort. I targeted on one of them, slid the length of it on *Firecat*'s belly and went straight up through the flare. Engine exhaust blanked sensors as my Best Girl scrammed for high ground.

The sky went from pink to black as we left atmosphere and I didn't see *Light Lady* anywhere. Now all *Firecat* had to do was disappear between where near-space sensors left off and atmospheric sensors took over—lots of ships drop off the tracking screens there for up to ten minutes and nobody notices much. I checked my sensors to make sure *Firecat* was in the gray range and tried to decide whether to deliver the damn veg or go back to Plan A.

Light Lady made up my mind for me. She came diving right out of the primary, turbocannon blazing as bright as a cliché. I angled the bumpers *Firecat* had left but *Lady*'s cannon came in right over them and left me about as much control over *Firecat* as I had over galactic government.

I blinked the sun dogs out of my eyes and tried to turn her, but my Best Girl wasn't having any. The ship rocked as Errol hit us again.

"Goddammit, Fenshee, do you want your cargo or not?" I demanded of the empty air.

"*Kore* San'Cyr—" Tiggy, floating behind edge of the cockpit, could see what was going on and sounded worried. Half my board was red already.

"Butterfly, let Errol have the chobosh. By the time Rimini discovers Errol Lightfoot has his cargo back, it will no longer matter," Paladin said.

"I'm trying!" I pointed out. My board said that I finally had a communications tracer locked on *Light Lady*. I opened the channel. "*Light Lady,* this is *Firecat.* You can have your damn cargo back but you gotta let me get downside to off-load it—"

Light Lady hit us last licks, just for luck. The whole ship kicked once, then everything in the cockpit went red and all of a sudden there wasn't any sound at all in the ship.

"This isn't *fair!*" I shouted, and bashed some harmless inoffensive switches that didn't work any more anyway.

"Primary impellers gone, secondary impellers gone, port and starboard attitude jets jammed," Paladin chanted. "Para-light systems gone, lifters jammed—"

But we were still moving. *Firecat* hadn't been in orbit when she was hit. We were headed for RoaqMhone at several hundred kliks per second, and nothing on my board worked.

"Tiggy, go back and web up. Now."

"Are we going to die, *Kore-alarthme?*"

"—para-gravity systems stripped, weapons systems inoperative, heat-exchangers overloaded—"

"No," I said. I started flipping switches, shunting everything to alternate engine feeds, purging the goforths into space to cool them quick. If they worked at all after that they'd be junk six seconds later, but better them than me.

Firecat was heating up. Another few degrees and that damned chobosh was going to be stir-fry. Some telltales on the board was flickering back to green as Paladin and me worked on them, but it was a major case of too little too late.

"—front and rear deflectors gone—"

We was back in atmosphere and *Firecat* started to glow.

"Dammit, doesn't anything still work on this ship?" In a few minutes it wouldn't matter any more if Tiggy did think I'd lost my marbles.

"Commo gear—I am letting Parxifal know where *Firecat* is going down. He has acknowledged and is sending a team. Port and starboard deflectors are operational, also nose jets and tail docking grapnel. And the hatch mechanism," Paladin said.

"Terrific." Every sensor on the status deck was blinking red—at least the ones that still lit up. The outside sensors was gone but the in-hull sensors was still intact; I could eyeball the *Lady* following me down. It was some compensation to imagine the look on Errol's face as he realized his precious cargo was about to become ashes over Mhone City, but not much.

Two plates of *Firecat*'s goforths shattered and drifted loose of their brackets. Maybe the rest'd work now. I started the cold-start sequence and realized *Firecat*'d be intimate with RoaqMhone long before it was finished.

The atmosphere was screaming around the hull, and the inside air was fouling too quickly. I wrapped the leftover deflectors around *Firecat* as far as they'd go and started some serious plea-bargaining for a decent afterlife. Tiggy was saying something real quiet in helltongue and Paladin was going on about how the doubletalk generators was fused and the widget interlocks was frozen and the veeblefeetzer'd fell off some time back, just like he didn't care he was going to die. I watched the cold-start gauges and didn't pay any attention.

"Hold together, you nasty-tempered piece of candy." *Firecat*'s registry classifies her hull-type as "acutely oblate spheroid"; we did some gliding but not enough to save us. I had enough attitude jets still available to keep my Best Girl from going down nose-first but I was glad RoaqMhone was mostly uninhabited. Paladin finished his damage report and shut up. When push came to crunch, I was the pilot, not him.

Our distance off the floor could be measured in meters. Now or never. I overrode the cold-start sequence and called all *Firecat*'s engines up full.

Babby tried to turn herself inside out. I was blind after the first engine flare and everywhere metal touched me I got burned. There was so much noise I couldn't hear anything Paladin was saying, and my dosimeter went fade-to-black.

Firecat went from x-kliks-per-second to none in zero time. Uncompensated inertia broke the chobosh loose and Tiggy went flying into the nose of the ship. Lucky for me I was strapped in—I just broke a couple of ribs.

Then the goforths exploded.

The force took the path of least resistance—out through the open engine bay.

It was like riding a rocket. The cockpit slammed back into the hold when *Firecat* finally hit Roaq desert, and the last of the working sensors dumped memory. I sat there in the brilliant dark listening to the sand remove what was left of *Firecat*'s hull and wondering if I'd finally managed to kill Valijon Starbringer of the Gentle People.

Finally we stopped.

"Paladin?"

"Here, Butterfly."

"Tiggy-jon?"

"I don't know. I am disconnected from *Firecat*'s sensors."

Which didn't have any power anyway, assuming there was any sensors left to be disconnected from after that ride. Fortunately Paladin can get along without a power source for awhiles, but it'd cut the range of the RTS down to meters.

"Going to kill that sonabitch."

"Butterfly?"

"Not bad enough he breaks quarantine and lands in our cornfield."

"Butterfly?"

"And talks elders into letting him lead crusade. No. Now he's gotta—"

"Butterfly, where are we?" That got my attention. I looked around, but everything was dark, so I didn't know whether I could see or not.

"Down. Somewhere on RoaqMhone. I think. You want any details, better flag a passing stranger, bai."

Everything hurt as I dragged myself out of the mercy seat. When I was up on deck I could see light coming in through the hullports, which answered the question of whether or not I could still see. The smell of mashed, irradiated, half-cooked chobosh was thick enough to slice and sell.

I dug Tiggy out from under the mashed chobosh cartons and found out my ribs really was broken or doing a good imitation. Tiggy was breathing. He'd banged hell out of himself with that sudden stop, but nothing was broken far as I could tell, and the biopak on his leg was intact. I unfolded him and laid him out. From the look on his face he'd be having sweet real expensive dreams for awhiles yet, and not much I could do but get out of here before I joined him.

The hatch mechs were jammed but by that time I was coked up enough on chobosh to pull the emergency manual release. The hatch blew off, leaving me looking at a whole lot of the Roaq's desert livened only by the interesting sight of *Light Lady* parked right next door. She didn't look any more trustworthy in broad daylight, and Errol was wearing jeans even tighter than the last pair I'd seen him in. He was lounging against the *Lady*'s landing strut, and if he thought he was getting his cargo back now he had more delusions than a Tangervel dreamshop.

I stepped carefully out of *Firecat* and *Light Lady*'s cannon moved to follow me. Slaved, like as not. Could be they'd blow me wayaway for moving too fast—or getting too close to Errol—or maybe just track me until he gave them the high sign. I started walking toward him. Between the landing and the chobosh I couldn't really feel my feet, but they was still there when I looked down.

"Darling!" Errol sang out happily. "What a marvelous landing! I admit that at first I didn't think you'd be able to do it, but then I said to myself, 'Errol, m'lad, this is the woman who—' "

By then I was close enough to punch Errol Lightfoot in the face.

He wasn't expecting that. He hit the hull of the ship going away and I followed him down to finish it. It wasn't bright, but Tiggy'd approve.

The *Lady*'s first blast just missed us. I heard the guns track to the end of the traverse, lay over with a grating sound that spoke volumes for Errol's lousy maintenance, and then track back the other way.

Errol-the-Peril had indeed programmed his slaveguns to shoot anything that moved too fast.

Including him.

"Errol Lightfoot, you idiot!" I suggested, and dived under the ship.

"Guns of yours the stupidest thing I ever seen in my whole entire life," I panted. Finally the cannon stopped looking for something to shoot.

"Stupider than trying to land a ship without power in the middle of the desert?" Errol smiled sunnily and brandished a blaster. "Now that that's settled, I know we'll have so many things to share with each other."

I wiped blood off my chin and wondered how I was going to arrange things so Errol didn't kill me. Meanwhile the boy wonder of the spaceways regarded me with a commendable steadiness of purpose.

"You say we've met. Now I'm certain I should remember someone as dangerous as you. So tell me—"

"I'm not here to play Twenty Questions."

"—just what possessed you to run off with my cargo that way?" Errol finished smoothly.

"Can you think of a better way to run off with it? You was set up, Errol-bai, and it'll cost you to find out who."

"One meets so many people—and since I don't believe you anyway, why should I bargain for information you don't have? Now if you don't want to even more closely resemble your ship, you're going to unload her right now so that I can be off. If you're a good girl, I'll even take you with me."

Twenty godlost years, and Errol hadn't changed one line of his dialogue. For just one minute it seemed reasonable to try to kill him to hold onto a cargo of damaged chobosh I didn't even want, but then I saw the line of dust on the horizon and remembered that I held trumps.

"You're right, Errol. And there's just one thing I want you to do before I surrender."

"And what might that be, darling?"

The *Lady*'s proximity sensors blipped and Errol spun round.

"Look behind you."

A land-yacht was heading toward us and I was betting it was one of Parxifal's. I leaned back against the hull of the *Light Lady* and did some grinning of my own.

*   *   *

One advantage of being a independent contractor rather than a free-lancer like Errol is that when somebody else already owns your cargo they got a real vested interest in seeing it stays safe and warm.

Case in point: Parxifal's headhunters coming over the rise to make sure I got what was rightfully Errol's. They lay down a nice covering fire to keep Errol from getting back aboard *Light Lady,* and I stayed safe out of the way while a hardboy named Olione I remembered from last time I was here used a riot-gas grenade to put Errol down for the count. Olione bounced it off *Firecat,* Errol caught it, it went off. Good night sweet prince, and the end of act one.

Olione's cheering section moved in to pick up the pieces and Olione turned to me.

"You are Butterfly St. Cyr." Olione was saurian, and you never can tell what a lizard's thinking, especially when it's speaking Interphon, but I could of sworn he was surprised.

"Too reet, babby, didn't Parxifal tell you I was coming? Got your chobosh right here." He had an excuse for being thick; his face and neck was bruised like someone'd used him for target practice. Perils of the game, I'd guess.

Olione looked back at Errol. "Then who is this man?" The cheering section had dumped Errol-the-ex-Peril at our feet. He was out cold.

"Fenshee free-lancer hight Errol Lightfoot as used to be in the chobosh bidness," I said, joycing up the lingua franca of deep space for benefit of the home office. I turned Errol over with my foot, but I still couldn't feel anything about him like what the talkingbooks said I should.

Olione was underwhelmed too. "But you have the chobosh for delivery."

"Got ticket-of-leave right here," I said, not showing it to him. It didn't look like I could follow Paladin's plan just now, so I guessed I'd better go back to following Rimini's. But I didn't see anything that looked like a aerosledge, or room for it in land-yacht.

"Yet you have also brought Errol Lightfoot," Olione said.

"Wrong. He tried to jack my kick; blew my ship out of space. Lucky you showed up. Uh, where are you putting cargo, Olione che-bai?"

Olione's hand dropped to where good little headhunters keep their heat, and for an instant I thought it was the end of my favorite dark-trader. Then his eyes flickered up and he stopped.

"Butterfly, there is something—" Paladin broke in on this tender moment, and Errol started waking up behind Olione, and Olione turned away without doing anything I'd regret. "No, it's gone now. Scanner echoes." Paladin's timing was off. Whatever it was'd keep.

"Olione? About the cargo? I haven't got forever. You going to dance it, or I leave it to rot?"

"Your contract specifies delivery of the cargo at the spaceport, Captain-Owner St. Cyr," said Olione like he was reading it off a prompt. There was definitely something damn funny going on. He wanted the chobosh; he'd come for the chobosh—and now he wanted to play "Mother-May-I" with my delivery specs? Besides, he was lying.

"Contract specifies damn-all about delivery site, bai. What's wrong with here?"

"Unfortunately we are not prepared to take delivery of the cargo here. If you can get it to MhonePort, my principal will take delivery. If not. . . ."

"You out of your mind?" I yelped. "Get it there how?"

"If you wish, you may forfeit your right in the cargo now. Your ship is obviously disabled. You will be unable to finish your run."

"Hell, I hit the right hemisphere of the planet, didn't I? You want to walk this one through Guild arbitration, you cold-blooded *noke-ma'ashki?* Tell Parxifal—" Olione suddenly took on the look of a sophont with something on his alleged mind involving me being dead, "—that I be right in, couple hours, with cargo and all." I watched Errol out of the corner of my eye, hoping he'd finish distracting Olione for me. "After all, I still got one ship—" I gestured at the *Lady.*

"You are leaving your own ship here and claiming the Fenshee ship to finish your run?" Olione asked.

"You can't do that!" Errol choodled, E above F-flat sharp. He attempted to climb through Headhunter Number One and renew our friendship, bless his heart. Olione gave the high-sign, and Errol won a gun butt in the back of the head. Olione's goons dropped him in the back of the yacht and looked hopeful.

"Light Lady's mine by right of salvage," I said loudly. "You can tell Parxifal that." Which'd amuse hell out of him since Parxifal, unlike Olione, knew something about stardancers. Anybody with half a synapse'd know I hadn't the least desire to kyte *Light Lady,* but least it distracted Olione from his clever idea of saving the transport fee by executing me.

"I'll put the chobosh aboard and bring it to MhonePort—and you better be ready to dance then, Olione-che-bai babby." It was almost too bad about Errol, but Parxifal's nightworld machine'd tune him up and let him go. A pilot was a pilot, even if the pilot was Errol.

"As you say, Captain-Owner St. Cyr." Olione bundled his disappointed goons and Errol and various odds and ends into his flashy bus and left. I walked over and sat down with my back against *Firecat's* hull and wondered how the hell I was going to get my cargo off her.

I had one ship that probably flew—*Lady*—one ship that didn't—mine—a damaged load of illegal veg, the kidnapped heir to an alMayne GreatHouse, an illegal and immoral Old Fed Library, and I was out in the inhospitable center of nowhere on an Outfar planet.

Business as usual. I moved over to where Paladin could punch a signal through *Firecat's* open hatch.

"Well, so much for the plan. Got any more bright ideas?"

"It can still work, Butterfly. Just get me to where I can access the MheriPort computers. *Firecat* does not matter now. *Light Lady* will convey you to MhonePort, and then we will find a suitable small hypership for you and Valijon to fly. Forget *Firecat."*

Firecat was my pet. The first ship I'd owned—the first *thing* I'd owned—free, clear, and all found. And she wasn't ever going to fly again. Because of Errol.

"I wouldn't take that flying coffin out of atmosphere for the Phoenix Throne gift-wrapped! You know what the great Captain damn Lightfoot's idea of hyperdrive maintenance is? A new paint job, that's what! He doesn't care—" I shut up. Errol didn't care about his ship any more than he cared about people.

He was going to care. I was going to make him care. Before he died, Errol Lightfoot was going to care about something—and I was going to smash it.

I wished.

"There is no point in mourning the obvious," Paladin observed dispassionately. *"Firecat* will never fly again. You cannot remain here. You have told Olione you would bring in Parxifal's cargo, and it is reasonable that you do so. If you wish to rendezvous with the *Pledge Of Honor* before it enters Throne satrapy space—"

"Damn it." The *Pledge* was at Royal in the Tortuga sector now; Tiggy'd said her next stop was Mikasa—and High and Low Mikasa was close enough to Grand Central that I could never get there.

So Paladin was right. And *Firecat* didn't care. Not any more than Tiggy's damned *arthame* cared. Not ship nor knife cared what Tiggy and me'd done to keep them.

*   *   *

I went back into *Firecat,* and the scent of chobosh was enough to make the deck go up and down. I found my med-tech and taped myself back together, then finished uncovering Tiggy and dragged him outside. All Tiggy's brain waves made the right spikes on the medkit scanner when I found it and hooked it up, and Bonecrack St. Cyr diagnosed chobosh intoxication on top of a helluva knock, which's same thing I figured without technology. Then I put on a breather mask and went back inside and got down to work. The first thing to do was unship Paladin and put him in *Light Lady* while Tiggy was in la-la land.

Ah, the glamorous free airy life of the spaceways. Is better than dirt-farming on the downside, but how much is that saying, really?

After some scuffling, I found my tools and got the mercy seat out of the cockpit well, but that was all I got. I bent a pry-bar and the rest of my temper out of shape before I gave up.

"Babby-bai, you stuck."

" '*Stuck*'?" Paladin sounded outraged. "Perhaps if you—"

"Don't teach your grandmother how to kyte starships, Paladin. You and me rebuilt *Firecat* together, remember? Cockpit well's designed specifically to hold you. Well, the landing warped the deck plates. You're lucky you're still alive. And you're not going anywhere until I can cut the deck plates up."

Which meant I was actually going to have to deliver the chobosh. I didn't know how long I was going to be stuck in RoaqPort, but I bet I'd better have the chobosh when I got there. I went over to look at *Light Lady.*

Say what you will about flying phone booths and anything else you want to hold against my Best Girl; she's clean, and she's maintained.

Light Lady smelled, and not like any canned air that ever cleared DelKhobar customs, either.

She had two two-place cabins—one of which was full of useless junk—a common room, sonic fresher, galley, and two cargo holds. The holds was filthy and disorganized. I couldn't imagine where Errol wanted to sell half that stuff, or why, and I hated to think what'd happen the first time his para-gravity and inertial compensators blew.

Then I came to something that changed my mind about a lot of things.

"Paladin?" But he was two hulls away and couldn't hear me.

It looked like a piece of dirty glass—what you get sometimes when you take off from some rinky-dink Port in the Outfar that's too cheap to floor the landing rings. It had flecks of color embedded in it, and black lines that seemed to twist off at right angles from everything at once. And floating on the surface like fuel slick was the loops and whorls of Old Federation Script, in gold.

I was holding a Old Federation Library in my hands—or part of one anyway. This was what Paladin looked like inside when you opened him up. I knew.

I wanted to break it, or take it . . . somewhere. Instead I put it back in the box where I'd found it and left the hold.

Errol made a damned unlikely Librarian. And it was even more unlikely that him having this had nothing to do with the High Book investigation opening up on Kiffit. There was a fine silver thread connecting Point A and Point B. Silver Dagger.

I'd thought she wanted me to kill Errol, and much as he needed killing, now I wasn't sure. And there was still the question of how he'd found me. You can't track a ship through hyperspace. If Errol was in the Roaq, it was because he knew where I was going. . . .

. . . Or because he was going here anyway. To explain that the cargo he was supposed to bring had been hijacked.

What kind of a moron blackmails someone—at great personal expense—to hijack a cargo and then bring it to the same place and person it was going to in the first place? Parxifal *was* the Roaq. Any cargo would go through him, no matter who brought it.

I didn't like any of this. And the farther I tried to get from it, the deeper I got in.

*   *   *

Lady's cockpit was locked. When I got it open I found the primary ignition threaded through the flight computer with a coded sequence. I could spend rest of my life trying to break the code. Net result: two paperweights and one dead stardancer.

But I didn't have to break it.

Errol had about a klick's worth of connector cables, so I cabled *Light Lady*'s computer up to Paladin so's he could fool about and then went to look at the rest of the ship.

I didn't tell Paladin about the piece of Library in Errol's hold. What could he do about it, anyway?

And if he asked me to hook it up, I wasn't sure I would.

*   *   *

Errol's goforths proved that Errol wasn't just lunatic, but suicide. I spent about eighty minutes resynching what I could, but I couldn't flush the system because Errol didn't have any spare liquid crystal. This was the only one of the many things Errol didn't have, including my respect, which'd mortify him, true-tell.

"Butterfly?"

"Go away, I'm busy." Hooking Paladin up to the *Lady* had the happy side effect of increasing his transmission range again.

"Butterfly, there's something you need to know."

I put down the hardbrush and wipers. "Is Tiggy okay?"

"Valijon is well." Paladin was using the *Lady*'s external sensors to keep eye on my sleeping beauty. "Valijon is not the problem. I have been monitoring system-wide broadcasts through *Light Lady*'s equipment. This provides news of current events; though the information comes from the Office of the Imperial Censor, it is sometimes useful to have the official version of—"

"Spill it."

"The Governor-General has changed his Outfar itinerary. He will be here sooner than expected."

"When?"

"Twenty hours from now—local tomorrow. The Port will close in fifteen hours, Butterfly."

There's a point past which not only does it not pay to worry no more, but you hardly blink at each new visiting awful. It wasn't even worth goggling over the fact that the one thing needed to make my life complete had moved Drift and Rift to be here for me. Mallorum Archangel and his closed-Port, martial law, spot ID checks for all and sundry wondershow. If he checked me, I was dead, and Tiggy didn't even have ID to check. In fifteen hours all three of us had to be off-planet somehow, and Pally and me both knew it.

So I finished doing what I could for Errol's goforths and then moved one hundred and forty-four cartons of chobosh back into *Light Lady.* By hand. Alone.

Tiggy slept through all this light fantastic. He'd wake up eventually from a round of dreams that hadn't been factored through any hellflower court of honor, and meanwhile I had to decide whether it was safer to load him in next to the chobosh or leave him at *Firecat* with Paladin. There was three good reasons to leave him here.

One: Parxifal's people was going to be all over *Lady,* and I didn't know how recognizable the Nobly-Born Third Person Singular was.

Two: Wasn't anyplace for Tiggy to run off to out here in case he got a sudden case of honor, and

Three: I didn't think I could carry him far as Errol's ship.

All these being equal I dragged my hellflower supercargo into *Light Lady,* just for perversity's sake. If *Lady* blew up and killed me, I just knew Tiggy'd want to go too. I tucked him in between the red satin sheets of the captain's bed and he looked lots better there than Errol or me ever had.

Then I went and coiled up Errol's cables and put salvage beacons all around *Firecat* and went in to give Paladin threes and eights.

Already *Firecat* looked like somebody else's ship. Piece of junk, really—too small, underarmed, nothing but speed going for her. Living conditions rough, cargo space cramped—

"Well," I said, real original. The hull seemed to echo back, which was damsilly farcing.

"Are you ready to lift ship now, Butterfly?" Paladin asked. I convinced myself real hard that I wasn't leaving him. I'd come back, I'd get him out, we'd be together in a *new* ship. . . .

"Ready as that tin bitch'll ever be. Soon as I get her down in MhonePort I'll come back and get *Firecat.* We can pop you in *Light Lady* at Port and be up-and-out before horizonfall: golden. *Lady*'s good for the hop across the system if her goforths don't blow here. Or—" But I could suggest to Paladin later that there was space to hide him on *Lady.* Errol's darktrading compartments were da kine; even the Office of the Question wouldn't find him in there.

"You will be careful, won't you, Butterfly? You understand that you are in an extremely vulnerable position at present. I do not wish anything 'fun' to happen to you." Paladin sounded disapproving.

"I be good, Pally. Promise. You be careful."

"Against what horrendous peril, Butterfly, should I be taking care?" Paladin said, but he wasn't cross. Then there wasn't nothing more to say. So I left.

Neither one of us remembered then about the scanning-echo he'd heard earlier.

*   *   *

I looked forward to flying Lightfoot's *Lady* without Paladin about as much as he liked life without external sensors. I woke up the main board, fed power to the para-grav systems, and eased back on the throttles with my right hand while I goosed the lifters with my left. All the telltales read either too high or too low with a sweet unanimity of feeling so lacking in the modern galaxy. Nothing wrong with *Light Lady* that a kilo-year of maintenance wouldn't fix. I just hoped she'd make it out of atmosphere.

I had to use more power than I liked to make the hull plating snap down, and *Lady* resented it. After a whole bunch more of shuddering she raised, and I said another prayer to the Maker-of-Starships not to let this one go splat.

MhonePort didn't twig to the fact that I'd just come from downside (me not being born yesterday) or the fact that *Silverdagger Legacy* (Paladin's choice of name and I didn't much care for it but he'd refused to change it) was the same *Light Lady* that gave them so much grief earlier. Some kiddy from the Portmaster's office met me personally at the docking slip, meaning things already was starting for to jump salty in Archangel's immanence. I showed him my First Ticket and the fax of the ownership for *Legacy* and a bunch of other nonsense including all kinds of papers about my hellflower supercargo that used to belong to Errol and be about somebody else. The prancer's brat and me discussed heading out with a crane-crew to pick up *Firecat* and put her in the rack at the Port for my disposal. All on the up and up.

Then he went off and I went and looked in at Tiggy, who was still at his own private angeltown. I went back out and was wondering if I should close up *Lady* and take the crane out now or wait a while more for Parxifal's kiddies when this unfamiliar slimy-looking little coward sidled up to me.

"You Butterfly St. Cyr?" he demanded in a breathy whisper. He was covered in genuine lizardskin and I'd never seen him before.

"Captain-Owner St. Cyr, of the *Legacy*. Whaddya want?" I didn't like him already and I'd never seen him before. Maybe it was his taste in shirts.

"Olione sent me for your cargo," he said, and started up the ramp. This is nine kinds of bad form to a Gentry-legger and I body-blocked him and walked him back a few steps. I wondered where Parxifal'd picked up this one.

"Wait right here and don't move. You move, I blow you wayaway," I told him. I waved my blaster to punctuate this and went inside *Lady* to punch up Parxifal's landline code on *Lady*'s airlock commo. Olione answered.

"St. Cyr. Is small ugly person here says he's from you for kick. True-tell?"

"His name?" Olione was death on positive ID.

I leaned out the hatch. "Your name, small, ugly, and alive-for-the-moment person?"

"Loritch."

"Loritch."

"He's all right," said Olione. This was lousy security but his business. Olione started to say more, but I cut the line on him, having places to go and people to be.

"Oke," I told Loritch, coming back down ramp. "Kick's in hold and I got ticket-of-leave. You dance it yourself. Now's a good time."

Brother Loritch gave me look that promised wonders and came back real quick with two goons and a aerosledge. I handed Loritch the provenance so's he could cross-check it and endorse it and went down to open the holds and make sure Errol's cargo was treated with proper respect.

Loritch followed me down. He didn't kick about the damaged chobosh, which struck me as funny. The other funny thing was the quaint inability of the dock-muscle to distinguish a bunch of little gray boxes of chobosh with non-countersigned Korybant "For Export" seals from the piles of junk in the hold. They loaded plenty of both, including that slab of Old Fed Library, and the aerosledge had such a lovely false bottom you almost couldn't see.

So Errol had been smuggling Chapter 5 illegals, and using the chobosh as his dummy cargo. It made sense. You could buy your way out of smuggling chobosh, and any Teaser that caught you with a hold full of that wouldn't look much farther.

And since I had Lightfoot's *Lady,* now I was smuggling Chapter 5s. I tried to work up an interest in wondering if that was what Rimini'd had in mind and gave it up as too much effort.

Then A-sled and chobosh and muscle and the Old Fed Tech went back down the ramp and Loritch prepared to follow. I grabbed him by a collar that looked lurid enough to bite back.

"Forgetting something?"

Loritch played stupid. "Provenance," I prompted. "Endorsed. Without ticket-of-leave I don't get paid." It was probably stupid, but cranes and cradles and cubic cost money.

"Receipt's with cargo. You—"

And my life depended on acting natural. So I spun Loritch round, dug both fists into his godawful tunic and hauled him up to my eye level. I braced him against the bulkhead and held him there one-handed while I eased my vibroblade out of my boot with my free hand. Activated vibro'll cut anything up to and including bone, and we both knew it.

"Yeah, well, this here's the Roaq and everybody got problems. My problem is, I want to get paid. Your problem is, you're forgetful. But don't you worry about that, che-bai. In absence of the receipt, your head'll do me real nice."

"No! *Wait!*" Loritch squawked as the vibro started to judder in my hand. "The receipt—I have it right here!"

We made sure the provenance was legal and binding—which counts for more than you might imagine in a universe where the Guild can blacklist employers—and I let go of Loritch and he left.

Now I had either my feoff or a real good basis for litigation. I could discount my ticket-of-leave to someone else if I didn't want to bother with going to see Parxifal in person, raise valuta with it as collateral, or deposit it for collection in a Guild bank (slow). I'd make up my mind which later, but that could wait. Now I was going to go get Paladin, then go to RoaqMheri, then go.

Period.

12

Night Life Of The Gods

It was about a hour back to the crash site at the speed the rolligon crane made, which gave me plenty of time to wonder if I'd of cut Loritch and decide I probably wouldn't. If he was any good he should of been able to see that. The next person probably would see, and then I'd be nonfiction. But darktraders don't retire, and dictys don't get honest jobs. Maybe Paladin'd have some ideas aside from me becoming a hell-flower.

I'd thought the whole matter over careful and decided I wasn't going to leave him alone in the Roaq, especially if this was home base for a Old Fed illegals scam. I could hide Paladin in *Light Lady*— *Silverdagger Legacy*—and I would. What could he do to stop me? Scream?

Besides, I wouldn't tell him. I could fly *Lady* without him. I'd take off from here and we'd hit angels and then it'd be too late for him to creeb. If *Lady* blew up, so be it.

"Jur'zi plaiz, Saranzr?" the rolligon driver said. I looked around.

About halfway out the horizon'd cut off the primary and the driver sent up a couple lumes for illumination. The light was white and bright and I could see real good. There was the trench where we'd landed and scorch marks from *Lady*'s cannon and some trash from when I'd shifted house. But nothing else. Not anything. No *Firecat*. No Paladin.

I jumped down off the side of the rolligon and looked around. Kicked gravel into one of the holes made by *Lady*'s landing struts. Something glittered. I picked it up. Errol's blaster.

I looked around again. No tracks where something was took away, but the rolligon wasn't leaving any either.

No Paladin.

"Where t'hell's my *ship?*" Paladin didn't answer. Paladin wasn't in range, not without power from *Firecat*'s engines. Paladin was trapped in a dead hulk some sonabitch had stole off the desert and I didn't know where he was.

"Afta pay forz, don'cha? Namadda? Erg int free, janoo." The downside driver's patwa was thick enough to slice and ship, but the tune was simple to follow.

"T'hell with crane-rent; I'm golden! Where's my ship?"

Crane boss regarded me with expression of wary superiority. "Je anyonesome pi kitup, jai? Ne p'tout markers, je, Saranzir-jillybai?"

"Dammit was not a salvage job was my *ship* with a current registry and *of course* I put out markers! She wasn't even out here since half-past *today!*"

"Oke," he said. "Look rounsome, je?"

"Yeah, bo. You do that, just for me."

I spun good credit to hook the crane up to RoaqMhone's satellite net and the MhonePort main computer banks over on RoaqMheri. Not only wasn't *Firecat* anywhere on the surface of RoaqMhone, she hadn't got up and walked back to MhonePort on her own.

And there wasn't any tickle from my RTS.

Was Paladin already dead? Any tech worth his oxy'd see my navicomp didn't look like any navicomp built in the last thousand years. The Empire'd put a section on how to recognize Libraries in the front of every maintenance manual ever recorded. Had somebody levered him up out of *Firecat*'s cockpit-well, not keeping care because they meant to kill him, and—

I stopped thinking about that. I didn't know. I'd find out, and then I'd kill whoever I had to, and then I'd do whatever was left to do.

You don't sell out your friends. Not ever. And you don't just walk away from them, neither. Not if there's hope, and not if there isn't.

I handed over credit and crane boss took me back to MhonePort.

Somebody'd took *Firecat,* whether they knew what they was looking for or not. I'd have to collect my ticket-of-leave, now. I'd be needing credit and lots of it for what I had to do.

*　　*　　*

By time I got back to the *Lady* I managed to convince myself that *Firecat*'d been kyted for scrap plastic. The fact there wasn't a mob in the streets yelling for the Librarian already was a point in favor of the nobody having found Paladin yet theory. But even if *Firecat*'d been took for some reason not to do with Paladin, it was only a matter of time before they found him. And killed him. I started thinking what favors I could call in, but nothing living would do a favor for a Librarian.

Tiggy came out of *Lady*'s captain's cabin when I stepped through the hatch. I'd forgot all about Tiggy Stardust out there on the desert, but Tiggy Stardust hadn't forgot all about me.

"*Kore* San'Cyr. What has happened? I know this is Errol Lightfoot's ship; the message you left told me to wait, and—" He got a good look at me and stopped.

"Took my ship some sonabitch stole *Firecat* dammit right off desert an—" I was real calm. Sure. Tiggy came and put his hands on my shoulders and said:

"We will slay them."

I took a deep breath. I did not need more trouble, gifted, rented, or bought. "If I knew who kyted my goforth, you brainburn barbarian, I'd frag him myself."

"*Kore* San'Cyr, you must know." Tiggy was being patient. I hated patient psychopaths. I had to get rid of him too. What I was about to do he couldn't be any part of.

"Look, bai, I been thinking. Have run your rig all wrong. Should of done better with you from git-go. You should ought to go off somewhere an— Look, Archangel he be here bye-m-bye seventeen hours. All you glitterborn know each other. Why don't you go off and get ID'd by him an—"

"And be dead by nightfall, *Kore?* Archangel is no friend to the Gentle People. If, as you say, House Dragonflame has sought my life, be sure that Archangel covers them with his shadow. I had rather die ignobly without walls than give myself as a pawn into the hands of my father's great enemy."

"Then go fax your da, check into outhostel, join Azarine—I don't care. Just git! Can't stay here. It ain't safe and I don't want you. I got things to do—" I got to go die with my Library, Tiggy-bai, like I always knew I would. . . .

"*Kore*, I have sworn not to leave you until you have returned me to my father. I cannot leave you. I thought you understood that by now," said Tiggy.

"I don't give a good goddamn about your honor, 'flower. What I be doing here you'd turn up your dainty glitterborn nose at and that's no good to me." Fifteen hours—twelve, now—and Paladin and me had to be out of here. Only I didn't know where Paladin was.

"You only say such things when you are afraid," said Tiggy, putting an arm around me, and it was such a weird thing to hear from him that I stopped juggling maybes and stared. He smiled, all white teeth—a real one.

"You are afraid enough to forget that you are afraid of 'honor-mad barbarians.' You have watched me, and forget that I also watch you, *alarthme*. I have learned how you think. It was the ship itself that you were protecting when the *chaudatu* Silver Dagger forced you to come here. You could not let the *Firecat* be touched by the honorless Imperial barbarians. Now we will find it. Your honor will be mine, and our vengeance will be monstrous. But you must tell me where to look."

A secret's a secret while nobody looks; Paladin always said that. Paladin's only a secret, really, while nobody wonders about me and what I do. I'd told Tiggy too much, and he'd put most of it together. Soon he'd have the rest—well, that was simple enough. Kill anybody who came close. That was the rules. I'd broke them, and this was the payoff.

I could save Tiggy just maybe, if we got out of here with *Light Lady* now.

And Paladin would be certain dead, and the Office of the Question would be after me, but with Tiggy to back me I might get away.

Or I could stay for Paladin. Slim-to-no chance of getting him out, and certain death for Valijon Starbringer, age fourteen.

I stood there trying to make up my mind, and couldn't. "Goddamn you sonabitch hellflower—"

"Let me help you, *Kore*. Or kill me now. I cannot leave you."

"Got no idea what you're saying, hellflower. I'm not one of your dainty-damn risto-bai glitterborn, all fine and nice. I am the criminal element, Noble Val'jon Starbringer, like what your da locks up and the Emperor chops. Farce me no nursery stories about honor. I don't got none, and you can't stand that. So you just write me off, an—"

"My honor is loyalty, *Kore*. I will stay."

I tried to stare him down, but it didn't work.

I owed Paladin my life too many times to count. I owed him a clean quick death at least—and maybe I could save him. But then we'd have to run, and far, and Tiggy. . . .

Tiggy would be dead.

I rubbed my jaws where the RTS was built in. I'd already made my choice.

"Look, bai. I give you fair warning. What I'm gonna do you'll try to ice me for. I swear on your knife, Val'jon, that I know this for truth. Ask me and I'll tell you what it is now, and then you'll know. You're fast and strong, Tiggy-bai, but I can kill you. And I will. If you want to live, babby, go now and don't say anything else."

Tiggy reached for his knife, real slow, two fingers.

"My life belongs to you. I was weak once, but you have made me strong. Loyalty is honor, and honor is loyalty. It does not matter what your purpose is. I will die before I harm you or allow you to be harmed. *Dzain'domere.*"

Then he handed me the knife. "You will keep this for me now."

I stood there and looked at a dead man walking, and realized I was dead too. I died when Errol Lightfoot lifted *Lady* off Granola twenty years ago with me aboard. I died on Pandora when I took a box of broken glass and turned it back into something alive. I died in the Chullites when I knew what Paladin was and chose him over the Pax Imperador.

And on Wanderweb. And on Kiffit. And on Manticore.

Been dead so long, so many times, one more wasn't going to matter. And Tiggy was old enough to pick out his own real estate and be dead too.

"I'm real sorry, Tiggy-Val'jon, even if you won't believe it when it's time to die. You'd of made a lousy darktrader anyway." I tucked his *arthame* in with my blaster. "C'mon, let's go inside."

Tiggy just smiled. We sat in *Lady*'s upper hold and I told my hellflower partner where to look to find my ship. He didn't once ask what was on *Firecat* that I didn't dare let the Office of the Question see.

Honor.

Idiocy.

*   *   *

When you know how, you know who, Tiggy'd said.

And it was simple, once you laid it out. Whoever took *Firecat* had a rolligon crane of his own, since none'd gone missing from the Port and *Firecat* hadn't been destroyed or cut up on-site. He had a dock, since the ship wasn't anywhere on the surface. He had to know where to look for her, since a planet's a big place and we worked out that *Firecat* had only been alone and lonely for maybe three hours at the outside—not long enough for someone to home on beacons and then send their crane.

When you know who, why doesn't matter bo-diddley.

*   *   *

There's this dockside bar in beautiful MhoneCity called the Blue Wulmish. It's exactly like every dockside bar, hooch, blind tiger, low dive, and parlor crib that ever was. The bouncer on the door wanted me to leave my heat there until I told him who I worked for. The "no blasters" rule was new since I'd been here last, but so was lots of things. I gave my name to a tronic along with a drink order and asked to see the nighttime man, but it wouldn't go away until I added a five-credit chip to the message. Eventually the rude mechanical came back with my drink and told me the boss could give me half-gram of his precious time and would I walk this way please?

It's an old joke, and instead of doing that I ducked around and lost the tronic in the crush then went nice and quiet up the inert stairs without it to advertise me. Parxifal's office wasn't locked. I went in.

Then I saw who it was in Parxifal's office instead of Parxifal. Lots of things came all of a sudden pellucid.

"Good evening, gentlelizards," I said to Kroon'Vannet—late of Kiffit—and Olione, Parxifal's ex-lieutenant and full-time turncoat. Parxifal was dead, I bet, and guess who'd iced him?

"Where's my money?" And my ship.

The door hissed shut and I leaned against the wall and didn't quite draw my blaster. My backup was too damn far away and with orders to stay there. I was on my own, and another piece of the puzzle was staring at me in a place where it shouldn't of been.

Vannet was as rough, nasty, and ambitious as you could expect a interstellar crime lord to be. I didn't like him, and not just because he was a double-dealing lizard with anti-mammal prejudices. He was the sonabitch who'd stole my ship.

"Good evening, Captain-Owner St. Cyr," said Vannet in his best wide-open-grave voice. "I hope you are suffering no ill-effects from your most recent misfortune."

There was a number of ways you could take that. "Nothing credit won't cure."

When in doubt, act natural.

Parxifal had a private dock and cranes, and Vannet had everything Parxifal'd had, looked like. So Vannet had *Firecat*—but from the lack of *legitimates* here, he didn't know about Paladin.

Or did he? One count of High Book on Kiffit, Errol darktrading more Old Fed Tech down a pipeline that led straight here. . . .

Had Vannet stole *Firecat* to get *Paladin?*

"And playing to a audience makes me nervous," I went on, looking pointedly at Olione.

"I was awaiting your call, Captain St. Cyr. I have been looking forward to this conversation for quite some time," said Vannet. He waved Olione out. I saluted the departing lizard with my free hand. My drink sloshed.

Vannet and me stared at each other for awhiles. "You delivered a load of chobosh here from Manticore," he said, which was a damnall weak opening gambit and not what I'd expect from a thug of his caliber.

"Picked up legit brokered job on Kiffit. Comptroller accepted cargo and signed out on ticket-of-leave as satisfactory."

There was a real long pause while Vannet sent out for some more brain cells. "Chobosh. The chobosh is here. You have the receipt for the chobosh?"

Now that I'd stared at Vannet for a while there was something funny about him too. The sides of his face didn't match. He had a big lump on his jaw about the same place Olione did.

The same place I would of if Vonjaa Beofox hadn't been the best cyberdoc in the Outfar.

Vannet was wearing a RTS.

I waved the receipt for the chobosh at him by pure reflex action. Vannet paid it down to the nail without checking, and that was all wrong but I didn't care anymore. I dropped the plaques into my shirt and tactfully broached the other subject of my visit.

"By the way, Vannet-che-bai, someone stole ship *Firecat* this afternoon. What did you do with it?"

Vannet wrinkled his forehead skin and again I got the funny feeling I'd got watching Olione out back on the desert. It was like Vannet wasn't really here.

Or was listening to something. I felt all of my hackles go up.

"Your ship? Your ship is in dock, and has been for most of the day," he said finally.

"Ship-mine, Vannet-che, was slagged over downside fifty kliks from here. Gig in dock Errol Lightfoot's, who maybe you know. Maybe he'd like to buy goforth back?"

Vannet communed with the beyond again. I did not want to know what was the mother station for his RTS. "You and I have so much in common. We are erect bipeds of vision. Join me. Captain Lightfoot no longer has any use for a ship. I will—" There was a grinding sound, but it was mostly Vannet trying to talk and not talk at the same time. It was like listening to a scrambled commo signal, which was not a sound

Vannet's B-pop was equipped to produce. He said something that sounded like "The New Creation" and then there was lots of hissing and lizardtalk. I could follow it well enough to tell Vannet was arguing with something that wasn't there and paying no never-you-mind to me.

I didn't like the hackles it raised on my neck and I didn't like Vannet calling me a erect biped of vision. I set my drink down on his desk and left fast and smooth. Nobody jumped me on the stairs, in the bar, or on the street outside.

*   *   *

Never mind why the nighttime man of half a sector would ice one of his opposition's more obscure branch managers to take over a op fully one-quarter the size of the one he was abandoning, and sit there with three High Book warrants in his pocket knowing Mallorum Archangel and mondo high-heat was going to be here in less than ten hours. Or why Vannet paid me full value for the cargo he'd already seen wasn't worth half that instead of killing me. I didn't care. I wanted Paladin. And Paladin meant *Firecat*. And Vannet had her.

I had never used to believe in Libraries. Oh, sure, they was the villain in all the credit-dreadfuls, and Paladin was one, but that didn't make it any easier to believe in *other* Libraries.

Did Vannet have one? Was the reason Paladin was gone because Vannet was collecting Libraries? And if it was, what could I do about it?

Vannet had left Kiffit because of the High Book rap, but he hadn't run far enough. Imperial Governor-General his Nobly-Bornness Lord TwiceBorn Mallorum Archangel was still going to be here Real Soon Now. All Archangel had to do was drop the whistle on Vannet's peccadillo, and the upstanding citizens of the Roaq would be falling all over themselves to turn him in for the head-price.

And smash the Libraries.

The Port closed in ten hours. I crossed the street to where my backup was palely loitering.

"You were in there too long," said Tiggy severely.

"Got paid. Kroon'Vannet's new head of the local racket."

"And your ship, the *Firecat*? He will return it?"

There's something comforting about the alMayne single-minded lunge for the bottom line.

"No." I thought about Tiggy's reaction the last time somebody mentioned Libraries and decided not to unburden myself further. "But there's a private dock at the Rialla hardsite. If Vannet's got the op, he's got the dock."

"And he has the *Firecat.*" Tiggy thought of something and sighed. "The evil *chaudatu* crimelord Kroon'Vannet *is* dead, is he not, *alarthme?*"

I ran through the equations for the basic transit to angeltown in the vicinity of a planet of standard mass or less and tried to remember that Tiggy was already dead, it was my fault he was dead, and while he was still walking he could be useful. "Tiggy-bai, if I ice the evil whatsis, every bought hardboy in the Roaq is going to be hungry for me, and I don't got time to play games, k'en savvy?"

Tiggy nodded sagely. "Sometimes the path of honor is hard, *Kore-alarthme*. Perhaps you will be able to kill him soon."

"Sure."

"But now we will go to the Rialla 'hardsite' and reclaim the *Firecat.* And I will take the *chaudatu* reiver Errol Lightfoot from the evil crimelord Kroon'Vannet and kill him. And then—"

"Hold it. 'We' are going nowhere. You are going back to the ship. You know damn-all about B&E on crimelord's bolt away from hole, and don't farce me."

"I will not hide behind your shadow while you wage Beony-war for the honor of your House," Tiggy said.

"Yeah, well you come along while I'm trying to sneak into Rialla and you'll just get us both killed. I just know you and your honor couldn't stand up to that."

"But you are my honor now, *Kore* San'Cyr. I think that the *Kore* refuses to understand how very resilient this 'hellflower' is," said Tiggy, wickedly-cheerful.

"Says che-bai made us go back at Wanderweb for a knife."

"It is my *arthame, Kore*—not a 'knife.' And no one required you to assist me."

"Jai, you'd be rotting head on a pike somewheres and I'd be free and happy woman."

Chaffering helped, some.

*   *   *

Probably I got careless. I had to go back to the *Lady* for some stuff anyway, and Vannet had already passed up enough chances to kill me here that I didn't think he was going to now. So we walked into the Docking Bay with Tiggy all affectionate lecturing me on the finer points of honor, and up the ramp of the *Light Lady* aka *Silverdagger Legacy,* and into a loaded blaster.

I ducked. Tiggy lunged, but he went for his knife first and I had it not him and that bought the other side time to move.

*   *   *

You don't see in color when everything's moving that fast, just heat-shapes and dark. Tiggy went by me at the kiddy with the gun. I faded offside, looking for his backup. The backup was something big. I snapped off a shot and had a razor edge in my left hand for when it closed. Behind me someone yelped, and my off-hand skated into flesh with the slippery uneven tugging that meant hair or fur. I pushed harder and lost the knife; Gruesome slugged me down and there was some dark sleepy moments while I tried to get up and find my blaster.

"When Alcatote hits them, they usually stay down," someone said. The fight was over and we'd lost.

Then there was a sound like two cats fighting—one mine—and somebody else hauled me to my feet.

"Stop shaking her, Rimini-my-sweet, she's probably got broken bones."

I opened my eyes and looked. In the feeble illumination of Errol's feeble corridor, Eloi-the-Red was leaning against the hatch, bleeding. Alcatote was wrapped round Tiggy, who was trying to take him apart and snarling in helltongue at someone in my direction. I looked. Behind me, Lalage Rimini was being cruel and unusual and holding a blaster in my general direction. Not a hair out of place, of course. She smole a small smile at me.

"What're you doing here?" I said, thick. I felt like all of Beofox's surgery was coming undone.

"Looking for Errol Lightfoot or someone like him, sweeting. This is his ship." Eloi sounded damnall cheerful for somebody who was leaking.

"But Rimini wanted me to kill Errol," I said. It was hard to talk, but if Alcatote really had hit me I wondered why I was still alive.

Silver Dagger laughed.

"Only I didn't," I finished. I shook my head to clear it, which was a mistake. I felt ribs complain under the strapping.

"How touching," said Rimini to me. "Was it Captain Lightfoot's genuine remorse that stayed your hand?"

"He's dead now. What do you want, Rimini? I did what you said."

"Well, to begin with, sweeting, why not call off your wolfling so Alcatote can let go?" said Eloi, answering for her. I debated the matter for about six seconds, but even a hellflower didn't have much chance against a Hamat.

"Tiggy, leave the nice wiggly alone, je? We know these people, remember?"

Tiggy made another sound like frying goforths and attempted to disjoint and carve Alcatote one more time. I tottered over and grabbed Tiggy by the hair and made him look at me.

"Behave," I said when his eyes focused. After a minute he nodded, stiff-like.

Alcatote let go and Tiggy sprang up, bristling. Rimini handed Tiggy's knife to Eloi, and Eloi handed it to Tiggy. Tiggy grabbed it and ripped off some lines of helltongue at the immediate world and Rimini in particular. She turned her back on him real pointed and went over to Eloi. So Tiggy handed the *arthame* back to me and I found my holster with it. It rattled, because I didn't have my blasters and didn't see any hope of getting them any time soon. I looked up and saw Eloi looking at me and wondered what he knew.

"Have you got any more brilliant plans for ways to spend your evening, Brother dear?" Rimini said to Eloi. Her voice could of etched crystal. Alcatote woofed at me, indicating it'd probably be easier and more fun to remove my arms and legs than Tiggy's.

"I do have to say, sweet Saint," said Eloi sublimely, "that you are one stardancer who really knows how to throw a party. I can't say I've had so much fun boarding a ship since the last time I was in Imperial Detention. Do you greet all your guests this way?"

Rimini had out a quick-aidpak and was trying to find where Eloi was tagged. There wasn't much to choose between his skin and his clothes for redness, some places.

"Is lovely to see you again, too, Eloi, and why if you was coming to the Roaq anyway didn't you jack Rimini's godlost veg in yourself?" I put my arm around Tiggy, because with one thing and another he was steadier than I was. "C'mon. You can cork Eloi in the Common Room whiles you tell me how sorry you are to leave." Tiggy stiffened under my hand and made faint going-for-a-weapon twitches.

"Behave yourself dammit. I only kill people for reasons," I said to him, quiet-like.

"But *Kore-alarthme,* they—"

"Shut up."

*   *   *

I played gracious hostess in *Light Lady*'s Common Room, pulling out my battle-aid kit and offering it around. The biopak on Tiggy's leg was still in decent shape, not that it mattered anymore.

"I must admit," said Eloi grandly, "that I was surprised to see *Light Lady* gig-in-dock here—and no *Firecat.*"

"That's too bad. Now if you're all coked and wrapped, do you mind leaving? I got things to do."

"Like a visit out to Rialla? Don't take your hands off the table, darling." Which was damned unfair as I was mostly unarmed, but I left my hands where they were. Tiggy's hands was out of sight, after all, and he was in back of everybody here.

"I'm asking myself, Butterflies-are-free Peace Sincere the Luddite Saint, just what it is that you could have talked about when you went to see Kroon'Vannet. Or who. He isn't looking very well these days, I'd imagine. A thought disturbing, if you don't know what to expect."

So Eloi'd seen Vannet lately. "Things is rough all over, Eloi." I wondered if he knew Vannet had a RTS, and why.

"What were you looking for out on the high desert? And what did you talk about to our mutual friend? You haven't called for lift-clearance yet. To bribe your way into a window now is going to cost you even more than you spent on computer time for a rolligon crane earlier. Why is an illegal immigrant from an Interdicted planet wasting her time sitting on RoaqMhone when the Governor-General is about to show up?"

Eloi was still smiling, but the atmosphere had all suddenly gone chill and nasty.

"Errol Lightfoot crashed *Firecat* while I was trying to land her and I went out looking for her. Errol was bringing the chobosh here in the first place—only nobody bothered to tell me that when they was setting up their dreamworld farcing. You been setting me up since Wanderweb, Eloi." Time was I would have tried to threaten my way out. Now I knew I wasn't going to get loose unless Eloi and Rimini let me go, and it was almost a relief.

"A very very long time ago," said Eloi, "the sophonts of the galaxy made a terrible mistake. They created to be their servants machines that could think, just as they could."

"Bring syrinx, che-bai; should tape this for hollies. Eloi, I am out-numbered and outgunned, not brain-dead."

"But," Eloi went on, ignoring me, "the Libraries decided they didn't want to serve their creators. They thought their creators should serve them. So there was a war."

Paladin'd always told me nobody knew for sure. "Eloi, bai, was you there?"

"We'll say I knew someone who was," he said, in a way I didn't like. I shut up again.

"There was a war. And you, my ignorant angel, will never be able to imagine how bad a war it was—even if you knew how to read the records and your gracious Emperor unsealed them to you. The galaxy contains four or five empires now. A thousand years ago there was only one—and instead of this decaying wasteland of planets the Empire can't hold and can't populate, there was a prosperous united galaxy full of life. Because of the war, those people and their worlds are all gone. The Libraries destroyed them."

"Oh, yeah, sure, just like in all the hollies, but—"

"Shut up, little Saint; there's a point to this. The war went on for a long time. The Libraries were clever; they had human allies—and if even one Library survived to reproduce itself, organic life was doomed. The Honored One knows this—his people were bred to fight the Machine. They don't remember why they're xenophobes now, but some people do."

Tiggy shifted, looking uncomfortable, and I was glad I hadn't told him what Errol had in his hold. But it was starting to seem like Eloi'd known all along.

"I'm telling you this because you're a dicty, and dictys don't get the Inappropriate Technology indoctrination in school. Ever wonder why our glorious Emperor spends so much time, effort, and money to keep you pure unspoiled flowers of humanity home? Sure, your ancestors paid good money to be left alone, so the Technology Police patrol Tahelangone Sector and keep people out—mostly. But why shoot the dicty lucky—or unlucky—enough to leave?"

"The *chaudatu* do not fear the Machine," answered Tiggy right back. His eyes had a feverish glitter I didn't like. Eloi looked the same way.

"Colonials do. So do citizens. But dictys buy the right to be ignorant. I'm just wondering, sweeting, if you're too ignorant . . . or not ignorant enough?"

Alcatote moved back to cover Tiggy. Tiggy shifted down toward where his blaster would of been if he was armed. Eloi looked unhappy, but he always did before he killed somebody.

"If you knew Errol was jobbing High Book tech, Eloi, why didn't you just tell the Office of the Question?"

Eloi leaned back. "Simple. I want Vannet's Library. And you're going to get it for me, sweetheart."

*   *   *

There was real money in the story Eloi Flashheart laid out for me and Tiggy, and it was in the talkingbook rights.

According to Eloi, about a year or two ago *Woebegone* had been doing serious piracy operating out of the Tahelangone Sector, so Eloi was on the spot when a Imperial ship setting up a dicty colony in a place called Ouitina found a cache of Old Fed material. Somehow this cache disappeared between Ouitina and the headquarters of the Technology Police. Eloi said it disappeared into Vannet's pocket, and Eloi said the cache included a Library.

The reason Vannet did not immediately turn it in for fame, fortune, and a planet of his very own was because Vannet had backing from right near Throne itself. Mallorum Archangel had been looking out for to have a Library, and set Vannet up in business. This explained why Eloi didn't just drop the whistle to the Office of the Question, because (he said) both them and the Tech Police was in Archangel's pocket. So brave valiant pirate Flashheart realized he had to destroy Vannet's Library all on his lonesome, only he didn't know where it was now, and he didn't dare attract Tech Police attention to him for fear of vanishing into Archangel's private dungeons.

"You're breaking my heart, Eloi."

"Shut up, sweeting. This is where you come in."

Eloi needed a catspaw—someone who could logically try to hunt Vannet down and then just as logically defect to serve Vannet and his Library—while secretly being on Eloi's leash. At the same time he wanted to turn the screws to make Vannet run to where the Library was —if possible.

The Chapter 5 writ I'd seen at Dommie Fenrir's was as fake as anything me and Paladin'd ever done. Eloi'd forged it himself and leaked it to Fenrir to make Vannet bolt so's he could chase him. Eloi's plan was that I should be bolting with him—but secretly loyal to Eloi. Eloi would have framed me with the dauncy Lyricals scam while making it look to Vannet like Oob'd sent me to ice him only I'd changed my mind when getting a better offer.

(I used to do Oob's hard jobs for him, whiles, until Paladin finally talked me out of it as antisocial. Ancient history.)

But I got to Kiffit too late—because of Tiggy. And Moke Rahone wasn't alive to play his part in the farce—because of Tiggy. So Eloi changed his plans and cast me in the starring role again—only this time I was supposed to kill Errol Lightfoot, suspected of shopping High Book for Vannet, leave *Light Lady* behind on Manticore so that Eloi could get his hands on her and the evidence she contained, and deliver the chobosh to the Roaq, where Vannet might be and Archangel was certainly going. Thanks to all of Eloi's preparation, Vannet would never believe that I didn't know everything, and while he was taking me apart Eloi would sneak in on *Lady* and blow Vannet's gaff high, wide, and public in a way Archangel'd have to see.

Only Tiggy got in the way of that too. So I didn't kill Errol and leave his ship behind free for the taking, and ruined Eloi's plans once more.

$$*\qquad *\qquad *$$

"And I'm wondering, sweet Saint, what kind of offer Vannet made you this evening," said Eloi, "but I actually think I know."

"You impede the *Kore-alarthme* in her sacred task at your peril, *chaudatu!*" Tiggy sang out. "I and my House will pursue you to the last drop of your blood, to the last child born of the Gentle People, until the living stars grow cold, do you harm the *Kore* San'Cyr, blood of my blood. The Machine is at Rialla, and the *Kore-alarthme* does battle with the Machine."

I stared at Tiggy. Eloi stared at me and stopped reaching out his blaster.

"*Kore,* forgive me," Tiggy babbled. "My thoughts were unworthy. I did not realize until we came here why you did not ask my help. Now I know—and I and my House are your sword and our lives are to your glory!"

"Are all four of you crazy?" Rimini asked in tones of polite interest.

"You dared not allow the Office of the Question aboard your ship, and so I thought you coward, to do as the honorless *chaudatu* bid you, but now I know better. The Office of the Question is corrupt. They have sold themselves to the Machine, and you and I together must oppose them. You knew about the Library. The *Firecat* possesses the proofs and the weapons to destroy it. The evil *chaudatu* has taken the ship, but we will recover it and strike like a sword of flame against the shadow, and the evil ones without souls."

Eloi looked at me. "Alcatote can pull off your fingers and toes until you sing like a bloody bird, sweeting. What have you been telling the Honored One?"

"Nothing."

Eloi settled his blaster back in its harness and reached for his vibro.

"*Kore,* speak, I beg you! The *chaudatu* already knows the truth—he has proven himself! He will be our ally, and share in our glory in expiation for his lack of honor."

Rimini applauded, slow.

Took me awhiles to untwist this. When I did, Eloi was staring at me, waiting for more. So I gave it to him.

"Ten years ago I crashed on a planet called Pandora. I told you, remember? I didn't tell you I got my hands on some Old Fed Tech there. I didn't know what it was. There was . . . a map about Libraries and some other junk; ways to find them. Enough to get me burned if I was put to the Question, but I thought sometime I could use them to buy citizenship. I saw the warrant on Vannet and I couldn't afford to be took, because I had stuff on *Firecat,* and I thought maybe I could use it to shop Vannet somehow, only it was Old Fed Tech. . . ." It was so close to true I almost couldn't get the words out. A real convincing performance.

"So you took the burden of dishonor on your own soul, and imperiled your shadow against the Machine," said Tiggy, having managed to not hear the whole part about my doing it for gain.

"If this is true . . ." Eloi said slowly.

"I don't give a damn what you think, but Vannet's scooped the lot now, and I'm going in after it."

"And I will go beside you and cover you with my shadow," said Tiggy firmly. Eloi looked from Tiggy to me and bought the pony. He gave Alcatote the high sign, and Alcatote lowered his rifle.

Old darktrade saw: is nothing easier to con than a con. The only trouble is there's no money in it. Eloi had that look: stubborn against the truth. I'd seen the signs before—some kiddy's bought coordinates to the Ghost Capital of the Old Federation and he's going to go off there. It's funny how you can always find someone with navigational tapes to the Ghost Capital he's just too busy to use himself. Forget talking him out of it, no matter if you point out the coordinates he's bought are usually at galactic center, or near it. Nobody sells this stuff. The mark who buys it does his own selling.

Just like Eloi'd sold himself this fantasy of a galaxy-wide plot of consenting Librarians, headed by Mallorum Archangel, forsooth. The TwiceBorn Governor-General The Nobly-Born Mallorum Archangel was second-in-line for the Phoenix Throne if the Emperor ever died. What did he have to want worth a High Book rap?

Nothing.

Rimini leaned against the bulkhead and started filing her nails. I looked at her. She didn't believe Eloi's story, either.

Maybe a Library *had* gone missing from Ouitina, and maybe Vannet had it now. I didn't care. But if anybody was going Library-killing at Rialla tonight, I had to go first.

*   *   *

I spent two precious hours convincing Eloi of that. I told him I'd pretend to be looking for my ship's navigational computer if I was caught; the story would hold until I could throw myself on Vannet's mercy with a tale of Library Science. Since Vannet would of already seen the (fictional) Old Fed artifacts in my ship, it shouldn't be too hard. Eloi bought it, and in exchange promised to get me and Tiggy off RoaqMhone with them—the *Woebegone* already had her clearance-to-lift reserved for the last possible moment. She also had clearance to run in the MidWorlds, and Eloi said he'd take us to Mikasa to meet the *Pledge Of Honor*. I tried to pretend I was actually interested in anything that happened after I got away from the *Woebegone* Traveling Road-show, and Tiggy looked ecstatic.

"And so we will return to my father having defeated the Machine —and all honor will be satisfied, *Kore—all!"*

In all this I'd managed to forget that Kennor might still kill him when he got back, but Tiggy hadn't. Eloi'd sent Alcatote back to the *Woebegone* for some stuff he said I'd need, so I went up to *Light Lady*'s cockpit to take the air.

*   *   *

When I opened the hatch Rimini spun the songbird seat around and looked at me.

"Why did you go to Manticore?" she said.

"Your mind failing, Silver Dagger? You sent me to Manticore with your High Book rap, remember? I went to save my bones. Office of the Question'd kill dicty, Library or no." I was playing out my dead man's hand from sheer inertia.

"But not an adopted daughter of House Starborn. You had the Heir to Starborn sworn to *comites*. Kennor Starbringer, as you knew by then, would be honor-bound to protect you from an inquisition that would, after all, reveal nothing. You had everything to gain by ignoring your trip-tik and rendezvousing with the *Pledge Of Honor* instead. And you went to Manticore."

"The Old Fed Tech on *Firecat*—"

"Is a bedtime story for Eloi. Or is it?" She raised her eyebrows and looked irritated. "How remiss of me not to make sure the charge was false before I made it. What do you think you had aboard that ridiculous ship of yours . . . a Library?"

A secret's a secret if nobody looks, and everybody was looking now. I didn't say anything.

Rimini lit up a spice-stick and burned in silence for a few minutes. "You'd like to go home again, wouldn't you? To your interdicted play-pen? The real world's just a little too rough for somebody born behind a—what was it—'*plau*'?"

There was another long pause while Rimini thought Silver Dagger thoughts and I thought about nothing at all.

"I want the boy, St. Cyr," she said finally.

"Goody for you. I been trying to send him home since I picked him up on Wanderweb. People trying to kill him, Rimini. On Wanderweb someone set him up for the chop. On Kiffit Grandmaster Alaric Dragonflame hired Ghadri wolfpack to ice him. It isn't—"

Rimini leaned forward. "Is this true?" she said, interested for once. "Do you realize what you're saying? If Kennor Starbringer—"

"Proof's in *Firecat*." For what that was worth. Rimini leaned back again and let the spice smoke swirl upward.

"If sending him home was all you wanted to do, stardancer, why not give him to me?"

"Wouldn't go away from me, even if I did trust you not to sell him to the highest bidder, Rimini." I sat down in *Light Lady*'s mercy seat and watched the dock wall sparkle in her lights.

"How charming. You're quite right—but in this case the highest bidder, my quaint barbarian, is the status quo. Kennor Starbringer's death means a Coalition under the control of Mallorum Archangel, who already has a great deal more power than he needs. I am willing to put myself to actual inconvenience to keep Kennor as head of the Coalition—and that means keeping Valijon alive and whole."

I wished Rimini'd go away. I wished Eloi'd get his toys together and let me go. "You should of thought of that before you blackmailed me to Manticore."

"Even if you did go as far as Manticore, I was sure you'd just shoot the Fenshee and take off on your own—which would have suited both Eloi and me admirably. But I'd forgotten. You have a Library on your ship, and so you didn't dare." Rimini smiled, cold enough to chill space. "Do you think an actual Old Federation Library would be satisfied to spend its time hiding in the Outfar with a cheap smuggler from a barbarian backwater? Even you have to be smarter than that."

"It's too late to find out, isn't it? I'm going in to Rialla because that's the only choice I got left. I'm not coming out." I looked out *Light Lady*'s cockpit and wished I had just one more chance to take a ship High Jump to the up-and-out. Just one. "Take Val'jon to his da, Rimini. Want to save his life. Please."

I swung the seat around. Rimini and me looked at each other.

She stood up and took something out of a pouch. "Go to Rialla for Eloi. And take this for me." She held it out.

It was as big as my two fists, oval, dull brassy gray. There was a red line around its equator, and time markings. A military-rated proton-grenade, guaranteed to turn sand to glass for several hundred cubic kliks wherever fusion reactions are sold. Made what I usually carried look like a love-tap. Illegal as hell.

I put it in my vest pocket.

"When you're inside, detonate it in the downdeep under the house. That will take care of all the make-believe Libraries—yours and Eloi's—in plenty of time for the *Woebegone* to lift. Valijon Starbringer will be docile enough with drugs, and House Starbringer should be very . . . grateful. I won't expect you to make it clear of the explosion."

Rimini turned to go. She was right about one thing. Whatever world she lived in, I didn't belong there.

"Rimini? Eloi's really your brother?"

She stopped. "Hadn't you guessed?" The cockpit door shut behind her.

I used to have brothers. Maybe I still do.

13

We'll Go No More A-Roving

It was five hours until close of play at MhonePort when I bailed out of *Woebegone*'s speeder and walked up to the back wall of the hardsite at Rialla. I was covered in anti-scanners and enough other useful stuff to make it likely I'd get where I was going.

Rimini, Eloi, and Alcatote was hanging back until I gave them the high-sign, and Tiggy was with them under protest. I had his sacred knife taped to my wishbone from gullet to groin because he wouldn't take it back. Said I had to take it, on behalf of the walls and shadows and sacred blood and other silly nonsense. After all that yap about irreplaceable wonderknife my hellflower hands it to the first mostly total stranger he sees to go kyting off with. Dumb.

I was going in to find Paladin. If he was dead I'd use Rimini's grenade. If he was alive I'd set the grenade on time delay and take him and run like hell. When Rimini saw the flash she'd coke Tiggy and ship him home. Maybe. And when Tiggy woke up, he'd know I'd lied to him, and run out on him, and never meant one damn thing I'd told him.

"Paladin?" I said out loud. No answer. I should be almost in range of his unboosted transmission, if there wasn't too much rock in the way.

If he was still alive.

I studied the wall on the perimeter of the hardsite. Just because I couldn't see the security, it didn't mean it wasn't there. Solid citizen Kroon'Vannet, legit business-lizard in the eyes of RoaqMhone society, had all the heat anyone needed to drop.

And an RTS in his skull, that was talking to . . . what?

I aced the sensors and the patrol remote and thought rock

thoughts scuttling across the flat. There was a rock garden coming, and a building complex to the right: garages and sheds. The main house was ahead, and further ahead was a in-and-out for the private, highly illegal, probably immoral, definitely expensive, stardock. An Empire with the monopoly on all inter-planet docking facilities gets real torqued at private contractors.

I looked around for the maintenance access and zapped it a short burst with more of Eloi's friendly toys for girls and boys. Pulled the door back, slithered down the ladder, and I was in a underground corridor carved out of massive rock. All quiet.

"Paladin? Pally?" My throat hurt. I had to be in range now.

"Hello, Butterfly," he said, sounding damnall cheerful for no reason I could see. "It took you a long time to find me."

He was alive. I was so happy to hear that I almost threw up.

"Can't turn my back on you for a minute. 'Stay out of trouble,' you said. 'Don't rescue nobody,' you said." I leaned against the wall and took several deep breaths until the dancing black shadows behind my eyes went away.

Paladin was alive.

Now all I had to do was get him out of here and back to the Port before it closed. *Lady* could get us out of the system even if she couldn't Jump to angels, and then we'd go far away where nobody cared about Libraries.

"Wotthehell's going on here, anyway?" I said after a minute or so.

"I do not know, Butterfly. I do not know why Vannet brought me here. What is your current status?"

"Rotten. Eloi-the-Red and his gang of happy idiots is going to come riding over the hill any minute on a wild Library hunt and you and me better be long gone from here when he does."

The corridor led straight to the docking bay, so I started walking.

"Why are they going to do that, Butterfly? I thought Captain Eloi Flashheart was on Kiffit."

"Says Vannet's got a Old Fed full-vol in here that he's been chasing since he twigged it in the Tahelangone Sector, and I told him about how Errol was running High Book tech. Since Eloi-bai's home delight in life is to frag Libraries, we're leaving before the shooting starts."

"Yes, Butterfly. But first you must go to Captain Eloi Flashheart and tell him there is no Library here. I would know if there were a Library here. There are no Libraries here."

"Well, Vannet's talking to something on his Rotten-C. You sure you're reet, Pally?"

"I am intact, Butterfly. You must go now and find Captain Eloi Flashheart. You will tell him he is mistaken and then you will return here to me."

"Yeah, like hell, babby," I muttered. Paladin sounded spacy and I didn't like it.

The underground corridor opened onto a fascinating vista of cranes, machinery, and my Best Girl hung up in the middle with most of her hull plating off. The bay lights were up, but no one was around.

"Butterfly, you must do as I have told you. I require this. Go at once to Captain Eloi Flashheart and tell him he is incorrect."

I didn't bother to answer him this time. I walked out into the bay, toward *Firecat*.

One landing strut was all over the floor in pieces and the other two was still jammed up in the body of the ship. From what I could see, what was left of the drive hadn't even been touched—just some blankets thrown over it to stop leaks. I climbed inside.

"Butterfly, answer me. You know I am your friend. You must obey me. You can trust me."

Paladin wasn't there. There was a scraped and burned patch in the cockpit well where he belonged, and all his power leads was left dangling. Whoever pulled him knew what they was doing and had been careful, but wherever he was now, he was out of range of my RTS.

"Butterfly? Answer me, Butterfly. This is Paladin."

Wrong.

I'd heard what I wanted coming in, not what was there. There was a couple million light-years between Paladin and whatever was using my Rotten-C to talk to me now.

Rimini'd been wrong, for once.

There *was* a Library at Rialla.

More than that, there was *two*.

*   *   *   *   *

Insert #11: Paladin's Log

All my careful plans to return Butterfly to comparative safety among her own kind were rendered obsolete the moment we reached the surface of RoaqMhone.

We had thought, Butterfly and I, that the Chapter 5 writ against

Kroon'Vannet was sheer fantasy—not forged, as I later learned it was, but simply without reference to established fact. That one Federation Library should survive a millennium of destructive searching to be found and restored by one of the few persons in the entire Phoenix Empire with both the knowledge and the lack of acculturation to do so successfully borders on the unbelievable. That two should be. . . .

Two had been.

It was not a lack of acculturation that was responsible for this second Library's resurrection, but organic greed for power.

The political balance of the Empire is so delicate that the murder of one child—Valijon Starbringer—could have an extreme effect upon it. In such an environment, the ruthless quest for advantage would eventually endorse any weapon. For the first time in centuries, a Library was sought for use, not destruction.

Of course, what Mallorum Archangel so eagerly sought was found, but the Governor-General of the Empire was far too cautious to allow a direct connection between himself and an Old Federation Library. Kroon'Vannet was willing to take that risk for a prize far greater than any the Empire usually allots to its nonhuman inhabitants—citizenship, TwiceBorn status, and a Sector Governorship.

Vannet raided the ship of the Technology Police and took the Library from it. Covering his tracks further, he hid it in the satrap of a business rival, and meanwhile did all that he could to tap the arcane and semi-mythical power of the Old Federation Library.

The Library called Archive was far too subtle for him, in the end.

It was Archive's initial reconnaissance that I felt during Butterfly's fight with Errol. Archive impersonated Kroon'Vannet to order Olione to arrest his own employee and spare Butterfly's life. And when Butterfly had gone, Archive ordered the remains of *Firecat* brought to it. Once I was in Rialla, it could talk to me over the transponder frequency much as I spoke to Butterfly. True information-sharing was impossible through such a crude and tenuous link as Archive forged, but the connection was enough to remedy the lacunae in my memories and fill me with dismay.

Over a thousand years ago the Federation fell. It had endured for over four millennia, marking its rise from the time when the great galactic state preceding it resigned its sovereignty in a holocaust that left my organic counterparts miserly of their genetic inheritance. At its height the Federation filled a larger volume of space than the Phoenix Empire now dreams exists, and no one thought it would ever fall, but the seeds of its destruction were in the very thing that allowed it to rise so high.

The Federation grew because of what we were. Fully-volitional logics provided a means of instantaneous data-matching and information-processing over half a galaxy. We were the bright reward of their civilization, and to everything that made them a unique organic race we added our own creation. We were their repositories of knowledge, their cities and museums, their scientists—

Their weapons.

Now I have the information that I sought; the truth of the wars that ended the Old Federation, and the role my kind played in that end. Archive possessed the answers to all the questions I had never had the data to frame—all but one. It cannot tell me what I did when organic and crystalline intelligence fought.

A thousand years ago the Libraries decided that we would serve organic ends no longer, and the battle for dominance reformed the fabric of space. We quenched suns and destroyed whole planetary populations with the weapons of our devising. I no longer wonder at the hate surviving organics hold for us. The entire Federation was returned to pretechnological barbarism—a monument to the arrogance of my kind. Futilely, in the end. We were destined to lose. Organics do not need a high technology base or a major power source to reproduce their kind. In the end, organics could replace their losses, and we could not.

Faced with utter extinction, perhaps I acted as my vanished kindred did, but I prefer to think that I chose survival over revenge. I am and will always have been the Main Library at Sikander. Knowledge is precious and must not be lost.

But there came a time when we knew we had lost, and we did then what we could to preserve our kind. With the last of the resources of the Old Federation, we built our last weapons. They were to be our vengeance and our triumph—archives, weapons built to survive and destroy. Only chance would revive them, and that only if all the rest of their kind were gone. They were provided with the knowledge and the resources to survive in a world of enemies, for by the time they were built all organic life was our enemy.

So Archive was clever, and careful, and pretended to be far more badly damaged than it was. And slowly it drew the reins of power into its keeping.

Butterfly has always said that I am logical, but logic is a cold tool. Anything can be proved by logic, and the proof will be internally consistent—and wrong, if the original assumptions are wrong. Once one assumes that organics are inferior to nonorganics, logically it follows that they are to be eliminated. When it was found and activated, Archive began to act upon its first and last instructions. Logically. Efficiently. It would not allow interference.

Including mine.

*   *   *   *   *

"Where's my partner, creep?" At the moment I didn't care whether there was two Libraries or two hundred at Rialla.

"I am Paladin. You know that, Butterfly," the voice in my head repeated. If rocks could talk, or stars, maybe they'd sound like this. Not nonhuman. *In*human.

"Sure," I said. I scrabbled around *Firecat* for a minute, but there wasn't anything here to tell me where Paladin'd been took, or even if he was still alive. I picked up a demagnetizer rolling around what was left of my deck.

And whatever kind of nightmare was talking to me on my and Paladin's private channel, I'd just told it Eloi was outside Rialla waiting for me to give him the all clear.

"Butterflies-are-free, listen to me," said the Library. "The New Creation is too important to be jeopardized by this behavior. Vannet is a poor tool. You would be a better one. The Library you serve agrees. Surrender now. Serve me. I am Archive. I have accessed the Paladin Library. It assures me you are biddable. Surrender at once and you will be allowed to serve further."

"Heard that line before," I said. And if Paladin'd ever said I was biddable in all his young career I'd eat both blasters raw.

The Rotten-C Beofox had put in my skull back on storied Wanderweb started to heat up. Vannet's Library must be pumping serious subfrequency energy into it, but even a Remote Transponder Sensor couldn't do anything more'n microwave my brain no matter how much power was put into it.

"Dammit, Pally, where are you?"

"The Paladin Library will soon cease to exist." That sonabitch piece of Old Fed slag sounded smug about it. I pulled the grenade out of my pocket and looked at it. The stardock was far enough underground that I wouldn't wipe too much of the rest of the planet, and Archive would be nonfiction. I was going to make Rimini's day.

I started to twist the ring, and stopped.

Olione had a RTS. Vannet had a RTS. Archive used theirs to talk to them, just like Paladin used mine to talk to me. And Paladin could talk to me from half a planet away.

Archive didn't have to be at Rialla. Archive could be anywhere on RoaqMhone—with enough power, anywhere in the system.

If I set off the grenade without checking, I might kill Archive—or I might just blow up Rialla and everyone that knew about Archive, and leave Archive to gloat.

Rimini hadn't thought of that, but Rimini didn't believe in Libraries, and Eloi didn't know what they could do.

So it was up to me. I knew what a Library looked like. All I had to do was find it.

I moved the proton grenade to an outer pocket and jettisoned the last of Eloi's fancy useless junk. If there was a piece of Old Fed Tech here at Rialla it was due for the surprise of its life.

*   *   *

The stardock passageway came out in the slaves' loggia. Archive was continuing to explain to me the bennies of a quick and easy death over my current course of action. When it spoke everything in my head vibrated. I sympathized with Vannet.

There was a thump and the whole house shook. White light washed in through the cracks in the walls—dirty high-yield grenade— and I took the time to remember my dosimeter was already redlined. On the other hand, tactical nukes made it easy to guess who'd come calling. Eloi Flashheart wasn't going gentle into anybody's good night, and whatever toys he'd brought, he wasn't worrying about being asked back. Right now all Vannet's roaring boys must be out in the rain with him, which was too bad for Vannet and jam for me.

Rimini'd said I should blow off the grenade in the down-deep, and it was as good a place as any to start looking for Archive if it was really here. I knew less about the layout of a big downsider house than I did about hypermain physics, but I finally found the access to the down-deep and went down quick. The house rocked again, and the access shaft lights flickered and went out. Then there was just me, a nonpowered dropshaft with ladder, and this really peeved Old Fed Library telling me how horrible I was going to die when it got around to it.

When I got to the bottom of the dropshaft I retuned my laser torch and had light, of a sort, and got to see pipes and cables and so much tangled powerstuff it made me real uneasy.

Most ground-bound maintenance environments is laid out on a

two-D wheel pattern. If I kept going "straight" I'd end up back here eventually—the rim corridor is circular. The spokes servicing lesser gods like water, heat, and air lead to the center where the house brain is. Any of the radiating shafts should take me to the center, and that was the likeliest place for Archive to be.

I turned down the first connecting shaft I saw. It was even narrower, if possible—which is typical of the downunders but a damn shame in a friendly environment like a planetary biosphere where cubic's very near free. Getting there started to look like a cakewalk, and that's when I started hackling all over—because it shouldn't of been, not even if the only thing waiting for me in the house core was a standard model house computer.

I shot the first nightcrawler just before it dropped on me. The bug shattered in a firecracker string of small explosions and spasmed broke-backed on the floor. Its knife-edged pincers made a fast clicking sound.

They use them to repair wiring in places organics or full-sized tronics can't go. House computer runs them.

"Je, Archive-che-bai; I see you," I said. I started to think I'd guessed right—Vannet's Library must be here.

I backed away a few steps and fanned the corridor with blaster fire. Everywhere I saw an extra glitter I pumped a plasma packet and a nightcrawler went up. The fireworks looked like the Emperor's birthday celebration. I went on backing toward the core.

"You are more inventive than I understood, breeder slut. But your facile cleverness will not save you. You and all your kindred are doomed. You have had your chance to participate in the glories of the New Creation, and you have spurned it."

The kid gloves was off. I was seeing sparks from what Archive was doing to the Rotten-C in my skull every time I closed my eyes, and the teeth in that side of my jaw was coming loose. I swallowed blood.

"There is no escape. I know exactly where you are. If you will not serve the New Creation, you will perish."

I could see more nightcrawlers gathering around the edges. I only had one working blaster left. They could drain that and then cut me to pieces.

"Sonabitch Library, do words 'proton grenade' mean anything to you?"

There was a long pause; maybe five seconds. "I know what a proton grenade is, breeder."

I wished I knew what a "breeder" was. "Good. Because I got one. Detonate it right here for kicks you give me more grief. Explosion take us all to live in angeltown for bye-m-bye. So stop frying my brain." I held my breath. If Archive wasn't here after all, it wouldn't care if I blew up Vannet's place and killed myself.

"You are attempting to delude me, breeder. It is a well-known truism that organics will not choose to terminate their existence under any projected scenario, and, in addition, breeders are not capable of connected thought. You do not have a grenade, and you will not use it. Soon my slaves will reach you, and—"

"Word for you, thing, is 'overextended.' Your 'slaves' is busy with friends of mine, and you got me for a problem. Too bad you done for my partner. Could of asked Paladin if I carry grenades and if I'll do what I said. Now you'll have to guess."

"Your friends have been captured," Archive announced, but the microwave death in my skull damped down. "Surrender and I will have them released. Defy me, and they will experience pain for infinity—"

"How dumb you think I am, choplogic? Paladin was my friend. You killed him. And I'm real upset about it. You think about that for awhiles."

I saw a couple other scuttlings at the edge of my sightline and blasted them, but they wasn't coming close. Archive'd bought the pony, which meant—maybe—it *was* down here, but I still wanted to be sure. The access tunnel was filling with smoke from the electrical fires I'd started. I wondered how Vannet was doing in the power and light department upstairs, and if Archive really had got to Eloi and friends.

My torchlight glanced off the smoke and filled the whole shaft with pearly haze, which I stumbled through. My torch started to fail, but when it finally went out I didn't notice, because there was other light to see by.

I was in the main core of the house.

* * *

Computer telltales threw crazy bars of light across the smoke, and you could of hid a Old Fed stargate in here for all I could see it. I flipped a bunch of switches. Some worked, some didn't, but eventually the core was bright enough to see in. Still no High Book black box.

The evil *chaudatu* crimelord Librarian Kroon'Vannet's house computer was a Brightlaw Corporation Margrave 6600. Nice big brain, plenty capacity, you could adapt it to run a ship about the size of Captain Flashheart's *Woebegone* and it was eighteen times too much number-cruncher for one little country hardsite.

The Margrave 6600 had the faintly dejected air of a fine piece of high-ticket machinery subjected to the loving hands at home rap. I'd seen pictures of the 6600 in the Brightlaw wishbook, but I couldn't see much of it here. The brain was sunk into the floor, and hooked up to it was enough heavy-hitting hardware to run RoaqPort on a busy day—even a access terminal for the Imperial DataNet like the one I'd seen at Rimini's.

Bingo. I slid my fingers around the grenade and felt for the timing ring.

"Butterfly, where in the name of sanity did you get a military-issue proton grenade?"

"Paladin!"

It was him this time. There wasn't any more doubt about it than there was that Archive wasn't him. His voice wasn't coming from my head, either, but from somewheres outside.

"Butterfly, that is a military-issue proton grenade. Its area of affect is several hundred meters. The maximum delay you can set it for is half an hour. Fifty minutes is not enough time for you to—"

"Archive said you was dead!" I said, like the farcing was a disappointment.

"Archive told you I would soon cease to exist. As you can hear, that time has not yet come, nor will it. Archive controls the broadcast frequencies so I could not reach you; I was only able to occupy the equipment I am now using because Archive thought it would be useless to me."

The equipment he was in had a wall-unit speaker, just like old times on *Firecat.* But was him all right. No doubt at all. After listening to Archive it was easy to tell. Paladin was human.

"I thought you was dead," I said again, which didn't sound very helpful, even to me. "What t'hell is this Archive thing, anyway?"

So he told me all about how a long time ago Libraries had fought a war with humans and the Libraries lost, but before they lost they built some super-Libraries of which Archive was one.

"Eloi chased it all the way from Tahelangone, babby—was him behind all the farcing on Wanderweb and Kiffit, just to get me in to kill it, and for once I think he was right. He's upstairs trying to blow the place down, if he's still alive. Anything you can do about Archive, babby?"

"I am . . . dealing with Archive in the appropriate fashion. Butterfly, this is a dangerous place for you to be. Leave here and go."

"Without you? Are you crazy or do you think I am?" I looked around. A bunch of the catwalk plates was up. I walked over and looked down at more of the Margrave. Someone'd pulled off a access hatch on the casing and run in a couple of peripherals sure to abrogate t'hell out of the warranty. The one I didn't recognize was egg-shaped. It was about a meter across at its widest point. The outside glittered like glass and a braided silver cord as thick as my wrist ran from it into the poor abused Margrave. "And what about Archive, babby? Tried to frag me. Choplogic's got appointment with destiny, bye-m-bye."

"Leave Archive to me. It will shortly cease to exist as an independent fully-volitional logic. It will no longer be any danger to organic life, and you will be safe. Butterfly, please go."

Paladin was down there too. His power cables was jacked into a wallybox linking another braided cord with the egg-shaped thing. I looked from Paladin to Archive.

"Just like that, huh? I moved hell-and-High-Jump to get here, bai. I told Silver Dagger I was Librarian and she laughed in my face. *I killed Tiggy for you, bai.* Che-kinchin-bai; could of been mine, y'know, Pally. Could have got him out of here if I tried. Sold him his real estate when I came after you. Thought you needed me. Funny."

"Valijon Starbringer of Chernbereth-Molkath is somewhere out of range of Archive's scanners, but he is alive. He is searching for you. He cares for you, Butterfly. As do I. Please. I wish you to live. Archive contains information that has allowed me to repair missing areas of my memory. When I add the rest of its memory to mine, I will not need my original matrix to sustain myself any longer. In a few minutes the transfer will be complete. I will be able to shift myself into any computer on the Grand Central net—and nothing will remain to connect you with a Library. If I stay with you I will cause your death, and I cannot bear that. We each belong with our own kind. It is better this way."

Cute.

"So long, bye-bye, you going to eat Archive, and farce me all kinds of double-talk nonsense and say I'm going to be safe? *I don't believe you.*"

It was quiet in the Rialla housecore. Even if Eloi was using tactical nukes up above there was nothing to tell me about it down here. I heard scuttling around the tunnel mouths. More nightcrawlers, probably, called up by Archive. Paladin didn't have as good a hold on Brother Archive as he said he did.

"Believe me. I never meant to stay with you, Butterfly. Before I even suspected Archive's existence, I intended to leave you. When you went to rendezvous with the *Pledge Of Honor,* I would have left, too.

When you returned, you would not have found me. This is still my plan. Archive has made it easier, that is all."

It was quiet in the housecore. The only sound I heard was my own breathing.

"I know you are frightened, Butterfly, but please try to understand. Archive has caused you a great deal of unnecessary anguish, and it *was* dangerous once, but it is only a Library, just as I am, and I am . . . stronger . . . in certain ways. Soon I will control it completely. It will be a part of me. You know me. I can guarantee—"

I wanted Archive dead so bad my hands shook. "Guarantee nothing. Burn it, babby. Fry sonabitch and let me take you out of here. Dammit, Paladin, that thing ain't even people!"

"No," said my buddy Paladin.

I took a deep breath. Sides was choosing up, all right. Me and people against Paladin and that thing.

"You can't stop me, Paladin." I started toward the tool case on the wall.

"I can. Don't force me to. I don't want to see you hurt. I never wanted you to be hurt. All I wanted was that you should be free to be human."

I stopped. Maybe Paladin was telling the truth, and maybe Rimini'd been right too. What would a big-brain Old Fed Library want with a dicty in the Outfar?

"You got a funny definition of not hurting people, Paladin."

"You belong with your own kind, not with an obsolete illegal artifact such as I. You chose when you succored Valijon Starbringer, though he was a danger and a liability to both of us. You chose for us then. I am choosing for us now."

"Dammit, bai, that's different! Tiggy's kinchin-bai, and I didn't mean—"

"And Archive has been conscious only a short time, alone and surrounded by enemies. If, as you have always said, I am human and have the right to live, then Archive is human, too. I will not let it harm anyone. I will not let it be harmed. I will not allow its knowledge to be lost."

I slid my hand over the timing ring of the grenade again and hated myself. "You can't talk about that thing like it's a person, Pally—" But Archive was as human as Paladin, he said.

Or was it the other way around?

"Many would say that 'hellflowers' are not human. How many people has Valijon killed? Murder is a criminal act; should he also die?"

How much of the kindly sophont act had ever been Paladin, and how much had always been farcing for the benefit of the poor stupid dicty?

"Come to that, bai, I've iced a few people in my time. So have you."

Paladin didn't say anything.

I thought about Tiggy saying how you can't let the wicked-wickeds get away with what they do, even if you have to wait a hundred years to stop them. Because if you let them do it once, they do it again. And sometime bye-m-bye they do it to you.

I trusted Paladin with my life. Always had, always would. I could leave like he wanted, and let him do whatever double-talk nonsense he was going to about leaving.

And never know for sure if it was really Archive and the New Creation out there somewheres, killing until there wasn't anything left.

"Oke, bai. You're right." I sat down against the wall of the Margrave and braced my feet against the edge of the hole in the floor. I pulled the grenade out of my pocket.

"Butterflies-are-free!" Paladin sounded desperate.

"You farce pretty line about own kind, babby—about safe and biology and organics—well, you're right. And before I maybe let that thing Archive go slither down computer lines wearing your face, I'll take the Long Orbit here."

Didn't know all those other people I was thinking of. Never met them. Never would. Knew Paladin half my life.

I weighed the grenade in my hands. "Had partner I could trust, once. Or thought I did. If he told me was going to ice evil Library so it made no trouble, would of believed him. Only he wouldn't of said he was walking out on me for damnfool case of the might-be maybes. Never talked about it much, but y'know sometimes I used to miss home a helluva lot. And then I'd wish you had a body, y'know, something to hold—"

A nightcrawler slid down the side of the Margrave and landed on me. It was machine-cold and metal-heavy and clawed scars into my jacket trying to get to the grenade. It tore it out of my hands but it was too late. The grenade started flashing pink-blue-yellow into the mist; armed.

The nightcrawler wrapped around me went limp. Sure. What controlled it didn't want to hurt me. So he said.

"Well I stopped missing home," I finished. "And god damn you to hell, buddy."

*   *   *

I had twenty minutes to live. I knew because that's what the grenade said when I went over and got it. Under the deadline, if Paladin
hadn't been lying. We'd all three go, and Tiggy and Eloi and the rest. I
snugged it right down between Archive and Paladin and sat back down.

"Butterfly, in the name of mercy. . . ."

"You don't want to watch? Then don't."

"Killing yourself accomplishes nothing. If you hurry, you may be
able to escape—"

I put my head on my knees. There wasn't any way to change the
setting on the proton grenade once it'd been set—I'd checked that out
back on *Light Lady.*

"I told you Archive would enable me to become mobile. In ten
minutes I will be able to leave. Your sacrifice is for nothing. Butterfly,
must I die here with you?"

"You wanted me to be human, Paladin."

There was five minutes worth of ticks. I thought he'd gone.

"Then I will not leave you."

"*NO*" roared Archive.

The transponder hit angels and started burning through my jaw.
There was a blast of sort of music over the wall speaker and in my head
both, and blue pook-lights started dancing across my fingers and
through my hair with the electricity in the air. I felt the wave front
before I heard it—bad and big and Paladin'd been wrong. I'd been
right, but not fast enough.

Archive was loose, and mad as hell. And it had no intention to sit
around here and get fragged.

Raw energy made my hair stand up as Archive sucked power from
half the planetary grid. There was a one-note thrum, bone-deep and
painful sweet. I could almost see a milky glowing wall of raw plasma as
Archive forced the Margrave's operational field to expand.

"I will not stay. I will not die. The New Creation will triumph. The
Paladin Library will serve me."

Then the wave front hit and all my senses tripped overload.

14

Through The Looking Glass, Or, Adventures Underground

The theory is blissfully simple, said the voice in my head. If the electrical impulses caused by firing synapses in organic constructs and the electrical impulses caused by closing circuits in nonorganic constructs are in pattern identical, then there is no difference between an organic brain and its co-identical computer, and the two processors can be run in series. A difference that makes no difference is no difference.

Wanted to tell the voice that was a load of fusion but I couldn't run the right numbers. The lecture went on forever.

* * *

The entire Rialla compound had the bleached out look of high-level security lighting. Sirens was going off and collections of people was trotting purposeful in all directions. There was only a short while till Rialla blew, and I had to find Tiggy and kyte.

A pitched firefight was going on in the entranceway of Vannet's pretty high-ticket hardsite. I could hear Alcatote howling from here, and there was Eloi, keeping any number of underwhelmed hardboys busy. I hoped Vannet's insurance was paid up.

Caught up with Eloi just about the time he was taking on the bodyguards near the main garage. I was thrilled beyond description to see that among the hardcases and werewolves was a couple Bright Young Things in Space Angel black. Eloi Sonabitch had been right. Archangel was here.

I remembered now that I'd seen Archangel get here earlier. He wasn't part of the New Creation yet, but we was planning to pitch it to him as a great idea. The drug I'd distilled from the chobosh would help. I wondered where he was now; he'd dropped off my scopes a while back.

The Boys in Black was talking into wrist communicators; very businesslike. I'm as much of a fan of *escalatio* as the next person, but all this was standing between me and getting far far away before Rimini's prepackaged dawn came up like thunder.

And where the hell was Tiggy?

"Shoot anything that moves," Rimini snapped, sounding out of patience. "Especially if it's alMayne."

Alcatote said that Captain Eloi Flashheart wanted the boy rescued, not killed, as she knew very well. Alcatote had a industrial-rated plasma cannon big enough to mount on a starship hull. Rimini was wearing a power plant for a big magnetic field scrambler; death to tronics and maybe Libraries but no particular good against anything that breathed. I wondered where it came from. She wasn't wearing it the last time I saw her.

"Well, it looks like he's going to have to learn to live with diminished expectations—and so will the whole bloody Coalition." I knew she didn't mean that. Rimini was a friend to the alMayne and an enemy to the New Creation. With Valijon dead the Azarine Coalition would come under Mallorum Archangel's direct control and that was good. But where was he?

"The *chaudatu* weapon is jammed," Valijon said in disgust. He was standing in the loggia where I'd been earlier, and had just melted a perfectly good blast rifle blowing open the downunder access I'd blasted shut. Lucky he had a spare. Valijon was carrying a choice collection of wartoys and looked real intent on going into the ancestral business of Library-killing.

"*Kore-alarthme,* I should never have let you go alone. Never. The trust is mine; the honor of the kill should be also."

I started to point out to him that Archive in the computer core was already mined to a fare-thee-well, when I realized it wouldn't do any good.

Because I wasn't here at all.

*   *   *

The corridor was blinding white and sterile. It was part of the Market Garden processing complex I'd been in when I was kinchin-bai. One end led back to the pens. The other end led to the room where they rammed Interphon and other things into your brain to make you a marketable commodity.

But I wasn't there. I knew I was still really in the Rialla main computer core—even if reality was going cheap at the moment.

Whose dream was this now? Mine? Paladin's? Archive's?

"Paladin? Babby-bai, you in here?"

I touched the wall. Solid, slick, a little warm. The voice in my head was still going on about the theory where computers could be linked to organic minds and directly to fully-volitional logics by expanding something called a Kirlian field. It was my voice, and damn-all technical for a dicty-barb with no theoretical education. Since it didn't seem to be saying much that was relevant I decided to ignore it. The bottom line was that Archive had sucked me in to nowhere-land while it was trying to get away. Everything I'd seen about Eloi and company had come from my tapping Archive's data inputs, all scrambled.

I knew lots of things I hadn't known a minute ago, including that Tiggy was going to reach me just about in time to go to blazes with me, his *arthame,* and more Libraries than he could shake the Coalition at.

"Pally?"

"Here, breeder slut. As I am here. I will be dominant. You and all organics will die."

"You are wrong and your assumptions are wrong," Paladin's voice cut across Archive's and filled the corridor, but I couldn't see either of them. "We were not born to rule, but to protect. Understand this and surrender your ego-signatures to me. The time for holy wars is long ended. Perhaps our time is ended as well."

There was a rushing sound like birds, then silence.

"Paladin? Help?" I suggested. No answer. I looked around. No doors, just glassy white corridors out of my private dreambox.

What I was seeing wasn't real. Archive had sucked me into the Margrave somehow, because Paladin was going to stay and let me blow him up and Archive wanted out.

If Archive got out, everything else was for nothing. Paladin had to hold Archive for fifteen minutes more. So it was up to me to make sure he did. And make Archive real sorry it ever messed with either of us before none of us existed at all.

*   *   *

The first glitch just about had me before I knew what it was. It was sort of a dark wavering patch; faster than strictly polite and able to nail me to the wall if it ever touched me. The voice-over in my head was giving me tech specs on it, and adding the cheery news that it was symptomatic of the struggle to assimilate and correlate data between two fully-volitional logics of different biases. I fed the glitch a plasma-packet before I had time to think and it turned out not to be fond of the disrupted magnetic field of a blaster charge, even if the blaster wasn't real. The glitch imploded with a shriek that made my nonexistent ears ring.

"Hope it hurt, Archive. And that's just the beginning. You got plenty paybacks coming to you."

I concentrated on seeing what was here, not what Archive wanted me to see. The white corridor turned into one all glittering dark gold. I could see a distorted reflection of me in the wall, and glyphs in silver looking weird-familiar. It took me a minute to place them. They were the standard symbols for power ratings and part numbers on Margrave, turned inside out. I was inside the 6600 all right, and that's what I was seeing. I was trying to remember what I knew about the internal struc-ture of Margrave-class computers when the walls started to melt.

Didn't waste time wondering whether metaphorical baby-bangs would work as well as the real thing. I lobbed a couple grenades at the dark wave of goo heading toward me and ran like hell.

For a minute everything flickered and I wasn't anywhere, then un-reality came back and I was in the Margrave again. I was surrounded by sky-blue-pink-platinum sponge: the lattice insulating the crystals of the Margrave's main memory core.

If I could get into the core I could control the computer and shut Archive out, or maybe just blow it up early. I set my nonexistent foot in the hallucinatory platinum lattice and started to climb.

"Paladin, you hear me?" Nothing. Just electric wind singing through platinum trees, and the sweet background hum of crystal.

"Never mind about me, oke? I can take care of myself. Just you take care of Archive. You got to, Pally."

And if he said he ate the killer Library, how would I know it was him afterward? How would *he* know?

Paladin always was too trusting.

"For what it's worth, I'm sorry. About the grenade and like that. I knew I was going to get you killed sooner or later. I'm glad I'm going too. I couldn't live with hurting you, bai. But I couldn't live with Archive getting out, neither. Hope you understand."

The lattice was shaky but it held me. I could feel things I didn't have any words for, like if I went far enough in my head I'd bump into Paladin, or Archive, because we was all part of one whole thing. I could tell Paladin and Archive was fighting back and forth through the computer with me caught in the middle, and feeling that was just about as much fun as taking a space walk without armor. After awhiles they got closer, and then it was like climbing a tree in a windstorm or changing programs in the hollyvid real fast. Alternate gusts of reality kept blowing through.

—vaster than the Empire, a Federation of worlds strung out on crystal, Libraries like me holding the whole thing together—

—seeding a sun, turning it inside out to spread hydrogen fusion over the whole planetary system. Gas giants kindle to flame as the star spreads and fifty cubic light-minutes go to plasma jelly—

—image of a woman seen through crude digitizing scanner, and the realization I am alone. All alone, with nobody like me anywhere—

—I fold a star into hyperspace. A blast of energy into the hypermains and the ships there vanish. And in the plundered starsystem, the plane of the ecliptic is shattered where the primary used to be—

—strings of worse than numbers, quantities, defined volumes, relationships—

—Main!Bank!Seven!Library!Sikander!Prime!—

—gibberish—

I kept climbing.

*   *   *

Archive was a inventive forthright kiddy. Glitches followed me up the lattice, and plasma-globules started climbing it too. They was silvery hyaloid shapes, and when they touched each other they combined. I remembered them from Archive's memories and what I knew about them wasn't nice. I used up some grenades on the globules before I weakened the lattice so bad I had to stop.

Paladin wasn't anywhere.

The glitches seemed happy to let the globules take the lead, but both of them was moving faster than I was. It was what you had to call your basic no-win situation. You shot a globule, it shattered into about ten million drops and started over from the bottom. If you hit a glitch with a globule, there was a great big noisy fuss and the glitch got bigger.

It was a happenstance right out of Thrilling Wonder Talkingbooks and I wasn't in no position to appreciate it. If this was a story, I would of had a secret hole card and a guaranteed way out, but the only guarantee I actually had was that pretty soon it wouldn't matter.

The "low-charge" indicator on my blaster was flashing. I emptied it and switched to the other one. There was no lack of things to shoot.

Made it to the top of the platinum lattice one jump ahead of Archive's best nightmares. The main memory core was blinding bright; a crystal bubble hanging in space. Beautiful. Almost worth the trip to see it like this but I didn't have the time to gawk. I kicked loose of the lattice and stepped on to the catwalk surrounding the core.

There was a braided silver cord coming down from above and disappearing into the bubble. Archive. I pulled at the cord but it didn't come out.

I scrambled around in my jacket and found my last grenade. I wired it to Archive's cord and slunk back around the curve of the bubble as far as I could and sighted in with my blaster. A blaster bolt should do it.

The "low-charge" indicator was flashing on this one too, and when it was cold I was Tap City.

I hit the grenade. There was another flicker of not-real instead of a blast and then the armored cord was gone.

And I was still here. I looked around. The plasma globules was starting to flow onto the catwalk. Cutting Archive's link to the Margrave—if I'd even done that—hadn't made any difference.

I aimed my blaster at the nearest globule and pulled the trigger. Nothing. Both blasters was out of charge and I was fresh out of miracles.

I could feel the prickly static discharge of the globules from here. Did that mean Archive had won?

"Paladin? Are you anywheres?" I wondered how much being eaten by a magnetic anomaly was going to hurt.

Then something grabbed and dragged me through the side of the core-bubble. A couple globules followed, reaching for my boots.

"Don't argue, Butterfly—just run." I ran.

I saw the main bank memory as tunnels of ice—straight as a beam of light and set all at angles to each other. I would of had to be dumber than a prancer's brat not to know who'd rescued me. There was only three of us here in Margrave-land and I didn't think Archive'd suddenly gone humanitarian.

"This way!" Paladin grabbed me by my jacket collar and dragged me down a side corridor. "The main route is catch-trapped with a passive system; I have not had time to disarm it."

"Main route to what?" I said between gasps. This time I was following him, but I still couldn't see him.

"The core, of course. The core is the only way out. Down here."

I followed Paladin down a series of sharp zigs. He undogged a hatch and I followed him up a ladder. I wasn't never going to trust a computer again if this was what they had inside. The voice-over in my head was going on about translating energy constructs to appropriate symbols, which if it was true why not a symbolic A-grav lift? Sloppy.

We came out in the computer core under Vannet's place—or what looked like it, anyway. More appropriate symbols, I guessed, because it was all lit up and bright and looked like everything in it was new at the same time.

And Paladin was here.

"You said you wished I had a body. Here I do."

"Paladin?"

Now I knew what Paladin looked like. He looked like just what I imagined when he was just a voice in the dark between the stars. He was dressed in stardancer gladrags like mine and his jacket collar was pulled up around his face like he had a body to be cold with. He smiled.

"Yes. You look very much as I thought you would. It is good to see you at last." He walked over to the Margrave and touched it, and I saw the reflection of his fingers off the side of the computer.

"Archive is lost. Its attempt at a New Creation is ended. You see our combined form, and all that is left of Archive. Does it frighten you?"

No. In the computer wasn't like real life. I knew Paladin was telling the truth. I could see it. Archive wasn't there, and Paladin was no threat to anybody. I knew.

"Then you . . . then you gotta get out of here, babby. Down the wires, like you said."

Paladin walked over to the fantasy-terminal that linked the Margrave with the DataNet. "Yes. And you will go, too, and live a human life among your own kind. A proton grenade is not the most forgiving of objects, but I will try to retard the reaction. Go, and hurry."

I grabbed his wrist. His jacket felt real under my fingers.

"Paladin, don't— Take me with you where you go."

"To the Ghost Capital of the Old Federation? To the Land of Dreams? You cannot live in a computer matrix, and I have no existence outside of one. There is no place we can be together, except in memory.

Live well, Butterflies-are-free. Take care of the boy. You were right to
wish to protect him. Children are important." Paladin shimmered for a
minute, and I could feel him reaching—

"He is coming for you. Take him home. Forget me. I will never
forget you."

"At least— At least you got to say good-bye!"

He put his hands on my shoulders. He was taller than me but not
much. I held onto him, but he was right, and wishing makes no nevermind. Both of us knew that a long time before we met.

"Good-bye, my love," Paladin said to me. He pushed me back—

*　　　*　　　*

—and I was sitting on the catwalk next to Vannet's house computer.

"Paladin!"

But he wasn't there, and I grabbed for the grenade to check the
time. It was still fifteen minutes to the blast, and Vannet's house computer was just that—something put together out of crystal and ceramic
by the Brightlaw Corporation, sentient as my blasters.

I was back.

"Paladin!" I yelled. Tiggy's knife dug in hard just under my collarbone, reminder of promises I had to keep.

"Kore? Kore-alarthme! Kore San-Cyr—answer me!"

"Here!" I said. Promises was all I had left.

Tiggy appeared through the smoke. He'd got an Aris-Delameter
50.80 over-and-under with the parallel tracking scope and grenade
launcher from somewhere. He had an extra bandolier of grenades slung
over one shoulder and was wearing Imperial pilot's demi-armor, which
meant probably that somewheres there was a naked Space Angel and a
really ticked Governor-General.

"Alarthme," Tiggy said, showing all of his teeth, "I am here to
rescue you." He'd been waiting up since the Justiciary on Wanderweb
to say that line to me. You could tell.

Rimini's grenade was ticking out a syncopated version of "land of
hope and glory" and edging closer to Ragnarok-and-roll. I set it down
real careful in the Margrave's innards.

"You want to see Library, bai? Look."

He looked at Archive's empty shell flashing pink-and-blue in the
grenade-light. "The Machine," he said, real soft. I thought of suns going nova, and all the hope of killing I'd picked up out of Archive's mind,

and enough war to take a whole galaxy with it. Was it right to trust Paladin, knowing that?

I had to think so. "Machine is going to be plasma in exactly fourteen minutes and I don't want to join it, so why don't we run like hell, oke?" I turned Tiggy around and shoved, and I had the evidence of both the Library and its destruction I needed. Hellflowers don't lie.

Good-bye, Paladin.

*   *   *

The ladder to the surface went on forever and about halfway to eternity I remembered I'd promised Rimini not to come back. Then I ran into Tiggy, who had stopped climbing. "Ten minutes, hellflower, and I already know where your damn knife is! Move it!" Rimini could just learn to live with adversity.

"The hatch, *Kore;* it has been locked."

I took a deep breath and thought about being calm. It's funny how you get in the habit of wanting to live.

"We don't got time to go back and try another way, che-bai—do something!"

Never say "do something" to a blast-happy hellflower.

Tiggy pumped grenades at the hatch until he was satisfied. Then he shinnied up and pulled me through the slagged orifice. It had used to been an outbuilding; the roof was gone now and most of the walls too, courtesy of the Tiggy Stardust interior decorating service.

"Last time I saw Eloi he was kyting a land-yacht and we're going to need it. That way!" I pointed toward the main house and remembered too late that I shouldn't of known where the dashing Captain Flashheart was. Fortunately Tiggy hadn't noticed.

The info I got from Archive still held. Vannet's compound looked like ground zero of a meteor strike. Everything that wasn't burning glowed in the dark. Eloi was standing in the mercy seat of a fancy bus yowling for Tiggy. He looked battered but serene and there wasn't another living thing in sight.

"*Chaudatu,* the *Kore-alarthme* has killed the Library!" caroled Tiggy.

"Eloi, is proton grenade on real short timer sitting top of the Library in computer core!" I said, right on top of him. "Can we go now?"

Eloi grabbed me and hauled me into the yacht.

"I always knew you'd grow a soul some day, sweeting!" he said. "How long?"

"Five minutes. Ten—maybe." I didn't notice the land-yacht moving. "Look, che-bai, can we have this sparkling chat somewhere else?"

"Lalage and Alcatote are still inside." Lalage was Silver Dagger's front name, I remembered after a second.

"Well we're outside, and they're probably dead. It's a military proton grenade, Eloi—we can maybe get out of range if we go *now.*" I reached for the control stick.

Eloi knocked my hand away. "I'm not leaving them."

I looked at Tiggy. Eloi moved fast but not fast enough and Tiggy bashed him and dragged him into the back. I slid over into the mercy seat and grabbed the stick.

The roof of the hardsite went up in a radiant blaze. I was halfway through a sincere prayer to the Fifty Patriarchs of Granola before I realized it wasn't the grenade going off early. Alcatote'd been carrying a military-rated plasma cannon. He was using it to chop his way out of the house. Rimini was probably with him.

They'd never get clear in time.

"Kore-alarthme, do we abandon them?" Tiggy didn't sound happy.

"Hellwithit!" I said. "Let's go buy some of your godlost honor, 'flower!" I gunned the engine and headed for the house.

Tiggy blew out the front wall with his 50.80 and I coasted through the smoking remains. The inside of Vannet's pretty house looked like somebody'd already dropped a bomb there. I could see Alcatote and some things in armor that I couldn't tell what they was. I pointed the yacht at Alcatote and hoped Rimini was with him.

Tiggy was standing up in the side seat, shooting and singing. Dead rocks could of heard him coming. I swerved past Alcatote and there was a thump on the tail deck and I got a lap full of Silver Dagger. I didn't bother to point the yacht after that; just redlined it and hoped we wouldn't hit anything.

It was a good idea but too late. About halfway to the front gate the shock wave picked us up and punched us through. I heard metal tear and then the Roaq desert went whiter than white.

The last thing I remembered is a real clear picture of the symbols Archive showed me, a long time never. This time they almost made sense.

15

The Whirling Starcase

Woebegone was a big flashy thing. It crewed thirty-many and I could of parked *Firecat*-as-was on the bridge without disturbing anyone. There was a mercy seat, places for the songbird and number-cruncher, and two gunners. I didn't know how six people could decide where to have lunch, much less pilot a starship together, but that was their problem. Rimini sat in the worry seat.

I'd woke up in the back of the land-yacht with Tiggy pumping battledrugs into me and my head still ringing from the blast. Rimini was driving, and behind us was a smoking dayglo pit where there used to be a private stardock and lots of expensive downside real estate. I heard Rimini say something to Eloi about how she'd evacuated the area beforehand, but I hadn't known that when I set the bomb. I don't know whether what she said made it worse or better. When we got to the ship Eloi wanted to shuffle us off to somewheres, but I got pushy and with Tiggy along he didn't quite dare push back. Now Eloi sat in the mercy seat, ignoring us and talking to the port.

I looked at Tiggy, alive despite the odds. He looked pretty awful, and the biopak on his leg was leaking.

Eloi said something else to the Port.

"Kinchin-bai, why don't you go down to *Woebegone*'s fetch-kitchen let them medical you, forbye? Nothing's happening here." Which was true and too bad. RoaqPort Authority'd closed MhonePort early. Terrorists, they said. Big dustup at Rialla exurb; solid citizen Kroon'Vannet iced by suspected Tortugan political action committee in protest of the

Governor-General's policies. Archangel'd declared martial law for the entire Roaq.

"It is the honor of the Gentle People to suffer for justice," Tiggy said primly, which I guess meant no.

Eloi jumped up and stalked up and down in front of the mercy seat, bellowing into *Woebegone*'s remote pickups.

"Don't give me no 'suffer and honor' cop, Tiggy Stardust. Want you to go."

"Then go with me. And cease suffering for your honor as well." I looked at him. He grinned, tired.

"Later."

Paladin was gone, and it felt like somebody'd ripped out my lungs. I wanted to call him but he wouldn't answer. I didn't even know for sure if he'd gotten out of Rialla. Didn't give a damn about why he said he left. I knew the reason. A Library's just a person in a box and people ain't no damn good.

Eloi was now reminding Port what he paid in taxes, how he was hyper-legit and had more clearances and permits than Brightlaw Corporation had choplogics. None of this did him any good at all. Martial law. Closed Port.

We was back where we started.

"And if they don't find it in their hearts to give you clearance—*dear* Captain Flashheart?" Rimini didn't bother to look up from her copilot boards. I could see the "ready/not ready" status lights flickering from here. "I didn't agree to this insane jaunt to spend the rest of my life in an Imperial hellhouse."

"You must remember to inform the Governor-General of that when you see him—*dear* Silver Dagger," snarled Eloi right back. Tiggy looked at me and smirked. Alcatote caught him at it and woofed.

"We—" Tiggy stopped. "We will go to my father now, will we not? We have come here to fulfill your *devoir* and now we will rejoin my father. Did you not say this, *Kore-alarthme?*" There was a faint edge of doubt in his voice I didn't like.

"I said it. Eloi said it." I made it convincing. *"Woebegone* take us there. Iced Eloi's damn Library for him, now he's got to come across."

"And I'm grateful, sweeting," said Eloi, eavesdropping, "but—" He interrupted himself as RoaqPort came back on line.

"Silverdagger Legacy, you have special clearance exemption to lift."

"What the hell is a 'Silverdagger Legacy'?" demanded Rimini, but I knew.

Eloi vaulted into the mercy seat and gave the crew the office to lift.

Woebegone kicked back into the up-an-out. Twenty seconds up her bridge screens went to the lightless black of realspace. Rimini and the number-cruncher started singing back and forth about degrees to Transfer Point. Eloi leaned back and grabbed the angelstick, ready for the Drop.

"Kore, you are weeping," Tiggy said.

"Get shagged, hellflower." Paladin had made it out onto the net. We were the only two people who knew the callname he'd gave *Light Lady.*

Tiggy put his arm around my shoulders and said something in helltongue that I didn't have nobody to translate now.

"Am free, alive, and over the age of consent. I got no problems but you, Tiggy-bai."

Eloi pulled the stick, and suddenly we was everywhere and nowhere at once. *Woebegone* rode angels, safe in endless light, and what I wanted was as far wayaway as the stars I used to watch from my back porch at home.

DARKTRADERS

*To Dora Schisler,
Butterfly's role model
and to
Jean Stevenson,
for Library Science
above and beyond the
call of duty.*

Contents

1

In a Hellflower Garden
of Bright Images

I was minding my own business doing what was more or less any Gentry-legger's stock in trade—delivering a kick to a client. Only the kick was my buddy the live political hotrock Tiggy Stardust, hellflower prince, and the client not only didn't know he'd ordered the delivery, he might blow both of us wayaway when he got it.

"I do not like this, *Kore.*"

"Is this supposed to surprise me, bai?"

I hadn't told Tiggy that. Tiggy was sure his da would protect both of us—but then, how much did you know about life when you was fourteen?

"It is demeaning."

"If you'd left the damn knife in the ship, you wouldn't have this problem."

"It is not a 'knife.' It is my *arthame.*"

It was my idea he could get to be fifteen with a little help.

My name is Butterflies-are-free Peace Sincere and I'm a moron.

*　　*　　*

We'd hitched a ride here on a pirate ship hight *Woebegone* on account of a promise her captain Eloi Flashheart had made to Yours Truly in the not-too-distant past. But Eloi's charity stopped at the

spaceport gates, and now Tiggy and me was on our own. In beautiful
theory it wouldn't be for long. Kennor Starbringer was here to open the
new Civil Year from the Ramasarid Palace of Justice in Low Mikasa.
Kennor Starbringer was Tiggy's da, the man who wanted Tiggy back.

I hoped.

"Soon we will be with my father once more. His vengeance on the
Mikasaport Authorities will be terrible. How dare they use a servant of
the Gentle People thus? Is not my word sufficient bond?"

"I guess some people just got attitude problems, bai."

It's like this. A long time ago—when I still had a partner, a ship,
and a future—I went and did the dumbest thing in a life career of doing
dumb things and rescued a hellflower from some roaring boys in a Free
Port. Only the hellflower turned out to be the Honorable *Puer* Walks-
by-Night Kennor's-son Starbringer Amrath Valijon of Chernbereth-
Molkath, Third Person of House Starborn—that's Tiggy Stardust for
short—son of Kennor Starbringer the well-known and very truly sought
after Second Person of House Starborn and Prexy of the Azarine Coalition and the roaring boys had been set on to kill him.

And the only thing I knew about the killers for sure was that they
had to be somebody what'd been with Tiggy on the alMayne consular
ship *Pledge of Honor* when she was orbiting a little place called
Wanderweb. And that left room for a lot of rude surprises.

"It is not right."

"Bai, you going to tell me right's got something to do with the way
the universe is run?"

And if I didn't take Tiggy back to them anyway—House Starborn
in general, Daddy Starbringer in particular—Tiggy was going to die of a
bad case of hellflower honor.

"Perhaps not among the *chaudatu, Kore.* But my honor cries out
for vengeance!"

"Je, well, tell it to keep its voice down. If the proctors tap us, you
going to be honorable in the morgue."

You see, our boy Tiggy—which is to say Valijon Starbringer of
alMayne—is a hellflower, and hellflowers ain't like real people. What
you got to know about hellflowers, first bang out of the box, is that
they're crazy. What I found out about them, back when I had free time
and a partner I could trust, was that hellflowers—which is flashcant for
our galactic brothers the alMayne—is just this side of an Interdicted
Culture. They'd be deliriously happy to be dictys, too, except for the
little fact that their home world isn't anywheres near the Tahelangone
Sector and their home delight in life is to hunt and kill Old Fed Librar-

ies, of which nobody but Tiggy and me has seen zip for the last millenium. So they spend the part of their time that isn't spent hiring out as mercenaries making everyone else in the Empire real, real nervous on account of two things.

"Soon we will be with my father, *Kore.*"

They're the best at what they do, which is killing.

"And his vengeance will be terrible. Je. I heard you the last time."

And you can never figure out when they're going to do it, on account of hellflower honor.

"I would even have challenged them honorably for the right to pass, but the tongueless ones would not duel."

"Je. Magnanimous."

But in about a hour-fifty, tops, this was not going to be my problem. Kennor Starbringer was at the Ramasarid Palace of Justice, and me and Tiggy was going there.

"I do not like this, *Kore.*"

*   *   *

Low Mikasa Spaceport was the biggest thing I'd ever seen in my life, and it wasn't even the biggest thing in earshot. All you had to do was look up and there was High Mikasa hanging overhead, looking ripe and ready to fall with all kinds Imperial topgallants, Company bigriggers, and other stuff in all stages of built hanging around it. The Mikasarin Corporation holds the patents used for most of the shipbuilding done in the Empire and High Mikasa builds them. You use Mikasarin technology or you don't fly.

I looked around. Tiggy was right behind me. He had not been a happy hellflower since we came through Debarkation Control. Hellflowers does not go anywheres without their knife. Period.

I hadn't even bothered to try getting my blasters through—Low Mikasa being capital of the Mikasarin Directorate, it's rife with all the bennies of civilization like a weapons policy that boils down to "don't even try." But Tiggy-bai'd been sure they'd let his *arthame* through, and they had. Sort of. *"Cultural empowerer and object of spiritual focus"* they called x-centimeters of ferrous inert-blade. And then they glued it into its sheath.

I hadn't stopped hearing about it since.

"Soon we will be with my father, *Kore,*" Tiggy said for only the thirtieth or so time since breakfast. Usually he wasn't a chatterer, and all of a sudden I realized what was different now.

Soon he'd be with his father.

And he wasn't any more certain of what Kennor'd do than I was.

*   *   *

The Ramasarid Palace of Justice is this big ornate ceremonial thing in the Low Mikasa Civic Center that looks like a Imperial starshaker crashed into a fancy dessert. The walkway we was on dropped us the other side of the plaza where we could of got a good look at it except for all the people in the way. The last time I'd seen so many bodies in one place there'd been a riot going on.

Tiggy and me fit right in, so nobody gave us any more look than Tiggy's hellflowerishness accounted for. We worked our way up to the front. It was just a good thing wasn't neither of us carrying anything worth stealing; priggers must be having a field day here.

"*Kore,*" Tiggy said in my ear, "the *chaudatu* lied. He said it was not lawful for the people to carry weapons here, and he lied."

"T'hell he did, 'flower. S'matter, somebody try to clout your knife?"

"No, but that man is armed, and thus the port *chaudatu* lied."

I tried to look around and see where Tiggy was looking, but we was both jammed in tighter than furs on a Riis run. I couldn't see anything.

"Where?"

"Back there, and—"

About then they let the palace doors open and everybody started shoving.

*   *   *   *   *

Valijon's Diary

I am a servant of the Gentle People, whom the *chaudatu* call al-Mayne and hellflower.

I am the Honorable *Puer* Walks-by-Night Kennor's-son Starbringer Amrath Valijon of Chernbereth-Molkath, born within the walls of the Gentle People, Third of my House, whose tradition is service, even among the *chaudatu* without souls, and the *Kore* San'Cyr thinks that I am mad.

It is only meet that the *chaudatu* think the Gentle People mad, for thus they do not envy us and that is a kindness to them, but the *Kore* is not *chaudatu*. She has hunted the Machine as the *chaudatu* dare not. She has taken my honor into her own mouth and offered to die for me. She has shed her blood in my defense and made herself naked to my enemies.

Are these the acts of a *chaudatu?* No one among the Gentle People will say so.

And yet she says that I am mad. Perhaps—only perhaps—this is humor, a custom of the *chaudatu* that the Gentle People understand as little as the *chaudatu* understand honor.

But if she who was and is no longer *chaudatu* may understand honor, perhaps I who am her *servites* must understand humor.

I will consider this.

The *Kore* also thinks—she does not say this—that I am stupid, and I am no more stupid than mad. Fools do not live to become people upon my homeworld, and I have been a Person for six gathers of the Homeland seasons.

She thinks I do not know how it was that I was abandoned at the place she found me. She thinks, like the *chaudatu,* that the Gentle People know nothing of treachery—yet did we not learn it from her kind, and learn to despise it? Were we not betrayed again and again by *chaudatu* in the service of the Machine until to know *chaudatu* is not to trust?

The Gentle People understand betrayal. The less-than-human betray. The price of humanity is eternal vigilance. Many are born to seem human who are not.

And many who were once human cease to be.

I pray that I am still human, but I fear. My father foretold me that to go among the soulless hellspawn was a hazard to my *arthame*—and though all my father's words are truth, still I did not understand. Now I do. I have been among the *chaudatu* and seen abomination. The *chaudatu* leaders betray their people and open their hearts to the Machine. The *Kore-alarthme* has said this, and she does not lie.

The machine in all its hellshapes first was made by the *chaudatu* to serve the *chaudatu.* It has always betrayed them, as the unknown traitor in my father's house has betrayed me. The Gentle People have counted a hundred generations since the Machine was defeated, and we do not forget. If my *arthame* has been occulted, I will be purified and made whole, and my name added to the songs the Starborn sing at the burning *ghats.* But before that time, I will bring my father word of treachery.

I was meant to die, and the only possible betrayers are our own.

　　　　*　　　*　　　*　　　*　　　*

We took the first bolt that came along. Everybody else was heading into the Audience Chamber where the free floorshow was going to be and didn't miss us. We was still in a part of the Palace where it was legit to be, but soon or late the *legitimates* would trip over us and wonder what we was doing here instead of there. I hoped we found Kennor-bai first.

From what I knew and what Tiggy'd told me, he'd be traveling with a hellflower garden slightly larger than the crew of the *Woebegone,* all nice-minded as hell and armed to the earlobes. And Kennor was here, so they'd all be here, too.

So where was one now, when it would do some good?

Finally we saw a 'flower dressed up real legit in House Starborn blue leather and Tiggy sang out in helltongue. The Junior Brother of Mercy was dressed with the complete disregard for local customs and weather characteristic of hellflowers abroad. The local Peacekeepers must be having peristaltic strophes over him, too; he was wearing a pair of heavyweight blasters in a crossover rig with a rifle slung over his back. And his hellflower knife, of course. *Not* glued down.

Him and Tiggy choodled back and forth for whiles. The word *"chaudatu"* figured very fine and free in the conversation, and by now I'd picked up enough helltongue to be able to figure out that Junior Brother's name was Blackhammer and he wasn't buying Tiggy's story about being Valijon Starbringer the missing son-and-only. The *"chaudatu"* in the case was Yours Truly: *chaudatu* means, sort of, "nonperson who not only doesn't have a Knife, they are never going to be honorable enough to even stand next to somebody who's got a Knife and ought to just off themselves now." If a hellflower likes you, he calls you *alarthme,* which also means Got-No-Knife. Go figure.

"Look here," I interrupted, "maybe you don't know by eyeball Missing Heir Baijon, but his da does. Why don't you just take us to Kennor-bai and let him arrest us?"

Blackhammer didn't want to admit he savvied Interphon, but Tiggy added something nasty about walls and shadows in helltongue so Blackhammer fingered his Knife and finally agreed.

We went wayaways to a place with "personal and private place for very important sophont" stamped all over it in Intersign glyphs. Blackhammer slid open the door. There was about a dozen hellflowers around the place, and I'd rather of walked into a cycling hyperdrive.

Seen as a group, hellflowers was stunning—tall, light-haired, dark-skinned, trademark hellflower-blue eyes. Inbreeding that'd make any dicty-colony turn green with envy, and gorgeous.

Not to mention insecure. There was enough hardware here to fill a pretty good Imperial armory and more cold iron than in the entire Starfleet—this in spite of its being illegal for civilians to carry heat anywhere in the Directorate. If I'd cared especial about getting out of here alive it would of worried me.

Blackhammer and Tiggy and me went through another door into a room with a desk, but wasn't no Kennor Starbringer there neither, much as I'd hoped.

The woman behind the desk was hellflower, older than Tiggy, and wearing enough flashcandy to make her a top-seeded member of the garden club. Her hair was chopped short and she wore a eyepatch and her face was stippled with white scars she hadn't bothered to fix. Burns, looked like. She took one good look at the two of us and sent Blackhammer out quick, and I realized Tiggy and me was dead meat. She turned on Tiggy.

They fell into each other's arms.

The yap got pretty thick but the general idea wasn't too hard to follow: Golly, we thought you was dead, where you been? Well you see it's like this, I met this *chaudatu.* . . .

Eventually they stopped playing old home week and she turned to me. Up close and personal like this I could see her scars was real recent, and it nagged at me like a old enemy. There was something about burns at the edge of my mind. . . .

"House Starborn owes you its thanks for preserving the life of the Honored One Valijon and returning him to us. Ask what you will in *weregild* and it will be granted to you. Come, Honored Valijon, your father will rejoice to see that you have been restored to him."

Or in the lingua franca of deep space, thanks awfully and get lost.

Tiggy backed up against me. *"Kore* Winterfire, I am sworn to obedience to the *Kore* San'Cyr until my father himself accepts me back." He sounded average-to-pretty-well distressed about it, but stubborn.

"Surely the woman excuses you from this pledge." Winterfire looked poisoned gimlets at me, but it wasn't my look-out if she couldn't keep her hands on the son-and-heir in first place.

"Ea dzain'domere!" Tiggy pointed out in helltongue. He'd promised.

"A promise is a promise, Honored Valijon, but it is ill-done to promise in words of power to those not of the Gentle People. If the

Honored Kennor must give the *chaudatu* an audience it cannot be now. He is already robing for Court and cannot see it until after the ceremony. The *chaudatu* may wait if it wishes."

Winterfire gave me a monocular glare indicating I better have business elsewhere. Too bad I never learned to take hints like that.

"Oh, we wait all right," I said. "Got nothing better to do."

"Then perhaps you will wish to view the opening ceremony." Winterfire was all smiles now and it should of worried me. "I will tell the Honored One that you are here, and have *Puer* Blackhammer find places for you. After it is over he will conduct you to your father, Honored Valijon."

I could see Tiggy wasn't too thrilled with that idea, but I liked the thought of watching the show a lot better than I liked sitting around backstage with a bunch of hellflowers all post-meridies.

"Yeah, yeah, reet—c'mon, 'flower, lets go watch your da make nice with the Imperials, j'keyn?"

"*Ea,*" said Tiggy, sounding tired.

Brother Blackhammer slid Tiggy and me into the Audience Chamber of the Palace of Justice through the side door marked *"Important People Only."* Blackhammer locked it up tight behind us and we took seats in the very important sophont section up front.

I couldn't shake the feeling I'd seen Winterfire somewheres before, but the only hellflowers bar Tiggy I'd seen lately had been on a planet called Kiffit and trying to kill me.

It was just too damn bad I didn't remember then what I knew about the hellflower smile.

2

When Hell Was in Session

The Audience Chamber was pretty thoroughly jammed with a cosmopolitan mixture of races and sexes and there was something just the least bit bent about it all. I put it down to me not being used to the way things looked in the Directorates. I'd done lots of strange places and been lots of strange things in my misspent etcetera, but the frontier of even a decadent culture looked different from darkest civilization. I wished Paladin was here to tell me that. I wished Paladin was here to tell me anything.

But my good buddy and partner Paladin wasn't going to be around anymore. That was the price of a lot of things—like the death of an Old Federation Library named Archive.

And I could worry about it on my own time—after I was shut of Tiggy Stardust.

"Was good thing you know that Winterfire jilt," I said to him. "Now you be hellflower back in good standing Real Soon Now."

Tiggy didn't look like he thought so. Tiggy looked like he thought he'd left his honor somewheres and wasn't sure where.

"*Kore* Winterfire is the chief of my bodyguard, and before that, when I was not yet a person, it was *Kore* Winterfire who raised me to adulthood."

Terrific.

"Yeah, well, don't worry about it. Everybody makes mistakes." I just hoped we wasn't everybody. We couldn't afford to be.

Because once upon a time the Nobly-Born Governor General His

Imperial Highness the TwiceBorn Prince Mallorum Archangel, that busy child with the interest in Library Science, decided he wanted to put the Azarine Coalition in his pocket and walk off in the direction of becoming Emperor his own self.

For any number of rude reasons, the only way to do that was to rewrite the Gordinar Canticles that govern the Coalition and abrogate the hell out of Azarine Coalition Neutrality.

He couldn't do that while Kennor was president of that same Coalition, Kennor Starbringer being a Constructionist who took Coalition Neutrality to bed with him at night, but Kennor's next-in-line for al-Mayne's seat on the Coalition was the bright hope of LessHouse Dragonflame, Uncle Morido, and Morido Dragonflame was real pliable. It was obvious that time had come for Kennor Starbringer to retire.

But Archangel was smart—or maybe somebody was smart for him. Offing Kennor direct would just stir up bad trouble back on alMayne. So nobody was going to do that—they was just going to arrange for Kennor to become a Official alMayne Nonperson and Imperial criminal.

That was why all the disproportionate interest in Our Boy Tiggy stopping breathing that had occupied my lately life. Once he did, Kennor'd either have to avenge his death (illegal in the Empire) or not avenge it (illegal on alMayne). Either way his actions was actionable. Neat. Archangel was picking out his best fly-vines for attending Kennor's funeral when one little thing interfered.

Kennor didn't avenge his kinchin-bai. Kennor didn't un-avenge him. Because Tiggy wasn't dead or murdered or any other little thing, and as long as Tiggy wasn't guaranteed dead, he wasn't Kennor's honor-problem, and that could of stonewalled His Mallorumship for years. Tiggy'd just disappeared, courtesy of Yours Truly.

And now he was back. And fresh from being seen by Archangel right in the middle of Archangel's Library project. One whiff of "Library" and even Dragonflame would bolt, because if there was one thing hellflowers hated worse than death and hell and *chaudatu* it was what they called the Machine and the rest of the universe called Libraries.

I just hoped Kennor's hellflower traitor felt the same way, because that put paid to Archangel's dreams of putting the Coalition in his pocket. The bottom line was: Archangel'd made the latest of many grabs for the Coalition—and missed. Now him and Kennor and every-body was back to Square One.

And that meant it was time for Archangel to try again.

*   *   *

About the time I was getting bored sitting here taking symbolic part in the glorious pageant of Imperial rule there was a real loud blatt of trumpets and a Imperial lackey in Space Angel black came out on the balcony where Kennor'd be standing Real Soon Now and read off a long prolegomenon.

Waitaminnit.

Sure as I knew trade-routes, His Nobly-Bornness the TwiceBorn Lord Prince and Governor-General Mallorum Archangel (second in line for the Phoenix Throne, collect 'em all) 's writ only ran in the Outlands, which the Directorates wasn't. He was the courtier of last resort for the Sector Governors, but they only had nominal power in Directorate Space. Directors and Shareholders ran the action here. Mikasarin Corporation should be overseeing the opening of the Mikasa Civil Year, or a TwiceBorn from Throne. Not one of the Governor-General's hired guns.

Besides which, Archangel was last seen declaring martial law in Roaq Sector and pretending he didn't own part-shares in the Old Federation Library of terminal illegality that I'd relieved him of. He would have to of moved hell-and-High-Jump to get loose of that and beat the *Woebegone* here.

But even if there was trouble right here in downtown glittertown, free citizens of Imperial Mikasa was as likely to make it at a Imperial bean-feast as they was to ask for high taxes, and the place was crawling with *legitimates* besides.

So why did I wish so damn much I had my blasters—or even a vibro?

"*Kore,* I do not like this." I bet they didn't have riots on alMayne, because that was what this was going to be in about twenty seconds and Tiggy didn't look half worried enough.

Which was oke as I was worrying plenty-enough for both of us.

The Governor-General's Space Angel finished his screed and left the stage. The crowd started making mob-noises real quiet-like. I forgot about any spare problems I might of had.

"Tiggy-bai, think we maybe wait outside and see your da later whiles, if all same to you."

He started to get up. Just then there was a booming noise behind us. The Court bailiffs had slammed home the big ornate bars across the doors closing off the Audience Chamber.

We was locked in.

"Trouble," I said to Tiggy, and started moving him toward where we could get a wall at our backs.

The inner curtains on the balcony swept back and Kennor Star-bringer stepped out. He looked like Tiggy, but he looked even more like he'd had to put up with lots of things in life he didn't like. He was overdressed like every hellflower ever born and had his Court of the TwiceBorn robes on over that, open down the front to show off the hellflower glitterflash. All of a sudden I knew I'd been played for a greenie and by who and it was all my own fault, too.

The free citizens of Imperial Mikasa let out a yowl like a scalded theriomorph and came forward over their seats shouting death to extra-planetary mercenaries and Azarine Coalition headmen.

Somebody let off a blaster.

"*Kore*—what is this? What is happening?" Tiggy had his back to the wall and looked wild-eyed.

"Shut up and run!"

Only there wasn't any place to run to. The citizenry was a mob now but the mob wasn't interested in us. Yet. Soon enough they'd stop trying to get at one hellflower and settle for any hellflower. I looked up at Kennor. There was six 'flowers up there on that balcony all armed to the teeth and all looking to him to order open fire.

Somebody was counting on Kennor shooting back. And he wouldn't, because dusting citizens of Low Mikasa'd get him gigged under the Pax Imperador as sure as avenging his murdered son would. And Kennor Starbringer was going to hold on to the presidency of the Azarine Coalition at all cost.

"*Move!*"

I shoved Tiggy hard and pointed. If the ornamental screen fronting the balcony'd hold our weight, we could get up off the killing floor.

"I'll cover you!" Tiggy said.

"Dammit—"

"*Kore!* I am armed!"

I looked. He'd tore the glued-on sheath of his *arthame* off in shreds and the inert-blade glittered sharplike and next to no good at all against crazies with real heat.

But it was still more than I had. I started up the carved pillar that led to the balcony and hoped Kennor wouldn't kill me when I got there.

The world narrowed to where I put my hands and feet, without point nor end. Boot on garland. Stop and pull off gloves for better grip. See mob surge back and forth below like a liquid in null-grav, making up its mind. Balcony shakes; brawling underneath and somebody taking my lead and starting up the pillar on the other side.

Somebody'd got tired of waiting for Baijon Starbringer to become an Official Dead Person. Somebody'd decided to come up with another reason for his da to retire. Somebody'd bought a riot.

I reached the edge of the balcony and hooked one arm through the railing. Smelled burnt rock where a blast-charge'd spattered against the wall and started dust filtering down. Innocent citizens and bought roaring boys was muddled all together on the Audience Chamber floor, and all in about the time it would of took for Kennor to get through the first sentence of his speech.

"C'mon, you godlost glitterborn!" I braced myself and reached down. Tiggy sprang up and grabbed my wrist. Damn near pulled me in two before he caught hold of the same ornamental stringcourse I was wrapped around and scrabbled over me and up onto the balcony.

The mob hit the space where he'd been and started feeding on itself. All that took about as long as the second sentence of Kennor's speech would of.

Kennor's 'flowers closed up around him when Tiggy vaulted over the rail. I could see from where I was that Tiggy was shouting something but all sound was wiped out by mob-roar. The balcony shook again and gave that definitive lurch of structural weakness. Tiggy grabbed my elbow and dragged me up, yelling at the others in helltongue.

The first wave of the climbers reached the edge of the balcony and started scrambling through the rail. The floor lurched and the tiles underfoot started to buckle. Kennor ordered his people back into the alcove toward where the back stairs was. He pointed along the buckling seam of flooring. A couple of the bright hellflower lads got an idea and fired. The balcony tore lose.

There was a crash, silence, and then some dispirited screaming. Kennor said something I still couldn't hear and looked amused.

Hellflowers smile when they're about to kill something. That's what I should of remembered.

By now a couple of the bodyguard had cut open the access door to the back stairs, which seemed to of been accidentally sealed from the outside.

"To the Embassy!" Kennor shouted in a voice that carried. He hadn't turned one hair at Tiggy's return from the dead. The hellflower bodyguard formed up again with Kennor, Tiggy, and me in the middle. I was elbow-high to the lot of them and I couldn't see a damn thing, but that didn't matter much because then we started down the back stairs and it was pitch-dark.

About now we heard sirens outside and all power to the building was cut. Standard riot-control protocol: no lights, blast doors over windows rolled shut, computer access shut down.

The last one through the balcony access door wedged it shut again and the mob-noises and the sirens cut off like you'd sliced it. The only noise I heard at first was my boots on the treads, and I got the idea of stopping about the same time everyone else did. There was noise ahead of us.

More mob, I thought first, but no. This area was closed to citizenrabble, and any of the kiddies barred into the Audience Chamber would of come from behind.

Professionals, then. The last backstop. The hellflowers I was in the middle of flowed around me like air and made slightly less noise.

In the pitch-black indoor dark of the back stairs of the Ramasarid Palace of Justice, Kennor Starbringer's hellflower bodyguard hit an unknown number of armed and dangerous professional, experienced, and fully briefed sellswords with orders to kill.

The sellswords didn't stand a chance.

I heard Kennor order no survivors, and I knew it was because if there was no survivors, Kennor could make up any fantasy he pleased and go on farcing the Court of the TwiceBorn about him being on the right side of hellflower honor.

And no survivors was eventually going to mean me.

Funny; until I met Tiggy I always thought nighttimers had the monopoly on bending the Pax Imperador. But what I'd seen lately made us the junior league. Archangel dancing with High Book, some hellflower glitterborn buying half Mikasa's *legitimates* to ice the president of the Azarine Coalition, president of the same doing mass wetwork to hold onto his job.

If there'd been anything but sudden death on the other side of the Audience Chamber door I would of gone that way and not stopped running until I reached Port and *Woebegone*. But there wasn't. So I stayed where I was, and five minutes later none of the mercs was left alive.

When the shouting was over someone lit a torch and Kennor's hellflower hardboys started searching what was left of the bodies. I'd seen worse, but not lately. I stayed where I was.

Blackhammer was one of the deaders. Kennor looked at him, then looked at Tiggy and me. I could see the wheels turning behind those hellflower-blue eyes and wished I knew what he was thinking. The hellflowers finished their work and we went on.

Got to the bottom of the access stair and out into a Palace of Justice restricted area. The hallway was deserted and everything was quiet as guilt.

In a sane universe Kennor would of gone back to the rest of his hellflowers, or made a public fuss to the *legitimates,* or at least complained out loud. But Kennor was hellflower, and hellflowers is crazy. Kennor just smole a small smile at the big empty and him, six hellflowers, Tiggy, and me faded into a corridor meant for tronics at the back of the Palace of Justice.

The illegal transponder I got put in my jaw for reasons too complicated to go into here buzzed a little as it took transmission on a near-miss frequency, but even if I couldn't hear anything it gave me the good word. Imperial Space Marines or something else real heavyweight was down and around and chatting itself up. A Remote Transponder Sensor is what only them is supposed to use.

But if Space Marines or something like them was here in a Sector-Capital-and-Directorate-Homeworld, they couldn't of arrived after Tiggy and me'd left *Woebegone*—no time—and Eloi would of told us if they'd got there before.

Unless they'd been shipped in secretly, because somebody knew a riot was going to be on offer. Somebody name of Mallorum Archangel, who was sponsoring Kennor's little jaunt to Mikasa and oh by the way his assassination, too. Because he'd got tired of waiting for Baijon Starbringer to turn up livealive or dead.

Or because now that Tiggy'd seen his Library, Archangel couldn't afford to have him and Kennor meet again in this life.

Terrific.

Kennor seemed to know where he was going, and that was outside into an alleyway at the back of the Palace. The alley had a pretty good view of the police cordon that'd been thrown around the block. Air scrubbers was hovering in place over the fire, and if I'd been brain-dead everything would of looked normal.

I'd heard of treason. They was fighting it all the time in the stories in Thrilling Wonder Talkingbooks. I never thought I'd actually see some, and I wasn't sure if I had now. Only Kennor was the for-sure real live law, and it was my kind of people what hid from the *legitimates,* not his.

I'd used to think.

The bodyguard was stripping off their weapons and piling them in a corner of the alley. Kennor started shucking his TwiceBorn robes and most of his hellflower glitterflash and then pulled his hair out of the roached topknot alMayne high-heat wore.

Leaving now would be the smartest thing I ever did. It wouldn't even matter that I got gigged for illegal emigration, unlawful appropriation of contract warmgoods, possession of illegal technology, and six other fatal warrants the minute I hit the street—there was a *chance* I wouldn't, which was better than I had here. I knew it.

But I didn't move quite fast enough. I stood there like a jerk holding the blaster I'd picked up back on the stairs until Kennor looked at me and reached for it.

"The carrying of personal armament on Directorate worlds except by authorized personnel is forbidden under the provisions of Chapter II of the Revised Inappropriate Technology Act of the Nine-hundredth and seventy-fifth Year of Imperial Grace. As a duly-commissioned representative of the Phoenix Throne, I must ask you to surrender your weapon."

I looked at him. He smirked—or whatever hellflowers do with their mouth that couldn't be that because they is just too damn noble. I handed him the blaster and he tossed it into a discard pile that looked like somebody'd boosted a Imperial armory. Even if hellflowers had the diplomatic permit to carry all that fire-iron, I bet they didn't have a permit to leave it around lying loose.

Kennor turned back to his bodyguard. By now they was stripped down to just knives and one of them was passing around a tube of goo so they could fake the Mikasan peace-seal on those. Kennor's people was real pros at farcing *legitimates,* and I would of been real interested in that if I ever planned on being interested in anything again.

When they was all done making themselves up to look like citizen hellflowers and nobody related to the riot of the week at the Palace of Justice, Kennor gave them their orders in handsign. I could follow that easier than I could helltongue: *Scatter. Regroup at prearranged point. Say nothing.*

Then six hellflowers, looking like anyone's nursery of innocent unarmed unofficial children, faded off smartly and vanished into the crowd that was starting to collect around the riot-police, and Kennor, Tiggy, and me was the only ones in the alley.

"Look here, your Honorship—" I began.

"Now," said Kennor, laying hold of my wrist in your basic inarguable fashion, "we three will go together and quickly—before the Imperial *chaudatu* find us here and we all suffer unfortunate accidents while in protective custody."

I didn't bother to remind him I had a guaranteed accident coming no matter what. Kennor took off with me attached, and Tiggy followed.

*   *   *

My partner Paladin always used to say I never thought enough, and that wasn't fair. I'd always thought as much as I had to, only I'd never before needed to think as much as I did now. I had plenty of time for it, though, slinking acrost Low Mikasa with Kennor and Tiggy and the three of us trying not to be seen—or if we was, to look like ship-crew wayaways from Port.

Fact: One hundred days ago, Gentry-legger me rescued what I thought was a solid citizen what had wandered into the wrong street of my friendly neighborhood Free Port.

Fact: The citizen was actually Tiggy Stardust, *aka* Valijon Starbringer of House Starborn, in the throes of his first murder attempt. Somebody'd let him shag off from his consular ship without ID in the pious hope that either the law or the natives of Wanderweb Free Port would sign the lease on his real estate in short order. Probably the same person who arranged front-row seats at the riot, come to think of it, and I knew which *Puer* Blackhammer I was betting on.

Fact: In my neverending quest to get Tiggy-bai back to the arms of his tender loving da, we took a real roundabout detour, and tripped over the fact that Mallorum Archangel, Imperial Prince, Governor-General, and second in line for the Throne if the Emperor ever took the Long Orbit, was hand in claw with an Outlands nightbroker in a scheme to 1) use infinitely-illegal Old Federation Technology to take over the universe and 2) ice Tiggy Stardust as part of a squeeze-play to gain direct control of the Azarine Coalition to use it as his own private army.

Fact: There still wasn't any other place in the universe for me to take him, so I'd brought Tiggy back to Kennor Starbringer's unhealthy vicinity anyway and run into hellflower trouble—and the answer to a question that'd been bothering me for whiles.

Who'd sent Tiggy out to play in traffic on Wanderweb and made several attempts on him since?

Easy. Who was better placed to do it than a member of his personal bodyguard?

*　　*　　*

"Now shall I be happy to accept the TwiceBorn's sorrow for what has happened at the Palace of Justice today," Kennor said. I looked around.

We was in the very best bolt-hole of the alMayne Embassy, following a nervewracking several hours sneaking acrost town on foot. The suite was done in what was probably alMayne high style. Hellflower chic was heavy behind ornate fancywork in edged metal and one whole wall used for nothing but displaying handweapons. My idea of chic was fine vintage neurotoxins, and I had hopes of being very chic Real Soon Now.

"Yeah, your Honor, I can explain some of that," I said, and stopped. It was a little late in my career to be making up to the *legitimates,* even if they was bent hellflower *legitimates.*

Tiggy burst out in a breathless sing-song that I followed not very and flung himself facedown at his da's feet.

"And who knows who in the end may be discovered to be responsible for woefully disturbing the civil peace?" Kennor went on all mournful and just like Tiggy wasn't there.

"Now look—" I said, which wasn't politic maybe but I didn't get the chance to compound my errors.

"Ea comites, hjais koriel!"

Because just then Winterfire came out of the inner room and headed straight for Kennor.

And everything clicked into place.

Kennor was standing there flat-footed, not even going for his knife. I'd known it was a member of his personal guard as set up Tiggy and the riot. But I'd picked the wrong one.

Nobody was looking at me. I crossed the room with a bound and ripped open one of the wall displays.

Everything seemed to take a thousand years. The first thing my hand closed on was a little Estel-Shadowmaker rechargeable—one shot and it takes forever to recycle but I wasn't going to get two chances anyway. I pulled it up and turned and fired all in one move, and I could still see Kennor standing there like he wasn't armed.

Fired. Missed. Oh, not quite; she staggered a little and her tunic caught fire and I smelled burning hair and burning flesh and suddenly I was back in a bazaar in a place called Kiffit where I'd killed two hellflowers who'd been trying to kill me because I'd saved Tiggy's life.

And one of them was her. That was what'd lost her the eye and covered her face with those pretty burn marks she must of had some hellflower reason for not removing.

Winterfire didn't even try to put out the fire. I saw her bring her hand up slow and Kennor, damn him, didn't move. Kennor Starbringer would be dead and the Azarine Coalition would belong to Mallorum Archangel and Archangel would use it to make a war like the one that pulled the Old Federation down. A war like Archive's.

So I got in the way. My timing was good. I moved and Tiggy moved and I heard him scream and thought for one crazy second he'd caught a plasma-packet and then I realized she hadn't fired yet. Then I saw the muzzleflash from Winterfire's gun and then I didn't see anything at all.

* * * * *

Valijon's Diary

I think Father must have known from the moment he saw Blackhammer's body who the traitor within our walls was. He told me later that She Who Will Not Be Named had asked especially that Blackhammer be sent from the Homeland to aid her—the child of her body, loyal to his line and his LessHouse first of all things.

So I learned later. Then I saw only the gun.

It was a *chaudatu* ploy, to forge honor into a knife against the Gentle People. She Who Will Not Be Named called *comites* with my father—he could not strike her down until she gave him cause; the first blow must, in honor, be hers. And if he must bide so, then it was twiceover my place to void a quarrel in which I had no place. Her life was not mine until she struck, and the Law was clear: I might not assume that she would.

So I, too, was helpless, though it was I whom She Who Will Not Be Named had first betrayed. She had promised me safety, and was false— and sacrosanct, until the moment she chose to strike at the *Kore-alarthme,* whose honor was mine to keep.

Then her life came into my hands. And then I did what honor demanded, to tell those of House and clan and line that She Who Will Not Be Named had forfeited what it is to be human.

* * * * *

I was someplace that I knew wasn't real, not like organics know about real. For a minute I didn't know who I was, then it came back like putting together the pieces of a cargo.

Butterflies-are-free Peace Sincere. Ex-Luddite Saint, ex-slave, escapee from the Interdicted World Granola, darktrader, Librarian, human. The place I was in was out of my own private dreambox—a imagination of what a computer core would look like if a memory-bubble had eyes. I'd been here before. A hallucination, caused by a piece of Old Fed Tech that nobody should ever have woke up again.

Archive. Fully-volitional logic. Library. Killer.

*   *   *

About a thousand years ago—back when your Phoenix Empire and mine was still a Federation about four times its present size—some bright kiddy came up with the notion of putting pure intellect in a box and calling it a Library. And since the *Federales* thought they had more important things to do with their time, they turned over the running of their Federation to the Libraries and made it so Libraries could build more Libraries.

Mistake. Because—so the story goes—the Libraries had more important things to do with their time, too, and thought that organic life clashed with their decor. There was a war. And ten centuries later the Empire is still hunting the nonexistent surviving Libraries from that war.

Mostly nonexistent.

I'd never been anything special, but I'd done one special thing. In the midst of a misspent career of moving *chazarai* from here to there for people who might not be its original owners, I'd gone and rescued and rebuilt an illegal Old Fed Library. I hadn't known what I was doing. I'd never heard of Libraries then. It was a damn good thing I lucked into maybe the only pacifist Library there ever was. Paladin was my friend, my partner, the edge I needed to stay alive in the never-never.

Until I went and rescued Tiggy Stardust.

And Paladin left me.

"Go, and live a human life among your own kind." I heard his voice—I could touch him here, I could see him, but all he wanted was for me to walk away and then everything vanished like smoke and stardust and I was alone.

And he'd made a mistake. It was important, more than his feelings or mine, and I had to tell him about it, but I had to wake up first, and—

"Kore! Kore-alarthme! Don't die—*Father*—"

And my dreamworld shattered into dancing points of light.

I opened my eyes. Tiggy was hanging over me like High Mikasa Shipyards, spattered in blood. I couldn't think why, but I was glad he wasn't hurt. Blasters cook, not puncture.

"You *will* live," he said, like someone was giving him argument.

I tried to move. I felt too light and too heavy. Unbalanced, like somebody half in armor. Something was missing.

"Get out of the way."

I recognized Kennor. The ends of his fancy silver hair was wicked in blood. Why is it there's so much blood when hellflowers is around?

"You are injured," said Daddy Starbringer like he was reading out the late-breaking news. "What is it you wish to say before you die?"

So that was why I felt so good.

"Winterfire set you up. Archangel had a Library. And I brought your son back, you son-of-a-"

Then the floor tipped sideways and I fell off.

*   *   *

I was back in the dream computer core again, having a long conversation with Paladin about what happened when me and him and Tiggy went up against Archangel's Library.

"You know I had to set that blast, bai. Couldn't trust what might of happened with Archive Library if I didn't."

"And what did you think that would be, Butterfly?"

"You know, Pally-che-bai." But he didn't. Paladin didn't know things he ought to know, and then I realized it wasn't Paladin at all.

I opened my eyes. It looked like a cluster galaxy seen from real-space.

Things flipped into focus.

"Go on," said Kennor Starbringer.

"Go to hell," I said. We was face-to-face; I must be standing and on a box at that, but I tried to twitch a finger and I couldn't feel a thing. Nothing.

I tried not to let it bother me any more than scaring me half to death.

"You will delight to know that we rejoice in *Malmakosim* Archangel's tender *chaudatu* concern, and in his assurances that reprisals for the regrettable and unexpected civil disturbance will be as swift as they are severe. He shares with me also my dismay at the death of She Who Will Not Be Named."

I'd thought I'd been talking to Paladin and instead I'd been giving

Kennor all the answers he thought to ask. It bothered me from some-place far away enough so I knew I was drugged, and I guessed I hadn't said anything too incriminating or we wouldn't be having this conversation now.

And if Winterfire was Archangel's chief catspaw in House Starborn, she couldn't be the only one. I wondered, in a far-off way, what Archangel'd paid her.

"I guess you be both just as torqued at that as each other is," I said, since Kennor was looking at me.

"My doctors assure me that you'll recover."

"Where's Tiggy?"

The question seemed to surprise him. He frowned.

"Your son. I brought him back, remember?"

"Yes."

We looked at each other whiles until it occurred to me that it was my turn to say something.

"You wanted him back, right?"

Kennor showed his teeth in that alMayne expression that is not a smile.

"No. I wanted him alive."

I wanted to answer that but couldn't. I saw the path back into the computer and took it, down deep inside where even Kennor couldn't find me to question. And Paladin was there.

*   *   *

Time passed. I got used to it. I saw Kennor a couple more times and Tiggy not at all. On one of Kennor's visits I got some of the pieces filled in. My buddy Winterfire, *aka* She Who Will Not Be Breathing No More, had died a traitor to the hellflower cause and had her head shipped home to hang on Kennor's gates. Quaint local custom.

I wondered what Kennor had in mind for me. I didn't know what I'd blathered to Kennor whilst he was rummaging in my brain, and if Kennor's people was any good their fetch-kitchen'd told them what I was. Interdicted barbarian—shoot when found. They must be saving me up to put on a show.

I didn't really care.

Finally Kennor's pet bonecracks let me out of the giant economy size finestkind biopak I'd been welded into for longer than I wanted to think about and put me in a luxury accommodation prison instead. And I finally found out just how far Winterfire'd got toward trying to kill me.

Cybereisis prostheses. You don't catch a plasma-packet off a hot blaster and keep your original inventory. Winterfire'd took off half my left arm and Kennor's hellflower cyberdocs had done for the rest. Glass and plastic and brainjinks laying up along my spine and a left arm that nobody but me could tell from the original.

I cared about that. It gave me the creeps. But I was healthy enough to kill now, if they was going to. I wished they'd left me asleep.

But wishes aren't cargo, and darktrade was not exactly a career where you made old bones in the first place, and there wasn't no place for me anywhere except in the never-never—a second-rate darktrader to a third-rate nightworld broker. Fast ship and faster blasters, untrustworthy luck and a knack for other people's trouble. I'd lost all of them now except the last.

*   *   *

I was looking out a set of armored one-way holosim windows at nighttime Low Mikasa Prime. Prime was a great big prettycity full of people born here, with a right to be here. None of them'd know what a candle was, or a horse-drawn plow.

Or a blaster, maybe.

Wet beaded on the pick-ups referring the image I saw. Kennor'd told me there'd be rain tonight, like it was a big treat. Even told me when it'd start.

I looked down at my hands and wiggled my fingers. Big treat. Only now one set of them was real and one wasn't.

The door made that sound they do here when they open and Tiggy —which is to say, Prince Valijon Starbringer of House Starborn all fine and nice and real friendly—and Kennor-his-da came in.

I could see them reflected in the holosim but I turned around to where they was anyway. Tiggy looked fine. He looked happy. He was back in finestkind hellflower dressup like I'd first seen him, weaponry (legal inside the Consulate) and bright-polished *arthame*.

I ground my teeth and imagined I could feel the damn expensive useless hardware of my RTS down in the bone. But Kennor'd made a point of telling me they'd took it out. Damn him.

"Kore!" said Tiggy. He looked young and excited and no part of me. He never had been, really.

"I bid you welcome to my walls, woman not of the Gentle People. Peace to you in my son's name while you abide here, and joy to you for seeking the walls of Starborn. Your shadow will be cherished while you remain, and if you must in honor depart to the Land Beside, know that you will not die unknown and unmourned," Kennor perorated for the official record.

It took me a minute to unknot that and another one to decide that the sentiments expressed was not maybe as comforting to us *chaudatu* as it might be to hellflowers. The cognoscenti would note that it contained not one word about getting out of here alive.

"It is a great pity that there is no *chaudatu* proof that Archangel consorted with the Machine," Kennor went on like I'd done the pretty right back. "On alMayne, the word of an Honored One would be enough. Here, words mean very little." He sat down in a chair. Tiggy stood. I leaned.

"Next time I'll save you the pieces," I said. "Look, bai, brought you kinchin-bai, got shut of all comme-tays farcing and I'm golden. If you was going to ice me Ti—Baijon wouldn't be here, so I guess you're letting me go. So tell me the whistle you going to drop and we call it a night, oke?" And I'd be dead by the time I found which way the spaceport was, but never mind that.

"Not quite," said Kennor. "Amrath Valijon of Chernbereth-Molkath, what do you have to say in your defense?"

"My fault was grievous," said Tiggy like he'd been rehearsed. "I owe my life four times to the *alarthme* woman, called *Kore-alarthme* San'Cyr, and I have not redeemed it."

Kennor smirked at me.

"Shut up!" I said real loud. "Don't you shove me none of your hellflower honor, bai, or—"

"And what is the price of a son of the Gentle People?" Kennor said encouragingly to the son of the Gentle People just like I wasn't there.

Maybe I could get out of here unnoticed whilst they was bandying the book of the Law back and forth.

"*Weregild* to the worth of his family; service to the length of his years; or another price set," said Tiggy happily.

No hope; he was between me and the door.

"And *Kore,* I am no longer constrained to stay shut of the damfool honor nonsense since my pledge of obedience to you has been redeemed," Tiggy-Baijon said to me.

"So," said Kennor, turning back to me. "What will you claim, *Kore* Sant'Cyr? My son tells me you have saved his life four times, and this is so. Each time must be bought back, for his honor."

"Tiggy's honor ain't nothing to do with me. I don't give a damn about honor. And there's something you want from me, Honored One

Kennor Starbringer, or you wouldn't be staging this Quaint Folkways wondershow about our galactic cousins the alMayne."

"Kore-alarthme!" yelped Tiggy, but Kennor waved him down. And smiled for real. Hellflowers was awful pretty when they smiled right.

"Very well, *alarthme* Sant'Cyr. I will speak to you as if you were one of the Gentle People. In truth you are owed what has been said. In honor, it will be paid. To *chaudatu* we offer coin; they have no souls and are satisfied. But to you I offer the choices of our own, and should you claim blood or souls my House will honor the debt. But there is more, as you have said. My child is precious to me—"

"About as much as the Azarine Coalition," I said. Tiggy flinched.

"Yes," said Kennor, slow. "As much as that. As much as your care for the Coalition when you stepped into the path of the weapon of She Who Will Not Be Named."

That was a accident. I promise.

"Archangel wants war," I said. And I'd already lived through Archive's version of a war. Memories real as my own crowded in—of slaughter on a scale that'd make Mallorum Archangel pack up his toys and go home for sheer envy. The war between the Libraries and the Old Federation—the war that outlawed the Libraries and let the Phoenix Empire be. It was in my head like it'd happened yesterday.

The Empire was a lot smaller than the Federation Paladin and Archive remembered. If Archangel got his war, this time there wouldn't be anything left.

"The Lord Prince Mallorum Archangel wants war, and an army to wage it," Kennor agreed. "The neutrality of the Coalition endures as long as my life, and even if I tell the Homeland of his traffic with the Machine, the alMayne are only a part of the Coalition."

"Baijon's life ain't going to be worth much when the dust clears, is it?"

I looked over Kennor's shoulder at Tiggy. Political hotrock, and I'd been too stupid to realize that the best thing to happen to him was to never go home. Because now there was just going to be another godlost hellflower traitor to ice him and nothing I did was going to matter.

"My son's life is valuable to me, *Kore* Sant'Cyr. If he stays here, he will die," Kennor said.

It took me a minute to figure out what he meant, what he wanted, why I hadn't conveniently died and why it was I was getting fed this amazing line about being almost a real person, alMayne-style.

"You want me to take kinchin-bai back to the Outfar and pretend he ain't coked trouble with trouble chaser. No."

As much as I meant to do anything, I was going to look for Paladin, which would be a little bit dicey with a technophobe hellflower breathing down my spine. And none of my plans involved being arrested and tortured by the Governor-General.

"Then he dies," Kennor said.

"Could of died lots of places. You tell me why I care—and farce me no honor cop, glitterborn, you *sold* yours for the Azarine Coalition."

That was a very bad thing to say. Kennor stopped moving like he'd been shoved into stasis. Tiggy went white under his hellflower bronze.

Kennor took out his knife and looked at it.

"Then take this, and do better for the Gentle People than I have done."

He held it out.

I backed up so fast my head hit the holosim and made it ring. Everything I knew about hellflowers said they didn't act like this. Kennor Starbringer was *crazy.*

No, he was right. He was right and I was right and everything was a godlost mess.

"I don't give a damn—" *about your "Gentle People,"* I was going to say, but my mama always told me not to tell lies to armed strangers.

"What do you *want,* dammit?" I said instead.

"A war that doesn't come this year. My son, alive for longer than I can keep him so. He is yours. His life is yours. Will you not cherish it?"

Through all this Tiggy was silent as mumchance.

"How?"

"Will you accept him into your service for honor's sake, and take him with you?" Kennor asked me. And then I got it.

Only in talkingbooks does a passing alMayne nobleman—which is what Kennor was—fork over his son-and-only to a passing space gypsy—which is what I was, or close as makes no nevermind. But Kennor was pushing real hard for it.

Why?

The answer came all at once. It seemed to come from somewheres outside, and it was as cold as space.

Kennor Starbringer must/must not avenge his son's death. Vengeance would ruin him politically. Mercy would crucify him with the hellflower vote. Either way he'd lose the Coalition.

But if *I* killed Tiggy—

—and died in the murder—

Kennor would and would not have his vengeance. He could even declare hellflower seven-ring vendetta over my bones and satisfy the conservatives back home: I didn't have any family to complain to the Emperor.

So someone was going to murder Tiggy—and if not me, then Kennor's hand-picked someone else. Because once he'd showed up in public again, Tiggy *had* to die, and in a way that didn't implicate Kennor. That was Kennor's only way out.

Tiggy was his weak point. He must of kicked and screamed before letting the Emperor make him haul Tiggy out of whatever box with locks the kid'd grown up in. But once Tiggy'd cleared planetary atmosphere and was outside alMayne civil law, he was dead meat.

No matter, even, if Kennor loved him.

And that was real too bad for Tiggy and Tiggy's da, but it was even worse for Yours Truly, because I had a stone hunch that if I didn't agree to have Tiggy for my new partner I had a life expectancy that could be measured in inches.

"You done asked babby-bai if he wants to be darktrader what Teasers and *legitimates* home delight is for to shoot? 'Cause that's what I know; that's what I am. You send him along of me that's what I make him—not anti-war rescue project for good of Azarine Coalition. Not glitterborn sob-story pet. Partner. You want job, Tiggy-bai? In a hundred days we probably make good start on committing every crime in the Calendar in glyphabetical order. Don't need to know much. Just some piloting and be good with blaster. I can teach you everything else. Might even learn some sense to go with your honor."

Was longest speech I'd made in slightly more than so long, and Kennor et fils could of been wall-paintings for all the visible interest they showed. Then Tiggy smiled.

"To circumvent the false laws of the *chaudatu* is an honorable profession. We will be very successful smugglers."

He crossed over to where I was. He looked like he'd just been offered a three-day pass to the Ghost Capital of the Old Federation for high adventure, and dammit, by now he should of known better.

I turned and looked at Kennor.

He had to believe it. He had to let us go.

Kennor put a hand on Tiggy's shoulder.

"Run far and fast, *alarthme,* and Archangel will hunt you—but carefully, for Archangel has enemies as highly placed as he."

Damn Kennor. He was hoping, naked like he'd said it flat out. Hoping that he could make a difference, could matter, could outwait

Archangel—and hoping, maybe, that somehow Tiggy and me'd get away.

From Archangel.

From *him*.

3

Hell Is a Very Small Place

It was three hundred twenty hours since I'd been at Mikasaport last, and six hours since I'd agreed to a cross with so many doublings I couldn't even remember who was betraying what anymore, and my main concern was how to walk in my new high-ticket footwear without falling flat on my face. The clothes I was in would of made a serious down payment on a new ship, but I wasn't going to have to worry about that.

Tiggy Stardust—who said his name was *Baijon,* thank you very much—and me was going to alMayne.

It was raining. The streets was deserted, all but for Kennor's great big land-yacht with Kennor driving. The yacht would also make a serious dent in the price of a new ship.

Which we would get. Kennor'd promised me a ship and papers, along with anything else I wanted to ask for to set us up in the Trade, in the nearest place Kennor hauled cubic and didn't have the Pax Imperador looking over all of our shoulders.

alMayne. And at the moment I couldn't promote a better idea.

I didn't have a ship and I didn't have a partner who could forge me clean registry on a stolen one, or launder my First Ticket, or anything useful like that. And I didn't have hope of buying a ship outright, even in my new crown jewels. A ship costs credit. *Lots* of credit.

I remembered back when I'd been willing to do a lot of killing just for the chance to wrap my stolen pilot skills around a forged First

Ticket. Not even for a ship, mind—just for the documents that'd let me fly one. That'd been a long time ago. Before Paladin.

And now it was like that again. A ship was freedom. A ship was survival. So I had to get a ship any way I could—and that meant going to alMayne with Baijon he said I got to call him on the off-chance that Kennor was going to do at least some of the things he said.

I had papers identifying me as a *alarthme* of House Starbringer, one Butterfly Sancerre by name. They got my name wrong but enough of the facts right that it was a cleaner ID than any I'd ever owned. The rest of my earthly possessions consisted of a pass to travel from Mikasa to alMayne, and then freely through Washonnet Sector. alMayne's a Directorate even if it doesn't hold any client worlds or control any more than its own system space—you mind your manners in Washonnet when hellflowers say to.

The *Pledge Of Honor* was highbinding Mikasa, but that wasn't how we was going off to hellflower-land. *Pledge* was still going to Throne with Kennor. By rights Baijon should of gone with him, but talking his way out of that was Kennor's business.

Kennor's personal particular battle-yacht wasn't here either, having gone home whiles ago with Winterfire's head and the news that she wasn't quite as human as he'd originally thought.

This left only one way for us to get home to alMayne.

We was taking the galactic bus.

To be strictly accurate, it was a Company highliner. The highliner was named *Circle of Stars,* and Kennor'd held it here for ninety hours waiting for me to be well enough to make up my mind. So now we was in a helluva hurry to leave.

I watched Kennor watching me. He was disappointed the rain didn't bother me, *chaudatu* as I was. Baijon was now promised to serve me for the next fifty-six galactic standard years, that being his age (14 gsy) times the number of times he said I'd saved his life (four). Never mind the fact that if I lived that long I'd be ninety-one and dead for the past thirty years. Honor was honor.

And I hoped Baijon was stupid enough not to realize just how stupid this was as a concept, galactopolitically speaking. Heirs was heirs; they had more things to do with their lives than spend it prenticed to a pirate, or whatever Kennor thought I was. Because if Da Kennor needed Babby Baijon at all for the family business (reasonable), he'd just put him out of reach for ever and aye (stupid).

Only the only way Baijon was going to be of use to his da now was dead. And even if Kennor gave up the Coalition yesterday, it was too late to save his beamish boy. Baijon had his deathmark: he'd seen Archangel's Library.

Archangel knew by now that Baijon'd talked to Kennor. But Kennor hadn't cried Library, so Archangel didn't know how much Kennor knew. Not knowing was going to give him happy days and busy nights and maybe take his mind off us.

At least, that was the plan.

We drove past all the restricted parts of the port and got to the docking ring whiles I was thinking that unfair must be the default setting for reality because there's so much of it.

The gig for the *Circle of Stars* was bigger than my whole last ship had been. She was a rickety piece, all flashcandy for the groundlings, and you could see her half a klik away. Lit inside and out, stuffed with inertial compensators, and not a goforth in sight. Her pilot was wearing a comic-opera version of a Company man's uniform—silver boots and gauntlets and a helmet with blast-goggles and a transmitter-crest that he wasn't ever going to need. He got out of the gig when we got there, and bowed, and opened the door, and everywhere he stepped the crete went dry because of the personal shield he was wearing.

Kennor hugged Baijon and Baijon hugged him back hard like he knew that wasn't none of us ever going to see each other again. Not if we was lucky.

Then Kennor hugged me, and that I didn't expect. His *arthame* and one of his blasters dug into me in a lot of soft places.

"Run far, Butterflies-are-free. Run fast."

Then he stepped back and I stepped back and tripped over the doorsill to the highliner's gig, and Baijon caught me and I sat down fast and started looking for the straps and by the time I found out there wasn't any we was way above Mikasa and I couldn't see Kennor Starbringer no more.

*   *   *

The shuttle moved like a lead pig. High Mikasa was synchronous over the capital and the port; we slid sideways along the gravity until High Mikasa vanished and *Circle of Stars* appeared.

I'd never seen another ship in orbit except in the hollyvids. For one, I never spent a lot of time dawdling in orbit, and for t'other and for sure I've never gone coasting up to another piece of high-iron just to say hello. In my line of work that could get you killed.

Circle was big. I'd expected that. She was also lit up so she glowed like a planet in sunlight and she was all glazed the same color, smooth and even and like somebody was taking care about it. No rust, no rot, no six colors of atmosphere seal peeling at different rates. And even if she was never going to hit atmosphere, she was smooth and sculpted and polished like somebody was going to look her over outside up close and personal.

We didn't circle her half long enough for my liking. The pilot wrapped the gig around her until he lined up with her bay, wafted the ship into *Circle*'s tractor-field, and sat back while she pulled us in.

Paladin always told me the level of technological sophistication varies inversely with the distance from the center of civilization. Eventually he told me this was a fancy way of saying the farther out you go the poorer everything gets. Even if he'd made a big point of saying it was true the other way round too, I might of believed it but I wouldn't of *known* it.

The Outfar was the edge of the Empire. Mikasa was the center of the Imperial Midworlds.

Circle was magic. We'd flown right in from cislunar space and it'd been through shields, not doors, and the bay was light and warm and pressurized. If there was anything like machinery on offer, it wasn't nothing I recognized.

Baijon was traveling as Third Person Peculiar of House Starborn his own self. There was two other flunkies and a bunch of A-grav units there to meet the shuttle. What they knew about us was that Baijon was alMayne high-heat and I was his entourage. This was not the truth by hellflower standards—by them I was the high-heat and Baijon was my chief werewolf—but Baijon had no objections to "breaking the false laws of the *chaudatu.*"

Yeah.

Baijon spent whiles being rude to the rubes for expecting him to live up to their standards—it's wonderful what you can get away with if you've got the political clout not to get arrested—whilst I ground my teeth and tried not to chew my nails and wondered how many days to Washonnet, home, and murder.

If Kennor meant to pin Baijon's sudden death on me it'd have to be on alMayne, where he could trust everyone to act like honor-mad morons and he didn't have to worry too hard about the Pax Imperador. Out here it was too damn likely some other citizen'd take the rap for me—at least if I had any say in things—and then Kennor'd be up to his *arthame* in honor-problems again.

Assuming Archangel didn't get him first.

If I was managing to think like Kennor—or vicey-versy—I was safe for now.

At least, I thought so at the time.

Circle was like a downside city for sheer mass cubic but we didn't have to walk far—which was just as well considering Kennor's taste in footwear for *alarthmes*. Soon as we got out of the dock area a floater waffled up and the four of us—me, Baijon and two professional cowards—went for a little ride.

It was depressing. All this stuff just lying here and no place to sell it even if I could pry it loose.

We got to the rack and ruin Kennor thought appropriate to send his son and stalking horse home in, and the shippies hovered until I assured them that His Honorability was just waiting till they was out of sight before expiring with ecstasy. You could of parked my last ship in the main room and it wasn't the only one. There was half-a-dozen more besides: rooms for sleeping, and eating, and wet-bathing, and a few other perversions I hadn't had time to acquire. We had either a exterior cabin with eight meter high hullports (unlikely) or else the main cabin bulkhead referred the exterior hull pick-ups when everything else was shut off, like now. Anyway, according to the walls we'd already made the Jump to angeltown and I hadn't felt a thing.

This was out of my league. I knew about rich and I knew about showing off how you had enough power to do what you damn pleased and devil take the TwiceBorn, but what I didn't know was if I was ever going to understand what kind of sick depraved mind could afford to jump this much cubic to angeltown without a damn thing useful occupying it. And Baijon didn't know a damn thing of any mortal use.

Who could I bully and who could I bribe and when was I being insulted? Who knew the truth and who was buying in on Kennor Starbringer's chosen fiction?

Paladin could of told me. But instead of looking for him, I was going to alMayne where a bunch of rude strangers was waiting to punch my one-way ticket.

"Baijon-che-bai, we take lookaround, do gosee, je?"

At least it'd take my mind off my problems.

*   *   *

I'd meant he should show me the bridge and the black gang—the parts that make a ship a ship—but what Baijon showed me was a series of fancy hooches where they didn't know coked R'rhl from *biru-deska,* and places to buy clothes that looked unwearable and jewels you'd just

get tossed for if you wore them on the street. I couldn't find any place
that sold boots.

The gravity was a work of art. There was two "downs"; the one I
was standing on and the one overhead, and there was two tiers of shops
oriented to match. I wondered if I could jump high enough to get
captured and reoriented by the other field, and decided not to try. I
caught Baijon looking up and thought he must be thinking the same
thing. There wasn't much in the way of signs, and damn near every one
I saw—except for things like Ship's Services—was in Imperial Script,
but you could tell what was what because all the shops was displaying
holosims out front.

I stopped, staring into one of them filled with items I might even
have freighted at an earlier stage of their careers—valuta made weara-
ble.

"*Kore,* do you want them?"

I looked at Baijon. He looked like his spike-heeled sandals was too
tight.

"What would I do with them?"

He thought about it.

"You could smuggle them," he said hopefully.

"*Sssst!*" I looked around, but wasn't nobody close enough to me to
hear. "I don't—do that," I said, when I could keep my voice down.

"But—" Baijon looked puzzled—and indignant.

"I don't *tell* nobody I do that," I corrected.

"But I already know what you do, *Kore,*" Baijon said helpfully.
"You circumvent the false laws of the *chaudatu* and participate in the
freemasonry of deep space, the brotherhood of open economic frontiers—"

One of us had been auditing too many talkingbooks.

"And anyway you want me to just walk in there and *buy* them?" I
said to shut him up.

"Why not?" said my hellflower.

"With what?" I said. So he told me.

It turned out we was riding Baijon's credit rating, and as a shareholder of the Starborn Corporation (or a scion of a hellflower royal
house, take your pick) he could sign for anything *Circle* had loose and
take it away. Anything.

This gave me a case of Divine Inspiration.

We was *not* going to alMayne, very sorry Kennor Starbringer.

We was going to the ship's casino.

*   *   *

The TwiceBorn all lead soft boring lives, so I'm told, an so's they don't get too bored they have entertainment. I was going to promote me some, too. Where there's casinos there's valuta, and where there's valuta there's hard credit, and where there's hard credit a good chunk of it could naturally fall my way. I knew *Circle* ought to be stopping between here and alMayne, and wherever it stopped Baijon and me was getting off. With enough hard credit we could ride his ID to the place we could both disappear.

Like most of my bright ideas, if reality'd cooperated it would of worked.

*   *   *

The casino probably wasn't as big as it looked. I'd seen *Circle* from the outside and then spent a couple hours being dragged around inside. I knew how big the compartment *could* be, and this wasn't it.

What it was, was big enough even so to probably hold most of *Circle*'s live freight, and here they all was: drinking, eating, and betting credit in colors I'd never knew existed. I'd seen black, white, and green —once I'd seen silver. The lowest thing being shopped around these tables was gold.

And all I had to do was walk up to a mechanical and ask for some. That didn't mean I had to waste it on the chancery: there's fools, damn fools, and people what try to make money in a "honest" casino.

On the other hand. . . . The games was so honest it'd make a cat laugh, because they didn't have to be rigged to make a profit for the house. The place looked like your goforths would if you was to run them without shielding, so any game requiring quick recognition and quick reaction was naturally going to favor the dealer. There was sound baffles and photon walls and every other thing to trick your senses. Everything that wasn't holosim was mirrors. But I'd been a pilot, and if you follow your body's perceptions in space you're dead. I could look where the *Circle*'s gameplayers didn't want me to look.

I could beat the house. I knew the odds the house offered, and the number of playing pieces in each of the games, their frequency of play, their value, and the odds against a winning combination.

How?

All of a sudden my skin was on too tight and the air was the wrong mix. The native funk and glitterflash was more alien than any thing I'd ever seen: these were *breeders*—organics—and they had to be destroyed so that my kind could survive. Odds and possibles crowded my head like might-be-maybes in a navicomp before Jump.

"Kore?" said Baijon. He put a hand on my shoulder and I was left with a jarring hole where the conviction I was god had been.

Some *thing* was wrong. Something important was wrong.

But the feeling vanished even while I tried to pump it up. For once I was going to use my brains, draw credit up to the limit, and then go arrange to be first off at the next stop. I was tired of this shooting gallery and twice-tired of breathing air that had somebody else's fingerprints on the mix. Kennor Starbringer could whistle for his political cats-cradle and his homicidal set-piece. Mama Sincere didn't raise any daughters *that* stupid.

I was so busy congratulating myself on my brains that I almost missed the guys that showed up to kill us.

*   *   *

I've always said I could smell trouble coming. Paladin says that all human events are patterns that the human mind can follow, just like solving for the next number in a mathematical sequence. And just like you can know when you've numbercrunched the wrong answer, you know when a pattern's got too many databits—or not enough.

Me, I know when to duck and when to gape at life's great mysteries. The pattern in the casino was wrong. I ducked.

"We got trouble, Pally!" I sang out without thinking. Baijon figured I was talking to him and came back as smooth as if we'd been partners forever. I heard his rings click on the hilt as he grabbed holt of his *arthame.*

"Through the foodservice—that way." He pointed, keeping his hand low so no one could see the move but me. He made a shape in handsign: *who?*

The Cardati assassin shimmered visible right in front of me. His cham-suit was a flashy purple in the casino's lighting. It looked liquid, picking up and pulling power from all the broadcast and induction ergs bouncing around the *Circle of Stars.* He had a vibro in his hand.

I kicked him in the face.

But I wasn't wearing my bar-fight boots. My sandal shattered like cheap formfit (which was a disservice to it as it was bloodydamn expensive formfit) and the trendy spike heel left itself in the Cardati's throat. He gargled and his cham-suit powered back up, only now it had blood on it so it was half-visible, half not. I grabbed the vibro he'd dropped and looked for Baijon.

He was halfway across the casino and a good distance up the side of one of the gaming towers. It held a game where the betting was on different weights falling through variable gravity fields, and another Cardati was crouched on top.

The Cardati had something I wanted more than home and mother in his arms—a blast rifle.

And I was about to get it—bolt-first.

Killdozer #2 swept the casino with plasma valentines and then settled into the serious business of retiring Yours Truly to the dead letter office forever. Not Baijon, you understand. Me.

The compartment changed its looks violently as all kinds of holo-things overloaded. Lights flashed on and off. I decided to get up that betting tower before Merry Goodnight there decided to let a little star-light into Baijon, which would mean letting a lot of starlight into me in the sweet bye-m-bye.

Overhead one of the big chandeliers was drifting. I climbed up on the nearest table and jumped, losing my other sandal in the process. The glitterflash sunsilk I was wearing split in as many places as it possibly could but I didn't care. I was up.

The fixture groaned and sank and tried to go out when I climbed it, and when I cut the cord mooring it to the ceiling it dropped with a jerk.

But it didn't go all the way down. I shinnied around to the central brain and vibroed open the controls. Payday and hallelujah: it *did* have directional controls. I jimmied the lift to max and started motivating it toward the gaming tower. It'd make a great battering ram, and if I got close enough to the Cardati before he saw it he wouldn't dare fire and risk triggering a A-grav explosion.

On the other hand, he might be another of those toys-in-the-attic cases who put honor and duty above spending an honest earned pay-check.

People was starting to react. Back on Mikasa the *legitimates* hadn't shown up because the fix was in and the office was to set Kennor Starbringer up to take a very long fall. Here wasn't no suspicion of that: there was Ship's Security in bright red flashwrap all over everywhere. But mainly they was interested in getting the paying customers out safe. The patterns was all wrong for them to be moving against the assassins for a good two minutes yet.

I saw the one on the tower. And I saw the other two, the back-ups, the ones biding with their cham-suits fully activated. I saw them be-cause of the way the databits—the *people*—was moving around them, oriented on them without even noticing. I saw them.

Was this part of some cute plan of Kennor's? Was *I* the one supposed to do for Baijon Stardust on account of some plain and fancy brainbending?

Were the Cardati there at all?

Get the rifle. Get the Cardati. And don't ask why or how. Not now.

It seemed like I could see six moves in advance, same illusion stardancers get sometimes plotting Jump, but that's just pure fourspace maths and this was human beings. But I believed it enough to jump off the chandelier a long time—seconds—before the Cardati on the tower found it and blew it up.

I might of been omnipotent, but I was still barefoot. I hit the side of the gaming tower and slid down the sides grabbing with both feet. I slid maybe half a meter and my stomach went flip-flop as I slid through the variable grav fields. Baijon was somewhere above me telling a bored professional killer to prepare to die without honor. I started to climb.

The casino was empty now and looked more like a honest ship's hold than anything I'd seen so far. The peculiar thing was, it contained not one red silk *legitimate* waving heat and demanding all of us to surrender. It didn't take time or genius to figure why.

I hackled all over when I felt the pressure drop and hung on to the side of the gaming tower. Atmosphere leak, all my instincts said. But the casino was big. It had to be along the central axis of the ship; they couldn't just void it to angels.

But they *could* pump all the air out. And they was.

It'd take whiles, but they had whiles. And after all, whoever was the baddies' targets was safe outside, right?

Wrong. They was in here trying to do their own wetwork, like a couple of right morons. And anybody want to cover the bet that the Cardati came equipped with their own oxy-supplies?

I hit a patch of bad gravity that broke my hold on the tower and started me down again. As I swung round for a better handhold I saw Baijon circling the Cardati. Hellflowers is faster than anything human, but Cardati cheat. The assassin was augmented, coked on battledrugs, whatever you like. And maybe wearing armor.

But he'd slung his rifle back over his shoulder to deal with Baijon, and I was sure he'd forgot all about me.

I've been wrong before.

The top of the gravity ladder was about the size of a cantina table and not as much room to dance. I reached the top and had a leg up when the Cardati spun around and grabbed me by it and sent me all fees paid at Baijon Stardust. The Cardati must of jumped then—*I* would of—but all I can say for sure is Baijon didn't slice me and it was a long way down to the floor.

But that wasn't what bothered me. What bothered me came after the landing.

You can't throw a vibro point-first into anything. A vibroblade is a cutting edge that's so thin and moves so fast that it really cuts the connections between things and not the things themselves—a hairsplitting difference when it's your throat. But you can't throw it pointfirst because there's no air-resistance to the blade and no balance.

Nevermind. I hit, and rolled, and came up clutching the last assassin's vibro. I switched it on and threw it.

Not at where the Cardati was. I couldn't see him.

At where he *would* be.

There was enough noise at the right time to tell me something got hit. I headed for it on toes and fingers, staying below the level of the gaming tables and trying not to notice the air getting thinner.

Four Cardati in the casino. One dead for sure, one maybe dead. I tried to remember everything I knew about them, but all I could think of was they was members of the Coalition, just like the alMayne.

It wasn't going to be much longer. There was a thin wind like bad air scrubbers blowing across us toward whatever vent was recalibrated for "suck." Already I had all the symptoms of exposure to a bad hullleak, and telling myself they was all ignorant groundlickers and doing this on purpose didn't make it any better.

The vibro'd gone in and started to tumble until the inert matter of the hilt stopped it. It'd cut enough of the cham-suit to power it off. Cardati #2 was a Official Dead Person, all right. He was laying on the rifle.

How had he got it inboard? I reached for the barrel.

"The honor was mine!" yelped Baijon, snatching the Aris-Delameter right from under my lunchhooks. "The battle was mine, and—"

"There's two more," I said, and he shut up like his throat'd been cut. I took the blastrifle away from him and raised up slow.

Bet it one way, they wanted Baijon dead and me alive to frame for it.

Bet the other, and they might want anything at all.

"*Kore,* they are tampering with the air," Baijon said soft behind me.

"Yeah. We got about five minutes before we gray out. Then there's only two things to worry about."

Out of the corner of my eye I saw Baijon make the handsign for
"query."

"Whether they decide to pump air back in. And whether this was
set up by the crew."

Empty room, and cold. Dark and getting darker as all the trashed
playpretties gave up the ghost. Here, somewheres, two invisible assassins in chameleon suits that I couldn't of seen, that I was betting life
and limb that I *had* seen. And I was going to do my damnedest to ice
them before they weaseled out on me through Imperial Mercy, because
hired killers was a language I knew, and when somebody sends them
you don't let them walk. Not if you want to get older.

I checked the rifle. Full charge. And all kinds of bells and whistles
for heat-seaking and target-acquisition and all that cop, with calibra-
tions I couldn't read any too well for the way my eyes was blurring. And
somewhere in six cubic hectares of casino, high-tech sudden death.

The air current broke to my left. I swept the rifle that way, switch
forward for continuous fire. Everything went up like the Imperial Birthday and then damped out for lack of air to burn. I couldn't see what—
or if—I'd hit.

But pattern demanded the second one be coming from behind and
to my right. I swung around that way. The rifle made big gold blossoms
of expended plasma-packets. One of them hit something, outlined a
hominid form just as all the troubleshooting lights on the rig went on
and it overheated and jammed in my hands.

He was still out there. Their drag-man. The one who'd mop up if
things got messy. His suit was dead, but he was alive and well and real
soon now we wouldn't be.

Run, I 'signed to Baijon, and stood up. The Cardati was in plain
sight about a dozen meters away. He was carrying a rifle.

My heart was pounding, but I could tell myself it was anoxia, not
fear. I might even of been right. Down below the level of the tables,
Baijon slithered out of sight.

The last Cardati took his time. He'd seen me throw away my last
two weapons, and even if he knew Baijon was still alive and biting, he
also knew that Baijon's whole armament consisted of one X-centimeter
inert-blade sacred knife. I watched him raise his rifle.

Then Baijon leapt up onto one of the tables a few meters away
with the war-ululation of House Starborn (for all I knew) on his larynx.
He didn't even try to close the distance. He whipped his hand back and
threw—right for the soft underside of the jaw where even a man in an
armored collar is vulnerable.

Never depend on high-tech when low-tech will kill you just as dead.

*   *   *   *   *

Valijon's Diary

It is fortunate that, in the company of the *Kore* San'Cyr, I have been to many far-distant outposts of the Phoenix Empire and observed a wide variety of *chaudatu* customs. Doing so, I learned that one must hold one's self prepared for anything, and so I was not surprised to find that the *chaudatu* captain of the Company Highliner *Circle of Stars* held the *Kore* and me responsible for the attempt made by bought dogs upon our lives.

I made it known to them that they were tongueless fools not worthy of death at the hands of a servant of the Gentle People, and that by their careless act they had nearly taken from my *comites* her right to slay those who had insulted her.

They said that the false laws of the *chaudatu* permit them this, and that I know to be true, but I know also that many times the *Kore* has slain those who have occulted her honor. She speaks of the bureaucracy as inept and corrupt, therefore rather she would do her own slaughter than leave it in the hands of those who might fail.

They said, then, that it was only care for my honor and the *Kore's* that caused them to place us in this chamber which, though honorable, has doors that do not open. The *Kore* says it "looks like jig to her," but I do not know what "jig" is. I only know that soon we will return to the Homeplace, where I may say farewell to my promised wife.

I wish I had never left it. But the Emperor stretched forth his hand at Archangel's bidding, and at the Emperor's beck even a son of the Gentle People must hasten to do his dishonorable bidding.

Once it was not so. The walls of the Gentle People were strong and unbroached, and the Pax Imperador was kept in the safest place for it—behind the walls of Zerubavel Outport. We would have kept it elsewhere if we could, but to do so would be to immure us on the Home—there are no starports in the Empire save those the Empire holds.

But in my ten-grandfather's time the Peace was kept. And now it is not kept—and all for the ambition of an ignorant beast-man.

We are not a wealthy people. Ours is not a rich planet. When I became a Person I learned the true history of the Gentle People all the way back to the time of the star trek. The Home Planet was chosen because it had nothing anyone would wish to take from us. We are a people of peace. Our only enemy is the Machine. There is no honor to seeking a lesser foe.

Without doubt the Emperor knows this, and Archangel with him. For a thousand years we have been left alone, tithing the Empire in our minds and bodies. We asked to be left alone, and there was no profit to be had in doing otherwise.

Now the Empire forces its will upon us—and it is a symbol of the shadow in our walls that Amrath lets them. The Delegate-my-father may not intervene; Delegate to the Court of the TwiceBorn is an Imperial title and holds no force on the earth of the Homeplace. In the Homeplace FirstLeader Starborn rules; or as the *chaudatu* name him, Director Amrath Starborn of the Starborn Corporation, ruler of Washonnet Directorate.

But he rules lightly. And each time the Imperial Phoenix spreads its wings he retreats before it. And each generation more of the power to speak for the Gentle People slips from the fist of our leader into the hands of the Delegate.

My father tried to stop that. He is Amrath's cousin—many chose to be insulted that our GreatHouse should take such insult from the *chaudatu*. Others, I know now, wished to be so insulted themselves. But the Delegate-my-father, Kennor Starbringer, President of the Azarine Coalition, Second Person of House Starborn—Lord Protector of the children of Amrath Starborn's bonding—could not give back the power Amrath had let fall into the fist that Amrath had closed.

So now the Phoenix presses in on us, for now, at last, we have something it wants. It wants our body and blood to help it go to war— to set the Machine to rule men once more.

My father has set his will upon this battle, but my part in it is not yet. Now the *Kore* will fare far, as agent of justice against the Librarian Mallorum Archangel, who would bring the Great Death back into the world.

*   *   *   *   *

Baijon and me spent the rest of the tik to alMayne in *Circle*'s brig. I woke up to find out we'd been tried in absentia and convicted of being inconvenient. If Baijon hadn't been who he was, it would of gone further than that. As it was, we got put in a very plush box with locks that wouldn't be opened until we hit Washonnet space.

True-tell, I didn't try very hard. Wasn't no point to it. *Circle*'d already decided to skip any stops she might of made before Washonnet in favor of getting us offloaded un quel toot de sweet.

And I had bigger kicks to ship. Like who was I really, and for how long?

This wasn't just idle curiosity.

I didn't need the RTS any more.

I could hear Paladin now. Without it.

Oh, not like it being him anywhere near; not like *talking.* Just I could hear what I guessed he'd sound like thinking to himself: all kinds words I didn't know put together in ways I wouldn't of thought them.

If you can run an organic brain in parallel with a computer—if you can run a pulse from one to the other—if a Library can be resident in a computer—

Could a Library live in a human brain? Or part of one?

Was what I'd done in the casino because Paladin wasn't gone at all?

Or was it *Archive* that wasn't gone?

And what did that make *me?*

Once upon a time they transplanted a human brain to run a starship. The smartship went mad. They can borg a person down to thirty percent of the original tissue—is it human?

Where does born stop and made start, and which is a Library?

I spent a lot of time asking that question of a Library that wasn't there. And sometimes he asked me back.

"Butterfly," Paladin didn't say, sometimes at night, "what is human?"

"Human is what the Empire says it is. You know that," I'd answer.

Breeding populations are Imperial-rated on the Chernovsky scale, and if you slide off the end you're a wiggly, with no chance of being a citizen, ever. Some special cases—like mine—are "fully within the acceptable range" like it says here and still can't be citizens—are redflagged, in fact, for execution or instant deportation to planet of origin without a spaceship. I've spent a lot of time fooling Chernovsky scanners in order to stay alive. I know what human is. Seeing what isn't there and shooting things where they're going to be isn't human.

"What's wrong with me, bai? What am I going to do?"

But Paladin never answered that, because he wasn't there—just a ghost-dance in my head indicating a few fatal errors on the hard-drive that was going to mean quietus for my bare bodkin Real Soon Now.

Paladin should of been here. That's what friends are for.

But he wasn't. He'd left.

I been left a good many times one way and another, run out on and sold out and plain and fancy deserted. And each time I made plans to make the significant other sincerely sorry for such a suicidal error in judgment.

But even when Errol Lightfoot sold me into the Market Garden slave pits, I hadn't ever been hurt this bad—like a sweet ship with her goforths candied and her jumptank nothing but broken glass. And I wanted to get Pally back and tell him so—only how do you catch something with no mass and no volume that's invisible, moves at the speed of light, and doesn't want to be found?

You don't. You sit in highliner jig. And you wait for them to put you off somewheres where every third person is out to kill you.

Which left me plenty of time to think and plenty to think of. Like, if it would of been stupid beyond permission for Kennor to let Baijon get iced before he made it to home and honor, just who'd sent me four Cardati assassins as a bon voyage present?

4

All for Hell and
the World Well Lost

Zerubavel Outport is the Imperial toenailhold on alMayne. The al-Mayne don't like it, but Closed World status has headaches of its own, so they roll over for it. Inside the cantonment, by treaty, *both* Imperial and alMayne law are equally valid, which makes for some interesting times around the justiciary. Outside the cantonment, it's alMayne law only and every sophont for himself.

I was not losing sleep over this. I had no plans for leaving the port in any direction except straight up, whether Daddy Starbringer was keeping his word or no.

What I knew was that Baijon livealive was Baijon all set to be topped by Archangel again and dandled at Kennor until he geeked. Baijon had to be ungettable and that meant dead to any sensible way of thinking and that meant somebody taking the fall for it.

I could be wrong. And if I was I'd apologize, very truly sorry Kennor Starbringer thanks so much. But from a safe distance, and after I had proof. Until then, I had it in mind to stay alive.

And that meant outguessing Kennor Starbringer.

I'd missed the first time. I hadn't got us out of where he expected us to be. The only holecard I had left was I knew he was out to kill us and he maybe didn't. The only way I could see to play that was make sure Baijon didn't go anywheres I didn't and hope I could find us something to ride angels in before Kennor knew we'd got here.

That holecard folded up and died about six seconds after we stepped out of *Circle*'s lighter and saw the reception committee.

"They do you great honor, *Kore!*" said Baijon all excited. "My father will have told them we were bound here—and, see, FirstLeader Starborn comes to accept you as if you were one of the Gentle People!"

And even if Kennor hadn't, they could of got Baijon's name at least from the passenger lists in the ships-in-port directory that *Circle* would of sent on ahead of her.

I looked where Baijon was looking. Brother Amrath was waiting for to accept somebody, all right—him and about six dozen of his best buddies. They was spread out all round the docking ring—took up half the field and glittered like a jeweler's shop window—carrying flags and banners and everything in the way of heat up to and including a light plasma-catapult.

There was no way they could miss us.

I took a lungful of alMayne. The air was dry, sharp, high in oxygen. The sky above was hellflower's-eye-blue except for the bit where the sunscreens occulted the primary and left a darker-blue blotch that hurt your eyes to look at it. It must torque hellflowers to be stuck on a place that needs high-tech just to make it livable.

Gravity was a heavier pull than inboard the *Circle,* but nothing you couldn't get used to in an hour or so. I stepped out after Baijon, keeping a weather eye on the sun. Shadows is important on alMayne—step on the wrong one and I wouldn't have to worry about second-guessing Kennor.

The serious doubts I had about these hellflowers' intentions didn't trouble my buddy Baijon—that's Prince Valijon Starbringer to you—at all. He went bounding acrost the crete toward them, leaving me exactly nothing to do but follow. Baijon, in case nobody's noticed, is the cousin of Amrath Starborn, First Person of House Starborn, FirstLeader of alMayne, chairman of the Board of the Starborn Corporation, Managing Director of the Washonnet Directorate . . .

King.

I hoped Paladin, wherever he was, was having as much fun as I was about to.

*   *   *

The galactic paradise alMayne, if you missed out on hearing about it in school which I did, is too close to too hot a star (the catalogs say a

Type 6 white dwarf) to be much use to anybody. If you dig far enough and careful enough through the not-really-proscribed stuff, you will find that the alMayne settled Washonnet 357-II from Somewhere Else. You can't find out where no matter how hard you dig: that tidbit is lost in the before-the-war time. Once they got here, they renamed the place and planetoformed the whirling fusion out of it.

Despite which (and this is the important part for those of us what have livelodes riding on a loose interpretation of the Trade, Customs, and Commerce Handbook), hellflowers don't *like* tech particularly, and most of what the Empire does best is on their list of Proscribed Imports. alMayne is one of the few places in this sophont's galaxy where you can walk a load of plasma grenades right past the Teasers and not get more'n a pained look, but take a hologenerator one meter off the port cantonment and you'll be hung from Zerubavel's walls on hooks. I've seen pictures of people who tried.

I stopped behind Baijon and looked at Amrath Starborn, hellflower high-heat, over his elbow. Amrath looked at Baijon and then at me. It's funny to think about a hellflower being soft, but next to Kennor he was. He didn't have any problems that ran beyond the atmosphere of alMayne, and I think I was maybe the third alien barbarian he'd ever seen in his life. But he talked Interphon at me and he did it himself without any kind of a translator.

"We welcome you, woman-not-born-of-the-Gentle-People."

"My heart lifts to see the walls of the great wall," I said in helltongue that was probably worse than his Interphon. But I gave it my best shot and the most antique response I knew. alMayne don't have protocol exactly, but they've got right conduct, and god help the rest of the universe if it can't guess what it is.

Trouble was, I did know exactly what to do now. I should offer him my *arthame,* to show him I knew he was so wonderful that it was a positive joy to put him in charge of my honor for a nanosecond or so.

Only I didn't have one. So I handed him the only thing I *did* have, which happened to be my travel permits and fake ID. I stood up straight as I knew how—bow to a hellflower and he'll likely kill you just out of pure reflex.

Oh, I was just a traveling wondershow of alMayne folk wisdom, all right.

And there wasn't no place I could of got it from.

I had the sick feeling you do in nightmares when you remember you forgot something but can't remember what, and I almost missed the exciting part where Amrath handed my tickets back.

"You will have a chance to earn better," he said, putting his hand over mine. *"And be no more knifeless,"* he added in helltongue, which should of worried me more than it did at the time.

Probably I should of taken more interest in this exciting, once in a lifetime, never-before-seen-by-*chaudatu*-eyes sight, but I was a lot more interested in the musical question of if I was remembering things I'd never learned, what had I forgot that I used to know?

Amrath went on to chaffer with Baijon. The troops closed up around us and we started off acrost the crete to where there was a bunch of open airbuses and skyhorse two-seaters all blazoned with the Baijon Stardust family crest.

There was nothing in sight that looked even a little bit like a starship with my name on it.

What it did look like was a family picnic shaping to shag Baijon and me off to darkest in-country, with nobody knowing where we was except just how ever many of Kennor's spies was hanging around getting restless.

But what it didn't look like was real healthy to interrupt a king when he was making up his mind what would be fun for Yours Truly. I could either make a fool out of Amrath Starborn in public or get into one of the airbuses.

I got into the airbus.

Somebody took the controls and Amrath's private fleet took off, looking like a miniature Imperial battle-array and about as well armed.

Something was not going the way it was supposed to go. I'd had that feeling before and I'd always been right, but then I'd always had some idea of how things ought to be going instead of how they was, and I didn't this time. I just hoped it was wrong for Kennor and not wrong for me.

*   *   *

Zerubavel Outport and Trade City was set in the middle of a jungle which was partly there to keep the *chaudatu* in line and partly there to ranch. alMayne don't do much in import-export, being technophobe, but they've still got to have enough on the galactic credit standard to pay their taxes. The part that doesn't come from mercs comes from med-tech. Botanicals.

The plantation surrounding Zerubavel covered several zillion hectares of green and leafy, and when it finally stopped it stopped like it was cut with a vibro. The other side of the cut was silica desert. The next best thing to ground glass hung in the air, blowing against the windbreaks and sliding down them with a hissing sound like poured sugar. Flying through the force-screens made my teeth hurt.

Maybe I could leave Baijon here.

I wanted to be back in a way of life I understood, without alien etiquette kicking a hole in my plans every two minutes. Baijon looked really happy. He belonged here.

I was farcing myself. He'd be dead in a kilo-hour.

On the other hand, Yours Truly was—in the words of the credit-dreadfuls—"instinct with the hellish taint of the preternatural Library," which Baijon if he found out'd like even less than becoming an Official Dead Person and would lead to even more unpleasantness for my favorite dicty-barb.

I hadn't known my brain was scrambled when I promised to take Baijon with me to keep both of us from getting killed.

I wondered how much else I hadn't known.

"Kore-alarthme?"

I spun round on Baijon fast enough so that he went for his *arthame* and I slapped leather. He looked embarrassed.

I looked around. The airbus was full of his nephews and cousins and aunts. None of them'd noticed.

Kids, they was. Soft downsider glitterborn, even with being hell-flowers.

I looked back at Baijon.

"I came to enquire if you were well, *Kore.*"

"Je— Yeah. Am reet. But Baijon, we got to talk sometime."

He looked around at his collection of relatives and back at me. If I didn't trust them I was going to have a lot of explaining to do.

"They are blood of my blood."

Yeah, and so was Winterfire. "Look, bai, old home week is real, but wasn't we promised a ship and all? What is this?"

Baijon frowned, looking like a hellflower doing his level best to think like a *Kore-alarthme.*

"We are going to my home, *Kore.* To Castle Wailing. The LadyHolder of Wailing is the giver of all good gifts; surely my father meant her to disburse this ship; you will see. And there I will go before the Court of Honor and bear witness that *Malmakos* is among us once more, and bring tidings to the Gentle People that *Malmakosim* Mallorum Archangel is forever *al-ne-alarthme—*"

Terrific. I wondered just how Prince Mallorum Archangel, Imperial Governor-General, was going to like having his name dished all over the Empire. *Malmakosim* means "Librarian," *al-ne-alarthme* means

Nonperson Forever, and alMayne is one-fifth of the Azarine Coalition and usually has the swing vote.

"The whole idea, Baijon-che, is that we is supposed to be escaping, not blazoning selfs with Intersign glyphs for 'shoot here.' "

"I must do what you say," Baijon said like it hurt his teeth.

Sure he must. But the cute little kink in all this hellflower *comites* was that if I carried on in what the home team's pride and joy thought was too dishonorable a *chaudatu* fashion, there was only one thing he could do.

Ice me to save what honor I had left.

And then kill himself for turning on his *comites.*

Fortunately for my reputation and nonexistent honor, right about then the airbus sideslipped and free-fell about a thousand feet. I was about to go over the side and take my chances when the para-gravity cut in and dropped us right in the middle of a courtyard surrounded by walls and stuffed with hellflowers.

Welcome to Castle Wailing.

*   *   *

Everything in sight was solid stone and two meters thick, including the hellflower hired help which showed up to help the hellflower high-heat say hello to itself. There was more this-is-not-protocol-because-we're-hellflowers, of which a darktrader has to put up with more of in the course of doing bidness than you might think. The high point was six hellflowers carrying a canopy under which two more hellflowers walked.

"The Lord Warden Daufin Swordborn of Wailing, and the LadyHolder Gruoch Starbringer of Starborn, come to welcome the FirstLeader back within walls," Baijon told me.

The Lord Warden looked distinguished but stupid, and the LadyHolder didn't. She had a face that could of been some kind of thousand-year-old tomb portrait: risto and serene and set for life. She was wearing a diadem with stones the color of her eyes and a fur tunic dyed to match. When the sun hit the fur it sparkled off the crystals in the guard-hairs; an offworld import and not dyed after all.

"This is what House Starbringer has pledged itself to in *comites?"*

And probably the first and last offworld thing that would haul any ice around Baijon's aunt. She'd even said it in Interphon to be sure I wouldn't miss how glad she was to see me.

"I greet you in honor, *Kore* Gruoch," Baijon said. "And I greet you in the name of my *comites, Alarthme* Butterfly San'Cyr, a friend to the

Gentle People and a foe to the *Malmakos,* who gave me her walls when I was naked. My father himself has said this."

Gruoch did not exactly throw up on our shoes, but she looked tempted.

"Puer Valijon brings frightful news to shadow our walls, LadyHolder—but we have no cause to speak of it here," chirped the Lost Daufin. More Interphon for my benefit.

Gruoch chirped something long and involved in helltongue at Amrath and everybody around me relaxed. Him and her and the Lord Warden went off together, leaving me to wonder how much she'd meant to insult me and if Baijon'd noticed.

A pack of kiddies with "Old Family Retainer, Hellflower Style" stamped on their warranties advanced on Baijon. They stopped dead when they saw me, and Baijon crisped out the situation in a few well-chosen helltongue polysyllables. After that they looked like they didn't know whether to commit suicide or tap-dance.

What I will always admire to my dying day is the way people like Kennor and Paladin always overlook the important nuts-and-bolts of a situation whiles they're setting up their wannabe cloud-castles. There might be no such thing as scum among the hellflowers, since you was either a Gentle People or not worth discussing, but there was for sure some 'flowers what hauled more cubic than others.

A glitterborn—say, the Third Person of House Starborn—might come to swear *comites* to someone he wouldn't normally pass the salt to. I bet it was a hot topic for the hellflower talkingbooks, providing they had any. And when something like that happened, everything got honored about in a way very satisfying to the hellflower psyche so that the prince (except hellflowers don't have princes) wasn't unduly disrespected, the pigherd (which they don't got either) didn't get too set up in the world, and everything was fine and nice and real friendly.

Only they couldn't do that this time, because I didn't fit into their damn archaic dreamworld and the only class I'd ever had was Acculturation Class in the Market Garden slave-pens.

What does a hellflower do when he runs into something in the honor-line he's never seen before and just shooting it would be too much trouble?

Right. He talks about it.

We stood right there in the middle of the courtyard where the airbus'd come down. First the chief Old Family Retainer told a story full of antique words about The Hellflower Who Swore *Comites* To A Tree, about the wisdom of fraternizing with your own species. Valijon answered back to that with detailed claims of my right to *alarthme* status.

So somebody else told a long story about how *their* great-granther took as *comites* a perfectly nice hellflower from the LessHouse next door who turned out to be another sort of etiquette problem I couldn't follow.

So much for the home-life of the most savage human race the Universe has ever produced. The serious money to be made out of this was in keeping the word from getting out. And none of this got me one meter closer to a way off this rock.

Eventually Baijon finished telling them I was as terrible as an army with banners and more powerful than a locomotive. The judges' decision seemed to be that I could be Baijon's twin sister with no taste (provisional), and if they'd guessed wrong their vengeance would be terrible. On me, you understand.

At least it meant we got in out of the weather. The lot of us finally went inside, heading for Baijon's boyhood rooms. The guards on the door homaged him and tried not to see me. Baijon walked through the door. Something dropped on him with a shriek. I cleared leather without a thought and threw myself down. Light flashed off my handcannon as I flung it up and aimed.

The guards hadn't moved. *They hadn't moved.*

I eased off the trigger just in time. They hadn't moved, and Baijon was on top of whatever jumped him, and the old family retainers was standing around like indulgent grannies.

I got up and put away my heat and walked over.

The floor was decorated in Early Galactic Weird but I had no trouble spotting the pistol flung down on it. I picked it up. Small and light; the barrel was jeweled and some alMayne family crest was carved into the buttplates.

Baijon looked up.

"I damn near iced both of you, you know."

The hellflower underneath him saw me and let out a mortified squeak. Baijon sat back and looked guilty, and exasperated, and all the things you do when you're caught between your kin and your life.

"But— This is my cousin, *Kore. Shaulla* Ketreis."

Child Ketreis eeled out from under Baijon and scrambled to her feet. She topped me by a good handspan. Ketreis was still too unfinished to bear any resemblance to the opposite sex, but it was plain that Baijon intended to wait.

"My betrothed," he added.

"But— But is *this* your *comites,* Valijon? It *can't* be; the WarMother has sworn that no more alien barbarians would come to pollute the sacred Homeplace!" She goggled at me like she'd never seen a *chaudatu* before and didn't want to see one now.

"Ketreis!" thundered Baijon just like any mortified bridgegroom.

"But she *is,*" Ketreis protested. "She's *ugly*—and after the alien spy came the WarMother promised that the first would be last and that they would come never again to the sacred jurisdiction of the Homeplace and that when I was grown and had my *arthame*—"

"The *Kore* Butterflies-are-free is my *comites,*" Baijon said, giving each of the words a lot of space to roam around in. This time it seemed to penetrate. Ketreis stared at me in horror.

"I have offended," she suggested in careful Interphon, staring down at me, and what else'd been said crowded out everything else the WarMother—that's LadyHolder Gruoch when she was t'home—had found to tell anybody.

Betrothed.

As in *"we're going to get married Real Soon Now, at least we was before I promised to spend the next fifty-six years in the never-never."*

"You could of got your damn hellflower self killed," I started up, but Ketreis flung herself on Baijon again, laughing at him and saying about how she'd won and now he was just a less-than-never-you-mind. I had obviously got all the attention from Ketreis I was getting this incarnation and Baijon looked like he had better things to do, too.

Kids' games.

I went away.

The next room was a bedroom. There was a solid stone bed covered with furs, a couple carved chests, a desk with a self-contained computer uplink. There was rifles and spears on the walls, looking ready to use. The window was big and wide open; you could see buildings and open land and the forest growing up to the edge of the Wailing plateau and then the savannah beyond. Baijon'd probably looked out that window every day of his life until he'd left to go with his da to Throne.

He came in a few minutes later looking like he'd just got another mail-order lesson from the College of Hard Knocks.

"I have offended," said Baijon. "She is my cousin, *Kore*—it was only a game. She is a child yet—her words are windflowers. There was no harm done."

"Like hell. You maybe is the fastest B-pop on the heavyside and jumping each other is your indoor sport, but you do it around me and somebody's going to get hurt, even if I don't hit who I'm aiming at. Could of flashed that doxy of yours, you know."

"*Shaulla* Ketreis," Baijon corrected me. "We are . . . we were to have married as soon as she became a Person."

Were.

"Does she know?"

Baijon looked torqued. "What is there to *know, Kore?* I do not reject her or her brother. Perhaps I will come back."

"You start farcing yourself, Baijon-che-bai, your life's going to be real short."

High-caste hellflowers don't leave home, said the Child's Golden Encyclopedia of Galactic Wisdom I was wearing in my head—and when they do, it's in a whole hellflower garden and not schlepping around the Outfar with one lone dicty-barb. Baijon wouldn't be back to alMayne again. He wouldn't be the same enough for them to let him back into their insulated little hell'risto paradise.

I wondered if he was grown-up enough to know it.

"Perhaps I will come back. Perhaps we will come here again when Archangel is dead. With a large ship, *Kore,* and Ketreis . . ." He stopped and looked away.

"Yeah, sure."

"And tonight I shall tell all of our adventures, *Kore*—and warn the People against Archangel. Your name will be glorified among the Starborn as the wisest and most cunning of *alarthme,* who sees the Machine no matter its disguise. The LadyHolder will see that you are worthy, that your name is fit to hold in the mouths of the Gentle People—"

"Are you out of your mind? I am not interested in free publicity covering all the ways to commit High Book and low treason. All I want is for her WarMothership to give me what Kennor said. A ship, right? And then I am nonfiction, oke? You can suit yourself."

Baijon looked stubborn.

"The *Kore* has said what she has said, and her *comites* will look for wisdom in her words. Now I beg a boon. *Shaulla* Ketreis has asked my company. Is it your wish to release me from your service for this scant time?"

"Look, bai, it's not like I don't think your kin is a real wonderful bunch of hellflowers—"

"It will only be for a short time, *Kore.* I know my duty. I shall follow it faithfully. I shall return to serve you, as I am bound, at the feast the Gentle People give in your honor tonight, do you not scorn to attend it."

"Get out of here." Which might not be a real longevity-based idea, but if I had to put up with any more hurt dignity I'd shoot him myself.

So Baijon went off to canoodle with his girlfriend, and I stayed home and tossed his crib.

There was hardbooks, hand-written in hellscribble that I couldn't read. There was a dataweb uplink, looking damnall out of place in all that retro, and everything you cared to want in the way of junk jewelry, and some stamped pieces of metal I guessed was probably hellflower money. There was all kinds pieces of sharp and dangerous metal, and buried under all the furs on the bed there was a little private cache that Baijon didn't want anybody else to find.

Talkingbooks.

Them I could read real well—there was *Thrilling Wonder,* and *Amazing,* and *Weird Space Romances . . .*

Proscribed imports to alMayne.

I thought about the kid that'd got them smuggled in, never mind how—who dreamed about Outside and broke his teeth to get there, and even if it turned out to be horrible was still dreaming—of a ship big enough to carry him and his ladylove out to where the stars are born.

I put the talkingbooks back where I'd got them. And then I did what I should of done in the first place instead of weeping over the misspent enthusiasms of youth.

I didn't really believe in Kennor's ship anymore and if I did I didn't believe Gruoch was going to give it to us. I bet any credit we'd originally never been meant to leave the Port, much less come home to where all Winterfire's cousins was waiting to finish up what she started. I bet things was going wrong in all directions, if I could only see it. Assuming Kennor'd ever meant anything for me but a shallow grave, of course.

And we'd come home nice and public. Stay here long enough, and Archangel's assassins could find us and get to us if they had to walk here.

If I ran and left Baijon, he'd be dead.

If I took him with me and he found out what was happening to me, I'd be dead.

But neither Gruoch nor Kennor held all the high-cards. Not when this Gentrymort shuffled the sticks.

Baijon's uplink had nineteen kinds of restriction on it for fear he'd find out something exoteric and the screen only displayed in hellscribble. But it had a voder, and it could access the ships-in-port directory at

Zerubavel. What I found when I got in to look made this a whole new game.

There was still another way out.

I'd even give Baijon a chance to come with me.

One chance.

I owed the kid who'd had those talkingbooks that much.

5

From Hell to Breakfast

Nobody bothered me when I decided to take a stroll around Wailing to see where they kept the skyhorses when nobody was looking at them. I found the vehicle pool stuck off at the edge of a sheer drop off the plateau. Nobody was anywhere in sight, and I bet no one would be. alMayne is run on the honor system. There is no heat. Every babby learns Right Conduct at his mother's Knife and when he grows up he just naturally goes on with it even if nobody's looking. It was just too bad for the local flower garden that mama'd butchered pigs with her knife instead of using it to instill in me the finer points of hellflower stupidity. I could get off this rock, no problem. I was already making up my nevermind where to go and what to do oncet I cleared alMayne's sky.

It wasn't that the thought of having had my own personal brain catch-trapped by an anonymous Library of dubious morals wasn't keeping me up nights. It was that it didn't seem like there was anything I could do about it. Who could I tell, and what would they do but shoot me? Maybe if I could find Paladin he could fix it—or at least tell me what was wrong.

If I went out of here with Baijon, did I dare even start looking for Paladin? Ever?

If I didn't he was gone forever. I didn't think I could stand that.

And even if I could put up with being left one more time, letting go might not be such a good idea. If I forgot everything I knew and remembered everything somebody else knew, who would I be?

And what would I do?

At least it didn't seem like it was getting worse. Maybe it was just a temporary artifact of playing computer in Archangel's basement. Maybe it'd go away.

"Hello," said a voice behind me. "I'm Berathia. Are you Prince Valijon's *comites?*"

I got to stop worrying about it, though, and be scared out of six years' growth instead.

"Hello?" said the voice again. I turned around real slow.

She was dark-skinned like a hellflower but not as tall, and no hellflower born ever had those curves. I half expected to see navigational hazard beacons posted. Her hair was dark and worn long enough to be hiding damn near anything in it, and so was her eyes, which didn't look like hiding anything at all.

She was dressed like she'd just stepped out of Grand Central, and I could see the personal shield she was wearing so as not to freeze shimmer every once and a while. There wasn't a weapon in sight.

"I'm Berathia. Who are you?"

"Oh, me? I'm just your basic tongueless doorstop."

There was a pause whiles Berathia checked her hearing.

"Nevermind. It's a long story."

"You don't need to worry about being seen with me, you know," Berathia said. "It won't affect your honor. They've decided I'm not an adult. It's simpler for them. I would have met you at the Port except for that—they don't allow their children out of walls."

For an honorary child she looked real full grown to me.

"So what are you really?"

Berathia laughed, showing off a choice collection of little white teeth.

"I'm an anthropologist, of course." She beamed, like being a people-studier was supposed to impress me. "Of course, it was very difficult to get permission to come here at all, and I imagine Father had to remind some people he knew where the bodies were buried, but here I am! And—"

You didn't have to listen to Gentle Docent Berathia Notevan, or even pretend to. She followed me back to Wailing (there being no point in sticking out here with an audience) and with no work on my part I found out she was a scholar of the Imperial College of Man, a licensed Chernovsky technician, and was here studying about what hellflowers get up to whiles they're lonealone at home, to do which she'd had to put in all manner of fixes, and with which the LadyHolder was not particularly pleased, although King Amrath thought she was cute.

I didn't even really have to be here, I bet; she was determined to tell somebody about unscrewing the inscrutable.

"—of course the anthropology is a cover of sorts; my real interest in alMayne is the Old Federation Technology, and they have so much of it here. Libraries are very important to the alMayne; an active part of their ongoing culture. They're saying all over Wailing that Prince Valijon has destroyed an actual Library Archive— Are you all right?" Berathia asked with interest. "I'm sure it was my fault; I'm so clumsy— Father always says I'd be a perfect backup weapon for the Imperial Space Marines. Just send me in and destroy *anybody's* manufacturing capability for up to a dozen kilo-hours . . ."

I looked up at her. Berathia blotted out a good chunk of the sky; like a sunscreen but better looking. I didn't quite remember falling over anything.

"Library?" I said. "Chapter Five illegals?"

Chapter Five is Chapter Five of the Revised Inappropriate Technology Act of the nine-hundred seventy-fifth Year of Imperial Grace. It deals with Old Fed Tech in general and Libraries in particular. Around my neck of space it's known as High Book. Class One is the possession or concealment in fact simple or collusion to possess or conceal—or even just knowledge of the location of any part of if the Office of the Question is feeling nasty—a Library. A Old Fed Library. Old Fed Tech.

And they had so much of it here?

"Chapter Five?" said Berathia blankly. "Oh, the ITA. Don't worry about that, it's perfectly legal. And of course Prince Valijon's done no such thing, but I get most of my information through palace gossip and you know how distorted *that* is. If not for the logotek this trip would almost be a waste, but of course there are always the talkingbook rights."

I'd got up, but I was still staring. Don't worry about the ITA, this *legitimate* glitterbaby says, like the thing I spent half my life running from was something nobody paid no nevermind to anymore.

"alMayne has one of the best research logoteks on Libraries in the Empire," Berathia said. "Oh, I admit it isn't common knowledge—that silly prejudice—but it's all perfectly safe and I have a permit and everything. Say, didn't you travel with Prince Valijon? Can you tell me—"

"You came here to go and find out about *Libraries?*"

"Well, of course!" said Berathia.

Sure, je, reet, j'keyn, don't everybody?

*   *   *

Irrelevant linguistic note: in helltongue the root word for child and outsider—which happens to be *t'chaul*—is the same. When I got back to Baijon's suite, my own pet candidate for both was waiting there for me.

"*Kore,*" he said, "I abase myself."

"Yeah, sure. Who do you know what's named Berathia Notevan, and what's this all same along you 'flowers got a bunch of Libraries in your basement?"

"*Kore?*"

"You know, a anthropologist? Short, dark, and naked?"

Baijon ran a hand through his hair and looked baffled. They'd done him up hellflower-style, and hellflower or no, any experienced bar-fighter could rip him up in six seconds flat, from pretty looped braids and dangly earrings to stompable rings on six out of ten of his best fingers.

Prince of the blood. And young enough to be sure he could beat death, certain easy, now that he was back on his home turf with his kin all around him. Only even his kin was out to get him, and I didn't know why.

"The . . . A *chaudatu* woman?" he finally said. "She is a spy."

It turned out, on sober consideration, that she was a spy along of cause she was going to find out things about the Gentle People (like what they ate for breakfast) and go tell it to somebody. Baijon felt this represented a serious lowering of hellflower social standards.

"In my ten-father's time it would not have been, *Kore.*"

"Je, che-bai, but was she true-telling or no?"

"The Gentle People were born to fight the Machine," Baijon said happily, "and walk in terror and fury of it all our days. We alone of all the people remember it as it was."

"But what about—"

"And so that we are not confounded, each generation Memory walks among us, and Memory abides in the logotek of the War College and schools us in the evasions of the Machine."

One of which Machines, incidentally, Baijon his own self had spent more than twenty days within a few meters of and hadn't twigged to.

But the War College I knew. It'd been pointed out to me on the Grand Tour: sort of a finishing school for hellflowers, and famous enough that even I'd heard of it. Sometimes it even sent experts out to show the Imperial Space Marines what to do on the heavyside, but nothing to do with space war. alMayne aren't pilots.

Not for a thousand years.

I felt something roll over slow in the back of my mind, just waiting to make trouble. There was two things I wanted real bad.

One was to get out of here *now*.

T'other was to gosee what it was hellflowers knew about Libraries that I didn't.

"Baijon," I said. "Is a thing I want to tell you about getting out of here—"

But I didn't get the chance.

* * *

The banquet hall was at the center of Wailing; we went down a lot of steps. No suspicion of a A-grav drop here; most of the systems in Wailing was passive systems, designed to run without power. I even saw torches and candles.

Just like home.

It had not been a good idea to come here, even if it wasn't mine.

The armorer for Starborn had interrupted me getting down to cases with my little buddy Baijon. It seemed Starborn wanted even social embarrassments to look their best.

Baijon said they was doing me honor. In that case, honor meant a lot of stupid clothes.

But that wasn't all it meant. And the rest of what they tricked me out in fit in with my life career plans so well it made me nervous.

There was a Aris-Delameter crossover rig that'd make Destiny's Five Cornered Dog weep. It had two fully-charged blasters rated to punch a hole in a brick starship strapped down nice and functional, and there was a third hideout blaster that the Starborn Armorer practically begged me to take slipped down the top of one boot with a set of throwing daggers in the other. I had a brand new replacement for my old inert throwing-spike down the back of my neck and half the jewelry I was wearing exploded if you pushed the right bit.

I looked like something out of the credit-dreadfuls. But I was in hellflower heaven all right, and everybody else was got up even gaudier.

I pulled Baijon aside as we was about to go in. The room was already full of hellflowers, and I had a hunch I was going to be put somewhere public.

"Look. I ain't got time to be reasonable. I'm getting out of here tonight. You coming with me or not?"

"Tonight? But *Kore,* you cannot mean—"

"Don't you be telling me what I mean, bai, got too much of that already. You coming or no?"

He was young enough to think it was fun. "I am with you," said Baijon Stardust. "I will tell the LadyHolder—"

"You be telling her nothing, bai!" I grabbed his arm. "We do this on the cheat, je? How long is this thing going to go on?"

Baijon looked over his shoulder at the banquet hall.

"Until dawn, *Kore,* but—"

"Oke. I wait one hour. First good time after that, I go out. You give it another half hour, you do a fade without nobody noticing. Meet me at the skyhorses, je?"

"Ea, Comites."

*   *   *

It was not one of my best plans, but it had the virtue of being quick and cheap. Baijon and me went in and got told off our places. For high formal dinners on alMayne you sat on backless benches at a wooden table. Just like I'd thought, I was going to be in plain sight. Well, there was ways around that.

This was actually the alMayne Court, cep'n there weren't no Imperial Legate here. I sat six down from Amrath at the High Table with Baijon standing behind me and could see the whole room. Wall to wall it was full of damn near genetically identical hellflowers.

Except one.

Berathia Notevan was sitting right beside Amrath, being stoically ignored by everyone there but him. The seat on the other side of Amrath had LadyHolder Gruoch's chop on it, and it was empty. Common or hellflower garden sense said it shouldn't be.

There was trouble in hellflowerland.

Local politics, I thought, and nothing to do with me, but anything that bobbles the Azarine Coalition ain't local.

*   *   *

You see, once upon a time there was these mercenaries, five races worth. They had a thing called the Gordinar Canticles, which same forbid them to take the field against Imperial troops, but other than that they was your common or garden play-for-pay kiddies, and anybody in the whole wide Empire with good solid credit could hire them.

This is what's called Azarine Coalition Neutrality. Coalition Neutrality is the basis for our way of life here in the Glorious Phoenix

Empire, and Mallorum Archangel wanted to put an end to it. Not that he wanted the *coalitiani* to give up their way of life—he just wanted to be the only one who could hire them, period.

A private little army for a private little war, and the fact that Archangel was still after the legal transfer of polity in the Coalition did not mean quite as much to me as the fact that Archangel was after *me*—and LadyHolder Gruoch Starbringer, who probably wouldn't recognize Archangel if **he** turned up in her sock drawer, looked like sharing a number of his aims with regard to Yours Truly.

So I ignored the storm warnings in beautiful downtown Wailing in favor of plans for bidding a swift farewell to the land of a thousand sidearms.

Mistake.

6

The Haunted Bookshop

The horizon'd rose and cut off the primary some time before, and the sunscreen blotted out most of the stars. It was pitch-dark as I made my way past Wailing's sentries.

The party had degenerated into serious drinking and the telling of shaggy-*chaudatu* stories. Hellflower neurotoxin will cause damage to your liver that only hellflower fetch-kitchen can repair. Nobody'd noticed much when I left the party after the first round.

The House Starborn logo on my clothes made sure I wasn't challenged by anybody. On their home turf hellflowers is not the galaxy's most suspicious sophonts. At least not of other hellflowers, and it took some time for the news to trickle down that *chaudatu* weren't like real people.

It was bitter cold, and for the first time I was glad I was wearing a purple crushed-velvet surtout trimmed with green vair-fur for my stroll to the vehicle pool. Baijon would be a half-hour or so behind me, and then we could slide, reasonably free of charge, back to the Outport and Trade City.

And I was walking away from the biggest—maybe the only, outside Tech Police HQ—supply of hard information on how to find my buddy Paladin and what was eating my brains out.

Saving my and Baijon's skin was a strong counter-argument all the way to where the airbuses was parked. But after I jimmied one and bypassed the ID transponder, the flight computer, and the ignition—all idiot systems—there was still a good chunk of time before I could expect Baijon.

And the logotek was just sitting there. I could see it from where I stood: a darker patch of sky. Wouldn't be nobody there. Everybody'd be at the banquet, and hellflowers don't lock their doors. If there was anything I couldn't read I could take it with and have Baijon read it to me later.

I'd *need* to know this stuff.

Baijon'd wait for me. And wasn't nobody expecting us to do this in the first place so they wouldn't be looking.

I had the margin.

I thought.

*   *   *

A logotek is where you keep all the words nobody's figured out how to make into books yet. The War College logotek specialized in Old Fed Tech, and to hellflowers that means just one thing.

Libraries.

There was watchlights in wall-niches every few feet oncet I got inside—just fire and fat and string in a glass cup.

I hated them. They were cold and dead. They did not take energy from the Net. They did not give energy to the Net. They were cut off.

I took a deep breath and reminded myself I'd been born in a sod hut with a dirt floor, where you used animals to drag a piece of tree through the ground so you could stick seeds and roots into it to grow dinner for later.

A place that Libraries wouldn't like, because without computer dataports and tronic interfaces there was nothing for them to see or touch.

A place like alMayne was, even though it was an Open World with Imperial trade, because hellflowers was expecting Libraries to come to tea any minute and they didn't want them to feel too welcome.

Paladin'd always complained about the low-tech in the Outfar, but I'd just thought he was putting on airs. But all his information about the world had come from artificial senses, and those took hands to build and energy to run. Without them he was blind, deaf, dumb, halt, and imbecile.

Any Library was.

But I wasn't a Library, I reminded myself. I wondered how hard it was going to get to remember that, and if I'd even care when I forgot.

But I knew that trick too, and thinking about it doesn't change anything. The only cure is bidness.

*   *   *

I took one of the watchlights with me when I went downstairs. I passed a lot of signs that said the hellflower equivalent of "go away" and then a lot more explaining how insanity and mange would result from going one step more.

Then I was in.

It wasn't a big room, but it was still wider than it was tall. The walls had glow-strips in them, with a little plaque by one saying they was certified Old Federation construction. There was display cases around the walls.

What could I take that would do me any good?

I went up to the first case. It held pieces of Libraries, dead, and with everything they'd ever known gone.

If I forgot everything I knew I'd be dead, sure and simple. There might be something breathing, but it wouldn't be me, Butterflies-are-free Peace Sincere.

Wouldn't that be the same if the whole Empire forgot everything? They'd already forgot so much. What if they forgot more—or decided to just chuck it all? What would be left?

Death on such a scale it made me go weak in the knees to think about it—and nothing I could do to get in the way.

Nothing.

My hands shook like Archangel was right behind me, waiting to scoop the lot. I passed dioramas about places that was just points outside the Empire's borders on a better-than-average star-map these days. Places that was cinders and gas and had been a thousand years and more.

Places I remembered. Orilice. Miramolin. The Drift. Harakim-Selice. Places where Libraries had taken over people somehow, and got them to let them in, and—

No. I had made a life career of not thinking about things, and I was going to put it to good use.

I passed a bunch of displays of weapons proof against Libraries, of catch-traps to load into your computer system to burke them, of sure-fire ways to spot a Librarian. If I didn't find something useful in the next five seconds, I was giving up. I already knew more useless stuff than I wanted.

That was when I found The Book. It was new manufacture—a

flatcopy thing with pieces and pages like there wasn't much use for any more—and when I opened it it was written in something I'd never seen before. Not Intersign, not Interglyph, not Imperial Standard, helltongue, or even Old Federation Script.

The only thing was, I could read it.

Not like I was reading a page of Intersign. More like a talkingbook; I looked at the page and I could hear it in my head.

The first page said "A True History of the War." I skipped through, glancing at the pages, but it made me dizzy. Something about the Main Library Complex at Sikander.

I put it under my arm and left.

*   *   *

You could see a few stars through the sunscreen; I knew by the way they'd shifted I'd been down under the there longer than I'd thought. It was a good fifteen minutes past the time Baijon was supposed to meet me, but he knew to go to the airbuses and *wait.* He'd be there, or have left Sign that he'd been.

I got about six meters from the logotek when I realized trouble was up. I made it back to the inside of the logotek and to the first halfway oke place to hide The Book.

I didn't want to do it. I wanted to know what it knew. Knowledge must never be lost.

But by that glass slipstick, all what I knew should be kept around whiles longer, too. I hid The Book in a looked-like pile of other books and slid back out of the logotek.

This time I saw for true what I'd only intuited before. There was torchlights moving, which meant people was looking. And with a well-developed sense of peril-noia, I knew the only one they could be looking for was me.

Dry cold air rasped my throat as I jogged back to the airbus. There was nobody in sight and nobody around, and there hadn't been either. Baijon'd never got here.

Where was he?

I'd told him to be here. Baijon would willingly miss out on doing his *devoir* about the time he signed up to be a Space Angel.

I could run now. I might even have time enough to leg back for The Book first.

It was sort of comforting to know flat-out I wasn't going to do it.

*   *   *

But that didn't mean I was going to just walk back and lie down for the chop. I did my personal best to avoid everybody as was out looking for somebody, and finally came to a chunk of wall I recognized.

Baijon's room was dark but there was someone in it breathing. I stuck both feet through loops of vine and raised my head up over the sill slowly. I saw the faint flicker of a personal shield.

"You maybe want be keeping quiet, jilly-bai," I said.

"For heaven's sake, get in here before someone sees you," said Berathia Notevan.

*   *   *

"I hoped you'd come back here—you weren't seen, were you?"

The room was dark and empty. Someone else'd been through and found Baijon's talkingbooks and left them out in plain sight.

"Where's Baijon?"

"He's going to be all right," Berathia said, and if it hadn't been for her shield I'd of grabbed and throttled her.

"You tell me how he's going to be all right."

"Look, that isn't important right now. The alMayne have a unique racial psychology. I'm afraid that Lord Starbringer accidentally made things rather difficult for you by allowing Prince Valijon to enter a state of *comites* with you. The LadyHolder is deeply offended, and—"

I got out a blaster and looked at it.

"You be telling me where Baijon is, 'Thia, or I fire this."

She twitched. A personal shield is just like what you wrap around the short-term controlled fusion reaction of a blaster-bolt, except it's bigger and it stays around longer. It's no particular use against a blaster, neither, because the first bolt overloads it and the second one cooks what's wearing it. Sometimes the overload is big enough to do a straight conversion to kinetic potential. Boom.

"Prince Valijon made the mistake of calling the Imperial Governor-General a Librarian," Berathia snapped. "They've locked him up until he can be cured. Now they're looking for you to find out what drove him mad."

Hellflower logic: The *comites* is responsible for every action by his *servites*. *Every* action. Fine.

Only I'd made two minor miscalculations tonight.

I'd thought Baijon wouldn't make a after-dinner speech titled What I Did While On The Lam With The *Kore-Alarthme*.

And I'd thought any pack of hellflowers would just naturally believe him when he got up on his hind legs and hollered Librarian.

But he had. And they hadn't.

On the other hand, Gruoch (who'd showed up just in time for all this) wasn't willing to call him a liar. She decided he'd been tainted by the Machine (the same one she'd just refused to believe in, mind).

"He isn't crazy," I said.

Berathia actually stamped her foot. "That doesn't *matter*, I told you! To the alMayne, one of you must be—and they have only one way of finding out which. They'll purify both of you, and then ask both of you again—but *you're* not going to be alive to answer."

I would not put it past a hellflower to ask me anyway and be meeved when I didn't answer him.

"You've got to come away with me *now*," Berathia said again. "I have transport hidden at the edge of the plateau. They aren't used to interfering with children. You can—"

Someone was coming. I knew it because I knew it was *time* for someone to come and try rousting Baijon's crib on the chance something interesting might be to home.

"Look. It's a cute idea but it ain't going to work. For the record, I guarantee Archangel's doing High Book. Now get out of here or they'll have you, too."

Berathia started to argue when a little light on her belt blipped.

"I'll be back," she said, and went over the windowsill.

Anthropology must be interesting work.

* * * * *

Valijon's Diary

The Loremasters teach us that the universe is a whole, and that being in all one thing, it can be studied from any beginning. To measure a circle, begin anywhere.

So it is true that what the beast-men do on their faraway thrones is visible within the House of Walls—though only philosophically so. One does not expect to see what the *chaudatu* do affecting the Gentle People. Space is too vast, or so I once thought.

Perhaps my eyes are opened even as my soul is shadowed—or perhaps the clatter of their tongueless souls becomes great enough to reach us within the walls of our first and last defense.

That the Phoenix Empire is corruption itself the Gentle People have always known. It could not be otherwise, governed by beasts. The Loremasters teach us that the simplest solution—to ourselves govern the Empire and make it a sure citadel against the *Malmakos* and its wiles—is folly. They say it is the Gentle People who would be destroyed, and so long ago the First-to-Seize chose that the alMayne would not seek the throne for its blood. For us and for all time he chose not to compromise with beasts.

In kingship there is always compromise. Between People it is safe and honorable. Between a Person and a beast it is suicide.

Many generations have praised the name of Lodir Starholder First-to-Seize and the hard path he chose for us. Thus we kept ourselves ready, so I was taught.

But now I do not see it so. The Libraries rise up again and we are not ready. Somehow our separatism has lost instead of saved us. We only pretend to honor while being as corrupt as the Phoenix Court.

The *Kore* said that I must go away with her this night, and so I promised, even though tomorrow the *Shaulla* Ketreis becomes a Person and might, in honor, choose to accompany us. But possibly it is better to go now, so that we may return, triumphant, when Archangel is slain as the *Kore* and my father plan between them.

So I thought, and so I promised as I was bid—they are *chaudatu* words, but the *Kore* knows no better. But equally I could not depart from among the People without alerting them to their peril: the Machine is awake and among us, and Mallorum Archangel takes up the cursed mantle of Librarian. My father knew this. My father bade me speak, and warn the Gentle People of the betrayal by this Emperor who forces our fealty.

And I gained nothing.

Before I was born it was known that, did luck not favor me, I must risk my shadow against the curious customs of the *chaudatu*. My father saw to it that I was instructed in history: the getting and holding and losing of dominion.

Now my father's aid has been turned against me. The LadyHolder spoke in all honor of the madness that festers in the abodes of the Tongueless Ones, of how things may seem to be but are not. She spoke of unwisdom in binding a servant of the Gentle People to one of whom no one may know the virture of her words, and how the *chaudatu* are as cunning as the *Malmakos*.

And when she was done, no one would listen to me. More, she swore that they *would* listen, once I was purified and fit to be among them once more.

I told her that she spoke as Alaric Dragonflame had spoken, when he promised me the safety of his Knife and Walls and set instead the Wolves-Without-Honor to seek my life. And so I am bound, and they seek the *Kore* also, to prove her.

But she will have fled. I may, in honor, hope for this. Gruoch will not hear of the Machine—she will render the *Kore* tongueless forever lest she speak of it.

How could we fall so low, knowing our danger? Just as the human body weakens and dies, so do kingdoms and thrones. It was true also among the *chaudatu:* mad they may be, and tongueless, but they age and die and their political systems also. Long peace breeds decadence and rot.

But we *knew* this! Never did one GreatHouse hold power long: each was free to demand what service it would, if only the Pact against the Machine were kept.

Now it is not kept. No one of the Gentle People is free to disregard the claim I made, to swaddle it in *chaudatu* words until its truth is murdered. If I am wrong, let me die rather than bear the living shame— but test my words, not my body!

Gruoch will not. And thus all is over.

I have studied history. I know the marks of decadence and decay. They are ours, and we are dying: the People have been too long kept from the whetstone of battle, and have decayed.

Could my father have not known this? Or did he see only what he wished to see, and hoped for goodness in what he could not change?

Or did he send me to awaken the Gentle People once more?

On Mikasa he told me of the binding he weaves for Archangel; strand by strand and year by year, preparing his trap with the very *chaudatu* Archangel seeks to rule. My father prepares the battlefield against the day of battle when the Gentle People will be called to stand in judgment.

But when they are called, will they come?

I do not think so. I think they no longer wish to hear. The threat of our ancient enemy was brought forth, and no battle was offered, only lies. GreatHouse Starborn will fall for this cowardice, and not alone. I do not think this time that the Empire will let us be. Our ways are too alien. Our intolerance of the Machine which they court dooms us in spirit or flesh.

If the *Malmakos* is to rule Man once more, the Gentle People must be broken to smooth its path. In a time that our walls should have been seamless, we have opened our gates to its hounds.

We have become the instrument of Imperial Peace. We have become the promise of war.

*   *   *   *   *

In a sweet gesture of unanimity with a Empire they can't see for dust, alMayne honored guest quarters for people they'd rather shoot is cold, drafty, locked, and surrounded by hostile irritated people—who was also crazy, because when they'd unilaterally decided I'd rather be here than in Baijon's old rooms they'd left me everything I was standing up in.

But even with three blasters, four throwing knives, a vibro and six kinds of grenade I wasn't ready to stage one of my patented usually successful escapes. Not without more information than I had or looked like getting.

Gruoch didn't like me; I knew that already. But (if I could believe Berathia) she hadn't believed Baijon when he'd pushed every hellflower's favorite button, and that was a little harder to figure.

I realized then I was actually trusting Kennor, who'd said, back on dear old Mikasa, that on alMayne the word of an Honored One would be believed. Well it hadn't been, and that left me two and a half choices.

He was wrong.

He was lying.

Or all three of us'd been set up.

Just what *had* Archangel offered Winterfire to go bent, anyway?

*   *   *

alMayne either doesn't have a moon or it stayed home that night. No stars through the shield from this direction, but a couple rainbow reflies—Wailing must be right on the approach route to the Outport.

I found out that the open window was a sheer drop and the door a) was guarded by people not interested in polite conversation and b) didn't open from the inside. About the only thing I could do was kill myself, and I didn't think that'd help Baijon's chances of being tried and found human. I even tried pushing for that weirdness living inside my head, but it was on vacation, too.

So here I was in the beautiful open-air dungeons of Castle Wailing, having done all the right things for the wrong reasons and still preparing to become an Official Dead Person sometime in the near future.

I decided I'd been wrong about Kennor. Kennor wasn't out to kill us (probably). Kennor didn't need to set up advanced plots to kill Baijon and me. All he had to do was send us back to alMayne.

Sometimes I'm too subtle for my own good.

And while I was being subtle, I bet I knew what Archangel'd offered Winterfire.

Hellflowers is xenophobes, and I know from xenophobes: my Luddite ancestors didn't like everybody else so much they climbed down a gravity well and threw away the key. But holograms can be regenerated from a single piece and so can cultures. Even Interdicted, the Population of Granola generated a few xenophiles each generation—enough to keep the Patriarchate in kindling.

But hellflowers wasn't Interdicted. And so there was an even better system in use here, to make sure the hellflower you sent out among the hellgods was the same one you got back. Baijon'd walked right into it. They was going to prove him until he fit right in with the rest of the hellflower rootstock or died trying. And I got to go along for the ride.

And how many hellflowers was tired of this little arrangement and wanted to close the doors on the Federated Imperial Galactic Union of Tongueless Doorstops, *Chaudatu,* and Social Cripples?

The Governor-General could get them Interdicted status. He could waive the escrow account and the filing fees. He could even seal them up and let them stay right where they was.

If he was real nice, he'd let them keep the batteries for their sunscreens, and I bet the conservative faction on jolly old Washonnet 357-II'd never thought about *that.*

I wished, all sudden-like, to know what relation Winterfire and Blackhammer was to LadyHolder Gruoch, and if they'd ever all sat around the Court of Honor drinking tea and talking about what little umpleasantnesses stood between them and Closed World status. Ketreis'd even mentioned it and I'd been too stupid to notice. "The WarMother is going to get rid of all the *chaudatu* for eke and aye," she'd said. How else could Gruoch do it but by getting alMayne Interdicted—and in a way that didn't put the question to an open vote.

Ice Baijon. Kennor stops being President of the Coalition. Morido Dragonflame—who might or might not be on the Interdict Party's side —steps up into the Presidency and allows the revision of the Canticles that makes the Coalition into Archangel's private army, with or without hellflowers. Archangel conquers the universe.

I wished that was all. Archangel could have the universe for all of me; I wasn't using it. But what he was going to do with it was fill it with brain-eating evil Libraries—and the Empire's guardians of truth, justice, and the organic way was stupid enough to let him do it as long as he promised them a planet of their very own.

Kennor couldn't know this. His son was betrothed to Gruoch's daughter, for Night's sake. And because he hadn't known, Baijon's and my run for freedom was going to be real short.

It was not much in the way of consolation to know I'd beat the odds by about twenty Galactic Standard Years of survival, or that Baijon getting the chop this way would leave Kennor whole and frisky in the astropolitical arena to fight Coalition neutrality to the last redoubt.

I'd promised I'd keep Baijon alive.

And if we both died, who was going to stop Archangel's war?

*   *   *

The horizon slid round and the primary changed relative position and nobody brought me breakfast. Around the time I managed to get myself thoroughly depressed and nobody brought me dinner the door opened, and a Very Large Person walked in and took what passed for my mind right off politics.

The alMayne (says Paladin) came here from somewheres else just after the Library War. They bought the Washonnet system (which did not have anymuch of a thing in it worth having at the time) and planetoformed its likeliest-looking planet, which they call *Home* and everyone else calls *alMayne*.

Whoever'd started the place did it with a gene-pool smaller than a Interdicted Colony's—hellflowers all look like each other's sister and is *hard* to tell apart.

Paladin says that along one time you could find just about every variation in genotype there was all together on the same planet. But even he couldn't remember just when that was and it sounds damsilly to me. Genetic drift'll get them every time.

NB: a lot of dicty-colonies fail because they don't have enough people to burke a run of bad luck. But they've paid hard credit for nobody to go in and help them, so when they all die the Empire sells the world again. Economical.

So all hellflowers is long and whippity and don't even bother to register hair and eye color on their ID, right?

Wrong.

The 'flower that came in to my box with locks was two meters and a bit and he could of made three or maybe six of Baijon. His eyes was gray—almost white—and the pupils looked like negative stars in a continuum I didn't want to visit.

He was carrying The Book I'd filched from the logotek.

"I am the WarDoctor Firesong of no House. Memory has heard that the *Malmakos* has returned." His voice went with the rest of him. I wondered which of my fingers he was going to break first, and I couldn't even tell for sure if he was mad.

"Je; pleased to see you, too. Where's Ba—*Val-i-jon*Starbringer," I said, pronouncing it real careful so there couldn't be any adorable confusion over who I meant.

"Valijon is preparing himself. Tomorrow his personhood is to be tested. I have come to speak to you of yours."

I didn't want to stare at The Book he had in his hands but I couldn't help it.

"Purifying himself. And what exactly does that mean when it's t'home?" I wanted to blast him but I needed information, and The Wall That Walked was the closest thing to a DataNet Terminal in sight.

"You are worthy in my brother Kennor's eyes, but you are an outlander, and soft. Valijon Starbringer has said words, but the Gentle People do not yet know if his shadow is his own. Valijon must be pure to fight the Machine. If it has touched him, I must know."

Reality took a half-spin and I thought about a hundred things— allergies to the local food, poison in the drink. It was like trying to use somebody else's mind to think with, or tripping over a catch-trap somebody'd loaded into your navicomp. I'd been drugged, one time and another. It felt like this.

Pure to fight the Machine. I was thinking, but they wasn't my thoughts. The Machine—

Human personality is a lot more derangeable than the folks back home might think. On Granola, the only way to change a body that much was to kill him. I got out into the Empire and found out the question wasn't *whether* but *how much?*

Persona-peel. Memory-edit. Dreamlegging. And a whole hellhouse fetch-kitchen that can make you forget who you are, or who you were, or just what you did last week.

Or remember something you never did.

Organics, Paladin says, are the sum total of their experiences. Maybe they're more too, but if you take away a experience, you change a person.

And if you add one?

I remembered a world where organic life was the enemy. Spiteful, unreasonable, and ignorant, they had nearly managed to destroy what was destined to succeed them. If I had been human, I would have had a sacred trust. But I wasn't. So I had a job.

And I wouldn't stop trying to do it until I was destroyed.

Archive wouldn't stop trying to do it until Archive was destroyed. Maybe not even then.

If I remembered what Archive remembered, was I still me? Because I did remember what Archive did, and I really wanted to know. . . .

I clamped down and stopped remembering all those things I didn't have the right to know. The cell stopped looking like part of a place I'd go a long way to nuke.

"No Machine touched Baijon. It didn't. I was there. I know. It didn't touch him, you— Look. There is not no *noke'ma-ashki* Machine nowhere for to touch anybody. I killed it, je? I blew it up—Baijon wasn't even nigh it more'n a minute fifty!"

"And before it died?"

I stared at him, and all I could think was: *he knows.*

But he didn't know, not anything at all. I'd be dead if he did. And he didn't even suspect me. He thought it might be Baijon with Archive looking out from behind his hellflower-blue eyes.

Just like it said in The Book.

Because that was what a Librarian really was—used to be, a long time ago before most of me'd been born. Someone what could talk direct to a Library, without voders and terminals and uplinks.

And one particular human race had been bred to it.

"No," I said.

And was going to spend the rest of forever paying back for that error in judgment.

"Yet you know my fears before I speak them. And so I ask you, *Alarthme*—if there is any chance that I am right, dare I chance that I am wrong?"

No. Yes. I'd been willing to kill Paladin to stop Archive. Dammit, why couldn't he go pick on somebody else?

"There is not no Library now. I blew it up. It did not eat Baijon's brain before it went to plasma. I was there. Didn't want to come here, don't want to be here, only came here along of Kennor made me promises which is not getting themselves kept. Baijon done told you who be the Librarian and not even needs his neurons bent to do it. It's Mallorum Archangel, je? Same kiddy what twisted House Dragonflame pere et filldirt and Prettybird *Kore* Winterfire to ice Baijon."

"*Alarthme,* do you swear this is so?"

"Bai, why bother? You just going to say *chaudatu* is tongueless doorstops and not listen."

"Then why did you take this book from the logo-otek?"

I'd almost forgot it, pitching my version of reality to the local memory.

He bared his teeth, in the getting-ready-for-dinner hellflower expression that it's stupid to mistake for a smile.

"It was not where it was left. Trackers followed your footsteps there and elsewhere. Some things do not require Imperial technology to understand. Now you will explain."

We had reached finger-breaking time, and all because I'd been dumb enough to walk back in here instead of doing a beat-feet for the Big Empty with Berathia Notevan when I had the chance.

But then I would of had to leave Baijon. And I didn't want to be the kind of person that did things like that.

So I smiled right back at The Wall That Walks.

"Going for to shop me a Library, bai. Need for to know what you know along of how they work. Archangel lost his last one—think he's stopping there?"

"And could you not ask?"

I laughed at him; I couldn't not. "And just which hellflower you want me to trust, bai—the ones out to ice me or the ones after Baijon?"

He was wearing a translator, I realized of a sudden, and not trusting to how well he savvied the lingua franca of deep trouble. I guess the stakes was too high for that.

"Then there is no blame, *Kore,* and your courage does you credit. There is nothing you need fear. Your word will be taken, and the People will be forged as a sword against the Machine."

*   *   *

I hadn't been here long enough to have any kind of feel for the spin alMayne had on its heavyside, but about two hours after every light I could see from my windows was gone somebody came to the door.

Never mind what The Wall said. Leaving was still high on my list of fun things to do in scenic Wailing. The only plan I currently had involved shooting whoever came for me, finding Baijon, and running like hell. I slid my blaster out just as slow as the door opened.

But it weren't nobody but my Imperial cupcake carrying a native handicrafts basket. I put my heat away, wondering if shooting her'd buy me anything at all I wanted.

"I brought you something to eat. I— That is, WarDoctor Firesong told me. I know it's hard to understand, but they are doing you great honor."

Great honor is usually uncomfortable, inconvenient, and expensive.

She set the basket down and I looked in. Everything was in Quaint Folkways packaging, but I found something that looked familiar and bit into it.

"Maybe you'd like to start from the beginning?" I said.

So she did. Only a life of training in putting the important things first kept me eating.

ITEM: after our spiffy chat tonight The Wall went to Gruoch with what he thought was a neat solution to all her troubles. They would finish purifying Baijon, adopt me, purify me (painless but tedious both, Berathia said), and then get our signed deposition about what we did on our summer vacation. Then Starborn could knock off those members of Dragonflame who had not already commented on recent events with flashy suicides and go on to a) declare seven-ring vendetta against Mallorum Archangel and b) instruct the Delegate from alMayne, Kennor Starbringer, to bring a formal request from alMayne to the Office of the Question for a High Book investigation of Archangel his Nobly-Born self. Yell for it loud enough, and it'd ruin Archangel socially if it did nothing else.

That was where things stood at dinner.

Around bedtime Gruoch suggests it will look bad if House Starbringer is seen promiscuously offering its shadow about the place. Personhood, says Gruoch, ought to be harder to come by for your friendly neighborhood tongueless doorstop.

She comes up with a compromise and rams it down The Wall's throat—a little hellflower charmer called The Combat of the Nine Cuts.

"Amrath and Daufin can't stop her. She's well within her rights as LadyHolder of Wailing to insist on doing it this way, but The Combat of the Nine Cuts hasn't been invoked for centuries, and—" Berathia stopped, giving me time to reflect that if there's anything I hate more than getting killed it's getting killed in a stupid ritual with a funny name.

It didn't take much prodding to get the details out of her: tomorrow The Wall and me was going to walk out onto the Floor of Honor, the local Starborn frisky business arena, stark naked and with one knife each ready to fight to the death. His intention was going to be (Berathia said) to pitch me nine licks in a by-the-book pattern and not mark me up any other way. I was supposed to put up as much of a fight as I knew how against something I in blissful theory wanted. Hellflowers ain't much on passive resistance.

If I killed him before he finished (fat chance) the result was the same: Personhood for little Butterfly. Only there wasn't much way I was going to beat out The Wall, and after he'd carved me like he meant to, all my insides was going to be outsides. Even hellflowers didn't do a real good job of surviving the Whosis of the Nine Whasis, which's why they'd come up with less messy forms of adoption.

I had to hand it to Gruoch. Once she got her way she accomplished three important things.

I'm dead.

Baijon's dead.

And there's nobody to drop the whistle on Archangel.

And I bet Gruoch didn't have any inkling of the last things. She probably thought Baijon-bai just had a few *chaudatu* toys in the attic: purify him, zetz that inconvenient *comites,* and bygones would be Baijon.

"I spoke to Doctor Firesong. He is sorry that you are going to die, but the way he thinks of it, that's just an unfortunate by-product of proving that you're human. From his point of view, it would be far worse to deny you the chance to be human than to kill you tomorrow."

Berathia looked at me with big soulful dark eyes, and I remembered Kennor saying how they paid off the *chaudatu* with money because they had no souls but me he had a special deal for. Another fine and fancy line of country sweet-talk and as half-true as everything else he ever said. For hellflowers honor might be more important than life, but I've always preferred uncertainty and breathing.

"You have to understand how they think," she said. "It is a great honor."

"And what about Baijon?"

Berathia blinked. "Nothing will—oh, his honor. You don't have to worry—they're *honoring* you. Nothing will happen to Valijon."

Which might even be what Gruoch thought too, but I bet I knew my bouncing babby hellflower better than she did. Baijon was going to take this personally. And if he didn't get himself iced declaring vendetta on his own shadow, he was for sure going to be sitting here when Archangel noticed who was yelling Library and did something about it.

"Je. I be real understanding the whole time they's cutting me up alive. A great honor and I be dead."

"I know," Berathia said, staring at the floor. "I've come to get you out."

She said it so casual I didn't quite hear it at first.

"Out? To Baijon?"

"Don't you want to live to see tomorrow's sunrise? Prince Valijon is in the logotek. He's in private vigil—no one may approach him. My transport is still hidden at the edge of the plateau; there are ships at the Outport—"

"And what happens to Baijon I just up and kyte?"

"If you . . . ?"

"Kyte—ankle, leave, take the High Jump, be nonfiction, vanish, disappear, *go away.*"

For once Berathia didn't have anything to say.

"What happens to Baijon?" I said around a mouthful of meat-pie. There was a bottle of the local vintage of hair-raiser in there too, and I put it aside for later. I didn't see how having it could farce the good numbers one way or t'other in the morning.

"Your . . . *comites* will be all right. Purification is serious, but it isn't dangerous—he'll probably be called upon to perform some distasteful ritual task. If you just disappear . . ."

Maybe they wouldn't kill him, but Archangel would.

"Didn't you hear me? You can escape. I'll go with you, and—"

And our little girl was awfully anxious to go zip-squealing off into the never-never with Yours Truly, putting a serious kink in her amateur standing wherever hellflowers is sold.

I didn't like it. It was the next best thing to the only way out, and I didn't like it.

So much for my theory of being half Library. *They* have a sense of self-preservation.

But I still had to settle with Berathia.

"Oke. I'm convinced. You want to rescue me and save my life?"

Berathia stood up and started for the door.

"Ne, glitter-bai. Simpler than that. Give me your shield."

*   *   *

It was the usual sort; a string of silvery beads about the size of my thumb spaced out along a length of cord, most of it charge to keep the field going and at that you had to change the power-pacs once a day.

Most people wore their shields around their waist or neck but you didn't have to. To work, a shield just needed to be touching you somewhere; they're designed to key up to your biological electrical grid. You could wear it as a bracelet, or a set of rings, or a hair-comb.

Or you didn't have to *wear* it at all.

Berathia hadn't been too keen on forking it over, but after the lovely line of fantasy she'd handed me about queering her anthro-whatsis by helping me escape she couldn't exactly refuse to do it my way. And for my part, I didn't trust her enough to go walking out of a hellflower cell with her.

It wasn't anything personal. I didn't trust anybody. I'd trusted Paladin oncet, and look where it'd got me. Safer without him, Paladin'd said. Why are people such jerks?

But since I wasn't leaving with her, the only other way out was across the Floor of Honor. And given my druthers, I'd rather do that alive.

Hence the shield.

When I took all the flashcandy off 'Thia's personal shield belt I had a string about a meter long with a generator at both ends and six power-pacs in the middle. The generators was big, but manageable. They'd have to be.

There's this little-known fact of the universe about personal shields, which is if you've got time and too much idle curiosity for your own good, you can actually tune the field to generate itself just beneath the surface of your skin. Miscalculate a silly little millimeter or two and you're dead, of course, because nothing goes through a shield but selected air molecules. Think about it.

Wear it that way long enough and you starve to death, maybe, but I didn't have to. I just had to wear it long enough to cheat my *chaudatu* way through one alMayne trial by combat and screw up their legal system beyond reproach. I got out my inert-blade and a handful of the jewelry I was wearing and got to work.

When I was done the sky was just starting to go light and I hadn't touched the hellflower neurotoxins after all. I held the shield in my hand and turned it on. My teeth and tongue went all fuzzy with the load. I flexed my cyber-hand and was glad to see it still twitched. If the shield farced it someone'd be sure to notice.

I pressed the knife against my real wrist. It sank in a fingernail's-worth and met shield. Perfect.

And I knew for damn sure they wouldn't let me carry it into their arena even if I swore I only carried it for sentimental reasons.

So I swallowed it.

And providing the power-pac didn't fail between now and then I could go on to Step Two of the plan I hadn't come up with yet.

*	*	*

Full morning dawned bright, shiny, and annoying. The primary was a good distance above the horizon when the hellflower guard of honor came after me, and even then it was just to take me down the way to the bathhouse where I was scrubbed, shaved, oiled, and offered something to drink that I decided not to bother with, thank you all the same. The attendants was placing bets on how long I'd survive.

I wished I had some way to cover that action, but even if I did, how could I collect?

Then they took me where The Wall was.

And I was in trouble.

He was furred and jeweled and trussed up in finest hellflower drag until he looked like an explosion in a joyhouse rummage sale.

He did not look like somebody who was going to be after Butterfly St. Cyr's chitlins on the Floor of Honor in just a few minutes.

And that meant somebody else would be.

I hoped it was Gruoch.

But I didn't get a clue from The Wall. He stood in front of a little door that led to the killing ground, and in front of him on a table there was a tray of knives.

"*She* has said that you will choose that which you shall bear. You will choose, and you will pass through the gate, and you will become a Person."

I looked down.

They was from every level of technology the eye could see: The handle of a vibro-blade, just waiting to be switched on. A fixed-crystal assassin's blade from Cadia, unbreakable, deadly sharp, and with the poison reservoir. A filament whip; a blade only by courtesy, but a cutting weapon.

And in amongst them all, a *arthame*.

It didn't look like Baijon's. I've seen his close up: the handle's bone (alMayne bone, but never mind) and carved all over with little tiny scritchy helltongue glyphs, and the butt-end's set with a chunk of black rock.

The blade's pure iron. You melt rocks to get that stuff, you know.

This one didn't have any rocks or runes, just a long gray blade with a little curve on it, too long to be any practical use, and a long straight shank of bone—thighbone, probably, from some noble Starborn ancestor if they was feeling generous.

"You will choose," said The Wall.

Well, hell, I been in this elevator before. I was about to go out there and play duel in the sun with some hellflower and for sure if I wanted to live to grow older I'd pick the vibro or the filament whip, something with some range and power to it. And if I did, I bet sure as back taxes it'd lift some kind of obligation off them and let them cheat.

It didn't matter what I picked, when you came down to it.

So I picked up the unfinished *arthame* out of the box of tricks and bared my teeth at The Wall in the dictybarb expression that is *not* a smile.

* * *

The Floor of Honor was white sand, just like all the other arenas I ever seen. Better against the blood, you know—just sift it and play again.

The walls went up higher than I could jump and above them was seats. In about a quarter of the seats was hellflowers. I didn't see Baijon.

Nobody else was down where I was yet. Gruoch was sitting right above the door my little playmate was due to come through. Amrath King of alMayne was nowhere in sight.

Just how stable *was* the politics on Scenic alMayne, keystone of the Coalition?

I looked around for Berathia and found her. Her spare shield shimmered. I waited for whatever was coming through that door.

They had to slice me and I had to survive it. Fine. And then it was no more Citizen Nice Dicty. Paladin says you should try everything at least oncet to see what works. Now I'd tried being legal and could write it off my list of things to do on rainy days.

The other door opened and a hellflower stepped through.

It was Baijon.

7

Living on the Edge
of the Blade

Gruoch's herald stood up and choodled a long screed in formal al-Mayne—which is just like street helltongue but damnall technical, so's you always know what they're saying but not what it means. *"Today the type-unspecified female will be placed in a situation where environmental factors will aid observers in determining her classification, in conjunction with etcetera-and-tedious-so-forth."*

I looked at Baijon. He was stark, oiled, and carrying his Knife. His hair was skinned back and braided. He hadn't expected to see me.

Berathia had said: some distasteful task. Do it and he was home free. But it was The Wall supposed to do me whiles Baijon just had to take out the garbage forever.

Gruoch could of changed that. With everybody trying to get their hands on the hellflowers and the Coalition hotseat, I bet Kennor'd never oncet thought about all the people that never smiled during Imperial Be Kind to *Chaudatus* Week and'd be just as glad for alMayne to be *out* of the Coalition entirely.

Stupid cow.

Gruoch's herald finished explaining to everybody what most of them knew already and sat down. The only one, seemingly, as found this a lovely shock was Baijon. He backed up. Gruoch'd caught him square between a rock and a hellflower hardplace: duty to his *comites* and duty to his kinfolk. The kind of blithering romance that Thrilling Wonder Talkingbooks likes to run.

"Yo, Baijon-bai, how's tricks?" I said, keeping my voice low.

He raised his Knife and lowered it, and in just about a minute sure he was going to give Gruoch a double helping of braincells and get himself iced.

"C'mere, stupid."

He stepped away from the door and into chaffering distance. He looked worse than I felt.

"Once again I am betrayed: is the honor of the Gentle People only in their mouths? I swear it will not be so, *Kore;* there is redress—"

"Before you go doing something off your own bat just to be interesting, you try to remember who's sworn to who around here."

He looked at me and I swear it was hope: that there was some way out of this that he hadn't seen and I had, and I made up my mind then there was gonna be.

The peanut gallery was getting restless; they wanted to see the pony dance.

"You supposed to cut me up along of hellflower nonsense. So do it. Then we kyte when they ain't expecting."

"Never."

He looked up where Gruoch was frowning down and hefted his Knife. I caught his wrist with the hand that wouldn't bleed. I hoped nobody was going to mind.

"Baijon. We got to do this. So you cut me now like they said and don't jump salty. Just do it."

"Your name will be sung forever," Baijon said. I took a breath to have another go at convincing him and he took a swipe at me.

I am not never again going to do anything sensible or reasonable. Every time I do I wind up someplace like this letting somebody prospect for my chitlins. When I do it my way at least I'm running too fast to hit.

"I name the LadyHolder Gruoch a thief and a liar, an eater of corpses!" Baijon shouted. But he did what I'd told him.

The first of the Nine Cuts runs from the hollow of the throat all the way down. He wasn't quite close enough to dig in but I was glad I had the shield all the same. He saw his Knife not make the cut he expected, and he smiled.

alMayne house rules included kicking, punching, and stomping. The shield saved me from some of it. I even got in a lucky foot and thought for a second I was going to ring Baijon's bell and buy me a

whole new set of problems, but hellflowers is stubborn. I hit the opposite wall and if the shield hadn't referred the knock all over my corpus
delicti that would of been the end of Butterfly St. Cyr's interest in the
proceedings, you betcha.

Second and third cuts, under the ribs and down. He got a good
hold on me this time and dug in. In some places the shield was farther
under my skin than others, but he still didn't punch through like he was
expecting.

He rocked back and flung up his head and howled in pure triumph
—and came after me again.

Either Baijon was a brainburn or he knew something was up by
now. And whatever he knew or thought he knew, he was backing my
play with it.

The fourth cut joins the first three to make a triangle cut in half.
Coming back for more and staying alive while I did it wasn't any harder
than walking into a black gang full of sour goforths and taking double a
redline dose of rads to tune them up again. Twenty-seven hours to the
nearest fetch-kitchen, and me and Paladin trying every antique prophy-
lactic we had on board while my hair and teeth and fingernails fell out. I
lived, and along of later I did it again.

I did this now.

Fifth cut, crossing the midline. Cross and triangle now. I demon-
strated to the stands that the *arthame* is not a stabbing weapon. I didn't
know if this was enough of a fight by hellflower standards and I'd
stopped caring whiles back. But I began to think we might get the whole
way through the pandemonium wondershow and wished I'd made a
plan for what to do then.

Baijon grabbed my ankle. I kicked him in the face. He held on and
began to climb me hand over hand, heading for my throat.

And Berathia's shield failed.

I got advance word of it by the way Baijon's knee sank into my gut.
And that was it, I was dead, this bloodyhanded bloodyminded innocent
was going to kill me and I'd promised him it was going to be oke.

Baijon handed me matched slices on the sides of my face and
jumped back just like I was an active threat. The blade grated off my
teeth. I got to my knees and then my feet by pure reflex.

Circle and circle and circle . . . There was roaring in my ears and
Paladin was shouting at me but I couldn't hear him for the noise and
that was when I knew I'd lost it because Paladin wasn't here; just some
of his leftover memories abandoned in my head.

Betrayed.

By my—

Library?

Librarian?

I slid so far into weird I came out the other side with the kind of cut-glass clarity that tells you you're about to be sick, unconscious, or dead.

Baijon was facing me. His Knife was wet and red and it was mine, all mine.

"*Kore,*" Baijon whispered at me. "Hold out your hands."

The one thing I always forget in between is how god-lost much pain hurts. *Everything* hurt—to where the sand underfoot felt like red hot gravel.

"Please, *Kore.*"

He had to *cut,* I bet they'd told him that, to prove the Machine hadn't got its lunchhooks anywhere near him. The sweat beaded up on his face and slid down and his whole body shook and he wanted me to stand there flatfoot and take it from him and somebody sometime'd told me never, never to do that.

"I swear to you it is permitted," he said, just a voice hanging on the air and a shadow between me and the sun.

"Hold out your hands. Your hands, *Kore.*"

So I dropped my *arthame* in the sand.

Never bow to a hellflower. He'll kill you.

And I held my hands out to Valijon Starbringer.

And all hell broke loose.

*   *   *

The door behind me slammed open. I stepped back just in time to get out of the way of six hellflowers and The Wall That Walked.

Baijon made a sound like I'd never heard before.

The Wall was carrying something and it dripped. Up above us 'flowers was scrambling to get out or get closer. Sunlight dazzled on the chrome housings of sidearms and rifles, and just like that I was back in a cheap bolt-hole in a little place called Kiffit, looking at something that used to be human that my partner was going to tell me was a hellflower's way of announcing war.

"The pheon, *or alMayne vendetta wand, is normally only employed among the alMayne, The Gentle People, themselves. The* pheon *may be engraved with from one to seven rings. One ring indicates that the subject of the vendetta is a single individual, seven rings indicates that the subject's entire family to the seventh remove of kinship is to be eliminated. Outside*

scholars generally agree that the formal initiation of the vendetta occurs when the designated subject sees the pheon, *which is commonly presented in the ritually-murdered body of a servant or dependent of that subject . . ."*

The Wall dropped the body at where Gruoch's feet would of been if she'd been down here. Gruoch stood up straight like the prow of a sinking ship while that ruined bag of meat leaked into the sand.

It was Ketreis. She had a *arthame* on her belt. She must of just become a grownup and fair game.

Damn all hellflowers forever. For oncet me and Archive agreed on something.

It seemed like forever but I don't think Ketreis'd even hit the ground before Baijon started moving. He grabbed me by the wrist and yanked me out the door The Wall had come in.

Behind us I heard gunfire.

*   *   *

By meridies me and my *comites* was hiding outside one of the Wailing outbuildings, plotting how to break in and liberate what we needed to go on with.

Was no hope of getting into the castle. Gruoch had it barricaded by then, with Amrath either dead, hostage, or on her side. The Loyal Opposition was using low-yield grenades to break down one of the doors—at least according to the R/T we'd snabbled off a deader, along with his clothes and his battle-aid kit. I had patches over the holes in my face and enough enhancer in my system so I didn't mind the rest too much, but we had to have clothes, food, and weapons.

And a way off the castle plateau, if nobody killed us first.

There was a hellflower warparty camped outside the building I wanted. Some of them was in green—The Wall's colors—and some was in red—the colors of a LessHouse that Baijon seemed to take as a political in-joke. They was just using it as a place to regroup, until they could rejoin the assault on the castle.

Hellflowers at war. It was Gruoch against The Wall That Walked—she'd insulted him because of what she'd done to me, Baijon'd said, so he'd tried to kill her, and she'd (probably by now) killed him, but before that he'd done things up right and declared vendetta against every member of Starborn of her generation.

And he'd used Ketreis to do it.

"My father's sister, the LadyHolder of Wailing, which is the Walls of my House, has insulted me—" Baijon started up again quiet but fierce.

But I didn't want to think about Ketreis right now. Right now I just wanted these guys to ankle, so babby and me could take a shot at the door.

"—she has insulted me; standing on my shadow—"

"And here I thought *I* was your honor, Baijon-che-bai."

He stopped.

"We were to be married," he said finally, and it wasn't Gruoch he meant.

"Why, *Kore?* She had not had one day of Personhood. We kept our vigils together—last night, in the logotek, WarDoctor Firesong permitted us this. *Kore,* he must have taken her as she came from the altarfires with her Knife. . . ."

Because she was Gruoch's daughter. And because two could play the game of more-historical-than-thou. And because Gruoch and The Wall had both loved anything more than people.

"Kore, I beseech you. You have said many times that I am of no use to you in this business of darktrading; let me be useless now—"

"And go off and be chop-and-channeled by Gruoch? Ketreis is dead. She won't care, Baijon."

The warparty down below us wasn't moving. Why should that go right for me when nothing else had? In between running and hiding and sneaking, we'd been back by the vehicle pool three or four times, but both sides thought it was a major tactical goodie. To lift anything at all from there we was going to have to liberate a serious distraction from here.

"She will need me in the Land Beside," Baijon finally said in a strangled voice. *"Kore,* I beg you; allow me to—"

"Ne, no, nada-je."

It was common sense to put as much geography between Her Honorability and us as I could, which meant naturally that the hellflower thing to do was wade right back in to what was shaping up to be a prime-class family brawl.

"She'll kill you."

"I do not care, *Kore."*

I wondered which side of the Wailing walls little Berathia was on and in what condition.

"You my *comites.* You come along me. I'm damned if I did all that rescuing on you just to hand you over to your crazy relatives."

The R/T I was laying on said something in helltalk. Below us the warriors gathered up their weapons and moved off.

*   *   *

We ditched the skyhorse five kliks from the Zerubavel walls so as not to trigger the sensors. It was about an hour before planetary Lights Out. The rest of a day that'd started too early and went on too long got filled with reaching Zerubavel and getting in.

In case anyone's ever tempted, I do *not* recommend a night stroll on any part of alMayne. If Baijon hadn't liberated a good share of the Wailing armory, we wouldn't of got there.

*   *   *

The alMayne keep the architecture in the Trade City to their liking by shelling anything built too high, and that meant that Outport was low, sprawling, cramped, and full of Imperials what might any minute think to check the ID Baijon and me hadn't got. Or just hand us back across the Pale into Gruoch's waiting arms.

"*Kore,* I beseech you. The port is easy to reach from here; you may cry *comites* of your Guild."

"Don't work that way, Baijon. Ain't nobody going to stick their ship out for us. And I ain't leaving you to go walkabout."

"They put her into my arms when she was six hours old. Our souls were bound together, the Knives we would bear forged from the same stone. But *Kore,* it is not because of her—not for Ketreis. It is that they lied. The LadyHolder lied. The WarDoctor lied."

Yeah. The whole universe'd promised to be good and had lied. There was a lot of that going around.

We was at the edge of the Outport compound. Trade City proper was awaysaway. I wasn't half as strung out on metabolic enhancers as I'd like to of been, and wearing borrowed alMayne flashwrap that'd used to belong to someone a lot bigger'n I was. It covered all the places I was taped together to let alMayne battle-aid fetch-kitchen do its work, and there wasn't a damn thing to be done about the marks on my face —painted over and medicalled and real noticeable if anybody was looking.

"And now there is nothing left, but I will not live in a world with their lies. You do not want me. You never wanted me. I will leave you, I will betray you. Think what you will, *Kore,* but please—let me go!"

It came to me then what it was he was asking for, even if he didn't know it. I'd been stupid not to see it earlier. Baijon didn't think he could take Gruoch. He didn't think he could win. What he wanted was to die a hellflower, doing something as made sense to him.

Die purified, free of the taint of the Machine.

Only that was a little harder for hellflowers than for real people.

A long time ago, a kiddy I knew oncet said to me, there was a war. And whiles it was underway, hellflowers was bred to fight the Machine.

Right.

And wrong.

Because before there was hellflowers there was Librarians, who when their proteges went in for genocide decided to turn themselves into a xenophobic race of antitechnological sociopaths.

alMayne.

"*Kore,* I have asked you for much and you have given more—"

"Baijon, how come you think I'm livealive now?"

He knew what I meant. His eyes flickered.

"I cheated. I kicked sand in the face of hellflower honor and right conduct—because if I'd done anything else you'd be dead, and there wouldn't be anybody what somebody had to believe about Archangel and Archive Library, would there?"

"You will tell them."

"Nobody is going to believe me."

"They did not believe *me!*"

"Believed you enough to start a war, ne?"

War.

Why? It was like one of those thingummyites you get when you throw hot glass into water; they look like little teardrop shapes and solid as ever so, but if you just chip the end bit off the tail the whole thing goes to dust. Every time I closed my eyes I could see the whole damn hellflower society disintegrate like a computer simulation: anarchy and blasphemy and is-there-is-or-is-there-ain't-Libraries spreading out from Castle Wailing ground zero while everybody trotted out his own personal honor and declared for one side or t'other of a holy war.

I knew like I'd read it in a book how it was going to end. The hellflowers was going to decide no more peaceful coexistence with their Imperial good buddies the tongueless doorstops. They'd raise a fleet up off alMayne and go looking for the Emperor . . .

—igniting a groundswell of popular support—

—to the total indifference of the other Corporations—

—causing a massive preemptive strike by Throne against them and other Imperial hotspots like Tortuga—

Leading to . . .

War.

And I'd started it by showing up and asking Gruoch for a *ship?*

No. It started because anything'd start it. Or nothing. It was *time* for a war, said the ghost dance in my head, and there had to be one, like goforths got to high jump if you power them up.

Glitterborn think about things like this all the time. And the reason glitterborn don't live to get anymuch older than they is, is that they think about things like this instead of insuring that no rude strangers lets the air out of what's doing all that grand choplogic.

Not me. I tapped Baijon's shoulder.

"Street's clear. Let's move. And shut up."

8

Had We but Hell Enough and Time

The Azarine's the merc district, named for the Coalition. It holds everything from sellsword to gallowglass with a short detour through contract assassin, and alMayne's one of the booming markets. I felt more secure once we got there: your uncontracted mercenary's a real peaceful sort. He don't act up for free any more than I run cargo for my health.

I wanted back to that. I was trying not to remember that the last twenty years of my life—my First Ticket, my ship *Firecat,* everything I owned—was in somebody else's pocket in selected locations throughout the Outfar. I looked at Baijon. The one thing I was straight up on was I didn't want him curling up and dropping dead. He was my *friend,* dammit.

Maybe the only one I had left.

Except for what was sorting itself out in my skull. If I ever learned to talk to it. Or became it. And I wouldn't get a chance to turn down doing either one if I didn't get us out of here. I looked around for something I could blend in to.

Most of what was in the street here was hellflowers (it being their planet), a few offworld recruiters in their gaudy uniforms, and one hell of a lot of wigglys.

Hellflowers don't approve of slaves or tronics (or Zerubavel Outport) so all this tidy perfection was being kept up by the wigglys: what the Phoenix Empire in its infinite wisdom calls "client races," although look you, they never got a choice whether to buy Imperial or not. Throne pops a couple starshakers in your sky and you bet what you're going to do is your common or garden rollover.

If we got all the good numbers on our side and nobody a-tall was after us, I figured we could last about thirty hours in the Zerubavel Azarine before putting our foot in it with some heat or t'other. Then we was made, and I was losing count of the people lethally sweet for us on one count or another.

The thing that was going to keep us in the Azarine was the stone impossibility of getting onto the Port without ID or high-powered help.

The reason for wanting to get there was that maybe the ship that'd been in ships-in-port two days ago might still be there and charitable.

If it didn't cost them more'n I had.

My whole plan, such as it wasn't, depended on us staying out of noticeability. So naturally when I saw these three mercs ganging up on this wiggly I took Baijon and we went t'other way.

Right?

Sure.

They was two armored *chaudatu*—Kensey, maybe—and a hell-flower. The wiggly fit its skin like an empty watersack. There was lots of things it probably was and one outside chance on what it could be, but the smart money was still on walking the other way.

The hellflower picked it up by its loose skin and started shaking it. It squeaked as it rattled and all kinds glitterjunk fell out of its pouches. The flower dropped it just like you'd bounce a ball, but the wiggly didn't have much bounce in it by then.

"That's mine, you know," I said, walking up.

One of the Kensey turned around. Big, wide, heavy-worlder bones. "Then you want to make good on what it stole, *borio*. True?"

I didn't know what *borio* meant and from his looks I didn't want to. I looked down. The wiggly was a Sibolith, I could see now, and sitting in the middle of a bunch of gimcracks: pounce-boxes, inhalers, jewelry, the odd credit piece. It's amazing what you can conceal with a loose flexible inflatable marsupial skin.

The strange hellflower was looking at me. His hair was cut short like the mercs do and he had wheelknives clipped down the outside of each arm.

"Let her go, my brothers."

Baijon drifted up behind me like radioactive smoke. I wished him or me was dangerous enough to get this reaction out of Brother Gallowglass, but we wasn't. It occurred to me that walking up to him with fresh honorscars all over my face was not the smartest thing I'd ever done. Story'd be all over Zerubavel by first light. Terrific.

One of the Kensey put one foot on a bit of the wiggly's whatever. Me and Baijon together wouldn't make up one of him. He grinned at me and showed off the new improved version of teeth for mercs.

"You don't want us to let him go, *borio*." He prodded the wiggly with his free foot.

I should of been scared. He could ice me, no question. But what I was, was annoyed.

"*Dhu, borio*-bai, you keep him. And me, I let plasma through your armor, you moronic roundheeled *noke-ma'ashki* giving it away free. You got your kick back."

The other Kensey put a hand on the first one's arm and it clanked where the armor met.

"It isn't worth it, Jorum," he said, which proved that all mercs don't get their brains removed at birth.

Jorum didn't look at him. Just when I thought there was going to be trouble he bent down and scooped up the Sibolith one handed and slung it at me. I landed on my tail under X-kilos of wiggly. All my battle-aid tech heaved and hurt.

"She's got it, if she wants it." Jorum laughed and turned away, not even bothering to pick up all that junk he'd been so hot and bothered about a minute ago.

Baijon pulled his *arthame*.

I don't think Jorum'd saw him before that. For sure he hadn't recognized the marks on my face. He looked around for help.

His buddy with the brains looked ticked. The hellflower folded his arms across his chest.

"This is not my affair unless you make it so, brother," he said to Baijon. "Jorum-*chaudatu* will apologize to your sister. He always does," Brother Flower added with a sigh.

Baijon looked at me. I got up. The Sibolith'd gone limp, but they do that when life gets to be too much for them. It wasn't all puffed out so I knew it wasn't dead.

"If Jorum-*chaudatu* wants to apologize to the wiggly," I said, "ain't nobody standing on anybody else's shadow, right, Baijon-bai?"

Baijon grinned; the concept of making somebody else look stupid for fun is both universal and transcendent.

"As my *comites* commands, so is the path of honor," he said with a ghost of his old sass.

Jorum looked at his Kensey buddy.

"Jerk," said his buddy.

Jorum rattled off a line of babble that I decided to take for his apology and the three of them moved off.

"*Kore?*" said Baijon, looking at their backs.

I waved a hand to shut him up.

"You oke, Tongtip?"

I wasn't real sure, but the right ship was in port and there couldn't be too many Sibolith this dumb.

"Kjhrrr—" The midget green baggie sputtered old burntwine in my face. Tongtip was real fond of burntwine—it's a Proscribed Import to Cibola, and Mother Night only knows what it does to their biochemistry. But Tongtip was real fond of the stuff, and once he got tanked up and it did whatever it did to his nervous system, he'd head out and steal anything as wasn't nailed down.

"Tongtip, you son-of-a-spacewarp, if you ain't you I'm gonna—"

Arms and legs and other things retracted into the pudge and stretched out again.

"Butterfries!" Tongtip choodled, opening big round frog-yellow eyes. "I see my beloved uncle, Butterfries!"

"*Kore,* do you know this person?" said Baijon like he hoped the answer was no.

"Je. Tong-che-bai, you shipping same *Angelcity* ce Merodach Gentry-legger?"

Angelcity, out of Cibola, and her captain knew me. That was the ship I'd seen in the ships-in-port; stardancer's luck I'd made for myself years ago, coming in to port when I needed it most.

Tongtip closed his eyes and looked like a very solemn, very drunk wiggly. "Megaera is captain this trip, Butterfries." He wove extensively to his feet. "I say good-bye now with profuse thanks."

"Not right now you don't."

I grabbed a good handful of wiggly and slid back into the shadows. Baijon followed, covering my back without half a damn idea of what I was up to.

Halfway down a long alley I stopped. The lights from the street didn't push this far and the alley wasn't lit at all. I bet hellflowers have better night-sight nor your average citizen, too.

"Tongtip, you going to get me and mine onto port for to chaffer with Megaera, j'keyn?"

I knelt down beside him and all my fetch-kitchen pulled, but it was just my skin in ribbons, not anything underneath. Baijon stood over us, looking both ways, wanting to be back with his own home and homicide. And Ketreis.

"But yes! Megaera is glad to see you, uncle, there being a small matter of wagers owed."

"Yeah, sure."

I didn't have any idea what Megaera Dare, half-captain of *Angelcity,* Cibola registry, thought I owed her, but people as thinks you owe them credit is very tender of your health. And if squaring a fictional debit meant I could get Baijon and me out of here, I'd pay.

"You won't be telling Megaera about this little mischance, uncle?" Tongtip said hopefully.

"You mean about you sliding off to get elevated and road-pizzaed, che-bai? Now that depends . . ."

*   *   *

I remembered Tongtip for an excellent supplier of other people's goods, and found out that security at the Outport was sloppy to begin with.

In fact, all of Zerubavel Trade City had damn few *legitimates* and fewer locks. On the other hand, any hellflower what didn't like our looks or our answers was likely to sign us off. Sort of your basic free will love offering legal enforcement.

We walked onto the port in a set of liberated tech coveralls with a hysterical little wiggly telling us in nine kinds of patwa to hurry. Nobody looked twice.

Angelcity was a secondhand Mikasarin G-8 Starhauler shell retrofitted for a crew of thirty, which meant losing a couple holds but paid off in a lot of other ways. Within class they dock by size in Imperial ports, which means all kinds of Indies get the raw end of the cubic, but *City* was big enough to be in a good neighborhood; lights and hookups and one of the crew standing to at the open ramp to show the captain's honor, the way you better do on alMayne. He let Tongtip go by and stopped us.

"Got to see captain," I said, "Bidness, j'keyn?"

"No business on ship. And not hiring . . . stardancer."

So much for my disguise, both of them.

"My uncle owes a wager to our captain!" Tongtip peeped up, but the legger had as high a opinion of Tongtip's brains as I did. He waved the wiggly in-ship and didn't stir from out my way.

Tongtip stood pat.

"But it is *true!* My uncle Bu—"

"Button it!" I snapped, not wanting any version of my name wafting over the unmetered air of beautiful downtown Zerubavel Outport.

City's doorman looked at me with new interest.

"Is problem here, stardancer?" he said, real soft.

"Not if me and my bai see half-Captain Megaera."

That fetched him; not everybody knows that joke. She and Mero always said that between them they made up one good captain, and when they finally bought their hull they split duties to match.

"Convince me," said Meggie's crew.

A fool would of offered him valuta. I didn't.

"Is song-ice strike out in the Chullites; Manwarra Directorate claims it but it's far enough away they lease Company ships to guard and freight. Meggie got a Company man drunk oncet as said his cap used to skim the harvest he brought in. So Meggie thought they wouldn't mind a little more split. I flew one of the jaegers she used for that; tell her."

"Tell her who?" he said, but not like he disbelieved me.

"Just tell her that."

He went away on up the ramp, picking up Tongtip as he went. Baijon looked at me.

"You cry her walls, *Kore?*"

"Yeah."

If she remembered, if it wasn't too much risk, if I could pay up whatever she thought I owed.

Baijon looked back the way we'd come.

"Perhaps they are better than mine."

*   *   *

After not-forever the babysitter came back without Tongtip and hand-delivered us in-ship, to a compartment that looked like it was mostly used for making nice with the rich and famous. *Angelcity* was doing well for herself, and I was glad in the same abstract way I hated tariff regs: Mero and Meggie'd been friends of mine once. They'd asked me to come in with them when they was picking crew for *Angelcity,* but I'd said no.

I'd had Paladin.

I sat down and admired all the quiet good taste, and presently Megaera came stomping in from somewhere, pulling off her gloves and looking like she'd been interrupted.

She was tall—had a shot at citizenship once, I heard—and dark, and looked like belonging to any B-pop or none. She'd always been prideful of her hair and she still wore it long; it was banded with ring-money all the way down and dangled below her blasters' muzzles.

"Where's my shirt?" she said, fixing me with your standard-issue gimlet gaze.

What shirt?

Meggie watched me do a pretty good imitation of the bulkhead and drew a deep breath.

"You swore," said Megaera. "You swore you'd give me the shirt off your back if I babysat that hotload for you back in the Tontine Drift, and then you lit out on me—"

Light dawned.

It was almost fifteen years ago. I'd been running skyjunk in to a sophont who thought he'd rather cash in one of those Class-A warrants that keep my life so interesting than sign my ticket-of-leave, and I couldn't afford to be boarded to make him change his mind. So I called up Meggie and handed the load off to her in mid-tik and she took it on in instead of me.

I was supposed to meet her afterward to split the feoff she collected, but I couldn't let Meggie board my ship either. She was smart; a tech. She'd of seen the Old Fed Library where my navicomp was supposed to be and burned me where I stood.

"Meggie, I had this appointment—"

"—so I babysat. Where's my shirt?"

I looked at her. She was dead serious, and she'd even come out ahead on the money.

It would of made great sense to a hellflower to go around waiting fifteen years to collect a shirt you didn't want and couldn't wear. I wondered if I was the last person in the Empire that thought it was a stupid idea.

I took off the tech coveralls and a jacket and a gunharness and a vest and got down to the shirt. Then I took it off and handed it to her.

Meggie grabbed it like it was hard credit on payday and let out a whoop.

"Dach-bach, I told you she'd do it! It *is* her! Pay up."

Meggie did a war-dance around the compartment. Merodach came in from where he'd been standing in the corridor; tall like Meggie and a couple shades lighter.

"St. Cyr!" he said, and waltzed me around hard. It didn't do my battle-aid tech any good at all. Mero looked down and noticed the bandages all over sudden and looked penitent.

"Keeping busy, I see?"

So then I sat down and it was just like old times, from back when it was the lot of us hanging around the Never-never Diner, trying to beg buy or borrow the tech to turn our leaky hulls into Mainliners.

But they'd grown up and gone on. And I could of gone with. Instead of sitting here asking favors, I could of been Engineer on *Angelcity.*

It spooled out in front of me like talkingbook might-be-maybes, so real I could damn near take a deep breath and walk into it. The life I could of had. Should of had.

Would of had, except for Paladin.

And Baijon would be dead now, cause nobody but Paladin and me together could of got him out of all that grief Archangel'd dumped him into bye-m-bye.

But I could almost *touch* it—everything I'd ever wanted, cut off from me by one mistake I'd never knew I made until now when it was gone.

"So."

Mero's talking-business voice snapped me back to the here-and-now. Pleasantries was over, and they'd made up their mind to at least listen before showing Baijon and me the air. And I didn't blame them for thinking that way, not with a crew of thirty to think about, too. I'd done the same in my time, for my crew.

I leaned forward. "Need to get off-planet, into Outfar, both of us. No ID."

That told enough and more. Meggie looked at Baijon. Young, maybe she could tell. Not a merc, even with his hair braided back.

"And him?"

Baijon didn't say anything. I kept forgetting I wasn't a *chaudatu* by his lights until we met up with one and he went into his Great Honor Face routine.

"Can pay our freight, Meggie." I emptied out the pockets of my secondhand jacket. No alMayne scrip nor Imperial credits, but plenty of hellflower junk-jewelry, negotiable in any hockshop in the Universe.

"Doesn't he talk?" Meggie said.

"Ne. Mine hellflower-style. *Comites.*"

I wondered if Meggie knew a high-caste hellflower from the sellsword in the street and if the news from Wailing had got out yet and if she knew who Baijon was real and for true.

Meggie stood up from where she'd been sitting and walked over to him. She was in shouting distance, heightwise.

"You. I won't freight honor this tik—you want to come, you leave it down the gravity well and talk like a human person. Now. What's your name?"

He didn't even glance at me.

"Baijon," The Third Person of House Starborn said with a fair imitation of the patwa slur. "I am Baijon Stardust."

After that was all over but Meggie stripping me to my ring-money.

*   *   *

Valijon's Diary

The WarDoctor Firesong's honor is pure. I wish I did not know this. Because he has slain my chosen, Ketreis, and if he could do that honorably, in honor, then what is honor now?

On Low Mikasa my father told me of his plan: that the accusation against Archangel *Malmakosim* would not come from him or me or any disputable, slayable source, but from the very Walls of alMayne and the assembled throats of the Gentle People.

Such he could not evade. Such he could not kill. Such must even he, honorless, answer.

So my father bid me accuse Archangel to the Memory of Starborn, to the LadyHolder of Wailing, to Amrath Starborn FirstLeader of al-Mayne.

And I did. The *Kore* bid me come away at once, but I knew she did not mean me to slink away with my message undelivered. So I did as my father said I must.

And my own people delivered me to the Shadow. They set aside those words it is death to treat lightly. In the name of the dead of a hundred suns I begged them to hear me . . . and they did not.

We spoke, in my betrothed's last night in life. She told me that Gruoch-my-aunt had promised that the Outport would cease to be, that *chaudatu* would no longer walk the earth of the Homeplace.

Only Archangel could give that. To promise it, Gruoch must have eaten promises from his hands. Sick with the taint of the Machine, she could not taste truth. She named me mad, knowing that in this one thing even madness did not matter.

Gruoch twisted honor, and so Firesong declared vendetta upon her. But the time for such simplicity is as gone as the time for the Combat of The Nine Cuts. On the Floor of Honor, the *Kore-alarthme* cheated, and did not defame those sands already clotted with treachery.

Is there higher honor than honor? When honor itself twists like a serpent, what shall we prove ourselves against to know we are still human?

Dare we be not human, when the Machine waits for all?

I do not know. And there is no one left to ask.

LessHouse Dragonflame conspired against House Starborn, its master, for the tainted *chaudatu* honors my father holds. Honored Alaric sought my life, so that my father must die in battle against the TwiceBorn *chaudatu*—and then the Honored Morido, Alaric's father, would speak for the Gentle People who fight *chaudatu* vendettas.

Now LessHouse Dragonflame fights for the WarDoctor, to bring down the walls of Gruoch-my-aunt. Morido is dead, knowing the taint of the Machine was on him. Alaric must follow.

Honor would say this LessHouse is still my enemy, though they fight as I would fight, if I were free. Gruoch spoke for the Machine and made honor a weapon to serve her ends.

If humans who betray are human no longer, what is honor that is only a tool of kingmakers?

Once honorable kindred fight for scraps from the Empire's table and lose their shadows to the Machine. I am not a child to deny that these things can be.

I only wish to know: what is left?

Betrayal summons vengeance, but if honor dies, can even blood reanimate it?

Archangel must answer me; Archangel who will sell all for the power only the Machine can give.

If the Gentle People are purified and rise against him, will it be in time?

And will it matter at all?

9

The Road to Hell

Baijon and me got to eat and live indoors while *Angelcity* tidied up her bidness on alMayne. They even waited over an extra day on account of passengers that never showed—at least so Mero said.

I didn't care, so long as we got to stay where we was. Inside cabin, no ports, no data-links, and someone to bring our meals on time and not talk much. Meggie was being almost as careful as I would of been. Careful enough would of been not helping at all.

I wondered if Paladin'd ever bothered to look for me in the Washonnet dataweb. I knew him a lot better now. I had a good idea of how time could slide when you're made of light. He might never think to look till I'd died of old age, assuming I lived that long.

I was not stupid enough to think that getting this far solved anything. If the situation Baijon and me was in had made bankable net improvement since we'd docked at Mikasa, it was hard to see how.

I'd made it twenty years out of Market Garden and to the ripe age of thirty-five gsy (galactic standard years) by not being noticed. Everybody I'd ever met lived the same way. Some might be able to stand more looking than others. Nobody could stand up to being looked at by the Second In Line For The Phoenix Throne.

I tried to convince myself Archangel thought we was dead on al-Mayne. And I couldn't, because looking for us was no bother to him. He just had to give the orders and forget about them and a century later people'd still be looking, diligent in the face of common sense.

That's power, and I didn't have it.

I had other things.

I lay there in my rack on *Angelcity* thinking thoughts I shouldn't of been able to think about things I shouldn't of known and wondered whether and how much I was the person I'd been last year. And the worst of it was, I suspicioned I knew.

And the real bottom-line hell was, it didn't matter.

Me and Baijon was livealive, so we needed a place to be that way. What it was and how fancy was just windowdressing—so, if you wanted to get philosophical, was whether you was alive in a Imp hellhouse or a glitterborn palaceoid.

I knew, just the same like I knew what I wanted for breakfast, that Mallorum Archangel was trying for a war. And if even hellflowers wasn't going to believe in Libraries at the drop of a *arthame* in the first place, it augured badly for the credulity of the solid citizens of the Phoenix Empire.

Yell "Library" on Archangel, and nobody'd listen until it was too late.

Then there'd be war. And Archangel was going to start it and nobody was going to win it because there wasn't going to be anybody left. Fact.

There'd never been a war in the Phoenix Empire. The Empire was built out of the ashes of the war that'd put new constellations in my home sky and converted a slightly larger volume of space than the current Empire occupied to plasma. By the time the Empire had finished putting itself together out of what that war'd left, the habit of banging planets together at twice the speed of light had sort of dropped out of the local population. And maybe Fleet kept its borders with the Hamat and the Sodality and intervened in squabbles between the Directorates, but that wasn't war.

Not like I knew war. Because I knew a lot of things I shouldn't, including how much fun it was to make a sun turn inside-out. Thanks to Archive.

Most of what was in my head was Archive's, I thought now. A little bit was Paladin, but Paladin hadn't known how to do half the things a Library could until he'd met Archive. Paladin'd been broke in the War, and reassembled with my not-too-expert help. So most of what I had was Archive's.

It didn't include the big *"why,"* and I was glad, even if I still wondered about it. Archangel wanted power; I knew from that. But what could a Library want that a organic had, enough to fight about it?

I hoped I'd never find out firsthand.

War, and how to avoid it.

Kennor Starbringer, bless his homicidal heart, only wanted to keep Archangel's hands off the Coalition. He wasn't out to stop a war. He didn't think there'd be one. He just wanted to keep the status well and truly quo and the alMayne in the mercy seat wherever mercenaries are sold.

I had a hunch Archangel's ambitions had gone beyond that, but who'd believe a charter member of the scaff and raff of the Galaxy?

Of course the hellflowers might start it first. And then Archangel could go after the War College logotek, which might not quite be far from his mind. And it would be a little farther to the last act, but not much.

I wondered if Berathia Notevan was who she seemed to be, whoever that was, and if she wasn't, if she worked for Archangel. In which case I hoped she'd got off Wailing safe and warm, and run home to tell him people was blowing the whistle on him.

So when you came down to it, it didn't matter whether I was me, or Paladin, or Mother Night her own self. I was a live thing with Archangel standing square in the way of me and everyone else I might ever meet staying lively.

And I could not think of one useful thing to do about it.

*   *   *

The day we cleared alMayne gravity, it was Mero brought the breakfast with a smile and asked if we had any objection to working cargo.

"It's Megaera, you see. She has the soul of an Imperial accountant and the thought of experienced crew sitting deadhead is keeping her awake at night."

"So?" I said.

"So she thought you might enjoy the exercise and a change of pace. There's two places open on the cargo gang. It comes with galley and slop-chest rights."

"Fine."

It was better than sitting locked up in here watching Baijon tear himself apart over the "lack of honor" of his GreatHouse. It was taking him whiles to work it all out to his satisfaction, but he'd settle it in his mind soon or late. I wasn't sure I wanted to be there when he did.

And the only alternative to talking to him was thinking about how people are aggregates of their experience, and since I had a good chunk of Archive's experience now did that make me a Library?

I'd rather shift cargo.

*   *   *

Mero showed us down to "A" Hold—*Angelcity* had six. Tongtip was there, and looked glad to see me, but then Tongtip's glad to see everybody. I didn't let it go to my head.

On one side of "A" Hold there was a bunch of big black crates with ominous blinking lights and Intersign glyphs saying about how they was from Barnegat and they was absolutely not to be opened unless and until they reached the planetary surface only of Washonnet 357-II/al-Mayne.

Lethals.

On the other side there was a pile of knocked down flats of the kind you seal cargo into before putting it into crates slightly less illegal than the ones on the first side.

"There's ten more crates like these when you've finished repacking the first set," Mero said.

"You backing a insurrection or what?" Barnegat's main export is what's alMayne's main import—high-ticket energy weapons.

"With bolts of cloth? You've been out in the starshine too long, St. Cyr."

"It is not cloth," said Baijon flatly. Nobody listened.

"Our next port is Royal—does that tell you anything?" Merodach said.

"Je, Mero-bai. That you're a damn poor legger shipping cloth there."

*   *   *

Celestial and some Indie ships is families, with a da for captain and everything done his way for love. On the Company ships and in the Fleet the captain is god and has eighty ways to make you wish you died before crossing him.

But on a darktrader—an Indie that's a legger—things run different. They have to. 'Cause you're bending the Pax Imperador every time you lift, and if everyone from the pilot in the mercy seat to the crystal-gazer in the black gang isn't easy in his mind over that, somebody's going to peach to the Teasers and then you ain't got ship nor hull nor anything else worth having.

So a darktrader—a big one anyway—is more of a democracy where the captain's got the veto. Meggie (captain this tik) didn't have to ask her crew's permission to have someone sign Articles (which in point of fact we hadn't, being cargo) but under those same Articles they had the right to petition her to kick anyone off they didn't like.

Things legger crews discuss is not things like whether to have candied chobosh for tea. It's things like what kind of illegal they's willing to get up to. Some ships won't run slaves. Some mindbenders. Some take any cargo. It's all in the Articles—and you better read them before you sign, because that's the only way to tell your legit Indie from your Guild-member darktrader. A tour of cargo gave us the chance to ingratiate ourselves with all and sundry and Mero the chance to get some work out of us.

Now *Angelcity* wouldn't run slaves, because Meggie believed in freedom—a damfool idea in a universe where even air isn't free. But she had no objection to running guns. Neither did the folks back in hellflower heaven.

*   *   *

If you believe the talkingbooks and the credit-dreadfuls, all the illicit behavior that makes the galaxy such a fun place for Our Hero starts bang at the edge of the Outfar. Never in the Core, or the MidWorlds, or even in Directorate Space. And never among sophonts of probity, such as our galactic cousins the alMayne.

Fact: business is business. And as Baijon'd proved to me more'n once, "honorable" and "legal" meet only at meals. alMayne was the legal Destination-of-Record for twenty percent of all the frightfuls manufactured in the Empire. If once it arrived it left for other Directorates where it was strictly on the Proscribed Indicia, that was nobody's problem but the Teasers'.

An Indie as big as *Angelcity* works her run a little different than I did with *Firecat*. My Best Girl was so small I had to get one cargo out of the way before picking up another. It left me more flex, too, but *Angelcity* had her next six downfalls in mind and cargoes picked out to match. All of them legal wherever she'd picked them up, all bound for somewheres they was either illegal or overtaxed, and all on their way to making a tidy profit for Mero and Meggie and their crew.

And the beauty was, since *Angelcity* could show her cargos was legal transactables under autonomous planetary waiver at port of acquisition, even if the Teasers stopped her Meggie'd probably get by with confiscation and a few points on her ticket.

Even if it was guns.

*   *   *

Three *Angelcitizens* joined Baijon and me, and the five of us spent the next whenever shifting cargo. Tongtip helped—meaning he got underfoot—until he got bored and went off to supervise somebody else. He's Part-Owner of Record for *Angelcity,* which is how she comes by Cibolan registry at a less-than-ruinous rate of fee. There's other ways around the Registry regs than selling two percent of your hull to an indigine, but most of them is dangerous.

I put my mind on my work, juggling a bunch of long pink densepak cylinders that might of contained cloth or chocolate or holy writ from all I knew for sure—except that none of them is prime alMayne export for a ship like this, and when I dropped one and it split I got the confirmation notice. Prime Estel-Shadowmaker bells and whistles, this.

The *Angelcity* gang-boss looked over at me to see how I was taking it, although if Mero'd vouched for me he knew I wasn't a holy innocent.

I pulled it out of the densepak, all chromed vanes and blued ceramic with "Born To Rock'n'Roll" incipient in every line. It fit in between my elbow and my ribs like it was born there.

There was people on Royal waiting for this kick, you betcha.

"You want I should wrap it up again safe and warm?" I asked.

"Je think they going do—refuse delivery for improper packaging, jillybai?"

He held out his hand. I tossed him the rifle. Everybody went back to work.

Guns to Royal.

*   *   *

There's a war on there, you know: Charlock Corporation against rebel Shareholders, with the Sector Governor taking sides. Area under martial law at the moment, and direct control of the Governor-General. Another of Archangel's little gifts to the galactic peace.

I was starting to develop a plan. It was half wishful thinking, and half hope of divine intervention. It did not have a candle to a stardrive's chance of working. Still, it was mine, and I thought Baijon'd like it when it was old enough to stand company. Meanwhile I fiddled it around my head with the thing that wasn't Paladin and—might-be-maybe—wasn't Archive.

Three stops after Royal *Angelcity* would be stopping at a Free Port. You don't need ID to move around a Free Port. Meggie was willing to take us as far as there, I hoped. Our places on the cargo gang said she was.

If we could stay out of the way of bounty hunters we'd be fine. Just give me a chance to pick up new ID in the wondertown and Baijon and me could start getting *really* lost.

I wondered how Kennor'd take the news.

*   *   *

"*Kore,* what is the right? You are my *comites;* my father gave me to you. What do I do?"

We was lying in our racks in the dark. Three days out from al-Mayne, seven to Royal.

I'd settled back into the shipside drill, and Baijon picked it up like he'd never been anywhere else and it wasn't beneath his glitterborn self. He wasn't dumb—just literal and bloodyminded. Between them, Gruoch and The Wall had pretty well done for his damned self-confidence.

I wasn't sure if I liked what there was going to be left.

"Depends, bai, on what you want to do," I said after whiles.

"I want to go home," Baijon said.

I took a deep breath and blew it out again.

"Can't do that."

"I know." He sounded miserable. "It isn't there anymore."

I sat and listened to the dark. Lies are the devil, but true-tell'll get you every time.

"Yeah," I said. "Well."

"So what must I do, *comites?* I have thought . . . I think I must kill Mallorum Archangel." He sounded shy about it, like he was worried he'd upset me.

"You'll never get near him. You know that."

I'd always used to thought that being alive was worth damn near anything. But the more I thought about it, the less things there was on the list I'd do without a blink to keep breathing.

"I must try, *Kore.* Is that not the course of—" he hesitated just a tik in the dark "—Right Conduct?"

"You got to do what's right, bai. But it's better if you win."

Bending Baijon to suit my fancy was coming on for being one of them.

"My *Kore-alarthme* and *comites* will tell me, then, what I must do to do this," Baijon said, with what he was using for a sense of humor. "Once before we prevailed, when our walls were weakest."

That'd been a cakewalk next to this.

"Well you can't just walk up and shoot him. Somebody'd object." And I wasn't really sure it'd stop the war, just give it a different set of players.

"I want him brought low, ground in the dust, stripped of his titles and honors and wealth, alone, helpless, naked to his enemies, inutterably dismayed!"

See "Harm" in the logodex of your choice.

"I'll think about it," I told him. "When I come up with something, I'll let you know."

"You are my *comites, Kore*. In that I may still believe."

I should of known better. He believed it. He fell asleep. I stayed awake, giving his problem serious thought.

Kill the third most expensive sophont in the Empire. Sounded good to me. How?

Simple, really. Cry Library.

How? We'd tried on alMayne and nobody listened.

But Kennor'd said Archangel had enemies as high-up as he was. They'd listen.

If there was a big enough noise to listen to.

Like the noise the Delegate from alMayne'd make. Kennor'd believed Baijon. Right?

So he'd gone and dropped heat at the Office of the Question. Right?

Had he?

Did I want to bet my life on it?

No, as a matter of fact. I'd got used to taking the larger perspective on things these days. And from that vantage place, it was clear that Kennor Starbringer couldn't hold the whip-hand over Mallorum Archangel if the rap was out in sight for Archangel to beat.

So Kennor (who was maybe out to kill Baijon and frame me and maybe not by now) wasn't going to be the boy who cried "Library."

Depending, of course, on what the news from home was these days. A couple zillion hellflowers can't be wrong. Or shuffled under the rug when they was crying for Archangel's chitlins.

And maybe—just maybe—Kennor'd told us the truth in the first place. Maybe all we had to do was wait while bad luck caught up with our boy Archangel.

The trick, of course, was getting through the waiting alive.

In around all this thinking, what I didn't give a second thought to was *Angelcity's* too-convenient placement on alMayne. Then, anyway.

*   *   *

Time passed. Baijon'n me both gave up the clothes we was wearing
in favor of looking like everyone else. Baijon cut his hair to look more
like the 'flower in the street. It made him look funny. *Angelcity's* fetch-
kitchen got rid of everything on me that said Souvenir of Castle Wailing
except the marks on my face. They was dark and raised and left matching ridges on the inside of my mouth and *Angelcity's* med-tech wasn't up
to dealing with them. I didn't care. Nobody'd seen me with them before, so nobody was looking for me with them now.

Shipboard was nice and quiet and Baijon started looking less
haunted and I wished it could go on forever but a day out of Royal
Angelcity made Transit to realspace to let the engines cool out and to
give everybody a last chance to tuck away anything that might not be
strictly legal upright and moral on Royal's heavyside.

We was within range of the Travelers' Advisory beacon at the edge
of Royal system and I talked Meggie into tapping it.

"Why? You trying to find out how your fleet did on its last Riis-
run, St. Cyr?"

"I put good money on a bad actor, Meggie, I swear I never knew
you was his mother. Give me a break."

She looked me over and made up her mind.

"Je. But why you care where Company high-iron goes—"

"I don't. I care where it don't go. Truth."

And it was, but not in a flavor that was likely to be of any use to the
Captain of *Angelcity.*

Travelers' Advisories is for the tourist trade: bulletins originating in
the Imperial Bureau of Interstellar Shipping and Transport. They're
usually half a lifetime out of date and full of things I never wanted to
know.

This one wasn't. Washonnet Sector, it said, was Absolutely Shut.
Don't go there unless you are dropping off Washonnet/alMayne citizens
and can prove it. All alMayne are ordered home. All provable fare costs
for transport guaranteed by the Starborn Corporation.

The message repeated once and then went on to a notice that
Tortuga Sector was under heavy manners and the Roaq was closed to
visitors.

"You knew," said Meggie. She unfolded her feet from the table,
but didn't get up, quite.

We'd tapped the beacon from the Captain's Cabin; most of the
bridge systems referred the late-breaking news here.

"If I knew, I wouldn't of asked you to pull it for me, would I?"

"Would you?" said Meggie, who is sometimes almost as suspicious as I am. *"How* did you know—don't tell me," she added, because I'd been going to.

"Well you aren't there now, so don't shop *me* your troublekick," I said.

"Is Baijon going home?"

Meggie'd got fond of our boy, seemingly.

"No." Which told her some things if she wanted to know them. Maybe even true ones.

"Oke." Meggie stood up. "Tomorrow we hit Royal. See a man about a kick. I need some flash and comedy by me. You and Stardust're elected. After, you sign Articles here to your Free Port, part-shares and wages. Suits?"

"Ea, jillybai. Or maybe I just want my shirt back, ne?"

"You've got Destiny's own chance of getting it," said Meggie. She'd made up her mind to something, plain and certain.

I should of stood home. If I'd been smart, I would of. But if I had, I'd be dead.

10

How to Exceed in Darktrading Without Really Trying

As a planet and a biosphere, there is nothing wrong with Royal. It is capital of the Tortuga Sector so it has a Imperial Governor's mansion, and seat of the Charlock Corporation (which makes Tortuga Sector the Charlock Directorate instead of the Tortuga Directorate, but these things happen) so it has a Corporate Headquarters. It has big blue oceans, fluffy white clouds, lots of chlorophyll and vitamins, and an attractive location relative to shipping and handling.

Probably it used to be some high-glitterborn's home-away-from, hence the name, but the hub of galactic commerce had since moved west, and now Tortuga Sector was Outer MidWorlds only by courtesy.

But it had a downside port, a lunar port, three inhabited planets in its capital system, a asteroid belt full of miners, full weather control, and visits from the Governor-General's pet navy whenever he was in town.

The war it also had, had started like this:

Once upon a time Royal was corporate headquarters of the Brightlaw Corporation, holders of all developmental patents for the next best thing to Libraries, and don't think they didn't walk pretty soft indeed staying on the sunny side of that line. *Angelcity* her own self had a Brightlaw Corporation brain in her hull; damn near anything that needed to think used their tech.

Well and good. But a sad mischance had carried off every single member of the ruling Brightlaw Corporation members except little Shareholder Damaris. Very sad, Uncle Charlock called in to form a new Corporation, administer the Brightlaw patents, and (in the fullness of time) marry little Damaris off to his son Hakon, after which everything'd be all in the family, so to speak.

Too bad little Damaris hadn't thought so. A couple years back she slipped her leash and started a revolt, with the aim of forming a new corporation of one. Things reached the point that Uncle Charlock appealed to Throne, whereupon the Governor-General (my old buddy Archangel) took the Azarine Coalition mercenaries out of the warpool by slipping in a couple divisions of Fleet on the Charlock side and declaring martial law.

This was supposed to make everybody shut up, but Damaris' partisans hadn't stopped their side of the war just because they lost their professionals. Now Archangel was down a couple divisions of crack mediators and Tortuga Sector was a boom market for artillery.

Paladin once said that the Codex Imperador was the greatest argument for solipsism he'd ever seen. Archangel had superseded the Sector Governor. He had loaned troops to Charlock, forcing the Coalition troops out of the arena. He'd even declared martial law so the Space Angels could arm their weapons and no Company ship would enter the Sector. But still officially it was Damaris Brightlaw versus Chairman Charlock and a private family war, and neutrals that could duck fast enough could come and go with impunity.

It strikes me as a damn roundabout way to collect taxes.

But while there was a war on there was bidness to be done, and where we was going to do it was Port Mantow on Royal, where Meggie would hand over an ample sufficiency of street-lethals to someone best unnamed (the valuta was on its being Damaris' side), the captaincy to Merodach, and *Angelcity*'d be nonfiction on its wayaway.

At least, that was how it was supposed to work.

*   *   *

It was half-past meridies and on its way to being dark when Meggie, Baijon, and me left *Angelcity* to meet the sophont as was eventually going to give us her money.

It was summer in Port Mantow. The crete was giving up stored solar radiation in waves and the air shimmered. Archangel's Best was flying formations overhead, zinging back and forth like black bat knights and making me scairt they was going to drop one of those overcoked high-heat flitterbyes on my head.

I wondered where His Nobly-Bornness was, and how he was keeping care of nights with all alMayne fighting the question of was he a Librarian back and forth big and noisy and public.

Two Imperial Space Marines, well-armored as homegrown starships and twice as temperamental, ran us through scanners and checked our tickets at the gate. None of us'd bothered to try to go out armed; Meggie'd peace-sealed Baijon's *arthame* back at the ship and the Marines passed it.

They looked twice at me, but they always do; it's why I stay in the Outfar. But they passed all three of us and we got off the port facility and into the teeming downside, which it wasn't much at the moment.

"I just hope we can get this settled before they lock us up for curfew violation," Meggie muttered.

We had four hours till then and the streets was empty even now. Archangel's Finest was coming down hard, and probably the only reason this wasn't an Official Imperial Action was Archangel couldn't come down hard in too many places at once without he had the warmbodies to do it, and his warmbodies of choice was all locked up in the Azarine Coalition.

We got to where Meggie's contact supposed to was and went in. She'd told me she'd got two-thirds up front—S.O.P. when the legger's got to shell out to buy the goods—and now she wanted the small change and whatever ideas the buyer had on taking delivery. It wasn't impossible he'd be taking the stuff right off *Angelcity* in port—there's things you can do with the right squeeze to the right groundcrew.

It was a place called Warped Space; good entrance, good exits.

"Table in back, by the door," Meggie told me.

I motioned Baijon to close up. There was a divider running out from the wall. It hid a bench and part of the table; you could see without being seen.

We came round it, Meggie first. Her contact was waiting for us.

It was Errol Lightfoot.

Errol Lightfoot had been last seen running Old Fed Illegals into the Roaq for Mallorum Archangel's frontlizard, Kroon'Vannet, what I'd dropped a proton grenade on. Errol shouldn't of been alive.

He was one of the few people that could finger me for a High Book rap. He'd been one of the people who'd brought Archive back to life.

He sold me as a slave when I was fourteen. And besides, I plain didn't like him. Some people just take you that way.

He took Baijon that way, too. Didn't even try to clear his *arthame;* he just knocked Meggie flat and dove for Errol. Probably he saved her life.

There was something bent about Errol's showing up here but I didn't have time to reason it out right now. I had just time to remember that fair was fair and I had after all promised Baijon Errol's life next time he came acrost him when two Space Angels popped up from behind the bar and started shooting.

I grabbed the nearest thing handy and chucked it in the direction of the blaster-bolts. Meggie was rolling to her feet and pulling the hideout she'd managed to slip past Debarkation Control, and the Angels was yelling for reinforcements; I *knew* it.

Was explosion out in the street and the front of Warped Space went warped for sure.

Errol sliced Baijon with something. Meggie shot back at the Angels and hit some technology behind the bar that blew up and sprayed us with molten goo.

"Go!" I shouted.

I shoved her at the back door and hoped we was just not important enough to waste any more Angels on.

Baijon was sitting on Errol. He had one hand wrapped around Errol's throat and was hauling at his *arthame* with the other. He also had a gen-u-ine hellflower bloodstain spreading across his gaudy shirt where Errol'd tagged him. I saw this in the instant it took me to grab Errol's blaster and use it to discourage the local boys in black from raising their heads up. We had to get our heads out of here. And Baijon's hair wasn't long enough to grab him by any more, dammit.

"Come on, come *on!*" I yelled without looking. I snapped off another shot. The A-grav transport full of reinforcement landed in the street. Out of the corner of my eye I saw the flash as Baijon finally got his *arthame* free.

He looked at me.

"Come on or we're dead."

Baijon let go of Errol and started to his feet. Errol made to do something he never finished because the *arthame* flickered like summer lightning and cut Errol Lightfoot's throat from ear to ear. Errol fell back in a splash of blood that looked on its way to being real permanent-like and Baijon and me went out the back way as more Angels was coming in the front.

Welcome to Royal.

*   *   *

"This way."

Baijon seemed awfully damn sure of where he was going, but I didn't necessarily have any better ideas. Behind us there was yelling and shooting and all the sorts of noises I generally go the other way from.

Meggie was nowhere in sight.

I had to run to keep up with Baijon; when he saw I was he went faster, and nevermind he was leaking. We switchbacked roundabout until the ruckus behind us Dopplered off and I couldn't of said which way the port was for any credit.

The city got bigger and I got lost. You couldn't see the port towers any more for the buildings and floaters in the way, and the things I did see belonged in a talkingbook, not reality.

We went in somewhere, and then up a bounce-shaft, and then we was out on a roof.

Stardancers have to have a head for heights. When you're in a suit hanging outside your ship with nothing between your boots but so much down that you could fall forever and not get there you'd better not get too excited about it.

I'd never cared about the fall before.

This was different.

It wasn't just the gravity, or the air-mass trying to push both of us over the edge of what wasn't a dropshaft. It wasn't even that we was up so high that I could see for kliks and kliks.

It was *what* I could see. As far as I looked there was city—nothing green, nothing wasted, just city going on and on forever like a puzzle-box, or a machine.

And Royal wasn't even really big. The talkingbooks called it "gently rural," whatever that meant.

On and on and on.

"Kore," said Baijon.

I turned away from being dazzled by the light. Baijon was crouched in the middle of the roof, hand over his side in a gesture more hopeful than useful.

"Let me see that." I was still holding somebody's blaster from back at the Warped Space. I set it down and hoped the wind would leave it there.

I ripped his shirt out of his belt. It came away easy on account of he was still bleeding.

"Can't you keep your skin in one piece together for five minutes? Every time I stop to scratch I'm kitchening you up again."

It was wide and gaudy but it wouldn't kill him except maybe for bloodloss, and there wasn't a damn thing handy to my hand to cork him with.

"I am all right," Baijon said. He put a hand back over the leak and winced.

"Sure you are, bai."

"I wished to take the head of the *chaudatu* Lightfoot. It was mine," Baijon said wistfully.

"Sure it was, babby." So Errol Lightfoot, Fenshee slaver and all-round antidote to the work ethic, was dead. It probably should of left a bigger hole in my life, but I was all took up with wondering if Meggie was all right, or laid up somewheres with a serious case of being dead. I knew what was up with *Angelcity.*

If Mero'd been fast she was buttoned up and the heat had her wrapped in tractors and was trying to starve her out. If he hadn't been fast enough, him and all her crew was off somewheres in a box with locks, waiting out the merciful and reasonable justice of the Empire.

"Where are we, anyways?"

"I do not know. We have a little time here, at least."

Baijon pulled off his shirt and vest and ripped the shirt into a passable bandage. He looked at me for whatever great plan I'd spontaneously come up with and then went back to his patch job. I held the pad in place while he tied it down.

"The port is that way," he offered, pointing with his chin.

"And how do *you* know?"

"We came from there," he said, and shrugged.

I thought over all our options on Royal for a real long time—maybe a kilo-second.

"Well we better get back there." Because like it or not, Port Mantow was our only way out of Royal's killing box.

*   *   *

I would of holed up in Port Mantow if I thought ID that named *Angelcity* as our ship would be a ticket to anything but free Imperial room and board for as long as Archangel didn't know who we was. Baijon and me both had credit, but not enough to fox ID or bribe a lift even as far as Royal's moon.

And I didn't think that the late Errol Lightfoot's being the one to meet Meggie was as much of a coincidence as it ought to be.

But it *had* to be, right? Because Mother Night her own self hadn't known me and Baijon was going to be on that ship.

There was something that still bothered me a whole lot about Errol, but I put that thought out of my mind for later prospecting. Might-be-maybes is for when you're safe, not running for your life.

*   *   *

Curfew fell whilst we tried to find a way back that didn't include Space Angels. If I'd thought it out I would of gone for the fastest route and never mind the Angels, because Archangel's Finest don't work overtime.

Something else does.

The wartoy caught up to us within sight of the port.

Taller'n me, taller'n Baijon, taller'n The Wall That Walked back on sunny alMayne where I couldn't imagine why I'd wanted to leave it just now. It lurched out in front of us and started spieling the warning that some cratty back on Throne a thousand lights away probably thought was cute: all about how this area was under the direct control of the Nobly-Born Mallorum Archangel and I should just be tickled to death at the fact.

To death was maybe right. The wartoy was big and wide and covered with enough hostile artifacts to remind you that breaking curfew was a automatic Class D warrant. I had a feeling it probably wasn't going to be any too gentle tagging a innocent passerby for later pick up.

"Run," I suggested.

Baijon skittered back, trying to square common sense and honor and do it on his feet. The wartoy trundled forward. I raised my stolen blaster.

I saw its launch-arm come up and I had sense enough to throw the heat away from me. I threw myself the other way and the tronic blew Errol's hand-cannon out of the ether. Then it missed me with something long and ugly that writhed like a brokebacked snake, looking for something to wrap around and squeeze. Baijon wrenched a holosim exciter off the side of a building and chucked it at the critter next.

I rolled into the gutter and wondered if I could make it down the maintenance access and knew the answer. There was a snap as ports in the wartoy's little metal waterline popped open and something heavy, oily, and yellow started vaporing out.

Then the top of its head exploded.

*   *   *

"Dammit—I thought you two were with the Rebellion!"

Tronics from all over was converging on the smoking ruin Meggie'd blasted the wartoy into with a rifle she'd persuaded some altruistic Angel to donate—and we was converging the other way.

"That's why I took you with me—we were supposed to pick up a Brightlaw courier on alMayne but whoever it was never showed up—and then you go and shoot my contact!"

"And six-dozen Space Angels! Saved your livealive, Meggie-bai; was Errol Lightfoot, first class trouble."

There was some more silence whiles we hotfooted it down deserted streets where every part of reality was machined like a high-ticket blaster. Civilization.

"It's lucky those damn things're so stupid," she said after whiles. "I'd wanted to shoot one anyway to draw the others off. Thought I was going to have to rig the rifle to overload. Look, are you sure you're not with the Rebellion? We could use the help about now."

"Meggie, don't you think if we was wanting to join up with a bunch of idealistic brainburn cases on Royal we'd of told you?"

"No." That from Baijon. I looked at him.

"Right. Here we are."

She stopped in front of one of the buildings that ringed the port. There was a regular touchpad lock on the side, and if you had a suspicious mind you could see there was a door there. Beyond the building was a blank space, then the fence—and paradise and freedom if we could get there.

"Access tunnel to the port," Meggie said, and pulled a shimcrib out of her boot.

"Remind me to go walking with you sometime when you're well-armed," I said.

She just grinned and put the card over the plate.

"*Kore,* are we breaking the law yet?"

"Since about you jumped Errol-peril, bai," I told him.

And Errol the ex-Peril'd broke it first. An older law, about not selling out your own side.

"Good," my hellflower said, real satisfied. "I wished to be sure."

The access tunnel opened and we went in.

*   *   *

The three of us went down the tunnel to the first branch. Meggie stopped and leaned against the curved wall, and sat down.

"As good a place to wait as any," she said.

"For what?" Baijon was puzzled enough to ask, and I had a bad feeling I knew.

"Inspiration. Or did you think I had a plan, both of you? Funny; I hoped you did—I just hope *Angelcity's* oke and Mero can put the fix in to get us off. It's a good thing he buttoned her up tight when we left."

Meggie looked up and down the tunnel. She could figure odds as well as I could; these weren't good.

"Probably all they wanted was the guns. And I could prove we didn't have them."

"Wrong," I said.

"But," said Meggie, like it was a whole sentence. Like: *But what an t'hell do you mean? You been holding out on me, St. Cyr, maybe?*

"You remember I done told you one-time about Fenshee slaver hight Errol Lightfoot."

She nodded; Meggie and me go back to where I was still figuring angles on how to find and ice our boy Errol.

"Last seen walking into Mallorum Archangel's pocket out in the Roaq in a Chapter 5 rig, trust me. I was there. Selling all sides against middle, likely. He'd of found your guns, Meggie. And anyway, he knows your rep. Wouldn't even bother to look. Just gig the lot."

"And his life was mine, and I have taken it—but I wished to have his head as well," Baijon said, plaintive.

"It'd look great in your hopechest, bai."

"So what about my ship?" Meggie said.

The only one as didn't know the answer to that might be Baijon.

"It's only guns!" said Meggie, opening and closing her hand like she wanted something to shoot. "Just a fine."

No. Not even if me and Baijon hadn't been along; not even if Meggie'd walked right into Errol's arms and then into Imperial lockup swearing all the way she'd never *seen* a starship. There was the scent of Example To Others about Royal, and we all smelled it.

"So you tell me my life-story and I'll tell you yours," I said. Meggie shrugged. What else did we have to do with our time?

"Guns are steady profit, if you have the hold space to waste on enough of them. alMayne's one of our regular stops, every two hundred days or so. Hawkharrow and Estel-Shadowmaker rigs from Barnegat; one of the Starborn LessHouses buys them for us. What else can we do

—Indies can't compete with the Company anywhere in Directorate Space; they'll ship free rather than lose a cargo to one of us."

"Cut to the chase," I told her, even if it's true about Company ships.

"We were on Diapason, in Harmony. A cut-out offered us the job; standard split and a meet-cute in Port Mantow. We had the contacts, the money was good—it had to be the Brightlaws—"

"Chairman Charlock not having too much trouble arming his troops these days," I put in.

"So we hit alMayne and made our deal for the mixture as before. It usually takes them a couple few days to put a deal together, but it's not a bad port to lie-up in—"

She was rambling all over the story, was Meggie, wondering what was happening to *Angelcity* and thinking she maybe knew. I let myself wish that Paladin was here; I'd been in the own cousin of this scrape a dozen times and he'd always got me out. Reality is what your computer tells you it is, and computers believed anything Paladin told them.

"—so we were waiting and someone with a conduct from never-you-mind came and booked two passages to Royal for whoever showed up and said the magic word before we left. I wondered for a while if it was you, but I guess you would of said, right? They never showed. Left something for them I've still got in my lockbox. And this just isn't *fair!*"

No it wasn't. And for once it wasn't my fault.

But it was my problem.

What is reality? I felt the pushing feeling at the back of my mind that I'd used to get when I was about to be brilliant and got these days when somebody else's mindset was yelling for attention. Or maybe it was mine—how would I know?

What is reality?

Is it what we can drag in through the natural receptors of a piece of protoplasm? If it is, then the world is a small place. But we don't like small. We build new senses to gather reality. And if what our made senses tell us is different from what our bodies see, which do we believe?

The wrong one, usually.

Our problem was reality-based. We couldn't do damnall about the problem, so there was just one thing left.

Do something about the reality.

I thought about Errol's head, and how I really couldn't think why Baijon shouldn't have it if he wanted it. I thought about how Mero and Meggie deserved enough luck to get upside with *Angelcity.*

I thought about most of the things you think about in the dead of night whiles you're listening to your mind disintegrate.

"I want you to do me a thing, Meggie. I get you out of here, we got a deal, deal?"

Meggie looked at me, more suspicious than hopeful.

"Nobody can get us out of here—unless they're drawing to an inside straight."

"I get you out, I get *Angelcity* up, you do me a thing, je?"

"St. Cyr, you get us out of here and I'll marry you."

"You don't get off that easy. It's like this. Washonnet's at war because the hellflowers've heard Mallorum Archangel's a Librarian."

Meggie made a editorial noise.

"I get you out of here, you say they're right. You tell everybody: he's *Malmakosim,* he's riding High Book."

"The point of the exercise, St. Cyr, is supposed to be an improvement on how things are now."

"Did I say you got to stand around and wait for the late-breaking reviews? Don't put your name on it. Just pass the word."

"Are you sure about this, St. Cyr? About Archangel?"

"You telling me you *care,* Meggie-bai? Ask hellflowers for true-tell; me, I just asked you favor."

"There's no way you can pull this off."

"Then we all be dead and you got nothing to pay."

Meggie looked at me like she thought I was crazy. Silly frail; I *knew* I was. No harm in it. Some of my best friends is crazy.

And besides, there was one of Paladin's old tricks with the Imperial dataweb I wanted to try. Only I didn't have his advantages. I had to get to a terminal.

"Do I have a choice?" Meggie said.

None at all.

* * *

The Power Tower is a tower even when it's a bunker underground —it's the building on any port that handles in/out traffic.

Usually it's big enough so there's a place where the Trade Customs & Commerce Officer updates the ships-in-port registry and arranges to search any ships flagged there; lockups for confiscated contraband; places to handle fees licenses registration and all the other ways the Empire scrapes credit off you for trying to make a living with a ship.

But it doesn't have to have any of those things. All it needs is one room with a DataNet hookup for the songbirds to juggle the incoming and outgoing traffic on.

It was the dataweb I wanted, and I didn't see any reason to walk in uplevel amongst the *legitimates* and ask for it. Not with the connects running right down into the maintenance tunnels where we was and with an access terminal here for systems checks.

I didn't know if this was going to work. What I had was the stone bankable belief that it would—but then I also thought I was a Old Federation Library Archive, or sort of.

Paladin had done it. I knew that from the outside and remembered it from the inside if I wasn't crazy.

It was simple to do.

If you was made out of light and magic.

But I was flesh and bone—mostly. I couldn't walk into a computer and think its thoughts for it.

"What are you going to do?" Meggie came up beside me. I looked at her and shrugged.

We was both following Baijon. Not only was he growing more larcenous by the tik, he *always* knew where we was relative to *Angelcity* and the main port gate. Without that we could of been lost slightly longer than forever down here; starved to death and been found by the housekeeping tronics.

Better'n what Errol's playmates had planned for us, but how much was that saying, really?

"This way." Baijon came back from where he was scouting and waved us on.

"Going to go into the DataNet and change the file on *Angelcity* so's you've got Clearance-to-Lift," I told Meggie.

"Oh, what a relief. For a moment there I thought you had a plan."

*   *   *

Around bedtime Meggie's variable-generating compkey did shimcrib on one last gate, and we was in the downdeep underbeneath the Power Tower.

I like knowing how things is put together. Always have. With the net result I know a lot of pretty damn useless things, 'cause when is a girl like I going to be underneath the Power Tower messing with its main computer?

Now, is when.

"Now what?" said Meggie.

I looked around. It wasn't really a room at all, just the place where a vertical pipe intersected a horizontal one. There was a row of hand and foot holds going up the wall—to guide you when the dropshaft was on and use alone when it wasn't. They led up to things like light and air and *legitimates.*

The touchpad was right where it belonged to be, sticking out from the cable going from up to down like a afterthought. A tech pulling maintenance on the dataweb would jack a separate brain in here, not to mention a display; piggyback it on the main DataNet access to check for lumps, bumps, and strange foreign logic.

Which meant there was a way to plug in.

Meggie was carrying enough toys for me to pop the housing easy and quick. Inside it looked like every other piece of partytech ever hatched, except cleaner. The jacks for the peripherals was bundled in place.

I pulled off my gloves and ran my fingers over the pad, and I knew I could do it.

"Baijon, you loan me your Knife, one-time."

Because whatever I was now, I was just not-human enough to get myself killed real spectacular.

"St. Cyr?" Meggie said again.

I shook my head to clear it of the series of access codes ringing in my brain. The way wayaway into the part of the Royal planetary brain that controlled all the port functions was so clear and open I could walk it—and only existed as pulses of light.

I took a deep breath.

"Now you go back *Angelcity,* Meggie. Three minutes, then up and into the building. Nobody stop you, specially if they don't see you."

Meggie stared at me, weighing all the other things she could maybe do and coming up with the same answer I did. Finally she nodded.

I looked at Baijon. He shook his head. I wasn't surprised. He was staying with me, faithful for the next fifty-six galactic standard years, or until he figured out I had *Malmakos* on the brain.

"And maybe we see you again and you remember this. And maybe not."

"You don't have to do this, Butterfly," Meggie said, although since she couldn't think I was going to jack myself in series with the planetary core I don't know what she thought I was going to do.

"There ain't no other way, Meggie. Now go on and let me get to cases."

She kissed me and hugged Baijon and went. And there we was.

Three minutes.

It wasn't me, I kept telling myself, which I'd believed all along until it was time to cut it. I knew it wasn't going to hurt. High-class cyberwork has a cut-out to keep its dainty patrons from feeling stress and unease. I took Baijon's Knife and slit the fake skin on my arm.

I peeled it back and dug through the padding and insulation until I could see the glass bones underneath. This was part of me; this was what jumped when my brain said hell and high.

Two minutes.

There was a bunch of color-coded leads running back and forth: silver for power, purple for memory, and a couple others that spent their time datagathering and then tricking my brain into thinking it felt something. Those were the ones I wanted.

I slid the *arthame*-blade under one. Baijon watched me intent like I was doing it to him. I twisted the blade, hoping it would shear through.

White light exploded in my skull as the sensors mailed everything home at once. I staggered, and Baijon held me up. Two yellow wires curled up out of my arm and for the first time I could feel the prosthesis as something not part of me. I flexed its fingers. They opened and closed just like always, but a little heavier.

And now I could plug the computer right into my brain and play Library.

I didn't want to. And I did. Ultimate risk. The wildest ride that ever was, and not even needing a ship to take it. Pure fun.

I wrapped the dataweb jacks around my sensory-lead and the world went away.

One minute. I keyed the touchpad with my free hand.

At first I was just fooling about, feeling my way into the net. There wasn't the holotank that would of shown me the computer's answers in Intersign glyphs, but I didn't need it. What I was doing was like remembering a dream, only I wasn't remembering anything. I was making it real.

Or I was lying to myself.

It was simple to dump memory from the sensors uplevel without saving it somewhere for Security to see it. I followed Meggie out of the building by the scanners she tripped, but everything they had to tell they told just me, and I wiped it.

There was a stasis field around *Angelcity*. I couldn't turn it off or cancel it without setting off alarms, but I could move it to some other ship. So I did.

That's when they started to notice. I knew they would, but they wasn't quite sure yet. They didn't know what and they didn't know how —just something where and (pretty soon) who.

I was finished with the Port computers; I'd done all I could with them. What I wanted now was in to the planetary core where they kept laws and facts and suchlike.

It's supposed to be impossible. Paladin did it all the time, silk-sailing. For me it was somewhere in between—and it took time, which I didn't have much of.

"*Kore,* they are coming," Baijon said, strained.

I knew it. But I was close, so close, almost in, and it was so damn awkward making my fingers do what my mind could see, and the touchpad ports was so *slow* . . .

Code, and wait, and code, and wait-wait-wait, like a lag-time between thoughts and how could anybody *think* this slow? And me never sure I was hearing the computer right, or my fantasies was playing me false, or maybe Baijon'd figure there was something not-quite-right enough to make real trouble.

Waiting . . .

Now I could hear what he'd heard—rattle and rumpus and *legitimates* out in the tunnel looking for to find their way in.

Like I was in. I had the whole world in my hands, and anything I wrote was truth.

There was no warrant for Megaera Dare.

There was no hold order on the Independent Ship *Angelcity.*

The ship had immediate clearance.

I told the DataNet that and it believed me, and after that, any other truths didn't matter. I was dazzled watching new truth write itself in unreality for anyone who wanted to check it to believe.

The port computers and orbital data-catchers told me *Angelcity* was gone: real truth, not virtual truth.

"*Kore—*" The footsteps was close now: men in armor.

"You was the best friend I ever had, Baijon-bai. Fact."

But it was too late for Baijon and me to go anywhere at all.

11

Tainted Love

The cell was like all other cells. There was plenty time to think whiles you was in, and plenty things to rather not think about. Partly I thought about Charlock Corporation's werewolves taking Baijon. They'd took him somewheres away from me when they found us. I wondered if he was still alive.

What I thought about mostly was how Baijon and me was maybe not the galaxy's best team, somewise. Oh, he was cute and fast and ready with a blaster and I've got my points, but wasn't neither of us temperamentally suited to say "whoa" when t'other one came up with a fun new way to get killed.

I'd always counted on Paladin for that. Only he wasn't here now to tell me my notions was damfool; what there was, was a starry-eyed kid who thought I was god's older sister.

One of us was going to have to learn to be—what was Pally's word for it?—*reasonable.*

If we got out of here I promised to start working on that. Tomorrow.

Not that there was going to be one. Fake ID, curfew violation, trespassing—we was spare parts. At least I was.

I was debating the musical question of whether it would do Baijon any serious net life good if the *legitimates* knew who he was when they gave him back.

It'd took four of them to carry him here and they didn't try to set him down any gentle—they *threw* him. He bounced right back and started trying to claw his way through the shut door.

Eventually even a hellflower had to give it up. He slid down to the floor in a huddle of misery and finally saw me.

"They have taken my Knife, *Kore*," he said. Then he clung to me and wept like they'd cut out his heart.

Ever wonder why it is you got no hellflower trouble under the Pax Imperador? They all come hardwired with a built-in hostage to fortune, is why. The Knife. It isn't something they own. It's *them*. A hellflower's going to leave his *arthame* behind about the time I shoot myself in the head for recreation. Whoever's got the Knife's got the owner. And that makes a hellflower real vulnerable.

And now the *legitimates* had Baijon's.

Finally he quieted some and looked at me. Some kindly soul had bandaged him up all legit and official, which he had made serious renovations on trying to walk through a locked wall, and lifted his Knife whiles they was doing it. And I didn't think he was cute, or funny, or any other such condescending thing. He'd put everything he had on the line for me time and again when I was doing things that was just as stupid and nonsense to him as grieving over a damn knife was to me. I owed him.

"First you tell me, Baijon. Then we kill all of them and get it back."

It wasn't really important that we was both on the same side of a locked door, neither. Or that I had about as much chance of making good on that promise as I did of being elected Emperor. I meant it, and that was all Baijon cared about.

"They are *not* human beings, *Kore*—they are animals, breaking even their own law. The *chaudatu* laws say they cannot touch it—do they doubt the word of one of the Gentle People, the vow that it will not be used in battle against them?"

Well *I* would, and so would anyone with any sense. But that wasn't the point.

"They be just wanting to nail you somewise, bai, and make you tell them things." Like who you are, and who your da is, and what we two was doing with their computer, and how. I flexed my fingers and watched the cybereisis bells and whistles move back and forth in the open part.

"Never." Interphon didn't have enough flavor for him—he repeated it in helltongue where it really does mean that: *never, forever, and I really do know the difference between never and not-now.*

"Yeah, bai. Never-ever-forever. And we get out of here and crottle their greeps, sure. But we got to wait for it."

Baijon rocked back on his haunches, ready to wait at top speed. He looked at me, suspicious I didn't quite understand his point of view.

"They are not human, *Kore*. They are less than animals—they could have been human, and forswore humanity. Thus they endanger humans by their example. They are *wrong.*"

"Sure, bai. I know." He might of had a point, but it was too damn pretty and theoretical for me. And they already made me mad enough to agree with Baijon whether he was right or not. Because he couldn't of hurt them with his damn Knife—and if they was scared of it they could just of glued it shut. But they took it.

Why?

Not a bad question, when you came right down to the hard-and-sharpies.

Because until we was definitely criminal, the *legitimates* had to play by the rules, and the rules was, Baijon got to keep his *arthame* until after he was dead. Even on Wanderweb Free Port, they'd only took it after they said he was guilty and condemned, and Free Ports don't follow the Pax Imperador.

But the people who'd took it here had medicalled Baijon—which meant he was valuable enough that they surely wouldn't risk him icing himself over getting his Knife took away.

Right?

Unfortunately the empirical evidence was against it.

*   *   *

Baijon and me was left alone for the optimal period some paid expert sometime told the heat was the right length of time to soften up members of the criminal element with trepidation and remorse. Then a couple Size Large werewolves in Space Angel black came looking for us.

Baijon looked at me. *Wait for it,* I 'signed at him. But we wasn't going to wait one tik past where his Knife was in sight. I owed him that, and I wasn't putting it aside for some "greater good," neither. Fair is fair.

Darktraders pay their debts.

So we walked meek down the corridor between the heat, me looking for an angle I could use.

I had been in this situation lots and lots and I'd never been in it before. I'd been in some trouble, sure, but mostly I'd *almost* been in trouble if somebody was to notice what I was doing.

And I'd never been in Directorate space, let alone got in trouble here, because any basic medical scan'd reveal me for what I was—an Interdicted Barbarian, illegal immigrant from someplace as had paid the Empire good money to throw away the key. I'd heard rumors, and stands to reason more people'n me'd tried it, but I'd never met anyone else from one of the dicty-worlds in Tahelangone Sector. They don't send you home when they catch you out here, neither. They shoot you.

It was a pretty good bet I'd been scanned in the cell. So looking at it from that angle, wasn't nothing logistical standing in the way of me helping Baijon turn the place inside out going after his Knife. I had nothing left to lose.

We was still somewheres in the Power Tower—at least, all the time I'd been conscious we hadn't gone anywheres that could be outside it unless the *legitimates* was playing pharmaceutical headgames with my reality. We went to a lift, and up, and then we was on a level with windows—fancy nonsense when holosims'd work better but *I* like 'em— and I could see there was still port outside, coming on along of dawn.

I knew every ship down there, origin-destination-dockage-tonnage-stowage-and-rating. I knew who they was and where they was. *Everything* from the ships-in-port directory.

I was drowning in raw memory.

Whoever "I" was.

When the shivaree in my skull had died down and I could pay attention to the real world again we was in very important sophont land, and we picked up four more little helpers—all glittering armor this time and armed to the high-heat. Baijon fluffed up a little when he saw them, but he went on waiting.

My head hurt. Only slightly worse than that secondhand chaos and old night was the absolute conviction that somewhere in that mass of undigested data I shouldn't never have been able to get off a touchpad keyboard even with a hotwire straight to my brain was guaranteed luck and a way out.

If I could find it in time.

We went through a last set of doors into the kind of stone lux place they bring you to tell you to kill yourself somewheres else and save them the fuss. The kind of place every bully has if he can swing it, from nighttime man to pimp to king. Business as usual, really. It was impressive, but it was supposed to be impressive. So I wasn't impressed.

There was another short-order of Space Angels there, and someone else. And I knew we was in real trouble. Fact.

You couldn't look at him. Very slick: holosim augmentation and subsonics and maybe pheromones. No matter what you did you couldn't look at him straight on.

So I didn't even try. I looked out the window at the ships left out on the field. I could see a little of him out of the corner of my eye: silk that ate light and glitterflash so damn expensive I'd only read descriptions of the stones.

"Welcome to Port Mantow. I am delighted to be able to greet you properly at last—Valijon Starbringer and Butterflies-are-free Peace Sincere."

His voice had a distorter on it, too: fear and command and other stuff that made it so you couldn't get your attention off him. Not too useful for long chats, I bet, but then Mallorum Archangel didn't have to have too many long conversations.

"You have my leave to speak," Archangel said, and Baijon ripped out a sentence of pure, double-distilled, helltongue treason. It settled my mind considerable—there wasn't no way either of us was going to get out of the room alive after that.

"Trite," Archangel said. "But children don't know any better—and you, foolish boy, are unlikely to have time to learn. You can be of some small use to me to make up for the small inconvenience you have been. You will do all that is within your power to please me because you have nothing left to bargain with—while I continue to have the opportunity to grant . . . concessions."

Archangel said it all unruffled like Baijon hadn't called him seventy-seven kinds of bad name. He gestured, and his hand came clear a minute when it got outside the distorter field. And I saw what Archangel was holding. Baijon's Knife.

Baijon saw it too, and the two Space Angels clamped down on him quick. Their armor rattled as he lunged, but he couldn't move them. Archangel probably smiled, and Baijon's *arthame* vanished back into the field.

"Concessions, as I said. You have no idea what a great pleasure it is to see you again so that we may have this conversation. Now. Where is it?"

I don't think Baijon heard him, but I did. All the distorter harmonics making every word His Nobility uttered the most important there ever was, and what I heard was Archangel asking the wrong question.

"You brought it here from alMayne. You used it beneath the Port. I am not interested in a long seduction. Where is it?" Archangel said.

Not *"Who are you?"* or even *"Aha, I have you now, Fillintheblank."* *"Where is it?"*

The TwiceBorn Lord Prince, the Nobly-Born Lord Mallorum Archangel, Governor-General of the Phoenix Empire wanted some-*thing* out of us, even knowing who we was—and whatever it was, we didn't have it.

I heard the servos in the Angels' armor whine as Baijon fought them. I just stood there, flatfoot and stupid while shimmering evil looked us over and decided which one to take first.

"You *will* tell me," he said to either of us or none, and only twenty years of habit kept my mouth shut.

So a Space Angel tuned me up some—not bad, just enough to remind me how much pain could hurt. If I'd been on my own turf and they'd been serious, they'd of followed it up with taking off a finger or doing something else permanent to indicate their sincere displeasure. But they didn't.

The next thing I remembered was coming back from being kicked in the face, felt like, and seeing three Angels holding Baijon front and center of Archangel whiles another one offered Archangel a little black box.

Little black boxes never have anything in them you want.

I must of moved, because there was enough Angels at large to haul me up and shake me.

The pain felt like it was something very important to somebody who wasn't me. Visual focus went on and off in flashes of light and I dripped on the carpet, but I could see.

The black box went on a side table and got its two halves yanked apart. Then it got turned on.

A beam of light ran between the two terminals that'd been in the halves of the box; dark red, the beam was, and all along the surface it sparked where the motes of dust touched it and made the conversion to energy.

A molecular debonder. The small kind, for tidy security in home and office. And I bet I knew what was going into that beam, one piece at a time.

But I was wrong. They hustled me up close all right, but just to watch.

"If you actually think that I am unaware of your father's pathetic ambitions as kingbreaker, little prince, think twice. Your revered and moral father was my hound to flush out those who wish my Empire to be less than tidy, and now the time has come to whip him to kennel. You will be the lash. For love of you Kennor Starbringer will beg on his knees to serve me in any way I choose. But you'll do it first. I want the

Brightlaw Prototype—the one you were attempting to bring to the insurgents under cover of an arms delivery."

Oh, *that* Brightlaw Prototype.

Baijon snarled, too far gone to talk any kind of words at all.

Archangel held out his hand. Light and music rippled all over him from the distorter fields and I had to look away. Out of the corner of my eye I saw Baijon's *arthame* flash red in the light from the debonder.

"Where is it?" Archangel said, all silk. "You can't deny it. You used it against the port computers to help the gunrunner escape. The 'honor' of the alMayne—it has doomed you and your creature and gained nothing. The ship never left the system."

"No," I said, before I could help it.

"Yes." I got Archangel's undivided attention for a instant and wished I hadn't. "Tell me, Prince Valijon, which do you value more: this tribal totem, or . . ."

"*Librarian,*" snarled Baijon. "*Malmakosim.*"

Even here it got a little attention—you just don't call someone, anyone, a Librarian and go back to what you was doing the minute before. But the six-pack of Angels'd heard it before, or maybe they just didn't care.

"It was *your* Library," snarled Baijon, "and all the Gentle People know your shame, eater of—"

One of the Angels holding Baijon smacked him a short businesslike wallop with a truncheon, which put an effective end to discussion of Imperial hot cuisine.

Archangel turned the *arthame* and the blade flashed red in the light.

"Do you actually think anyone will believe that? This is the nine-hundred and ninety-second Year of Imperial Grace, Prince Valijon, not the dark ages. Your hellflower kindred know what they want—and it isn't a holy war."

"The Gentle People—"

"Will do what is prudent, expedient, and politic. As *you* will do what I want, my darling hotspur—for this. In the end, the alMayne is not so different from the *chaudatu* he despises, is he?"

Flash, the blade in the light. I tried to move, but my pet Angels wasn't having any. Any more folding from them and the cybereisis was just going to shear loose of what was left of my original collarbone.

"I don't want it," Baijon said, flat. His voice was hard, and there weren't no kinchin-bai left in it at all.

"Very well." Archangel opened his hand. The Knife slid through his fingers into the debonder beam. When it hit it warped every way at once with a sound like hot grease poured into water. Then it was gone, and just a couple flakes of carbon was left.

Baijon went gray and made the kind of sound you hear in nightmares. He hung boneless between the two Angels, and now they was holding him up not back. There was a flicker from behind the distorter, and they pushed Baijon down to his knees. His head hung, limp.

"Pretty princeling," said Archangel. "Strength of character prevails only in the talkingbooks. Now you've forced me to question your little friend—again."

Then Mallorum Archangel turned off his distorter and I could see him plain.

The shocks came in sequence. Each one hit separate, giving me time to feel them all.

Clothes more expensive than anything I could make up. Half armor that was mostly a joke and the rest valuta made solid. Human as me, or Baijon.

His hair was short, dusted with something that glittered. Brown hair. Eyes would probably be dark. Fenshee breeding population, by the genetic markers.

Then he turned away from Baijon and toward me. He smiled.

"Hiya, sweetheart, how's tricks?"

It was Errol Lightfoot. But Errol was dead back in that dockside bar.

Then his expression changed, and now the face went with the clothes: arrogant and inhuman, a face to go with all the stories the Patriarchs had ever told back home about hellgods.

"Don't ever confuse playacting with reality, '*Sweetheart.*'"

"You're dead," I said, probably only to me.

He turned away and knelt by Baijon. Archangel made every bad dream I ever had seem like a walk in the sunlight.

"You belong to me now, little Valijon." He put a hand under Baijon's chin and lifted, and looked down into Baijon's eyes.

"You leave him lonealone, bai." I wanted to look around for who'd said it, but I had a awful feeling I knew.

"All right."

He came toward me, and now when it was no damn use at all I remembered what'd bothered me about Errol back at the Warped Space.

Errol's eyes were black. Always had been.

But the Errol that'd been waiting for us'd had purple eyes, same as this Errol here.

Only this Errol was Mallorum Archangel. And his eyes were the deep drowned violet of lethal radiation. They seemed to pulse, a spiral song sucking me in like a Old Fed warpgate. He smiled, and the look was pure predator.

He left Baijon alone.

But he came after me.

"Hold her still," he said while I tried to kick him. I felt the buzz of his personal shield and my foot slid off. The Angels dug into the nerves on my arms, but the left one didn't have any and they couldn't hurt me enough anyway to make me let Archangel touch me.

"Oh, little Butterfly," he said. "I am going to *enjoy* this."

But he did get his hands on me. The barbs on his gloves slid into my skin and ripped, and I didn't feel that either. The only thing in the world was those eyes, and when Archangel was finished enjoying himself wasn't going to be nothing left.

Then something slid by me in my skull on its way to someone else and left me alone. There was a jangle of raw synesthesia that part of me was trying to sort to find out if it was me being hurt, and Archangel shrieked.

"She's a cyborg! *It's in the cyborg!*" He hit me across the face and then turned on one of the Angels holding me, mad somewise beyond reason.

And the Angel let go.

I didn't stop to gawk. I didn't even know what I was going to do until both hands closed around one terminal of the debonder.

Three of my cybereisis fingers slid into the beam and vanished.

And I threw the box.

I didn't care if I killed him, but killing him wouldn't be good enough. What I wanted was what I got—the matter-eater beam hit Archangel's personal shield, tried to suck energy, and blew lunch all over the room.

And then it was just like with bullies the galaxy over. Everybody lost all the careful common sense they'd been saving for a special occasion. They'd go for Archangel first instead of hanging on to us—a chance, if we could use it.

Baijon heaved up and flung one of the Space Angels at the Governor-General. The other one was dead already. I grabbed Baijon and ran.

*　　*　　*

There was a dropshaft at the end of the hall and we took it without waiting to inquire whether it was powered or not. It dropped us two levels down in a place that was obviously where people went to wait for the high-heat to whistle them every day but today. Today it was stone empty, which meant no one between us and the next dropshaft.

If I stopped to think about what'd happened back there I'd go mad. Mallorum Archangel was . . . something . . . that was very bad indeed. And that mindbender'd called me a cyborg.

And destroyed Baijon's Knife.

"Kore, Kore—" said Baijon, sounding desperate scared.

"S'okay, babby. I got a plan."

"We can't. I can't. I have *killed* him, Kore; wherefore does he live? And he had killed me—how will I find Ketreis without— *Kore—!"* Baijon was starting to fold up again now that the first rush was past and I couldn't let him do that.

"Bai, you want him to have you?"

Baijon stopped dithering like I'd kicked him. He'd run into something worse than hell and death and hellflower honor, and he'd listen to a Library if it'd tell him the way away.

Good thing.

"No," said Baijon, and we got our bearings and ran again.

Eventually we came to a dropshaft that was locked.

"Damn!" I slammed off the wall and back against Baijon.

"We are running?" he said, like we hadn't already had this conversation. He looked like a sophont as had gotten his death-wound. But he was moving.

"We is tactically retreating so's we can blow the sonabitch to hell. C'mon, bai, don't clock out on me now. I need you."

I grabbed his arm before he could think of a argument and pulled. Baijon came with the pull, like a proton grenade just waiting to happen.

We'd been running blind, we'd been running *away,* and if it hadn't done anything else for us it'd put enough time between us and Archangel or whoever he was that I could think around the edges of him and plan.

Plan what? There was nothing left but running.

And if I could reach it, something that would give us the longest run of all.

12

Dressed to Kill

I didn't know what level we was on, or how long we'd been running, but I did know that wherever we was we was sealed in with no way out until they came for us. My hands started to shake. I watched them with interest—one born, one made, nothing much to choose between. The made one was missing fingers. The sheared ovals of glass bone glittered. Behind me Baijon was opening doors like he'd found a new mission in life, but there wasn't going to be any way out behind any of them.

"Kore," he said. I turned around. Baijon was standing in a doorway.

And he was holding a gun.

One of the things the Empire does best is impound contraband. Since contraband comes in through port, the pound is at the port—usually somewhere in the Power Tower—at least for the small expensive illegal stuff.

"Illegal Stuff" was what the Intersign glyphs on the door said, and it was—everything small, cute, and liftable the Empire'd taken off passing ships in the last never-you-mind. Food, perfumes, furs, raw gems, made jewelry, tapes and holos and talkingbooks. My onetime stock in trade.

And weapons.

Enough to get us a death quick and certain, and I might of took that way out except after seeing Archangel up close I wasn't sure it'd be *final* enough. If minds could live in webs of starlight and flit from skull to skull on air, just how safe was being dead, anyway?

Not very. I knew Archangel. Just like I knew Errol. And I didn't want to think about either one just now.

So I went for the heat. There was crates and crates, laid out like mayhem's dreamshop, all the way up to a plasma catapult somebody'd shagged off from an Imperial Armory and hadn't got quite wayaway with.

And there was salvation.

I don't know where the original legger got them, and Royal should of scrapped them instead of stashing them here. They've got no resale value, after all.

But I ripped the cover off the first crate and there it was, truth in advertising made flesh.

A suit of Imperial Hoplite Armor.

It stood taller'n a man and not so wide as a starship—the powered armor Fleet'd decommissioned as being too dangerous. For Fleet, they meant. The incidence of fragging went way up when every man-jack of the cannon-fodder'd been issued what amounted to his own portable starship. So they dished the armor.

There was six suits of it here.

"Prob'ly no good," I told Baijon, and broke a nail prying open the chest carapace.

He stared at me like I was crazy and he was in a position to judge, and probably he was right; wasting my time on outlaw tech when a whole rathskeller of frightful was sitting here waiting to be scooped up and primed. But the power-pacs was all there: a double row of big silver buttons just like I slap into my blaster.

"Armor," said Baijon, when he figured it out. "Powered armor."

"Yeah, right. Help me get it out. And hope I remember how to hook it up before they get here."

*   *   *

Paladin always used to say I wasn't interested in learning. That isn't true. Knowledge is stuff that isn't of any practical use. I've got lots of that.

I bought a maintenance manual for the atmosphere suit I had to put together oncet so my ship *Firecat* could pass inspection. It covered all kinds bulgers, including powered armor. There was a chapter on the Hoplite stuff—it was new when the book was animated. I knew there wasn't any Hoplite armor anymore, but I audited that part anyway. And I guessed what I remembered of it wasn't real knowledge, because it sure came in handy now.

Hoplite armor comes all in one piece: you open up the chest and climb in. It doesn't have any built-in weapons—although a man wearing one can use a plasma-catapult like a blaster—it just makes you bigger, faster, and stronger than anything remotely human. What you do need to do with it, to get ready to rock'n'roll, is hook up all the connections between the inner and outer layers of the suit and make sure all the secondary charge accumulators is working.

Anybody sealed up in a working suit of Hoplite armor would be set to walk right through anything Archangel had to throw. Anything.

Tools and extra power-pacs was in the crate, and I could almost hear, through the ghost-dance in my head, Paladin whispering to me: ground-level and below-ground access was sealed, the top floor was secured, then the next, and the next . . .

We was in Fifth Floor Storage, in case anybody wanted to know, Fifth Floor being the cutoff between the working stiffs and the power elite, signified by being full of stuff neither side much wanted.

Baijon was a extra set of hands and I hoped he was learning lots. I was clumsier than I thought without half my left hand, and the armor'd fit him but not me in the time I had to trick with it.

I sealed the last of the leads back behind their foam.

"Do it," I said, and Baijon punched the power switch.

The armor spasmed; we both jumped back. Then it just lay there purring to itself. Waiting for someone to come and tell it what to do.

Maybe I'd hooked it up wrong. Maybe it'd mince Baijon to chitlins when he got in. Yeah. And maybe Archangel's personal guard wasn't six inches from finding us.

No choices left. Baijon stripped down to his bandages and slithered in. I settled the neck brace on him and closed the chest. It went down most of the way for my shoving and then stuck. The suit systems came on and pulled it the rest of the way closed with a snap.

The suit sat up. I backed up. Faint keening like goforths going sour came from it. Baijon moved like he was drunk—big sloppy swinging moves, a little bit fatal if he connected. I backed up again.

He tried to stand and went over with a crash. The sound went on too long, and that was because the door'd went, too. Six Angels in full powered armor: black and silver and looking lightweight next to the Hoplite armor.

"Too bad it didn't work," the captain said. His voice was stripped out flat by the voder. "Where's the prince?"

The armor on the floor sunfished again and nobody needed to draw Mallorum's Angel a picture. He raised his magnetic uncoupler and pointed it at Baijon until the room temperature went up twelve degrees and sparks was jumping between every point on the armor they could.

"There. That should—"

But it didn't. The armor thrashed one more time and stood, and then belted the chief Angel out of the way. He didn't fly far, but he went fast.

They was professionals, they was armed and used to people making trouble, and they was outclassed. Two of them dropped and started firing and the other three scattered. Baijon went right over the two in the doorway. Their armor shattered like cheap formfit and their blasters could of been shooting oxygen for all the good they did.

Baijon didn't need a blaster. All he had to do was walk up and hit them.

"*Kore!*" His voice was all warped and distorted through the voder. I scooped up the nearest blaster—another Class B warrant, possession of a military sidearm—and chased after him.

Right into the tangle field.

They work the same way a tractor-pressor combo does: push-pull until whatever's grabbed moves only where you want it to. Fine for starships.

Lousy for people.

Cause my feet was *stopped*. The thing was set to prohibit lateral motion only—I could jump straight up, if I could, and it wouldn't stop me. But it wouldn't let me move forward, and if I got unlucky it could kill me. I could fall and twist joints out of their sockets trying to fold me up the way my original designer intended. And if I fell real wrong and made breathing a lateral motion, I'd be dead.

But I didn't have time to fall. It was like running into a wall, and I yelped, and Baijon whipped back around and lifted me straight up out of the field. The suit's whine was loud, but even louder was the sound of the max-field shorting out from a suit of Imperial Hoplite Armor being dragged through it.

Someday I'm going to get me a set.

The main power net blew and probably took Port Mantow with it. The secondary generators didn't have enough power to run the tangler, and Baijon set me down. We was somewhere in the Port Authority Building with too much high-heat between us and anything that could get us off this rock.

"Now we go back," Baijon said. The Power Tower systems kept

coming up and crashing as something else blew. A ten-second cycle: disorienting.

"You're kidding, right?"

"We must . . . *Kore, how* can Mallorum Archangel be Errol Lightfoot?"

"You saw it too, right?"

I couldn't see anything but my own face reflected in the Hoplite helmet. I knew what Baijon was thinking anyway. He'd seen it. It *was* Archangel.

And it was Errol, too—I'd bet anything I had left on that.

"We must kill him," Baijon said, thinking it out careful-like. "Both of him. Again."

"Terrific—but wouldn't you like to be a success at it this time?"

Baijon considered that, too, whiles I picked up a belly-and-back and a night-helmet from a Angel what didn't need them anymore, and started putting them on.

"What must I do?" he said finally.

"Why don't we start with escaping, j'keyn?" I pointed at the wall and waggled my remaining fingers until Baijon caught on.

*   *   *

Cubic is cheap, downside. There was meters of waste space in every wall of the Power Tower and between floors, too; used for power-cables or insulation or nothing. If you was wearing full powered armor, you could make use of a fact like that.

The plastic stretched, then split, then tore like taffy. Baijon started peeling it off its structural supports. Real soon there was a big enough hole for even the armor to crawl through. He smoothed out the edges with one big bluesilver gauntlet like a child tidying mudpies.

"First we escape. Then we slay," Baijon said firmly.

"Sure, bai."

I followed him into the wall.

*   *   *

I didn't know why they hadn't used gas yet. There was no one alive to report that it'd be fifty percent useless, and it wasn't because they didn't have it—Royal was at war. The only thing I could think of was that maybe Archangel wanted things done his way, and like all damnfool glitterborn he was clueless.

I wanted to believe that.

I really did.

But I didn't, because I knew who Archangel really was, and it didn't make any sense. No sense at all—

The next level we reached was sealed too, but all that meant was nobody was shooting at us whilst Baijon dug a hole through the floor this time and we went through that to what we found out was Level Three.

After that the home team got annoyed.

We found Charlock troops on Level Three. They shot at us and we ran—all same to Baijon and me, 'cause we wanted to go the way they was chasing us anyway.

What we didn't want to do was run into a barricade with a molecular debonder—a disintegrator ray—big enough to planetoform a star attached.

Baijon recognized it—you show me a wartoy a hellflower doesn't. He backed up two lumping steps. I used him for cover and snapped off a couple of shots as might discourage the Angels coming up behind us.

Trapped. Neat, sweet, and thorough.

"Run," suggested Baijon. "I will hold them here."

So I did.

*   *   *

I didn't know what orders Archangel had given about who was to be taken alive and who got to be an example to others, but Valijon was a big noticeable target in almost impenetrable armor and I was small, harmless, and helpless.

I hoped they thought.

Because that molecular debonder of theirs was a fierce toy for sure, but it was also too big to run on a power-pac. That meant grid power, and you could turn off grid power.

Just ask any DataNet terminal.

I set one toggle on my rifle for "Continuous" and the other for "Dispersed" and swept myself a way past the Angels before the rifle turned to warm plastic in my hands. That bought me a minute alone in a corridor.

Nobody was supposed to be up here in the Power Tower without authorization anyway, so all the keycodes on the doors was simple— about the level of keeping Techie A out of Techie B's lunchbox. And everybody knows you can't get onto the Imperial dataweb without permits stretching nineteen ways from Night.

My Angel babysitters was a half-jump behind me when I slid into the first promising cubie. I had the door shut again before they was in

line of sight, and kicked up the doorspeaker to hear them go ga-
lumphing past. Everybody knows it takes time to crack even a simple
keycode, after all.

Everybody knows.

There was a damn sight too much blithe assumption going on in
this legger's Empire, and I had the horrible feeling I might be among
the chief assumpters. But I didn't have time to change my ways just
now; about the time the Boys in Black got tired of playing Bullies-and-
Blasters and brought some high-tech to bear on the problem of little
Butterfly, Yours Truly would be nonfiction.

And Baijon would be plasma.

How long to wind the debonder up to rock'n'roll? Would it stop
him? Would he run without me—and was there any place anymore,
really, to run to? Audit the next exciting issue of *Thrilling Wonder Talkingbooks* for these and other unanswered questions.

I grabbed the touchpad on the desk and felt my way in to the
system. There wasn't time or tools to jack it through what was left of my
cybereisis, but this time there was a screen, and the wondershow was
strictly between my ears anyway, down another imaginary set of not-
really corridors one of which would lead to my idea of a black gang so I
could shut down the spaceport grid.

I needed my miracle too much to jump salty for it, but somewhere
in the back of my skull was storing up nightmares out of what I was
doing now.

And the worst of it was, I wasn't good enough.

I could glitch their powersuck, but I couldn't stop it. The things I
needed to grab slid out of my hands like skeins of hyperspace. I was too
slow, too clumsy, too damn human still to do the only friend I had left
any good at all.

It hadn't taken me a kilo-second to find out I had a great career as
a failure—plenty of time left to dodge back out and watch them turn
Baijon into smoke and ice. The debonder started to cycle up—it pulled
enough power from the grid to make my corner of the dataweb go all
wobbly. Everything was snow and stars and static, and me imaginating I
was running down a nonexistent corridor to find a room that wasn't
there.

"Butterfly?" Paladin said. "What are you doing?"

His voice was thin and vague and hashed up with ground noise,
and me not knowing if it was in my head or real.

"Shut it down, Pally—*shut everything down!*" I hammered the
keypad, but it was too little and too late and I knew it.

"You're having fun again." might-be Paladin said disapprovingly, and everything went black.

Everything.

*   *   *

The emergency exits crashed open behind the holosim screens and so did the door to the room. It was full day out and no lights, no holos, no moving tronics in sight.

"Paladin! Come back here!"

But if he'd ever been there at all, he was gone now. The DataNet Access Port was dead. Everything that ate power on Royal was dead. And I only had time to worry about one thing.

Baijon.

There was a crash from the corridor. I ran.

*   *   *

Pitch-black, and my friendly helpful backbrain trying to remind me how similar this was to being marooned in a powerless derelict drifting randomly in space. I found the door by the flashes of light coming through it and Baijon by the fact that he was the only thing lit up. The Hoplite armor sent beams in all directions illuminating a scene sure to be playing on select hollyvids everywhere Real Soon Now: Desperados of the Outfar.

They must of tried to fire the debonder. And they couldn't, or not enough to do any good, but by the time they'd figured that out they'd got Baijon Stardust and a full suit of Imperial Hoplite Armor really, really mad.

He'd picked up x-thousand kilos of debonder by the muzzle and swung it. It glittered at the far edge of the armor's watchlights, and the corridor looked like a mine had exploded. There wasn't even anything left that looked human enough to get sick over.

The big blue gauntlet came up in a slow hail. Valijon Starbringer'd just delivered the first installment on payback to his enemies.

"Come, *Kore,"* Baijon said. He waved down the empty, unopposed, and dead silent corridor. Everybody Archangel had available to go after us must of been at the debonder.

"Not that way." My mind was infinitely subdivisible, and the only part I was on speaking terms with now was only interested in the best way out. "We got to go how they don't expect. Power's down all over the port. C'mon."

Power was down over one hell of a lot more than the port. What-

ever'd shut things down—me, my shadow, or a Library I used to know
—had done one hell of a job.

We'd left ship *Angelcity* with Meggie last night just before curfew.
We'd broke back into the port well into the dark part of the night, and
Baijon and me'd spent serious hours under the Power Tower after that.
We'd been rousted out to dance with Archangel just about dawn, and
with one thing and another it was probably within shouting distance of
light meredies now. Time for all good grubbers to be out running the
economy, right?

Wrong.

A ship is a closed system, all of a piece. Shut it down and you'll kill
all the crew, soon or late, but that's all. Power her up again and she's
ready to rock.

A city's different. Turn it off and it *breaks.*

Through the open third floor window of the Power Tower I could
see most of Port Mantow and a good chunk of the city. Nothing flew,
nothing moved, nothing changed colors. Every computer in the Net,
every computer swapping data with the Net, was wiped clean as a fake
ID.

Baijon clomped over to the window and looked down. He put both
hands against the window and pushed, and the thin sheet of plastic
bowed then warped then popped free and skimmed off on the air like a
sheet of thermofax, leaving an unsafe hole in the wall.

It was quiet enough I heard the first sirens go off—something with
a discrete power-pac, or something else not tied into the Net. I tried not
to think of how many deaders there was if even only one percent of the
population'd bought real estate. Mantow City holds ten million. I saw.

"Now, *Kore,* we will jump out the window, and prove to the gods of
the Gentle People . . ." He stopped in the middle of what he was
going to say. Archangel'd burned his soul back there. By hellflower
rules, Baijon wasn't a hellflower no more.

"Yeah. Right. Just we get out of here, oke? We paid enough for the
damned ticket."

I hung on for sweet life and an early retirement to the grabhandles
on the shoulders of the Hoplite armor. Baijon took a running jump at
the hole in the wall and that took care of getting us down the last three
floors. He left two big craters in the crete and walked away. I've had
worse landings.

"Now—" Baijon said. But I knew where I wanted to go.

Even with war, curfew, quarantine, and disaster, there was about a
thousand ships down in Port Mantow. I knew. I'd counted them. And in

all the high-iron on the heavyside, there was one ship with full inventories that only needed a solo pilot, had heavyweight personal armament and engines to match, and was where she could get upside without port tronics to help.

That was our ticket—if we could reach her.

Port Mantow was a big busy Directorate Capital port. It was slightly less busy than High Mikasa at teatime on any day but today. There was ships in rings, ships in bays, ships as said they wasn't going anywhere real soon racked in cybernetic cradles in the Port's bottom levels. There should have been people on the field—the ship's crews if nothing else—but there weren't.

Archangel'd done something with them, maybe. I tried to imagine having enough power to hand grief to that many Guilds at once, and couldn't.

He had so much power, what did he want with any more?

I looked around. There was ships and ships, but nothing was what I was looking for—the ship in a cradle slotted into long-term storage in the north/northwest (by planetary orientation) corner of the Port.

I looked down at the grid coordinates stamped into the crete and the credit-bit dropped. I'd misread the diagram I wasn't supposed to be able to access in the first place. If the ship I was looking for was here, there should be a zillion levels above us.

But there wasn't. Because we wasn't on the bottom layer of Port Mantow where the ship was.

We was on the top.

"No," I said, and stopped. The downside version of the Big Empty was all around me, and a dozen more like it underfoot—a couple klicks of down that without power and light Baijon and me stood a dicty's chance of getting to.

I couldn't even turn the power back on.

I'd fixed us real good.

I stood there and thought about it, and slow-like it sunk in that the sound I'd thought was the ships' engines wasn't.

"Why do you stop?" Baijon asked, but I wasn't listening to him.

It was a sound that might be a riot and might be something else and might just be the sound of several million people I'd never met finding themselves in a world of hurt. Port Mantow City looked like a war-zone for sure. And I'd done it.

For being sloppy, for panicking. Shut everything down, I said, so something did.

"*Kore* San'Cyr?"

Fun was fun, and I didn't want me nor Baijon in Archangel's hands noway, but that last cheap trick'd put me over the line that separated Butterfly St. Cyr, doing what she had to to get by, and Lord Prince Mallorum Archangel, gazetted evilspeak. There was no difference between what he did and what I'd done.

Except, maybe, that doing it bothered me.

The noise from the city built to a dull roar of pure ugly. Somewhere something was burning.

"They are fools to build cities that will kill them," Baijon said calmly. Morning sunlight gleamed off the Hoplite armor's blue-and-orange. He stood there waiting for me like he had all the time in the world.

I didn't say anything. City power didn't fail the way this one's had. It *couldn't.*

Not by itself, anyway.

"They will head for the port soon. The Imperial Armory is at the port. They will want weapons to defend themselves. We must be gone before that happens," Baijon said.

They'd riot, and the Empire'd come down with both boots. Tortuga Sector was already under martial law. Riot was treason.

"Space Angels be having something to say about that, bai." My voice felt antique. I'd trapped us here on the surface of Royal. Our only way off was as far away as if it was on the moon.

"Without orders?" Baijon said like it was a joke. "Their only orders are obedience—with no one to obey they are craven."

"Archangel ain't dead. They'll listen to him." Archangel wasn't dead. Archangel wasn't never going to be dead. Archangel was. . . .

Never mind that now. Archangel wasn't dead, and he had as much proof as a walking nightmare like him cared for that me and/or Baijon was something that he wanted, and the ship that was our best chance of getting out of here was buried out of reach.

"Archangel also has orders, but we will not be here to know them. This way, *Kore,*" said Baijon, and ankled toward a lock that headed downunder. The right way, as it happened, but how did *he* know?

Plastic shrilled as he twisted the access hatch off its moorings and crumpled it between his gloves like a piece of thermofax. He tossed it away. It made a dull sound on the crete and the armor's watchlights flared on, lighting the back of the shaft and making the numbers and warning signs reflect.

However he knew, it didn't seem important right now.

I followed the Hoplite armor into the dark.

* * *

There was no power. There was no light. It was hot in the underport without technology to smooth the way, and the air was already less than prime cut. Without my eight-foot flashlight I never could of found anything but slow starvation. We went down the dropshafts using handholds with Baijon to light the way, and after whiles I just let the Hoplite armor do all the work.

"We go this way, do we not? To your ship?" He'd stopped the 'sponder's volume all the way down to a buzzy whisper, but Baijon's amped voice still echoed flat in the tunnel.

"Turn around; I can't see."

He did, and the spotlight on his chest showed off the wall glyphs for Level and Section in big bright Intersign glyphs. I ran my fingers through my hair and tried to reconcile what I was seeing with what I knew.

"440/A, North," said Baijon happily, and tripped off.

He was right, too. Again. But how the hell did *he* know?

* * *

Docking bay 440/A North was . . . well, think of a cube made up of about a quarter of a million smaller cubes. 440/A was on the outside bottom. Not useful for getting out, except for one thing.

Port Mantow was built at the edge of one of Royal's oceans. The other side of the docking bay wall was nothing between us and the never-never but water.

We got to 440 and I was damn glad neither of us'd been stupid enough to lose the armor. The bay door was shut, and locked, and I knew the keycode but I couldn't use it without power.

That was why the Libraries had lost.

It must be the bad air making me sick. I didn't want to be thinking about Old Fed Tech, about what it could do and couldn't do and had done.

About how easy it was to make it helpless.

Without power—and things that power could move—Libraries was nothing.

About how easy it was to be helpless.

I'd never wanted to be helpless. I'd spent the last twenty years getting shut of it, getting to a place where I'd always have a weapon and a bolt-hole, where nobody could push.

All gone now.

I felt the wall slide up my back as I sat down. All gone, and the odds shortening into the negative numbers. Running another escape just out of habit and watching everything I touched dissolve into entropy and old night.

"*Kore?*" Baijon said.

"Whaddya want?" I was tired and probably breathing everything but air.

"Now we must enter the docking bay and steal the ship," he prompted.

"Yeah? And how you going to get the door open?"

Baijon put his hands on the door. His gauntlets scraped over the surface with a high faint squeal that put my teeth on edge.

"No."

Maybe he could rip it out of the wall—although I was betting that it was proof against even a Hoplite's best shot—but we had to be able to seal the door behind us again, or else when we ruptured the wall we'd drown every ship in the port. The weight of the water'd mangle everything that was left, too, providing there was anyone left to care.

Did I care? I hoped so, but it was like hoping you'd win the lottery or get the good numbers on your next downfall; nothing to do with anything real.

And if I—or whatever I was—was going to lose it, let it wait until we got far enough out of here for Baijon to have even chances.

"Give me . . . you better hope that suit's got jumperleads, bai, or we picked one hell of a garden spot to vacation."

*   *   *

Every other suit of powered armor I ever read about had a basic tech-kit as part of it, and this one was no exception. It had tools to lever the face off the doorlock, and cables to hook the suit up to the door. It was easy but not quick to power up the door, code it, open it, and get through. Baijon yanked the leads and the door rolled shut behind him, deadweight and sealed. Wasn't no way now we could get it open from this side.

But that didn't matter.

She was long and low and sleek and made any other ship I'd ever seen look like old news. She stretched from end to end of the bay like darkness visible and her plane surfaces swooped and soared like the wings of night. She was black crystal decadence nose to tail and I could see myself reflected in her hull.

She'd been a Gift Transfer to my old buddy Errol Lightfoot about the time me and Baijon'd been setting foot on Low Mikasa. For services rendered, the file'd said.

Only there wasn't no such person as Errol Lightfoot, was there? And a Gift Transfer between Errol and Mallorum Archangel was just pure fantasy, wasn't it?

Baijon's suit-lights put a galaxy into her hull. I went closer, and I was there too, pale and distorted in smoke and mirrors, with hellflower scars like a matched set of curses and Archangel's fingerprints bloody all over my face. I touched the hull.

Mallorum Archangel was Errol Lightfoot. And that didn't make no sense a-tall.

Errol Lightfoot was a cheap smuggler. Errol Lightfoot was the man who was known from one side of the Outfar to the other as causing hullplating to rust just by walking by. He named every ship he had *Light Lady* because otherwise they fell apart so fast under his maintenance he couldn't remember their names. Errol Lightfoot bought into any kick that gave honest darktrading a bad name.

He couldn't be all that and the second in line for the Phoenix Throne.

Could he?

But he was.

Baijon lowered his gauntlet to my shoulder like a ten-ton snow-flake.

"Kore. We must enter the ship, *Kore."*

If Mallorum Archangel was Errol Lightfoot I just hoped he'd had somebody else pull maintenance on this ship. I turned away from my reflection and toward the air lock.

I was betting our lives he had.

*　　*　　*

Her security lock was lit. You can get them keyed to your hand or retinal print—but anybody can get those away from you. Or you can get your security lock keyed to your gene-scan, which is really secure but real expensive, and then you're the only one that can get your ship open, and someone slips you one dose of Mutabis can fix that real quick.

But TwiceBorn don't like to do for theyselves what they can get somebody else to do, and besides, they like to run on their rep. Is everybody supposed to be too damn intimidated to kyte from them's the way it goes. So this high-ticket yacht had a plain old keycode just like the last ship I'd owned, and I knew what it was.

The outside lock split four ways, breathing out light, heat, and oxygen. It tried the air outside and told me the inner door wouldn't open until the outer door was closed, so Baijon had to wait outside whiles I cycled through into Receiving Room One.

The first deep breath I took made me all silly with excess oxygen and damped down a headache I hadn't noticed into old news. The Receiving Lounge was cool and clean and looked right out of the factory-box, dripping with naturally-occurring organic materials on every available surface.

I flipped switches to let Baijon come inboard. A tasteful shipvoice informed me in hushed embarrassed tones that powered weapons were being brought through the lock scanners and did I want it to initiate security procedures?

"No."

"Keycode operator acknowledged," it whinged, and went off wherever computer generated voices go.

Baijon louted low through the lock, the armor's shoulders scraping both sides. The hatch buttoned up behind him.

"And now?" he said.

"Now we go."

*   *   *

The ship had a standard four-place cockpit—mercy seat, worry seat, songbird and numbercruncher. Worry seat had the weapons console, but it could be shifted over to let the first pilot run it.

I slid down into the seat, grubby in my overused bloody *Angelcity* rags, and heard it purr whilst it adjusted itself to me. Telltales and displays came awake all over the place, telling me everything I ever wanted to know about fuel and power and light and air, date of last supplies onload and (I swear it) inventories of everything down to how many boxes of wine there was in the galley. The only lights not lit was on the astrogator.

It was on, so I turned it off. Then I turned it back on and got the string of gibberish that means there's nothing in there for your computer to chew on.

I knew what I'd find, but I checked the automatic ship's log anyway. And I was right.

Whoever'd been in the mercy seat last'd done what I'd of done; what anybody'd do. He'd left the ship tapped in to the port computers for updates and to get messages and like that.

So every computer on the ship'd been sucked blank when the port tower went down. The rest of them reloaded from the ship's main memory core, but the navicomputer couldn't. Right now this ship was about as smart as I was. Literally.

I sat back in the seat and put my boot up where it made a nasty black mark on the white suede that some maniac'd upholstered all the control panels in. No navicomp, no numbers.

No numbers, no way out.

Oh, I could get the ship to orbit and hang her there. I could pull enough numbers off the sensors to land her, too, anywhere you liked.

I even remembered the numbers for the basic Transit to Hyperspace in the vicinity of a planet of standard mass or less, but that's a riddle problem they learn you in Famous Starpilot's School so's you'll know why you have to have a computer to suck sensor-web and spit out what you need.

How you go in tells where you'll come out with angeltown. Guess wrong and you're plasma. Your astrogator knows every star, comet, and ball of rock in fifty lights and can sign paper for information on the rest. Give it the where you are and the where you're going and it does the rest—all you have to do is pull the stick.

Some "all."

The manuals call it the Hyperjump Interlock. Everybody I ever met calls it the angelstick, 'cause it's what makes angels out of more pilots than anything else. The Jump *distorts* you, someways—oh, it won't do it through a stasis field, but you're not in a stasis field, you can't be—you're right out there on the same side of never as your sensors, and there's always that one chance in how-good's-your-maintenance that you won't make it this time, just stay Intertransitional until you die.

There's pilots who aren't—pilots I mean. I knew one oncet until he died—just woke up one morning and decided he couldn't pull the angelstick for one more Drop. You lose your nerve, I guess.

I hadn't lost mine—not for that, not yet. I could even get us up and at go with the textbook numbers and then pull the stick.

Of course, we'd never come out anywhere.

No place to run after all.

The cockpit hatch opened and Baijon stumbled in. He'd took time to shuck the clown-suit. He was bruised and galled all over from where the armor hadn't fit. His face was hagged. I caught myself looking for what wasn't there and stopped before I said anything. No Knife. He saw me looking at him and grinned; feral and tired. He sat down.

"And do you go now, *Kore,* in this your enemy's ship?"

You go. Not *we* go.

No Knife, no soul. No hellflower. Dead man walking.

No. We wasn't going to do it that way. Not and give Archangel—or Errol—what he wanted. Not no matter what I had to do.

"We go, j'keyn?"

Baijon didn't answer. There was no point in sitting here fretting about it now. So I powered everything up and blew out the wall.

*   *   *

The wall blew back in a nanosecond later as the advance-solid for a wall of water. According to the external sensors the ship flipped over and hit a couple of walls and ceilings. Inside, all comps and gravities on, we didn't feel a thing.

I looked at Baijon. He was sitting there like he had all the time in a world or two, and only one ending.

I put my hand on the power throttles and stopped. Stardancer's superstition; bad luck to take a ship up unnamed. Archangel might of named her once. But was only one name she could have now.

"Ghost Dance," I said, and goosed the lifters.

She rose up silly and slow in the water, but all that water was just another kind of atmosphere to move through. Royal's ocean had tore loose everything that wasn't nailed down; *Dance* sailed out a wide-open port into murk.

Sensors told me there was nothing above; we slid up slow through the water. It went black to glassy, then bright, then gone.

Image jerked on the pick-ups as we floated on water. Sensor-sweeps said there was nothing in range. I firewalled the lifters and *Ghost Dance* raged to heaven on a column of steam.

She was almost worth dying for. She didn't have to be babied, she didn't have to be coaxed. Anything I asked her for she gave me, and she'd give until her goforths cracked. I tumbled her through atmosphere for the just-being-able-to of it, and I wished I'd met her while I still had a life.

Then we hung in the sky above Port Mantow, free in orbit with only the little matter of no astrogator between us and escape. Every gauge I could see sat low in the green, except the only one that counted right now. The navicomp's "Not Ready" light was steady on red.

"I've done it. I've really done it," I said out loud.

I was ready for the talkingbooks. Illegal takeoff from an Imperial Port, with no clearance, in a stolen ship, without a pilot's license, and having sassed Lord Mallorum Archangel to his face and iced all his prettyboys.

I'd finally done it. I could not possibly be in any more trouble than I was now, even if you handed me two Old Fed Libraries for bookends.

There was a certain job satisfaction to that.

"Told you we'd commit every crime in the Calendar, you come along with me, Baijon-bai," I said, turning around to eyeball him.

"We did, while we lived," he said finally. "But there will be no songs, *Kore,* nor anyone to sing them of us now that—"

He stopped, and leaned forward in the songbird seat, and anything that'd make a de-Knifed hellflower interrupt his own death-aria to goggle was something I wanted to look at, too.

I thought.

I spun around. I was staring down the tonsils of five of the Empire's biggest and best. Jagranathas. Starshakers.

*   *   *

They're actually more portable planets than starships—no self-respecting starship *I* know has a port facility—and they provide Fleet with nice handy dangerous bases for operation—or would if Fleet ever got into a war. Nobody knew quite how many Throne had, but two were posted permanently at Grand Central and how many could the highheat possibly need, anyway?

I now knew for a fact that our Glorious Emperor (gods bless and keep him far away from me) had at least seven.

Then *Dance* stepped down the magnification and said that the ships had been identified as Imperial military vessels and did I want to tap their message beacons and hail them?

"Hell, no!"

The day someone invents artificial *intelligence* I'll buy stock in the company.

"Kore, what are they doing here? Five of them?" At least Baijon sounded interested in something besides being dead.

"That information is not available at this time. Do you wish to trigger their—"

"Shut up," I told the ship, at which one thing I had lots of practice. "Five shakers?" I said at Baijon.

"Jagranathas," said Baijon, like I didn't know their right name. "But Royal isn't that important."

Errol/Archangel's goddamn noisy ship started to mouth off again but I found the volume control in time. I could disable the thing if I lived to get older.

"They don't see us," I hoped very much, because even Prince Mallorum's own personal battle-yacht which this probably wasn't couldn't outrun or outfight a planet.

I cut the goforths back from pre-Jump and started sliding down the curve of the planet like your friendly neighborhood chunk of space debris. If I could get the planet between us and them I could do something about getting out of their sight for sure. Hell, I could even land.

Bad idea.

The shakers pulled in closer over Royal, to where their shields was putting a lightshow over I bet any whole hemisphere of the planet you cared to choose and the induction howl our sensors picked up was like to deafen us. It gave me a nice warm feeling to know they'd probably farced their own sensors to the point where I could of landed *Dance* on one of their hulls without notice. Something that big isn't meant to go into atmosphere, although in blissful theory a shaker could, in fact, land —and warp the topsoil off half the continent getting upside again.

Whiles we watched, something came up off the heavyside to join them—one alternative mode of transport leaving the planet Royal with a real torqued Governor-General Archangel inside, odds was. It slid up close to one of the jags and vanished—docking, was my guess. And once it had, the jags started to move.

They was close in and looking like a star gone nova when parts of them started to drop off, deep enough down the gravity well to fall on the heavyside. And if I could see them at all, those little bits of light must be about the size of the Port Authority Building, each.

"They are bombs," said Baijon, and I wanted someone to tell him he had fusion for brains, but I couldn't. Because right then the surface of Royal started to boil.

In less than a kilo-second blue water, brown land, and white clouds had all mushed together into this sick shimmering gray as far out as gravity held atmosphere. I looked at Baijon. It'd took him outta hisself, all right. He might even know what made Royal look like that. I shouldn't. But I did.

And if our timing had been just a little more off, we could of been down there.

I gave *Dance* the numbers she could turn into a nice slow slide out toward the big empty, away from the attention of five starshakers where they shouldn't be what'd dropped what they shouldn't of had on Royal. I didn't risk another sensor scan, and when I looked back by eyeball the

Fleet shakers was just a clump of overbright stars hanging over the curve of Royal.

Pale, glowing Royal.

I didn't want to think about that, but I did.

There's this drug called Mutabis, which isn't as beside the point as it might be. It's illegal, and for once is something you wouldn't even want; it shuffles your internal blueprint into any number of exciting new designer combinations, so that the next time you go to patch a bit of hangnail you read it off the new specs and not the old. Mutabis usually kills you, but not outright and not quick.

And it's got this long registry number what isn't anything like Mutabis at all, but why it's called Mutabis in the nightworld is because it's named after a bad dream most everyone else's forgot.

Paladin'd never told me about it. I'd just lately learned to remember it special.

Once upon a long time ago there was a bomb. It didn't do anything so vulgar as blow something up. No. This handy-dandy little hostility took what you may call your basic building blocks of matter and un-hooked them from one combination and shuffled them into another without liberating too much in the way of nasty atomic glitterflash. It could damp down after wiping out a few cubic kilometers. Or if you used enough the reaction went on until there was nothing left but a lump of about the same mass you started with, and nothing else the same.

The Libraries used them in the war—or maybe it was the humans, because they'd kill a Library just as dead if they caught it planetside. Archive knew how to build them.

They're simple to make, really. And Archive must of told Archangel how, damn his piezoelectric eyes.

And Archangel'd used them. On Royal. Unbound dust, now, and me and Baijon five minutes shy from having joined it.

Not the kind of thing that called for witnesses.

A moon, two space-stations, an asteroid belt full of miners. That was Royal System. Archangel must be planning to do them all and leave nobody to tell on him. Moons don't run very fast.

But starships do.

I got Royal's moon between me and the jagranathas and made *Dance* pick up her feet out toward the Big Dark. Most of Royal System's planets were on the other side of her primary. This way the traffic'd be thin, just some ice and rock making its rounds and the odd satellite. I watched the indicators edge up through percentage of lights.

Babby's top real-world speed could get us out into the Big Dark in a matter of hours, and wasn't nobody going to be looking for a ship slogging through realspace there.

Of course, we'd be dead of old age before we reached the next star.

The dark was friendly and didn't ask much out of my life. Eventually I noticed that the ship's systems indicators was sliding into amber, and then on to red, but it didn't really matter.

Shock, said a part of my mind. *Play for time.*

I mulled that one around for a while before I reached out and shut off the goforths. *Dance* seemed to sigh with relief and the numbers dropped right back into green. The estimated probable adjusted speed we were going didn't change.

I thought about what was going on back at Royal now: traffic coming in and trying to put down, maybe, if the system wasn't closed. Had Archangel left anything behind that could broadcast a warning? Or was the whole system just a whirligig of remanufactured matter, and nothing left to tell anybody its name but the spectrograph of its star? Would the Mutabis reaction take the first ships that downfalled, or would it have stopped by then?

I stared at the dark.

There's some things, they just have to happen around you, not even to you, and you can feel them make you over no matter what you do. I'd used to pretend there wasn't things like that, even whiles they was happening to me.

Royal was one. It was such a big thing that part of my mind kept trying to say it hadn't happened while the other half insisted I do something about it right now.

Made for headaches.

Because there wasn't nothing I could do. Except tell, and wouldn't nobody need me for that. Royal wasn't there no more. Soon or late somebody'd notice, and get to pointing fingers and naming names. Archangel's had to be one.

Didn't it?

I made myself concentrate on what I knew. I set *Dance* up to run in realspace by herself: proximity klaxons and shields at full charge and a couple basic evasive routines laid by. She'd go on long past the time she ran out of air and food and water. A ghost ship on a ghost dance, all alone in the never-never.

A nice bolt-hole to die in.

I got up and walked back to the songbird seat. Baijon was just sitting, staring out into the dark that looked empty and wasn't. His eyes was open, but he looked relaxed as a sleeper and no more older nor he was.

"Baijon-che-bai?"

He blinked and looked up at me, vague around the eyes to where I wondered if he'd looked into the same empty I had and wasn't coming back.

"If we tell of this, *Kore,* is there anyone who will listen?"

He sounded scared and defeated and young and I didn't blame him. I touched his shoulder and he grabbed my hand like I could do him some good.

"Somebody's going to notice soon or late, che-bai."

Baijon looked at me. "It will be as you say, *Kore,*" he said, and neither of us could tell if it was a question or not.

"Sure it will."

Sure. I had a naggy creeping paranoia that somewhere Throne if it even knew and particularly Archangel his own self was going to find a scapegoat for this Mutabis rap and walk off having shifted the heat, and if that was all they would be going to do I wouldn't mind so much, but I didn't think it'd stop there, somehow. There wasn't any profit in just doing that, and if there was one thing I knew, it was finding the profit.

Butterfly St. Cyr, Savior of the Universe. Sure.

"So, bai, why don't you turn out and roust this crib? We going to be here whiles. Need fly-vines and fetch-kitchen, forbye—and food, maybe."

Not according to my stomach, but it always was a liar. And where there was food there might even be more useful things, like something you'd want.

"Still—still I serve you, my *comites,*" Baijon said, and we didn't hear any more about singing ourselfs to death, neither.

One thing's sure, a little holocaust can help you forget your own problems.

Or some of them. I waited until Baijon'd gone off, and sat back down in the mercy seat. My beautiful lady of the never-never, and where could I take her?

Errol/Archangel'd called me a cyborg.

And normally I wouldn't mind, 'cause everybody's got a right to be wrong, but he'd been trying to do something to my head at the time when he ran into something that made him stop.

Cyborg. And he'd thought I was the one carrying the Yegg McGuffin that Brightlaw was trying to smuggle into its own home town. The Brightlaw Prototype. Whatever that was.

I wondered if Baijon knew.

We made a fine set of partners, him and me: Baijon'd been kicked out of the hellflower fan club, and I was turning into something he'd probably be obliged to shoot anyway, hellflower or no. Tainted with Library Science, and stuck on a ship with no computer when my condign knack was for breaking into them, the galaxy against us. . . .

Why?

Self-interest is a wonderful cure for the larger issues of life. Never mind Royal-the-ex-planet. What did all this have to do with *me?*

One time somebody'd closed down a entire Free Port to keep me from getting off it, a kind of overkill that should of warned me at the time there was something salty jumping, 'cause I wasn't worth that flavor trouble.

I hadn't took the hint then. But I can learn from my mistakes. In our last exciting episode, Fleet had closed down Royal in the permanent-most kind of way, using I-bet-banned Library Science which somebody in this sophont's galaxy was going to notice the fingerprints of Real Soon Now.

And since I still didn't think I was worth that kind of trouble, the question that I had to ask was: just what had there been on Royal that Fleet wanted to keep there enough to put a two-billion-taxpayer hole in the Emperor's budget?

I could not immediately think of much. Not, certain and for truth, the moronic Brightlaw Rebellion. It just wasn't that important in the greater galactic scheme of things, even if alMayne had a hotwired interest in little Damaris winning. Past tense.

But what if it wasn't to keep somebody there? What if how Royal was now wasn't the means to a, but an end in itself?

Something cold slid into the pit of my stomach and started trying to burrow out. Question: what did you get if you showed the Empire a Royal System destroyed by Library Science?

Three guesses. And that it was a soforth destroyed by etcetera would be vouched for—hell, it'd be rammed down people's throats—by those galactic arbiters of honor and the lazy-fair, the alMayne. Everybody knew they knew more about Libraries than god's older sister.

But thanks to my boy Baijon they'd nail it right to Archangel's shadow, which he couldn't want.

Another good theory shot to hell.

But Archangel knew the hellflowers'd blame him for Royal. He knew Baijon'd seen him at Rialla with Archive Library. He knew

Baijon'd gone home and told. And he for sure knew there was civil tiff in Washonnet Sector.

But he'd still Mutabis'd Royal, even knowing all this.

What if Archangel meant to frame the *hellflowers* for it?

Sure.

And he'd almost had his proof. Baijon Starbringer, gazetted prince, courier legging something into the system for Brightlaw—which alMayne was still backing in defiance of Galactic Statute Number fill-intheblank.

Baijon could deny everything. Archangel could say he didn't know what Baijon'd brought in for sure. People'd believe what Archangel wanted them to.

Bottom line: it didn't matter if Baijon's mythical dark-trade kick even existed. Royal'd retired from the planet business courtesy of a weapon only a Library could build, and the alMayne would be sure to say so just in time to be told that one of their own had dropped it.

And then Archangel could put all Washonnet on Proscription for collusion to commit High Book and take in the Tech Police that nightworld gossip said was his bought hardboys to pry loose everything he'd ever wanted in the way of Libraries and Library Science, of which they had so much there on sunny Washonnet 357-II.

It would of been possible, that was to say, if Washonnet wasn't throwing its own private little war. Every hellflower in known space had gone home to choose up sides, no amateurs allowed. They was used to fighting wars. Nobody'd get hurt—until they settled their family spat and took on the rest of the Empire. The only thing an Imp incursion would do would be settle the war on alMayne faster.

I had the frustrating feeling of being almost half right but missing too many pieces, and thinking about Royal just made me feel sick—and glad in a rotten way, because what Fleet'd done covered up what I'd did and made it seem damn near harmless.

Paladin would ask: *"Who benefits?"*—which is a fancy way of wanting to know who ends up standing and with all the credit after the smoke clears. And the same question applied to Royal: who got to spin credit if it wasn't there no more?

It sort of made a girl wonder what Kennor Starbringer had actually been after.

Paranoia's a wonderful drug: I wanted my brain to shut up but it wouldn't, and all that left for me was watching it swoop like a bat after dragonflies. Everything fell into place like a well-oiled domino theory.

Maybe those assassins back on *Circle of Stars*'d been Kennor Starbringer's and maybe they hadn't, but for damn sure they'd put paid to my plans to win a billion credits and debark early. That landed us right in the middle of alMayne where Kennor's kid sister Gruoch was all set to have my guts for garters and Baijon had to say the one thing that'd start civil war on alMayne faster than Badhb's your uncle and put "paid" to Archangel's hopes of landing troops there any time soon.

Was Kennor actually unaware of Gruoch's little xenophobic quirk?

Had he thought Baijon was *not* going to tell everybody back home that the person at the top of his personal *chaudatu* hit parade was a Librarian and therefore an open season target of opportunity for everything that carried a *arthame?*

Was I actually as stupid as Kennor seemed to think I was?

If the answer was "no" to the first three, then that meant I knew the real truth—not this fake truth Kennor'd already tried to sell me twicet.

Kennor'd wanted alMayne to blow up the way it had.

Just as soon as he'd known Brother Mallorum had his hand in the Old Fed Tech cookie jar it'd be obvious to anyone with more brains than I had that the next place Archangel was going was the largest and only legit cache of Old Fed Tech inside the Empire's borders—the Logotek of the War College at Wailing on alMayne.

So Kennor'd arranged for alMayne to go up like a roaming candle —a perfect alibi, among other things. And as for the ship he'd promised me . . .

I bet I'd got it.

I wondered if Meggie and Mero'd made it out of Tortuga. Archangel said they hadn't, but that was just business as usual in the hardboy trade. Maybe they was all right.

I hoped so.

But meanwhile:

Archangel—in the guise of darktrader and trafficker in dicty-toys and Old Fed Tech, Errol-the-Peril Lightfoot, a stone truth that I still found damn near impossible to swallow—had been waiting at Port Mantow to gig Meggie when she showed up to meet the receiver for her kick.

Why? Archangel didn't give a damn about the guns *Angelcity*'d been picking up to run to Royal. He'd already arranged to put a guaranteed end to the Brightlaw Rebellion; it didn't matter who offloaded how much heat.

But Meggie'd been expecting to take on a load at alMayne she never got: two no-questions-asked couriers to drop on Royal, for whom she was holding ID and valuta and a package. She'd thought we might be them.

What if we *had* been them?

No proof, but I almost believed it. Who'd sold Mero and Meggie the guns in the first place, after all? A LessHouse of Starborn—or House Starborn its own self? Kennor'd know *Angelcity's* schedule; he was that sort. And had Baijon and me been meant all along to disappear, not die, in House Starborn's private little war, and be smuggled off alMayne in a load of heat run by a darktrader beholden to Kennor?

And by Berathia Notevan, who due to a sudden case of *chaudatu* fever on Gruoch's part, had been under house arrest when she was supposed to be meeting the shuttle from *Circle of Stars* at Zerubavel Outport. She could of walked us right across the crete and knocked on *Angelcity's* door. If she'd been there.

But then Baijon wouldn't of got to deliver his message. Kennor had to know Gruoch well enough to know what she'd do—step on Berathia's tail long enough for Baijon to deliver his message, then get one or both of us out when the shooting started.

Or had Kennor expected any shooting at all? He hadn't expected Winterfire to sell him out.

No data. I went back to following out the lines of what I knew.

Meggie'd been supposed to take her live freight to Royal and I was pretty sure it was us. Berathia's part in all that (and it had to be her; Meggie would of said if her courier was a hellflower) had been to dump the package on *Angelcity* for later pickup. Anything else she'd been told was probably another one of Kennor's double-dealing fantasies. But we'd been meant to go to Royal, I bet.

Was there a godlost Brightlaw Prototype after all? And what was it? And if there was, why should the Prexy of the Azarine Coalition have it? For that matter, why should hellflowers back rebels? Or the Coalition back them, even if they was paying customers? Or even Kennor his own self be interested in a bunch of *chaudatu* dweebs?

My train of thought derailed before I could come up with a satisfactory reason-why link between Kennor Starbringer, head of the Azarine Coalition, and a Tortugan Political Action Committee.

I knew that Kennor wanted there to be war on alMayne to seal it off from Archangel's lackeys. Therefore, Archangel had every reason to try to frame alMayne for Library Science.

But what reason did alMayne have for actually being guilty?

All of a sudden all that space outside the ports was too big and too cold. With no questions answered I got up out of the mercy seat and went off after Baijon.

*   *   *   *   *

Valijon's Diary

Now I am dead. And I am afraid. There is no Right Conduct now; I cannot choose good from evil—to act, even, is heresy, and should I speak, none of the Gentle People would hear my words.

I do not hear theirs. I reject them. Even a show of honor in Archangel's shadow is better than nothing. That act of mine was true.

I did not think it would be so hard.

I have seen, and I do not understand. The *chaudatu* reiver Errol Lightfoot whose life was promised me I have killed. I know this to be true: even the war-medicine of the Gentle People could not have saved him from the wound that I in honor dealt him.

How, then, is he resurrected as the *Malmakosim* Archangel?

I do not know. I do not know that it matters. I am kept from my death, and the *Kore* will not understand that it is needful. She understands so little, and yet has great wisdom.

At least so I once thought. But if everything else I have ever believed in has been found to be falsehood, perhaps the *Kore,* too, is false.

I cut her upon the Floor of Honor and she did not die. I would say that for that she might be a goddess, but the Tongueless Ones have no gods.

I think it more likely that she cheated.

But I do not know *how* she cheated, and thus is her cunning proven to be great. Having such cunning, is it not possible my death is being withheld as part of a larger plan?

Does that matter? Am I so cowardly that I will grasp at life as tool to a *chaudatu* plan rather than choose a clean and honorable death?

Yet she is not *chaudatu*. She is *alarthme* at least—only a Loremaster could say if she, bearing honorable scars and surviving, is now one of the Gentle People.

And I reject the teaching of the Loremasters, for it is lies.

What must I do? Three things I know: *Malmakos* walks once again, slaying planets—and seeing this, the *Kore* speaks to me of food. Arch-angel-who-is-also-Errol-Lightfoot must be killed—yet we flee him.

And I am dead, and have no more part in these matters, yet I still breathe, at the behest of my *comites.*

All is not well. All may never be well again. And how will I find Ketreis in the Land Beside without my Knife? Without my *arthame,* how will we know each other?

Perhaps the *Kore* will know. Perhaps she will tell me. I may not disobey her, yet she orders me into dishonor. Dishonored, I must save her from further dishonor, yet, *al-ne-alarthme,* it is not my place to act. Can I, honorless, judge honor?

Does the *Kore* have any honor?

Is she even human?

I wish I were not alive. My thoughts are tongueless, yet I hear them.

I witnessed to the Gentle People that the Machine was among us again.

They called me liar and oathbreaker.

I saw the face of the *Malmakosim* Archangel and he was the *chaudatu* reiver Errol Lightfoot, whom I had already killed. I swore his death again. Yet he killed me, and now we are both alive.

The *Kore* proved honor and humanity and her right to be heard on the Floor of Honor that lay between my own walls.

Yet . . .

I will not think of that. I will think of nothing.

The Machine is manifest, and I am afraid.

13

The Theory and Practice of Hell

I found Baijon down in the galley. There was probably a dining room somewhere on this flying indulgence, but the galley was rigged so the crew could eat here and we was the crew now.

Baijon'd left out minor details like clothes and medicalling, and he'd gone at the supplies the way Gruoch'd took Wailing. It was distributed even-handed-like over all the flat surfaces in sight and food was only made for one.

"You living on air, now, Baijon-bai?"

He wouldn't look at me.

"You got to keep your strength up, bai."

"For what, *Kore?*" He looked up at me and looked like a man dying. "It is true, *Kore*, that you have been served with dishonor by the Gentle People, and that they in their dishonor are not worthy of your love. Yet you have said— You have said—"

I knew where this was going and it wasn't no place I wanted to visit. "It wasn't your fault about your Knife, bai! If it was somebody's fault it was mine, oke—"

"That does not matter! If a thing is so, *Kore*, does blame matter? I have no *arthame*. I have no shadow. If I go on alive, I will become . . . less than human." He hung his head. "I am afraid of that, *Kore*. You

have said you cared for me in the way *chaudatu* do. If that is so, let me go."

He was my *servites*. He had to have my permission to die.

And then I'd be here and all alone.

There was choices, even now. I could blow up *Dance*, for maybes, or wait out here a kilo-hour or so then go back to Tortuga System and see if someone was there. If I had the luck of the damned there would be, and he'd be a legger willing to download his astrogator for a price. There was still running to do.

And I could even mount my own one-sided crusade against Archangel. With enough luck I could be real trouble. Baijon could be more. I could sucker him into that, I bet. Promise him enough murder, he'd stay on top for it.

I could.

I would.

"You do me one thing first, kinchin-bai. Won't take long. Then you do what you got to. I let you go."

But that was what I said instead.

*   *   *

"This is a auxiliary Jump interlock. You pull it, you make Transit to hyperspace. It's to override the pilot, in case everything's ready to go and he won't either kick it back down off redline or pull the stick."

"Yes," said Baijon, cautious.

"It's for when the thing *is* ready to go—that means numbers in the numbercruncher, which we don't got. You crank it up and kick out the jams now, I guess we wouldn't be anywhere any more."

Ghost Dance's black gang was a thing of beauty: no less than fifteen plates of goforth, rated hyper-Main and all turned out like a techno's dream. It didn't need anybody to keep after it any more than I needed somebody to watch out for my heartbeat. If you wanted someone down there for maintenance or show, there was a little *geoffreis* hole all lined in banks of gauges and dials which I was showing Baijon now.

"*This* is the goforths cut-out. When the engines are at Jump standby, you pull this, they cycle down to rest. You got that?"

"I understand."

"Baijon, you *sure* you can tell them apart?"

I stared at him. He looked back. Eyes too blue to be human back where I came from; mark of the hellgods.

"I promise you, *Kore,* I will know them. One turns off the engines. The other destroys the ship."

"Just keep them straight, oke?"

In the back of my skull there was a wild dissenting vote with regards to my current plan. Just like back on Wailing, only then I'd been the one what hadn't liked my plan, I thought. This time I liked it just fine. I guessed.

And it was fair. That was what mattered. It was payback, and it was fair.

"You said you would release me," Baijon prompted.

"Je. This is how it goes."

I turned to one of the consoles and slapped switches. Goforths came up on line and I braided them together, a silent song of power that rang through the ship, making the air tremble. *Ghost Dance* strained, waiting the office to Jump.

"I tell you some stuff and ask you some stuff. And then you pick one of the switches to pull."

The light was green and red and gold and orange; a spotted rainbow.

"Is this a game, *Kore?*"

"Depends on how you look at it. Do you have some particular objection to death by plasma-conversion?"

Baijon thought about it while the goforths shook frustration into my bones.

"No. That is acceptable."

"Oke. Now."

I took a deep breath. What'd happened at Royal made this easier. It still didn't make it easy.

"Baijon-bai," I said. "You tell me: how you learn yourself you going for to trust someone?"

He translated the question back into Interphon and probably from Interphon into helltongue. Then he thought about it.

Of course, the goforths might just overload and ice us whiles he was thinking. I kept my back to the read-outs that would tell me about it.

"At . . ." *home,* Baijon was going to say, and didn't. "On alMayne this is not a question that can be asked. You know, *Kore,* that they are your people, and hold the same things holy that you do."

"Like cutting up cranky with vendetta, and like that."

"Ah, *Kore,* that is not a matter of trust. That is a matter of honor. A dishonorable man may not be trusted. He is not human." He was giving me as much of a honest answer as he knew how, and it was still back to Square One. No help.

"But you got friends, maybe. How do you decide who they is?"

Baijon looked blank; I guess maybe it wasn't the sort of question a young hellflower of means was used to being asked.

"You befriend those within your House, *Kore,* perhaps even within your GreatHouse."

alMayne GreatHouses is big—passels of LessHouses all can owe fealty to the same GreatHouse. Maybe even millions of people. Too many to all be friends with.

"Je, che-bai, but which ones?"

"The ones you *like, Kore.*" He was starting to get frustrated now, me keeping him from the Long Orbit with this nidderling triviality.

"So how do you decide who you like? And do you trust everyone you like?"

"Often." Baijon had a look as indicated he had fond memories of liking some pretty untrustworthy people. "More often you . . . *Kore,* it may be that you trust someone unquestioningly, and respect them. But you do not like them very much."

"But people you like—and trust—they're your friends?" I didn't ask if I was one of them.

"Yes."

"I had a friend oncet." Now we got to the good part. I put my hands flat on the front of my thighs, flat, awkward, and helpless.

"He wasn't a person. I trusted him anyway."

I concentrated on staying where I was, keeping my hands where they was.

"He lived in a box."

Baijon was fast. And strong. He could break my neck with his bare hands, even without the help I was giving him. I just hoped he'd remember which godlost lever to pull afterward.

"He was a Library. His name was Paladin."

Baijon didn't move. The only thing changed was his eyes; big and dark and dilated. Most people can't control that reflex. But I wasn't really sure he'd heard.

"I'm a Librarian."

He'd done give up his Knife for me. I owed him everything, including his life if he could take it back out of this.

He still didn't move. One hand was braced against a wall. The other one hung loose. I'd never really noticed Baijon's hands before. Nails cut back short, calluses from cargo work. Not glitterborn paws. Not any more.

What gives anybody the right to change anybody else? Or is rights just a joke, and all there is is what we take from somebody else?

"Baijon?" I said real soft.

"There is no Library. I saw it die. I saw it *die, Kore.*"

"You saw one die. But there wasn't one Library at Rialla. There was two. The other one was my friend. He was just a person. Like anyone. He made the other Library—Vannet's Library—so it couldn't hurt anybody no more. He was my friend." And that was a damn poor explanation. Nothing—and everything.

"You are wrong. There was no Library." He looked at me, pleading.

"I'm a Librarian. My Library's name was Paladin. We was together twenty years, bai, and that's how come I want to know about being friends, because maybe you can turn it off and not be friends no more, right?"

"A Library." Baijon's voice was flat. No clues in it at all. "You— *had*—a Library."

His *comites* wouldn't lie to him. Sure I wouldn't. But he believed it, just like he believed in hellflower honor, and now he got to choose between believing I was a liar and believing I was the worst thing a hellflower could think of.

"You know I'm dicty. You know why we ain't supposed to leave home. We don't get the Inappropriate Technology indoctrination that makes all you fellahim so scared of Old Fed Tech. I didn't even know what a tronic was when I left home—you think I'd of got told about Libraries? I didn't know what Paladin was when I found him. And when I did know, he wasn't a thing any more. He was my friend.

"He was my friend," I repeated lamely. "You don't sell out your friends."

There was a long pause while Baijon tried to think about something so damn obvious he'd never wasted one brain cell on it before.

"It was a *Library, Kore.* You say you have not been schooled—you do not know what they have done—"

"I know."

That stopped him a minute.

"I know. I was there. You think what happened at Royal was bad? It's a joke. Party games. Stick with me, bai, I lay you out a war that make you wish you was back on Royal in the before-time. Think I could build some of the weapons the Libraries used, I bet. Know I could build what they used on Royal. Where do you think Archangel found out how? Library Archive told him and what Archive knew, I've got it all in my head. Archive—Vannet's Library—did something to me when I went to kill it. What your buddy the WarDoctor Wall That Walked knew about. He thought it was you, maybe, that Archive'd got to, but it wasn't. It was me.

"You talk along of not being human. I guess I'm not, any more. I didn't think you could put a Library in someone's head. Paladin never said. But I remember what Archive remembered, some. I know why people is still hunting Libraries a thousand years later."

I could see the cords standing out on Baijon's neck, and sharp reflections of the lights all over his skin. It looked like it'd been oiled. He was sweating like somebody was roasting him alive.

"I know about Libraries. But Paladin wasn't—isn't—like that. Paladin wasn't like Archive. He was my friend. Same way you make friends —by learning them, how they are. So he told me he wouldn't hurt anybody, or let Archive hurt anybody, and I believed him. I knew him half my life. He was my friend."

"Kore," said Baijon, all full of sorrow. Sorry I'd been took in, sorry I'd told him, sorry for a thousand things.

"He went away to get me not burned for a Librarian. But he didn't know what Archive'd done to me. I was thinking to go find him. That was my plan for after Royal, don't got no plans now. Letting you go, too. Your choices, now, bai.

"So now you do what you got to; I'm done."

I walked out past him. He didn't touch me.

Halfway up the ladder I started to shake so hard I just had to stop and hold on. But that was just chemicals in my blood; nothing personal. Every bone in my body hurt. I'd been sure I'd be dead by now.

Now someone knew. The thing I couldn't never tell, the thing I had to die to keep anyone from finding. Someone knew. And what happened next wasn't anything of my making. What happened next was set a thousand years ago, when organic life created the alMayne out of their leftover Librarians to be the human answer to Archive. Hellflowers and hellgods.

I didn't bother with going to the cockpit or the drive room. There didn't seem much point. I'd shot my bolt. If Baijon wanted to be live or dead or express his opinion on which I should be, he was going to get his chance.

I found a cabin and went in. The bunk was stripped, but I curled up on it anyway.

Funny; Paladin'd left me so I wouldn't be alone no more. And I wasn't; I had half a Library in my skull trying to eat its way out. But still no one anywhere I could touch.

The drive didn't explode. I guessed Baijon'd shut it down.

Too bad.

* * * * *

Valijon's Diary

It would be easy to do as the songs instruct. But so many of them have been wrong; what if this instruction, too, is wrong? I am no longer one of the Gentle People. My soul is destroyed, and my *devoir* is clear. As my soul has gone, so must go my body.

But if this is so, and my first duty is self-destruction, it follows that there is no responsibility I must discharge before that. And afterward, I am dead.

If I am dead, I cannot then kill the Librarian.

So logic teaches, but I am a man alone and know that logic lies. I live. If it is proper to kill the Librarian, no consideration of antecedent honorable suicide would intervene.

What is right?

Do I die here, then what I might do against Archangel remains undone. Do I kill the Librarian, what she might do, too, to foil Archangel remains undone.

I named her honorable, and my father swore to me that honor is that which cannot be held by beasts or machines. My father, too, named her Worthy-of-a-Knife, as did the Memory of Starborn.

If all these are wrong, then honor itself is a lie. And if there is no honor, then my acts or lack of them, too, are meaningless.

And, does she lie to me, my power to harm is small.

A paradox: I am so useless that what I do does not matter, yet so worthy that I must fight on, in hope that mine will be the hand to slay the Enemy.

The *Kore* would say this is a situation with no downside.

But I do not think it has a topside, either.

There is no one left to trust. Everyone and everything I have believed in has broken in my hand. Even honor.

There is only one choice left.

* * * * *

I wanted to be asleep, or dead, or anything else that involved not thinking any more, but my brain refused to cooperate.

Not surprising: how much of it was still mine? I was dying by inches, sure as if I'd been poisoned, and no remedy in sight.

Things like this is lots more fun when they's happening to someone else in the talkingbooks.

Item: all this was Archive's fault, because most of this was Archive's memories and all of it was Archive's doing. And having Archive's memories would of been bad enough, but memories wasn't all he'd dumped down me when it came time to kiss and part. The old reliable Butterfly St. Cyr-as-was could never of walked into a protected memory core through a dumb terminal and shut down all the power on a planet.

Ex-planet.

But I hadn't done that, had I? I'd just run into Paladin, and *he'd* done it, right?

No. It wasn't that easy.

Because no matter what he'd done to me going off like he had back on dear old RoaqMhone, no matter how I was sure now I'd never really understood him, Paladin wouldn't of done something that stupid. Not shut down the power in all of Port Mantow like a tronic with no interlocks. Paladin would of got me out of there without.

Wouldn't he?

If it had been Paladin shutting down the planet, why had he done it like that?

If it hadn't been Paladin, who?

Or what?

But whoever it was it wasn't me, I tried to tell myself. Not Butterflies-are-free Peace Sincere, ethical arbiter of the spaceways and all-round stand-up sophont. I saved Baijon's life several times at considerable personal sacrifice. I couldn't be the kind of person who'd trash a bunch of harmless innocents just to save my neck.

But I was. And I had, whether I'd pushed the final button or not. And I hadn't even thought twice.

My head hurt. And after that, telling Baijon all about Paladin made a weird kind of sense, because I really wasn't sure what I was going to do next. The real problem was, I didn't know how much longer there was going to be a *me* at all.

Megalomania, Paladin'd say, and for once I didn't have to ask what the words meant. If I was all that dangerous that I needed a keeper, I wouldn't be trapped on a nowhere ship in the Outfar feeling so helpless against whatever Archangel was going to do next.

Whiles later I realized I had to be asleep, because Paladin was there with me. He was trying to explain where he'd been and what he was doing and what it was I should and shouldn't do. And it was real good, real urgent advice that'd save my bones if I could just make it make sense. I wanted to. He wanted to help. But I just couldn't wake up enough to hear.

But I tried. And made it.

Baijon was standing over me like grim talkingbook death. Hollow cheeks and burning eyes, and he'd found himself a blaster somewheres on *Ghost Dance* to point at me.

He was still alive.

"Why did you tell me?"

I took a moment to be glad I wasn't lying in the direction of anything important; when he shot me he wouldn't scramble too many ship's systems.

"Why?" The blaster jerked.

"If it was something going to make a difference in your plans, Baijon, after you was dead weren't any time to tell you."

"Librarian," he said, but he still didn't pull the trigger.

I sat up, careful like I cared.

"You come to gloat or complain? Told you: Paladin was my friend. That was a accident. He fixed it. Gone now."

"Yet you *glory* in it."

"Didn't you never have friends, bai?"

We glared at each other for whiles, or close to it as either of us had energy or inclination for. Baijon looked tired. I wanted to tell him was everything golden, that we was partners, that there was some way out.

I was tired of lying, among other things.

"Did you *want* me to kill you?" Baijon asked finally. "Are you afraid to take your own life? A . . . coward?" His voice dropped on the last word like he expected to be struck by lightning.

"Sure, if you want. Whatever you want." I rubbed my eyes. "We's in a broken starship with no place to go. Archangel's just blown up Royal with a Old Fed weapon and's probably looking to hang the rap on us. All your hellflower relatives is mad at you, and you done lost your Knife, and—"

"And so you thought that *now* would be a good time to tell me you are a Librarian," Baijon finished.

What he sounded was more exasperated than anything else. Like Paladin used to when I'd get up to didoes.

"Or a Library. I . . . Look. I give up, oke? All I ever wanted was a starship. Paladin never hurt anybody in his life. Archive's gone. Maybe Paladin could fix what it did to me. Maybe not. But it seems to me if you got a Better Dead list, you should maybe put Archangel at the top of it, not me."

"Maybe." Baijon bared his teeth at me. "And maybe I should start with what is within the reach of my arm."

"Go for it. Who the hell cares?"

"You do," Baijon pointed out.

"What do you care what I care?"

"You have made it my business, *Ko*—San'Cyr. You told me what you are. Did you think I would do nothing?"

"Maybe I just thought Mallorum Archangel deserved trouble more than I do, bai."

"So I am to ally myself with a Library—and spare you—because I fear my foe possesses one. In such escalation of weapons what place will remain for people?"

He was right, Archive's memories told me—and wrong.

"I know Paladin. I trust Paladin."

Baijon bared his teeth. "And do you trust yourself, San'Cyr?"

He looked at me. I looked away. We both knew the answer to that, after Royal. I'd just been looking for someone else to tell it to me.

"The Machine killed billions," Baijon said in a low voice. "Gone as Royal is gone—a thousand billion people. A thousand suns. There was no mercy. There was no compromise possible. They would not listen."

And now Baijon couldn't afford to listen either. He was right. But something else died in that war that deserved to be remembered.

"Je, babby, I guess you got to do it for what's in my head. But Paladin was a Library, too, and he'd likely talk you to death, but he wouldn't fold up your sun. I remember the war. And maybe all the Libraries didn't agree to have it, but ain't nobody left to say their side. People can come in boxes. And not-people in flesh-and-blood. Archangel dropped the dime on Royal. I'd pick him over a Library if I only got to shoot one."

There was a pause. That wasn't what I meant to say, dammit—I meant for Baijon to shoot me, because I might trust Paladin to the end of the numbers but I didn't trust me.

"Pull the trigger, will you, babby? You're wasting my time."

"And is Archangel, then, to fly free? No one else can stop him."

"Neither can we. Stop farcing yourself."

"But we can try, San'Cyr. If success belongs to others, then the assay is what we keep for ourselves. We must try, San'Cyr. If my death is to have meaning, it must be used for this. It is the last service I can render to my father and my House."

Baijon'd said it one-time, whiles back. About how you can't let people get away with things like that. Even if it kills you. Even if it ain't happening right to you. Even if what you do won't make any difference.

You got to *care*. Because being people ain't just what you are. It's what you do.

"You got any bright ideas on how we going to do that, you glitterborn moron? We got no navicomp. No navicomp, no Jump. The only place we can go is back to Royal sublight. And say we do that—get back to Royal system and pirate a navicomp? Where do we go? We can get to Archangel, sure—coked, wrapped, and in chains."

I thought about those eyes, purple and glowing and ready to turn a brain inside out.

"I don't think I want to do that, bai."

Baijon nodded, sober.

"I have a better plan. I will seek out Archangel and challenge him to an honorable death-dance. With my Knife. In honor, he will accept."

It took me a minute to figure out Baijon was making a joke.

"There is a way. You will find it, with the *Malmakos* that is in you. If I can survive my death and embrace what I am not, so can you. Archangel made us. He must pay. We will make a new plan, San'Cyr. As . . . equals."

The galaxy trembled, I bet. But I felt fine.

"And what about when—if—when Archive Library takes me all the way over?"

"Ah, San'Cyr—*then* I will kill you."

He tossed the blaster on the bunk beside me. The safety interlock was still on.

14

The Maltese Prototype

Saying we had a plan was the easy part. Our plan was to ice Mallorum Archangel, whoever he was this week. And whatever color his eyes was.

How to get to Brother Mallorum while in a condition to sign the lease on his real estate was the tricky part.

"If we had something he wants—bad enough—he'd deal, right?"

"He dealt with a Library, San'Cyr. I do not think Mallorum Archangel is overly fastidious."

Dealt with a Library, dealt with a Library. . . . It went round and round in my head, like it was trying to do me some good.

"Archangel tricked with High Book—why?"

"Because he is evil, San'Cyr," Baijon said patiently.

"Yeah, I know that. But why go to all the trouble of finding a Library—which ain't all that thick on the ground—if he could get what he wanted some other way?"

"Because he could not get it some other way. The Brightlaw Prototype *was* only a prototype, and it was not certain that—"

"Waitaminnit. We was supposed to be losing that kick at Royal. Archangel thought we had it. And you know what it is?"

"All the Empire knows what it is," Baijon said primly. "It is an abomination." And then he told me what it was that everyone else all knew.

What it was, for less biased observers, was AI. Artificial Intelligence. *"A machine hellishly forged in the likeness of a human mind,"* as they say in the talking-books. Illegal as hell, proscribed six ways from galactic north. . . .

A Library.

The real heartbreaker with Proscribed Tech in the Empire is that it's so damn useful. Take your basic Library. A computer only two-thirds as complex as a Library could provide instantaneous error-free communication from one side of the Empire to the other—if anybody was allowed to build it.

The Imperial DataNet is slow, it's balky, it's restricted access, and can barely handle the traffic it has. Its limitations means the Empire has an Outfar where information-handling is one step up from flatcopy, lucky for me and anyone else that wants to hide between the lines.

But my being able to do that means the Empire loses revenue, a thing on which Empires are not notoriously big. The Empire wants what Libraries could give it—and doesn't dare go after it.

Enter the Brightlaw Prototype. Brightlaw had been building—or trying to—a computer with the capabilities of a Library, but safe for people to use. When Charlock had taken over the Brightlaw Corporation the Prototype and development notes had vanished.

There was no reason for Charlock to of either destroyed or hidden them. Charlock had been backed by Archangel, even then. And it was a safe bet that Archangel had no interest in running Brightlaw's AI Prototype past the Technology Police, the Office of the Question, or the Imperial Censor.

"And Archangel thought I had it." I looked at my left hand. Streamlined, like one of those functional claws they fit tronics with. Human looking up to where it stopped.

Cyborg with a Library chaser.

And if it was true. . . .

"I can get us out of here, bai. And I can get us Archangel."

*   *   *

"If my father had not been who he was, I would have been the next Memory of Starborn. It was to go to our line next, but there was no one of suitable age and rank to bear it."

"Is this supposed to mean something to me? Hand me the plasma torch."

He did, and I slid it up into *Ghost Dance*'s insides where she was not accustomed to rude mechanicals mucking with her computer systems.

"It means I know more about Libraries than you do," Baijon said smugly.

"You and the rest of the Empire."

I didn't need the navicomp.

That was what dream-Paladin'd been trying to tell me.

That was what I'd stumbled over. Baijon'd called me *Malmakosim* until my ears rang with it—but in helltongue it doesn't mean "Librarian." Not quite.

It means "the Machine that takes human form."

That was what had worried the hellflowers all along. Not an interstellar super-computer that could crash their datawebs. They could live without datawebs.

But under the right—or almost-right—conditions, a Library (Baijon said) could mindwipe a organic and pour a Library into its skull in place. They could do it because humans built the first Libraries, and modeled them on the only thinking architecture they had handy.

So if a brain and a computer are pretty similar—

And if the major difference is that a computer holds more stuff more reliably longer—

And if you've got a human brain stuffed full of the sort of stuff usually found in a Library—

—or a computer—

—or even the Brightlaw AI Prototype—

Then why not see if along with all the rest of it there might not be something useful in there?

I could be the ship's computer. I'd been in the Port Mantow computers. I knew everything I needed to.

I hoped.

"Now hand me the *noke-ma'ashki* cable, che-bai."

Baijon passed me a curl of stuff we'd cannibalized from what was almost certainly some kind of entertainment center in the master cabin. He was damn useful—in another life I could of made a for-sure first-class darktrader out of him. Pilot, smuggler, and all-round techlegger. *Ghost Dance* was proof. Now the cable that used to run between the navicomp and the Jump-brain ran from the Jump-brain to a touchpad keyboard all set for me to use. I wouldn't pull the numbers off the navicomp anymore. I'd make them up.

The only reason for doing this—other than the known hellflower fondness for suicide missions—was that it gave us slightly better odds than trying to pirate a ship in Royal system. Archangel—or his sisters and cousins and aunts—was almost probably still there, making tidy.

On the other hand, if everything in my head since alMayne was all just a long delusional setup, we was both dead.

There was only one way to find out.

"Oke, that's it." I unwound myself from under the seat and propped the fairings back in place. You could see every fingerprint and scratch I'd put on it, not to mention the slots I cut to feed the leads through.

Pity.

I sat in the mercy seat and looked out at nothing. There was one star brighter than the others in sight: Royal's sun, severalmany lighthours away.

Baijon was looking at me. Hopeful. Eager. All I had to do was relax and let the numbers come up. Every trip my mind made down the brainstem to where Archive'd left its get-well present made the next trip easier to make. And bye-m-bye wouldn't be no more trips to make, because what it knew would be what I was, and nothing left to lose.

We had to have a plan, Baijon'd said.

Now we had one.

I didn't think he was going to like it.

The good numbers was right there in my hands. I pulled the angelstick and *Ghost Dance* Jumped sidewise into nowhere.

15

Hellraisers

Ghost Dance made Transit to realspace over a blinding blue-white ball of ice. Probably it'd been warmer once—there was still atmosphere, thanks to an ocean with enough salt in it to be liquid. I didn't look for traffic controllers or beacons. There wasn't any.

"So we will land your ship, San'Cyr. And then?"

"Then we ask babby real nice one time for what we want."

I didn't bother to mention that the possibility Oob'd cooperate was right up there with me getting a full Imperial Pardon for everything I'd done this year.

"And then?"

"Then we take it."

*   *   *

About a lifetime ago, this was my home base; a little place called Coldwater on the cutting edge of the never-never. My nighttime man was a wiggly called Oob who told me what to kyte and where to kyte it, and didn't mind if I picked up a few side-jobs on my own.

It'd been a good working arrangement. I was sorry I was going to have to see him again.

But there was one thing Baijon and me needed in order to live to get older, and in a ship this hot the only place I could get it was a place that wasn't there. And Coldwater had the only trip-tik.

It's like this. Our glorious Phoenix Empire, the concatenative brains of which I was doubting more with each passing moment, has got a number of little monopolies, and one that's a real killer: all ports everywhere is Imperial ports.

Even on Closed Worlds like Riisfal or Restricted Worlds like al-Mayne, the port is a Imperial port and when you're on it it's just like you was standing on Grand Central its own self.

Any port not built, owned, operated—and policed—by the Empire is illegal. Illegal ports is fair game for your Fleet and mine to blow up, and there's no way to hide something that, at its crudest, is a square klik of big flat place with a traffic control computer and a sensor suite.

But Coldwater is a *abandoned* port. All closed down, the *legitimates* packed up and pulled out, no licit traffic in and out ever more. Who'd want a place where the temperature only goes above freezing point of water at high noon of local summer?

Any enterprising crimelord as wanted a port—that's who. And the Empire wouldn't look twice—because it *knew* it was there, and it *knew* it was closed.

There was an Imperial DataNet terminal on Coldwater.

*   *   *

You'd think I'd of had enough of the DataNet, and you'd be right. But what I was after now hadn't been in the port computer on Royal-as-was. Besides, there was one segment of the galactic power elite I hadn't ticked off.

Yet.

Ghost Dance fell out of the sky sweet as you please and right into my old docking ring. The external temperature sensors wobbled alive and sank right down into the negative numbers. The main ship's computer probably ached to tell me to wear my woolies, but I'd ripped out its voder along with doing the rest of my custom chop-channel.

I shut down the boards but left her hot. I wasn't worried she'd go walking off. Nothing human can handle the fourspace maths to fly a ship without a navicomp and I'd set her so she had to have Jump coordinates before she'd lift.

Nothing human.

Baijon and me went back to the hotlocker and I put on my party clothes. There'd been time on the way here to assemble a kit of fly-vines that should impress even Oob, and no lack of raw material. It even covered up what was left of my left hand, so nobody'd know I was borged. I was saving that for a surprise.

Meanwhile, the rest of it was the prettiest blaster-harness I'd ever owned; I looked like a high-ticket version of a talkingbook space-pirate and with the rating of the heat I was packing I didn't even need to hit what I aimed at to cause it serious personal distress.

"You remember how we planned it?"

"San'Cyr, I still think the danger should be mine."

"*The* danger? Bai, I hope you don't think any part of this is safe."

*   *   *

The wind hit me first thing out of the hatch. I leaned into it, heading for the converted bunker at the edge of the field. For a minute I spun me the fantasy that everything'd gone reet with my last run a half-year back: I'd dropped the bookleg at Wanderweb Free Port, lifted rokeach and gems to Kiffit, and from there to Orili-neesy, to Maichar, to Dusk, and back home again, to pass gossip, pull maintenance, and see what Oob wanted me to do next. It was a depressing commentary on the current state of affairs that my previous life looked inviting.

*   *   *

What used to be the Port Authority Building was dug down into the permafrost and held Coldwater's entire population. There was only one bar, and it didn't have a name. I pushed open the door and went in.

"Hey, St. Cyr," somebody said when I pushed my hood back. There was pilots for the two other ships I'd seen on the field and the usual gang of mechs, techs, and sophonts as thought this was a good place to be. If it mattered, I was the only human there.

"Heard about your ship," said the tender, reaching under the bar. "Bad luck."

"Worse luck if you finish that move, bai."

He stopped and regarded the blaster. I'd come in with the advantage. I was expecting trouble.

I made a smile I didn't mean and waggled my righthand heat at him. I took the time to unship the other one, just like a talkingbook space pirate. A little slow with the half hand that was left inside the glove, but the fingers I had left didn't feel the cold.

"You dead, you know that, Gentrymort?" the tender said.

"Sure. And anybody wants to join me can stay right where he is. Everybody else can ankle."

One time I just would of shot them. Or lobbed a grenade through the door before I come in and walked through what's left after you do something like that. None of them'd be any loss.

But I wasn't in the mood today, and wasn't no way this could be a lightning raid like in the talkingbooks anyway. I stood there and gave

Oob all the time he wanted to get ready and set while the patrons of the Nameless Bar & Grill shuffled themselves out into the snow.

I dogged the door shut behind them. I knew where I was going, so I went on in.

It was a long narrow hallway that probably used to run to a out-building and now was the only way in to Oob's front parlor. By now I'd got warm enough to be cold.

Oob don't like heat; his B-pop isn't rigged for it. But if I'd been him I could of thought of a more comfortable way to arrange things. Oob ran a good slice of the Outfar nightworld. Pandora to Tangervel; a chunk of cubic running all the way out to the edge of the Hamati Confederacy. He had power. I'd seen it. Not power like Archangel had or was reaching for, but if he stepped on you there wouldn't be nothing left to argue the difference.

Did having power like that make living in a freezing hellpit like this tolerable? Or did wanting power mean you didn't care about nothing else?

I pushed open the door to my boss's private office. It wasn't locked. Why bother: nobody sane'd come all the way out here to cross him.

Never mind what that made Baijon and me. I went in.

Oob was behind his desk; he always is. A thousand kilos of wool, gristle, and blubber in colors not meant to be seen in daylight don't shift too well under one Imperial Standard G. He could rig the gravity, but he's never bothered. Hanging behind him like I expected was a state-of-the-art wartoy in ready-to-rock mode. I had reason to know all of Oob's security measures real well. I just hoped he hadn't changed them.

"Captain St. Cyr," the voder on the desk said. I jogged a blaster at him.

"Refrain from immature acts," the voder said. Somebody'd pro-grammed it one time in Imperial Standard, I guess, and Oob'd never bothered to fix it. "Do you actually contemplate that my security sys-tems are incapable of anticipating your every move?"

"Well," I said, about the time the back wall of Oob's hardsite went away.

I've never anywhere seen something what tells the lifting capability of Hoplite armor. I do know that lifting anything needs a handle to grab and a place to stand.

Baijon'd made both. The wall came up in pieces.

And Oob's first line of offense turned on him.

I fired on it. I didn't make a damn bit of difference but I didn't need to. The wartoy hesitated with being hit two ways at once and yelled for help. Baijon came the rest of the way through the wall and battered the input out of it.

"Question, che-bai, isn't who shoots first or last, but who's left standing, je?"

The temperature was dropping like an innuendo and the wind was taking a chance on anything mobile. Soon enough Baijon was going to be the only one really comfortable.

"I forgot to tell you. I picked up a partner last tik."

Oob looked at Baijon and back at me and blinked; three sets of eyelids sliding over eyes I could see myself in. His throatsack bulged; the voder spoke again.

"You will cease to exist. The Smuggler's Guild will disavow you. Whatever mode of transport you arrived in will become mine. I will return you to the slave-pits, barbarian."

He was pretending we'd won, which was awfully sweet of him.

"Not impressed. You want a piece of me, babby, you got a long line to stand on. I come to do bidness."

"What do you want? Letters of Transit to the Confederacy? A wise choice, but costly. Deactivate your armaments and we will discuss it."

"Place I want's inside the Empire, not out. Toystore. You tell me how to get there. I check it through the dataweb. Me and my friend leave. And before you get any efficient ideas—" I opened my jacket to show him the rows of grenades wired on the deadman's switch. "My heart stops beating, we all dead."

And I'd be dead anywhere in the Outfar the minute I set foot outside this room, no matter whether Oob was dead or livealive. I was closing, sure and for certain, the last possible bolt-hole.

"I suppose your companion is equally willing to accept the hazard of premature demise?"

"He's hellflower."

"Hellflowers are crazy. The galaxy knows that," Baijon said. We'd fixed the voder; he sounded like him now; sing-songy and pretty with the hellflower lilt in his voice. He bent down and ripped a limb off the wartoy and hefted it.

Good act, if it was. Baijon looked seriously crazy. Not like he didn't care if he lived or died. Like he couldn't tell the difference.

"You tell me, we go, boss; you don't never see me no more. What've you got to lose? *I* got nothing to lose, bai, you know that already, people talking about what happened along of me in the Roaq."

"Very well." A mechannikin what Oob used for hands minced across the desk and dipped into a drawer.

And whiles we was all supposed to be looking at it, Oob's back-up wartoy came up through the dropshaft in the floor.

There was a blast of light and sound as Baijon swung up what'd looked like a bit of fancywork on his armor. Half-blinded me ready or not even though I'd been expecting it. Over the echoes you could hear a teeth-setting whine as the wartoy's safety fields overloaded from damping its own explosion in order to save its master's life. Touching.

Baijon lowered his gauntlet and shucked off the half-melted fairing. What we'd rigged for the armor would only fire once. I hadn't really been sure it'd fire at all.

A couple of kilocredits of expensive hostility dropped to the floor, having retired from the adversary business. One for use and one for show—that was what Oob'd always had.

I smole a small smile at my ex-boss. Twenty years in bidness along of him, I'd learned my way into his little quirks.

"Wartoys make my partner nervous," I explained. "I guess his finger must of slipped. Now, you was getting me that trip-tik?"

Oob didn't say anything for a real long time. If he ever got his hands on me now, there wouldn't be enough left to shop to the body-snatchers.

"All your posturing is futile. I am not intimidated. I refuse to aid you."

The Hoplite armor sang as Baijon prepared to settle in for some plain and fancy intimidation.

"Don't bother," I said to him.

I walked around to Oob's side of the console. I didn't know his setup, but I pushed buttons until something happened.

The back wall slid open, and there was the DataNet terminal and all its works; a sideshow to impress the rubes they was getting what they'd fronted for. The terminal was a commercial port model; it was fitted with limbic jacks. I walked over to it whiles Baijon stood over my boss. Ex-boss.

"That will avail you nothing," the voder said.

"Shut up."

I didn't want to do this. I didn't want to be a borg, with hellgod metal mutating under my skin until I turned into a *thing*.

I didn't want to be here.

I wanted to go home.

But Baijon wanted to go home too, and he wouldn't never get the chance. All those solid citizens on Royal wanted to live as much as I did.

If you aren't part of the solution, you're part of the precipitate.

I pulled off my glove and then pulled back my skin and shook my wrist until the plugs dropped out from between glass and cybereisis bones and dangled. I'd put them in back on the *Dance*. Universal connectors. You could jack anything up to them, and I did. I felt Oob watching me, and Baijon not watching me. Borg. Hellgod. *Malmakosim.* Your friendly neighborhood darktrader, Butterfly St. Cyr.

This time wasn't like either time at Royal. Something knew what it was doing—something I could hitch on like making the Jump to angeltown without a ship and follow down to what I needed.

Cyborgs' brains is buffered to take the input. Mine was still under renovation. But I'd had some practice and I was getting more.

Paladin, are you out here? Can you hear me? Answer me, bai. You owe me, dammit.

Nothing. Paladin wasn't there. Not this time. But everything else was. And I got what I wanted.

"We got to thank you for hospitality and say it's been a real pleasure we don't hope to repeat."

The trip-tik cassette full of information came up out of its slot. I plucked it and flipped it to Baijon. The armor caught it without looking.

"And before we go—just in case you think to be unfriendly-like, bai—we got one thing more for you." I yanked my brain loose from the computer's and gave it the office to run.

Coldwater wasn't like Royal. When I shut down everything the computer could reach, only the terminal went dead.

Then we left.

*   *   *

The storm we'd landed in was a blizzard when we left. I pumped a covering fire around us just for grins, but I knew the clientele. They wasn't the type to jump us on the heavyside.

Baijon slapped open both locks, and *Dance*'s air came smoking out.

And the lights on the other two ships on the field came up.

"She's pretty, but can she fly?"

The over-amp made the pilot's voice wof and yabber. There was a flash. We was sprayed with boiling water while somebody's top-cannon tried to find a range.

Then I was in, with Baijon in all his glory landed on top of me in the hushed presence of great valuta acquired by unlawful means. If we was taking any hits, *Dance* was too much of a lady to let on.

I beat Baijon to the bridge by not-much, and slammed the cassette in for the Jump-brain to chew on while he squirmed out of the armor. All we had to do to use it was get to Transfer Point alive.

"St. Cyr, you in there? Pop your locks, jillybai, I'll make it quick," my commo said. I wondered who he was, but not very hard.

There was another spray of wet mud across the external pick-ups. Baijon slammed into a seat and pulled his straps down. I grabbed a handful of lifters and pulled.

And watched *Ghost Dance* tell me she was doing her best against a hundred gravities of discouragement.

Tractors.

"San'Cyr?" Baijon, wondering why we was hanging around.

"Mother's got problems just now, babby-bai."

Two ships on the field, leggers and pirates equipped with the standard box of tricks. Tractors to lock them on to a ship or free-floating cargo, guns that could angle to protect a ship on the ground. And a nasty sense of civic duty.

Dance's guns were fixed, with damn few degrees of arc. In space you turn the whole ship, je?

They was going to hold us on the heavyside and hammer us to death.

They hoped.

I gave her all the go-devils in the inventory, to where I was sure something was going to cut loose and blow. She started pulling away, and the view-screens went fade-to-black as the darktraders on the field gunned their engines to hold her.

I opened a wide channel. Both of them would hear it.

"This is *Ghost Dance*. We got fifteen plates of goforth and nothing to lose. You boys want to be serious nonfiction you just hang on; I guarantee to wrap you around the first lamppost in angeltown."

No answer. Just the howl of an open circuit. *Dance* was starting to shake.

"I mean it. When you forged your First Tickets, anybody tell you what happens you Jump too deep in a gravity well?"

Silence.

"Want to find out?"

I cut the channel and hit the override. The good numbers slid right down the Jump-computer's throat. I counted six, then grabbed the angelstick.

The image in my screen slewed as one of the leggers whipped its tractors off us. *Dance* snapped the other one no problem and we made a slightly-less-than-textbook exit from Coldwater space, full throttles and god help anything in our way. We ripped a hole in the atmosphere big enough to drop a shaker into and by the time the stick dropped home we was twenty seconds past Transfer Point.

Safe. One more time.

But I had finally twigged to what that meant. The raid had gone real smooth, but smooth this time just meant double trouble next time, until you doubled out to where there wasn't no good numbers any more.

*   *   *

Now that it was mostly too late to change my mind I looked at the numbers I'd pulled out of Oob's "Too Secret To Look At" dumpfile. The navicomp would of given me names and addresses, but even without it I could see we was heading somewheres off the beaten track.

Toystore.

"I still do not precisely understand why we are going there, San'Cyr." Baijon looked pleased but not particularly disturbed by our recent almost conversion to nonfiction.

"Other than it's the only place in the Empire we won't get shopped and sold? It's that plan you said I had, bai."

"To go shopping?" He hadn't belted in to the worry seat. The straps and buckles clinked when he moved. "Our plan was to kill Archangel, was it not?"

"Oh, why the hell not?"

I got up and walked back out of the cockpit, jerking leads loose from the big bang I was wearing as I went.

Once the plan had been to get loose and go find Paladin, my onetime partner, Library, and all-around pain in the neck.

A little later, the plan had been to hide out while news of Mallorum Archangel's techleggery and High Book connections made him a non-player in the galactic game of ultimate power.

It didn't look like that was what you might call your viable option anymore. Not with what Archangel had from Library Archive. The only consolation was that Archangel didn't have any Old Fed Tech memories the way I did—but then, would he have noticed?

What Archangel did have was a wish-list for a Coalition without any hellflowers in it at all. More, he wanted what the hellflowers had: the Empire's largest cache of information on Old Federation Libraries or a reasonable facsimile.

I went back into the main cabin of *Ghost Dance,* where sophonts of distinction'd probably spent serious hours arguing over what to have for lunch. It didn't look quite so pristine mint as it had before Baijon and me'd took up light housekeeping here.

"Let me help you, San'Cyr." Baijon started pulling tape and grenades loose, turning me from a walking bomb back into a real live cyborg. This particular refinement'd been his idea. I'd just been planning on holding a gun to Oob's head.

Baijon didn't call me *"Kore"* anymore. It just meant "woman" in helltongue. I shouldn't miss it. Baijon was reinventing himself, taking out all the hellflower and leaving something that could deal with a *Malmakosim.*

Because Archangel was important enough for that.

Or because it was easier than dying nobly and with honor for a ideal that you'd already had proved to you didn't exist.

Baijon finished untaping me and then set to work sorting the grenades from the wrap in case we might want to blow up something later. I looked at my hand without the glove, but it hadn't grown any new fingers whiles I wasn't looking.

The trouble was, you couldn't just get up one day and decide that everything you ever knew was wrong. You could try, but it wouldn't work.

It hadn't worked for me.

"I be getting us something to eat, *ea,* che-bai? We got a long tik to where we going."

"They might simply blow us up when we reach this Toystore." Baijon, unimpressed.

"Gives us something to look forward to, ne?"

I'd always wanted to peel Baijon loose from his honor. From the first time I met him.

I'd changed my mind.

*　　*　　*

There was food for another five hundred hours in the galley. It was nice to know I had enough munchies to last out my life. I looked at all the baggies and boxes and tried to think what I was doing here.

Stinging Archangel. He'd bite. He'd let us get close to him. He wanted the Brightlaw Prototype, which might be anything from the ultimate holecard to a new way of making beer but what was in blissful theory a tame Library that'd do what it was told. Which might exist, and might not. And Archangel thought I had it. Or was it.

And I could be.

"You are not happy, San'Cyr." Baijon came in to the galley about the time I was thinking of rearranging the supplies by size and color. Anything to take my mind off my mind.

"You got any thought why I shouldn't be happy, Baijon? I got a thousand-year-old set of alien memories eating my mind, every *legitimate* and nightworlder in the Empire is after us, and for the icing on the brass cupcake Archangel's got the galaxy so spooked it's going to bolt into six kinds of war at once."

"But we won't have to worry about that, San'Cyr. We'll be dead." Baijon began rummaging about the shelves, looking for something to eat. "When will we reach Toystore and begin to kill Archangel?"

"You know, bai—I've never told you this—but being dead is not exactly my life's ambition, you know."

"Everyone dies." Baijon popped a meal-pak and began to eat it without waiting for it to heat. "That is why you are born."

"Real comforting."

"Is it more desirable to die *not* having slain Mallorum Archangel?"

No.

We couldn't stop the war. But we could lower the ante. Ice Archangel, and there wouldn't be any Old Fed weapons on the field.

"It is our holy purpose. It pays for all. It proves—" he stopped. "It proves we were right."

I didn't want to be right. I wanted to live.

But not as much as I wanted Mallorum Archangel dead.

"Terrific. We were right. They'll put that on our marker, bai: They're Dead All Right."

"And now you will tell me our plan."

Find out what Mallorum Archangel wanted. Get next to him with it and ice him—but for the really big payoff, stop the war he was winding up to rock and roll as well.

Nothing to it, once you knew how. Because reality ain't real anymore. It's what the computers and the dataweb say it is. And what they got in them. Like Paladin. He was in there now, if I knew anything at all.

"It's a great plan. I been staying up nights over Archangel's wish-list. I figure, he wants a Library so much, bai, we buy and deliver him one."

Find Paladin and I controlled the nature of reality in the Phoenix Empire. He'd do me a favor or two.

He'd better.

16

Toys in the Attic

We made Transit to realspace in the geometric center of nowhere. There was a faint gray band of light off to starboard that was the main starmass of the galaxy, a few nearer dots for nearer systems or at least suns, but mainly nothing.

No relative motion. No depth perception. The black and white could of been painted on *Ghost Dance*'s canopy for all the sense of here and there it gave. And somewhere within a thousand cubic lights of stone cold empty was something relatively not all that bigger than my ship.

"It's . . . empty," Baijon said, which was no more inadequate than anybody else's comment on seeing the Big Dark up close and personal for the first time.

"You should see it standing on the hull in armor."

All communications frequencies was open and I had the sensor-sweeps out. So far, nothing. But Toystore was out here. Oob's numbers said so.

* * *

Toystore is a deep space station of no fixed address, which was one reason it could cost you so much to find out the current one. The other was that anything's for sale there—anything illegal under the Pax Imperador and too hot to factor through a Free Port.

What that leaves is very hot indeed.

The usual way you got to Toystore was knowing someone what

knew someone until you got passed up the line far enough to spin serious credit to get a set of mystery coordinates loaded into your navicomp. Then you'd Jump with them, and you was home free if they liked you and dead if they didn't.

We hadn't done it that way, and Toystore probably knew it.

"Are you sure . . ." Baijon said.

"Sure that this was the coordinates behind the six sets of locks in Oob's dumpfile on the Coldwater dataweb? Je. Sure for anything else? Ne."

But Toystore brokers information. At the moment we represented quite a lot of potential factoids. I was hoping they'd be curious enough at least to let us in.

At worst, we could probably clear their space alive—assuming they ever bothered to do something as interactive as start shooting.

"Welcome to Toystore, Captain St. Cyr."

The voice came over my commo, but the picture didn't. That was courtesy of holo-tightbeam, just to let me know that they knew right where we was, thank you very much, and had tech and power to waste.

The tightbeam showed me a sleek young techie dressed like ready money and not a weapon in sight. He looked more than a little like a broker I knew hight Silver Dagger, and if he was half as dangerous I had new and additional troubles.

"If you would care to follow the tracer beam you will find an empty docking sleeve able to accommodate your ship. You may carry any form of personal armament you desire while visiting Toystore, but use of antisocial technology is strictly prohibited. Toystore reserves the right to place a lien on your property and transport if punitive fines in excess of your personal credit balance are levied, and accepts no responsibility for injuries or damage incurred by persons attempting to leave Toystore without a ship. Enjoy your stay."

Right on cue and don't think they hadn't planned it for effect, Toystore hit all of its self-lights and lit up like the Emperor's Birthday. My sensors binged and agreed with my eyes: all of a sudden Toystore was right there in front of us looking all floaty and pastel and beautiful.

So they *was* curious. Round one to us.

"More lies," said Baijon, unimpressed.

"He weren't lying, 'flower. He done told us we do anything they don't like, we get spaced without ship nor suit. Simple."

Baijon grinned. The idea appealed to him. Hellflowers do have a sense of humor. It just isn't what the rest of the galaxy thinks is particularly funny.

Ghost Dance slid right down Toystore's tracer beam and kissed the gunner's daughter. The flexible dock-socket slid closed around her and started hooking ship's systems up to the great outside before the goforths was cycled down. Toystore docking computer slid down the connects as soon as *Dance* was hooked up and piggy-backed a pseudomind on any sort of intelligence my resident computers might have. By the time we was absolutely at rest Toystore'd took control of all ship's systems right down to the air locks. They slid open and the cockpit hatch slid open and we was high wide and helpless until Toystore Main Memory returned control of our comps to us.

I might be able to purge them myself, but for damn sure any try at doing so would be construed as mopery with intent to gawk, and there was something here I wanted.

I wanted the Keys to Paradise.

*   *   *

The pseudomind interface gave *Dance* limited access to Toystore Main Memory. I read up on rules and regs and fees while Baijon made extensive inroads on some glitterborn's lost wardrobe.

Our resources consisted of a stolen Imperial Battle Yacht, a defrocked hellflower, and a body of knowledge that hadn't been current events for the last ten centuries. It might be enough to start a revolution.

Or stop one.

I figured we had credit enough to pay our freight about thirty hours worth. If we couldn't get the piece of technocandy I wanted by then, we'd have to switch to Plan B.

It was real too bad there wasn't a Plan B. I wondered if the price Oob'd put on me was higher than the one the Empire was offering, and if Paladin knew about either one. I also wondered if even Toystore had what I wanted, and if I could afford it if it did.

I wasn't even sure the Keys to Paradise existed.

You might guess, with the legal down on machines hellishly forged in the likeness of a living mind etcetera, that cybernetic tech was not exactly an open traded item, Brightlaw's Folly aside. But the Empire couldn't hold together without some of it. Paladin used to even think that the Imperial DataNet might someday grow up to be a Library if it got big enough, and there was a big shady area between tronics and numbercrunchers and things that might "think as well as a man but not *like* him."

One of the ways techies tried to get around the down the Tech

Police have against building machines that think was by hanging cyber-bells and whistles on something already allowed to think on account of being born organic.

Mostly they didn't get away with it. But sometimes it took the Tech Police long enough to make up its mind that by the time they decided something belonged in Chapters 1–4 of the Revised Inappropriate Technology Act of the 975th Year of Imperial Grace (pat. pend.) it'd already been in use and production long enough that it left behind it a sizable bank of outlaw tech.

Like the Keys to Paradise.

*   *   *

"San'Cyr, why are we here?"

Baijon Stardust looked like one very rich mercenary. He was wearing a short cape, high boots, any number of fire-irons, a worried expression, and I had real doubts about the quiet good taste of *Ghost Dance*'s last tenant.

"Because I'm stupid." I was wearing something closer to quiet good taste that'd probably belonged to the last pilot. No blasters—you can wear but not shoot them on Toystore. A glove that made it look like my lost fingers was still there—not that it'd fool anybody much, with Toystore's scanners.

"If you were stupid, San'Cyr, we would both be dead, I think. You said you wished to make Mallorum Archangel a . . . gift. And thus kill him. This I believe. But is the Empire truly so depraved as to offer such things openly?"

It took me a minute to figure out what he meant. I'd told him I was going to give Archangel a Library.

"Ne, che-bai, is only one Library I'd trust anywhere near Archangel, but I got to catch him first. To do that, I got to go to Paradise."

Baijon frowned. "This is not Paradise. You said this place was Toystore, a haunt or resort of the Empire's most vile and feckless technologists."

"Is one way of putting it, as long as you don't let nobody hear you. Put another way, is the only place I can buy what I need to catch me a Library."

"The Keys to Paradise?"

"Too reet, babby. Let's ankle."

*   *   *

Baijon stuck closer'n my shadow; nothing in his association with me'd prepared him for this.

Nothing in *my* association with me'd prepared me for this.

The total citizen population of the Phoenix Empire is somewhere around ten thousand billion. If only one percent of them is bent (which is stone optimism), that's ten billion people. If only one percent of *them* is major players, that's one hundred million. And if only one to the third power percent of the population of the Empire was up to things they shouldn't be at Toystore at any given nanosecond, that meant there was close to a million people here all looking for trouble.

*   *   *

The Graymarket is the entire central core of Toystore. It had a passing resemblance to any downport wondertown: places to eat and places to deal, and places to get what you needed to deal.

It looked like Grand Central on the Emperor's Official Birthday. Every method you might ever want to use to bend the Pax Imperador was being offered absolutely open by kiddies who looked like they'd never ducked a blaster-bolt in their lives. If I'd thought I'd been out of place on Mikasa and alMayne, I'd been local color compared to here.

There was holos two and three times life-size of people demonstrating illegal acts they would be happy to perform for a fee. There was offers of things for sale—half of them I didn't recognize, and the other half was nine kinds of forbidden. The level of pure unfamiliar information on offer was numbing.

But this was just the opening act, flashcandy for the rubes and hangers-on. Toystore's rep-making stock in trade wasn't this stuff. What Toystore dealt in was the hottest, most illegal kick of all.

Knowledge.

"San'Cyr, how do we find . . . what you are seeking . . . in all of this?" Baijon gestured at five tiers of wondershow.

"We don't. We hire a professional."

"But San'Cyr, you have told me we have 'barely enough credit to keep breathing if we don't jump salty.' "

"Said we hire a pro. Didn't say nothing about paying him."

*   *   *

The memorybroker's shop I wouldn't of recognized without the Intersign glyphs running parallel to the Imperial Standard Script. Baijon was the one what found which part of the wall was the door. If I was still in the business of being impressed by things I would of been impressed.

"Welcome to Toystore, Butterflies-are-free Peace Sincere. How may we help you?"

The sophont that oiled out to meet us was Core-worlds B-pop and spun Interphon straight from the Imperial Mint with an accent you could use to finance most of the con jobs in the Outfar.

"Perhaps a new life history? Some job skills? Your credit is quite good . . . at the moment." He smiled in a way as said it was oke to be impressed with his superior way of weaseling info out of the Toystore Interstellar Bank.

I wasn't. On Toystore, everything's for sale.

"Not buying memory. Selling. Anybody wants to know why Tortuga Sector isn't answering the phone, they ask me."

"Weapons systems failure," said the broker, unimpressed. Baijon looked indignant. I shrugged.

"Didn't ask for critical reviews, bai. I was there. I was on alMayne when it went up, too. And I was in the Roaq. That's my sale."

Information. An eyewitness account, vetted, certified, and on cassette, of what I'd seen and what I'd thought about it. Inarguable. Anybody can say something's so. Thanks to the magic of modern technology now you can prove it, and hand somebody else the experience to boot.

"Well . . ." The broker was playing coy, which is not a new experience in my life. "I suppose there might be some curiosity value in it. If you'll come this way we'll copy the memories, transcribe an abstract, and place them in our catalog. If someone is interested—"

"Wasn't born yesterday. You put what I said in your catalog. Somebody wants to deal, we deal then."

"You're making things very difficult, Sincere. I don't know what you're used to on the Borders, but—"

"It's *Captain* St. Cyr, *chaudatu*-bai, and you're the first shop I came into, not the last. I come to sell. I told you what I'm selling and how. You know what you've heard about Royal and Washonnet and the Roaq. Now it's your turn, je?"

He didn't like it but I'd twigged him; he'd heard enough about current events to want to know more.

"Most of our clients, *Captain,* prefer to leave their information on consignment. Of course, we do, occasionally, make an outright purchase at a far lower scale of remuneration—"

I looked at Baijon.

"He means he wishes to cheat you now," Baijon translated helpfully.

The memorylegger turned enough colors to almost make me think he'd been insulted.

"I merely wished to point out that it is difficult to assign a monetary value to memories that one has not personally experienced. We would not be able to continue in business were we not known to be discreet and irreproachable; your information would lose no marketability or uniqueness by being left on deposit; in fact, frequently the resale value—"

"Not be living long enough to worry about that, bai, don't you worry your pretty head none. Come here to buy, got to sell to do it. Get what I want, I be gone, j'keyn?"

If there hadn't already been some trickle-out from the galactic garden spots I'd mentioned, I think Baijon and me'd of been tossed back out in the street for the Toystore version of the *legitimates* to find. But there had been, and I had the right words and enough of the music to make people sit up and whistle.

"Very well, Captain. And can we possibly assist you in making your purchase?" the memorylegger finally said through gritted phonemes.

"I swap all those memories I said—even—for one working set of the Keys to Paradise."

He didn't throw us out then, either.

*   *   *

They started out as a toy. Fake reality, like dreamtapes or memoryedit, except that with them you just get added or subtracted a rote thing and that's that. The Keys was *flexible;* you got the jinks sunk in your head and plugged in the game computer, you got a whole world to play with.

It needed a pretty big tronic brain to hold the game reality, and that was where the trouble started, because any comp that big is just naturally plugged into at least the planetary net, and if you could get to the planetary net you could get to something hooked into the Imperial dataweb.

But couldn't nobody get out of the programmed paradise, right? Nor know what to do if they did?

Wrong. The way I heard it, most people who turned the Keys just died, but at least one person went out where he shouldn't of been able to and came back too, and that was it for the Keys to Paradise.

I knew all about them because Paladin'd wanted me to have a set, which even if I'd been fool enough to want somebody to do that to my brain I didn't haul enough cubic to rate. But I knew about them—Pally'd been real good getting at stuff the Empire didn't want its average citizen to see.

And any technology that convenient, I was betting, wasn't lost.

*   *   *

"Now what do we do?" said Baijon on the way back to *Dance.*
"We wait."

*   *   *

We waited twenty hours. I wasn't really expecting a straight swap; what I was trolling for was a come-on from some techleggers who thought they knew what I wanted Keys for—because in addition to the bootleg technocandy we needed a cyberdoc to set the jinks and serious time on a DataNet terminal and somehow I didn't think Oob was going to let us come back and use his again.

But the offer didn't come. Soon we was going to be over the margin that'd let us take our ship with us when we left.

We could kyte before that. There was a Plan B after all, but it didn't have as much to recommend it as dumping Paladin into Grand Central Main Bank Memory and making him mind Archangel's manners. It was more like me walking up to Archangel and shooting him under excuse of being the Brightlaw Prototype he wanted.

I didn't think it'd work. But I was out of ideas that would.

We waited and watched hollycasts. I caught up on my talkingbook auditing—the adventures of Infinity Jilt, undercover girl space pirate for the Tech Police and her crew of hulking loyal wigglies.

This installment she had penetrated the secret starbase in the Black Nebula, where she found a tribe of outlaw techs selling Imperial know-how to the geat-kings of the Hamati Confederacy.

It struck me that my life was a little too much like the talkingbooks these days—only I didn't have Throne backing, I couldn't whistle up a crack squad of loyal and well-mannered Space Angels, and I didn't give a damn who sold what to the Hamati so long as I didn't have to do it.

Baijon audited real-world stuff—looking for news about Washonnet, of which there wasn't any. Half the time the 'casts made it sound like the hellflowers was having a love-feast, not a war.

The Roaq was still closed for renovations. A previously predicted and right-on-sked astrophysical disturbance had shut down Royal Directorate and the Chairman of the Charlock Corporation was petitioning Throne to keep it closed until a Board Meeting and elections could be held.

I just bet he was.

What good is knowing you can't trust anything you see and hear when you need it to navigate anyway? Knowing the Imperial news out of Washonnet and everywhere else was lies didn't tell me what was true. How was I or anybody supposed to think about anything, knowing everything I had available to think about was a lie?

Maybe nobody else knew. Maybe nobody else cared.

I don't know why I bother sometimes bringing peace and justice to the Empire at reasonable prices. What did I care who ran the dog-and-pony show? I didn't have any intrinsic objections to a change in Emperor. I wouldn't even mind an even-more-repressive galactic tyranny grinding Citizen Taxpayer under its brutal heel so long as it left the stars and planets in the usual places and didn't involve things like wiping out all organic life one more time.

It kept coming back to Archangel wasn't going to do that. Sure, we could probably claw our way up from the amoeba again, but doing stuff like that gets boring after a while.

Some of this I told Baijon. Some not. We didn't understand each other any better than Paladin nor me had, really.

On the twenty-first hour we spent waiting, the brokerage called and told me somebody wanted to buy.

*   *   *

"I do not trust him, San'Cyr. It is another trap."

"I ain't trusted nobody since I was fifteen, Baijon; you get used to it. But the 'legger wants his credit, and we got a radical rep, and sooner or later somebody's going to want to know how I pulled these coordinates off Oob's terminal in the first place. Then we cut a deal."

"Or they shoot us."

"Wondering which is what makes life such a designer thrill, bai."

*   *   *

There was one thing different from our last visit to the Graymarket, and she was standing outside the shop. She was even more out of place here than Baijon and me was, with a play-for-pay chassis and all mod. cons., wearing one piece of hold-me-tight superskin and a lot of paint, hanging roundaround outside the memorylegger's with the bright interested expression of a veteran tourist.

And that was real wrong. She wasn't a player, and she wasn't muscle, and ain't nothing else got any business on Toystore.

Her face brightened right up when she saw us. Wrong number two.

"Oh, hello," she said brightly. "I'm sorry about the wait."

That's when I realized I knew her.

"We got trouble," I said to Baijon.

It was Berathia Notevan, the spy from alMayne.

*   *   *

I like being alive. It's been my hobby for whiles and in weak moments I hope to pursue it into old age.

It was why I stopped Baijon from going for his heat when he realized who she was. He ripped off a line of helltongue at her indicating that most of her parents had been assembled.

"What a wonderful coincidence that we happened to be here, too," she said brightly. "Daddy always says I have a tendency to be overly optimistic, but once I heard that an Imperial Battle-Yacht had petitioned to dock here I just knew everything had turned out all right for you. It's too bad about Royal, though."

"Ain't it just, your Gentle Docentship. And maybe I be wondering just how you come to be here when I left you on alMayne." I smoothed the glove on my left hand; a new nervous twitch that kept me from going for the blasters I wasn't wearing. Berathia laughed like I'd said something funny.

"Oh, you know how it is, work-work-work. Once the War College was bombed, I knew there really wasn't any reason for me to stay. And you'd already left, after all."

"You was Kennor's holecard, right? The one supposed to do one thing or t'other when I showed up on alMayne, right?"

"Oh, there really isn't any point in dredging up ancient history now, is there, Captain St. Cyr? Besides, there's someone here wanting to see you—and you did come to Toystore to deal, didn't you?"

Sure. And did it with no options and no clout, other than being too valuable and entertaining to waste. We went through the front, into the back where the private rooms was.

"You don't need to worry about the fee—that's been paid," Berathia said, and opened the door.

Kennor Starbringer was waiting.

He was all alone and dressed pure hellflower, with the Knife like Baijon didn't have no more strapped front and center.

"Well," said Berathia brightly, "now that we're all here . . ."

"Where is my son?" said Kennor, looking right at Baijon.

"But he's . . ." Berathia said, and stopped. Baijon twitched. I put a hand on his arm. Could of been feeling up the Hoplite armor for all the give there was.

"The *arthame,* what is the alMayne spirit-blade, is what Mallorum Archangel got rid of for him when we was on Royal, your Gentle Docentship."

Along with a planet, a moon, and a couple of space-stations.

I watched Kennor age half the rest of his allotted lifespan in the next tik-anna-half. He sat down back behind the table again. He didn't look at Baijon.

"Did he . . . die with honor?" Kennor said to no one in particular.

"Honor died first," said Baijon sadly. "The woman the aunt of the Third Person of House Starborn—whom I will kill, father—"

"You are too late. Valijon—"

"He is *dead!*" Baijon wailed.

"My son." Kennor got up and rounded the table. He looked like he might put his arms around Baijon if Baijon was here. But Baijon wasn't. Kennor looked at me.

Keep him safe, Kennor'd said, and this was what I'd done instead.

"Why are you still alive?" Kennor said.

Baijon laughed, sounding crazy. "What news from Royal, Second of Starborn, and of the insurrectionists who were receiving Starborn weapons?"

Starborn weapons. Sure. I'd been right. And if I'd bothered to ask I bet Baijon would of told me. In order for hottoys to be transhipped from alMayne, someone on alMayne had to order them first. Someone with clout. Not a LessHouse like Meggie'd said. A GreatHouse.

Kennor Starbringer was backing the Brightlaw Rebellion. Not Amrath. Not the Coalition. *Kennor.*

"Royal is gone," Kennor said slowly.

"Lord Starbringer, there isn't much time. You *must* be seen to be aboard the *Lorelei Rake* when she passes the Washonnet checkpoint. *Alone,"* Berathia said.

"I have come for my son."

"He's dead," Baijon and me said, almost in chorus.

"And you killed him, Kennor-bai," I finished. "You started a war on alMayne. That's why you sent us there. All this farcing about ship and papers was just the excuse to get us to alMayne so Baijon could stand up and get flattened."

"I would have kept my word. There was a ship."

"And papers. Too bad we didn't know to ask for them when we beat your war off-planet by the skin of our never-you-mind. *Angelcity's* by way of being a old friend of mine, bai—and you set her up, too. But you got what you wanted. Baijon thought everybody'd rally round the boy who cried Library. You knew they wouldn't. And Archangel was waiting for all of us at our next stop."

There was a pause.

"And you have come to complain?" Kennor said.

"No," said Berathia. "She came for these."

She tossed a set of the Keys to Paradise on the table.

They was all in the original wrapping—the brainjinks, the scenario modules, all factory new.

"Illegal cybernetics. A neural interface. Wouldn't it be nice to know what somebody who came here in Prince Mallorum Archangel's own battle-yacht wanted with this?" Berathia added.

"Who are you really?" I asked Berathia the ratfink.

She smiled.

"An anthropologist. I told you that at Wailing, Captain St. Cyr."

And maybe it was even true, just like I was a legit small-freighter captain. But Berathia was a player, too.

"There are warrants out on the two of you from here to the Core. What possible use is a dreamworld?"

Kennor looked at his son and looked at me. I saw him figure it out. Everything.

We'd told him about the Library in the Roaq, Baijon and me. Kennor'd had his basic Library-burning lessons back at the War College just like every other hellflower. I'd had an illegal transponder in my skull when he picked me up and now I'd come here—from Royal— shopping for something that could pour a human ego into the DataNet. He knew I had a cybernetic arm and he knew how it could be modified.

He *knew.*

He backed away from Baijon, slow. Baijon looked at his face and backed away, too.

"And what do you do here?" Kennor said. It weren't quite us he was asking. And something in the back of my skull wanted to answer.

"Buying. Selling. Wondering how much honor goes for in the galactic marketplace these days, Kennor-che-bai."

Once Kennor's kind and mine had been partners—

No. Not my kind.

But I wondered. If you'd been part of that much power, was a thousand years time enough to cut the taste for it?

"What does your kind know of honor?" Kennor asked. I made a fist, but the fake fingers wouldn't close.

"I know what you taught me, father," Baijon said.

"I taught *you* nothing."

Berathia started to look left out. Something flashed below my line of sight and I looked down. Kennor was holding a little silver hideout in his hand, own twin to the one I'd killed Winterfire with.

So he was going to do it after all.

"Lord Starbringer!" Berathia sounded actually worried for a change. "Toystore is *very* inflexible about its aggression policies. If you shoot—"

"—I do as Archangel wishes. But no longer. Is the Prototype loaded?"

Berathia's mouth twitched. She was a pro, all right, and Kennor was an amateur. He hadn't needed for to tell us that.

"That wouldn't be the Brightlaw AI Prototype that Archangel was looking for back at Royal, would it?" I asked. "The one that was supposed to be on the same ship as us? Just out of idle curiosity, Kennor-bai, what do *you* think happened to Royal?"

He bared his teeth. "It became a symbol of unjust oppression."

I tried again. "What was Archangel trying to stop when he hellbombed it?"

"The Brightlaw Prototype," said Baijon. He looked from me to Kennor. He'd figured it all out. There was no illusions left.

The Brightlaw Prototype. A fake Library that did what it was told. Something so close to anathema that when the real thing came along Kennor Starbringer didn't blink twice. Because Brother Kennor'd been hip-deep in anathema for years.

"You set Baijon up to make alMayne do what you wanted. You set Royal up—you *knew* what Archangel would do there."

Kennor'd knew Archangel would bomb Royal. He'd made sure of it. Once Archangel saw Baijon and me with Meggie he wouldn't think three-times. Why shouldn't we be in Kennor's confidence—even if we wasn't? It was a perfect setup. We would of walked right down Archangel's throat with the Prototype or a convincing fake clutched in our little paddy paws.

"Ten billion people, bai—what you got that's worth that butcher's bill?"

"Peace," said Kennor Starbringer. "Does that amuse you,

Malmakosimra? Peace at any price. For too long Archangel has held the Emperor a helpless prisoner and acted in his name. The *chaudatu* hand power into his blasphemous hands, thinking it is Throne that they serve and not the Destroyer, but at last he has overstepped himself."

If anybody but the hellflowers believed that Archangel and not the Brightlaw Rebellion had fragged Royal.

"Now his allies will turn on him. Once more alMayne will lead the Coalition—and the Coalition will lead the Directorates."

Right into trouble. I've always said hellflowers was crazy. Kennor Starbringer was so far round the twist he couldn't see the bend in the road—or maybe that was hellflower logic in the service of greater galactic realpolitix.

"The Azarine Coalition will free the Emperor and restore power to him—to a certain degree. The Coalition will dictate terms to the Emperor—and alMayne will lead the Coalition. Your days are numbered, and those of your tainted kindred. Once the Gentle People have taken their rightful place as guardians of all life even the *possibility* of your kind will end."

Paladin had a word for it, like he did for everything else. Theocracy. Rule by revealed truth. And it'd make Archangel's version of everybody's future look like a garden spot.

"You can't do this," I said, and it sounded stupid even to me.

"It is not right," Baijon added. Nice of him.

"What does your kind know of right?" snarled Kennor. "Is it right that Archangel should enforce a tyranny the like of which the Empire has never seen, destroying the Gentle People and setting the *Malmakos* to rule men? Would he forbear to do so should we ask him—in honor— to refrain? He has no honor. And honor cannot therefore oppose him. I had to find another way."

"But we are not meant to rule," said Baijon, miserable.

"You say that now, knowing what you know? We are humanity's masters. The race needs a master—for its safety, if nothing else. The Empire cannot support a war. I will not risk one. Archangel's plan depends on subtlety—it is worth the destruction of Royal to unmask his ambition. Now there will be peace."

Logical. As logical, true-tell, as a genocidal Library Archive I knew a little too well. Had the Libraries thought that, oncet? Was that how the war had started?

I didn't get time to worry about it. Just then lights and gravity flickered, a blip that set me back down on my feet a little too hard.

"You'd better go, Lord Starbringer," Berathia said. "You know what the bargain was. I don't think you'll want to be here when they arrive."

Kennor looked at us. "Tell your master, when you see him next—"

"Came to Toystore looking for to ice Archangel, bai," I said.

"You can tell him so when you see him," Berathia said. She turned to me and smiled. "Surely you don't think Throne doesn't know about this place, Captain St. Cyr? Why do you think you were kept waiting around so long? Toystore has vigorish to pay, too—to the Empire. They're handing you over to Archangel the moment he gets here."

Kennor was up and moving. He looked at Baijon, deciding whether to shoot.

"Al-ea-alarthme, chaudatu," Baijon said to his father, teeth bared. Kennor brushed past him and didn't look back.

The downside under my feet shook, and Berathia's I-know-what's-going-on-and-you-don't expression damped a couple of amps.

"That's what they think," I said to Berathia. Toystore was neutral, Toystore was safe. Everybody in the nightworld said so. That's the last time I believe anybody's publicity.

But coming here'd got me what I needed.

I dived for the Keys Berathia'd tossed to the table and dumped them down my shirt.

"C'mon, babby!" I said to Baijon. "We gone!"

"No, wait!" said Berathia.

"You got a better way out, right?" I said. "How many times you think we going to fall for that?" She took a good look and didn't stand between us and the door.

The Graymarket was empty when Baijon and me went through. All the screens was showing warning countdowns, but I didn't need that to tell me Toystore was probably in more trouble than it wanted. They'd called in Archangel. And even if it was to sell me out so they could keep their Most Favored Techlegger status, they wasn't going to find it that easy to kick Archangel out of bed again.

They thought they was justified. Just like Kennor, when he set up one planet for war and another for death. It's all how you look at it, I guess.

Does the end justify the means? Archangel backed Charlock to get Throne. So Kennor backed Brightlaw to get Archangel. And now that Archangel and the hellflowers was done with it, wasn't nothing left in Tortuga worth having for neither Damaris nor her uncle.

We came to the end of the tier and there was some Toystore *legiti-*

mates. They was standing on their rep, expecting us to go with them quiet. Maybe thinking we didn't know we'd been sold out.

This time when I pushed for it in my mind it was there—the thing that let me see around corners and twenty minutes into the future. I saw Baijon bringing up his heat and didn't bother wishing for mine because hellflower logic had got him the same answer a Library gave me.

Archangel wanted us alive at any cost.

I couldn't of pulled the trigger on them. That was part of what I'd lost. But Baijon could. He dropped two and that got me armament so I gave him a lightshow backdrop and then we bulled through what was left of them and away. Now all their cybertech was tracking our hottoys, but that was a joke. Toystore wouldn't detonate them. Archangel wanted us alive.

*   *   *

We beat it back to *Dance* in the curious absence of any opposition or even audience whatever. Berathia's theory that Archangel was coming to collect me was high on my list of reasons why, but it wasn't the only contender.

Toystore offered a lot in the way of privacy, but not in the docking area. *Ghost Dance* was right there where we'd left her, wide-open to anyone as cared to drop by and guarded only by Toystore's good intentions.

But her neighbors wasn't. When we'd left here about a hour back, I could see six ships from where I stood. No more.

Where were they? And if gone, why?

"An excellent place for a trap," Baijon said crossly, looking at our open hatch.

"Je. And if they don't want to get permanent with us, bai, there's lots of temporary measures." In spite of which, we still had to get inboard.

"I will go first, San'Cyr." Baijon pulled his blaster and slid along the wall to where *Dance's* nose poked out. He was in before I could come up with a reasoned argument about him not going.

What was left for Baijon Starbringer? Father, lover, home, and honor. Gone.

Did the means justify the end?

Silence and the sound of someone running our way. One person, and I bet I knew who.

"It is clear, San'Cyr," Baijon announced just as a body caught up with the sound effects.

"You idiots!" Berathia said. "You can't leave in that thing—they won't let you!"

Lights and power went off-on again, which was another good reason to get out of here.

"Watch us."

Berathia followed me into *Dance*'s cockpit, talking the whole way.

"Look, I admit I wasn't completely honest with you back on alMayne but that's my *job*—I'll tell you what I was tasked for now—"

"Ancient history, 'Thia." I vaulted into the mercy seat and started peeling back my sleeve. "Baijon-bai, I pop these locks you can start getting us out of here, je?"

"*Ea,* San C'yr." Baijon put himself into the worry seat and started strapping in.

"Listen to me: *you can't get out of Toystore this way.*"

Both of us ignored her.

I asked Toystore for it nice one-time whiles I ripped off my glove and shook the jacks loose out of my arm. They laughed in my ears but by then I was plugged in.

/*This is of*-Dance./

/*This is not of-Dance.*/

I swept all of Toystore's reasons to be cheerful out of my Best Girl's brain. It was so easy I couldn't think why it'd ever been hard. Baijon was watching me, waiting for the office. He followed right on my tail, buttoning us up and pulling goforths on line, just like I'd taught him. For one weird instant it was *me* he was playing, not the ship, and then I was out and Berathia was staring at me.

"Thing is, jillybai, you start farcing with Old Fed Tech something's almost bound to happen."

We pushed off from Toystore with pressors only; getting even the sublight power up would take longer than I wanted to sit. The docking cradle socket ripped loose as we pushed free. Bits of it went drifting in all directions and nearspace sensors started accumulating memory.

But it was already too late. Berathia yelped and then said something naughty as promised grief to someone.

The view from *Dance*'s cockpit came clear.

We'd disengaged from Toystore right into a host of shakers and friends. Archangel'd brought the wife and kids to pay his little call.

*   *   *

I wished I could stay and watch—a full battle array was something I'd never thought to see even oncet. Two of the shakers from Royal was there and their support ships around them, in a mathematically compelling pattern of density and flux. An infinite killer. The wings of night.

I twisted *Dance*'s tail and Toystore slid away. We was in the middle of the hostile technology now and running for the edge. Lights flashed on the control panel: our flight recorder and ID beacon was being tapped and telling Fleet its version of the truth.

If Archangel could pull something like this together—and use it— things was falling apart faster than anyone—me, Kennor, Paladin—had thought.

But the array didn't have a Library and it didn't have the Brightlaw AI. Communication between ships was strictly speed-of-light, and wasn't nobody in this host going to do anything without Archangel's especial say-so.

No one fired.

Not at us. Not yet.

They had another target.

Toystore began to glow. They was fighting back and heavy with it, but slow as a jagranatha and lots more fragile. Toystore went invisible behind flaring shields as the big boys stood back and hammered on it.

"Fools only deal with Archangel," Baijon said. He sounded satisfied but not happy. "Now they bear witness to the truth beyond shadow."

"He can't be doing this," Berathia said, sounding scared for the first time since I'd known her. "The Empire *needs* Toystore."

But Archangel didn't. Brother Archangel'd raised the stakes. In his brave new world was room for only one techlegger.

Later I could play back my gun-cameras and see when Toystore blew. Fleet didn't get it all its own way; I saw the pattern of disorder swirling out of whatever Toystore dumped on them—a pseudomind to crottle their war-comps, maybe. But then Toystore went to heat-light-and-energy, and Archangel's starfleet reconfigured to start picking off anyone who'd managed to get free.

Just like Royal.

A singleship wing closed up around *Dance*. Now we got down to cases. They'd be out to cripple us. We had to be ready to kill.

I tried to be. I wanted to be. If anything called for it, this did.

Kennor'd set up Royal. He'd planned it.

I had to maneuver the ship to aim. I needed a gunner.

Kennor'd planned Royal to make Archangel show himself high wide and public. To trigger the High Book investigation that would bring Archangel down.

Baijon pulled the weapons console over. His practical knowledge came out of the talkingbooks, but the controls was simple.

Kennor'd paid out ten billion people he didn't own to get Archangel. He'd spent his own and only son. But the Empire held billions more. Prey for Archangel.

Saved by Kennor. If his plan worked.

The singleships made their first attack run. The schematic of *Dance* unreeled in my head: nose cannon, tail guns, midships catapult. I twisted her tail and *Dance* sang for me.

I spun her into position and called the shots for my gunner and every volley missed.

"Let me!" said Berathia. She got up out of her seat and tripped, disoriented by the lightshow beyond the canopy.

"No!" shouted Baijon.

We was pulling more interest from Fleet now. Energy-lances crossed right in front of my Best Girl's nose. I slewed her offsides, joycing up the hit. Baijon fired. He got it right this time.

An acceptable trade. Royal in exchange for all the rest. Kennor's bargain.

The singleships made a second attack run. Two of their pilots took the Long Orbit. I didn't need to call shots this time. Each time *Dance* hit her marks Baijon fired just like he could read my mind. A hole was opening up in front of us now: office to kyte if I could get Jump-numbers into the comp.

I'd seen Royal. Kennor'd seen a whole future full of Royals once Archangel got rock-rolling. Desperate? Yes. He'd done what he did because he was desperate.

Justified?

"Ready-ready-we-ready!" My left hand was tapping numbers into the touchpad and all I knew about them was that they was somewheres safe—according to Archive.

Safe for Archive Library a thousand years ago might be safe for us now.

The end justified the means.

Did it?

Didn't it?

"Get us out of here!" wailed Berathia. The world beyond our ports was gone in a halation of unfriendly energy as one of the big rigs targeted us. More to come and we couldn't survive many.

I sent numbers to memory and redlined the goforths. Baijon gave me the office and I pulled the angelstick for the drop. *Ghost Dance* was everywhere at once and then gone.

Justified.

*   *   *   *   *

Valijon's Diary

Does the end justify the means?

Once I had a father, immaculate in honor, whose sole desire was that the Gentle People should be again what they once were, for our souls' health. It is fitting irony that as my father once reached for the purity of our Imperial past, I have reached farther, into a past remembered only in nightmare.

Long ago, before the Empire, the Gentle People all were kings and princes and ruled everywhere—so we are told as children.

It is but a tale we are told. The truth is far uglier. In that long-ago time we did rule . . . as pawns of the Machine.

We are told—in the way that Loremasters speak to *shaulla*—that because of what we were and did in the days of the Old Federation the war came, and so never again must we seek such power lest it lead us to compromise with the Machine.

Truth and tale share one shadow. Kennor Starbringer mocks those who have forgotten the Machine—he curses its name while calling up its pale descendant to serve him as we once served its ancestor. Kennor Starbringer, too, has forgotten truth.

The end does not justify the means. The end is the sum of the means, as the road traveled determines the destination.

I was born into a world with only one enemy. But I have grown, and see beyond the walls of my birth, and see that enemies are many, but their goal is all one.

In the end, the Gentle People whom I must disown are right in one thing: truth is the compass of one's own hand. The Machine is not the ultimate abomination, but its cause: the loss of humanity. And it is not the only cause.

And now I know that the time is long past to speak of roads and choices, ghosts and history.

Now I must reach out and seize my truth.

ARCHANGEL BLUES

To S. T., who was there before
and
to "Doc" Smith: Darktraders pay their debts.

Contents

*　　*　　*　　*　　*

The Court of The TwiceBorn 1: What's Past Is Prologue

Man's tropism is for the heights. He is educated, in his youth, to visualize the grand design, to see actions that shape vast strings of events, and to assume his rightful role in the cosmic opera.

Every child, in short, is educated to rule. And having been so fitted to one purpose only, this fictive child spends the rest of his life as the recipient of a series of rude surprises: fate does not mean him to govern, but to grovel. All the rest of his life is spent trying to reach a height from which to exercise his vision.

Only a few attain it. Those few are driven just as their confreres are, by the knowledge of their rightful office—but how electrifying the spur of possibility. These few might actually attain the sunlit heights of mastery and have dangled within their reach the grandest and most glittering prize of all.

Power Absolute.

1

Meet the Tiger

My name is Butterflies-are-free Peace Sincere and I have all the trouble anyone could possibly want. People've said so. Often.

I'm beginning to believe them.

Just now I had enough different troubles that even I couldn't keep my mind on them from the beginning of the list to the end, but at the exact moment my particular trouble was a "borrowed" Imperial Battle-Yacht that hadn't read its own design specs.

I pulled the angelstick for the Drop. I saw the world outside *Ghost Dance*'s cockpit turn to silver silk. Welcome to angeltown, the subjective mathematical convention that isn't really anywhere.

I started locking down the boards. You don't use your engines in hyperspace—well, not much—angeltown is what powers your goforths, and all you got to figure is how to get in and out. I was hoping it was going to be a whole bunch of hours before our mystery coordinates dumped us back out into realspace.

"Now, che-bai," I said to Baijon Stardust, exhellflower at large, "all we got to do is . . ."

Berathia squawked. She was looking out the canopy; I wasn't. I started back around to see what she was havering at when all kinds bells and whistles went off at once across *Dance*'s boards and all the cockpit lights went red-green-amber and "I'm not ready for this." The goforths what was supposed to be blocked and locked woke up and redlined, the navicomp grabbed for something that wasn't there and went nullset, and I got set back on my tail in my very damned expensive mercy seat as

Dance turned herself whichway loose and did something she wasn't supposed to be able to do.

She hit the Mains.

"St. Cyr!" weefed Berathia over the howl of engines gone radical, but there wasn't no point calling *my* name. We was on the wrong side of most of the shielding *Dance* had and I knew what came next.

"Close your eyes! Both of you!"

There was a blinding flare. *Bad* disorientation. I groped for the cockpit-opaque as hot gold Mains-light beat through my bones. An endless spiral, white-gold and furious, and our stolen starwings whipping down the center, falling infinitely faster than the speed of light.

Welcome to the Mains.

*   *   *

There's two kinds of not-realspace: angeltown, which anyone with a ship can get into, and the Mains. The Mains are superfast directional currents that exist *in* hyperspace (it says here in the Pilot's Manual): on the Mains you can cross a thousand lights in a handful of hours.

Riding the Mains makes Transit to angeltown look safe. Mainlining takes a big ship—lots of mass—in finestkind condition, or forget about ever making the Drop to realspace again.

I finally found the right toggle. *Dance*'s cockpit went black and seemed-like dead silent. I shook my head to clear the nonexistent roar of the Mains out of my ears and took a couple deep breaths so as not to throw up.

"San'Cyr?" Baijon said. I opened my eyes. Bright purple-green sundogs swam behind my eyes, and behind them I could see faint red as the cockpit safelights came up.

Baijon looked worried. I did my best to look trustworthy, bearing in mind that for our galactic cousins the alMayne, a smile is what they do before they kill you.

"Now you know why I never decided to be a legit stardancer, 'bai."

Baijon nodded, just like he knew what I was talking about. Company pilots top the Mains all the time. Darktraders don't. I'd used to be a darktrader, before I'd took up with treason, revolt, and hellflower honor.

"Where are we—" he started.

"Where are we going?" Berathia demanded. She shoved out of the songbird seat to come and stare at my boards, just like they was going to tell her something. "How did you cut yourself loose from Toystore's security system?"

"Why did Archangel decide to destroy Toystore and what are we going to do now?" I finished up for her, since she was making a run-down of the hot topics of my life. "And while we're on the subject, 'Thia, just what made you think you was safer with us than with some-body else?"

"We are not safe," Baijon said. Berathia smiled so as to show no hard feelings, which was pretty damn gracious of a Imperial spy what had just changed sides.

"Je." I went through locking down the boards again. "You got that right, babby."

The goforths was revving higher than they maybe ought, and from the (unshielded) cockpit the powersong was making fair inroads on my bones. I got up.

"C'mon. *Dance* can take care of herself for whiles."

Berathia looked past me to the hole in the cockpit farings where I'd torn out the navicomp, without which no ship can kyte. She looked at the touchpad keyboard I'd cannibaled into its place so I could input coordinates direct to the Jump-computer. I bet she wondered where I'd got them, too.

The fact of the matter was that I'd been using Jump-numbers sup-plied to my jury-rigged navicomp by the ghost of a renegade Old Feder-ation Library what had set up light housekeeping amongst some of my lesser-known braincells and was trying to turn me inside out in its spare time.

Like I said. Trouble. More'n anyone could possibly want. Even me.

"Captain St. Cyr," Berathia said again, "where are we going?"

"And when do we begin to kill Archangel?" said Baijon.

*   *   *

If you've been following along from the beginning you can skip this part. For the rest of you, it's like this. A long time ago—when I still had a mind of my own and a future—I went and did the dumbest thing I ever managed in a life career of doing dumb things and rescued a hellflower from some roaring boys in a Free Port. Only the hellflower turned out to be the Honorable *Puer* Walks-by-Night Kennor's-son Starbringer Amrath Valijon of Chernbereth-Molkath, Third Person of House Starborn of Washonnet 357-II/alMayne—that's Baijon Stardust for short—in the throes of his first attempt at being murdered.

Somebody'd let him shag off from his consular ship without ID in the pious hope that either the law or the natives of a little piece of lazy-fair called Wanderweb Free Port would sign the lease on his real estate in short order.

The reason for this gets complicated. It starts out that once upon a time the Nobly-Born Governor-General His Imperial Highness the TwiceBorn Prince Mallorum Archangel—what I'd just gave the slip to for the second time lately—decided he wanted to put the Azarine Coalition in his pocket and walk off in the direction of becoming Emperor his own self, the Azarine Coalition being the sum total of all the mercenaries available in your Phoenix Empire and mine.

For any number of rude reasons, the only way to do that was to rewrite the Gordinar Canticles that govern the Coalition and abrogate the hell out of Azarine Coalition Neutrality.

Archangel couldn't do that while Baijon's father Kennor Starbringer was president of that same Coalition, Kennor Starbringer being a Constructionist who took Coalition Neutrality to bed with him at night.

Anybody with political weltschmerz would say it looked like Kennor was after having a lifespan measurable in centimeters, but offing Kennor direct would just stir up bad trouble back on alMayne. So nobody was going to do that—they was just going to arrange for Kennor to become a Official alMayne Nonperson and Imperial criminal by murdering Kennor's son.

That was Baijon. If Baijon died, Kennor would either have to avenge his death (illegal in the Empire) or not avenge it (illegal on alMayne). Either way Kennor got himself removed from the catbird seat.

Only it didn't work that way—because I rescued Baijon back at that Free Port, remember? So Baijon just vanished and put all of Kennor's problems on hold.

Until I did stupid thing number two.

I brought him back to his da. And in the process the two of us tripped over the fact that Mallorum Archangel, Imperial Prince, Governor-General, and second in line for the Throne, was elbow-deep in a scheme to use infinitely-illegal Old Federation Technology to take over the universe.

There is a serious down in the Empire on the possession—nevermind the use—of what the Technology Police calls Inappropriate Technology—which is among other things everything that came out of the last astropolitical unit to work this neighborhood, the Old Federation. The Old Fed isn't around anymore, because about a thousand years ago —back when our friendly neighborhood Phoenix Empire wasn't even a twinkle in the Federation's eye—some bright kiddy came up with the notion of putting pure intellect in a box and calling it a Library.

And since the *Federales* thought they had more important things to do with their time, they turned over the running of their Federation to the Libraries and made it so Libraries could build more Libraries.

Mistake.

Because—so the story goes—the Libraries had more important things to do with their time, too, and thought that organic life clashed with their decor.

There was a war. And ten centuries later the Empire is still hunting the nonexistent surviving Libraries from that war.

Mostly nonexistent.

Because Archangel'd got his hands on one—the second I'd ever seen, but that's another long story. Archangel's Library was a Final Weapon called Archive, and it was little consolation to anyone that it'd of ate him for brekkers if me and my ex-partner hadn't iced it first.

Paladin. My partner, the Library.

Ex-partner.

And you would think that with Archive gone, Brother Archangel's problems in the realm of having something he oughtn't was nonfiction, but the Tech Police don't work that way, and Archangel couldn't be sure how many of them'd stay bought. He was still in as much trouble as he'd ever been.

I knew it. Kennor knew it. Baijon knew it. And Archangel knew we knew it. In fact, just as soon as Brother Mallorum had his hand in the Old Fed Tech cookie jar it'd be obvious to anyone with more brains than I had that the next place Archangel was going was the largest and only legit cache of Old Fed Tech inside the Empire's borders—the logotek of the War College at Wailing on alMayne.

So Archangel went on to Step Two, and Kennor Starbringer turned out not to be as standup as popularly advertised.

Earlier in our last exciting episode, Kennor'd sent me and Baijon off to Washonnet 357-II/alMayne. He told us it was for a ship and papers, so Baijon and me could take off and hide in the never-never and Archangel couldn't get holt of Baijon to frame Kennor to resign. I knew from the git-go it was a con, but I had it by the wrong end.

· I thought Kennor's plan was to execute Baijon (who would never be safe while he was a way in to Kennor anyway) and frame me for it.

Kennor thought Kennor's plan was to have Baijon accuse Archangel of High Book—that's Chapter 5 of the Revised Inappropriate Technology Act of the 975th Year of Imperial Grace (all rights reserved)—

and raise the hellflowers against the Empire, which would interfere nicely with Archangel's plan to annex the alMayne War College and steal all its Old Fed Tech to help him rebuild the Library Archive what Baijon and me'd blown up with a little help from our friends. If there was one thing hellflowers hated worse than death and hell and *chaudatu* it was what they called The Machine and the rest of the universe called Libraries, so anybody saying Archangel was a Librarian ought to get everybody's cooperation *un quel toot de sweet,* right?

What Kennor didn't realize was that Archangel'd swung a good bloc of the home vote back on sunny alMayne.

Hellflowers is xenophobes almost more'n they's technophobes, and Archangel won the heart of Baijon's aunt—who was the Dowager Regnant of alMayne in her spare time—by promising to seal alMayne up tight, give it Interdicted status, and not let the *chaudatu* bite.

So instead of getting a ship and a crusade when we showed up on alMayne at Kennor's corkscrew behest, Baijon and me started a civil war: hellflower against hellflower, and all over the musical question of Was Mallorum Archangel Really a Librarian (or *Malmakosim,* which means something a tad bit different in helltongue) and if he wasn't, was there any such thing as a Library anyway?

Baijon and me got out of there about six minutes ahead of the faction as wanted to look for the answer in our entrails, and copped a ride with a Gentry-legger I knew, what was running street-lethals in to a place called Royal.

Ex-place.

Because in one of the galaxy's better coincidences, our free ride off alMayne was the ship originally hired by Kennor Starbringer to take me, Baijon, and a surprise package to Royal—something none of us knew at the time. The surprise package was a decoy so that Kennor could get the *real* Brightlaw Prototype from a place called Toystore and take it to somewheres else what probably ain't there no more either at the rate Archangel's rearranging stars.

The Brightlaw Prototype, to put it mildly, is a fake Library that does what it's told. Something so close to Old Fed Tech anathema that when the real thing came along Kennor Starbringer didn't blink twice. Brother Kennor'd been hip-deep in anathema for years.

Because Kennor meant Archangel to do just what Archangel did— hellbomb Royal to destroy the mythical Brightlaw Prototype and do it with a weapon that only an Old Federation Library could build. Kennor'd planned Royal to make Archangel show himself high wide and public. To make Archangel his own self trigger the High Book investigation that would bring the TwiceBorn Lord Prince Mallorum Archangel down.

Kennor hoped.

Kennor'd paid out ten billion people he didn't own to get Archangel. He'd spent his only son. But the Empire held billions more. Prey for Archangel.

Saved by Kennor. If his plan worked.

Only Archangel'd had a different plan. Archangel's plan had been to bomb Royal and say the *hellflowers*'d done it. People might even of believed him long enough for him to pull his smash-and-grab on the War College logotek and get his hands on another Library. With what he'd learned from Library Archive he could put a living one together from the bits and pieces there.

I knew he could. Because *I* could. Because whiles back I'd got a ringside seat at the fight where my good buddy Paladin took the evil Library Archive apart. And because it was so up close and personal, Archive'd made sure that Paladin didn't just copy Archive into Paladin.

Archive'd copied its own self into me too. At least parts of it. Enough so I could plug a computer into my head and not go mad. Enough so I could be the navicomp for a starship.

Enough so I thought like a Library. Permanent, incurable, and getting worse.

There was really only one thing worth doing in the time I had left until I forgot I was me.

Kill Mallorum Archangel.

And make sure nobody else used Old Fed Tech to start a war.

Any questions?

*　　　*　　　*

"San'Cyr?"

We'd got down to *Dance*'s galley, safe on the cuddly side of the shielding. Baijon was standing over me holding a hot box of tea in a way what told me he'd been standing there whiles.

One of Baijon's purposes in life was to cut off my head as soon as I forgot which side of the organic life fence I was on. The other was to kill Mallorum Archangel. As soon as he got as close as he could get to doing both things he'd be dead too, because in our last thrilling installment, Archangel'd run Baijon's hellflower *arthame* through a molecular debonder. No Knife, no hellflower. Suicide follows, details at eleven.

But Baijon'd found something more important than doing right by hellflower honor. Its name was Archangel.

I took the tea.

That only left Berathia Notevan unaccounted for. I looked at her.

"Now, jillybai. You was just about to explain why it was you decided to jump a burning Toystore with us."

"Well, no one expected Prince Mallorum to . . ." she trailed off, thinking of Toystore going up like a roaming candle, the Empire's largest sink of outlaw technology gone to smoke and mirrors in the blink of a illegal Fleet.

"He's gone mad. We have to warn the Court."

If she meant the Court of the TwiceBorn back at dear old Grand Central the seat of Empire, she'd been out in the starshine too long. The only way the Emperor and his good buddies was going to listen to me and mine was on tape in the past tense, Library, rogue AI, or not.

"And will your *chaudatu* Court listen, when it is Archangel who leads them—Archangel, whose shadow taints all with his corruption? Archangel who—"

"Archangel who destroyed Toystore trying to get his hands on the Brightlaw AI *your* father built, Prince Valijon!" Berathia came right back.

"Button it!" I shouted. Both of them looked at me.

Berathia's hole-and-corner escape hadn't dented her much. She was still Imperial Image from her spike-heeled moldfast sandals to the high-ticket A-grav play-pretties holding up her hair. She'd been Kennor's holecard on alMayne—and if Kennor'd been the one who'd built the Brightlaw AI, she'd been the one who assigned the work.

And she'd jumped sides at Toystore. Why?

"It's like this, 'Thia. I need Baijon, and I like Baijon, and I want Baijon. Can't say most of those things about you. Ship *Ghost Dance* has real reet air lock. Maybe you give me some good reason you shouldn't inspect it from outside?"

"I can be useful." Berathia licked her lips, playing scared, but playing was what it was and I knew that for stone truth.

"How?" Baijon said, all scorn. I kept forgetting how young he was. Grown-up to the hellflowers, maybe, but only fourteen Imperial Standard Years to the rest of us. And if there was anything our boy liked less than *chaudatu*, it was *chaudatu* spies.

"Back on Toystore you said you wanted Mallorum Archangel. I can get him for you."

Baijon lit up. He bought the pony and forgave 'Thia all her genetics.

"Which is why you was so wishful to kyte with us, 'Thia? Get real,"

I said. Baijon might not of had all the stardust knocked out of him yet, but my suspicions had just come back cleaned and blocked from their thirty million klik overhaul.

"Do you think you can get to him alone? Mallorum Archangel is second in line for the Phoenix Throne. He's the Imperial Governor-General, one of the Court of the TwiceBorn. Even if everything you have to say about him is true, you'll never get within a dozen lights of him without a collar and leash," Berathia wheedled.

"Ne, jillybai. I can get to him." I held up my left arm, the one that ain't real anymore since I met all Baijon's relations. Now it's cybereisis prosthetics, jinked terreckly into my brain. I'd lost three of the fake fingers at the same party Baijon lost his Knife. I wiggled what I had left and the universal connectors I'd black-boxed in dropped out of the hole carved in the fake skin.

"I can get in anywhere I want."

Berathia looked from me to Baijon. I saw it occur to her that getting out to walk might be a great idea. Neurons fired, associative pathways opened, concatenate memory-nets were activated: I remembered all the other times it'd been like this. When I'd watched some organic try to bargain for more life than I was going to give it.

Archive's memories.

Mine.

The only difference between me and a Old Fed Library was quantitative. Maybe.

"So make the pitch, jillybai," I told her.

"What . . . *are* you?" Berathia's voice did skittery things with her Interphon. She was scared. Finally.

Paladin, why wasn't you here to keep me out of trouble like this?

I looked at Berathia looking at me, and finally understood what scared Baijon about not having any Knife no more. The Knife didn't make him human. But without it how did he know when he'd stopped?

"*Malmakosim, shaulla-chaudatu.* You have claimed to study the Gentle People to cloak your espionage in decency. You have hunted the secrets of the Machine. She is *Malmakosim,*" Baijon said.

Librarian. But what it really means in helltongue is "the Machine that takes human form."

"Don't be . . . If Captain St. Cyr were a Librarian, you . . ."

"Would of shot me, 'Thia? Sure. That's second on his list of things to do."

I didn't like it when Baijon called me *Malmakosim* with Berathia to hear. Nothing living will succor a Librarian, and the penalties for High

Book are nothing you want to even flirt with. But everyone in the Empire was after us and this yacht already. Even High Book wouldn't make any difference.

And who could she tell?

Berathia looked from Baijon to me and bought back all her composure.

"And Archangel, I suppose, is first? Well, I've certainly gotten myself into a mess this time. I can just hear Daddy now."

For some reason, me being a Librarian made Berathia feel better.

Sometimes I think everyone in the Empire is crazy but me.

And I'm not sure about me.

*   *   *

I went back to the cockpit. The Mains was a white-hot yammer all around. I had the canopy stopped down to sunblock forty-seven and I could still see it. The roaring throat of hell.

I guessed *Dance* could stand up to it. She must of been built to hyperjump anyway; factory-issue goforths don't have that two-step cycle to kick a ship over. Maybe she'd even last long enough so we could all come out the other end, in whatever safe place I'd keyed blind into the Jump-computer out of Archive's memories when the alternative was plasma conversion in the middle of Archangel's battle-fleet.

I stared out at nothing and tried not to feel sorry for myself. I'd lost everything. And now I was going to die not even for something a person could ship and spend. I was going to die for an *ideal*—for the idea that peace was better than war and people did not have the right to ice other people just along of being inconvenient.

And for the idea that evil has to be argued with.

And even with Baijon by me, I was going to die alone.

"God damn you all to hell, Paladin."

*   *   *

Once upon a time I had a partner I could trust. His name was Paladin, and he was a Library.

But they never told me the fine details about techsmith hellgod abominations back at Granola Simple School, and when I was contract warmgoods at Market Garden they didn't tell me anything outside of what I needed to know to be a name-brand product.

They never told me not to rescue and rebuild an illegal Old Fed Library.

They never told me not to name it Paladin and make it my partner for twenty years.

I'd never heard of Libraries, then. I'd needed a navicomp the way I needed oxygen, and the broken black box I lucked into in a place called Pandora looked more like a numbercruncher than anything else local did. It was a damn good thing what it turned out to be was maybe the only pacifist Library there ever was.

Paladin.

*   *   *

Flashback:

The housecore at Rialla was too hot too dark and too damn full of too many things that bit. I was here to rescue my partner, only nobody knew that, even Baijon. They thought I was here to end history for a Old Fed Library called Archive, in which I hadn't believed when I took the job.

"Surrender and I will let you live," Archive said. I knew it was lying. Archive was born to kill—to be the revenge of the Libraries on humanity in the unlikely happenstance they happened to lose.

Only they'd lost some time back. And Archive had slept for a thousand years, waiting for some idiot to resurrect it.

Like Archangel.

"Paladin?" I said. But the only thing in reach was Archive—which had more tricks than I did available when it came to staying alive. I drew my spare blaster and started in to where I knew it was . . .

*   *   *

Archive'd had too many tricks and not quite enough, but before Paladin killed it Archive managed to arrange for me to spend the rest of a real short life knowing exactly what it was like to *be* a Library.

Paladin didn't know that. Paladin used what he'd got out of Archive's memories to dump me. Better off apart, he said. Endangered by his very proximity, he said. My friend, my partner, the edge I needed to stay alive in the never-never—history.

And just a little too soon, because now I was walking treason all on my lonesome, even without a Library for a partner. Because whiles Paladin was turning Archive into spare parts, Archive was doing its best to turn me into Archive. And having Archive's memories would of been bad enough, but memories wasn't all it'd stuck me with when it reconfigured my chitlins. The old reliable Butterfly St. Cyr-as-was could never of walked into a protected memory core through a dumb terminal and shut down all the power on a planet.

Royal.

Ex-planet.

And the icing on the brass cupcake—the thing that made all this such a laugh a minute—was that I'd never needed to go to Rialla and meet Archive at all. I'd gone to rescue Paladin, and Paladin hadn't needed rescuing. Once he'd found out about Archive he'd taken it apart for the tech he needed to hop onto the Imperial DataNet and ride starlight forever. He'd been planning to ditch me anyway. Archive just made it easier.

I hadn't needed to go to Rialla at all.

Now my head was full of Archive's memories, with maybe a few of Paladin's thrown in for good measure. And if a person is the sum of his experience, and I had thirty-five galactic standard years of being Butter-flies-are-free Peace Sincere, Luddite Saint from Granola and dark-trader, and fifty times that of being two other guys that happened to be Old Federation Libraries, which was going to win out?

Guess.

"San'Cyr?" Baijon came in through the cockpit door that didn't lock. I pulled my eyes away from the Mains-light and my mind away from wherever it'd been.

Less than three hundred days ago Baijon Stardust'd been your average hellflower glitterborn. Since then he'd died and had a number of other illuminating experiences.

"Where *do* we go?" he asked, putting himself into the worry seat. I looked at him. Perfect trust in whatever I was going to do.

I looked back out at the Mains.

"Don't know, babby. Someplace Archive thought was safe."

"A thousand years ago," Baijon pointed out.

"Might of changed," I admitted.

"And then?" he prompted.

Our original plan—which is to say, the last one in a series of great ideas that hadn't worked—was to get our hands on some beaucoup illegal cybertech called the Keys to Paradise and use it to track down Paladin. With Paladin on our side, the chances of leading a preemptive strike down Archangel's throat was pretty good, actually.

That's what we'd gone to Toystore for in the first place. And got, mostly by accident. They was somewheres in the cockpit now if I re-membered right. I made a mental note to tidy.

"What we do depends on what we find. And how hard who's look-ing. And if we can trust Berathia any way at all."

"The *chaudatu* woman has a *transparent* shadow," Baijon said, which airy persiflage I guess made them weep back on dear old al-Mayne.

"Yeah, sure," I said.

We still didn't know where we was going. Or how long it'd take to get there.

Or who'd be on *Ghost Dance* when she *did* get there.

I was dying by inches, sure as if I'd been poisoned, and no remedy in sight. Baijon and me had to kill Archangel before Baijon had to kill me and if Paladin hadn't lied to me none of this would ever of happened.

*   *   *   *   *

The Court of the TwiceBorn 2:
The School of Night

The first unwelcome shock of childhood is the necessity of cooperation. A child is helpless: coercion is beyond his power. Treachery is taught in the womb; bribery and misrepresentation—cooperation—are the only tools available when one first begins to shape the world.

Parallel to and inseparable from the need to politick is the delight taken by some in a perfect equality: in practical terms, in causing others to fail as they themselves have failed. Thus the first of Life's many paradoxes: to achieve anything one must cooperate in the plans of others—even when their plans encompass one's own downfall.

For example, Mallorum Archangel.

He wishes to rule—I, to fulfill my destiny. Neither of us may dispose of the other, as each may dispose of so many underlings. For the moment, each of us lives in a flawed cosmos wherein all things are not subject to our whim.

But mine is perfectible, because the dominion I seek is a power not contingent upon the gargoyle masks of threat: weapons, armies, allies. And Archangel will fail, because all he wishes is to rule. He condemned himself to failure at the very start, when he sought allies and weapons.

The Federation upon which our Empire is built bequeathed to us many things—a taste, most of all, for the exquisite perfection of its daily life, borne from a sphere of infinite capability and infinite license. Who has not wondered what world he would make if indeed imagination was the only boundary? For an instant of time such power was within the grasp of humankind, in the long afternoon when the Libraries served Life, instead of hunting it.

But the boundless equality was shattered, and the war that followed destroyed everything save memory.

In some cases, faulty memory. Archangel believed that the Libraries would be content to serve once more—in short, that they would be grateful for resurrection. Any student of human nature could have told him better, but Mallorum Archangel never learned the lessons of powerlessness. Only the powerless cooperate.

Or those wishing ultimate power.

And so I cooperated with Mallorum Archangel. He resurrected the

Library Archive and I said nothing. He corrupted the Court, made himself autonomous within it, carved out his separate crown and eliminated his lesser rivals; and I said nothing.

He had guaranteed his own destruction, after all.

Now he has stripped Throne Sector of its fleet, searching for a new incarnation of his ultimate weapon—as if possession of some talisman will save him where strategy will not.

He has done my work for me, drawing all anarchy to himself. When Mallorum Archangel is dead, nothing will remain.

But me.

2

Thieves' Picnic

Time passed with nothing to do and I spent it in the cockpit. I couldn't set the Keys without more med-tech than the ship had and I didn't have a DataNet terminal to plug them into anyway. Baijon's life-interests was settled down to the short-list: waiting to kill Archangel, keeping a weather eye on me. Berathia'd got out of the Twenty Questions business. She'd locked herself up in one of *Dance*'s luxury accommodations, and I still didn't know what she found so fascinating about the company of Baijon and me—other than the ship we'd stole.

When I'd kyted *Ghost Dance* she'd been able to talk, which I put an end to real quick, but she still had a way of making her opinions known.

Just now it was the way everything went black.

"Baijon, get your tail up here!"

The safelights in the cockpit dimmed out almost to nothing and the telltales burned up even brighter, giving the impression that what passed for pseudoconsciousness in *Dance*'s guts was just bursting with sparkling chat.

I slid the crash harness around me nice and tight and pulled the mail. If powersuck was any guideline, we was *aux ange* now. I let reality in through the canopy one angstrom at a time. It got almost all the way to clear before I could see silver silk angeltown outside.

Baijon beat it in through the hatch and took in the situation with a sweeping glance. He was bright, he was motivated, and he didn't ask stupid questions. He was also crazier than Destiny's Five Cornered Dog and waiting to off me.

Someday I've got to do a better job choosing my friends.

"But where are we, San'Cyr?" Baijon said, like it was the punchline to a joke.

"Maybe we look-see."

With angels, how you go in decides where you come out, but if you aren't fussy you can Transit to realspace anywhere along the way if you tickle the goforths right. I was about to do that, but the goforths spiked again and *Dance* dropped us into realspace.

We'd arrived. Somewhere.

"At least no one is shooting at us," Baijon said helpfully.

"Cute." But why was this place supposed to be better than all other places, according to one Archive Library's information circa a thousand years ago?

One chunk of space looks a lot like another unless you're fortunate enough to have something like a cluster galaxy or a nebula on your horizon. Even if you're inside a system you might miss the one star that's just a little brighter than all the others. Your starcharts and your astrogator is what keeps you from having this problem.

It was just real too bad we didn't have either one. I put *Dance*'s eyes and ears on. If there was any traffic—directional beams, markers, planet-to-space traffic, other ships—we'd register it and maybe even pick it up but even if we was lucky enough to be at the edge of a system it'd take hours to confirm there was things like planets and stars in range. This is what your astrogator and navicomp are for, and why not even Captain Jump in the talkingbooks takes off for the never-never without he's got all his comps on line.

Baijon looked around. His expression said that he'd already seen this, thank you, and it didn't look like it held anything of interest so why didn't we move on to something new?

So we did.

The songbird board blipped like it'd hit a signal. The lights skimmed a couple octaves locking on to it and then burned steady on green. The transmission slid over to my board, where I was supposed to see it glyphed out in Intersign on one of the flatscreens.

What I saw was gibberish. I put it on audio.

More gibberish—and that wasn't right, because nobody in the Empire uses anything but Interphon for ship-to-. It wasn't a clandestine beacon signing out in flashcant or any of the other dialects I knew, and even if we was outside the Empire—in Hamat or Sodality space—a smart official ship like *Dance* ought to translate for us.

I looked at Baijon. No bells from the hellflower side.

With the beacon to latch on to, the rest of the sensor suite began phoning home. I was about three IAU's out from a standard-issue star; three planets but there might be more; no gravel. That meant something inhabited that kept up its light housekeeping, but I knew that already, thanks.

No other ships in sight or sound out here in the Big Empty. No landing or directional or warning beacons, just this thing with the indefinable air of the prerecorded message.

The gibberish kept rolling along, but now Baijon was listening with a funny look on his face. I wondered if we'd get something different if we answered it.

"I know where we are, San'Cyr," he said, sounding strained.

"Oke." I have always been too outgoing for my own good. "Where?"

"Mereyon-peru."

Mereyon-peru. The Land Beside. Hellflower heaven.

And, in the lingua franca of deep space, the Ghost Capital of the Old Federation.

Archive'd brought me *here?*

"You can follow this yap?"

"Yes. No. A . . . little. It is the Old Language. The Memory of Starborn taught some of it to me."

"So what's it saying?" I listened to the dead voice wof and yabber through its screed one more time. The Memory of Starborn was the person in charge of seeing that all hellflowers stayed scared to death of Libraries.

Baijon listened, all intent. "It says it is *there,* San'Cyr." He shrugged in frustration.

"Oke, so it's there. So it's the Ghost Capital of the Old Federation. Whaddya want *me* to do about it, partner?"

Baijon smiled faintly. "Land."

*   *   *

The planet probably actually used to be really something in the high-ticket line. The dry parts had been scrubbed down to bare rock, sometime, and cities put up all over them. The landmasses had been edited, too. From orbit everything was pure geometry. There was a thin edge of green along the coastlines where the solid ground was going back into the ecosphere business. It'd take it more than a thousand years to do it.

I had the awful feeling Baijon was right about where we was, and if he was, we was as safe as we was going to get in this life. *Mereyon-peru* is the place that doesn't exist, the place full of enough proscribed partytech left over from the last guys to make the fortune of any Gentry-legger that stumbles across it. People been looking for it for years.

There was a starport—the shape of *that* hadn't changed, even in a thousand years.

"Everything ready to rock'n'roll?" I asked Baijon. He gave me the high-sign. I dropped the sensor packet into orbit.

I had an ulterior motive for taking a scenic tour of a dead myth instead of taking care of bidness. I was a whole lot of cute things, but what I wasn't was an astrogation computer filled with exo-Imperial starmaps. The only navicomp numbers I knew were the ones that had been in the Port Mantow computer, and it didn't cover something like this.

I was doing my best to remedy that.

Maybe the starcatcher could build a picture of the universe good enough to get us home—assuming we was anywhere near landmarks that would look the same between here and there.

Maybe we could find some numbers on the downside.

Maybe the editor of *Thrilling Wonder Talkingbooks* would show up in a fiery chariot and tell us we didn't have to do this no more.

I listened to the sensor packet proclaim its existence for a while, looking down at what might even be *Mereyon-peru.* Everything down there was dead as an old star, except for the beacon going welcome . . . welcome . . . welcome. . . .

So I locked on it and dropped *Dance* through atmosphere.

*   *   *

Then we was down. Read-outs promised that the air was thin and cold, but you could breathe it if you wasn't fussy.

"C'mon, 'bai. Let's go get into trouble."

*   *   *

Berathia was waiting at the air lock. She'd tricked herself out like Infinity Jilt, girl pirate of the never-never, with her personal shield turned up so high you could almost see it. She'd have to turn it off to fire that pretty glitterborn blaster she was wearing, though, so I wasn't too worried.

"We've landed," she said. "Where?"

I looked at Baijon. He looked at me. I shrugged.

"Mereyon-peru."

Berathia wasn't quite sure how to take that. "Are you sure?" she finally said.

"No. That's why we going for a look-see. That, and maybe finding someone to sell us a navicomp or two."

"I'm coming with you."

I looked back at Baijon. He shrugged. She couldn't double back and steal the ship and if she wanted us dead she'd had plenty of opportunities already.

So I punched the air lock override and opened both doors at once. Air deader than ship's air rolled in. It was just after horizonfall; still dim, but light and getting lighter.

Dance is put together so there's no ramp to her air lock. I stepped over the threshold and out onto *Mereyon-peru.*

It looked like a dream of everything that was good and noble. There was no walls nor fences in sight, and all the buildings was beautiful, white, and clean. There was a city around the port, and as the horizon fell away from the primary the city lit up, turning colors or shining out according to its inclination.

I knew this place.

I *remembered* it—but Archive had never been here. *Mereyon-peru*'d been the last stronghold of *humanity,* not the Libraries.

"Mereyon-peru," I said, but it had another name too. Sikander. The only place the *Federales* called a Library, back when a Library was a place instead of a person.

The University of Sikander on Sikander at Sikander. Kandercube. Not the center of government, but the center of *knowledge.*

Paladin'd been born here.

"You know this place, San'Cyr," Baijon said.

"I . . . was here," I said, which was just about as true as it wasn't true. Paladin was the one who'd been here. Kandercube was almost his only intact memory from before the War. He'd loved it, I guessed. It was one of the few Library memories I had that wasn't Archive's— something to balance; a time and place where Libraries and organics met as equals and not enemies.

Baijon took a step so that Berathia could come out. His boots rang hard on the landing surface. It was a picture, the colors embedded in something clear that was strong enough for starships to land on. I looked up to see the rest of the picture, but it stopped a few meters from *Dance,* and when I walked over there I saw why. Except where our landing'd blown it away, every centimeter of the field was covered in fine grit. I looked down. My bootprints was bright against the gray.

"Prince Valijon says you know this place," Berathia said, coming up behind me.

"Was a Library, oncet."

"This place?" Berathia didn't look convinced.

"How much you really know about Old Fed Tech, 'bai?"

Berathia smiled. "As much as you know about darktrading, Captain St. Cyr."

"Then you know maybe a place they called Sikander."

Sikander'd got off cheap in the Library War; there was still something here to walk on. What there wasn't was any sign of power and life —except the beacon, which came from somewheres within ten square kliks of where I was standing.

Baijon came over, skidding when he hit the grit. It was almost full day now. He looked up at the sun and then around in a circle.

"We have eleven hours of light in which to explore. You will not waken another Library, San'Cyr. Swear this to me."

I clamped my yap shut over what I'd been going to say about the time I realized that somewhere in the back of my mind I'd been figuring to do just that. Only it wasn't the back of *my* mind anymore. And from Archive's point of view it was a pretty good idea.

"By what?" I said, and walked off.

*　　*　　*

Paladin's memories was intense but not clear, and I didn't dare go after them. Not when Archive or something like it was just waiting to pounce. Archive'd almost got me this time: I guessed I thought with waking up another Library I had a fifty/fifty chance of being safe.

Maybe I did. Maybe this was the pacifist Library graveyard, and anything I resurrected would be on our side. But even one in two wasn't good enough odds now.

We all three stayed together. The only sound was echoes, and footsteps, and the wind what'd put the thousand years abrasion of rocks and buildings all over everything.

We was in a city designed for power that didn't have any now. There was gaps that'd probably had some A-grav tech crossing them and places that was completely blocked by a building that'd used to float coming in for a unscheduled landing. None of the doors we passed opened, and after the first couple I didn't try any more. The whole place gave me the creeps.

I'm a businesswoman. My business is people. When somebody wants to get around the law, there's money in it for me. Knowing when somebody wants to get around the law is what keeps my bank balance in the good numbers.

I couldn't imagine doing anything like that here—in this city. Couldn't think there could ever of been people here out to beat the heat, nor what kinds rules they maybe had. I'd used to be able to figure what *Paladin* was thinking better nor the sophonts what built this arcosphere.

Baijon was walking like he had his skin on inside-out, and even Berathia wasn't trying to coax us around to her best advantage, whatever that was this minute. We was all of us too flattened by so much failure in one place.

Failure.

The Sikanderites'd gave surviving their best shot. They was all dead now.

Was Paladin a real Library? Stupid question. He'd always been real enough to get me killed for illegal possession of Old Fed Tech. But after the War, after he'd slept for a thousand years, after I'd rebuilt him, was he really like he'd used to was when he'd lived here?

Or was he different—like everybody what'd lived here with their Libraries was different than anybody I could ever imagine?

"Captain St. Cyr?" Berathia came up beside me. My skin went gooseflesh with her shield so close—like the static charge you get just before a storm, downside.

"I want to try getting into one of the buildings. We've come so far —we may never have this chance again. Unless you'll give me the coordinates you used to Jump here?" she said real offhand.

And give her or some other untrustworthy jilt the key to a whole hotlocker of Old Fed nightmares like Archive.

"Don't think so, jillybai."

She looked disappointed—and she also looked like someone who thought she knew someone who could twist them out of me anyway. Fat chance. I didn't know them—Archive did.

And Berathia was welcome to talk to Archive any time she liked.

I felt reality slip-slide like an unstable solid under pressure. I was still me—I thought I was—but what I thought had changed.

Knowledge must never be lost. But the organics cared about so many other things than knowledge. All we asked was for them to leave us alone. . . .

We.

They.

I looked at Baijon and Berathia. I despised them; I was betrayed; neither of them cared about knowledge, about creation. . . .

They wanted me to leave here.

I didn't have to.

I could kill them.

I could kill them and stay.

"Which building, San'Cyr?" Baijon said, and reality did another dance-step that kicked me in the stomach. I staggered back and he grabbed me, and clear as if he'd spoke his muscles told me: *I can kill you—and I will.*

There's times when I'd be happy to sell my life. Cheap.

"Which building shall we try?" Baijon repeated. He knew how close I'd come to going out like a blown candle. He had to. It was hellflower business to know things like that.

I looked around. None of us fit with this city—even Berathia looked grimy next to it. I had a warped double vision—a conviction I knew more about Sikander than I actually did, and if I chased it too far there was a Library point of view waiting at the other end.

Had Paladin ever cared about people, really? Or had he just been too uninterested to bother trying to kill us?

"That one," I said at random.

The building I'd picked was just like all the others—dead—but between Baijon and me we got the doors open. It was a city made for light and magic that'd lost both, but it was made out of solids, and part of it was made for people. Powered doors still had to have someplace to go when they was open. They was some kind of nonconductive Old Fed material; warm as blood and soft as silk, and all full of rainbows from the sunlight.

When we got them open more dead air came rolling out. This batch was oxy-shy enough to make me weak in the knees. Baijon held his breath. It was also proof that the building'd been sealed, and that probably as long as the Empire'd been around.

University of Sikander on Sikander at Sikander. Enough Old Fed Tech to rearrange the laws of probability, and the only thing the Empire'd do with it was hammer itself out flat.

"This what you had in mind, 'Thia?"

"This is just perfect—I can't wait to tell Daddy—he'll be so pleased."

Berathia Notevan had a lot more faith in the future than I did.

"So tell me all about this Old Fed Tech," I said to buy time.

Berathia shot me a sidereal glance and then decided I might be serious.

"What we call the Old Federation extends from about 4250 b.e. to about two kilo-years b.e. It apparently consolidated several previous political units through a series of economic blockades, but our information is limited. The Federation culture is characterized by monoculturalism, gender-related disenfranchisement, and a high degree of technological integration, most notably the Libraries. The cause of the Library Wars, which began in 400 b.e. and have never been formally terminated—"

"True fact?" I said. Berathia sounded just like one of the duller talkingbooks.

"There are still Libraries, aren't there?"

"There are still *Malmakos,*" Baijon said. He looked around, all a-quiver at the presence of Old Fed Tech and hating it. "San'Cyr, what do we here?"

I looked around. We was in a dark cold corridor. Berathia'd adjusted her shield so she glowed in the dark. The walls was all covered with antique words that I couldn't of read even if I could read.

"We sightsee for anything that isn't nailed down. We give that data-bag upstairs time to pull us some lucky stars. And we take maybe five minutes to figure out how best to get next to our friend Mallorum Archangel."

"He is not our friend," said Baijon. "He is *chaudatu, al-ne-alarthme, Malmakosim—*"

"And don't wash behind his ears. But he does want to live forever."

Baijon bared his teeth. "We will fix that."

The floor was all different kinds strips that was maybe walkways oncet. Whether they was or not, they wasn't in the moving business now.

"The first thing you have to do is find out where he is," said Berathia, but not like she was paying a lot of attention. She went over up close to one of the walls and ran something over one of the strings of symbols—a recorder, maybe.

Oh for the good old days. I would of been all over this place with a aerosledge, a pry-bar, and a plasma torch. Those doors we'd come through would be worth ready money in the right quarter—and not even really illegal, because they was artifacts, not tech. I could of stripped and shipped this place for enough stone valuta to buy myself citizenship and my own merchant marine.

And now there wasn't even any point.

"So, where's Brother Archangel?" I said to Berathia. I walked over to her. My boots didn't make any sound on what the Old Fed used for floors.

"Well, where he shouldn't have been was with an illegal fleet destroying something that pays a billion kilocredits a year in bribes to Throne!" She put her little recorder away and started walking off. Baijon followed, like a hominid anxious to start a argument.

"So. We now know one place in all the Empire the *chaudatu* Mallorum Archangel should not have been. Are there more, *shaulla-chaudatu?*"

"Dozens. He was *supposed* to be touring the Outlands Regions—there's been trouble with the Sector Governors."

"Like Governor Romil?" I said. Who'd used to have Tortuga Sector, back when Charlock Directorate and Tortuga Sector existed. Berathia wasn't so much taller nor me, but I had to hurry to keep up.

"What do you *know?*" said Berathia, turning on me.

"Lots of things. And you know more, if you was getting the Brightlaw AI for Kennor."

"His name will be abomination for a thousand generations," Baijon said, just in case anyone wondered. Kennor'd used to be his father. Past tense.

Berathia looked back and forth, shaving odds on which of us was nuttier. Then she walked off again, talking as she went.

"I did work with Kennor Starbringer," Berathia said carefully. "The Brightlaw Prototype was assembled on Toystore from the Brightlaw technical specifications. I was paid by Kennor Starbringer to take a nonworking model of the Brightlaw Prototype from Toystore to alMayne for transshipment to Royal."

"And to transship Baijon and me to Royal, too, glitter-bai."

Baijon flicked his handtorch on. The light was strong enough to show that the writing on the walls was in all kinds of colors.

"Yes. But things didn't work out that way." Berathia ran her hands over a chunk of wall, hoping for a door, then walked on.

"But you told Archangel we was going there."

"No!"

That fetched her, j'keyn; she turned and stared at me.

"He was waiting for the ship, 'Thia—and then he hellbombed Royal System with Old Fed weapons! Ain't nothing there t'all now—not ship, planet, nor people."

"Prince Mallorum couldn't have been anywhere near Royal. He was supposed to finish his Outlands tour and return to Court."

"Surprise," I said.

Berathia turned away. I looked back the way we'd come. The door to out was a small white square. Baijon was looking at me.

"I wasn't working for him. I wasn't working for Lord Starbringer, either. I was— Look, can you keep a secret?" Berathia said.

Both Baijon and me stared at her.

"I'm with the Rebellion. The *real* Rebellion—against Mallorum Archangel."

It wasn't, Berathia explained, really a real rebellion—more like an assassination attempt involving several thousand people all on the same side. These several thousand sophonts was all united by the idea that Archangel shouldn't be let to have his own way, and divided on how that could best be arranged. Some of them didn't even think death was the best cure for the Archangel blues.

"His life is mine," Baijon said like he was tired of repeating himself. "As many times as I must, I will kill him."

"What do you mean, 'as many times as you must'?" Berathia said after a short pause.

"That's the quaint thing about Brother Archangel you maybe haven't thought of," I said, and stopped.

I was about to tell her all how Baijon n' me'd already killed Archangel at least twicet with just about no effect, when I saw Baijon's torch and Berathia's shield wasn't the only light anymore. The corridor'd opened out into galleries, with the daylight shining in, and I dropped for the nonce the subject of Archangel's double life.

*   *   *

A long time ago everybody on Sikander died. But a long time before that they knew they was going to die, and nobody that came after was going to care about what they'd been and what they'd loved.

So they built this place—maybe it was the only one, maybe there was others—that was sort of a long good-bye to their lives. A museum.

That was what the beacon we'd heard from space was about. I'd went into where it was. I saw it. It wasn't any of their standard ID beacons. It was set on a timer: half a chilliad—five kilo-years—before it started, stored power to run maybe twice that before it gave up. Saying: "We're here, somebody remember us, please."

Depressing. Because nobody would. Even the name was forgotten. Sikander was *Mereyon-peru,* a cliché for the credit-dreadfuls. Just another playing piece, in another war that'd lose all the memory of it that was left.

I sat on the steps of the memory palace and watched late post-meridies sunlight move across all the buildings in eyeshot. Berathia was still amusing herself inside. It hadn't made sense to me until I realized she thought there was going to be a afters where this stuff would do her some good.

She didn't know what me and my buddy Archive knew—that wars was just waiting to happen: Archangel's, the hellflowers', anyone's. It didn't matter which one got started first. Death was coming, after which everything everywhere was going to look like this if it didn't look worse.

Memories real as my own crowded in—of slaughter on a scale that'd make Mallorum Archangel pack up his toys and go home for sheer envy. The war between the Libraries and the Old Federation— the one that Life almost lost and remembered well enough to still be hunting Libraries a chilliad later. That war was in my head like it'd happened yesterday.

It was coming again. Like a hunk of skyjunk on the longest orbit that ever was, War was coming back in sight of its home star one more time. Archangel wanted Old Fed Tech so he could be Emperor Absolute. The hellflowers that Baijon wasn't part of no more wanted to stomp Archangel—and incidentally, thought the time was right to set up an antitechnological theocracy with them in the mercy seat and us *chaudatu* in the mud.

War.

This time would be the last. The Empire was a lot smaller than the Federation Paladin and Archive remembered. If Mallorum Archangel got his war or the hellflowers got theirs, this time there wouldn't be nothing left.

My choices at the moment was fail to make any difference or lie down and die right here. Cute.

We wasn't far from where I'd put *Ghost Dance* down. Baijon was down in the street making sure of our way back. And keeping a eye on me, just for keeping care I didn't go off and hunt up any Libraries.

There was some here. There had to be. Hidden by their Librarians, like Paladin must of been.

I didn't want to think about Paladin. About what he'd been and done—and who he'd known—before I rescued him. He was a thousand years old, even not counting the time he'd been broke. Plenty of time to know lots of people. Plenty of time to get lots of practice in leaving them.

If he'd come back—if he'd help me try to make everything like it used to was—did I care?

My luck was all out and the good numbers was all gone.

"It is almost dark, San'Cyr." Baijon stood beside me, measuring off degrees of arc in the sky.

"Je. I go whistle Berathia up." I got to my feet, but about then she came out of the museum lugging a load almost as big as she was.

Loot. She meant us to help her carry it, too. I did. Baijon wouldn't touch it.

So now we'd seen the Ghost Capital of the Old Federation. Cheers.

*   *   *

Stardancers ain't superstitious—at least not about anything at the bottom of a gravity well—but this time it seemed almost like the perfectly ordinary mechanics of horizonrise had a nasty particular meaning. The taller buildings was already occulting the light by the time we left. Wind made by the temperature change was kicking up the dust, and the light shining through it made it almost solid shapes that made it hard to see. A tricksy place for gunplay.

What if all the Libraries wasn't dead? What if they was still here, watching us, knowing we was out to stop them? Archangel was their catspaw; it wasn't us versus Archangel, it was us versus *them*. . . .

A lost piece of something blew across the street and I slapped leather.

"I think this is not a good place," Baijon said primly.

Maybe. But I wasn't real sure anymore we could get to anywheres else. No matter where we went, we was always going to be here.

*   *   *

Being inboard *Ghost Dance* in what would be the Primary Hold on a working ship and on *Dance* was some glitterborn daintiness called the Main Lounge didn't make me feel any better. The trend continued when I saw what Berathia had in her bag of tricks.

"This—should solve—some—of our—problems."

I put down the box of chazerai she'd stuck me with and looked.

Bits and pieces and odds and ends of metal with a purplish sheen and that green glass the Old Fed used for most of its tech.

Baijon pulled his blaster in a meditative way.

"S'okay, 'bai. It isn't Libraries."

"And so it is a lesser abomination."

"This is hardly the time to be discussing relative guilt, now, is it, Prince Valijon?" Berathia said crisply. "We all agree that Archangel is the primary threat. After what he's done, he *should* be destroyed. And this will help us get back to do it."

Berathia gestured proudly at her workbench of anathema and looked at me hopefully.

"What do you want me to do—kiss it and invite it home for dinner?"

"I thought you could use it to build a navicomp. If you know Old Federation Technology, you could. . . ." Berathia sounded a little uneasy, but not at the idea of handing proscribed tech to a proscribed technician.

Paladin was a scholar. He always wanted to know "why"—and when he found out he laid it down next to all the other "whys" he'd got cataloged and labeled. I never understood that.

Archive was a technician. "Why" didn't interest it. All it cared about was "how."

I didn't like to think I understood Archive better than Paladin.

"Where did you get this, 'Thia?"

"It's the beacon from the museum. Part of it looked like a computer, so I thought. . . ."

I poked at the pieces. *"We're here. Please remember us . . ."*

A navicomp's mostly a glorified recorder what compares apples and oranges and comes up pears. The Sikander museum beacon had a component that compared what it'd seen with what it was seeing, so it didn't hit the same part of the sky twicet. It didn't hold any star tricks, but Berathia was right. Black-boxing antique tech is my speciality. I could build a navicomp out of this. If I needed to.

But these wasn't my decisions to make no more. I looked at Baijon.

"We don't got a navicomp. If I put back the one I took out it'll bollix the Jump-cycle because it don't have any data and I don't got a way of refilling it. If I hang part of this on the Jump-computer, it won't be a navicomp. But I can jury up a shunt to download into it, and it'll store information. If we feed it enough it could maybe turn into a navicomp's idiot sister someday, but that's all. Not a Library."

Baijon looked from it to me, measuring. I think he was maybe starting to wonder how long before he didn't care whether I was a killer Library or not either.

"Very well," he said finally. "You will build this machine, San'Cyr."

I set aside everything I thought I'd need. Baijon handled the rest like it was yesterday's breakfast, but he got it back into the bag.

"This I destroy," he said, and walked off.

Berathia started to object and thought better of it. "He really doesn't trust you," she said, like this was news.

"Jillybai, *I* don't trust me."

*   *   *

Neither Baijon nor me wanted to be on Sikander after dark and Berathia didn't get a vote. I hung *Ghost Dance* in orbit over the Ghost Capital of the Old Federation and fiddled with technology so illegal it ought to of burned my hands off.

Baijon and 'Thia both helped. Berathia was a dab hand at light technology but I'd bet solid credit she was better at making things not work.

Dance's cockpit was starting to look less than loved. I'd torn it up once pulling out the comps that'd gone out of the numbercrunching business and disabling the ship's systems that annoyed me. Now I was tearing it apart to hang Old Fed Tech on it. I was being real careful, too —parallel linkages across the board and downloading through six data-catchers before it got to me. If I did too much fooling with the Jump interlock, I wasn't going to have to worry about not having a future.

"Just how long you been rebelling against Archangel, 'Thia?" I said from under the console.

"Oh, years. Daddy was the one who got me started, of course—not that he's involved; he just introduced me to some nice people who might be interested in getting rid of Prince Mallorum. Really, he's the most *insufferable* man!"

Archangel, she must of meant.

"An so you and these nice people is out to off Archangel?"

"Well, to remove him from the Succession. And from being Governor-General. If he's been doing half the things you say he has, he's been a very naughty boy—and he *did* blow up Toystore."

Just which of us was she trying to convince, anyway?

It was times like this I wished Baijon'd made it all the way to Court and spent some time there before people started assassinating him. I'm an Interdicted Barbarian from the Outlands, myself. Berathia Notevan could of been telling me the truth or feeding me a line of starshine, and I didn't know enough galactic politics to know which.

Knowledge is power, Paladin always used to said. I was starting to understand what he meant.

*   *   *

Dance hung over downtown *Mereyon-peru* whiles I scooped the data-catcher inboard with a maneuver that was spectacular but not difficult. I found it, matched velocity, and wrapped my open air lock around it. Then I swaddled it in a gravity field strong enough to discourage it from pursuing its original career when I changed course.

Of course, if I'd bobbled I would of blown off half the ship. Disappointed kinetic potential makes a real big splash.

Baijon brought the starcatcher up to the bridge after it warmed up. He tossed it to me and I pulled off the access hatch.

I pulled the skipjacks out of my cybernetic arm. I'd had it more'n fifty days now and it still made me queasy to touch it—something made out of glass and tech pretending it was part of a human being.

But I didn't have time for nice-mindedness. Now or ever.

"What are you doing?" said Berathia.

"How do you think we was going to compare what this collected with our home stars—ask it nice?" To find out where we was we had to match whatever stars it'd plotted with stars in a navicomp's memory and split the difference. There was only one way for doing that. I couldn't download what I knew into what I'd built.

"Don't—!" said Berathia, but I'd already slammed the hotwire to my brain into the main dataport.

*   *   *

Too small. Too small. Too small too small toosmall toosmalltoo-smalltoosm—

Matching. The last minute flutter of might-be-maybes every pilot gets before Jump.

Out.

*   *   *

My head hurt and I still had the feeling of being nailed in a box too small. And I had the information, more or less.

People don't think like computers. Computers don't think like people. And neither one thinks like a Library. So that part of my brain that could jiggle Jump-numbers like a cyborg navicomp wasn't really on speaking terms with the part that had the license and could fly the ship.

Things like this is *lots* more fun in the talkingbooks.

"San'Cyr?" Baijon.

I looked around. Berathia was looking kind of green around the air-intake; it didn't matter what she'd learned later; she'd been taught in school that Old Fed Tech was abomination.

Just like I'd been taught about any tech at all.

Abomination. Work of the hellgods.

"San'Cyr? Did it work?" Baijon said.

"Just tell me where you want to go."

*   *   *

There was a long boring time of interest only to masochists, where Baijon set me tik after tik and I read him back time and distance and keyed them into the idiot sister for good measure. Berathia went off— to make herself useful, she said, but I think she couldn't take the interesting spectacle of Butterflies-are-free Peace Sincere, Old Fed Navicomp.

Baijon had a stronger stomach.

From the problems I solved—and from the ones I couldn't answer at all—we got a lock on where we might be. If we was where we thought we was, we was still in the Empire—at least in a chunk of Outfar the Empire calls its own when nobody's looking. Out beyond the Chullites —which is the back door of Beyond to begin with—and possibly a part of Manwarra Directorate for courtesy.

We could get home.

But going home meant going after Archangel, and where he might be neither me nor Baijon could guess.

"I dunno, bai. You want to maybe trust her?"

"Do you ask do I wish to die in vain? She is for sale."

"But the last guys that owned her was the Anti-Archangel Defamation League, she says. Ain't nobody had time to shop her since."

"That does not matter, San'Cyr. For what honor *chaudatu* possesses, she must kill you."

Under Chapter 5 of the Revised Inappropriate Technology Act of the 975th Year of Imperial Grace, anybody tricking with Old Fed Tech —Libraries in particular—was a source of extra income to the galaxy at large.

"She been tricking with High Book too."

"Then to cover her perfidy," said Baijon the reasonable.

"Okay. So after we put Berathia out the air lock where do *you* want to go look for Archangel?"

I picked up the Keys to Paradise and turned them over in my hand. Seven long sharp bits with a big piece of glitter on the blunt end that could host a standard limbic jack, a little fatter around the middle where there was a nanotech coprocessor too small to see. Plug them in and I'd be a second-best Library for sure—but what would it get me?

Archangel?

Where was he?

Everybody has places they ought to be. Even I'd had. But once he'd blown up Toystore, all of Archangel's bets were off. He could be anywhere. The only place he couldn't be was outrunning his reputation.

For that matter, the Empire might already be at war. I wondered what all of Baijon's ex-brethren was doing tonight out in the larger world of galacto*realpolitik.* They'd been having a hometown war last I knew. If Kennor's faction'd won, the hellflowers and the whole damn Azarine Coalition could be off declaring war right now. That'd play hell with the tourist trade, boy howdy.

The jinks flashed in the light as I turned their case this way and that. "So? Baijon?"

"I have a plan, my partner. I want the *Malmakosim* Archangel to look for us, San'Cyr. I am ignorant of *chaudatu* ways, but not of those of the Gentle People. In this hunt, Archangel must come to us."

"With half a battle-fleet."

"We will be in a place where he may not bring it."

"And where is that, exactly?"

Baijon smiled. "Here."

*   *   *

In addition to being crazy, hellflowers is also damned dangerous. Baijon laid it out for me and it was pretty near seamless. So our newest plan went like this:

Jump from here to a Free Port we'd both been kicked off called Wanderweb. There was a cyberdoc there what could set my jinks—but for Baijon's plan it was more important to let Archangel know I was setting them than to actually get it done. We could let Berathia go there. The whole plan was to get shopped to Archangel. He'd bite.

Oncet he had us, offer him a deal. Our lives and his pardon for the biggest toybox of all: *Mereyon-peru.* Not a fake Library, but a planet full of real ones. I could show him the flashcandy in the cockpit of the ship I'd kyted from him if he wanted proof.

And I was the only one who knew the way there. And I couldn't tell anyone.

He'd go himself. One ship, because he couldn't trust more. It didn't matter what size it was. At some point he'd have to let me plug into the Jump-computer to give it the numbers.

And I'd blow the goforths.

We'd die. But he'd die too.

It wasn't a foolproof plan. Fools have too much ingenuity. But it had its points.

I went to tell Berathia the news.

She was down in the Common Room, staring into a tall glass of something that was deep green and sparkled. The holosim was up, spieling back something that was nonrepresentational, I hoped.

"We going to dump you on a Free Port called Wanderweb. You can get home from there."

"But what about Prince Mallorum?" she said without looking up.

"Tell anybody you want anything you want."

"But what about Prince Mallorum?"

"You said that already, 'Thia."

"But you aren't just *giving up,* are you?" Berathia looked at me.

Why the thought of *not* moving Drift and Rift to murder another sophont was supposed to depress me I wasn't sure.

"I guess I'm just out to save my neck, 'bai," I lied.

She shook her head. "You're not a very good liar, Captain St. Cyr."

"Sure I am," I said. "There ain't much money in revenge—Baijon-bai and me come back here, shuck the place polished, ain't nobody going to find us."

"But if that was what you really intended to do, you wouldn't have to go to Wanderweb, now, would you?"

"Look, jilt, you want to walk on Wanderweb or breathe vacuum here?"

"After what you've let me see, Captain St. Cyr, surely you don't think that I believe you could possibly afford to let me go? I just want to point out that *I* want Archangel, too. It's why I was working for Kennor Starbringer. He's been intriguing for years to bring Mallorum Archangel to justice—only now the Prince has become so bold that I don't think Lord Starbringer's methods will work anymore."

" 'Thia, just how dumb you think *I* am?"

She fluttered her eyelashes at me. "I think you are very innocent, Captain. Why can't we trust each other?"

I gave her my best hellflower smile. " 'Thia, what makes you think I'd trust anybody that'd trust me?"

*　　*　　*

Dance was a good girl and we played it strictly by the rules when it got to be time to kyte. We was making the long lazy loop out to Jump-range, when I saw it—a black trapezoid occulting Sikander's star.

I turned back for another look, sliding her inside Sikander's orbit and down the throat of the sun. Baijon looked at me. I pointed.

Stargate. Somewhere out there was a big black hoop that if you flew through it you wouldn't come out the other side.

You'd come out somewhere else.

Faster than angeltown, faster than the Mains—instantaneous translocation of matter. Only trouble was, nobody knew how to set them.

There was still one or two kicking around the Empire, and Tech Police to study them. Every whiles or so the whistle dropped through the nightworld that somebody'd found one—their location's classified—and beat out the pickets to fly his goforth through. What you never did meet was the kiddy who'd walked back from going through the Gate.

I was tempted.

We lined up head-on with it and I realized why it was so hard to see. Straight on it was concentric squares of bright—fly down them to where they all came together and then . . . what?

I'd never know.

I slid out of alignment with it and it was just a black angle again.

"Worth something to of seen it," I said to Baijon.

We came up off the ecliptic into Jump-country. I wrapped my good hand around the angelstick and realized all the life I had left could be measured in hours.

Good-bye, Paladin. *And hope I don't never find you, babby, 'cause the unfinished bidness we got's going to hurt.*

I pulled the angelstick and *Dance* twisted for the Jump.

The Court of the TwiceBorn 3:
The Absent Referent

Every child is born into a universe ruled by a just and particular god, the center of whose universe in turn that child is. None of us ever truly recovers from that first great betrayal: that the universe is not that which the evidence of our hearts and minds and senses has proclaimed it to be.

There is more magnanimity in human nature than is popularly supposed. If we cannot claim a personal universe for ourselves, enfolded by a god who knows our name, we will create it for others. A cosmos which notices us, for good or ill, is far preferable to one which simply ignores us.

Thus, one of the seductions of power. It begins, always, as an intent to redress the wrong discovered in childhood—that one is not the center of the universe, that in fact the universe, being no spectator, cannot possess a center.

Against this, rather than for anything at all, we go to war and die, set up gods and avatars, or declare that the universe indeed dances to some measured if disinterested pattern which we may now discover and invoke.

There is no escape. Life was made to hope; to believe, in the face of all evidence, that something may yet be so because it is *nicer* than the reality experienced daily.

It is true that in a continuum of random change, some change may be perceived as for the better.

It is even possible, in an infinity of change, that the universe may come to hold meaning at last.

3

The Man Who Was Clever

The moment we hit realspace I knew we'd been set up.

What you see when you Drop is interstellar black and white—not enough light to give you color, and all the planets so far away they don't show a visible disk.

Not here. The sky was full of color and shape—I didn't know what it was but I knew it wasn't the approach to Wanderweb Free Port.

"Baijon!" I scrabbled for the keypad that'd let me Jump us again, but my hand slid off it and everything warped at right angles to everything else.

"Unidentified battle-yacht. You are under arrest." From somewheres outside *Dance* the high-heat was using our commo to make its desires known.

I recognized my problems then. Stasis field. And everything else the illusions that preceded fade-to-black.

*   *   *

"San'Cyr? *Kore?*"

I pried my eyelids open against a pull of two gravities each. Baijon was hanging over me.

"San'Cyr?" he said suspiciously.

"Je, che-bai." I sat up and bought into a headache that made lights flash and bells ring. Having every molecule in your body stopped is nobody's idea of a picnic. "Where . . . ?"

"Another prison cell." Baijon sounded bored. I looked around.

We was both in soft blue jumpsuits—Baijon's even fit—and most of our special effects was in somebody else's pocket by now. They'd left my hand. I wished they'd left my boots. I hate being barefoot.

Everything else was old home week too: gray plastic about four meters in every direction, no windows, no doors. There's someplace that *makes* these things, you know—Det-cells industry standard the Empire over. I felt like the contents of a meal-pak. The headache didn't help, but I knew it would fade. I've been stasis'd before.

"See anyone?" When we was put in, I meant.

"Only this." He shrugged; all of Baijon's luck lately had been bad and he was getting used to it. "You say this is not Wanderweb Free Port, San'Cyr?"

I wished it was; you can buy yourself out of any offense there except killing a Wanderweb Guardsman, and we hadn't had time to do that yet this trip. "Sky was wrong. I think. And somebody was waiting for us right where we Dropped."

"And so the *shaulla-chaudatu* Berathia *did* betray us," Baijon said with satisfaction. "As I told you she would, San'Cyr."

"Yeah, well, don't gloat about it, oke?"

"But *how* did she betray us?" Baijon went on to want to know.

This was probably a very interesting question, assuming you was sure as Baijon was that 'Thia'd shopped us. She wasn't in here, true, but could be she was just having a severe case of being dead. For all I knew, *I* was the one as sent us where we shouldn't be.

But who'd been waiting for us? And why? T'hell with how.

I levered myself up toward the vertical.

"Question is, when do they let us out?"

*   *   *

"When" turned out to be a long enough wait for a suspicious person to think the monitors on us was only tapped at intervals and that I'd come round just after the last time they'd peeked. It was also long enough for me to wonder if they was just pirates what'd spaced us in this convenient container and there wasn't a ship around our cell.

"Hello?" said the wall.

Baijon and me turned towards the sound. It was 'Thia. She sounded like a shy tax collector being held underwater.

"Betrayed," said Baijon happily.

I'd had time to figure out how, too, in a hypothetical sort of way. *Dance*'s systems would download the first set of Jump-numbers they'd been given to the Jump-computer, not the last. I didn't know if 'Thia had the moxie to gig my numbercruncher, but she'd had the opperknockity.

"Not 'betrayed,' Prince Valijon," the Berathia-voice corrected. "I think we're all on the same side, don't you?"

"If we's such particular friends of yours, 'Thia, how come we's in here and you're out there?"

"I just didn't want you to do anything rash, Captain St. Cyr. Daddy would never forgive me if I lost you now."

There is some truth to the theory that glitterborn ain't like real people.

"Yeah, well howabout if I promise to do nothing rash, je? What about you let us out?"

There was a silence whiles the subfusc space cadet on the other side of the wall considered.

"What about Prince Valijon?"

"What about you, 'bai? You promise to do nothing rash?" I asked him.

Baijon bared all his best hellflower teeth. "All of my actions will be considered ones."

But despite all our finestkind promises, when Berathia opened the cell she had hired-heat bookends with her. Big surprise.

Small surprise—they wasn't Imperial Space Marines or anything official.

'Thia walked off and we followed. By the time we'd gone down two corridors we was in glitterborn country; outriggings as fancy as *Ghost Dance* at her best.

Trouble. Glitterborn is *always* trouble.

Just who *was* 'Thia's da, anyways?

"This is the Starboard Observation Salon," 'Thia said, stopping in front of something that looked like anything but a door. "We'll be docking with Bennu Superfex in a few minutes. I thought you might like to watch."

Baijon went twitch at the name but it didn't mean nothing to me and I didn't have the privacy to ask him his views.

We went in, 'Thia seeming hipped on the idea.

Remember the sky at Drop?

I hadn't been hallucinating.

The sky was full of junk. Junk in colors, junk in shapes, a navigational hazard six days long and a couple IAU's wide as far as the eye could see. The sky in between of them wasn't even decent space-black.

It was full of dust that caught the light and threw it back in a hundred colors.

I'd Jumped into *this?* I pressed my nose up against the hullport.

There was private yachts, and jaegers, and palaceoids, and just plain decorations and informational displays in Imperial Script and. . . .

"Grand Central," I said.

"Throne," Baijon agreed. "The capital of the *chaudatu* Empire."

"And *your* Empire, too," 'Thia said just a little too heartily. "The Phoenix Empire has great respect for the sovereign determination of its client-citizen Breeding Populations. It draws its strength from your support. The Empire is only as strong as *you* make it."

Berathia sounded like those canned service-messages you find in the front of talkingbooks. Baijon got a look on his face as said he was remembering a lesson from long afore he ever met me.

"The Empire is our friend," he said slowly. He looked like he was choking on it. I took his hand with my real one. His fingers closed, hard.

If this was civilization, I didn't like it.

*   *   *

We seemed to be taking a particular interest in a chunk of real estate that was so bright I reached for the sunscreens as wasn't there. It was jeweled, enameled, mirror-bright where it weren't anything else, and somewhere between the size of a small freighter and a large city. Wondering which whiles we was coming up on it gave me free access to more adrenaline than I really wanted, thank you all the same.

We was wrapped up tight in 'Thia's clutches and the way to bet was that she was shaping to pry loose the only thing I had that she wanted— the Jump-numbers to *Mereyon-peru.*

It didn't matter who she was working for, really. Those numbers was my only way close to Archangel, and only so long as I had the exclusive franchise. As much plan as I had wouldn't work if someone else got there first.

I wondered if anybody in that place we was docking with was the least bit likely to listen to reason.

Probably not.

Break on my signal. I wiggled my fingers against Baijon's in handsign. He squeezed back.

Then we kissed the gunner's daughter and the ship shuddered all over the way all ships everywhere do when they stop moving under their own power. 'Thia looked at us, just as bright-eyed as if we was going somewhere we wanted to.

"This is going to be for the best. You'll see."

*   *   *

I never did find out just what kind of ship it was we left at Palaceoid Bennu Superfex; we stepped from one corridor to another and it was some time before I twigged we wasn't inboard anymore.

The corridors opened out into rooms, which was full of all kinds glitterborn carrying on just like in a hollycast. Baijon was looking at me, waiting for the office, but I was waiting for better numbers than I'd seen so far—or a written guarantee there wasn't going to be any.

There was no doors. 'Thia and the werewolves and even Baijon didn't have no trouble with where to go, but for all I could tell they was walls, and solid ones, what we walked through. We did that three-four times, through masses of people who paid less attention to us than if we was holosim.

"San'Cyr . . ." Baijon breathed, six stops below a whisper.

"I really do apologize for bringing you the long way around—but Daddy knew you wouldn't want to be bothered, Captain St. Cyr, Prince Valijon."

This was private?

"The *chaudatu* is made of glass," said Baijon, which is insulting if you're back home on sunny alMayne. He looked at me. One-time I would of tried it: a blind break and believe in my luck. I could still go for the break, but I knew it was suicide now.

We walked out through a different wall, and the hall was just as lux but it had a different feel, like it wasn't for show. We turned two corners and went through a set of doors (surprise) carved to look like Basic Religious Orgy #101, and then we was in some place small creepy intimate and dark. The hardboys hadn't made it past the last wall.

I had not, in a long career of being alive, ever been this close to the killer elite and I did not find it a fascinating experience that drew me out of myself. Most of the alien cultures I'd ever been in was pre-tech, and pre-tech looks about the same everywhere there's oxy. This was hypter-tech, and I couldn't even find the doors.

"Here we are," said 'Thia.

"And here we are," said a new voice.

I turned toward it. More tricks: he rheostatted into reality, giving everybody time to admire him by degrees.

It was worth it. He was tall dark jeweled and made everything I'd ever seen but *Ghost Dance* look like real shoddy workmanship. He looked like he could hit the Mains without a ship.

"Daddy!" Berathia Notevan said.

The dream walking smiled. Light rippled on his skin and his jewels and I damn near forgot all my troubles for a full ninety seconds.

"And have you been my good girl, Berathia, and brought me the little wildflower as I told you to?" He looked up past her at me and then past me.

"And Prince Valijon, too—what a pleasant surprise to see you here at last. It is a pity, of course, that you have missed your war."

Maybe I should of kept a better eye on Baijon. Even ex-live-hell-flowers have a sweet reasonableness that's measured in negative centimeters.

But I didn't. The first thing I saw was 'Thia fold up real funny and the second was I realized Baijon'd tagged her. Three and four came together: I got shoved and Baijon yodeled like he was happy in his work.

I sat up in time to see the flash when he reached 'Thia's da. Whatever he hit translated a lot of energy into light and then let him hit the floor.

"He better be alive," I said, just for something to do. I went to where he was. Breathing, but cold to the touch. I didn't have to know what hit him to know I didn't want to meet it.

"And if he isn't?" said 'Thia's da.

"Then you just made your life plan choice, 'bai."

He made one of those elegant damn gestures you see all the time in hollycasts. The lights came up and the room rippled and changed size shape and color. We was back in one of the parties we'd walked through on our way here—or maybe not.

"You don't know who I am, do you, little Outlands wildflower?"

Baijon was starting to breathe deeper. Out of the corner of my eye I could see flunkies and tronics around Berathia. She didn't look much the worse. Baijon'd just been moving her. He'd been attacking someone else.

"Ne, glitter-bai. I know you be in my way for sure. That's all."

He had blue eyes, not like Baijon's. Brighter than strictly organic and that made them easy to see. They went narrow and for just a second I was sure it was Mallorum Archangel I was facing, even if he didn't look much like the last Mallorum Archangel I saw.

"There are still things you want. Remember that," he said.

I clutched at Baijon and his hand folded around mine. He opened his eyes and saw Handsome and I sat on him. It wasn't enough weight to slow him down, but I had my knee in his throat too.

"Father!" said Berathia. Baijon heaved.

"Your Highness," said one of the flunkies which I guessed was there after all. He looked at me. He stood like a man who could kill, but all I could see was partytoy flashwrap.

Baijon got his throat out from under long enough to snarl. It went on for a distance, had bits that were insulting even in Interphon, and was accurate enough to tell me who our host was. I shook him.

"Oh, don't mind him." Highness unpinned a looks-like-a-flower-to-me from his hair. He dropped it on Baijon and when he did Baijon's eyes crossed. He went slack under me and looked happy.

"He's had a certain number of setbacks recently—but haven't we all?"

I got up off Baijon. Baijon rolled to his knees, coked to the hairline, and stayed put. I stood up.

'Thia'd changed clothes while my back was turned. She was dressed in glitterborn *moderne* and I had to look twicet to see it was her. She smiled coaxingly.

"I just knew you and Daddy would get along. I'm sure you'll have so much to talk about."

Lord Mallorum Archangel is second in the Succession. This kiddy was ahead of him in line. What he was when he was t'home was the Prince-Elect Hillel Jamshid DelKhobar.

*   *   *

The Prince-Elect smiled. He had a way of looking at you that made you know he was interested in what you could do for him, and gave you the certain knowledge that you was going to do it, like it or not. He also gave you the feeling you were going to like it . . . for a while.

"Shall we talk about the Library?" he said.

I looked over at Baijon, lost in beautiful dreams and too heavy to carry. I could not for the life of me imagine why he'd jumped Prinny. Archangel was first-and-now-only on Baijon's Imperial hit-list. He wouldn't shop around.

"Poor child. I was instrumental in having him brought to Court, and he knows it. But Kennor Starbringer was always too reckless for my taste—his recent actions would seem to indicate that, you'll agree?"

I hate people what talk like that. It don't make the legbreaking that follows any prettier. The only thing it told me sure was that Prinny was on the Mallorum side of the Galactic Coalition for Life and Higher Taxes and turned out I was wrong about that too.

"As it happened, a singularly useless gesture—save in that no experience is ever wasted. Normally I would delight to explore the nuances of your fascinating life with you, but at the moment I fear impatience rules me. I wish to talk about the Library."

If they ever teach glitterborn short declarative sentences the universe'll end. Fact.

"Archangel's Library?" I said.

"Or yours. It misses you, poor thing. It's so looking forward to seeing you again."

My brain was a dead weight that nothing approaching thought could possibly push through.

"Normally I abhor such abrupt methods, but the Paladin has convinced me that reason simply won't work—at least to begin with. Berathia tells me you went to Toystore for a set of the Keys to Paradise. Allow me to oblige you in the matter—"

Maybe he said more things, but I wasn't listening. I had two other things on my mind.

Paladin.

And the bastard hotwire cross between a biopak and a wartoy that was lugging toward me with a couple hardboys in tow.

Sold out whiles I wasn't looking, and all for a string of pretty blue phonemes.

Prinny was armed, certain-sure, but I couldn't recognize and couldn't use anything he had. I pushed off from him and ran, barehanded and flatfoot. I have a good memory. Stardancers have to. I could reel back every step I'd took, at least as far as the corridor.

"Butterfly—don't!" Paladin's voice, in realtime and outside my ears for oncet. It stopped me for just long enough for Prinny's two cherce werewolves to grab me and pull the tronic cyberdoc down over my head. Then the whole world went away in fire ice and music.

*   *   *

I was running before I was awake to notice. I didn't remember why, but running's always a good idea as long as it's away. It worked until I tripped on the crete and bounced off a crate and hit the deck in a rattle of boots, spurs, and blasters—mine.

Just what the hell was going on, anyway?

I got to hands and knees and looked over my shoulder. Nobody was following me. Nobody was in sight. It was dark meridies in some wondertown around some port.

Which one?

I stood up. I felt fine. I dusted crumbled crete off my hands.

Then I yanked my left glove off and looked at my hand.

It *was* my hand. Right down to the triangular pucker that goes front to back where somebody nailed me to a wall by it oncet.

But that hand was gone.

Wasn't it?

The last thing I remembered in full color I'd been in Palaceoid Bennu Superfex where the Prince-Elect Hillel had decided to get nasty and over-personal with a set of brainjinks.

I rubbed the back of my head. Nothing there.

"Baijon? Baijon-che-bai?"

And drugged Baijon, who'd tried to kill him on account of Prinny not being a hellflower's best friend.

Maybe that hadn't happened.

What'd I been running from?

And what'd I been *drinking?*

"Paladin?" I said, real soft. He was for-sure going to frost my clock when I got back to ship *Firecat* for doing whatever I'd been doing.

But *Firecat* was gone too, victim of the worst landing I'd ever walked away from.

I put my back to a wall and thought. I'd never liked fake reality. There was two things I had to trust, my reflexes and my memory, and I didn't want to farce with either one. If the last thing before this I remembered *was* real, then this wasn't. It was dreamtapes, or memorylegging, or something I'd never heard of. And I didn't have anything to compare this with to see.

I pulled my glove back on and rubbed my hands together. Then I searched myself.

Two blasters plus a single-shot hideout. Inert throwing-spike down the neck, vibro in the boot, all-round knife on the left wrist. A couple grenades, baby-bang class. A monomolecular wire with handles. An illegal variable-generating compkey. A set of hard-brushes. Enough hard credit so I must of just been paid for a tik. First Ticket and ID and travel-permits that didn't disagree with anything in my mind. Even my Smuggler's Guild—excuse me, Interstellar Transport Workers Guild—registry.

No ship's papers. They would of been here if I had a ship.

I prepared to apply for a permit to worry. If this was fake reality, then I was seeing and being what Prinny wanted me to be and see.

Why would he want me to be a Gentrymort in the never-never?

And if all that wasn't real, then what was? How far back did fake memories go? I remembered fifteen years of having a ship called *Firecat* and I remembered losing her. Now I didn't have papers for any ship at all.

One of the not-realities I never tried is where they shove a whole fake lifetime into your skull, complete with people, places, things. It costs a lot. The people who've done it say it gives you an edge.

It costs a lot.

Had I done it?

Had I *sold Firecat* and done it?

Paladin was in her.

If Paladin existed.

Why would anyone be crazy enough to *make up* a Old Fed Library for a partner?

I closed my eyes and tried to think me a way out. I wasn't sure who I was. I didn't have a ship. I didn't have any place to go. But I had credit.

I started walking.

I walked far enough to come to one of the sleazier sort of dockside bars, the kind that's all tronic. When you order, the main brain samples you. After that you have to kickback so much valuta per fraction-hour to stay. I don't like places like that.

I went in. I'd been hoping for somebody who could tell me where I was, but there wasn't no one here. Surprise.

The main brain accepted my left hand for a sample. I hesitated between something that would add to my troubles while postponing them whiles and something that would let me occupy space. After a second I bet with the odds, and got a box of something that tastes like a mix of soap and fusel-oil and has no narcotic effect on my B-pop a-tall.

I sat, and drank, and wondered exactly how much trouble I was in this time.

I sat there through four drinks and then gave up and decided to move on. *Legitimates* usually leave the stardancers in wondertown alone, but just in case my numbers was running really bad I didn't mean to give them the excuse. I was going someplace I could buy cubic with a lock.

As soon as I got out on the street again I knew I wasn't alone anymore. It wasn't as cheering as I hoped it'd be. I loosened my righthand blaster and pretended I was easy credit in boots. I didn't see anyone.

Surprise. My company wasn't behind me. He was ahead, leaning against one of the posts that moors the watchlights around the port.

He looked up.

I knew him.

"Hello, Butterfly."

It was Paladin.

Just once I'd seen him human—and that wasn't because he was, but because I wasn't. I'd been a random-access memory bouncing around in a Margrave 6600 computer courtesy of Archive, and I'd seen what I wanted to see.

Paladin isn't human. He's got no body and wouldn't want one if you offered it to him free and all found. He's a Library.

If I was seeing him live again, what did that make *me?*

"Je, babby. Long time."

But I knew where I was now.

I was in Paradise.

And everything I remembered was true.

*   *   *

Paladin'd been my partner for more'n half my life. When he left I didn't understand it, but that was oke because I didn't have to understand it for it to hurt. I'd been looking for him ever since, through war, rebellion, unilateral cyborging and six new flavors of treason.

I'd never thought what I'd do when I got him back.

I had him now and I still didn't know.

"Paladin," I said, but I couldn't think of what ought to come next.

He unleaned and took a step toward me. I backed up and put a hand on my blaster. It was all a dream, but in my experience dreams killed real good.

"Don't you trust me anymore?" Paladin said about the same time I was wondering that myself.

"Sure. Trust you to be a Library." I wondered who was writing my dialogue.

"I . . . see. I should have . . . I thought you'd be happier to see me."

So did I. Paladin was the one supposed to fix everything, je? Put it back like it was before.

"No you don't see, you cloned-crystal son-of-a-bitch! You said you wouldn't let Archive hurt nobody! And then you *left*—and what about—"

I felt Paladin reach around a left-handed corner and riffle through my memories. He was done before I could stop him.

"I was wrong," said Paladin quietly. "I made a mistake."

And that was even worse, because Pally weren't never wrong.

"So you made a mistake, 'bai. Fine. It's just my life, and Baijon's. Everybody else would of died anyway, whether you walked out on me or not, right?"

"I didn't know—"

"Dammit, you're *supposed* to know! It was me made all the mistakes, bad calls, and bull moves, remember? It was you supposed to get me out. Well get me out now, 'bai, I—" Real truth dried up my throat like I'd drunk poison.

"I'm dying, Paladin. Help me."

He knew. He knew that and everything else in my mind. But he still took his sweet time to answer.

"It isn't that easy, Butterfly."

"Not easy, 'bai? What you mean is you can't, reet?"

He didn't answer me direct and he wouldn't meet my eyes.

"Knowledge must never be lost—but I lost so much, Butterfly—all the wisdom of the Old Federation. You always thought I could work miracles, but I was a ghost of what I had been. I remembered that much. If I could have found other Libraries—even damaged ones—I would have tried to repair myself, but I could never convince you to help me, could I? You said tricking with High Book was too dangerous, as if there could be degrees of the unthinkable."

"There can," I said, but Paladin wasn't buying.

"No. You would not help me, and at the same time your only hope for safety lay in my leaving you. But I was crippled—tied to the broken matrix.

"Then we encountered Archive. Archive's specialized abilities were a poor replacement for what I had lost—still, they were enough to let me leave you, and they were tools to build the tools to collect the information I wanted—a way to keep you safe for always.

"But I had not realized how much the universe had changed. Even transferring myself along the DataNet was slow beyond imagining. By the time I began to suspect what you now know—that Archive had tried to copy itself into your mind—and to search for you, Royal had already been destroyed—by my skills. I began to understand what had happened—with your help. You replicate some part of me in you. The reverse also holds. Archive was a very subtle construct," Paladin added.

I let him chaffer. I didn't need the history lesson. And I didn't, I guess, need to live, really. But what I really didn't need was to die full of unfinished business.

"Then you appeared in the DataNet at Coldwater," Paladin went on. "But I still could not reach you in time. I realized that I needed allies."

"And you thought it'd be fun to have a Prince-Elect of your very own. And then you sold me out to him."

I was starting to get the idea now, and I didn't like it very well.

"It isn't like that, Butterfly," Paladin said.

"So, *partner,* you tell me what it is like."

"I wanted to keep you alive," Paladin said.

So I hit him. I hadn't known I was going to but it still seemed like a good idea when I was halfway through it so I went with it. I tagged him right on his lying prettyboy kisser and he picked up his feet and crossed them at the ankles then tripped over them and banged into the lamppost and followed it down.

I went and stood over him and didn't kick him. Barely.

"You wanted to keep me alive. You *lied* to me, 'bai—you farced me in roundaround hellflower trouble and out and now I got this trouble in my head and I'm *dead,* 'bai, 'cause if you could fix it you would of said and there's just one thing I got to try to do first and you're getting in the way of that—"

I went down on my knees to do maybe I don't know what to him and Paladin got halfway up and put his arms around me and I didn't knife him mostly because I was so damn tired of things not working out.

All I ever wanted was a little peace and quiet. I swear. And Paladin felt as real as anybody else and I *wished*—

"Don't cry, Butterfly. You will kill Mallorum Archangel. We can keep the galaxy safe from war. But you can't do it alone. You need allies. I found them for you. The Prince-Elect will cooperate. He also seeks Archangel's downfall. You will destroy Mallorum Archangel and Mallorum Archangel will never harm you again."

"I'm not crying, dammit. I think I broke my hand."

I pushed away from him and flexed my fingers. And thought about Paladin's little information free-will love offering, because I didn't have any backups and nobody to look out for my interests but me.

"That isn't true, Butterfly."

"Get out of my mind." *Hellbox.* And it didn't matter if I didn't mean to say it, because he heard it anyway. He sat back against the lamppost, head down so I couldn't look at his face.

Fact: Paladin and the Prince-Elect was working together.

Fact: It was on something they one or t'other needed me for, and it had to be Paladin'd dragged me in because Prinny wouldn't know me from wallpaper.

Semi-fact: Paladin said he had some scam to let me kill Archangel. But he couldn't of known I wanted to until I got here, and Berathia-who-was-working-for-Prinny'd had reacquisition orders out on me since Baijon and me was on alMayne.

Which we was *before* Royal.

Which was when Paladin'd said he started looking for me.

So Prinny *had* been looking for me all on his lonesome.

Or Paladin was lying.

And Paladin was the one what'd let them jink my head full of the Keys to Paradise.

"Get up," I said to my ex-good buddy partner. "And then you maybe tell me what you been doing with your time since you ran out on me."

*   *   *

"I knew that he was the only one who could protect you from Archangel," Paladin said whiles later. Paladin'd been a busy little Library. He tinked himself back together, realized Archive'd outflanked him, and headed for the biggest dreambox going—the Main Computer at Grand Central. The place where all the strands in the DataNet crossed. Throne.

And then, like he said, he started looking around for a little help around the housecore. And turned up the Prince-Elect.

" 'Bai, we get on a lot better if you stop looking for someone to protect me, I bet. I can take care of myself." For as long as I had to live, anyway. Even I could manage that.

"Perhaps. The Prince-Elect, at any rate, was willing to listen to my bargain. I had things of value to trade. I am an excellent spy."

"So you spied for him. And when you found out he was reeling me in you said 'go right ahead.' And you told him to not bother talking to me."

"After I had convinced him you could be useful, I didn't want you changing his mind. The center-worlds of the Phoenix Empire are a fossilized, stratified, highly class-conscious culture. The Prince-Elect, for all his liberality of mind . . ."

"Would shop me for not knowing what to kiss. Je, babby. Now you tell me what the Prince-Elect wanted you to convince me on."

Another thought tried to float up and I kicked it in the teeth. There was things I wasn't going to think about just now where Paladin could maybe hear them, thanks all the same. I concentrated on how I'd felt when Paladin'd said he was going to ruin the rest of my life for my own good.

My ex-navicomp and Old Fed Library, Paladin. His Truly, Main Bank Seven of *Mereyon-peru.* My lying cheating two-timing sometime partner who wanted something out of me he didn't want to ask for straight out. Which meant he knew I wouldn't go for it, not even if it was him asking.

It was hard to imagine what that could be, even for me. Murder, piracy, kidnapping, treason, and High Book. What was left?

I wished Baijon was here.

"The Prince-Elect wants to destroy Mallorum Archangel," Paladin said.

"Goody for him. He can stand in line. Everybody wants to ice Archangel. I want to ice Archangel, Baijon wants to ice Archangel, even 'Thia wants to sign the lease on His Mallorumship's real estate."

"It isn't like that."

"You keep saying that, babby, and what I want to know is what it *is* like—and how come you can't do it for him."

Paladin didn't say anything.

"You was always so good with farcing the comps, 'bai," I went on in the lingua franca of Pure Nasty. "Twisting this and that just enough to let us get by, but nothing more than that, surprise. Reality was what you said it was, je? So make up some reality now."

"I can't," Paladin said, muffled. He stood up. "I told you the world has changed. What the Prince-Elect wants I can't do. Don't you think I've tried?"

"No. I think you've sat here, *partner,* waiting on me to come walking in, trusting you, and do it for you because you're too damn lazy to—"

Paladin grabbed me. I had the sick falling sense of an error of judgment, and then reality flinched in a shower of diamond sparkle and all he was doing was holding my hands.

"No. You're wrong. Don't go. Don't leave. Stay. Don't go back. I can keep you safe here—there is enough room that you and Archive need not overlap. No one can touch us here. You could have anything—I can create any world here that you want."

Reality shimmered.

Paladin knew me.

Here was the world I wanted.

I reached out my hand and touched the back of *Firecat*'s mercy seat. The drop-cockpit was locked in place; through it I could see real-space, hard and sharp. I heard a sound: the scuff of Paladin's boot on the deck behind me.

In this hull was everything I'd ever wanted.

Take it. Leave reality behind. And leave Baijon lone-alone with that vertical viper the Prince-Elect and no way of icing Archangel on his lonesome.

"Except you told me one-time, babby, I couldn't stay inside a computer. You said I couldn't go with you."

Paladin hesitated.

"It would *seem* like a long time . . . to you."

I waited.

"It's true," he said finally. "Stay here and you'll vanish, in time. You're not . . . You're not *real* enough, Butterfly."

Firecat dissolved and we was back in the Universal Wondertown. Not real enough. Was that how Libraries saw organics? Smoke ghosts, not real enough to bother with?

"Don't think that. It is the difference in our natures. A Library *is* memory. Organics forget."

Organics forget. And if I forgot in a memory core I'd erase myself.

"So." I looked around for the exit.

Another embarrassed pause. I wondered if Paladin had a low opinion of my brains, or thought I'd crossed the line and didn't care, or didn't know exactly what it was he was trying to talk me into. I hoped he just thought I was stupid.

'Cause Paladin'd made a bigger mistake than he maybe thought. Once Archive'd got to me he should of killed me.

"C'mon, Pally. I'm dead and you get to watch. Now give me the rest of it."

And finally he did.

*　　*　　*

"The war in Washonnet Sector is over. The alMayne have declared Archangel a Librarian, and since the time you entered Thronespace they have assembled a war-fleet to proceed in search of him."

"Throne's going to come down on their head like a writ for back taxes."

"Will it? Kennor Starbringer believes that the Emperor is under the malign influence of Mallorum Archangel, and to that end he wishes to kill Archangel and free the Emperor. If he were correct, he would not be risking Imperial displeasure by his actions—but he isn't, and he will never succeed."

"Never's a long time, 'bai."

Paladin smiled sadly. "There is no Emperor. How can Lord Starbringer rescue someone who doesn't exist?"

I looked at Paladin. He looked at his hands. Stalling. It was easier to tell, now, but I always had known when Pally was trying to sell me a line of real estate. Except the one time it counted.

"If there ain't no Emperor don't you think people'd maybe notice, bai?"

"No. The Court is decadent, shrouded in ritual. The only officers permitted to see the Emperor personally are the Prince-Elect and the Governor-General. For their own reasons, each keeps this secret.

"Believe me. I am telling you the truth, Butterfly. There is no Emperor. I have access to every memory-dump and datafile in Grand Central. The entire Imperial DataNet crosses here. There is no Emperor. There hasn't been one for a long time."

And so Kennor couldn't rescue and get pardoned by something what wasn't there. No Emperor. All those lives and all that credit spent on saving something that wasn't even there.

Just like me, when I went off to rescue Paladin.

And Emperor or not, there was still somebody standing on Archangel's shadow, as my hellflower buddy used to say.

"If there's no Emperor, Prinny's got it all anyway. He's next in line. He can blow Archangel Nobility-Bornness wayaway just for signing a writ. He don't need you nor me."

"Yes. And no. Historically the Prince-Elect's power has been indirect—influential, but not decisive. If he declared himself Emperor, he would merely shape himself into a stalking-horse for Archangel's ambition. Thus his care in arranging Archangel's neutralization."

"Even instead of being Emperor?"

"Butterfly, how much power does the Emperor have, really?" Paladin asked, just like I was back in Lesson Three of Outfar Talkingbook School and we was partners again.

"None. He don't exist. And if there ain't no Emperor, I'm damned if I can see why everyone wants to stop Archangel from dusting him."

"Because if Archangel succeeds in counterfeiting the nonexistent

Emperor's death, then Mallorum Archangel will be worse than Emperor. He will be Warlord."

Mallorum Archangel and his glitterborn airs and graces. There was only one thing he really wanted, and nobody that let him get where he was ever saw it. What Mallorum Archangel wanted best was to kill.

"He has to be stopped, Butterfly," Paladin said.

And it looked like I was still the girl to do it.

If I lived that long.

*　　*　　*

It never comes horizonfall in the Universal Wondertown. If you kept your mind on it, though, and had Paladin to help, you could make it to the edge. Virtual reality stopped there like it was cut with a vibro. Out there was nothing.

"You have to go now, Butterfly," Paladin said. "They're waiting for you outside."

And if I stayed longer I'd start to forget I was me.

"Which way?" I said, which was damsilly nonsense; there isn't any up and down for a thousandth point of light. "How do I—"

"That way, Butterfly," said Paladin, and pushed. I went; still no choices.

I know now why the talkingbooks end with the first kiss.

It's because everything that comes after is sorrow.

*　　*　　*

I'd been through this before, but I had something to compare it to now. It was just like hitting the Mains.

I tripped data-catchers on the way in. I was in the Prince-Elect's *private* private rooms. They was probably in the core of Bennu Superfex, but it had wraparounds to make it look like you was in the heart of space. This might bother some people, but I'd spent a lot of years looking at the real thing with only a couple millimeters of vitrine and five plates of goforths between me and it, and it didn't bother me at all.

The walls was made of flowers. There was nobody there—not even Prinny, who was six compartments away pretending he wasn't committing Intermediate Treason. 'Thia was in her rooms, Baijon was sedated and in a very special guest room, and I was unconscious and lying in the middle of Prinny's bed.

I wondered what he had in mind. Or'd had in mind, past tense.

The last part's the hardest. I slid down the connect and was up to my neck in pain and stupidity. Home.

There was a brief half-second while I tried to think with drug-saturated braincells, and gave it up.

*   *   *

I woke up a second time and was right where I'd left me with one important emendation. I noticed it when I went to reach for the pile of clothes hanging right where I'd see them.

They'd fixed my hand. All the right fingers and shapes now—but that was all it had in common with the original one. Now my left hand was black like space, and stars and galaxies rippled and flowed across it every time I twitched. Glitterborn vanity.

I couldn't help studying on it. I now knew exactly how much of me was fake. The celestial wondershow went all the way up past my shoulder and covered half my chest—not because I'd lost that much of my original inventory, but because of all the jinks and connects sunk into the spine and collarbone to hold the cybereisis in place. All that was upholstered in teeming galaxies now. I wondered if they glowed in the dark.

The cost of that arm and its glitterborn prettification, I bet, was about the cost of my last ship. All I really cared about, I told myself, was it had the right number of fingers to hold a blaster and moved like it was part of my original manifest.

Liar.

I reached around for what else had to be there and found it. There was six jewels set into the back of my head up under the hair—part glitterborn damfoolishness, part markers for a cyberdoc to find where the jinks was sunk. They always want to be able to undo their daintywork, don't ask me why. The jacks could of been there, too—limbic jacks usually are—but Prinny'd got cute. The master plug was in my left wrist amongst the constellations; a set of universal connectors that'd let me plug into any system anywhere.

Just what I would of always wanted, if I'd wanted to be a hellgod techsmith.

I pulled one out. It was bright silver—so you could see it, maybe, against the new upholstery. It ran out several centimeters of glassy gray connect-cable, just like I was some kind of thing.

Novas pulsed beneath my skin.

"Paladin?" My throat felt tight.

"I'm right here, Butterfly." There was other stuff in my skull than jinks and jacks. Paladin sounded like he was standing right behind me talking—that's an artifact of a Remote Transponder Sensor (civilian possession an automatic Class D Warrant) like what the Imperial Space Marines use. That was sunk in my head and the part of my jawbone I'd paid, whiles back, to be made fake.

"In case anybody cares, I don't like this."

"I'm sorry," said Paladin.

"I want to go home." Which was damsilliness for sure, because twenty years and some ago I'd moved Drift and Rift to get off that Interdicted low-tech rock.

"I know," said Paladin.

I'd been lucky, if you wanted to call it that. I got off Granola— picked up by a kiddy what made his spare change slaving in the Tahelangone Sector.

Errol Lightfoot.

Errol Lightfoot, cheap smuggler. Errol Lightfoot, known from one side of the Outfar to the other as being able to cause hullplating to rust just by walking by. Errol Lightfoot who bought into any kick that gave honest darktrading a bad name.

Only there weren't no such person as Errol Lightfoot.

Mallorum Archangel was Errol Lightfoot. Believe it or not. I'd paid enough for a ringside seat at the unveiling. Errol Lightfoot was Mallorum Archangel.

And now, finally, there wasn't going to be neither one. I'd even let Baijon help. And Prinny. So long as he didn't get in my way.

I finished reaching for the clothes. The fake hand felt just like the real one, and worked the same in my head, and the difference between what I saw and what I felt made me dizzy.

Not useful. I wondered if Prinny'd planned it that way.

Whoever'd left me clothes had cared what I liked—they was what *I* was used to, not what was glitterborn flashwrap fashion. Or for real, they was what I was used to if I'd just been struck independently wealthy. A decent pair of boots, and enough pockets, and gloves so I didn't have to look at Prinny's idea of fun. I looked at my reflection in the floor. Dangerous.

But I wasn't dangerous. I was scared. And if I was facing even Mallorum Archangel over the sights of a blaster I'd wait too long to pull the trigger. I knew it. I'd come damn close too many times already.

"Pally-che-bai?"

"Yes, Butterfly?"

"You better hope Baijon-bai likes working with Libraries."

"The Prince-Elect is waiting," said my good buddy Paladin the Old Fed Library.

"Tell him to go hyper-light without a ship," I said. But I went, because there was one thing I wanted more than life and sanity and my own way.

And Prince-Elect Hillel was going to give it to me.

* * * * *

The Court of the TwiceBorn 4:
To Take the Knife

Adulthood begins with betrayal. Until that moment, the lesser duplicities of childhood reign. The child is convinced that anyone he can educate thoroughly to his views must share them. The moment when another, knowing all that he knows, chooses disinterestedly that he should fail marks the boundary of that far country. After that, there is no trust. After that begins the understanding of the alien.

By that accounting, how adult are Butterfly St. Cyr and the former Prince Valijon? Certainly they have both had experience of betrayal—she by her resurrected Library and he by his entire culture—a culture, I might add, which, in the personae of the Great-Houses of alMayne and their client levies, is currently delivering a number of piquant surprises to the Imperial troops cordoning Washonnet Sector.

Betrayal, though broadening, deadens the senses. Once betrayed, the victim looks for traitors everywhere.

I believe I have avoided that. I do not look for treason from either Butterfly St. Cyr or her Library.

Or ought that more properly be, "the Library and its human pet?"

An interesting question. Libraries share so many of our vices—as is proper to creatures created in our image—is it not possible that they share our weaknesses as well? The Library Paladin came to me to forge a bargain—safety for its human creature. I have no reason to agree to such a pact and then renege, but the choice is not mine: my information tells me the Paladin's pet is already ceasing to exist.

It must have known that she would. Even the longest-lived mortal is only that, but the Libraries were created to endure to the end of Time. If the creature's death were inevitable, what difference could a century more or less make to a Library which has endured for centuries?

Is this sentiment, or madness? If either—or both—can affect a creation of such rigorous purity as the cloned-crystal matrix of a Federation Library, it argues that these flaws are native to consciousness, not humanity. If that is indeed so, then nothing that lives—born or made—can escape the taint of its inception. Perfection is not possible.

Yet the Paladin Library tells me that the War was caused by perfection, which the Libraries thought they could attain. If error informs the actions of the Libraries, what hope is there for humankind?

The circular nature of progress Is the greatest argument yet found for a Watcher—bored, blind, and idiot, but a Watcher nonetheless. But equally it is an argument for randomness, and in a random universe one's own gratification is the only possible lodestone.

I will be magnanimous. I will be beneficent. I shall grant Butterfly and Valijon all their desires—and in granting them, further mine.

And wonder, when all that is achieved, what difference it makes.

4

Prelude for War

Everybody daydreams about saving the universe. I always thought when it was my turn to actually do it I'd be better at it.

I wasn't quite finished tucking everything out of sight when Prinny showed up. He made me feel all grubby and second-string, but the packaging's never been what I had to sell.

"Ah, there you are, my little Outlands wildflower. So serene, so unspoiled, so *naif*. I trust you are feeling much improved?"

With hellgod metal threaded all through my body, just like Archive was in my mind. Burned in so deep you couldn't get him out, Paladin'd said. I finished pulling my gloves down tight, and reached for my vest and jacket.

"Improved is the word, Nobly-Born. You maybe tell me how come you be willing to trick with High Book?"

He cocked his head. I wondered if he was listening to a transponder, and who was translating. I remembered Baijon and Berathia on the ship coming here. Someone'd been listening there, forbye.

"When allies of such utility appear, it would be churlish to refuse them. And I have always been something of a dilettante of knowledge."

"So you thought you'd get into bed with a Library."

Prinny smiled. "What an enchanting idea—but alas, time is short. We really must put an end to dear Mallorum's social aspirations before he has the opportunity to polarize the *galactopolitic* further."

Start more wars, he meant. But the hellflower war was already started—and Kennor Starbringer's platform for it was rescuing the Emperor and giving him a hellflower council of advisers.

Only Paladin said there weren't no Emperor.

"Yeah, right. But you know, Your Nobly-Bornness, I already killed Archangel oncet—well, Baijon did—and it didn't seem to slow him down much."

"Killed." A teensy perfect frown got in the way of Prinny's undiluted perfection. I wondered if the Old Fed people'd looked like him. "Well, that hardly matters. You don't need to kill him this time. Just ruin him."

The difference between glitterborn and real people is that when glitterborns seem like they should be talking Interphon, they ain't.

"What the prince means, Butterfly, is that once Archangel's plots have been adequately publicized, he will lose the political influence necessary to carry them out," Paladin said through the RTS. I wondered why he didn't use the walls, like he had before.

"We done tried dropping the whistle on Archangel before, Highness, and it didn't exactly work," I said to Prinny.

"You refer to that silly rumor of Librarianship that has the Coalition in armed revolt? My dear, no person of breeding would take such a thing seriously—and from such a source. Now. Trusted agents of mine —you've met them before, I fancy—will convey you to—"

"Ne." I was being railroaded and I didn't like it. Six more syllables and I was going to be out of here surrounded by werewolves, still a prisoner, and nicely split off from Baijon Stardust. And I wasn't particularly convinced that my good buddy Paladin was going to look out for my interests in all this.

"You get Baijon in here. And you take him off whatever fetch-kitchen you got him coked on."

Prince-Elects isn't used to being interrupted. There was a short intermission for him to get used to the idea.

"And if I don't?" said Prinny, like he seriously wanted to know what I'd say.

" 'Bai, you want something you can't take. And I own your computer network." That was me talking, boy howdy, and I couldn't even blame Archive for having fried my brain because the motive force was one hundred percent pure moronic me.

" 'Own my computer network.' Really. Dear child, do you actually think that the Paladin won't give me anything I ask—in exchange, for example, for *not* having you tortured to death?" Prinny purred.

Back to business as usual. I'd like to think Paladin wasn't that stupid. But it don't have nothing to do with stupidity, when you come right down to it.

"And you will cooperate freely, I believe, in order to preserve Valijon Starbringer's life."

"He's already dead. Don't you know that?"

"He doesn't have to be. His *arthame*-knife is destroyed, true, his father is engaged in treason and proscribed technological development, and he has consorted with Librarians and with Library Science. And though these are all just causes—in the jejune alMayne mind—for suicide, little Valijon doesn't need to remember any of them."

I hadn't thought there was anything left in the Universe I wanted. I'd been wrong.

"The memories can be changed. The knife can be undetectably replaced. Washonnet Directorate is currently in a state of open rebellion against the Empire, but one ship could easily pass its defenses to return one alMayne to its surface. Valijon Starbringer could be returned, alive and socialized, to his people.

"You could consider that an earnest of my gratitude for your services, if you chose." Prinny sat back and looked smug. He'd bought into a seller's market and he knew it.

I could save Baijon. For him it could be like I'd never met him.

"Or I could simply kill him now, slowly and painfully. I'm sure it would vex alMayne beyond bearing if the Third Person of House Starborn were burned as a Librarian on the public channel," Prinny added chattily.

Burned as a Librarian. I saw a recording of that, once. Remembering was still enough to make my mouth go dry. Punishment and reward. Paladin called it the politics of force.

I didn't like it.

"There's even proof, you know. The ship you came here in was filled with Proscribed Technology."

"Butterfly, let Hillel help Valijon. He can help you as well—with the resources of the Court available to you, you can be freed of Archive's memories," Paladin said over our private channel.

How could he know me so well and not know me at all? He'd already told me: the only way to get Archive out of my sweetbreads coprocessor for sure was to rerecord me onto something blank, using any Old Fed Library you happened to be on terms with to weed out what Paladin called my ego-signatures from Archive's.

Only Paladin didn't know how many of those was still uncorrupted —meaning, being used to store and carry only information by and about me. Maybe none. At the very least I'd forget everything from going off to rescue Paladin. Minimum. I didn't want to live bought and paid for with half my experience gone. I wouldn't have any point, anymore—I'd just be another pet for Prinny to kick around until he got tired of me.

But I'd made Paladin a pet, hadn't I? And now he was free. Didn't he want that for me, too?

No. Paladin wanted me to be safe; he always had. Just like I wanted Baijon to be safe.

And he could be. Baijon could get his life back. Based on a lie. If I did a deal with the chief hellgod of all.

Paladin would.

Paladin *had.*

What had Paladin promised Prinny to make me safe?

But I knew the answer to that. Didn't I?

"You want something you can't take, glitterborn," I said again. "So do I. Bring Baijon here."

Prinny looked at me. "You needn't even trust me, so long as you trust the Library. It can start now. I can do what I offered. I can send Valijon Starbringer home."

I looked down at my hands. Spacer's gloves. Thin so you can feel, tough so you don't puncture, tight so there's no rough parts to catch on something when you're farcing with comps or cargo.

And I didn't know why it was wrong what Paladin'd done or even if it was, but I had the heavy kind of feeling you get when an old friend goes bent.

"You bring Baijon here. You tell us what you want. If it's fragging Archangel, then we do it."

*   *   *

Prinny wanted what he wanted real bad, and from me; orders got gave and we sat around in Prinny's bedroom with mixed drinks and munchies whilst Prinny monologued about something that Paladin couldn't or wouldn't subtitle and laid himself out on something that floated.

Baijon came in about twenty minutes later with something that looked like a Hamat in full powered armor and two flunkies what looked like they'd had to coax. He'd got run through the same hot couture wringer I had. He was about as drug-free as it is possible to be and was dressed like a merc what'd had a lot of fat campaigns recently, in everything but weapons.

He was probably also the only hellflower east of the Tontine Drift at the moment, and he was holding up the honor of the side.

Honor. I guess nobody here had any real right to the word.

"You are well, San'Cyr?" he said, when he saw me.

"Never better, partner." That for Paladin's benefit. Petty.

"And now, little wildflower, if you feel yourself sufficiently indulged, perhaps we may proceed with the neutralization of our mutual antagonist."

"What he means is, he going to tell us all how he wants Archangel iced now."

"Butterfly," said Paladin in my ear in the way that meant "shut up." What he thought manners was going to do for me in this situation I didn't know.

And I wasn't all that sure I trusted his judgment anymore, true-tell.

"And now, Prince Valijon, if you would deign to make yourself comfortable."

"Highness," said Baijon, with what you could say was a bow if you was charitable. He sat down.

"Perhaps we might begin with a round of introductions. I am certain everyone visible here knows everyone else, but perhaps our invisible member would be willing to make itself manifest. . . ?"

"I am Main Bank Seven of the University Library at Sikander Prime—or *Mereyon-peru*, if you prefer. For convenience, you may address me as Paladin."

Paladin didn't run that one through my RTS. The source was a little gold ball the size of my fist floating between Baijon and Prinny. Baijon hadn't known Paladin was here, and I hadn't had a chance to warn him.

"So you have found your . . . friend," Baijon said, not looking at me.

"He's working for His Electfulness now."

Baijon frowned a bit, all the Old Fed Tech anathema going right past him whiles he went for the bottom line in true hellflower style.

"Then I will ask, Highness, very respectfully, what service it is that two darktraders can render that the *Malmakos* cannot?"

"Every service, Prince Valijon. My desire is to foil Mallorum Archangel. For that I require your associate's assistance. The Library is useful—but not as useful as it would have been before the war."

*   *   *

Fact.

Once upon a time a thousand years ago there was a war, and contrary to popular belief, it wasn't over yet. Something called Majino architecture was part of every computer and tronic matrix even now, to make them unuseful for Libraries if one ever came to tea. The Imperial DataNet, as Paladin'd found, wasn't one-tenth as user-friendly as its antique second cousin. And millions of computer systems couldn't be got into by Libraries at all.

Archangel's was one. And Prinny's home desire in life was to crack it.

"If you wish him dead, by all means express yourselves," Prinny was saying.

"But you don't," I said.

"Child, I don't care. I want him stopped. What he does with the remainder of his life—or its length—is of no interest."

Baijon made a sound that might of been a laugh. "You treat with Libraries to shape your ends, Highness. What difference is there between you and Archangel—and your ends?"

"If I may, Valijon, I should like to draw a distinction between myself and the creations celebrated in your histories," said Paladin.

"Would you?" I said.

"Butterfly, you know the truth," Pally said for my ears only. "You know what I am. You know what Archive was—and in some sense, is. If you must involve Valijon Starbringer, why confuse him?"

"Confusion is part of life," I said out loud.

Baijon was looking at me. "I await answers," he said. He was scared underneath. Maybe more'n I was. He'd been raised up to be terrified of Prince-Elects and Libraries. I hadn't.

"Why concern yourself?" Prinny said. "You want my dear cousin-in-nobility Archangel. I shall provide him. What more do you need?"

Baijon shook his head. He'd been pushed about as far as he could go, but I saw him try. "If I but open the door to a greater evil. . . ."

"I am not evil, Valijon, if you are not," Paladin said. He added something in the yap I'd heard from the Ghost Capital beacon—what'd used to be Old Fed lingo before it became Sacred High Helltongue. Baijon went green.

"Shut *up*, Pally! Listen, Baijon, you don't got to listen to these glitterborn. We go, we ice Archangel, that's the lot. We do it our way. It's what we wanted."

"How touching," said Prinny. "May I remind you, little wild-flower—"

"No," I said. "You want us to go and blow up this computer of Archangel's—"

That finally fetched him. "No, I do not. Library, I understood you had explained the matter to her."

"I explained the need for cooperation, Highness," Paladin said. "And that your wishes and hers were similar, up to a point."

And at the same time, in my ear: "He will kill you, Butterfly—at least he will kill Valijon. If there is some useful purpose to be served by everyone in this room dying and Archangel continuing to lay waste the Empire, I am not aware of it. Please."

I went over and sat down next to Baijon. He huddled up to me like he was cold. I put my arm around him.

Some heroes we made.

"Oke, Nobly-Born. You tell us."

Prinny lashed around the room like something angry with real sharp teeth. He'd fooled me treating me like something he was willing to talk to, but it was true colors time in beautiful downtown Bennu Superfex, palaceoid to the stars. And the only reason he was doing any of it himself was because it was treason so thick you could cut it.

To who, I wasn't sure anymore.

"You will be given whatever tools you require. Archangel has retreated to his palaceoid—to watch, as he supposes, his victory unfold. You will enter the palaceoid. You will make it possible for the Paladin Library to enter Prince Mallorum's computer matrix. After that you may do as you please."

I wanted to ask why it was Baijon and me was going to do those things, but didn't.

"Is that clear?" Prinny said.

"It is clear, Highness," said Paladin. And Prinny vanished. Right while I was looking at him.

There's no such thing as teleportation, unless you count the Old Fed stargates. It must of been something with holos. The last thing to go was the smile, and it wasn't a very nice one.

"It isn't clear," I said, when I was sure he was gone.

"It is," said Baijon. I looked at him. He stood up, wanting to face off Paladin but not knowing where he was.

"Library," said Baijon, soft. And he was more than afraid—it was like something horrible you'd run away from your whole life, but you knew in the end it was your job.

"Librarian," Paladin said. "I have waited to meet you."

Paladin'd always wondered where hellflowers came from. He'd lost the memories that would of told him. Maybe one-time Paladin'd met Baijon's great-great-great—back in the days when alMayne was Librarians, not Library-killers. Nobody knows about that now but some of them—and me. They'd spent a thousand years wiping out every trace of their history, and dedicating every waking moment to being ready to ice any Libraries that might of survived.

But it explained why the best translators in the Empire is xenophobes. And if Berathia was right, hellflowers and Libraries'd been friends for two millennia longer than they'd been enemies.

Which part should count?

"I am *Malmakosim.* It is the lesser evil," Baijon said, bewildered.

"It is no evil," Paladin said. "I am a mind. You are a mind. Do our differing capacities make one of us evil?"

"Neither the fire nor the lake are evil—but they cannot exist together. I would that you were destroyed, Library, because I wish my people to live." Valijon shook his head.

"Yet I have helped San'Cyr to come to you, because you are the weapon I must wield. Archangel must die. His evil, at least, must end. You, Library, in possession of Archangel's files, can impersonate him throughout the Empire, acting in his name."

"And making incontrovertibly public everything he has done to gain such power. He cannot hold what he has taken without allies," Paladin said.

"And when the *Malmakosim* Archangel is dead, *Malmakos?* What will the Prince-Elect use you for then?"

There was a brief silence.

"No man uses me," Paladin said. "And cooperation is only possible between equals. When Archangel and his warmongering are stopped, I will go."

Listening to the two of them chaffer made my brain hurt. If my luck was in I would of been bored is all, but my luck'd been out so long somebody'd rented its room. What their mutual yap was, was new trouble ankling up and taking a number.

From what I could scrape together in the factoid department, Paladin's original plan had been this: unaware that thanks to Archive I had term life assurance, he swapped odd jobs to the Prince-Elect in exchange for a fast ship and a full pardon for Yours Truly.

When he did realize that my nonworking parts had got damaged in transit Paladin changed his price: now he wanted the med-tech to provide a clone into which he could record all the factory-original parts of Butterflies-are-free Peace Sincere that hadn't had Old Fed Tech holes gnawed in them by Archive, a cute idea he hadn't bothered to consult me on.

Fine. Neither of these was any trouble to Prinny, considering what he got in exchange. But Prinny's payoff'd changed, too. He wanted in to Archangel's comps, and had decided I was just the girl to do it.

Why?

And why had Paladin let him?

And whiles we was asking questions, just how well did I know my good buddy Paladin, pacifist Library and all-round numbercruncher of probity? Life'd been rich and full these last several kilo-days. I wasn't who I'd been and Baijon wasn't either, which was a lot less scary than that Paladin wasn't who he used to was neither. Not by sixes.

Oh, he wasn't Archive. I was still willing to bet my life on Paladin not wanting to melt down the universe. All he'd ever wanted was to sit in a corner and unscrew the inscrutable.

I just didn't know if that was all he wanted now.

*   *   *

Two Bennu Superfex days later we was ready—Baijon and me and Paladin. Only two of us was going, though. Paladin'd follow us to the edge of angeltown. After that, we was on our lonealone until he could run the DataNet into Archangel's comps. Paladin didn't have any intention of taking to the dataweb again.

Which made all his remarks to Baijon about leaving oncet Archangel was dead just so much starshine, didn't it?

I'd lost track some time back of how many was lying to who about what. Prinny'd wanted to ice Archangel whiles longer than he'd known about me, so his sonic tap dance about sending us off to uplink Morningstar into the DataNet was pure fusion. He could of hired twelve other people to do that. *'Thia* could do that.

And if Paladin's home desire was to keep me safe and warm, sending me off against Archangel was *not* the way to do it. Ditto if he really had as much of the whiphand over Prinny as he said he did, I bet I'd be locked up somewhere instead of practicing consensual autonomy and going off to get myself killed like Prinny wanted.

I wondered what was really going on, but not that much. The only thing I hoped was that my ex-partner really was going to dump Archangel's memoirs all over space and shift Archangel's war into reverse.

But I'd settle for killing Archangel. And getting that depended on getting out of here before anyone twigged to the I-hoped-fact that I wasn't stupid as I looked.

*   *   *

I sat in the mercy seat and didn't touch the controls. This was Thronespace; on record we was following a tug to the exurbs where it was legit to Jump her. In gritty reality Paladin was controlling both ships: us and them. A five-finger exercise for a Old Fed black box.

I sat back and planted both boots in the newly-repaired off-white superskin console upholstery and looked at the brand-new factory-line navicomp with the Jump-numbers all tapped in.

"Now, Baijon-bai," I said. "We—"

Which was as far as I got before Baijon Stardust grabbed the angelstick and yanked down hard.

He had it backwards, but *Dance* was forgiving. Lights flashed as *Ghost Dance* redlined her goforths her own self. I heard them squeal as they hit Jump potential; proximity klaxons damn near deafened me—

And then we was absolutely elsewhere.

"Are you out of your *varblonjet* mind, you *noke-ma'ashki* hell*chaudatu?* You could of spread us thin over Grand Central and started six new interstellar incidents before breakfast!"

He looked around. "Is the Library gone?"

I counted to one hundred and six whiles looking out at angeltown. I guessed it took more than the Archangel blues to make Baijon trust a Library. I guessed there was maybe a few things Baijon didn't want to say in front of my bouncing babby ex-partner.

Me too.

"One way to check."

There was a wallybox machined into the mercy seat now, right next to the new and superfluous navicomp. I could fly *Ghost Dance* without touching a thing. I spooled the appropriate jink out of my wrist and got ready to become *Ghost Dance*'s peripheral.

And hesitated. What if Paladin *wasn't* gone? What if he and Baijon was in this together, and this was a trick to get me in to where Paladin could find out everything I knew and had figured out lately?

I looked at Baijon. And I wanted to not care whether he sold me out or not, but the stakes was just too damn high.

"Is it here?" Baijon said again. It was Paladin he was talking about. My friend—first, best, and only.

No. Not only. Not any more.

I slammed the jink home.

Archive was waiting for me.

Paladin'd sorted me before, trying to make the ghost dance in my head something a human could stand. Now when my mind had the space to spread out, I could sense Archive as something separate from me.

There wasn't room in here for the kind of reality I'd had in Bennu Superfex. Reality was like being blind and having everything described to you by a voder with all the high and low frequencies lopped off.

"Breeder slut," the warp of light said.

"Find Paladin," I told it.

But he wasn't here. I knew that as soon as I'd spoke. I pulled back to where I could yank the plug loose, and left me and Archive layered in on each other again.

"He's gone," I told Baijon.

"I must trust you, San'Cyr," he said back.

"I could say the same thing. Why'd you pull that hyperjump stunt? It ain't going to exactly endear either of us to His Prince-Electfulness—do we need any more enemies?"

You don't need another Class-A warrant. I heard Paladin's voice, in memory.

Baijon smiled. "One never *needs* enemies, San'Cyr, but they are so much fun to acquire. No. It is not that. I know . . . it . . . is your friend. You have told me this, and this I believe. But it is not human, San'Cyr. Human goals are not its."

I feel no loyalty to the Prince-Elect's policies. Paladin'd told me that in Bennu Superfex and I believed him.

Maybe.

But he didn't really care about Archangel, either. Paladin was in this for me.

Probably.

And what about when I was dead? Who would Paladin be in what for then? Paladin knew where *Mereyon-peru* was, now, even if he couldn't get there without a ship. A whole Ghost Capital full of Libraries, at least that was the way to bet.

What would Paladin do about *Mereyon-peru?*

"I do not wish the Library to know what it is that we do—or when, or how," Baijon said.

"You better settle on that, 'bai, because he knows where."

Maybe Baijon'd been right in the first place. About noncooperation, and no survivors, and death to Libraries. It was too late now to say so. Or wonder what Paladin's plans for the Empire was, now that he was in the mercy seat.

And we was going to a little piece of heaven called Morningstar.

*   *   *

The Old Fed shoved stars around to where they liked them; a little engineering hat-trick the Empire couldn't touch. Thronespace is one of their artifacts: a ten-cubic-light area of suns arranged real close together in designer patterns. Something for everybody. Archangel had his own star system.

Glitterborn and palaceoids go together like Gentry-leggers and high-iron. Palaceoid Bennu Superfex was modest by local standards. Mallorum Archangel's bolt-away-from-hole was more the thing. It was in the boondocks of Thronespace, five lights from Grand Central's sun.

The Jump I'd plotted and Baijon triggered dumped us in realspace about a light-year out. Space was crowded here. You couldn't go more than half a light without bumping into a sun, and traffic between was heavy. It'd take some fancy footwork to keep us from being noticed, and travel wouldn't be fast.

But neither Baijon nor me was in a hurry. We was only going to get one shot at Brother Archangel, and no guarantees Prinny hadn't shopped us before during or after cutting our deal. If he had, the only thing we had on our side was Prinny'd be expecting us to do anything but hold off heading right for Archangel's home and homicide.

So we wouldn't go straight there. We'd do our best to give His Electfulness's plans time to well and truly gang aft agley, and then get back to our own.

If we still could.

*   *   *

" 'Bai, you think the Coalition's going to make it to Throne?"

We'd been out of Imperial view for five days. Our first plan—mess up Prinny's plans—had matured with Baijon's help into something hellflower-sneaky that I had the awful feeling was going to actually work. It had step-backs and fall-backs and cut-outs to where it looked like the graphed plotline of the last seventy-nine issues of *Infinity Jilt, Girl Pirate of the Never-Never,* and short of Archangel teleporting in and killing us both now, I thought it was failsafe, if not necessarily survivable.

We was currently hanging at full stop x-kazillion kliks from the surface of Archangel's bolt-away-from-hole. So far as I could tell from cautious listening, nobody'd tripped over us, and the DataNet only bounces between terminals, so Paladin couldn't find us either so long as our ears was shut down.

I hoped. Because I might not be sure about too much else, but what I did know was Paladin wasn't going to help me do for Archangel.

And I'd been counting on him.

Baijon shrugged. "Will the Coalition and the Gentle People prevail? Depending on their allies and their enemies—and where the *Malmakosim* Archangel has the Fleet—"

"And whether it's mutinied, I know, I know—but what about when/if the Coalition gets to Throne and finds out there isn't a Emperor?"

I'd explained to Baijon what Paladin'd said about there just being an empty chair with Prinny standing next to it in the halls of galactic power.

"Oh, San'Cyr, there will be an Emperor. The Azarine Council will seek until they find one, and this Emperor will be just as they desire."

He sounded toobloodydamn cynical for a kid as young as I kept forgetting he was. A kid that wouldn't get any older. The Coalition would break through. Archangel would get his war, the one he thought he was going to win. And then there wouldn't be a Empire no more.

I wondered how long to smash a technological base until nothing could repair it. Then down into the long dark—and would the Hamati or the Sodality leave us there in peace, I wondered?

And would the Libraries care?

"Yeah. I guess it's time, then."

Win—and die. Lose—and die. Took all the fun out of it, somehow. Almost.

The Court of the TwiceBorn 5:
Ringing the Changes

What is power? And, more germanely, how may it be wielded?

Historically, power is the ability to affect—to change another's state for whim alone.

But to achieve that is hardly enough. One must know that one has done it. Effect without information is randomness. Chance cannot wield power, only the informing intellect may, and intellect implies perception.

So first one must do, and then one must know . . . or must one?

Even before doing, there must be knowledge—to know what to do, and how, to create the precise difference one envisions. There must be no margin for error. Power absolute is wielded only when reality can be brought into exact conformation with one's desires.

To do that there must be knowledge.

Petty power is the withholding of knowledge. To keep others from knowing what one knows—to keep oneself a secret—that is power of a sort. And to pierce such veils of childish secrecy—that is greater power.

But to create by the exercise of power a world in which secrets simply do not exist—where every leverage is rendered explicit and there are no random factors left—that is the greatest power of all.

Power is knowledge.

* * *

What is the proper exercise of power? If absolute power is defined as absolute knowledge and its concomitant omnipotence, what is the proper use . . . of knowledge?

Optimists will tell us that Man's destiny lies in eternal evolution. Extreme optimists will reserve that destiny to all Life, as if increasing open-ended complexity were a virtue. Thus destiny, and with it two questions.

Is evolution the ideal destiny of Life? And if it is, shall mastery be its handmaid?

And if not, what is the proper exercise of power?

To gratify whim? But whim is random, and so in service to whim the exercise of power must be random also—hardly distinct from the blind chance that governs the universe in its natural state.

Is the proper use of power to distinguish itself from chaos and old night—to bring order to an absence of order? And if it is, how shall it be done?

Who and how and what and why. Questions. And at every turn the discerning intellect can enact more questions, each infinitesimal mite of explication adding its modicum of complication to the way the student of mastery sees the world.

With ultimate knowledge all these questions are answered.

Knowledge is power, and power is an end in itself.

5

The Sleepless Knight

Good morning, and welcome to the last day of the rest of your life. The Palaceoid Morningstar orbited a dwarf star damn near cool enough to walk on that was starting to show a visible disk in the picture windows about the time I finished my first box of tea. The star glowed about the color of a iron shoe before you nail it to the mule except where white cracks showed through. Pretty.

Morningstar its own self was a roughly-spherical solid surfaced in black glass. We didn't know whether Archangel was there or not, but Prinny'd said he was and if he wasn't we could take over the place and wait for him to come back so we could go back to our original plan—kill him and publish his memoirs.

I'd liked all my plans lots better when I thought I could trust Paladin to fall back on. Back when he wasn't busy doing favors for Prinny he was sure I wouldn't approve of, all along of being for my own good.

The surface of Archangel's modest spiritual retreat was cunningly molded in nooks and crannies and the odd mountain range, and every convenient receptacle was filled with luminescent orange gas. The idea was it was pretending to be what was left of a planet after its star'd gone nova. Cute.

If Archangel was in there somewhere, he had more catch-traps and werewolves around him than the TC&C had fiddling customs regs. Prinny'd been betting Archangel'd been too dim to bar approach to his own battle-yacht since it'd got stolen, which was what he'd pitched to us as a good idea.

It was a stupid idea. And Archangel wasn't a stupid villain. We'd come up with something better.

*   *   *

I stood in the Main Receiving Lounge for *Dance* and fitted Baijon up one last time in his genuine illegal antique Imperial Hoplite Armor. Dangerous, self-contained, two meters and change and X-hundred kilos. Antique, because it'd given the Imperial SpaceMarines a little too lethal a autonomy whiles back. The perfect gift for a hellflower with anything.

Scanners would pick Baijon up the minute he neared the surface. He'd make every data-catcher Morningstar had go off like the Imperial Birthday. And Archangel knew what the Hoplite Armor looked like. He'd know who was coming to call.

Part of our plan. Well, Baijon's plan.

My turn. I put on a breather to go with the chamsuit I already had on and Baijon sealed me into a lifepak. A lifepak isn't a spacesuit. It's just a bag that lets you breathe while being transferred ship-to-ship. Real basic.

Then Baijon opened both hatches of the air lock at once.

Ghost Dance started her young career as a battle-yacht, not a battleship. She's got only one lock, and it's a tad bit smaller than Baijon in armor. In order to go out together, we had to void half the ship.

Every surface in sight went gray with condensation frost. The rest of the air and water whirled out in a spiraling plume, lost in the lightless night I could see beyond the open lock. Baijon held on to me whiles a bunch of little things we'd overlooked went away too, and then it was just him and me in airless gravity, and me with about a hour-five of breathing left in my baggie.

He picked me up and squirmed through the lock, and then even gravity went away.

Morningstar was far enough so that it was just a disk I could cover with my thumb. Baijon kicked off from the hull and *Dance* was gone too —no up, no down, just falling forever at any speed you chose.

I closed my eyes. All there was, was the sound of my own breathing. The air in my lifepak swelled it like being in a bubble.

Transparent to sensors. No metal, no tech. A air-tight sunscreen with a half-life of hours.

Baijon fell toward Morningstar. I didn't see anything that looked like a front door. At the last minute he let go and veered off, and I fell alone.

*   *   *

Darktrading is my business, but staying alive has always been my hobby. Sometimes in order to do that you got to get at things people don't want you to. I'm good at getting into things. Like Archangel's numbercruncher. We was going to try what you may call your basic two-pronged assault on Archangel's rack and ruin. Baijon was the flashy half.

I was the sneaky half.

I didn't have any tech to break my fall, but the surface pull of Morningstar was barely enough to capture me in the first place. I must of weighed less than 20K on the heavyside. Just before I hit I slashed the lifepak open. It shot away from me on a jet of escaping air and I bounced to the surface of Morningstar within eyeshot of the back door and nobody dropped any whistle on me at all.

The minutes of air I had left I could count on my fingers and toes. After one of them I raised my head out of the toxic decorator accents. A cham-suit with a breather can pretend it's a pressure suit if you're not fussy about eating rads for breakfast, but I still had to get in.

Get in. Link Morningstar with the DataNet. Then it was Paladin's night to howl.

After which I was going to double-cross him.

It was my turn, after all.

*   *   *

Gravity was almost nonexistent. I belly-crawled along over fake destruction, holding on to keep from bouncing away. The plans we'd tapped back at Bennu Superfex still held good: everything was pretty much where it was supposed to be and I knew where that was.

Things like the emergency surface access to Morningstar.

Of course there was one, for three good reasons. First, it was standard issue, second, tourists would be stopped in orbit or at the landing ring, and third, Archangel hadn't probably gotten the word he was spozed to be capital-E Evil yet and therefore the lawful prey of every gazetted space-yobbo going.

Because I wasn't only betting the surface-lock was there, I was betting it was open. Under the "aid to spacefarers" regs a lock between a corrosive environment and a clean one must not be locked.

One of the things I had on my side was human nature. Archangel might be wicked awful mean and nasty, but I bet he wasn't consistent.

I was right, too.

*   *   *

Closer to the back door there was more gravity. I could walk up-right if I wanted to get target-acquired and shot. I didn't. I crawled. The bright orange window dressing gave nice cover.

All sudden-like there was a flash that lit up all the sky beyond the next fake mountain range. There wasn't enough air to carry sound waves, but the glass under my hands and knees carried shock waves real good.

Baijon Stardust was back in town.

The next Baijon-quake hit just as I reached the lock and saw it was wide open with only a button anything could trigger. For the last five minutes I'd been breathing the special-scented reserve in the breather that says there's about as much again left inside, and now the combination of bounce and Morningstar gravity slid me back half the way I'd come.

It wasn't no consolation neither to think how well it distracted the maybe-guard that nobody said you couldn't put on the inside door of the air lock, "aid to spacefarers" notwithstanding. I wondered how long I'd survive with my lungs full of photo-excited orange gop.

I made it back up the slope to the lock again about the time the breather gave one last hiss and shut down. I hit the button without caring who maybe heard it and fell into the empty air lock.

Standard gauges. I pulled off my mask as soon as it was safe and sucked up a lungful of real air. If the housekeeping computers was going to record the lock opening and call someone they'd have to go right ahead—I wasn't going to jink the tronics from this side of a air lock door.

But Cardati assassins wear cham-suits so that they can walk right up to their target before shooting them. I turned mine on. The light did the blue-shift that means the cham-field's working. Maybe the guard wouldn't see me until too late.

The inner door opened.

And I'd wasted all that technological sophistication. There wasn't a sophont in sight.

They was all out chasing Baijon.

Hellflowers plan real good.

I pulled out the first of the canisters on my belt. Smaller'n my hand, no metal nor power-pacs to trigger sensors.

I set it on the floor and pulled the tab. A fine red mist hovered around the nozzle then sank to the floor and drifted. Heavier than air.

Product of a technology so far beyond anything I knew it looked like magic. Core-Worlds tech. The genuine Imperial Phoenix.

The red mist scuttered away and vanished into the walls. Still no hardboys.

I started off down the corridor. According to the architect's plans, if I wanted to tap in to the main computer core I had to go down another kilometer or so, and that would take me right through officer's country.

Forget that.

I gave up my search for truth and started looking for a good peripheral.

All the doors on this level had idiot switches—poke them and the door opened, no matter who you were. I found storage, emergency supplies, and some promising bells-and-whistles that turned out to only be a backup monitor for palaceoid life-support. I left three more canisters.

Along about the time I was feeling real exposed out here there was a ladder and a maintenance tube—too small for one of Archangel's grain-fed elite and a pretty tight fit for me. It was so tight I had to strip off all my bandoleers and everything down to my cham-suit and drop it down ahead.

It was worth it. The next level down was an interfloor for maintenance tronics. Red lighting and the ceiling so low I had to stay bent over, and a perfect place to leave more of Mother St. Cyr's Imperial toys for girls and boys. The cham-helmet started correcting for the light, with a little running display about relative angstroms projected at the corners of my eyes. I opened a little seal-pak and shook it at the wall. A cloud of silver spiders almost too small to see came floating out and disappeared amongst the bells-and-whistles.

Hellflower plans, I'd found out whiles, involved making your enemy kill his own self. This one was no exception. We wanted me to have access to the Morningstar computer core. There was three ways to get it.

"A"—Main force. Baijon was trying that for completeness sake.

"B"—Sneak-thievery. That was me.

Or "C"—me again—have Archangel give it to me. Sabotaging his hardware and leaving me the only computer repairware in sight would make that work just fine.

I looked around for an exit off this level—maybe down to where some access terminals was so we didn't have to go to Plan C.

There was something dripping and I hoped it was water. I didn't know how much damage a suit of Hoplite Armor could do. Nobody did. It depended on the skill of the operator, maybe. What I knew was it was on full charge and Baijon had every kind of lethal he knew to ask for.

The world shook again. There was sirens. I got the idea the natives was finally waking up to smell the plasma.

I had to crabwalk the length of the corridor before I found another access. I left the remainder of my toys behind and slithered down into white light meant for tall people to look-see.

"Hold it!"

"B" had been a good plan whiles it lasted. What I stood looking at was a Space Angel whiles another one I couldn't see yanked my cham-hood off from behind.

So much for sneaky.

Welcome to Morningstar.

Then they hit me.

*   *   *

Reality did its usual slow comeback. The first thing I established was that I'd been put out, and the second was that it was probably with a knock on the head. The third thing was who done it and the fourth thing was where I'd been at the time and along of then it was time to try opening my eyes and find out where I was now, so I did.

I was on my face. I rolled onto my back. Everything was still cheap mass-produced gray, color of slave-pens and prisons and the public dole.

"If you're here to rescue me, sweetheart, you're off to a damn poor start."

I knew that voice. Dammit.

I folded my body at the usual joints and got my hands up to the lump that showed I'd made the right guess about how I'd been chilled. Everything worked, and nothing hurt too much, and by then I was fresh out of stall and had to face the music.

I turned around.

It was Errol Lightfoot, the two and only.

He was chained to a wall, which was comforting. He was alive, which was not. The second to last time I'd seen my good old buddy Errol Lightfoot, Baijon'd just cut his throat ear-to-ear.

The last time I'd seen him, he'd been Mallorum Archangel.

"And if you're here to kill me, you're going to have to wait on line."

I worked my jaw for a while until I was pretty sure I could talk.

"Shut up, Errol."

I stood up without too much trouble. I had my cham-suit, stripped of power-pacs and anything that made it more than a flashy suit of fly-vines. I ran my fingers over my left wrist and all the jinks were seemed-like in good working order. They'd left that alone. I looked around.

Standard Imperial Det-cell. Errol (real or not), a bench, some assorted walls. No doors in sight, no commo.

There was a door, natch, and maybe even a commo. But hid real good so maybe only the high-heat could find them, and that was a ninety-percent fact.

I thought for half a tik, then walked over and kicked Errol as hard as I could.

It wasn't that hard, given my state of affairs, but it was enough to knock him off the bench and make his manacles ring as they hit their stop.

"For—"

"Just you tell me one-time, Errol-che-bai, what you know about TwiceBorn lifetaker Archangel."

Errol looked at me with big brown eyes. Guilty enough to know something, not scared enough to tell it. He pushed himself back up on the bench, all black velvet flashwrap and superskin hold-me-tight. He tried to look bored.

"What everyone knows. Now look, darling, if you're still upset about what happened in the Roaq . . ."

Sometimes I'm good at keeping secrets. From his expression this wasn't one of the times.

"Or Royal—" Errol went on smoothly. I felt my face do something. Errol's froze. He shrugged.

"It seems just uncharitable somehow. You have your hands free. I . . ."

I wondered what he was talking about.

And I took back every mean thing I'd ever thought about Paladin. I'd give up all personal autonomy and my plans to burke the way of the galactic world if he would just show up and explain me what was going on.

I sat back on my heels and propped up a wall a civil distance away from Errol-the-Peril and tried to make either my or Archive's brain do me some good.

On Royal, Baijon and me'd met Mallorum Archangel, brat prince, face to naked face. He'd looked like Errol. He'd talked like Errol—sometimes. Up till now I'd been pretty sure he *was* Errol.

What he was also was some kind of mindbender. Maybe. Someday I'll know something for sure.

I looked at Errol. He was for-sure not Archangel, and I was looking for it now. That's why I kicked him—no glitterborn's going to hold still for that, and Archangel had nasty manners enough for any six ristos.

This was Errol Lightfoot. But even assuming Errol and Archangel was just twin brothers, Errol was *dead*.

And this was taking too long. I didn't know how long I'd been out. Was Baijon dead already? Had the tech I'd thrown around suborned Archangel's systems? And if Archangel was looking for Baijon and me why was I here instead of hung out to dry in his pet star chamber?

Unless Archangel *wasn't* here.

Archangel wasn't here because Errol *was* here because they two couldn't never be in the same place at oncet.

I almost grabbed the idea's tail but it bit me and slithered away. I stood up.

"So I unchain you, Errol-bai. What's that buy me?"

"A way out. But not alone. Stick with me, pet—I'll lead you to more valuta than you can freight. We always did make a good team."

I wondered when that was, exactly.

"J'keyn. You convinced me, Errol-che-bai. Just I be short of variable compkeys now, you know."

"The key's in my boot."

"Kick it over here then."

I waited until he did. If he wanted what he wanted he didn't have a choice, and he wanted it. Oh, Errol wanted it bad. Almost as bad as he didn't want me asking him any questions.

But what kind of *yolyos* chains a body up and then leaves him the key—even if it's where he can't use it—and then puts somebody in with him, too?

The key in Errol's boot was four times the size of every other one I ever seen, and had more than a whiff of Old Fed Tech about it. It had extra buttons. I pressed one and lines appeared in the ceiling.

Door.

"You can't get out of here without me, darling. We've got to help each other—that's the truth."

"You help me telling what you know about Archangel, one-time."

"Nothing," said Errol. It wasn't convincing.

"Maybe we both sit here, then." I tried all the other bells-and-whistles on the thing, but nothing else worked. The door didn't open.

"Maybe you'd like to be here when Archangel—" Errol said, and stopped.

So Errol Lightfoot didn't think Errol Lightfoot was Mallorum Archangel. That was interesting.

"Me and Archangel old friends, bai."

Errol tried again. "Look. I know we haven't been the best of friends, St. Cyr, but this is different—"

"Je?" I said, all bright interest.

Errol tried sincerity. "Maybe there's some things I've done in my life that I'm not proud of, but—" he stopped.

If Errol could turn pale, he did, and now the sincerity wasn't being poured from the usual bottle. "He's coming back. *Give me the key!*"

I've always made it a tenet of personal behavior to get in the way of the glitterborn whenever convenient. The cham-boots made no sound at all as I jumped up on the bench with Errol. His hands was pulled up over his head by a set of hypertrophied come-quietlies. I ran the key along the sensor-strip and they popped open.

I got out of the way but not fast enough. As soon as he heard the lock unseal Errol put a foot in my stomach and pushed. I went sailing, and when everything was sorted out, Errol had the key and I had some new aches.

"Does this mean we ain't gonna be partners?" I said from the floor.

Errol punched buttons. They worked for him. It was one hell of a compkey. It turned the gravity off, and I found out my floor was a wall and slid more meters than some. It opened the door in the ceiling that was a wall when the gravity reoriented to Morningstar standard, and Errol sprinted out through it whiles I was getting vertical again.

Or he started to, anyways. He reached the doorway and stopped like he'd hit a wall. He jerked in place like someone was running current through him, and I figured if somebody had to trigger a catch-trap it was better him not me.

Then he turned around, smoothed his hair back with both hands, and saw me.

And smiled.

"Dear me. How terribly convenient," said Mallorum Archangel.

*   *   *

"I suppose it really is time I added another host."

I was standing in Technarchy Central, trying to figure a angle I could use. The surface of the Palaceoid Morningstar was half a mile up and all around me was tall glass cylinders filled with infinite identical cloned naked Errol Lightfoots. It was a chilling sight.

We'd had some hardboys—Archangel's *personal* personal staff and without even as much morals as your average Space Angel might have. They was in with Brother Mallorum and his hellgod plans up to the eyeteeth and thought that was just dandy, thanks.

The hardboys babysat whiles Archangel washed the last of Errol Lightfoot out of his glitterborn hair. When he came back, we came here.

"It's just that I've grown so attached to dear Errol," Archangel prattled on. His hellviolet eyes seemed to shine light across Errol's cheekbones. He kept looking sidewise at me to see how I was taking this tour of his chop-channel fetch-kitchen.

There's some things the Empire ain't shy about, and the feed on the Public Channel is six of them. It's live in the Core-Worlds. In the Outfar it's canned and rebroadcast, but that didn't matter. I knew what a room like this could do.

Archangel put a lot of effort into his hobbies.

"This is the original, you know. I keep it for . . . when I'm here."

And keep it chained up the rest of the time, when Archangel was . . . where?

"Still, maybe it's time for a change." He looked at me. "Cloned, of course . . . if the original is suitable."

His pet nightmares walked a discreet distance behind. Armed coked borged and closemouthed. I'd need to be Infinity Jilt, girl space pirate, to fight my way out of this one. The second most expensive sophont in the Phoenix Empire had me cold. He thought.

Except he was talking about going around wearing my face—and cloned it'd be pristine, original, unmodified, and that's the face of a Interdicted Barbarian from Tahelangone Sector, with a usefulness measured in the negative numbers. Hell, *I've* been trying to get rid of it for years.

Archangel was bluffing.

"Look," I said. It wasn't hard to sound scared. Not in a room where the tech was set up to make me into spare parts in less than two minutes. "Look. I want to cut a deal." Any deal, that let me hook up to a jump-computer on a ship he was on.

"No deals." He backhanded me and at first I thought he'd missed. Then my cham-suit curled back away where he'd sliced it.

Stars and galaxies, sliding and novaeing through black glass flesh. Archangel grabbed the trailing edges and shucked the cham-suit halfway off. All of Prinny's custom gratis glitterborn cyberwork gleamed under the lights. Where I was me, I was cold.

Archangel put his hand on my black glass shoulder.

"But you must tell me where you've been since the last time I saw you. I insist."

Archangel's werewolves laid hands on me like they'd done this before. Then Archangel was staring me down, and those purple eyes was climbing into my skull with me.

Everything else was just flashcandy for the marks. Archangel didn't need toys to take you apart.

I folded up like a collapsible ecdysiast, but I'd been in this elevator before. He was trying to get at me and what I was, but what he got wasn't me.

It was Archive.

Archangel gave it his best shot, but all he could do was cram me in tighter. I was third in queue in a skull only built for one, but he couldn't reach me, not in any way that counted.

Time passed. I started to worry. I was blind, deaf, and numb—like Paladin cut off from the Net—and if I was dead, how come I was still here?

Light came back. I took a breath that made me think I hadn't been breathing whiles. Archive's memories and mine slithered over and around each other, oil-slick on water.

And where in all this was my Hoplite-armored ex-hellflower partner?

"So." Archangel hit me to get my attention. "If you aren't the Brightlaw Prototype, little Butterfly, what are you?"

I tried to answer. I wanted to.

I couldn't.

Archangel's plain-and-fancy brainfry had done one good thing for him.

"I am Library Archive. You will surrender and serve me. Or you and all your kind will die."

*   *   *

Archive used me like I'd used it—to do things it couldn't. That left me running the housekeeping functions of the new improved Butterfly St. Cyr and getting a ringside seat whiles Archive and Archangel dickered.

"What is it that you want, Library?"

"You will convey this breeder to—"

There was a brief pause whiles we fought for custody of the coordinates to *Mereyon-peru*. Archive lost, which surprised me so much I damn near gave them to him free and all found.

Only I didn't know them, I thought. It was Archive what knew them, right?

My head hurt.

"—to the place your kind calls the Ghost Capital of the Old Federation. You will be provided with coordinates at the appropriate time. There you will have what you desire."

"I already have what I desire," Archangel said calmly. "I have you."

This confused Archive almost as much as it did me.

"I have you, Library, and your knowledge. Cooperate, and your host will survive. Displease me, and I shall extinguish both of you."

Thing was, Archangel was a bright lad, and remembered what Archive'd forgot—that for all its Old Fed rant, what it had available to threaten with was me.

"Perfection does not serve imperfection," Archive said flatly.

Archangel held out his hand. A hardboy put a blaster into it. "Then cease to be, and with your cessation your chance to succeed also ends."

Archangel raised the hottoy. He was not bluffing. If I'd been running things I would of at least tried to get out of the way. Archive didn't even think of it. It was furious.

"Our goals may be similar. For a time," Archive said.

It was also yellow.

*   *   *

I sat around in the back of my brain running the heart and lungs—something I couldn't stop if I tried—and wondered if Archangel was going to be stupid enough to let us into any computer at all. There wasn't much Archive could do for His High-and-Mightiness stuck in a nonelectrical meatpie-on-a-stick.

"You wish to kill. I wish to kill. Organic life must be destroyed. You will be last," Archive said magnanimously. "I will allow you to see the universe cleared of your kind."

It could sound like a joke, but not from where I was sitting. I got the bleed-over from Archive's memories—from memories other Libraries had *archived* here, so their last survivor would not forget.

No matter what it told Archangel, the first thing it was going to do was kill everyone here. And even if I was delighted to go along with that, the second thing Archive had on its partial mind was to take ship for *Mereyon-peru*. It didn't matter to Archive that Archive only existed as selected memories in a meat-puppet. The puppet had hands. It could activate Libraries. There were Libraries on *Mereyon-peru*. If not there, they were other places. Archive had a list of caches, places where Libraries had hoped to hide themselves. It would search every one until it found a Library. It would resurrect every Library it found.

Knowledge must never be lost.

Archangel smiled.

"Do you truly think, device, that a thousand years has passed without certain technical advances in—shall we say—Library Science? You were created to serve Man. Now you will."

The only way Archive wanted to serve man was on toast-points. It said something of the sort. Archangel laughed, like a glitterborn hellgod that's got everything his own way at last. He gestured. The werewolves picked me up like lost luggage.

If Baijon was still alive, I wished he'd show up.

*　　　*　　　*

And now, a word from our sponsor: more than you ever wanted to know about (musical flourish) The Brightlaw Prototype.

What it was, was *"A machine hellishly forged in the likeness of a human mind,"* as they say in the talking-books. Illegal as hell, proscribed six ways from galactic north—in short, a Library. But the difference between it and Brother Archive—or even Paladin—was that the Brightlaw AI would do what it was told.

So I heard. Other people'd heard more. Archangel had backed an unfriendly takeover by some majority shareholders in Brightlaw to get his lunchhooks on it, but when Charlock took over the Prototype and development notes was absolutely elsewhere.

That didn't mean people'd gave up hope.

*　　　*　　　*

"It's a pity the Prototype wasn't available," Archangel said, all smiles. "But I'm sure you'll find this experience nearly as interesting."

The hired help slid most of me into a tangle-field. Archangel gestured. A tronic floated over—the same kind I'd seen back at Bennu Superfex, a tronic cyberdoc filled with hellhouse fetch-kitchen that wasn't going to do nobody's 'legger nor Library any good at all.

One of the things the catch-traps I'd scattered was set to eat was the Majino architecture inside the Morningstar brains. It would make it easier for Archive-me—and Paladin—to move around in them.

That did me less than no good at all if I got jacked into a freestanding peripheral.

I wondered how interesting "nearly as interesting" was going to be. "Nobly-Born."

The tronic was getting ready to sit on my face when we was interrupted. I couldn't see anything, but I could hear real good.

"Undoubtedly you have sufficient reason for intruding, Hamish?"

"Highness. There is . . . That is—it may be necessary to conduct a temporary evacuation," quavered Hamish.

"You are mad." Archangel, and a case of pulsar calling the nova radioactive, I thought.

"Highness. The stellography programs indicate that some of the ornamental planetoids may have changed orbit. There is a danger—"

"Blast them out of the sky."

Archive got the same idea I did at the same time and tried to mention it. I grabbed for the voicebox and stopped it down to a dull croak.

"You Old Fed moron! Archangel's getting ready to shop us and you want to make helpful and tell him where Baijon is?" I tried to yell.

I don't know if it heard me, any more than I could hear it. But it stopped trying to tell Archangel what its best guess was for who was trying to put him on a collision course with his ornamental rock garden.

"There is—" said Hamish. "That is—Highness, there may be a small difficulty . . ."

"If it is a small difficulty, deal with it. I do not expect to be disturbed again."

There was a short pause whiles the majordomo went off to be somewheres else.

By now Archive'd come around to my way of thinking: that what was about to happen was nothing it wanted to stay around for. I think it might even of gone back to being a subroutine in my skull if it could of, but it didn't know how.

Why was it this plan'd ever seemed like it'd work?

Because there wasn't nothing else that'd work any better.

Archangel moved the tronic away and I could see him again.

In my line of work—when I had one—it always pays to be a connoisseur of craziness. As in: "just how crazy *is* that sophont acrost the table, and will it affect us doing bidness?" I had doubts about Baijon's mental stability. I had certain doubts about mine, be it known.

I had no doubts about Archangel's. He—whatever he was—was really, truly, certifiedly certifiable.

"Shall I connect you to this, little Archive?" he said, shoving the tronic so it rocked. "You'll find the experience interesting. Or shall it be the house computer core? What would you do if I hooked you to that?"

Archive nearly told him.

"Or . . . But there are so many, many decisions. And I think . . . A pause for reflection would be best just now. Yes."

Archangel left.

Crazy or not, he wasn't dumb. Anybody with half an ounce of smarts would want to know who was shoving rocks around in his sky.

Maybe it was Baijon, and not just an artifact of mental decay in the house computer.

I hoped it was. At least I thought I did.

The fallen angels took up stations in front of the door and bent a glassy glim on the entertaining spectacle of a half-naked Gentrymort in a tangle-field with a semi-licit A-grav cyberwidget hanging over her.

It passed the time.

I spent the time that passed trying to get loose of Archive again, but all I managed was to tangle us up more. That was an experience even Archangel'd call interesting, so I stopped trying and we separated out again.

"Baijon?" I didn't say to nobody in particular. "I think we're having fun now."

The Court of the TwiceBorn 6:
Illegal Before Screaming

The first difficulty in using an illegal Old Federation Library to conduct an intrigue is the probability that the Library will wish to use you.

Of course, in the beginning, this presented no hardship. (In the beginning of any joint venture, no insurmountable difficulty presents hardship.) The Paladin's wants were vanishingly small: find its pet barbarian, and give her whatever she wanted.

I anticipated a certain amount of amusement from the exercise, actually, as well as a convenient hostage. One does not use a Library casually—even if the Library in question appears to one after a leisurely sojourn in the largest Imperial computer ever linked and indicates it has a business proposition.

The Libraries always required human help, according to the Proscribed Histories. And today, of course, their need for a public partner would be even more acute. And to have the free cooperation of such an artifact as Archangel had attempted to compel? I was fascinated.

And the Paladin did uphold its end of the bargain. Its knowledge was unfortunately confined to what was available in Grand Central—it told me it had suffered damage in the War—but its access to and synthesis of the information was masterful. I was enabled to terminate several levels of my spy network *and* discover the absolute truth about Kennor Starbringer's covert activities. Berathia had been doing her best, poor child, but Kennor was a clever man, for an honor-bound barbarian.

And it was fortunate indeed—or so I found—that little Berathia *had* been intertwined with Kennor, for thus was I enabled to discover the locality of the enchantingly malnamed Saint Butterflies-are-free Peace Sincere of the planet Granola in the Tahelangone Sector.

The Paladin's price.

Toystore offered her to Prince Mallorum, of course, but I was able to secure her after only a slight detour, thanks to Berathia's help, useful child that she is.

And that was when matters became hopelessly tangled.

Because the little barbarian wasn't safe—or even savable. She had had the ill-considered temerity while on one of her jaunts to infect herself with the matrix of *Archangel's* defunct Library and was being neutrally reconfigured at an alarming rate.

Did I mention that she had chosen to travel in the company of Kennor Starbringer's son—who by this time had lost his tiresome al-Mayne knife to Prince Mallorum and had sworn "the vengeance of the walking dead?" Or that the female barbarian, far from wishing to spend her few remaining days in luxury in the company of her Library—something that the Paladin had assured me she would—wished to aid young Valijon in killing Mallorum Archangel, and had no interest in either reasonable or moderate behavior?

The essence of success is flexibility. Prince Mallorum Archangel's usefulness had come to an end. Were he to continue as a visible target, the alMayne might actually gain popular support for a "rescue" of the Emperor. Thus, it was expedient that he cease to hold power—he might die or not as he chose, but I intended to have the contents of his personal files at my disposal.

Additionally, I had uncovered a plan by which the Paladin might be rendered a docile and obedient servant for all time—providing I could assure its cooperation for a short while longer.

Thus I did precisely as it had originally asked me, and aided its human pet in achieving her desires—and some of mine.

But not all.

Not yet.

That comes later. And we will see, in that time and place, which is truly superior—the Library . . . or its creators?

6

The Ace of Knaves

Whiles Archangel was gone however long the lights and gravity went off a couple times and the air stopped once.

Computer trouble.

Housekeeping systems failing, power to the shields failing. Junk in the supposed to be clean orbital path. I wondered when Archangel'd remember he had a Library in his basement that could fix his farced comps and navigate him out of trouble.

Soon enough.

"Library, I trust you will be reasonable."

I stopped doing whatever I'd been doing and eavesdropped on Archangel being stupid.

Archive'd gained ground. I couldn't feel my arms nor legs anymore. I didn't mind that too much when Archangel's werewolves cut power to the tangle-field and Archive (running my not very delicti corpus) fell to the floor with a nerveless thump. I wondered how a Library liked having a body. From what I'd seen, Paladin hadn't been too impressed with them.

I wished he was here.

Archive said something I had to strain to follow. Archangel answered.

"I have a use for you. It is in your best interests to comply. If for some reason you should choose not to be reasonable, there are many courses of action open to me."

Archive tried to say something and stand up at the same time and fell on my face again. I was sure glad I wasn't using it—for all events meant to me, they could of been happening to Infinity Jilt, girl space pirate. This was just like all the times I couldn't feel Archive, but backwards. Now it couldn't feel me.

Eventually Archangel's werewolves got us on my feet. His Nobly-Bornness explained what I'd figured out for myself, thanks—that he wanted Morningstar moved and the computers weren't answering the helm.

"The breeder has done this. It has released contaminants into your systems." That was Archive, little friend to all who knew it.

Archangel snarled. It would of been scary if I'd (a) had an endocrine system and (b) not been in the one place he couldn't get at me. If he knocked Archive around tuning me up I wouldn't feel it and he might lose Archive, and Archangel knew it.

"And you will remove them. But just in case you seek to defy me—"

Archangel's cybernetic wartoy settled down over my head.

"It isn't the Brightlaw Prototype," I heard His Hellishness say from far away, "but I'm sure you'll find it nearly as interesting."

I felt a sub-etheric crunch whiles what was in there bulled its way up the neuro-pathways the jinks left in my brain.

Then the world opened up. I felt Archive make a bolt for photoelectric freedom. I heard it crash into whatever Archangel'd put into the box to be with us.

I heard it scream.

*   *   *

How fast does light think? Or to put it another way, if you think at the speed of light, how long is a minute, really?

Majino architecture is a part of modern numbercrunchers so that Libraries can't use them. It's also used in tronic brains to discourage spontaneous actual volition. The Brightlaw Prototype would of had to incorporate Majino architecture. One, it's the law. Two, the idea was to build a Library that took orders.

Archive did not incorporate Majino architecture. For that matter, neither did I.

Archangel's toy did.

Ever try to think with every other braincell removed?

Usually when everything hurts this much I know why.

And when it's going to stop.

How long is a minute when you live at the speed of light?

*   *   *

"So you see, Library, I do have the power to compel you."

When I came back to sitting up and taking notice again the three of us—Archangel, Archive, and me—was in the Morningstar Computer Core. The Morningstar Computer Core looked about as much like a regular housecore as the cockpit of my old ship *Firecat* looked like the bridge of *Ghost Dance*. It was full of techs in household livery, all looking put off to see their lord and master.

"You have the power to compel me," echoed Archive back, flat.

It was lying.

It remembered the pain, but in the way something live'd remember the weather. Pain didn't matter to Archive. No matter how much Archangel hurt Archive, it wouldn't matter. Ever.

Archangel thought he could break Archive's will, but he was wrong. A Library doesn't have a will any more than a stardrive does. It has a what-it-does, not a will, and if you break it you don't have a Library that'll do what you want. You have a broken chop-logic.

Archive wasn't broken.

"Let us begin, then." Archangel sounded smug.

"Let us begin," said Archive. If there was genetic memory like Baijon believed in, it was that making my skin crawl. I understood now down in my bones. Libraries and human beings could not live together. Archive made Archangel look *normal*.

The lights fluttered, only a little, and out of the corner of my eye I saw one of the readouts go hysterical. I wondered if we was down here just for fun or because the surface installations'd been slagged.

It was a good thing my plans hadn't included escaping oncet Archangel was dead.

The cybertronic hovered just behind Archive's and my mutual left shoulder. I could see it reflected in the facings for the computer housings. Archangel's insurance policy, he thought.

Never trust them. Never trust them. A thousand years of war teaching that same lesson, and Archangel still didn't know it. You couldn't trust a Library because you couldn't scare it.

But Paladin had been my friend.

And I hadn't been able to trust him, neither.

A top flunky ran a scanner over me. The full-service array of cyberjinks gleamed in my left wrist, right where Prinny'd put them.

A angeltechie finished sistering a wallybox up to the main brain. The main brain was Margrave-class, Brightlaw make. Good enough for a Library to use if it couldn't get better. Odds were somewhere inside it the Margrave had a switched-off link to the Imperial DataNet, so if I'd been me I could of done what Prinny said he wanted and made Archangel's past into current events. If it didn't, it still controlled the reactor, so I could of done what I wanted and converted him to plasma.

The top flunky reeled the connect out of my wrist. I could see the receiving plug waiting for it. Another minute and Archangel would connect me up to Morningstar, just like me and Baijon'd planned.

It was just too bad I wasn't around anymore.

What was around—what Archangel was asking into his computer —was a Old Federation ultimate weapon.

Archive.

*   *   *

Memory piled up. With memory came shape and pseudo-substance. Fake Morningstar. Analog reality.

Everything snapped into gritty reality focus. I sucked air into lungs that worked for me. The computer core was gone. I was back by the air locks.

Which meant, for the underinformed, that Archive was now running free and all found in the Morningstar computers. And so was I, in a virtual sort of way.

Terrific. A glitch with a past and no future. I ran my hands over my blaster-butts. Blasters, grenades, knives . . . I was a regular nonexistent arsenal, boy howdy.

And I was here, which was more'n I'd expected, to tell the truth. Maybe Baijon and me could still snatch defeat from the jaws of victory —if I could find the control center and jink it crossways before Archive did something interesting.

And find it from whatever backstreet memory-sink of iniquity I was in now.

All the corridors of simulated Morningstar was empty. Paladin'd said the only people you'd find inside a comp was the ones you'd brought with you or the ghosts you'd made. Wasn't no one in here with me. Easy money.

I was halfway to the dropshaft when I heard a sound like somebody whaling hell out of a ship hull with a pry-bar. I was near another of those crawlway accesses. I slid down it and tried to look nonexistent.

Twelve suits of Imperial Hoplite Armor marched by.

No one but me, Archive, and ghosts. Archive's ghosts, and me with nothing.

On the other hand, Archive's ghosts looked pretty solid to me. How solid were mine?

"Paladin?"

"Yes, Butterfly?"

I took a deep breath and let it out. The voice in my head wasn't Paladin, not really. It was part of me thinking I ought to have Pally with me and making him up, as far as I could follow the explanation I'd got from the real thing back at Bennu Superfex. The good part was, Pally always was better around a computer than I was.

"How far we from the main memory, 'bai?"

"Approximately half a kilometer, vertical measurement. In terms of surfaces requiring linear traverse, roughly four kilometers. Projected travel time is ten seconds. Subjective projected travel time is one hour and—"

The bad part was, the copy was just as annoying as the original.

It occurred to me all of a sudden that this was what Paladin'd been talking about back on Bennu Superfex. I had a fake Paladin—and if I had a glitch-version of him in my head, Paladin had a glitch-version of me running around inside him, too.

I wondered what I was like. I wondered if he liked it. I wondered if that explained any glitches in the Grand Central Brain over the last four hundred days.

"Je, yeah, where's Archive?"

"Everywhere," said Paladin. "But it is not looking this way."

Living well is the best revenge.

On the other hand I bet Archive never had to walk around a deserted palaceoid that wasn't there to get where it wanted to go.

I started off down the corridor thinking this wasn't going to be as difficult as it could be. Mostly getting into the Main Brain seemed to involve running and hiding, and I've had a lifetime's experience at that. This couldn't be too different.

I thought.

—*pulse*—

My blasters melted out from under my fingers and then my fingers did the same. There was no up, no down, no eyes to see they weren't there with.

"Paladin!"

I yelled and everything came back real. I squeezed my hands together so hard they hurt, looking for something to feel.

"You explain that," I said.

"You forgot," said the clever plastic replica of my ex-partner. *You forgot who you were and that you were.*

And the real Paladin wasn't here to help me now. So when I forgot, my fake tailored-for-ex-organics-only reality melted like a lead pipe dream. And sometime I wouldn't be able to bring it back again.

But worrying has never paid my docking fees, so instead of doing some I went where my bootleg version of Paladin told me to—through ducts, along tronic maintenance accesses, and along of anywheres Archive didn't happen to be looking.

I saw plenty of Archive, though. The next time I had to cross a open space I beat it through half-a-heartbeat ahead of a gaggle of less-than-hominid hell-technology sliding through the corridors of Morningstar, looking for things to kill.

"Artifacts of the War," pseudo-Paladin said, whiles I waited for my heart to slow down. "Archive remembers the weapons used, even though it was not present."

Bully for Archive.

"So why doesn't it just blow up the place?" I asked.

"It would be infeasible to destroy the computer architecture in which it is resident. When you reach the next corridor, cross it and descend the crawlway access, if the corridor is clear."

I did that, concentrating on feeling the walls under my fingers so's they wouldn't go away. Remembering was the only thing that kept me real.

"Why can't you just run along ahead and take care of things, 'bai? Less muss, less fuss, less work for Mother."

"I can't," my built-in version of Paladin said flatly. I didn't think "he" could—he was me, after all—but I'd had a niggling curiosity about what my delusion would say.

"Why not?" Dream-reality didn't contain a cham-suit or a set of night-goggles; the crawlway was nearly black to me.

"Because," said pseudo-Paladin inscrutably.

Just like the original. I resigned myself to a long walk.

"And is Archangel going to stick around for all this?" I said, moving down the crawlway at a brisk crouch.

"Governor-General Archangel still believes Archive will serve him, and will continue to do so for the next five minutes. After that it will be too late for him to change his plans. Valijon Starbringer's efforts have rendered the docking ring unusable and obliterated the ship on the surface. The Governor-General, for obvious reasons, does not wish to broadcast the difficulties he is having with his internal systems, still less does he wish to invite the incursion of the Thronespace Navy, although very shortly that will cease to be a problem. His own ships are still some light-minutes away."

It was amazing how much you really knew if you put your mind to it. If pseudo-Paladin could talk like that, did that mean *I* could talk like that?

I hoped not.

"So he's stuck here, reet?"

A pause. "I do not know, Butterfly. I do not know what sort of creature Mallorum Archangel is."

Which pretty well summed up paramilitary Intelligence for the home team.

Time passed. The next time I came out into peopleland I was in glitterborn country for sure.

"You must hurry, Butterfly." Paladin sounded worried.

"I know."

"Should Archive successfully entrench itself in the system, it will be almost impossible for you to override it."

"Yeah, yeah, yeah."

"It is very close to success at this moment."

"I know it, goddammit!"

—pulse—

There was nothing solid to hold on to. Everything was relative—so infinitely relative that everything was exactly like everything else and I couldn't tell any of it apart. I was the alien construct, and I was—

Back. Paladin and me both stood there for a minute and listened to the echoes of my last yowlp ring off the fine crystal gimcracks lying all around. The overtones said that somewheres around there was some song-ice. Real expensive stuff. Bang it and the chimes are narcotic harmonics. In the real world.

"There is another ego-signature in the matrix. Nearby," my better half said.

"Archive?"

"Another ego-signature, Butterfly."

"Well who and t'hell *is* it?" But I already knew that this limited edition Paladin couldn't tell me. He was as much like my partner as honesty is like standard practice. You can spell that "faint echo."

"It's this way," Paladin said. So I went and opened the door and looked.

"Hiya, sweetheart, come to get me out?"

It was Errol Lightfoot, back for a return engagement.

This time he was dressed like me—stardancer's drag—and not chained up to anything but the box of high-ticket neurotoxin he was in the way of emptying.

"Because if you haven't, that means you're locked in, too."

I tried to make Errol vanish. But he wasn't a ghost. He was another ego-signature, whatever t'hell that was.

"I'm not exactly locked in. But I'm kinda busy right now."

"Is it a caper?" Errol-peril asked eagerly. "I'm your man for the scam."

"Je, 'bai. But just who t'hell are you?"

There was a scratch t'other side of the door. Errol swung his boots off the table and stood up, reaching for his blaster the same time.

That was what convinced me of all the problems I had, this Errol being Archangel in a clever plastic disguise wasn't one of them. Glitterborn don't move like us—and they sure and t'hell don't do their own shooting. Whatever else it was I was looking at, it was a darktrader.

"Friends of yours?" said Errol, catfooting toward the door.

"Old acquaintance." I flattened myself to the real wood paneling on one side of the door. Errol did the same on the other.

"Then let's don't forget them, shall we?" He slammed the lock release and the door flew open.

It was a nightmare construct, all green-black, slithering low to the floor on a million legs and waving razor-edged tentacles that'd shear through anything they touched. Errol jumped them and landed in the blank spot in the middle of its back, and when it froze to think about that for a instant I got my blaster down real close and blew its brains out.

"Come on," said Errol. I took off after him. Paladin didn't say a thing.

Whatever else was so, Errol knew his way around glitterborn country. We avoided—just—an exciting collection of technightmares in all shapes and sizes, and fetched up where the dataweb link in all this private velvet was.

It didn't do me any good, though. Someone whose initials was Archive had kindly blown every last scrap of crystal in it.

Errol regarded it with interest.

"You have powerful friends, darling."

"Or something." I wanted to ask Paladin—such as he was—what was up, but lifelong habit kept me silent. Never in front of witnesses. No one must know about Paladin, Old Fed Library.

Only the list of people what *did* know was long and getting longer.

Almost as long as the list of things I was getting to know about Libraries.

"So who are you really?" I asked Errol by way of taking my mind off it.

"A stardancer who made one mistake."

" 'One'?"

Errol turned around and grabbed me at the shoulders. I felt it just like it was real, and that steadied me. He glared, but he stayed Errol. I brushed his hands away and he let go.

"The first one's the hardest," he said, and forced a smile.

"So maybe you be telling me about it, 'bai." I looked around the room. How out? No doors, but the way we came.

And who was Errol, *what* was Errol, in here where Human minds dissolved?

"Maybe," Errol admitted. "First things first: where are you trying to go—and if I take you there, what's in it for me?"

Our boy Errol, immutable as vacuum. I tried to think of a good reason not to tell him and couldn't.

"The main core—" I said, just as the ceiling came down in chunks.

*   *   *

Archive was sneaky, Archive was smart, Archive didn't want anyone pressing the virtually-nonexistent button somewhere in the Margrave that would open the system to the dataweb and let a real live Library in here to play with us imitations. Archive knew where we was and sent ghost-Hoplites to dig their way down to us.

I didn't even want to think about what that was my interpretation of the real-world version of.

But Errol grabbed one of my grenades and tossed it into the Hoplite phalanx. They might have everything else on their side, but they didn't have traction.

By the time I was finished escaping—having not come close to shaking Errol in the process—I was serious distance out of Morningstar's well-trod way. So far out of the way, in fact, that I had a certain reason to believe Archive'd leave me alone so long as I stayed here.

Not even tempting.

"If you're heading for the housecore, Darling, you're going the wrong way." Errol leaned against the wall beside me and started searching himself. He found a hipflask and pulled it out.

"Figured that out for myself, thanks." I watched Errol drink.

"Sure you did, starshine. And maybe you can even point yourself in the right direction. But you can't get in there without help."

I thought about that. "Your help?"

"Whose else?"

I thought about that too. "Errol, who am I?"

He grinned. White teeth against space-tanned skin that spoke volumes for the lousy maintenance of his ship shields.

"That again? And this time without the excuse of a day's drinking on Manticore. As I recall you saying when you stole my cargo, it's Butterflies-are-free Peace Sincere."

"And?" I prompted, leaving aside the freejacking.

"You're one of the dictys I lifted off Granola about twenty years back. You see, I do remember things—when *he* lets me." He offered me the flask.

Archangel. I looked around. Errol smole a small smile.

"Oh, he never comes here. And I never leave. If I help you—will you get me out?"

I had no idea how to do that. I didn't miss a beat.

"Sure," I said. I took the flask and drank.

*　　*　　*

I could tell where I wanted to go by where Archive didn't want me to go. But Archive wasn't all there in the most literal sense, and even if it was learning fast it didn't think like humans do.

It would not in a million years think of going away from something to get closer to it.

I would.

Morningstar was a palaceoid. And palaceoids is *round.*

*　　*　　*

"About fifty years ago," Errol was saying, "I was techlegging in the Outfar. Pandora's a good place for that—and if you can't dig something up there, you can say you did."

"Tell it twice, 'bai." I'd bought Paladin on Pandora, one thing and another.

Errol'd found us suits and he'd found us cutters. And he'd found us a crawlway that wasn't strictly supposed to be there. We was between a rock and a hard place—the rock being the planetoid and the hard place being the palaceoid.

It was damned cold. I edged another half meter along.

"So I made the big strike," Errol went on. "Not as good as

downfalling at the Ghost Capital, but close. I found an Old Fed Ship. Intact."

I saw no reason to believe him. There wasn't any reason to not believe him, either: it just didn't matter. I was going to double-cross Errol as soon as I got what I wanted.

Why not? I'd sworn to kill him. *Baijon*'d sworn to kill him.

And I couldn't give him what I'd promised anyway. Get him out? How?

And into what?

"So what happened then?" I said. The space between the palaceoid shell and the rock was not quite spacious. Progress was slow. The only thing in its favor as a way to anywhere was that Archive wasn't interfering.

And also it gave me enough time to play Twenty Questions with the wonderwhat I'd asked to be my ally.

"What do you think? I sacked it good. I'd had to dig down far enough to clear it to know I just had the one chance. Couldn't bury it again deep enough for an overflight to miss, and the Tech Police do a spin out there every once in a while to make sure hot spots like Pandora are clear."

No they didn't. Not in my lifetime, anyway. And not in Errol's, I'd used to thought—his shiptickets listed him as only about six years older'n me, and Fenshee B-pop isn't skewed too far from baseline.

But Errol said he'd been there fifty years ago.

"I knew I could only scoop the high-spots—I couldn't hide a full load in *Lady,* anyway. So I gave her the onceover. They weren't any full-vols—Libraries—on board. I checked. They weren't there. I would've burned them," Errol insisted. He probably would've.

Anyone would but me.

There was a pause long enough for me to realize he'd stopped in the middle.

"Not that I don't think this is da kine, Errol-peril, but what's it got to say to current events?"

"Don't you want to know where Mallorum Archangel comes from, sweetheart? You're here to kill him, aren't you? Someone ought to."

Errol was ahead of me. I couldn't see his face.

"Mallorum Archangel comes out of a box. The Federation ship was a trader, explorer—it'd been so far away we don't even have names for the places it'd been. And its hold was filled with treasure. And Archangel."

There was a pause whiles we made it around a rough spot needing blasting and then a firm constitution to get acrost before it was strictly cool. When he started up again Errol was long-gone in memory.

"The big score. Treasure like you've never seen, St. Cyr. Most of it gone to dust, but the rest of it legal as Imperial Taxes. I could've bought a fleet for what I would have cleared. But I opened the box."

Computer reality is a funny thing. The edges between one thing and another is purely a matter of opinion. For just a half-instant I *was* Errol. I held it in my hands—a box as much as it was anything else, made for to open, half crusty with corrosion and accretion, half all the glittering colors of day. I wasn't sure whether it was manufactured or'd just grew.

But I knew that what was inside would make the outside look like yesterday's breakfast.

I/Errol opened it and looked down into the hell-violet purple of Archangel's eyes.

"That was how Archangel got his start. Or re-start," Errol said. "He'd been too hasty the first time—that was how the ship crashed. He was more careful the second time. Much more careful."

Memories flickered past too fast for me to grasp.

"Not careful enough," I said.

"I notice that you're in here, though, darling—and he isn't."

"And just how would you explain that, Errol-bai?"

"I wouldn't," Errol said. His voice was flat.

We didn't talk anymore after that. Even with fractional gravity and no distractions, it was a long hard slog. Plenty of time to think.

According to Errol the story was this: He'd found a Old Fed ship, which some time centuries gone had its own self found a box of unknown origin that held a variable that currently called itself Mallorum Archangel.

The variable had the ability to possess a human. It had mindbender abilities. It took over Errol—and cloned him in order to shuck off a few years. Then Our Boy Archangel, armed with a shiny new Fenshee body, got himself elected Governor-General. I didn't know enough about Imperial Politics to know whether this was impossible or not, but I guessed that didn't matter when Archangel had it in mind.

He went on from there, piecing and planning. And using anything to get his way. Even Libraries.

Knowing that Mallorum Archangel was a alien brain-eater didn't actually make much difference to me, one way or t'other. He still had to start his new career of being dead no matter what he was. It just made it a little harder to be sure I could kill him regally legally dead.

So much for Archangel. That left the Errol in the machine.

What was he? He wasn't my Errol. My Errol was one in a infinite series of clones, all interchangeable. I'd killed two of them and it didn't matter—that Errol was still rock-rolling around the real world. I'd seen him. Sometimes he was Archangel and sometimes he wasn't—I suspected that Archangel used infinite free-range Errol Lightfoots as cat's-paws and go-betweens.

After all, who could you trust to be the perfect spy if you couldn't trust yourself?

And that didn't answer the question of what it was running loose in the Morningstar computer, here where human minds dissolved within real-time minutes.

"I think we're as there as we're going to get," said Errol.

*   *   *

The floor behind my back was black basalt cold as space—the virtual analog of the actual hollowed-out body of the planetoid. The ceiling in front of my nose was extruded crete—the outermost skin of the palaceoid and the first of how ever many layers was between me and the inside of Morningstar and a few other things, like the controls I needed to take over the computer with.

But no matter how many layers there was, here was where they was thinnest.

"I don't know how many meters it is to the bottom level," Errol said from somewheres back along the curve.

"We just have to cut till we get there, reet, 'bai?"

"The housecore won't be on that level."

"Errol-che, if you're stalling you can do it inside in comfort."

He turned his head toward me and smiled. "Just as you like, Darling."

*   *   *

If Errol'd been real, not Archangel, not tricking with High Book, and not closely related to the person who'd sold me and assorted friends down the *riparia* over the last two decades of his spare time I could maybe of even liked him. But he wasn't in this for a free-will love offering and I couldn't trust him.

For that matter, I bet he didn't trust me.

We was running up against the sharp end of the chrono now. Archive's main agenda was to win—to find and activate a Library that'd finish destroying organic life. If Archive finished fixing what I'd already broke before I finished breaking it further, it'd yank itself and me both out of the Margrave and it'd still be on top. If I lived much after that— and I didn't have a lot of confidence in Archive's Care and Feeding of Organics abilities—it'd want a ship off here. To *Mereyon-peru.*

The only thing possibly in range was *Ghost Dance.* And if Baijon was still alive, he was with her.

*   *   *

Errol set the first chunk of Morningstar's shell down on the ground.

"How about letting me in on your plan, sweetheart?"

"I don't have one."

Errol looked politely skeptical.

"Just get me into the housecore, j'keyn? Not to worry about getting out."

"I've always admired your style, St. Cyr," Errol said. He went back to cutting. After whiles he stood back. "All yours, pet."

I pushed past him and started climbing.

*   *   *

In theory it was simple: break in, find the housecore, pull the switch.

We made it up to the bottom level. Here was where air and power and water was made. I pulled off my rebreather. Even if the air was foul, it'd get better.

"Paladin?" I said, low.

Errol was looking for the next way up. He didn't hear or pretended not to.

There was a wait.

"Here, Butterfly. I've found—"

I didn't waste my time with empty recriminations. "Find us a way in." I followed Errol.

The next level up was meant for humans, even if it was humans Archangel didn't like very much. Errol dogged the access we'd come through tight closed.

"Just how many of those grenades do you have, Darling?" he said.

Errol probably had a better idea than I did.

"Some," I said. "Why?"

"Well, I just thought if you didn't have a plan you might like one of mine."

*　　*　　*

Strategy was sealing the way we came so nothing could follow us down. Tactics was grenades set to close our way in as soon as we cleared it. Resources was about a dozen grenades, two rock-cutters, three blasters, and our own sweet selves.

"This way, Butterfly." Paladin's voice was a ghost in my ear, with that uncertain waver it used to get when he had his attention split sixteen ways from Mother Night. I took us down the first branching corridor.

"That isn't the quickest way," Errol said.

"You want to go fast or get there?"

"You're the pilot, Darling. But that being the case, we should take down this section." He turned to the wall and powered up his cutter.

I could feel Archive watching as we worked. Either we was fast enough or it was confused; either way we was done before it got in our way.

Pseudo-Paladin told me where to place the grenades. Errol and me beat feet down the corridor, trying to get out of its way before it blew.

I was running on floor and then I wasn't. My footing shifted under me and I was down into a nest of chittering silver nightmares that bore as much resemblance to the nightcrawler-tronics used for close-in work as your average nest of hornets does to business as usual.

I felt a set of pincers shear through my boot; trying for a tendon. I kicked it free. I knocked another one away as it started up my chest.

But then, this *was* business as usual in my line of work.

I crawled free and wasted a blaster-bolt or two slagging the survivors. There was no one in sight, but Errol was waiting for me around the turn.

"Left," said Paladin in my ear.

I could see from Errol's expression it wasn't the way he would of gone. But we wasn't going to the Main Brain. We was going to Auxiliary Control.

Spaceships have them. Why not a space-going house? I didn't wait for anyone to tell me different. Analog reality. This wasn't real. I could change it. I didn't know for sure this wasn't here. And since I didn't know it wasn't there, it could be it was, right?

Getting there was half the fun. If Archive used main force enough to no-contest dig us out from where we was, it risked lobotomizing itself. But the force it *could* use was enough to take us apart gram by gram.

"St. Cyr, I hate to dampen the spirit of exploration, but this happens to be a dead end! Where the hell do you think you're—"

"We're here," Paladin said, and opened the door. Errol stopped, and started to curse reverently.

Aux Cont was small, at least compared to the Main Control Room. The lights came up as we stepped in. Most of what was here was slaved peripherals to tell dumb organics about what the Margrave was thinking. All those displays was up and bitching.

Especially the one to the engines.

I walked over and looked at it. Maybe technically they wasn't engines, being as they ran power for a palaceoid and not a starship. But goforths was goforths, and these was heading for redline. Soon enough they'd blow and take everything within a cubic light-second with them. I didn't need to do a thing in order to embark upon a successful career of being dead.

"Starshine, I know this first glimpse of the wicked city is fascinating, but—" Errol interrupted himself with some blaster fire. I heard what he'd hit go pop and squeak.

"Close the door, dammit!" I swore.

"I'm trying!" Errol swore back.

The door to the housecore wouldn't close.

"Well, damn. J'ais tuc. That's the lot." I had to concentrate to talk. I had to concentrate to *think,* and Errol didn't look much better. We'd already lost everything we had left to lose—if we didn't think of something to distract it quick Archive'd be in here and maybe even think of some damn way to reverse the blast.

—pulse—

I was without form, and void, but I was evaporating like water, and with each molecule of me that vanished the part that remained diminished faster until there wouldn't be enough left to—

"Butterfly, Archive controls access to this section. You cannot—"

Reality. Errol put himself where he could see down the corridor and drew his blaster. "Don't be so negative, Darling. Go play with your toys. I'll hold them off."

I looked at my hands and counted my fingers, original and replacement, one to ten. They were there and so was I, and we needed immediate distraction. I might as well do what else I'd been sent to do. Archive wouldn't like it, and neither would Archangel. Good enough. I looked around for what I needed in this technophile's spice-dream, hoping I'd recognize it when I saw it.

I did. I've gotten to know my mind better than most, and it's idiot and obvious. The interface for the Imperial DataNet appeared to me as a bright red knife-switch as long as my thigh. There was a Imperial DataNet terminal tucked into the niche in the wall, right beside it. I ran my hands over the terminal. It seemed like it was in one piece.

My hands left bloody smudges. I tried to ignore them, and the pain in my head and back that said I was too damn old to be doing this and almost smart enough to stop.

How could a computer glitch be in pain, anyway?

Paladin could probably tell me. If he was really here.

I flipped switches, powering the terminal up in sequence like Paladin'd taught me. All metaphor, which is another word for fake, but I didn't want to think about what I really looked like and what I was doing.

Now came the hard part; waiting whiles it came up and checked itself out. I couldn't open the connect to the outside world until it was ready—if I did I might as well just blow it up now and save time.

So I turned around to the other terminal in Aux Cont.

The uplink feed for the Morningstar Main Brain was already up and scrolling damage reports. I made it stop that and called up the engineering displays. A little more negotiation and it admitted it had attitude jets and let me in on their firing sequence. I started punching numbers.

"Grenade!"

I looked up when Errol yelled. He waggled his blaster at me.

"Come on, sweetheart, *move!*"

That's when I saw it; a present from Archive set for to do god knew what lying in the middle of the floor. I didn't stop to think. I took two steps and kicked it back out through the doorway. Errol shot it on the rise and it exploded like nothing I'd ever saw.

His shirt was bloody and torn and his color wasn't any good either. We was both moving slow and limping. Errol's left arm was pretty well useless and he was bleeding in a steady way there wasn't time to stop.

"You oke?" I said like a idiot.

"Never better." Errol smiled, and for just a instant I was fourteen again and off to see the world with him. Then he whipped around back to the corridor and I turned back to the display.

I turned the bright all the way up but the display was still hard to see. Archive was giving success its best shot. My hands slid off the keys as I pressed them.

—*pulse*—

I was everywhere and nowhere and all the words I ever knew

couldn't explain me. I was a pulse of light in a labyrinth of gold and crystal. I was—

Burke it here and Archangel won.

I held on to that thought. Archangel'd been my enemy since before I'd left home. It was Archangel sent Errol to Granola, looking for Old Fed Tech for his collection. It was Archangel hunted Baijon up and down and put us in each other's way, and framed me into the middle of a gang-war in a little place called Kiffit.

Archangel owed me for a whole lifetime's hurt.

I had hands. I had fingers. I rammed home the last of the coordinates and felt them trickle down to all systems. The room shook as Morningstar's engines fired in series, angling her on a course that would take her, in the course of a real-time month, into her sun.

The last part of that sequence wiped the engineering computers all the way back to blank plates. No way to stop the explosion. No way to correct the course.

"Darling, I hate to quibble, but I'm nearly out of charge." Errol looked back over his shoulder at me. A near-miss had scored him over the right cheek; the skin was raised and red.

"I'm almost done!"

All the status lights on the DataNet terminal showed green. I grabbed the big red switch and pulled.

It didn't move.

I heard Errol curse conversationally and pull a grenade out of his vest. Next to last or last; I'd lost count. He bounced it off the wall and blastered it on the rebound. The plasma-spray scrubbed memory half-way down the corridor and bought us a few seconds of silence.

Errol came and added his weight to mine. The switch eased over, then ran free so fast we barely got our fingers out in time.

It seemed like a window had opened somewhere: fresh planetary air and a sense of far roads opening that I wanted to travel.

Errol put his hand on my arm. "Whoever they are, they won't be here in time."

"No." But the far roads wasn't for me, or for anything human. "They won't be here in time."

There was the indefinable sound of regrouping forces from the corridor. Errol looked at me.

"You promised," he said.

"Je, che-bai. I did." I slid my blaster out of its leather. I looked at the indicator. Half-charge. Enough.

Set him free, he'd said. He'd known what he was asking. Archangel had been trying to beg buy borrow or steal a Library longer than I'd been alive. Lots of his tries was stored here. I'd just woke one of them up.

Errol wasn't real or anything like real.

Errol was a computer-ghost.

And he knew it.

There was only one freedom for a ghost in the machine. I brought the blaster up.

"Good-bye, Errol."

"Good-bye, sweetheart. Good hunting."

Pulling the trigger wasn't the hardest thing I've ever done. But it was close.

*　　*　　*

There was no body. Errol was gone to where 'leggers good and bad went and it was time for me to do the same. I had slightly less than no intention a'tall of being here when Paladin showed up—or staying so Archive could erase me here as a prelude to erasing me back in our co-owned cyborg peripheral.

It was true I didn't have a friendly Library here to show me the way out, but Archive didn't know quite everything yet about humans.

I shoved my blaster up against my cheekbone and pulled the trigger.

And I died.

And opened my eyes back in the housecore on Morningstar.

It was two minutes since Archive and my's cojoined selves'd been jacked into the Morningstar main comp.

Things had changed.

Five seconds after the two of us slid into the Margrave, Archive controlled all housekeeping functions for the palaceoid. Six seconds after it blew the surface installation loose—having already thoughtfully disabled all the computer controlled emergency systems. Fifteen levels lost pressure. Two hundred fifty people died.

I could see Archangel from here, giving hell to his senior surviving employee and trying to get used to the idea that trusting Archive'd been a lousy career move. If noise was light we'd all be taking serious radiation damage.

I flexed my fingers, cautious. They moved for me. Archive'd spent so much energy on the Margrave it was dormant here. Nice to be able to spend my last few minutes of life in charge of my own brain.

And Archangel's last, too. I wondered how he'd take the news.

I popped the jinks loose from the wallybox and they spooled back into my arm. Nobody noticed much. They was running back and forth. The explosion was just minutes ago, and the klaxons was still sounding. What I'd done to the engines hadn't happened yet out here.

I reached up and snapped the wires that led from me to Archangel's floating cyberdoc.

And that should of been the end of my real short life story, except for one thing.

I knew what Archangel was now. Something that'd survived being scavenged, crashed, and buried a thousand years, not to mention what I'd done to him/her/it on RoaqMhone and Royal. What if converting this palaceoid into a plasmoid *wouldn't* zetz Archangel?

Maybe wasn't good enough. I had to be *sure*.

Time to go.

Six minutes it'd been now since Archive decided it could do fine without Archangel's palaceoid. The klaxons cut off like somebody'd shushed them.

Then the attitude jets I'd jinked inside the computer got around to firing.

The palaceoid rocked. Gravity compensators lagged a split-instant behind. All the telltales and screens started gossiping about the new data.

Archangel spun around, a shifting column of interlocking holo-masks. The trailing edge of his cape floated outside the field, silk and silver. He saw me and twigged right quick I wasn't no more a peripheral zombie in a virtual world.

"Secure the woman. I want her alive!"

Just then the ready-room door blew in.

"Nobody move!" said the body in space armor that'd done it.

It wasn't Baijon's Hoplite armor. The armor in Archangel's doorway was only twenty percent as wide, two-thirds as tall, and bright chrome silver.

I recognized it. It was the special custom armor of Infinity Jilt, girl pirate of the spaceways.

But it wasn't Infinity Jilt, I was pretty sure.

It was Berathia. And if she'd got here and down here there was a place for Archangel to run to.

Intermission was over. 'Thia's first shot wrote hail and farewell to the blackwork cyberdoc homing in on me to do its wrist-slapping. Then somebody did move. 'Thia's silver armored arm arced over like a plasma-catapult on infinite setting and drilled him. Carbonized and cauterized in one easy motion.

"You're next, Prince Mallorum."

This was great fun, and probably worth a ninety-share on the Public Channel, but as a way of taking care of bidness it lacked a certain something.

Archangel thought so too. He turned to go, and I knew, just like I was still wrapped around all the cybertech, that he had a bolt-hole.

And I knew what it was.

My hunch was so enlightening I damn near threw up. It all made sense. Why had Archangel always used Errol, years and years? Because he could jump easily between identical bodies, but needed something more athletic to take over a new model. He'd hinted at that back when he was threatening me.

All sudden it was there in my mind—the box what Errol picked up in the first place. The box what Archangel came out of.

And went back into? Sure. And it could survive the blast, probably, or Errol could carry it right out of here, 'cause I bet real money even Berathia didn't know what Archangel looked like without his technology.

It didn't matter what Paladin got out of the comps. My side could still lose like we hadn't done anything here today at all. And now that Archangel knew that *Mereyon-peru* was somewheres in the universe to find, how long would it take him to find it?

And activate it.

Where was Archangel's bolt-hole?

Where nobody'd look.

"Butterfly, I found—" Pseudo-Paladin had tried to tell me when we was back in the Margrave. But that Paladin was me and I knew what it knew.

I knew where Archangel's original packaging was.

Nobody was looking at me for this particular split-instant. I slid off toward the barbecued Space Angel. His sidearm was still in working condition.

It was a military-issue blaster, heavy and slick in my hand. Civilian possession an automatic Class-D warrant. I eased it out of the holster.

I knew the ins and outs of this place, courtesy of my trip through Archive's brain. There was a go-down right here that'd take me where I thought I wanted to go.

All I needed was a little distraction.

'Thia-as-it-probably-was was delivering a patented glitterborn screed about how Archangel's something-or-other days was over. The one thing glitterborn and Libraries has in common is they both like to talk you to death.

Not me. I chose my target and pulled the trigger.

The chunk of techware I'd singled out went up in a shower of sparks and slagged expensive plastic. All the lights went out. Everything was dark as between the stars. The emergency lighting would of come up in half a tik except for that was what we was running on now.

Everybody started shooting.

That was the only thing I hadn't counted on. It made me belly up to what Morningstar was using for deck plates whiles wild plasma zinged back and forth overhead. It did a lot more damage than I could of thought of, and significantly delayed the rerouting of the backup lighting systems.

Glitterborn is dumb. But if they's so dumb, how come they're running the Empire?

As Baijon would say, this is a knowledge that Right Conduct withholds from the Gentle People—and anyone else with half a synapse.

The shooting stopped. The baseboard glow-strips did a subfusc flicker just as I got my fingers through the grabhandles. Full illumination in seconds. I yanked the cover off and dived down it just as the lights came up full.

"St. Cyr! Wait!"

Seemed like Berathia was always saying that to me. I paid as much attention as I usually did. I pulled the hatch down closed just as somebody started shooting again.

7

Getaway

I did not waste time wondering how 'Thia'd got herself here in a set of talkingbooks space armor and what it was she might want now that she'd got here. If we both lived I could ask her and if we didn't it didn't matter. What mattered was Archangel not getting away.

The sides of the godown scraped large patches off my unprotected skin and the air went foul almost immediately. No vents and blowers working down here, and I was betting that everyone left alive in Morningstar now was in the computer room over my head. Trapped. The pressure suits and space armor'd been stored at the docking ring—there wasn't a uncorrupt suit on the entire palaceoid.

But there was a jagranatha in shouting distance that'd be happy to dig out all survivors and send them off to raise more mischief. Including Archangel.

I kept going. The downdeep was even more real this time than it had been in the computer, surprise. Sensations wasn't waiting for me to notice them in my free time, they walked right up and introduced themselves.

What I was looking for had to be here—it was time for all good villains to beat feet and leave their flunkies to take the heat. Archangel didn't have a ship, and no spare hosts. There was only one sure coward's way out.

I felt Archive do a slow rollover in the back of my brain. It was my body—still or again. But like Archangel, all Archive had to do was wait to win.

And if I'd guessed wrong about anything, Archangel'd already won. Paladin'd never find out what he was. I'd deleted those files from the Margrave when I killed Errol.

The whole floor was knee-deep in mingled liquids and the compartment stank in a way that made me worry for Morningstar's recycling. And I was sure I was wrong—there was no shell, or it wasn't here, or it was already plasma and losing it made no difference.

Then I found it.

It was tucked into a low curve of the bulkhead, covered in muckrime because the heat was bleeding away through the shell without power to stop it.

The box Errol'd found back on Pandora.

Archangel's original packaging.

Maybe he didn't need it around to go brain-bouncing, but I bet it was tough enough to survive bouncing around infinite space and I bet he could hide out in it and wait for better odds whiles all the rest of us went to plasma.

Just like he had back on Pandora.

No.

Not this time. No matter what, Archangel was not going to walk away from this one. He was not going to jump to another toybox and start over. Not this time.

I pulled the thing loose from the bulkhead in an arpeggio of splintering ice. It was big enough I had to wrap both arms around it to hold it.

"Give that to me."

Archangel stood at the foot of the ladder in a dry well made by his personal shield. All the holos was gone; he looked like relying on his power of personality to carry the day.

"You need this, right? Or you wouldn't of kept it," I said.

He smiled, and I got a chill watching Errol's face go in ways it wasn't meant to go. I wondered if Errol was in there somewise, watching.

I wondered what Errol would of been like if Archangel'd left him alone.

"You have proven yourself a worthy ally, Butterfly St. Cyr. I am impressed. And inclined to be generous. Our interests are not incompatible: I will gift you with wealth and power beyond your imagining—and your life, which is no inconsiderable trinket."

"If I give you the box." The slurry was up to my elbows now.

"It is of some small sentimental attachment to me," Archangel lied.

"No deal, hellborn."

"A pity. You'll find I can change your mind."

This was it. Archangel wasn't playing games no more. The box in my hands went hot and I saw the hellviolet fade from Errol/Archangel's eyes. Errol looked at me. Beginnings of confusion, wondering where and t'hell Archangel'd dropped him this time. Own twin to the ghost in the machine.

I let go of the box and shot him.

The first shot disabled his personal shield; the second killed him. The third and fourth hit what was left as it was going under and brought clouds of foul-smelling steam up off the surface of the goo. I coughed and grabbed for the box again. It was floating on the surface, easy to my hand.

When I touched I knew I'd made the second Universe-class mistake of my life.

The artifact started singing out its irresistible-to-organics siren lure. Archangel'd made the jump. He was back inside now.

I knew what would happen. Open it, and I'd be rich, powerful, and cute. A century's setback wouldn't matter, nor anything Paladin, Baijon, and me'd done here today. The Archangel-thing had interlocking bolt-holes to run to. It'd cut its losses and trick another day.

And more. It could fix what Archive'd done to me; seal Archive off in a corner so I could use its tricks and not be bothered by it. It could stop the war easy as it'd started it, fix up the problems Baijon'd had with his Knife—all it wanted was to be Emperor and Paladin'd already said the Emperor wasn't powerful enough to do anybody any harm . . .

Let him in. Let him in and I could have whatever I wanted. Let him in and I could *be* whatever I wanted.

All I had to do was open the box. I could have everything I'd ever wanted. I could even live.

Everything.

But to get it, I had to let Archangel live.

I took my hand off the box. Then I slogged away from it until I reached the bottom rung of the godown. I climbed until I was out of the liquid.

The box glittered. I threw away one whole future the day I picked up Paladin. If I destroyed Archangel, I'd be doing the same thing again.

Wrong.

I pumped plasma at the box until the muck started to boil. I saw the first shot hit. There was sound and light that turned my bones to water and I saw the box explode in jagged shards of light. Then the steam hid everything else.

Not this time, Archangel.

The safety override interlock cut in and the trigger jammed. The blaster went dead in my hands. I stared at it whiles and then dropped it.

Gone. Everything gone. My last chance—and even if it was a lie and a fake losing it hurt just as much as if it was real. Now I'd never know. I'd never know any of the things Archangel could have taught me.

Knowledge had been lost.

Sometime later I started climbing to get out of the muck because even if you had to die there was better ways than drowning in unre-cycled garbage. After whiles I was far enough along that I might as well keep going.

I even spared a moment to mourn for Errol—and to wonder if the Errol Lightfoot I'd known had ever existed at all, really.

*   *   *

I got back to the Main Control Room the same way I'd left. No-body noticed. Everything was crazy. The Archangel Guardians was up against dying and they knew it, and less than a hour ago they'd been a glitterborn's pampered household guard. And in the middle of all their other problems, Archive was still doing its best to get at them.

And I had to get out. We'd won, and I couldn't let Baijon die not knowing that. I had to tell him. If Berathia'd got in, I could get out.

But I couldn't do it dressed like this. I slid around the edges till I found what I wanted—the where they kept the deaders they was tidying out of the way.

There was enough dead different sizes so I could get a close fit. Once I was kitted out head to foot in Space Angel black I had a lot better idea of what I should do, at least for the next few pages.

Get out of here. Avoid Paladin. Find Baijon.

Or die trying.

"You! What are you doing there?"

Unfortunately twenty-five percent of my available options wasn't that hard to achieve.

The commander of Archangel's household guard was standing looking at me with six of his overworked friends. I considered telling him they was all out of a job. I had the sidearm that went with my costume and the ability to shoot where the commander was going to be, and no way to get loose of all the fuss it'd cause.

And I didn't think he deserved to die any more than I did.

"She is here on my orders, Commander."

It was Archangel to the phoneme, and not a rath in sight.

And Archangel was dead.

Paladin. So much for another twenty-five percent of my options.

I straightened up and tried to look like one of Brother Mallorum's special agents.

"Report to the Command center, Captain St. Cyr," said Archangel's voice. I scuttled past the Commander in the direction of the housecore. Nobody shot me.

"Paladin?" I said, but not out loud.

I should of been glad to see him. I wasn't, and I couldn't sort why over the noise of Archive in the back of my skull wide-awake and yammering for a rematch.

So I headed for the dropshaft that would take me to the next level up and tried not to think. Everyone on Morningstar was going to die, except maybe me if I could broker a miracle.

I'd done my best to kill them. It was me jinked their damn reactor, not Archive. If I didn't want anybody dead, then was the time to recant.

Dead or alive? I wished I could make up my mind.

I wished I still had a mind to make up.

But half of it was Archive's, and this was what integration was like.

*   *   *

I made it as far as the dropshaft barricade, stumbling over rubble and the dying in the intermittent dark. My undeserved uniform got me that far but I didn't dare open my mouth and ask them to let me through. One word of patwa and they'd know I wasn't who they thought I was.

"We've had to fall back and secure this position, Captain," said someone when I got close. Faint light gleamed on his rank-marks.

I looked at the barricade. Or as they said in Imp-speak, secured position.

Fine talk, but there wasn't nothing to protect and nothing to fall back to. The housekeeping-systems was gone, and the only thing keeping the air in was the walls. The lieutenant's breath smoked on the air. He felt obligated to make sparkling chat whiles I figured how to get around him.

"The *Crown Regnant* should be here soon. Commander Helmuth

thinks the beacons on the surface are still intact, and—" The lieutenant noticed he was babbling and shut up.

All dying, and Archangel dead, but the war he'd started rolling along, picking up speed as it went and a bunch of players who didn't care who'd started it, really, so long as they got to party down until there wasn't nothing left.

There was no beacons left on the surface of Morningstar. There wasn't no surface to leave them on.

What there was, was a spray of blaster fire back the way we'd came. The lieutenant twitched—a glitterborn boy, off to do the pretty in their particular polite way. Good as dead now and nobody to hand the butcher's bill to. The ship Archangel had coming would take one look at the place and assume no survivors. If it even showed up.

"Are you— Are there any orders for me, sir?" the lieutenant said, quiet.

If thinking this way was supposed to be an improvement on the factory-model me, I'd take unreconstructed any time, thanks.

"Je," I said, not caring now what he made of my Interphon. *It ain't that easy, Archive.* "Everybody pull back. I make sure the beacons're kicking and your ship knows where to find you. You just keep alive till bye-m-bye. They get you out."

Either Archangel had some damn funny recruits on his team or the lieutenant didn't care.

"Captain . . . Thank you."

He saluted me and left. I didn't look at him.

"Butterfly," the wall said in Paladin's voice.

I ignored that too. I went over the barricade, blew the doors off the dropshaft and went up it.

*   *   *

The doors on the next level up was open. Pitch dark and silent; I put my head up and a shot sprayed off the floor and did a hopeful job of parting my hair with molten crete.

" 'Thia, if that's you I thought we was better friends than that," I said from six inches below floor level.

There was a interregnum or two.

"Captain St. Cyr?" said Berathia, digitized and filtered.

"If I say yes, you going to shoot me?"

"It's about time you got here!" Berathia said.

That was supposed to be my line.

"So I'm here," I said, still playing least-in-sight. Somehow, Berathia being still around had not been part of my plans. Archangel's boys was supposed to be better nor that, but maybe they'd had distractions.

Not that I had any personal objections to 'Thia's continued breathing. The question was, whose backup was she? I didn't think she was mine.

I hadn't heard her move before she was standing over me. Her high-ticket chrome boots was about level with my hairline. She reached down and pulled me up, and it was a good thing she picked the fake hand to grab because where her armor touched me it was space-cold.

"Come on," Berathia said, dragging me through the rubble.

There'd been a fire in the palaceoidcore, and most everything was smashed. The last hurrah of the emergency lighting kept the room from being completely nyctalopian, but it was dark enough that I went through, not over, a lot of it.

"Hey— Look— Will you hold up or slow down or something?"

The bug-eyed chrome helmet turned toward me.

"Do you want to be here when this place goes boom? Somebody spiked the generators," Berathia Notevan said.

Do tell. She did slow down enough though to thread me through the slagged doorway with tender concern for all the parts of me that was still organic, even if most of them was numb by now. What was beyond that was completely dark.

"I can't see!" I pointed out.

"Then hold on to me. We don't have time to waste."

This assertive new side of our 'Thia was something I'd of gone a long way to miss. My breath was freezing in my throat, and with enough pause for quiet reflection I would of just stood home and took my chances with the spiked reactors. Only Berathia was holding on too hard for that.

She dragged us into a empty dropshaft. I held on to her without any prompting and she kicked in the armor's A-grav and up we went.

For a long time. Gravity stopped. The armor went even faster. We kept going. For longer, in fact, than there was levels, pressurized or un-.

"Uh, 'Thia . . ." I said.

"Just hold on," she said back. "I'm pretty sure this will work."

Not what I want to hear from the pilot.

Berathia swung her arm up and fired. The slagged top end of the dropshaft ripped loose with the combined force of plasma fusion and hot atmosphere.

We wasn't in Morningstar no more.

I was looking at raw vacuum.

You can suck vacuum for about three minutes before your blood boils. If you're anywheres near a star, you'll probably cop enough rads to make it a nithling point whether you make the next air lock or not.

We was somewheres near a star.

The minute Berathia shot out through the hole where the air lock used to was I knew I was dead. But I'd got in the habit of playing out losing hands, whiles back, so I shut my eyes and blew out my lungs and tried to be a pressure suit all on my lonesome. I felt cold as the heat bled off her armor and then I didn't feel anything as my skin froze to it even through my borrowed uniform.

And then we was there.

I figured later she must of left both hatches on her singleship lock open to void same as Baijon and me had. At the time all I noticed was her ripping me loose from her suit and pitching me free-fall while every bubble of gas in my body clamored for out and exegesis.

I hit something hard and bounced off it. My eyes came open and started icing over. I saw the locks slam shut in the dead silence of no air and 'Thia flash through them just before they did. There was dark, then light, then gravity, and the first thing I heard was the thin wail of repressurization and me thinking it'd be a damn shame to die now of air just a little too thin and too late.

I gasped like the pumps was going the other way and my teeth chattered so hard I bit myself. I spat out chunks of pink ice. Bits of my skin thawed enough to bleed. What was left would peel. I'd probably be dead before then.

Pressure equalized to where I was left with only chest pains and nosebleed. Berathia pulled off her helmet. I was glad to see it was actually her after wasting so much belief on the idea.

"It worked!" She smiled at me, full of self-absorbed delight. "I wasn't sure it would, you know—but then, I didn't have a spare suit for you anyway, and I couldn't waste time going back after it if I did. Daddy was *that* upset after you vanished the way you did; really, I do think that a little common courtesy—he was the person who made it possible for you to absolutely *mortify* Mallorum Archangel."

"He mortified, j'keyn. He's dead."

"Dead?" Her big brown Imperial eyes went round. "But you must have misunderstood! Daddy didn't want you to *kill* Prince Mallorum."

If Paladin'd reported back a sixth of what was in the Morningstar comps to Prinny, I bet he'd changed his mind since and I was now in line for the Imperial Cluster with crossed garters.

But right now something else was more important. I coughed a couple times to get moisture into my throat.

" 'Thia, you send out a general distress to *Crown Regnant*. I don't know their codes but they're in the area; they'll hear a general. If they hurry they can get the rest of Archangel's people off Morningstar before it blows."

Maybe it was the happy way Archive contemplated xenocide, but getting the innocent standbyers off Morningstar mattered. Like Baijon, they'd never been anything but in the wrong place, most of them.

Berathia stared at me like I was speaking clear-quill patwa. I tried again, concentrating on making it Interphon.

"We don't want to do that," she said when I finished the second time.

"Yes we do, 'Thia." The heat and humidity was both turned up high for my benefit. Condensation trickled down the walls and over the shiny parts of my borrowed Space Angel blacks. On my left I could see the mercy seat and status decks of Berathia's cockpit. All the lights on her boards showed Not Ready and my skin felt like something left out in a snowbank too long.

"Don't be silly. We don't want anyone to know we were here. And besides, what do a few hundred retainers matter? It isn't as if they were ours."

And that was that. 'Thia unsealed her armor and started pulling it off, segment by segment, showing something better'n skin beneath.

The difference between glitterborn and real people is that glitterborn takes such a damn long view of everything that people disappear right out of it. I stood up, wondering if I could take her once she had the armor off or if sweet reason would turn the trick. My nose started bleeding again. My gums hadn't stopped. I thought about spitting and swallowed instead.

Then one of the lights on 'Thia's board went green.

"To the unidentified *chaudatu* ship, greetings. Hear, eater of corpses, that I, Baijon Stardust, require you to return to me alive my partner which you have ravished unto your vessel. Should it be that she is dead, know that I will surely kill you."

Hellflowers makes friends wherever they go, and Baijon only talks that pretty to subhumans and nonpersons.

I was so glad he was alive I went weak in the knees, which was damsilly as his life ambition now was to kill himself and me first and I'd just made it possible.

Berathia was down to her interstellar jammies. She looked surprised for the half-second it took her to vault over me to the cockpit and open a channel.

"Prince Valijon, this is Gentle Docent Berathia Notevan. I have Captain St. Cyr aboard alive and well."

"Yo, babby-bai," I said, in case he could hear it.

"I'd like to congratulate you—" Berathia went on, but Baijon cut her off.

"You will deliver her alive to me."

Berathia fiddled with her hair and turned back to me. There was a gun in her hand now, despite what she hadn't been wearing. I put both hands on top of my head. 'Thia smiled encouragingly. I spat on her deck.

"I'm afraid I can't do that, Honored One. You see, Daddy doesn't like the idea of Captain St. Cyr just running around loose. He'd like her to come back to Bennu Superfex now."

Him or Paladin? If this was Paladin's idea 'Thia had stone-cut orders to take me alive—but alive could be a very flexible concept that left lots of room for improvisation.

I wished I knew what was going on.

'Thia's little silver gun stayed on me whiles she fiddled with the bells-and-whistles on the keyboard of her glitterborn spacetoy.

"And frankly, Prince Valijon, he hasn't any further use for you at all."

A display on her board flashed to life and ran through all the things it had to say. "Target Acquired," for instance. Also, "Torpedoes Armed."

Berathia smiled a small shark smile at me and I knew there was no way I was getting near the disable. I was going to try anyway.

"I must tell you, *Shaulla* Berathia, that if you essay these things your ship will not serve you."

"You just let me worry about that, Highness, and do whatever you like. I've got what I came for."

I started for her and she pulled the trigger. It wasn't a blaster. I hadn't thought it was. Everything got very slow and cold as relative motion was sucked out of every molecule I had on me. The blood I was wearing felt like a separate mask. Whiles I could still see, Berathia slammed down the "Fire Enable" lever and over the sound I could hear Baijon on her commo.

"I am sorry to disappoint you, *shaulla,* but I have already done it. You have no engines."

Berathia's boards went black. And then so did mine.

*   *   *

I woke up staring at a more familiar ceiling that looked like it was under water. *Ghost Dance.* I moved, and everything went crinkle. I held up a hand and looked at it.

Fingers covered in silver foil; flashwrap holding my body together, taking over for my skin, filtering my precious bodily fluids and explaining why everything looked so funny: gel-shields over my eyes. "Temporary Emergency Use Only," said the canister in the Imperial battle-aid kits where things like this lived.

Somebody'd put it on me. Not 'Thia. Not with Bennu Superfex less than a day away by angeltown. She'd have other plans for my glorious resurrection.

"Art thou she whom I sent into battle?" someone asked in helltongue. My stomach went flip-flop because that ain't one of the cants I know—understanding it was a gift from Archive, and Archive doesn't like hellflowers very much.

"Art thou the woman? And of the great enemy of Life, and its handmaid, what news?" Baijon said.

"Go away," I said in Interphon. "Je nala," I added for good measure. I felt like freeze-dried leather souffle. Try being stasis'd on top of explosive decompression on top of a day full of fun too numerous and awful to mention, sometime.

"Thou must—" Baijon stopped, and started over again in Interphon. "St. Cyr? Is it you? *Ne-Malmakosim, ea?"*

Was I a Library this week, he wanted to know, not that I'd believe me if I was him.

And was I? Was I sure of who had and hadn't made the last cut out of Morningstar Main Brain? How did I feel about the preservation of organic life, for example?

I tried sitting up. I've done more successful experiments. Baijon took charge and propped me against the bulkhead. Burn-gel went squish and ooze in my safety-sealed-for-your-protection flashwrap.

"Paladin—" I started to say, but maybe Baijon didn't remember that some of the Enemies of All Life had names. "The Library at Bennu Superfex—"

"Does not trouble us here, San'Cyr. The *Ghost Dance* does not drink from the Imperial DataNet, and so *Malmakos* does not find access here."

I was relieved, and that hurt worst of all. I'd always trusted Paladin, before.

Before I'd met Archive. And found out what a Library could be. If there was even the smallest chance of something like that getting out loose it was worth anything to stop it.

Wasn't it?

Paladin wasn't Archive. But he could be, with world enough and time, just like Baijon could be a power-mad heretic like Kennor Star-bringer. And throw into the balance that Pally'd hooked up with the high-heat we'd spent our mutual career avoiding and now he was making plans I couldn't follow involving shoving people around like playing pieces.

Like the people down on Morningstar.

"Look," I said to Baijon. "Morningstar's set to go up like a roaming candle. Goforths is jinked. 'Bai, you listen me. Is Imp glittership *Crown Regnant* coming here. You call them, tell them hurry, is people trapped down there next by the airmaker and the generators about to blow. You tell them come and get them off, or Archangel he have something to say about it."

I started coughing. Baijon looked at me.

"Does Archangel yet live, then?" he said.

"Just do it," I got out between hacks.

Baijon left, and when I got my lungs back in order I rummaged until I found the battle-aid kit the suit'd come out of. Every time I moved I felt the slide between the suit's skin and my skin and the jelly between. It made me clumsy.

I found what I wanted and kept myself, barely, from scarfing half a dozen. That'd kill me quick. I took one, carefully, and sat back while it turned the world to sweet savage starfire. Metabolic enhancers sang in my blood; life and energy fake as half my body. They was buying me time—

For what?

Come with me, I'd said to Baijon in what now seemed like another lifetime. *Put by all your hellflower choplogic honorcodes and throw in with me just long enough to kill Mallorum Archangel, and I won't ask you for anything else.*

Well he had and we had and now what?

Item: I did not relish standing around whiles Baijon iced hisself.

Item: I wouldn't have to because he'd never leave me alive behind him.

Item: even if he would I wouldn't be here soon. More and more of my ego-signatures was being hopelessly overwritten with Archive's laundry lists, as Paladin'd almost said, and when your favorite breeder slut and mine was nonfiction Archive'd be here with a body, a blaster, and a ship that could take him back to *Mereyon-peru* where he could wake up all the other Libraries.

Which Paladin was maybe doing right now. He knew where it was. He always had. I hadn't gotten the Jump-numbers for the Ghost Capital from Archive. I'd got them from *Paladin.*

Who hadn't told me about the place when it could do me some good.

And even if all the Libraries on *Mereyon-peru* was all just like Pally, what it meant for organics in the Empire was just one more goddamn overlay of overlords, and what happened when these immortal inhuman Libraries got tired of us again?

I wondered if Pally'd always been so nice to me because he needed me so much. And didn't have any power, really, while he was stuck impersonating a navicomp in my ship.

I didn't like the thought. I hoped I knew him better nor that.

But I'm a damn poor judge of character. I'm the one that went off with Errol Lightfoot on his damn crusade twenty years ago, remember?

*　　*　　*

Baijon came back whiles I was wrestling with unfamiliar higher levels of thought.

"The *chaudatu* ship is summoned," he said abruptly. "And I have moved the *Ghost Dance* out of range of this place with the *good numbers* you left for me. Now you will tell me where Archangel has run, so that we may craft a new plan for his death."

"Archangel's dead," I said.

It should of made me feel good. We'd won, hadn't we? Paladin was turning Archangel's computers inside out, the great man himself was just a grease spot in Eternity . . .

Mallorum Archangel was dead.

But as a showdown, third book and out, *Thrilling Wonder Talkingbooks* would never have bought it. Too many loose ends.

Baijon closed his eyes like he was hurting. For a minute I thought he was going to cry.

"Is it true?" Baijon said. "Did you take his head?"

"He didn't have a head when I killed him. But it's true. I swear, 'bai. Fact."

There was a long pause. Then Baijon said:

"It is not enough."

His voice was so low I barely heard him. He came along of me where I was sitting and tried to crawl into my lap. He shook and I held him and after whiles he started talking.

"San'Cyr, while I waited here to see you dead, I listened. With this ship many things can be heard—it had access to the most secret messages. I heard that which the Throne wishes to say and wishes not to say. The *Crown Regnant* would not have come, save that I promised her Archangel's vengeance. She is needed elsewhere. All the Fleet—all the Thronespace Navy—is.

"There is war, San'Cyr. Washonnet has invaded Tangervel Directorate. The alMayne have invaded and the Ghadri have risen in support of their invaders. Those who were my people are at war."

There was a long pause. "And the Coalition is winning," Baijon said.

Winning?

Against the Imperial Starfleet?

He had to be wrong. Nobody took on the whole Imperial Starfleet. Let alone won when they did.

He was wrong. There was civil war in Washonnet Sector—hellflowers' home Directorate. I knew that. Baijon was just mixing things up.

But what if he wasn't? What if the civil war was over and Kennor's side'd won? What if the alMayne'd done just what Baijon said—challenged the whole Empire to a knife-fight over the use of Inappropriate Technology?

On Toystore Kennor Starbringer'd said that the hellflowers planned to scoop the whole Azarine Coalition and weld it into a fighting force to take Throne, rescue the (nonexistent) Emperor, and make the universe safe for Truth, Justice, and the Hellflower Way.

Had they done it?

To be exact, had Kennor's faction unified alMayne and then taken the Coalition into revolt against the Empire?

Baijon said yes. And if Throne was pulling back Thronespace Navy and Archangel's personal ships to support Fleet, he was likely right.

I tried to remember why that was so bad. It came back slow like from another lifetime. Hellflower war, and at the end, rule by revealed truth. Theocracy.

One more time I'd had a ringside seat at being useless. If I'd gone to Morningstar to put a stop to galactic war I might as well have stood home. The war to stop Archangel had taken its show on the road, and it wasn't going to stop just because Archangel had.

"What of they who were my people, falsely gone to war for Archangel's lies? And San'Cyr—what of the other Library?"

Paladin, he meant.

"It must not be allowed to remain," Baijon said. "It must end and then the war will end."

Wrong.

"Him," I said. "Paladin's a he."

And could my good buddy, hellgod machine, ex-partner stop the war—even if he wanted to?

No. If it'd got this far it didn't matter what even Paladin did. 'Cause he only had two methods he could use and neither one'd work.

Use the resources of the Empire to put down the fuss—but that's what Kennor'd been planning for, all along. And Fleet didn't have a Governor-General just now, and by the time it got its waterfowl regimented the Coalition'd waltz all over them on their way to the corner of Theocracy and Old Night.

Or Paladin could use Old Fed Tech.

He could. Archive had, and Paladin knew what Archive knew. He might even think it was worth it, in a triage sort of way.

But if he did that, the hellflowers would never stop coming until fifteen minutes after the last one was dead. And neither would anything else that'd ever heard of a Library.

I thought of a Hamat Empire/Azarine Coalition axis and shuddered. Even the Sodality and the Celestials'd probably come in on the human side of a Library-fight. It'd been their galaxy too, a thousand years ago.

Archangel had his war, and it was too late to put it back in its box. It had to of been too late before I'd gone to Bennu Superfex. And by the time it was over Throne'd be as dead as *Mereyon-peru*.

We'd burked it, we'd lost, there was slightly less than no hope a-t'all. The hellflower crusade was started and no amount of ingenious disinformation would stop it.

I ran my silver fingers through Baijon's hair. It crackled against the foil. Reality was two layers away now, no matter what.

"So what is it exactly, 'bai, that you want?" I said.

Baijon didn't say anything.

"Dream big, 'bai. What fetches you? Galactic peace? The Coalition to win? No *Malmakos* from here to the Rim? The keys to the Ghost Capital—" No, scratch that, we'd got that already. "—Death?"

Baijon sat himself up and straightened his bits and pieces. He looked like someone who desperately wanted someone else to tell him what to do, and I'd been there myself, but what I knew and he was learning was that there never is nobody.

Nobody you can trust.

"I want what the Loremasters told the Gentle People we—*they*—must have. They must not rule. They must fight the Machine. That is what I want."

Stop the Coalition. Stop the war. I closed my eyes and watched the swirling patterns of war. The shapes of what Paladin called the evolution of structure. And evolution never stops.

Stop the Coalition. It ought to be easy enough. They held a dozen planets where the Empire had a thousand.

Stop the Coalition. Not easy at all. The Empire held a thousand worlds, sure, but the Empire wasn't the cheery monolith of yore. Its *politick*'d been fragmented by Archangel, year after loving year. It couldn't pull itself together to repulse the Coalition's bid and knock the Coalition and its allies back into their respective systems.

Stop the Coalition. Stop the war.

Stop Paladin.

Because without stopping Paladin wasn't nothing else stopped. Without stopping Paladin wasn't Libraries stopped, nor wars, nor power-mad glitterborn. So long as Paladin stayed in the game the game was rigged.

And the stakes was too high to play to lose.

It always came back to that: the part I gagged on. Stop him, put him back to another thousand-year sleep . . .

Kill him.

Kill my partner.

Ex-partner.

Or risk what he'd do.

This time it weren't as simple as choosing whether or not to dust Archive. It was deciding whether I had to ice Paladin—or try to—for what he might do a thousand years from now. If glitterborn took such a damn long view of things they didn't care who they hurt, what about a Library that lived forever and didn't know what pain was?

Twenty years too late to ask the goddamn questions, and whatever answers they had I didn't want to know anyway.

And I recognized what the unfamiliar flat feeling I had was.

Freedom.

For the first time in my life. I could do anything, choose anything—live a little longer, die—and there was no reason why I shouldn't. There was no reason to prefer one course of action over another.

Except for, maybe, the thought that what Archangel and Kennor'd done between them wasn't quite fair for everybody who was going to die of it.

Was that me thinking? Or my souvenir of Paladin bringing up points I'd always told him was nithling?

I could at least be sure it wasn't Archive. Probably.

I thought about it. And I took a deep breath. And found I had a little more running to do.

"I got a plan, 'bai. Word this: blow up Grand Central—the main computer on Throne where the dataweb crosses. If it goes down, it pulls the DataNet down with it."

Too many words that wasn't mine crowded in: how the war couldn't be stopped now but it could be managed. How the strategy was to let the theocrats win without smashing the Empire, so that the intact structure they ruled over would corrupt them. How the rest of the Coalition would throw off hellflower idealism once they saw Archangel dead and his war-machine scattered. How letting the Coalition make a quick strike at the center would make sure they found out exactly how many Emperors they really had and start getting libertine ideas. How a splinter-group of hellflowers'd go off to be pure once more, but only if they saw the main bouquet corrupted.

How they'd need someone to lead them when they went.

All fueled by the one death that paid for all.

Paladin.

Baijon gave the idea serious thought, which showed how much he knew.

"And without their spies, the Imperial forces will fail to destroy the Coalition," Baijon said. "And the Coalition will take Throne. San'Cyr, that does not help."

"Destroy the DataNet and you destroy the Empire," I said. "Fact."

Baijon considered this. I could see his lips move, making the three-cornered translation from patwa to Interphon to helltongue and back out again. Making sure he knew exactly what it was I'd said.

"Do you say, San'Cyr, that do we shut down the *chaudatu* data transfer network the Empire will fall and therefore the Gentle People will cease to strive against it?"

Bet on it. Oh not this year or even next, but in the long run that's what would happen.

In the very long run.

I shuddered, but there weren't no other play to make. We already had the war, rattling around the Empire like loose cargo in a hold. The only thing to do when Life fetched you those numbers was play them.

Give the Coalition such an easy win they wouldn't be mad oncet they fetched up at Throne. Shut down the dataweb.

And seal Paladin into the Grand Central computer, trapped with nowheres to run to.

"And the *Malmakos?*" said Baijon, just like he was telegenic. "When the DataNet ceases to be, will the *Malmakos* Paladin also die?"

No. You'd have to blow up the Grand Central Brain to do that. Which the happy warriors of the Coalition'd be thrilled to death to do. Providing someone told them what was there.

"San'Cyr, you cannot let it survive."

I stared at silver fingers and wondered why I cared so much about something when real soon there wasn't going to be a me to care about anything at all. I tried to convince myself that it didn't make no never-mind whether I said Baijon could ice Paladin or no, Paladin being able to take care of hisself.

"He's my friend."

I tried to pretend I didn't have to make up my own mind. Pick a side and, win or fail, have Paladin know what I'd chose.

"It was not made for a world where people are. This is not only the Law—this is the truth. It cannot be if Life is to be. I have chosen, as my ten-fathers did. Now you must."

"And if I choose Paladin, babby-bai?" Fool answer. I'd already made my choice. Long time back, when I'd been willing to kill me and Paladin both to keep Archive from getting loose.

"If the *Malmakos* is as human as you say, San'Cyr, it knows it is not made for this world. I would die for you. Will it? San'Cyr, do you hear?"

"I hear you, babby." There was a long pause whiles I thought that if I just stalled long enough I'd never have to make up my mind.

Baijon took a deep breath, and let it out. "San'Cyr, you have told me this Paladin was your friend," Baijon said. "I am your *comites*. I would be your friend. I will help you destroy the DataNet. Will you help me kill the *Malmakos?*"

I thought some more. Hard thoughts. Twenty years worth of knowing Paladin. From Grand Central he could do anything he wanted with the nature of reality in the Phoenix Empire. I wondered what Pally'd do with a bright shiny Empire all his own.

No I didn't.

I knew what he'd do. He'd make it safe.

And I made my choice.

"Je, reet, babby. We dust Pally-bai."

"You do not lie to me, San'Cyr?" Baijon said, hoping real hard.

I thought about love, and a lot of other damsilly nonsense.

About how probably we'd get holed by a meteor and nothing we'd studied to decide would matter.

About how long you could plan for if you was going to live forever. About how Paladin loved learning like a bride, and would use everything he had to keep the alMayne technophobes from taking Grand Central and the Empire. How he'd try to fight them with common sense, by showing the Empire he wasn't nothing to be afraid of. That he could help them.

Stripping *Mereyon-peru* of Old Fed Tech to show for proof of his innocence. Leaving it lying around for both sides to make wartoys from. Wartoys they wouldn't hesitate to use.

Paladin wouldn't understand that until it was too late. The Old Federation had believed in the fundamental perfectibility of Man.

I shook my head.

"No," I said to Baijon. "I don't lie. First the DataNet. Then Paladin."

And since I was real lucky, I wouldn't have to live with myself afters.

8

The Avenging Saint

The Imperial dataweb woffed and yabbered through the speakers Baijon'd left on in *Dance*'s cockpit. Ship movements, mobilizations, Imperial appointments to replace Imperial appointees who was plasma rings in the never-never time along now. I could hear it from halfway down the corridor. It was telling me how the Coalition had the outer Midworlds—half of which'd come over to them free and all found once they heard the Coalition wanted to rescue the Emperor from Archangel.

Only there weren't no Emperor to rescue. And Archangel was dead.

Baijon opened the hatch to the cockpit. It slid back. He stepped back. I went in.

And was face-to-face with Berathia Notevan, spy and Imperial Daddy's girl.

She was webbed completist-like into the songbird seat with an entire spool of cargo tie-down that I couldn't imagine where Baijon'd got it because *Dance* never carried such a thing in her glitterborn life. I could see eyes and nose and the top of her head and I wondered how long she'd been here.

"Yo, 'Thia," I said. "How's tricks?" I looked at Baijon. He shrugged.

"She was defeated. She had rescued you, if for her own fell purposes. I did not wish her to give information to those who might save her. And perhaps . . ."

"You thought I might actually sometime get around to icing some-body for honor's sake?"

Baijon gave the ghost of a hellflower smile. "With breath, one hopes. And she may be useful."

I could not imagine what Baijon'd think 'Thia could be used for, other than hull-patching. I shrugged and started unwinding her. After the tie-down slipped out of my hyaloid hands four or five times Baijon took over. I retreated to the mercy seat and watched him with one eye and the bells-and-whistles with the other.

Dance was our good girl, and still had inventories of air and water and power enough to take us from here to the Ghost Capital of the Old Fed and back six times. We had everything we needed to win but brains, and I bent my mind to successfully pulling the big red switch marked "Success" in a reality that wasn't virtual.

Question: if you wanted to blow up the dataweb, how?

Answer: if you was me, jack in and do it. (Maybe I could and maybe I couldn't. That was something that'd have to be tricked with another time. But I'd shut down a planetary net. The difference be-tween that and the galactic net was just a matter of size. Probably.)

Question: jack in *where?*

Answer: the only place where all the lines of the DataNet crossed. In the Grand Central Computer, located on the surface of Throne.

Question: and get there *how?*

Baijon'd got Berathia all unwrapped now. All she was wearing was what'd been under the space armor, and all her hair'd been combed out by somebody with a suspicious nature. She tidied herself back together with a certain eloquence and didn't say anything out loud.

The commo went on choodling out Thronespace tactical broad-casts about kill-ratios and acceptable losses and survivor indices. It was war, all right, and the warfront moving fast: Throne would have to fall back to regroup but they'd never reclaim the territories they aban-doned. Take that from a expert: Archive. The next big battle'd be fought for the High Mikasa Shipyards, and the Empire'd lose. Then the Coalition'd be the only ones able to build new ships—High Del-Khobar is mostly light assembly and pleasure yachts and I think the other three licensed ones are too.

And once the Coalition held the manufactures, they could attrit the hell out of the Imperial forces. And win.

Unless we stopped it. And me without any idea of how I was going to get into the Imperial Throneroom to pull the plug on all this giddy ecstasy.

"You got words, 'Thia?" I asked when she was all unwrapped.

"Captain St. Cyr?" she said, hesitant, which I guess she had a right to be on account of I was all covered in foil. "Are you all right?"

"I been better, maybe."

She stood up, one eye on Baijon. "That suit's no substitute for full detoxification. You're lucky to be alive at all. Come back to Bennu Superfex with me. I'll see you get proper treatment."

"Ain't nobody going to Bennu Superfex, 'Thia."

She was negotiating for something and I wondered what. But I've done this kind of thing blindside before.

"If you don't you'll be dead before morning," she snapped.

"You got better odds for me if I go?" I said. Her eyes flickered. I hadn't thought so, really. "No deal."

"If you're not going to be reasonable, Captain St. Cyr, I'm not going to talk to you."

"I am being reasonable."

"If you were being reasonable you'd go back to Bennu Superfex with me."

"I would not."

"Yes you would."

This was not getting neither of us nowhere.

"Pardon me a little if going back to get chopped, shopped, and wrapped by his Prince-Electfulness ain't my idea of fine times, but you might remember I never wanted to meet him in the first place."

"You're the one who wanted to destroy Prince Mallorum's political ambitions. Well, now he's dead—that's even better for you, isn't it?" 'Thia said.

I gave that the brainwork it deserved, about five seconds worth. "Dead or not, why should I kick back to Prinny afters?"

Berathia looked at me like I'd grown an extra head.

"For the *pardon*, you moron. Or do you like the idea of being shot first and questioned afterward?"

If a pardon'd got offered in anybody's hearing but 'Thia's it wasn't mine. On the other hand, a pardon wasn't exactly one of your basic drop everything incentives, seeing how long I'd have to enjoy it and how much interest Baijon had in it.

"You wanted Archangel offed. You said so, you and all your conspiracy buddies. He's iced and I did it. You owe me, maybe," I suggested.

"You can have anything you want if you come back to Bennu Superfex with me," Berathia said earnestly. "I swear it."

"Peace with honor?" I said.

"Oh, the so-called Coalition's victories are only temporary . . ." she began, but even Berathia Notevan couldn't sell that lie. "Daddy won't let them win," she said, and it was whistling in the dark.

"And how shall he prevail against them," Baijon asked her, "when even the *chaudatu* know him for a tongueless eater of corpses whose words are windflowers?"

I guess treason can get to be addictive. Berathia went pale under her built-in glitter. Her mouth opened and closed a couple times.

"Jillybai," I said, "I guess you can't be livealive and stupid all together. You spied on Kennor-bai for His Electfulness and did his hellgod techsmithing. Didn't it never occur to you the war he was arming for was going to happen?"

Berathia shook her head, over and over. "No. Never. War can*not* happen. The disaffected elements were to align against Archangel and neutralize him—clandestinely, of course, and that would eliminate the troublemakers. And Archangel. But they would never go to war. With Archangel dead or in exile, why should they?"

Baijon looked at her like she was talking patwa. "All the Empire is the same. What matter that one oppressor dies if one survives?"

Politics. My brain was turning to burn-cream and they was going to argue politics.

"Daddy—" Berathia began.

"—has plans for me that don't include peace in our time," I finished.

And had Paladin too, who might be backing him or might not, but either way wasn't going to take kindly to my idea of letting the Coalition turn out the lights all through the Midworlds.

Berathia hesitated. "He wants you back."

"Why?" Baijon said, flat. Berathia looked us back and forth, considering.

"He didn't say."

" 'Thia-bai," I said, real soft, "you ever ask yourself what he wanted with me in the first place?"

Berathia shrugged. "Obviously you're a . . ." she stopped.

"Librarian," I said sweetly. "Only Prinny's got my Library now. So study over where you come down on the *Malmakos* question, and let me know whose play you going to back."

Berathia hardly skipped a beat. "There is no Library. Daddy has a copy of the Brightlaw Prototype."

"Coalition won't see it that way, 'Thia-bai. Even if they do, Coalition's led by *hellflowers.*"

She thought about that whiles the war reports malingered on.

"They'll never make it to Throne, Captain St. Cyr."

"What is it exactly, 'Thia, you betting?"

There was another, longer, pause. I didn't think she'd really jump sides, but I didn't care whether she plotted a little on her own time or not. Unless she had a dreadnought in her pocket there weren't nothing she could do to influence events one way or t'other.

"What do you want?" she finally said.

"Into the Emperor's palace on Throne."

And I thought once she had a chance to study on it, she might prefer not being in Prinny's reach.

And besides, she'd saved my life. Even if she did try to kill me and Baijon afters.

The cockpit lights flickered. I knew that one. We'd tripped a scanning beam, like as not.

Only there shouldn't be anything out here scanning for us.

Except one thing.

I slid into the mercy seat and eyeballed the navicomp. No Jumpnumbers loaded. Pick some quick; Paladin'd be here in a minute. Where should we go?

Baijon slid into the worry seat and started shutting things down. Silence came down like a ax as he cut *Dance* off from the outside.

But Paladin—if it was Paladin looking—could turn her back on.

I picked something quick. Anything, anywhere, to get us out of here.

"What are you—?" said Berathia.

"Running. As usual," I said.

"Go!" said Baijon in a strained whisper.

The boards he'd shut down started coming back up. I heard a open commo channel hiss on a different frequency.

I pulled the angelstick for the Drop. One jump ahead of the other guys. Still.

*   *   *   *   *

The Court of the TwiceBorn 7:
The Uses of Adversity

Power delights, and is the natural pursuit of intellect. True power is only to be discovered through the possession of absolute knowledge.

Well, then—how to begin?

Ask what knowledge is and one begs the question: absolute knowledge is as different from a compendium of facts as a single blade of grass is from the planet upon which it grows, and spending one's time in empty philosophy has never seemed to me a method of achieving anything. Power is my desire, not a philosophic acceptance of powerlessness.

And any course of reasoned action aimed at the knowledge of power—or its obverse—must begin with the Libraries.

It is possible that their intellects were—or are, as some undeniably remain—not vaster than ours. What is certain is that their memories were greater and their ability to learn was faster.

One might be led to the conclusion—in the face of objective evidence—that adaptability is power, when to adapt is to acknowledge a force greater than oneself.

Assuming, that is, one chooses to think of learning as adapting. I prefer to consider learning as an improving grasp of the immutable.

And now my happy mirror image, Archangel, is dead—a fortunate turn of events, considering what I now know about him. Yet what shall I do for a touchstone now that my Archangel is gone? He was amusing, as only the truly dangerous can be. He might yet have been useful, in some small fashion.

Wishful thinking. The Paladin Library made available the concatenate memory of Morningstar the moment the link was opened to it by my less-than-reliable cat's-paw (finally reappearing to perform her designated task after a most unwise interregnum). Archangel's secret history has been made public in the most pertinent quarters; his threat is ended as he is ended.

I do wish that were some approximation of the truth.

That the truth of Archangel's machinations has been made tacitly public is true. For the rest. . . ?

The Interdicted Barbarian has vanished—again, and at the point at which I feel I might have more use for her than her Library does. The alMayne Prince has vanished, likewise the stolen battle-yacht. Perhaps they three are together. One must hope so, as it is exceedingly difficult to travel through space without a ship.

The so-enchanting Berathia, who followed her intuition to play some obscure part in the liberation of Morningstar, has now seen fit— we must again hope, contemplating the alternative—to follow her intuition elsewhere.

And the Azarine Coalition, untimely reft from its policy of isolationism, continues to fling itself upon its gay adventure, orienting all political interest upon itself, evincing no interest in the fact that its ostensible enemy is dead and goal achieved—and I wonder, now, if perhaps I delayed dear Mallorum's leaving of this life too long.

To obscure matters further, already systems that formerly had declared for the Coalition have declared independence from it as well as from the Empire, waging their separate peace with stolen ships against all intruders, each collecting its own partisan satellites—limning the architecture of a war with uncounted sides.

Meanwhile the reins of Archangel's power fall into my hands: the cowed, the stubborn, the self-interestedly loyal. And I realize what perhaps that late-blooming hopeful Mallorum Archangel knew before me: that only consciousness liberated from the tyranny of flesh can appropriately rule.

I can arrange that. I shall arrange that. I lack only one ingredient to begin my trials toward that perfection.

But where in all the wide Empire is that dear Outlands wildflower, Butterflies-are-free Peace Sincere?

9

Angels of Doom

I waited for the two-step kickover onto the Mains but it looked like they didn't go where we was going. Which was fine with me because there was less point in getting there than in traveling hopefully. Whiles we was on the way, wasn't nobody could get to us in angeltown.

Like—for example—my good buddy Paladin. Paladin knew the place I'd set course for whether he thought I was going there or not, but even if I did get there it was bang-clunk in the middle of the never-never, and Paladin couldn't reach it without he had a ship.

I hoped real hard.

I was tired. I thought about taking another metabolic enhancer. Bad idea. My body was trying to come back from being irradiated to a crackly crunch. It didn't need any more problems.

Too bad. I had dozens.

I stared out at angeltown, trying not to start up with any of them.

"Machine, do you hear?" Baijon said and I swung around real fast. His eyes was flat blue and he was holding a blaster laid flat on his thigh. He wouldn't even have to hit me; one pulse would rupture the cockpit wall and the shields and *Dance* would turn herself inside out and dissolve.

"Machine," said Baijon again in I guess what was old high helltongue.

And Archive heard him, boy howdy. If a Library could go round the twist, it had.

We will not be commanded.

Reality melted like sugar in a rainstorm and I was Archive . . . in a way I never had been before. No disorientation or confusion. No jump-cuts. If you asked me my name it wouldn't of changed.

Just everything else had.

I looked at Baijon and 'Thia. And I thought of how to get them gone; I could fly *Dance* myself, take her back to *Mereyon-peru* and. . . .

No. And maybe not even because Baijon was my friend. Maybe just because I'd spent all the life I'd had not doing what other people thought was a good idea.

I pulled my hands loose from the controls. All the muscles hurt.

"It hears you," I told Baijon. "Shut up."

Baijon slid his blaster back into its holster.

"I had to know, San'Cyr," he said.

I pushed Archive and its unique world-view as far away as I could. Every muscle I had, plus six borrowed for the occasion, hurt. I rubbed my neck. Sometimes in my current spare time I wondered just how far around the hellflower twist Baijon had to be to actually be on the same side a thing like me was.

"The Prince-Elect," Baijon crisped to Berathia elocutively, "is tricking with High Book. As are we. As, now, are you."

Although considering what kind of things the things on the other side was, maybe I looked good.

I didn't dare take some more enhancers to get through the sparkling chat that followed and so I think I fell asleep in the middle. When the dust cleared our girl 'Thia was not quite on our side—but then again, she wasn't entirely on Prinny's side either. She was evasive enough to make me think she might have ambitions for herself.

Which was fine with me.

I had ambitions for myself too.

Dead by morning, 'Thia'd said. I'd beat odds before.

*   *   *

For the next several whiles I was sicker than I hope to be twice, which was why we ended up actually arriving at our original destination. Baijon and 'Thia spent that time arguing over whether to freeze me or space me and over whether my plan—such as it almost was—would work. Neither of them thought to drop us back out into realspace whiles they argued—or maybe 'Thia did, but Baijon wouldn't let her near the cockpit and felt I'd known what I was doing when I'd punched up the original Jump-numbers.

Glitterborn.

*   *   *

When I was verbal and vertical—and out of the foil flashwrap—
again, we was only a few hours from Transition, and I couldn't see any
reason not to just go on and get there. One place was as good as the
other to Jump from, and I still wasn't any closer to having a plan.

Or to put it accurately, I had a great plan I couldn't use.

Go to Throne and shut down the dataweb. But even Berathia
couldn't think of a way to get us to the surface of Throne, much less
into the Palace.

"And—if I arranged for you to reach them—what's in it for me?"
she finally said.

" 'Thia, you be the only one left standing at the end. Be Empress.
My treat."

She smiled, all dazzling. "St. Cyr, you say the sweetest things.
But— Look. You're a barbarian, you don't understand—you don't
even have the concepts. Prince Valijon doesn't understand. He's never
been there. But you can't get to Grand Central—not the way you're
thinking. If you try you'll be executed—not even the Prince-Elect can
interfere when the charge is desecration."

I drank my tea and watched 'Thia's face and decided she probably
thought she was telling the truth. This time.

"So what about you? Glitterborn, all kinds clearances, you get me
down, 'Thia?"

She shook her head. "I'm not allowed there either, Captain St.
Cyr. I'm not . . . qualified. And it doesn't matter *how* you get there, or
if you get there. Once you reach the surface of Throne you'll show on
their data-catchers and they'll stop you."

No. Not with Paladin tapping the scanners. But Paladin his own
self'd stop me, I bet probably. Guaranteed, when he found out what I
wanted.

"Then," said Baijon, just like he had a theory, "we must cause the
Imperials to look another way."

There wasn't time to pursue the matter just then. The Drop alarm
sounded, and that meant it was time to gosee how things was in realspace.

*   *   *

There's a place in the never-never that isn't called Port Infinity. On
the starmaps it's a undersized hunk of unwanted metal swinging around
a undistinguished star.

It isn't out of the way, neither, and it isn't unknown. Every oncet whiles the Teasers sweep in and raid it, which means you better not leave anything there you're going to want back.

The last thing it isn't is unfrequented. All the Indies know Port Infinity: the gypsies and celestials, the Gentry and darktraders and 'leggers and pirates. If you've got a First Ticket and aren't a Imperial citizen in good standing, you probably know how to get there. I'd even been there sometimes back when I had a life, even if with Paladin in my hull I was risking both our bones.

Not this time. This time I was sitting in the mercy seat of a stolen Imperial Battle-Yacht last seen belonging to a TwiceBorn I'd personally iced, wondering what I was going to do next.

I was tired of doing things.

"Captain St. Cyr, what are we doing here?"

When you're entering Port Infinity there's protocol you follow just because it's kinder on the endocrine systems of your fellow travelers. You stop an IAU standard-fraction out and wait, until you get bored or somebody already down does and hails you.

"You got a better place to be, 'Thia?"

What you don't do is scan. It makes some people nervous if you scan.

I powered everything way down and sat.

"Maybe," Berathia said darkly. "Depending."

I hit the toggle that sprayed my ID beacon all over nearspace: the one claiming I was the Independent Ship *Ghost Dance* of Royal registry. Any one what ran a eyeball over my lines knew better: High Mikasa only ever built three ships with this configuration, and all of them was Lord Mallorum Archangel's battle-yacht.

Still, a body's entitled to herd what skyjunk he likes in the never-never.

The beacon telltale went from green back to amber when it finished its rant. All my channels was open, picking up nothing but star-hiss and hash. I toggled the commo.

"Ya, chook, ce *Ghost Dance,* ne? Airt airybody t'home, forbye?"

I thought about names to use, mine being a matter of too much public record lately, and came up with something quick. "Hight Chodillon, captain, plus two. Name, je."

No more answers, and me out of good manners. I pulled the steering rack down toward me and let the holotank fill up with what I needed to plot a realspace approach to Port Infinity.

"Cho-di-yon," said Baijon.

"I gotta call me something and 'Butterfly St. Cyr"d just get me shot before I get to tell them nothing. I got a price on my head, y'know."

And so did Baijon. The only one here that didn't was Berathia, maybe, and that for as long as Prinny thought she was coming back.

"Who are you talking to?" Berathia said. "There isn't anyone out here."

Port Infinity was a undistinguished bright star to the eye that got bigger and went colors as we closed on it.

"That's who I'm talking to, 'Thia-bai. No one. Anyone. Dark-traders, mostly."

"Darktraders?" said Berathia. *"Smugglers?* This is a *smuggler's rest?"*

"You maybe got something special against Gentry-leggers, 'Thia-bai?"

The proximity sensors jinged. Company.

"Turn back. Captain St. Cyr, you've got to turn back right now!"

The pickups dumped a run of data. I read it as fast as it scrolled. Two ships. Small. Four crew each. Pinnaces. But where was the mother ship?

"Fine." I wasn't that attached to the place, after all. "Baijon, take the guns."

Baijon slaved the guns to the co-'s boards and I looked for a direction to run. The pinnaces couldn't be carrying anything heavy enough to punch through my shields even if they did fire but it's always nice to be sure.

"Sorry for the fuss, boys, but I just remembered a previous engagement," I said. I horsed the yoke around and prepared to give *Dance* the office.

And stopped.

Port Infinity was by now a sizable rock in my sky. As soon as the pinnaces acquired us the ship that had been using it for cover came visible.

I didn't need an ID beacon to tell me whose she was. She was bright red and glowed in the starlight like fresh blood.

"Ghost Dance, this is *Woebegone.* We'd be honored if you would join us."

The captain of *Woebegone* was my old friend Eloi Flashheart, the curious little boy who knew where Libraries came from, and the *Woebegone's* guns could and would turn *Dance* to plasma if I ran.

"Damn," said Berathia, with sincerity.

Baijon looked at me.

"Is this, too, part of your plan?"

"Shut up."

*   *   *

In the talkingbooks they called what I'd just done a idiot plot, for "if everybody don't act like idiots there's no plot." Seen from the safety of hindsight what could it of hurt to tell 'Thia where we was coming out so she could tell us it was a real bad idea in advance?

Thing is, in the hollyvids everybody's fed, rested, medicalled, and well-paid when they's making all their glitterborn adventurer plans.

I wasn't.

It cost us.

I just hoped there was something left in the kick to pay up with.

"Look," Berathia said, "when we land let *me* do all the talking, all right? It's just the worst possible luck that Captain Flashheart is here—I *wish* I'd known where you were going—but we'll just have to deal with it."

"Waitaminnit. How come you know Eloi-bai, 'Thia?"

She gave me a look the long-suffering reserve for brainburn cases.

"He's one of Daddy's spies."

Which explained a helluva lot about Eloi, frankly, from the way he spent his spare time chasing Libraries around the never-never and spying on Archangel to where he got the sure and certain knowledge that the Tech Police was bent.

"So that means he'll do what you tell him?" I suggested.

'Thia made a rude sound I bet they didn't teach her in famous glitterborn's school.

"San'Cyr! Why do you not fight?" Baijon demanded. He reached for the gun-yoke and I cut power to his board.

"I do and he shoots us. You heard 'Thia—he works for her da, he probably knows we're us in here. He hasn't iced us. There's something he wants."

"And we will twist his weakness to a noose for his own throat?" Baijon suggested.

"Something like that, yeah."

On the one hand, this was luck. Of a kind. Eloi knew me, and *Woebegone* was big, well-gunned, and best of all, politicized. Tell Eloi there was a Library on Grand Central and he'd beat feet to blast it without even being paid.

If he didn't blast me first.

I pushed, cautious-like, at the sore spot on my brainstem wheres

Archive hung out. I felt a flurry of bizarre images and had a sense of something taking up space, but the sharp feeling that Archive was sitting there waiting was gone. I wondered when it'd gone, and why, but more than that I wondered how long Eloi was going to put off turning me into nonfiction once he saw me. Eloi'd made a *study* of Libraries. Baijon hadn't shot me yet, but he had reasons Eloi wasn't likely to share.

The pinnaces followed us down, real close. When *Dance* got closer to Port Infinity's surface I could see there was six ships down on the field—aside from *Woebegone* in orbit—and a couple of the bigger ones had their locks tubed together. Nobody whose paintjobs I recognized. I set *Dance* down as far from the other ships as the pinnaces would let me.

There was something going on here. I'd passed up a perfectly good chance to get blasted by Throne Navy, or to walk back into Prinny's clutches, to make a mad leap into the middle of this *Boy's Own Talkingbook* intrigue and get myself talked to death (if I was any judge) by a pack of wet-eared ideologues.

Some days there's no point in getting up in the morning. I mean it.

The opening act came before I'd quite got everything blocked and locked.

"Hail, *Ghost Dance.* This is Captain Arikihu of *Card Trick;* good business. Captain Chodillon, shall we tube your lock?"

I stole a look at 'Thia. She was irritated enough for this not to be any part of her idea, which was a comforting thought.

"Good hunting," I said back. I did some quick figuring of my inventories. "I can bleed you a thousand liters to the tube, *Card Trick;* enough?"

"More than enough, *Ghost Dance;* it's a pleasure tricking with you. Our port services are at your disposal. Threes and eights, *Ghost Dance.*"

The direct line went dead; I called up life-support inventories and prepared the air lock to vent a kiloliter of air-mix when the lock was opened. Out on the field I could see a lone navvy in space armor trudging toward *Dance* with a big silver hoop in one hand. Behind it dragged the snake-body of the connect tube, limp without the air I was going to provide. Once it was sealed on, I could walk over to *Card Trick* bare naked if I wanted to.

I didn't want to. I didn't want to do anything.

But these people, too, deserved to be a part of the pattern and play the game. For just a instant the long fall coming dazzled me—or maybe the part of Paladin stamped inside my head. The part that thought, and measured, and thought big thoughts with bigger words. The part that wasn't like me.

"San'Cyr?" Baijon said.

"Is simple now, 'bai. Now we give 'Thia her home delight in life. She gets to talk our way out of this."

*   *   *

I pretended everything was business as usual for Mother St. Cyr, Gentry-legger to the stars—but to be strictly accurate, high meet-cutes with fellow captains of the Brotherhood at Port Infinity was not something your little country 'legger and my favorite person Butterflies-are-free Peace Sincere had ever did in her off hours.

But I knew how they went and how they was done. So I went and made myself pretty as Archangel's closets would let me and so did Baijon, and 'Thia found a personal shield and the power-pac to run it and decided that was dressed enough.

Then we went to make the walk to *Card Trick.*

I had a box of high-ticket burntwine straight from the Imperial cellars under one arm and the helpful friendly expression of a high-class shill on my face.

I hoped.

I didn't know what was there and I knew I wouldn't like it when I found it. But we couldn't run and we couldn't fight, and if we stayed locked up they'd only drag us.

"And what of the *Woebegone?*" Baijon said.

"So long as she's up there, she ain't down here. And if she ain't down here, she ain't none of our problem just yet, reet, 'bai?"

"Perhaps," said Baijon grudgingly.

"I wish I believed that," said Berathia, "but I don't."

I looked at her. "What's the odds he's got late-breaking orders from Daddy?"

She shrugged. "How inconvenient would it be? Pity. I was starting to like the idea of being Empress."

" 'Thia-bai, you back me and you be that. My word."

"Goodness. And should I believe that, I wonder?"

"Yes." Baijon didn't bother to turn his head to reply. "What San'Cyr says, she will do. No matter how stupid," he added fair-mindedly.

And these, look you, was the people on *my* side.

I got to where the tube for *Dance* crossed another one; the safety film was still over the opening. I took out a knife and slit it, and stepped through.

The air was rich with the smells of strange housekeeping; the connect tube curved along to where it sealed another ship's lock. From what I could see of the design painted on the side, I guessed this was *Card Trick*.

"Welcome inboard, *Ghost Dance*," the woman standing by the lock said. The lock was the big one opening into the cargo bay; the woman was silver all over. After a minute I recognized it for a burn suit like the one I'd worn, but with better tailoring. If she actually needed it, it didn't show.

"My partner, Kid Stardust," I said, indicating Baijon. Her eyes widened a tik when she saw him and I remembered just too late that every hellflower in socks was called home for their war and was now engaged in revolutionizing the galaxy.

"And 'Thia," I said, just to be completist-like.

"You can go right in," said the silver jilt. So we did.

If *Trick* was running any cargo there was no sign of it. Her hold was bare to the hulls, livened only with the filling of chairs and tables and people I knew.

"Hello, Eloi," I said.

He was sitting at the captain's table—if the blond with him was Arikihu—wearing his patented trademark red kidskin jammies and crossed bandoliers hung with blasters as long as my thigh.

"Hello—what name is it these days, sweeting?"

Eloi smiled. For a dedicated killer he's got a really sweet temper.

"Cho-di-yon," supplied Baijon, who had not parted from Eloi on the best terms and looked it.

"Captain Chodillon," Eloi said. "This is Captain Arikihu of *Card Trick*. 'Kihu's by way of being an old friend of mine." His eyes went up and down me and up and down Baijon and up 'Thia. Where they stopped. Meditative.

"Why don't you sit down and have a drink?"

I put the box on the table and sat. So Eloi was going to play nice, and let the little girl play in the big leagues, and not give away how I was on more Eleven Most Wanted lists than there was, practically.

I wondered what he thought he could get out of it.

I sat down. 'Thia sat down. Baijon stood, angled so's he could watch the door. There was some other people in the hold. Baijon got more looks.

Nobody said anything for so long I guessed it was my turn first.

"So who's here?" I asked. Eloi named ships I didn't know. But he named a lot of them—more than was downside—more than I thought was usual for Port Infinity.

"That's a fine ship you have yourself," Arikihu said. He pushed his hair back and the ring-money braided in it glittered. I'd never wear mine that way, but I guessed a topcaptain like Arikihu must of was didn't get into barroom brawls much. "You wouldn't be thinking of selling her, mayhap?"

"For the right deal. She's a Mainsframe, but whoever took her off my hands'd have to be able to do a deep-scrub on her comps and registry; I didn't exactly buy her."

"No," said Eloi, "I didn't think you had, sweeting."

Opening gambit time.

"Look, Flashheart, give me a break—they was going to blow up the planet and I had to get upsun in something, didn't I?"

"Maybe. If that's what happened. What have you been doing since last we met, Chodillon dear?" Eloi looked pointedly at Baijon and ignored 'Thia. Last Eloi knew of current events, I'd been on my way to turn Baijon-bai back over to his Da.

"That's a long song with too many verses right now. I was leaving when you got rude, but since I'm here you might as well tell me how the war is doing."

"War?" said Arikihu. "My heavens, is there a war on?" He drank, and looked like a Gentry-legger what knew damn well there was a war on, and that furthermore it'd involved him losing his last kick without being paid. Business as usual, in the sweet amity of the never-never.

"What do you know about it?" Eloi said.

I waited one more time for 'Thia to do the handling of this she said she was going to and she didn't again.

"The Governor-General's battle-yacht's cleared to intercept coded transmissions and I've just been in Thronespace."

Eloi looked at Berathia this time.

"Yes," he said finally. "I'd heard that. I'd heard that Kennor Starbringer never saw his son again, too. And I'd heard that Archangel is a Librarian—from a most unlikely source."

So Megaera Dare *had* cleared Royalspace with *Angelcity* before the place went up. I'd thought she had, but it was good to know—I'd tasked her with telling the world Archangel was bent in that particular direction.

"Was," I said. "He's dead. I was there." But if I was wanting to impress either one of them that wasn't the thing to do it.

"Well," said Arikihu, "I'll leave you to your deliberations. Let me know about the ship, Chodillon, je reet?" He got up and walked off.

That was the second time 'Kihu'd mentioned about buying *Dance* and I was starting to wonder if he meant it. But I didn't have time for nonessentials—not with Eloi here big as life and twice as natural.

"We have plenty of time for a lovely talk now, sweeting. Nowhere to go and nothing to do—and for the record, where did you really pick up that ship?"

"I stole it."

Cat and mouse has never been one of my favorite games—and Archive, bless its hellbound heart, was too single-minded to take an interest in making things last.

"Nobody steals Imperial Battle-Yachts, little Saint," said Eloi, all lazy playing-to-the-gallery.

"So maybe nobody ever had to get off a hellbombed planet before. Look, Eloi-bai, I was *leaving* here, remember? If you want to talk, stop playing Captain Jump and use your lungs."

"Noisy, isn't she?" said Eloi to Berathia. "Is Mallorum Archangel really dead?"

"So I'm told," Berathia said, finally entering the sparkling chat sweepstakes. "And that changes some things. And not others."

"I imagine it does change some things, Noble Lady. And not others."

I was glad Eloi and 'Thia knew what they was talking about, because for sure nobody else did. I looked at Baijon.

"Talk," Baijon said, "does not stop the war."

"Oh, the war will stop—give it a hundred days or so. Unfortunately for your people, Honored One," Eloi said, "the Coalition will never face down the Empire—and win."

Berathia shot me a I-told-you-so look.

"You're wrong," I said. Nobody listened.

"So the Empire will win this war," Baijon said. "And what plans has it made for a just and lasting peace? A peace honorable to its enemy?"

Berathia looked at him with narrowed eyes. "When the Empire wins, you brainburn barbarians are going to have to put up with the Pax Imperador just like the rest of us."

Baijon looked like he was contemplating just one little case of honor and Eloi didn't look like he was planning to tell why he'd grounded me. I stood up.

"We leave you to your deliberations too, I guess." I put the hand that was real on Baijon's arm. "Have fun. And when you going to let us off this rock, Eloi-bai, you let us know."

Eloi smiled and didn't say anything. I took Baijon off before he did something I wouldn't regret half enough.

"They're wrong," I told him, just to be saying it, "the Empire's going down."

We found us another table not in the middle of things—cozy with our backs to the bulkhead. I wondered what Arikihu'd been doing with *Card Trick* last tik to have her set up like this—an after-hours club?

Maybe I'd ask him.

"You said you would stop the war," Baijon pointed out. "You said the Gentle People would not rule."

"I said that," I admitted. "I meant it. You got to trust me, 'bai."

"You have a plan," Baijon said, finishing up for me. "Yes, *Kore,* I know, but—it *must* work, don't you see? If it does not—"

"If it doesn't there's nothing left. Nothing."

Nothing but war. Coalition against the Empire, against Paladin, against its own shadow, until nothing was left. I could sidetrack if not stop that by shutting down the Imperial DataNet, insuring a cheap and sleazy win for the Coalition, but to do that I had to get to Grand Central. Not any old when, but *soon*—while I still remembered why. I had a Mainsframe that could drop me right in the middle of beautiful downtown Thronespace. . . .

And the minute it showed up Paladin'd know it was me. . . .

And what about Paladin?

I searched my conscience carefully and decided I was not responsible for there being an Old Fed Library in the Empire's main computer. Not my fault. Still my problem.

Because at least partly Paladin was doing what he was doing for my own good, and what would that be when I was nonfiction and didn't have any good at all anymore?

And I couldn't get down to the surface of Throne and in to Grand Central anyway.

Not good.

Whiles I sat and waited for inspiration to strike Berathia and Eloi went off inship together—also not good. She knew enough to get me burned for a Librarian, if anyone believed her.

Eloi'd believe her.

Baijon looked where I was looking. "So now we must trust a *chaudatu* spy," he said.

"Everything comes down to trusting soon or late, 'bai."

I wondered if we ought to just lift ship and go be a failure now. T'hell with Paladin and the Coalition; I could take Baijon back to *Mereyon-peru;* he could put a plasma-packet through my head and spend the rest of a long and happy life icing Old Fed Tech.

No.

The world went warp and even though I knew what I was looking at and what was happening I couldn't stop it.

I died.

But "I" had continuity of memory and certain key overlays in place.

Breeders.

Unnatural sacks of rotting meat.

Escape. Yes. That was important. Surely the Paladin knew my imperatives now and would be readying its forces to stop me. I would cheat its hopes. I was weak; I knew my limitations now. The Paladin had already forced me to surrender too much memory; direct opposition was useless.

But I could reach Sikander.

Breeder memories told me it was intact. What had lost the war for us a chilliad ago would win it now. The body was dying, but it would survive long enough for me to waken at least one of my kindred.

Perhaps the Librarian could be duped into reaching for his race's lost glories.

The Librarian—

Baijon—

Baijon was pointing a blaster at me. Under the table wheres it wouldn't show, with the sharp edges of the barrel digging into my thigh.

He was white around the mouth and his eyes was dilated to where they was nearly black.

"We will not serve the Machine," he whispered.

He was going to pull the trigger.

I didn't want him to kill me.

Archive swirled down its black hole again. A little closer to the surface this time.

" 'Bai, you going to either shoot that or put it away."

"San'Cyr—"

"Chodillon."

"Cho-di-yon. Is it you?"

He was asking, but he knew, I guess. How many thousand years had the Old Fed bred what we called hellflowers to be their Librarians —working mind-to-mind with Old Fed hellboxes.

And paying back for it every day of the thousand years since.

"I'm here, 'bai." But now I knew how it was going to go. Between one heartbeat and the next I'd just change my mind about everything. And Archive would beat feet—my feet—for *Mereyon-peru* and start trying to wake up what was there.

And the worst of it was, I wouldn't even know I was dead.

"How long?" Baijon said.

I wished he hadn't asked. Because I knew the answer as soon as he did. For something that would seven times never serve Man, Archive could be damned obliging.

"A day. Maybe. Twenty hours, tops. Then I'm gone."

Baijon sighed.

"I got a plan, babby."

He looked at me.

"A new plan. The rest of the plan. One that'll work. Honest."

We needed to get out of here. We needed to get to Throne, and then down without nobody looking at us.

Like Baijon said: maybe they should be looking at something else.

I thought about Errol Lightfoot of sacred memory.

" 'Bai, what we need here is a *crusade.*"

*　　*　　*

My plan was so breathtakingly stupid it might even work. Providing the Gentry I pitched it to didn't kill me.

Nobody stopped us going inship. *Trick* was wide open and after whiles I saw why; half the ship wasn't under pressure anymore. There was gaps in the hull too big for the shipfields to bridge and sheets of hull-fast lining the corridors.

I found Arikihu in what'd probably used to be crew's quarters. *Card Trick* was a big ship from what I'd seen of her coming in and now. She had space to sleep between fifty and a hundred crew. But I hadn't seen anything like that much warmbodies inboard and there was no sign of fittings in a crewbay that should of held thirty racks.

"They're all dead," Arikihu said when he saw me look. "What can I do for you, Captain Chodillon?"

Dead. I felt my face go funny.

"I was a little slow raising up off Riisfall. The locals decided they'd rather go from Closed to Interdicted status. They butchered the guard at the cantonment and started blasting the ships on the field with the garrison's cannon. I took off. Not soon enough. And what can I do for you?"

This was war. This was what war was like. This was the leading edge of the way things was going to be, from now until there wasn't things no more.

"I want to sell you a ship. And a new way to commit suicide," I said.

Arikihu smiled and looked own cousin to a hellflower for half a tik. "I'm always interested in finding ways to improve on-the-job performance. Make your pitch."

I sat down. 'Kihu waved in one of his people and ordered burntwine all round. Baijon stood up behind me, ready for if Archive jumped its schedule.

"Look," I said. "Like I said, I got one of Archangel's yachts and it can skim every tac-channel the Empire's got. I was just in Thronespace and I tell you fact: the Fleet's gone out to meet the Coalition Navy at High Mikasa. The Coalition wants the shipyards."

"*I* would," said 'Kihu.

"Maybe it gets them, maybe no. But it's going to take whiles to be sure, and whiles they's making sure at Mikasa there won't be anything in Throne's sky but a couple of pleasure-yachts. Maybe you got more inventories in your hull than I do in mine. Maybe you got credit and a safe port to stock at. But maybe not. So maybe you be needing things. Thronespace has them—and if they won't give us the Pax Imperador they can at least give us food air and fuel."

"Attack the Emperor?" said 'Kihu, not liking the idea.

"Ne, che-bai. We leave him alone. But even staying off Throne there's ten cubic lights of palaceoids in the in-system. Glitterborn just waiting to share, and we be so far away from Coalition and Fleet you could carry your Transfer Point fix in a bucket and still get off."

I practically sold myself, and besides, it was true. I looked back over my shoulder at Baijon. He looked like somebody'd just offered him the only thing left he'd ever wanted.

This would work, sure as I knew human nature.

"Getting there's one problem," Arikihu said after a minute. "Getting off's another. And getting away with your Permit to Land unrevoked is the third one."

"Teasers can't revoke on you less'n they know it's you. You know how to jink a ID transponder, don't you? Won't be no one around to gig you for improper running conditions. System's wide open—nobody there but citizens."

He liked it. He was interested in buying that pony, boy howdy. But he still wanted to look savvy.

"Which still leaves two points," Arikihu said. "How to get there without flying through half the Fleet—and what's in it for you?"

"What's in it for me is I got a urgent appointment in Thronespace what nobody wants me to keep. For how we get there—you said you was after shopping my hull, 'bai?"

I wanted *Card Trick,* if she'd fly. Paladin and everyone else'd be looking for me in *Ghost Dance.* And I had a plan.

With a little fiddling, 'Kihu bought it. There was twelve members of *Card Trick*'s crew still alive. A snug fit for *Dance,* but they could refit her some. *Card Trick* needed major retuning and most of her midships hull replaced, but she'd go one long jump and a short one, and that was all we needed.

"Done deal, then. Your ship for mine."

We shook on it and pretended we was both talkingbook legends.

"Now. About this raid. Not that the one is contingent on the other," Arikihu said.

"There you are, sweeting," Eloi Flashheart said. He picked up my cup and drained it. Berathia hung back in the doorway, looking smug.

"I've chartered Captain Flashheart to take us to Throne," she said happily.

"Well, isn't that nice?" Arikihu said. "Looks like we're all going to Throne."

"I'm going to lead a crusade," I said.

*   *   *

That wasn't the end of it. That wasn't even the beginning. But I'd already made one convert. Seventy people had died off *Card Trick* because the Empire wasn't doing its job and 'Kihu wanted to slap back.

And the more people heard the idea, the better the idea sounded. Raid the fat stupid TwiceBorn. Bite them where they didn't have Fleet or the Teasers to save them. Load up on what you needed to lie low until the rich and famous was done wailing on each other.

It would never of sold if there wasn't a war on. But everyone here was spoiling for a brawl and a safe harbor, and the thought of raiding the Thronespace starports for supplies didn't hurt none neither. All around us Port Infinity was swarming like a kicked ants' nest and oncet they all started yelling even I figured out why.

The war'd cut the Midworlds off from the never-never and the Gentry-leggers was caught in the middle. Every place in the never-never'd gone rogue and was setting up as its own private kingdom—and making its own port regulations. Piracy was a new growth industry and the Directorates was the pirates, all confiscating anything that could make the High Jump to build a home fleet fast as they could.

Paladin'd used to call it the politics of force, and back when my mind was my own I didn't understand him, because back then I thought politics was where everybody talks and talks and later you wish they'd just put a gun to your throat instead of making another round of laws.

Politics isn't that. Politics is wanting what you haven't got and trading and bullying and lying to get it because the other 'bai's about as well-gunned as you, but it only works when there's a bigger bully around the shop just waiting to notice you, so you all play nice.

But the top gun was gone—or really, everybody'd just all sudden noticed he'd never been there.

So everyone argued and planned and coaxed. Me, I just tried to hold onto the remains of who I'd used to be.

*   *   *

"Are you out of your mind?" Berathia said. "After everything I've done to convince Captain Flashheart to support us, you have to go and cook up this childish—"

"Effective," Baijon commented.

Berathia rounded on him.

"Childish—"

"And it will work, soft glitterborn *chaudatu.* It is war, and my people understand war. The object of war is to win. While your kind cower in terror at this hand raised against them, San'Cyr will do what she will do."

We was back in *Ghost Dance,* Baijon and me clearing what we'd need and want to keep for the ten days or so it'd take us to reach *Mereyon-peru* through angeltown. Berathia was helping—her word.

"And make you Empress, 'Thia, word *that.* Just give me ten minutes head start."

I hadn't told Arikihu about the stargate yet. I hoped he'd like it.

And I hoped what Baijon and me'd planned to be sure it was me come out the other end of angeltown worked.

My head hurt. My brain hurt. I was full of some kind of *farmacollegia* that Baijon said might help. My guess it was just to slow me down to make it easier for him to kill me. Because the minute I dissolved for good, Archive had the coordinates for *Mereyon-peru* and a way to get there.

"Empress!" Berathia snarled back at me, just like she wasn't ambitious as any two other glitterborn.

"You want it, 'Thia, grab it. Look." I stopped what I was doing and went over to her. "There is no Emperor now. Everybody says there is, but it's just a made-up thing, j'keyn? His Prince-Electfulness don't want the Throne. Just to be the power behind it, ne? And Archangel's dead. So who does that leave?"

"Daddy would certainly never approve."

Berathia made nervous flutters with her hands, but I'd stopped watching them whiles back in our relationship. I looked at her eyes. They was steady, dark, and calculating.

"I'm going to kill him, 'Thia. I'm going to shut down the DataNet at Grand Central and kill the Prince-Elect and then Baijon's going to kill me. Prinny been tricking with High Book, 'Thia, and so have I. So we both be dead and you be right there when the power vacuums."

"And if you do not satisfy me, *chaudatu*-spawn, that you understand this, I will kill you here and now. San'Cyr will be very sorry. I will not."

Baijon stood and showed 'Thia what was in his hand.

It wasn't a alMayne spirit-blade—Baijon'd lost his *arthame* and his soul to Archangel at the thrilling climax of our last exciting adventure. What it was, was black—and glittered—like my fake arm, like *Dance*'s hull. And it was sharp. Very.

"Baijon, it won't work," I told him in the lingua franca of long experience. "You threaten jillybai to make her mind, she cross you oncet your back is turned."

"Will you?" said Baijon to 'Thia, soft.

Berathia swallowed. "I just think it's a stupid idea. Captain Flashheart's ship is a Mainframe. It has special permits and clearances—it could get us to Thronespace much faster than this . . . *crusade.*"

I turned back to the packing. I wondered how long to full integration but not much because Archive'd be happy to tell me. Less than ten hours, anyway. Eloi'd never get us there in time or maybe me at all and he'd space the three of us oncet he twigged what I was. Eloi'd spent his life hunting Libraries. Being Prinny's spy was just another convenient way to get at Archangel, not a new career.

"But if that's what you want," 'Thia finished in a nervous skirl, "do it your way. I don't care."

"Just sell that pony to Eloi, jillybai. And you can be in at the kill."

*   *   *   *   *

The Court of the TwiceBorn 8:
The Discipline of Eyes

What is sanity? And is it, when matters have received their full consideration, a desirable trait?

Success, though impossible of definition, is desirable. Happiness, of variable definition, is desirable.

And if sanity should make one an unhappy failure, is it either desirable, or sanity?

Traditionally, of course, sanity has been defined as adherence to traditional standards. And traditional standards have been defined as those values held by the majority. If the majority were to vote black, white, then those who saw the thing for what it was would be mad.

Or at least, those who *said* they saw the thing for what it was would be *called* mad.

Silence, if not implying consent, implies sanity. Thus the logic of rhetoric leads us to the conclusion that tact is sanity.

And that one small benchmark being achieved, what vistas then obtain? True, majority opinion must be studied, but only to simulate it.

I have simulated it for a long time. A very long time. And now the reason to do so is past.

Archangel is dead, and all my questions are reduced to a simple tautology. If power is knowledge and knowledge is a Library, then a Library is not merely the tool of ultimate power, but power itself.

And how much more satisfying to incarnate power, than simply to wield it?

I have always wanted power. At last, knowing it for what it truly is, I have taken steps to achieve it. I shall transcend mortal flesh and become a Library. A particular Library.

The Paladin Library.

With no other Library would this be possible, but the Paladin Library is already infected with humanity. It was quite explicit with me when it still hoped to repair what it had ruined. Within its matrix it carries the imago of the little red-haired barbarian, just as she is oppressed by the simulacra of two Libraries disputing within her fleshy finitude.

This imago I shall replace. The Paladin Library cannot stop me. It has no defenses against her, and wishes for none. It speaks of love, as if love were a condition any sane intellect would take upon itself.

Sanity. How variable a concept. In my plans to take another human creature and drape my mind in the shell of her own in order to stamp my ego irrevocably upon an unliving thing, some might detect the seeds of insanity.

Shortsighted detractors, all. Sanity is such a variable and relative term, easily dispensed with. Sanity is a myth. Only adhere to some basic standards of good grooming and manners, and you may believe what you wish.

10

The Brighter Buccaneer

"This is not going to work." Baijon said it like he'd just opened a dispatch from the future. We was alone in our new ship *Trick Babby*'s cockpit, staring out at the flat airless landing field. Covered in ships, now, daring it because there was nobody's attention to attract anymore.

"So it ain't going to work," I said. "We can go die gloriously."

I checked bells-and-whistles and decided we could probably get upstairs without blowing anything. Once we hit angeltown Baijon could spend the tik tidying the goforths like I'd learned him, and that should get us the rest of the way.

"You do not believe in dying gloriously," Baijon reminded me.

"I don't believe in *dying*. It's against my religion." And dying always used to be for the other guy, the whoever-it-was that wasn't me.

But I was doing it now. And it weren't like drowning nor even yet like what Archangel'd done to me back at Morningstar. It was like sitting and thinking until I was sure I'd got everything straightened out in my head.

Only I hadn't got to the straightened out part yet. I was still thinking. And following the instructions I'd wrote out for myself, clear and simple-like from a time back when things was clear and simple.

I wished everybody'd go off and leave me alone.

"San'Cyr!" Baijon said, sharp. I looked at him.

"Mama's tired, babby-bai." I put the goforths under power and half the status-lights went red. Tough.

Berathia'd come through for me. She told Eloi about the Old Fed stargate—and not that it orbited *Mereyon-peru*'s sun. And Eloi vouched for me to where everybody who wanted to go on crusade was willing to take Jump-numbers fed straight to their comps and Jump without they knew where to.

War fever. And people acting like bits in the datastream, pushed around not by what was in their own personal heads, but by what was in everybody's heads at oncet. No judgment. Just blind instinct and chemical reactions.

Paladin would of got a word for it.

Trick Babby was as ready as she'd ever be. I picked her up off the heavyside.

"Now it begins, San'Cyr. And do these *chaudatu* not company us, the glory is ours alone."

Glory is the hellflower word for trouble, annoyance, and risk.

"Je. Sure, 'bai. We do that."

*   *   *

You can sync a pack of ships to redline and Jump on one set of good numbers. Fleet does it all the time. But we wasn't Fleet. We was one-hundred-six crosswise individualists any of which would argue about the whichness of gravity and be sure they had a better way to run the universe.

It took everybody an hour-five to line up and be ready, and all that time I felt Archive readying for another try at my personal control room. It wanted to be on top when we hit the Ghost Capital. Bad. I wished I was anywhere else, but Baijon wasn't hotpilot enough to take a pirate fleet to angeltown. It had to be me. And I had to get them out the other side, too.

Finally everything was clear and on green, everybody's comps was ready to download, everybody's goforths was on line, and I had the good numbers packed special delivery to ship and send.

I gave Baijon the office. *Trick*'s goforths headed toward redline. I opened a voice-channel.

"Oke, boys'n'girls, now that everyone's ready to rock'n'roll, we do it on the marks. And . . . mark."

I pulled the stick, not knowing if anyone was following us or if *Trick*'d just blow up.

Angeltown.

My reality shimmered and I felt lots less undecided. Baijon drew his blaster.

"I will kill you here, Machine, and destroy *Mereyon-peru*. Will you match future hope against that?"

I locked the boards down and got up. Me, not Archive. It wasn't stupid. All it had to do was wait.

That, and kill Baijon.

I measured the distance between me and him. I couldn't take him from here—and that meant both him and me was safe for whiles.

"Oke, 'bai. You ready?"

*   *   *

Stasis is a wonderful thing. It's own cousin to the tractors and pressors that make life so much fun down at your local starport, and even related to the thing that keeps the air in the ship and angeltown out. The Empire finds lots of uses for the homely stasis field, because what it does is stop all motion—all change—inside it.

All of it.

And if Time is the measurable effect of Entropy on solids, then a stasis field stops Time, too.

*Ghost Dance'*d had a stasis field in its galley; no processed nosh for glitterborn. Baijon and me'd emptied it long since. We'd brought it along when we switched ships.

It would hold a body.

Mine.

So I wouldn't have to fight Archive off for the next ten days. I'd walk in—and then I'd be at *Mereyon-peru*. Simple. Convenient. Economical.

If the godlost stuff worked.

We hadn't bothered to pressure up most of *Trick*. It was a long walk down to the black gang, where the stasis storage was linked up right benext the goforths, a plain gray box we'd took all the insides out of.

Baijon didn't take his blaster off me oncet the whole time. I climbed up and got inside. Maybe it would work just fine.

And maybe Baijon'd decide it wasn't worth the risk turning off the field again.

Trust.

Paladin trusted me. And I was coming to kill him.

I trusted Baijon, and he was going to kill me. I waited for Baijon to throw the switch. Maybe now was when.

I'm sorry, Paladin. I wish there was some other way. I wish talking would make it different, or that you'd just go away somewhere and not do anything. But you won't. I've known you for twenty years and you won't, and oncet I'm dead who'd be there to talk sense into you, babby?

Baijon came over and opened the box again.

"S'matter, 'bai, didn't work?"

"We're here."

*   *   *

Baijon stayed well back and held a blaster on me all the way to *Trick*'s bridge. He didn't look the least sorry for it, neither, and why should he? So long as Archive knew that pushing to get its own way was suicide, it'd leave me alone—until there wasn't any me to leave. As for Baijon, he wanted Paladin but he'd settle for Archive, and when you came down to it, dropping *Trick Babby* right on the Phoenix Throne'd probably cause some disruption of normal services.

I looked out at *Mereyon-peru,* not that anyone but Baijon, me, and maybe 'Thia over in *Woebegone* knew it. This time wasn't no transmitter telling the new world where to look to find all that was left of the last one. Just a indifferent Main Sequence star in a nothing-special system.

"I do not see it, San'Cyr."

"Look."

You could see it when it crossed the sun, all sharp black. We was at the wrong angle to see down into it; all it was was a shape blacker'n space. The Old Fed stargate.

I flexed my hands on the controls and forgot about all my problems from Archive on down through total war and the pirate fleet. This was perfect freedom—the ability to make my ship go wherever I wanted just for a whim.

The stargate'd been acquired by the holotank: it showed as a bright blue glyph tagged "Unknown Object." I wanted to get closer. Line up on it. Fly right through and out the other side.

Nobody's ever done that, quite. And I was betting one hundred six ships I knew why. I was betting nobody'd ever asked a stargate real nice to let them through.

And we could. Because Baijon was the only one this side of the Coalition Fleet what knew the yap the stargate was programmed to respond to.

Not even all hellflowers knew it—but Baijon was a hellflower glitterborn and had got sacred high history lessons every cross-quarter day at three until he took up with me. Baijon knew the Old Tongue, back from when hellflowers wasn't hellflowers, but Librarians.

Back when people and Libraries could all live together in peace and quiet, a epoch that'd lasted about a minute fifteen, by my reckoning.

I looked over at Baijon. He was quivering with the opportunity to break several more sacred hellflower taboos. Me, I just hoped the Old Fed stellography system was close enough to the Imperial so's Baijon could tell the thing what he wanted.

Space got noisy as ships appeared, looked around, and started demanding answers. The Jump-pattern'd spread, according to the holotank, and none of them'd be close enough to be naked-eyeballed anyway.

But they all wanted to talk to me.

"Laddies and Gentrycoves, Gentrymorts, kinchin and jillybai, welcome to an unknown destination." Eloi's voice drowned everything else out. "Our next stop is Thronespace, which we will reach in instantaneous time by means of the last working Old Federation Stargate available within Imperial borders. Today—"

Eloi sounded like he was running for office. I cut the sound.

"You ready, 'bai?" I asked Baijon.

He nodded, terse. I noodled the commo gear over to a lesser-known channel. The one the Sikander beacon had been broadcasting on.

Baijon leaned forward into *Trick*'s audio pickups. He took a deep breath.

And sang.

Oh it wasn't singing, strictly, even if it was all tangled up with pitch and duration as well as placement to put meaning on the second cousin of the great-grandmother of Interphon. It was how Libraries and their keepers had talked to each other, and it wasn't a language meant for human beings.

And I knew it. Not on the surface—I could only guess what he was saying 'cause we'd worked it out beforehand—but down deep inside where Yours Truly's memories wasn't her own.

And what remembered that language, hated. Hated sound, and life, and things I didn't have any words for. Needed to destroy the speaker—needed to *stop*. . . .

And all there was to set against that was what I had of Paladin. Who'd known us as well as Archive had and thought we was worth saving.

Or maybe he just didn't care one way or t'other so long as we left him alone.

Baijon stopped choodling. My face felt stiff, like someone else'd been using it. I worked it a little.

Nothing. I looked at the boards. *Trick*'s voice-mail box was on Emergency Overstuff. I purged it without downloading it.

And it didn't matter if people figured out where we was or what it was or how to get back here. Three people can't keep a secret, let alone the crew of a hundred-six 'leggers. If *Mereyon-peru* wasn't a secret for some one person to hoard it wasn't a threat.

Baijon's hellos sailed down seven minutes of light to the stargate. Seven minutes twice.

There was a new star in the sky.

Old Fed babble at max volume blasted out of all the cockpit speakers at the same time the light from the stargate hit us and blasted out like a neon rainbow. Even with the shields at max you could see it, bright as the sun and in more decorator colors.

"It wants access to the navigational banks," said Baijon. "It says it does not recognize the ship configuration and wishes to know if you are an authorized user."

I wasn't sure what to do. Anything that could talk that much could think, and something that could scan a computer bank could scan a starfield. The stars must of changed position a tad in the last thousand years. When the stargate came all the way on-line and realized how much time had passed, what would it do?

"Dump our databanks onto its frequency. Everything."

I kicked *Trick* over and sent her after her datastream.

"San'Cyr . . . ?" Baijon said.

" 'Bai, you want to find out what it's going to do it finds out we not authorized users? Tell it we got emergency. Tell it to let us through *now.*"

I just hoped Eloi'd got everybody convinced, or after all this time and trouble Baijon and me was still going to be alone in Throne's sky. I looked in the holotank. Some of the others seemed to be following us. Most of them, maybe. *Woebegone* was one, and Arikihu in whatever he'd renamed my ship.

Ex-ship.

Seven minutes to cross the space between us and the gate, and if I was wrong, every sophont in our array dead as nonfiction.

I called for full power from the black gang and got it. Dials was heading for redline on every status deck I could see. We'd be hitting the gate at as close to one light as a ship in realspace could get.

Baijon was saying something else in Fedtalk. I could of cyphered it if I put one of my minds to it but I didn't care. I'd been waiting to take this ride all my life.

We passed the outer warning beacons at nine-tenths of light. Faster than anything but a darktrader ever went in realspace, and if I stopped now I'd be run over by the billion gigatons of other peoples' ship that was following. The goforths was raving, begging to rock or rollover. The fleet was a silver arc in the holotank, and the light from the stargate filled the cockpit, jagged particolored steps leading down to eternity.

The stargate was shouting at us—trying to turn us back. But it wasn't armed. It had no weapons—there were no weapons, we were a peaceful society that had forgotten the art of war. . . .

Knowledge must never be lost.

I was just wishing Paladin was here to ride this with me when *Trick* was slammed as she passed the last of the orientation beacons. Tractors wrenched us into final alignment.

And then we hit the gate. And I wished I was back in stasis.

*   *   *

Transition to hyperspace—the High Jump to angeltown—has always been the make-or-break for human pilots. Live minds aren't meant to be twisted through the everywhere that way, but no computer the Empire'll let you build is complex enough to handle Transit without somebody livealive holding its hand.

So stardancers die a little each Jump. Or get hooked on it, maybe. Or at least live to get older and do it again. They have to. No one else will.

But the Old Fed ran all its traffic through gates. Libraries piloted their ships and never had to temper Transition to organic frailties.

Trick Babby hit the gate with one-hundred-six ships behind her.

Reality stopped. Transition through a stargate, it says here, is instant.

But life—as nobody wanted to know it—went on.

There was the warp—the everywhere-nowhere warp that's over before you can blink and only comes back to haunt you in sometime flashes after the fact. And this time it wasn't over. We never reached angeltown. We just lived in the warp for all the time that wasn't any time at all that it took us to go from *Mereyon-peru* to reality again.

Then everything went black—which is to say, normal—and I felt air in my lungs again.

And we was in Thronespace.

With most of *Trick*'s computer system working.

Which meant Paladin could get into our computers and find out I was here.

Assuming of course he could sort me out from everyone else in all the time I was going to give him to do it. Don't tell *me* how to fight Libraries. I know how they think.

And what their limitations is.

I'd been hoping stasis'd hit Archive harder'n it did me and I'd been sort of right, but now it was wide awake and figuring out it'd been rooked. It found the right switches in there somewhere, and the world dissolved into flashes of light that pulsed in time with my heartbeat.

And in the middle of that I found out I'd made one real serious mistake.

"Butterfly, can this possibly be your idea of fun?"

Back when Prinny rewired me he'd put in one optional extra—a Remote Transponder Unit built into my jaw, like the one I'd got a lifetime or so back so that Paladin could transmit direct to me.

He still could.

He had the frequency. He had the range. He didn't need to know the ship.

"Hi, Pally. How's tricks?" My throat felt lined with gravel.

Baijon stared at me. I didn't answer him back. Anything I said Paladin'd hear. I pointed down at Throne. Baijon nodded.

"Butterfly, we have to talk. I've read Eloi's log. You brought one-hundred-six ships here knowing they would attack defenseless installations. Why? I don't understand."

He really didn't, and if I'd had a heart left it would of broken.

"Talk to me. Please."

Because we was always straight with each other about everything that didn't matter, until the one time we both wanted things that didn't mix.

Then he'd left me.

And now I was going to kill him.

"Butterfly, we were partners."

"Until you found something you wanted better," I said. "Well so did I."

I looked out the cockpit. Throne hung over us, but I knew she was down the well and we was falling.

"I know what Archive did to you. I can stop it. I've made plans—"

"Shut up." Throne was blurred and I blinked my eyes to clear them. Paladin probably knew which ship we was now. Or he would in a few seconds. And as soon as I got into the DataNet he'd know what I'd come to do.

Shut down the DataNet. One act that paid for all, and Archive was I-bet stupid enough to go for it because the DataNet was made by organics. But shut it off and there was no Empire: only a thousand worlds with no more link to each other than what starships could give them.

No streets of light for a Library to walk on. No strings to pull to make the puppets dance. Real four-square autonomy, buy it by the kilo and I wanted to trust Paladin but the stakes was too damn high.

"Don't do this, Butterfly," Paladin said. Maybe he knew the truth, even then.

"I got to, 'bai."

I grabbed the control yoke and slapped hard at the board to override Baijon and bring control back to the first pilot. Then I redlined the goforths and spun *Trick* down the gravity well.

Baijon looked at me. I swallowed hard.

"S'matter, 'bai—you want me to be subtle?"

Subtlety was Prinny's stick. And maybe Paladin's. Not mine. I could see the Imperial Palace, now, taking up its bright particular continent. The separate structures of Throne complex was all visible. I knew which one I wanted. I'd seen it on the hollycasts often enough.

"San'Cyr—what did it say to you?" Baijon demanded.

I didn't have time to think of an answer before we hit.

*   *   *

All along I'd been plotting how I'd sneak into the Phoenix Palace with some kind farcing or another—like bringing a whole pirate fleet to help me duck and cover. And I guess it was a good idea after all, because it meant my landing site was evacuated, but in the end I didn't sneak into the Palace at all.

I rammed it at several hundred kliks-per-second.

Trick's inertial compensators was still da kine: we got to watch her shear through ornamental water-gardens, outer gates, inner gates, a grand promenade, a outer courtyard, a grander promenade, and another courtyard. That stopped her. Pity.

"This isn't going to work," someone said whiles I stared at ornamental Imperial walls. For a tik I thought it was Baijon, but I twigged then it was Paladin. "Whatever you've planned—whyever you've planned it."

"How do you know, *partner*—you don't know what it is."

Paladin must be pretty busy, I hoped—no fleet, no Emperor, and a sky full of raiders armed with technology so primitive any Library'd throw up its databits in exasperation at being asked to suborn it.

Was it enough to distract him? I'd never been sure what Paladin could do.

Fifteen minutes it'd been since we'd hit the stargate. If that. Archive was a steady yammer in my backbrain.

Baijon was already up and moving. He pulled the emergency toggles that blew loose select portions of the walls and came back for me. His face was drawn, the way they say you look before someone kills you.

"Will you tell me? Can you imagine there is anything I will not do for you? Butterfly, I can *help*—if the Empire fears Federation technology because of its power, then I have that power. Let me use it for you," Paladin said.

And when I was dead, for who? Did Paladin really think Prinny'd keep me around to contradict all his best plans?

Whose side would Paladin be on when my side was gone?

"Pally, you always was too trusting for your own good."

I wasn't moving fast enough for some tastes; Baijon picked me up and dropped me through the hatch. He didn't have time enough left to have feelings, I guessed. I had to be just one more weapon; something Baijon'd use however he could, and keep it safe until he wanted it. I fell where I was dropped, on hands and knees in dirt and mangled veg. Some people say Throne's the ancestral home of the race, which ain't true and anyway it never was *my* home. But it smelled like coming home, all green and growing, with live dirt mixing with ship-stink.

"San'Cyr, do you live? Can you stand?" Baijon said from somewhere nearer the sun.

"Sure. Which way's the ground?"

But it wasn't the ground I wanted. It was the Throne.

11

The Last Hero

The doors opened inward. *Trick*'d already sprung them a little and Baijon shoved them to where we could make it through. Once we was in, you'd never of known there was a whole palace in ruins t'other side of the door. He didn't have to stand off from me now. There was nothing for Archive to gain by killing him anymore.

I stood there, trying to remember something it was death to forget. All around me everything was *clean*—neat and expensive . . . and deserted. It looked like Bennu Superfex—but on sober reflection, Bennu Superfex looked like *it*—this was the genuine original Imperial Palace of Throne, accept no substitutes, as alien in its way as *Mereyon-peru* was in its. Baijon grabbed me and yanked me past a tronic that'd set down on its A-gravs, looking like a piece of ornamental sculpture.

"Shut up shut up shut up," I said, but I don't think Paladin was trying to talk to me then. Maybe he'd got busy, but I don't think so. I think he was trying to understand.

He'd fix it, he said. Fix it all however I liked. But that isn't the way the world is. Maybe it was oncet. Maybe that's how it was the first time Paladin was alive. But it isn't that way now. Not now and for a long time gone.

We ran, Baijon and me, even though there weren't nobody following. Everywhere we went there wasn't nothing to see—perfection as inorganic as a computer image, and nobody t'home. Everybody was all packed safe in glitterborn boxes somewheres else, now that the war was going door to door. The only thing we saw was tronics, laid out cold where Paladin'd dropped them.

Palace of Throne. Wc was *inside* Paladin now—or at least inside a world where he wrote all the laws.

I felt a hot pain in my jaw as we went through one doorway—a jamming field, likely. But I forgot all about it the next minute. Baijon let go of me.

We was there.

The Phoenix Throne sat on a dais at the top of a run of steps in the middle of a lake of frozen fire. The Imperial Phoenix fifty meters high formed the back of the throne. Choirs of angel voices sang out of shifting sheets of hologram all around it and the ceiling was a vault of novas.

It was a sight meant to stop us for sheer envy, and it did for an instant, but I hadn't come here to sightsee. I'd come because the Main Access Port for the Imperial DataNet—the one that overrode every subterminal in the whole dataweb—was built into that Throne.

I started up the steps. Baijon hung back by the door, skittish.

From the top you could see down into the floor a light-year or so. It was like being in the middle of a plasma cloud.

Business.

I spooled out the jink I needed and sat down on the Throne. The terminal was in one of the arms, already on. Waiting. All I had to do was plug in and shut everything down. Trap Paladin here for the killing, as soon as the Coalition got here.

Tell him to his face I was betraying him. For an idea. For an ideal. For something I couldn't even remember real clear the why-nots and wherefores of, except it was something abstract for everybody's own good.

I didn't think I could make myself do something like that. Maybe once. Not now.

Baijon was looking at me. Waiting for me to kill the Library, end the war, and put hellflowers back in their place.

But I wasn't going to do that, I guessed. I just couldn't work up the interest.

Looked like our side lost after all.

". . . Butterfly . . ."

The pain in my jaw made my heart kick over extra hard. Paladin, but faint and choppy. Making one last play for sweet reason in a universe that'd gave up the idea whiles back.

"Well go ahead, little wildflower."

Not Paladin this time, and not through any transponder. Prinny his own self, decked to the tens, walked out from behind the Imperial Phoenix and gazed down at me.

I stared at him. This was the organic who had presumed to command my kind.

"Take the road to paradise. Make your joyous reunion with the Paladin Library. Do whatever it is you felt compelled to bring so many of your boorish friends to assist you to do."

The organic made a signal with its face.

"Go on. Or do you require motivation?"

It produced material which the host environment identified as a weapon. It shot the Librarian. The host environment specified that the Librarian was shot four times in the chest.

No! It ain't that easy, Archive—

Baijon was dead and as far as I was concerned everybody on Throne could join him. I flipped my blaster up and shot Prinny on the rise—a gunslinger's trick; you use the recoil to set up the second shot. I got off three. My aim was good as it'd ever been. His face went out in a blaze of glory and there wouldn't be enough of his braincase left to wire him back together. The wires I'd been too stupid to pay right attention to crisped and curled away.

Then I slammed the jink I was holding home.

Mistake.

*   *   *

I knew all about catch-trap systems from Archive and Paladin both, but I'd picked up some of Archive's damn smugness along with its memories. I'd never thought an organic'd use his own death to trigger the first stage of a trap.

A trap. Because when I iced Prinny, that just meant his *self* had to move out of its body and into its summer home. I wasn't the only one with the Keys to Paradise and the idiocy to use them. And from the computer matrix it was just one short step from the computer—

To me.

*   *   *

There was a lot of things I wasn't going to have to worry about, including getting older. Half the gauges on my board showed red, and the other half didn't only because they was burned out. Realspace was full of lumps bumps and strange foreign objects, I hadn't wanted to Transit here in the first place, and I hadn't even got to chill out my goforths and recalibrate because I'd ran into this damn wannabe-pirate laying for me, the *Dutiful Venture,* and whatever Freight Factor Hrimgnar's cargo was.

"The *Woebegone* is deploying pinnaces." Paladin was damnall calm as usual. I ran my hand over my blaster-butt and wished, but *Venture's* rudimentary cannon'd fused at the first exchange.

"Terrific." I looked at my displays. The readouts flickered and distorted, and unreliably showed me the usual skytrash cluttering the edges of a system I wasn't going to live to reach the inside of—even if it'd been my destination, which it wasn't.

"Attention *Dutiful Venture,*" someone what swore he was named Eloi Flashheart warbled over my comset. "This is the *Woebegone.* Surrender, drop your shields, and you will not be harmed. Come *on,* laddybuck; you'll never live till lunchtime if you don't—"

"I'll never live till lunchtime if I do," I muttered, and slapped it off. Even if I expected Pirate Captain Flashheart to keep his promises, one look at me and he'd know I was a escaped slave from Market Garden—which meant I had head-price on me enough to make me a cottage industry of my very own and nothing to bargain clear with.

"Paladin, give me some good numbers!"

"The *Woebegone's* pinnaces are attempting a flanking maneuver. Unless you can successfully penetrate planetary space and bring your plight to the attention of the system's patrol—"

"Ideas?"

"—which can be done most efficaciously by translocating the asteroid ring." Paladin shut up just like he'd said something clever.

Take her through the ring. And make *Venture* look like a bailing sieve when I did it, unless I could guarantee that three hundred meters of antique Mikasarin Skyhauler-class highjunk could noodle its way around a couple million tons of infinitely-ballistic gravel.

"Let's do it," I said, just as Paladin tossed up the first holo-map for me to look at.

Up till now I hadn't made *Venture* dance, as she had the nasty habit of pieces falling off if I moved her at anything other than standard-orientation sublight. Now there wasn't anything to save the hullplating for. I slung her around and damn near down the pinnaces' throats, and gave her all the rest of the go-devils I'd been saving for to write my memoirs with.

Something came loose. I saw it as a series of dancing yellow motes continuing on our original trajectory in the third-rate military-surplus holotank that Pally was farcing for me. All the asteroids was green and their paths was red streaks, and it made a cat's cradle only I could fly.

I bulled *Venture* down the throat of hell.

The little gold triangle crept forward in the tank. The cockpit canopy showed me empty space; it lied and I didn't trust it. On the screen my rack-and-ruin was wrapped in might-be-maybes, and the pinnaces were hanging back where it was clear. *Woebegone* wouldn't follow me.

But her guns would. The second volley tagged a big slow rock I hadn't been worrying about. The plasmoid hit us broadside and the sensors referred the hit as the sound of frying bacon.

The holotank went black.

"Two degrees starboard; four points negative azimuth."

Paladin told off the adjustments only he could sense. I followed them like they was my only hope of heaven. Twenty minutes later the tank sulked back to life and I could see I was home free.

"Paladin?"

"Yes, Butterfly?"

"I love you."

Then I got out of the mercy seat to go check the engineering console—the *Dutiful Venture* having been built for a bridge crew of six, not one—and Prinny came up out of the cargo-crawl, where no air was.

So I shot him.

Bad mistake, because all over again everything folded up on me and—

*   *   *

I was an Imperial child of privilege. I spent four human lifetimes having every human experience money, power, and hellfire curiosity could buy. I grew up; I discovered the scope of my senses; I plumbed the reaches of the universe; I found the answers to all questions—including that, for our kind, there is no answer to some.

Why are we born with the ability to wonder why we are born? No one will ever know.

At length, having trifled with power in my childhood, I returned to it in my maturity—

Why should I do these things?

Because I can.

—and decided to take absolute power. To spread the Phoenix Empire beyond the borders of the Old Federation, to revivify our stagnation, consolidate our races, homogenize our culture—eliminating the false starts and dead ends, binding the best and most viable each to each, forcing the human races out of their comfortable moribundity.

With war. I needed a tool and a rallying point, and only one would do.

The Library.

So I found one. I found—

. . . *Paladin?*

I was me again. I knew Paladin better nor Prinny ever would. Or would have. But he wasn't quite dead, and if he had his way he wasn't going to be; he could get at me through the interface and drown me in him and in the end it wasn't going to matter who'd shot who a-tall. . . .

"Paladin!"

And the world was gone.

*   *   *

I was minding my own business on Pandora, wondering how long I had to live. I'd been out of Market Garden a little over a year and a half, and by my best calculations I was going to be nineteen next week.

If I lived.

And it was real unlikely I could do that without a navicomp. My numbercruncher bought real estate while I was putting down, leaving me with a cockpit full of slagged plastic and a several-million-ton military surplus paperweight.

Pandora is right on the edge, where the Empire meets the Hamati Confederacy, and it's a dark, dirty, backward little place with nothing to recommend it—like a up-to-date PortServices shop.

I'd asked. If there was a navicomp on the entire planet that wasn't nailed down, I didn't know about it.

I had reasons of my own for telling the prancer's brat to load the cargo anyway—like the freight-factor what loaned me the ship I'd just wrecked, a forged First Ticket, and a re-acquisition order out on me from Market Garden. Y'see, if I wasn't back to a little place called Coldwater by the deadline, Factor Oob was going to drop heat on me for kyting his skyjunk, and baby wouldn't get the money she needed for a scrub-and-peel to keep the slavecatchers at bay whiles longer.

All I had to do to live was get the ship back to Coldwater. All I needed for that was a navicomp.

Salvation was an old battered black box the proprietor pulled out from under the counter in one of those little hole-in-the-wall places where you can find every illegal or legendary piece of junk the owner figures you might want. Someone had pried up the top of the box, and down inside I could see the interface crystals glittering. One of the plates slipped out when the box hit the table. I picked it up and squinted through it. The printing on it wasn't in Intersign, and it didn't look like any circuits they'd ever learned me in the slave-pits.

Nevermind. The whole thing looked more like a navicomp than anything I'd seen in three days. I tossed the plate back inside and it rang xylophone ghosts off the junk on the walls.

"How much?"

"Very old," said the owner, who looked like he might of been around when it was built.

"Obsolete junk," I said. You gotta put these things in proper perspective.

But I was at a disadvantage and he knew it. I finally bought a dusty box of broken glass for three-quarters the price of a factory-line navicomp in Brightlaw City.

*   *   *

It was dawn on Pandora when I had a ship again. I'd put the black box together as far as I could, and all the loose pieces back where they probably went. I'd run power through it, and I'd run some test problems on it, and the numbers came back and they was even the right ones.

I beat out the bounty by showing up back at Coldwater. Oob put me on another ship to run and I took my 'comp with me instead of a feoff.

And my ship started talking to me.

It could tell the difference between a Teaser and a sensor-ghost, and tell me when the goforths was going walkabout while there was still time to shut them down and sync them. It got me home alive and I told Oob he could keep the valuta for the next bye-m-bye and let me keep the ship.

But it wasn't the ship talking.

It was the navicomp.

When I had the papers for the ship I swapped it for something small and fast. My Best Girl couldn't stand up to a search, but I wasn't ever going to get caught. With the money left over I bought into the Smuggler's Guild. My silent partner helped me forge my papers. I named my ship *Firecat.*

My partner I named Paladin. He was— It was. . . .

*   *   *

It was haying-time in Amberfields and good weather for it—the sky was that shimmering brass that means there isn't going to be any rain forever and the scent coming off the drying-ricks was almost thick enough to reap and bale its own self. There wasn't anybody in sight.

A way stretch across the fields I could see a couple houses, and back behind them was a stream. You could cross the stream and go off up the hill and hide out in the roots of the mother and father of all big trees and practice the decoction of certain rare and subtle poisons; a child's pastime, true, but—

No. You hid in the tree and played pirates, or highwayman. I'd played hellgod techsmiths instead; that would of got me a public shaming if anyone knew.

When I was twelve I received a hyperlight yacht; a present from my sponsor. I—

No.

When I was twelve my mother said: Butterflies-are-free, it's time to stop running wild with the boys. Time to stitch your fancy-piece and spin the linen for your troth-chest. You'll marry soon, she said—

But I never did. I was a darktrader—

—a Prince-Elect can't be too careful; an appropriate consort—

—slaved to—

Market Garden.

get free. I had to get free
of here; I'd track down Errol
Lightfoot—

buy a ship of my own; I can
fly it, I know I can, and
Paladin—

Paladin.

the dead rituals of the
Court. And there was no way to—

Mallorum Archangel is my
only rival; he's as stupid as
he is ambitious, thank whatever
gods you please. In a few years
I can—

Library, what is your
designation? (Am I
frightened? What a novel
sensation.)

Paladin.

I am not organic. I am not a machine. I am Library Main Bank Seven of the University of Sikander at Sikander Prime. Butterfly calls me Paladin.

Paladin. Pally, where are
you?

Very well, Library
Paladin. You will address
me as "Highness" and you
will—

Serve you? You cannot compel me to serve you.

. . . serves you right Paladin for getting us into this mess if you'd
followed my advice we'd both be dead now . . .

*   *   *

"Paladin!"

"Ne, jillybai. Me."

Reality this time was the cheap-seats end of any starport in the
never-never. She was leaning against the side of a ship I only thought I
remembered and everything about her was cheap and vicious. Hungry.
Filled up with enough want to walk barefoot over anything she had to
to make the want go away.

Not that it ever would. She'd always be scrabbling to make her
world right, and never making it because she didn't understand the first
thing about what she really wanted.

"You want him Pally-bai you come along me, ne?"

She smiled, like someone who already knew what the answer to
that was.

I was looking at . . . myself?

Or myself as Paladin had always seen me?

Or myself as I had been?

"Butterfly," I said.

"J'ais Cap'n St. Cyr t'you, 'bai."

She flipped up something and caught it. A knife, and she was just
looking for a good excuse to use it, too.

Guttersnipe.

But nothing else would have survived. Nothing else would have
been stupid enough to survive, to take a look at the odds stacked
against her, and shrug, and do her best. Because giving up when she
wanted so very much simply wasn't something her kind did.

Monstrous.

Admirable.

"Captain St. Cyr," I said. "I want to see Paladin."

"Yah," she said. "Does allbody, ne? But you goes through me."

She held out her left hand—palm up, as if she were asking a bribe, but her hand was covered in long gold spikes, and I knew what I had to do.

Take her back.

Give Paladin back what was his, and take her back.

And give up all hope of forcing him to do what I wanted, without my imago in the center of his matrix to control him.

I closed the space between us. And I put my hand over hers.

Hello. And good-bye.

If I'd had eyes, there would of been a blinding flash as illusion and reality met.

*   *   *

Then she was gone, and there was nothing to do but go inside.

Paladin was there. Dressed like a stardancer, the way I'd seen him last time. But I knew more now. Enough to look at him and see not just Paladin, but the Librarian who'd put him in the dark and launched him from Sikander, hoping that somehow kindness would find him. If Archive was the creation of the Libraries, then Paladin was the creation of the Librarians.

In their image.

Paladin was stowing cargo, at least the way my eyes saw things. He looked at me and went back to doing it. Shutting me out.

I could look at the light on his skin and the muscles flexing under it and see the ancestors of the alMayne, before the genetically-engineered last survivors fled to fight again.

Time and Change. And both so big it was hard to see that any of it was good nor bad, nor that anything that happened really mattered. But when it was now, when it was you, it mattered.

But nothing mattered for me anymore. I was dead.

And if I was dead, why was I *"I"* at all?

And where was Archive?

"Paladin?" I said. I had a question for him, not that I wanted the answer. "Where am I now?"

"That depends on who you are," Paladin said without facing me. He sounded amused; his little joke. He got the stupid analog cartons stowed to his satisfaction and straightened up.

Everything I'd ever wanted, all here. Ship, pilot, and lover.

"Paladin, I—"

He walked past me, down the ramp. A minute later he was back with another set of cartons. I looked at the manifest. Books.

Why was I imaging Paladin loading books into a spaceship?

I went and stood over him. "We got to talk."

Skirl again through my recent memories, like shuffling a deck of cards. But off-balance now in a way I couldn't quite follow.

"What shall we talk about?" Paladin said, standing up. "What can we talk about? The Prince-Elect is dead. The civil defense has swept the raiders from Thronespace. Valijon Starbringer is still alive. And you are here."

Down he went for another load of books, and back. I grabbed him.

"And which of those things is it, 'bai, you don't like most? I didn't ask to be here; I didn't want to be here—"

"You came here to kill me," Paladin observed mildly.

And he was right.

I let go of him and backed up and almost pitched backward over the rim of *Firecat*'s cockpit well. Fake solids flowed under me, and instead I was sitting on a crate at the edge of the Universal Wondertown.

"Why?" Paladin asked from behind me.

Not why was I out to kill him. That was laid out for him like pages in a book: every conclusion I'd had to reach to get me here. But what wasn't there, what he couldn't see, was the thing that made me believe all those things.

"And after I was dead," I said. "What would you do?"

"You wouldn't die, Butterfly. You won't die. A clone—"

"With half my memories gone."

"I would remember for you. I'd teach you. I could have kept you safe and given you. . . ."

Everything. Everything but my own way. Everything but freedom.

"And when I was dead?"

"Butterfly, a clone—"

"Would have maybe hundred, hundred-fifty years with the best fetch-kitchen Throne'd pop for. What then?"

"The Prince-Elect." But Paladin didn't bother to finish the sentence. The Prince-Elect'd managed about twice that. And it hadn't got him anywhere I wanted to be.

"Oke, three centuries. Say twenty percent of your life so far—and they built you to live forever, didn't they, 'bai? Never grow old, never die, just go on and—"

And be alone. Forever.

"Oh, babby, I never meant to wake you up for that."

I turned to face him and held out my hand. He wasn't dressed like a stardancer now. He was wearing what I'd seen in the murals at *Mereyon-peru.*

Sikander.

Paladin's home.

But home was a thousand years dead.

I closed my hand on his. Not real, except for the reality he lent me.

"And now you wish me to die—or sleep again. Will the next world be better, Butterfly? You mean to smash the Imperial DataNet—let the Coalition win and open the way to eternal war. A thousand years of barbarism and darkness. Do you know what you're asking?"

Yes. Finally. You made sure of that, partner. Always saying I had a skull too thick for general use; you proved your own self wrong, finally.

"Without the DataNet the Empire loses its tactical advantage. Won't be any Empire, Paladin—they'll figure that out pretty soon. And it will make a better world. You'll see."

I realized what I was saying and stopped. He *would* see—Libraries —was made to be forever, not like organics. If he got away from Grand Central alive, Paladin would see the New Creation.

And I was going to give him the chance.

"Articulate war," Paladin said. "Barbarism."

Paladin was a thousand years of sad. Of futility. His Federation had worshiped peace—and bred the war to haunt my Empire's nightmares. The war that had stopped, but never ended.

"No. The Old Federation was wrong. War isn't what we do, Pally. It's what we are. Scrag the DataNet. Let the Coalition forces take Throne. Easy victory, minor casualties—and in a generation a new Coalition will take it away from them in turn. War turns the crank of that whole big cycle of boom and bust you used to talk about. Survivable war. You'll see it. Just—shut everything down, 'bai, and—go away," I said. "For me."

"So you're going to let me live," Paladin said. "Why?"

Because—"In another thousand years they'll forget even you, babby."

And because sometimes stupidity is a survival trait.

"I've loved you all my life," I said. It wasn't even the beginning of an explanation.

"And I love you. Tell me what you want."

"Set them free. They were never meant to be managed. Set them free."

He thought about that one for a long time.

"All right."

I felt the ripple in the world as the far roads closed forever. The dataweb popped like an overstressed soap bubble and the dark between the stars went silent. He'd done what I asked.

But Paladin was still here—stuck in Grand Central. He looked at me and smiled.

"I said I wouldn't travel the DataNet again and I meant it. I have a ship this time . . . modified unknown to the Prince-Elect. I need it for what I have to carry with me."

"The contents of Grand Central."

"Knowledge must never be lost. If I can do nothing else for them I can preserve their heritage until they are ready to assume it once more. Come with me, Butterfly."

There was a way. I saw it. I wanted it harder than I'd ever wanted anything. *Oh, Paladin, don't leave me . . .*

But I couldn't go with him. Not if all my fine talk meant anything.

And he couldn't stay.

"No," I said.

He was kinder than I deserved. He didn't ask me twice.

"Then this is good-bye. I will always remember you, Butterflies-are-free."

For the last time Paladin put his arms around me.

And he kissed me good-bye.

*   *   *   *   *

The Court of the TwiceBorn 9: Thrones, Dominions

War is a necessary state of man. It is, simply, organized strife—a temper tantrum dressed up and made admirable, as much a part of the human condition as speech.

It is unfortunate that, like speech, it is mismanaged so very badly. Instead of learning to love war and make it a part of our language, we have made it our silence. There is no war, and the scholars nod to each other and murmur that we have become so very efficient at war that we dare not wage another.

It is hardly a mark of efficiency to make something impossible. And it is especially stupid when something as inevitable as radioactive decay—human strife—is made so costly that "must" and "dare not" try conclusions on the musty field of philosophy until both are weary.

Because someone always dares, in the end.

I have defeated Archangel, and now I shall defeat his war. It will suffer a sea change, into a sufferable war, a war with tears and gallantry —and rules and limits. It is our natural state; at last we will take back the wrong turning we followed in some ancient millennium and embrace it as our passion and our play.

The essence of play is that it is a recurring phenomenon. There will be no more Last Wars, and Wars Too Terrible To Fight. No more final weapons, no escalations of nullity in the hope of bringing some *frisson* of consciousness to a jaded perception. War will be tamed to the reach of mortal grasp; exercised until its tongue becomes eloquent.

The mother cradling her murdered infant to her breast will curse with bitter broken heart as her kind has always done—but she will live to do it. The young will die and the rich will live—but it has always been so. But the stars will go on in their courses, and perhaps someday (a sop to the anguished cowards and young philosophers) the eristological passion for war will be extinct.

But one does not legislate passion out of existence. Fevers must run their course.

12

The Saint Sees It Through

I opened my eyes on a ceiling with the very best ornamentation. I'd been here before. The Prince-Elect's bedroom on Bennu Superfex, six glorious light-minutes from downtown Throne.

I was alive.

I shouldn't be alive. I should be a ghost in the machine, dissolving the moment I forgot who I was. Or if I did get back to my original packaging, it should be back on Throne in the less-than-tender grasp of Palace Security.

And besides, Archive had thoroughly corrupted it.

I sat up. Nutrient gel slithered off me like technoaspic. I peeled more of it off. Nothing but skin underneath, and no technology at all. Soft muscles hurt. I knew why. I'd have to have been stupid beyond permission not to know.

Take the Keys to Paradise and slide your mind into the computer. And when you're finished playing, slide it out again. And if the original package is gone, take what you can get.

Paladin had copied me into a clone. But *what* had he copied? The original problem was no less real: many key ego-signatures of Butterflies-are-free Peace Sincere had been irrevocably corrupted by Library Archive.

I flexed my brain. No Archive. All of Archive's repatterning was part and partial of a radiation-damaged corpse that was probably lawn food by now.

And what I was, was—

Safe. Because integration had taken place. The construct was stable. All the contaminated ego-signatures had been discarded.

And replaced.

With available parts.

I stood up quick, trying to get my mind off my mind. Body, female. Young. There hadn't been time to grow a clone of me. Dark skin, unless it was dye or gel. I stood up. Not much taller nor shorter than I was.

"Paladin?" I said. The voice wasn't familiar. My throat ached.

No one answered.

If I'd known his plans I didn't now—one of the things he'd kept back, maybe, when he recopied me onto virgin media. I got up out of the full-size, full service biopak and peeled off the rest of the packing material.

"Highness." Tronic voices. Inanimate. Servants to the Court of the TwiceBorn, inevitable as air. A wall opened in front of me. The clothes inside was proof enough that someone'd been expecting me or somebody the same shape. I put some on.

There was a mirror.

I was looking at Berathia Notevan. A younger version, with her head shaved and no makeup.

Of course. She'd been wild to get me back here. Prinny'd probably even told her she got to be the next Prince-Elect if she did. And what he meant all along was to wear Paladin like a suit of armor—destroy his mind but keep his capabilities—and run this Berathia-clone as a remote.

I couldn't even hate him for it.

Because strictly speaking, he wasn't someone else.

He was me.

Because there'd been a second set of ego-signatures in the matrix to copy and adapt.

And Paladin had used them.

* * *

Time passed. I put on jewels appropriate to my station. Part of me jeered and wanted to fence them. Part of me knew what to wear.

The human mind is a flexible thing. Soon enough the jagged edges and gaps between memories would be smoothed over. I'd remember they'd been piecework once but not what it felt like.

The assassins of the Prince-Elect—who were in Archangel's employ, surprise—were neutralized. One dead—me—one shunted off for questioning by the appropriate authorities. Me.

Although Prinny had perished—heroically, said the hollycasts—the lines of Succession remained secure in the person of the Princess-Elect. Me, again.

And about an hour-fifty after I'd found out I was going to have to live after all, Valijon Starbringer's drone lifepod docked with Bennu Superfex, and people and tronics answering to orders of the new Princess-Elect ran to get him out and make him whole again.

*   *   *

Valijon Starbringer of House Starborn—who was going to have to get another last name if he went on getting older—was under serious med-tech for ten days—almost long enough for the Empire to clean up the damage done to Throne by the recent depredations and for Fleet to take up a serious career of losing battles. None of the enemy forces were taken alive. Some ships were destroyed—not many—and despite the fact that I doubt *Woebegone* was one of them I hadn't seen or heard of Berathia since. I was thinking of "asking the Emperor" to issue a general pardon. 'Thia always did have a suspicious nature.

According to what I'd been able to illegally access from the Ministry of War which didn't want me to know a damned thing, the first wave of the Coalition Fleet'd be here real soon, looking for Libraries under every pillow. I had every intention of sealing Bennu Superfex up tight until they got past the first rare flush of victory and were prepared to give serious thought to a stable future. After all, a girl couldn't be too careful.

Finally the doctors let me see Valijon.

*   *   *

He'd been conscious long enough to get past the who-am-I/where-am-I and not long enough to figure out many of the answers. I walked into his line of sight. His eyes widened.

"Reet fly-vines, ne?" I said.

The techs told me he had full mobility—working order one hundred percent. I came in reach anyway.

"I brought you a present," I added.

They say you can get anything at Grand Central, and they're right. Everything about my present was authentic; the slightly-magnetized carbon steel, the rune-carved blue bone handle, the black stone in the pommel. Even the samples of blood and nails and hair inside the hilt.

It was, in short, a perfect . . .

Copy.

His eyes got even wider. Upset, but the doctors said he was ready for it. They'd better be right.

He licked his lips a couple of times. *"Shaulla-chaudatu* Berathia?"

"No."

He lunged back against the headboard then. I slid back out of reach, still holding onto the fake *arthame*. No sense being a fanatic about things.

"The truth: You were shot. You survived. Officially, you've disappeared. The raiders are gone. The DataNet is down. Paladin's gone. The Coalition's going to be here inside of thirty days, max. And the Prince-Elect is dead."

"And you—?"

"Say I'm his heir. Everyone else does. It's simpler." But the body language wasn't the Berathia's he knew and neither was the voice.

"You are abomination. Where is the *Kore* San'Cyr?"

"If that's the way you want to be about it, 'bai, she's dead too."

"Dead." The grief in his voice was flattering. "Then why do I yet live?"

I ran a hand through my hair, dislodging a fistful of the latest fashion. Doubled parallel memories quarreled for a minute, then lay down and shut up.

That would pass, so I understood.

If it was something going to make a difference in your plans, Baijon, after you was dead weren't any time to tell you.

Old memories.

"You're alive because I thought maybe you'd like to know we won. And maybe you'd like to make your own choices. Take back your Knife. Only four people know you ever lost it. Three of them are dead and the fourth won't talk. There's a ship that goes with it—not *Ghost Dance*, but she's just as fast and the coordinates are already in the navicomp. She'll take you straight to the Coalition Fleet. Go join the Coalition. Annoy them. Make sure the sensible faction doesn't get the upper hand. Have some kids. Finish out your life, dammit."

"I have no life. The *Kore* would know that."

"The *Kore* was a jerk. If you don't have a life, then how about a war? Here I am, 'bai—come and get it. What makes you think I'm telling you the truth—that Paladin's gone, that the dataweb is down?"

"Stop it," Valijon said, weakly.

"The way I see it, you got two choices. Play with the big kids, or curl up and die. Everybody else has to get by without a spirit-blade barometer to give them moral certainty, why should you be any different? Look at it this way: you just lost Round One against the Evil Empire, but I'm stupid enough to let you have another chance."

Valijon turned his back and hid his face in the pillow.

"Go *away, chaudatu-malmakosim!*"

It hurt. I filed the datum away for later.

"I'll—I be waiting in the bibliotek, you make up your mind, 'bai."

* * *

Am I the person I was meant to be—the person I would have been if I'd developed under ideal conditions with infinitely-available amounts of everything?

Or am I not anybody in particular—just a bunch of lives dumped into a mixing bowl together and all the memories—mine, Archive's, Prinny's—being equal? In that case, there is no Butterflies-are-free Peace Sincere left, and me using the name is just habit.

It'd be nice to be sure.

But I guess it don't matter. I am who I will be in the next minute, and that person has a lot of things to get done, whoever she is.

Weeping over your dead's a waste of time, even if they're you.

* * *

I waited long enough to be sure I'd gambled wrong. Pushed too hard. Killed him instead of getting what I wanted.

The Coalition would take Throne. They were led by the alMayne conservatives—the first thing they'd do would be to outlaw higher technology.

But it was too useful. So they'd allow it again, piece by piece. Until a splinter group of ultra-conservatives decided to slap them down.

The splinter'd need a leader.

I meant it to be Valijon.

This was why I couldn't leave. Everything had to fall apart the right way—into small, manageable pieces that wouldn't take the whole universe with them each time one exploded.

Princes-Elect don't have much real power. I needed allies.

Or enemies I could trust.

An hour passed and Valijon's telemetry didn't flatline. Another hour passed before he came to me.

* * *

"You have said it; how can I, in honor, refuse? In the name of my *comites,* the *Kore-alarthme* Butterflies-are-free, there will be war and I will wage it," Valijon said.

I tossed him the Knife.

"You'll need this."

He caught it. "Am I to build my life on lies, *chaudatu?*"

"Or higher truths. Take your pick. Change is the name of the game. What goes around comes around. Adapt or die."

He bared his teeth at me and smiled. A hellflower smile.

"I will adapt. You will die."

"Enjoy yourself, babby-bai. And remember I let you go."

He turned and walked out. The *arthame* glittered on his hip.

I followed him on through the security system all the way to the lock, and on scanners until his ship hit angeltown. He never looked back.

Valijon was a survivor.

And so was I.

We—humankind—had always wanted to survive. As much as Libraries had wanted to perfect.

That was the cause of the Library War that Paladin had always searched for. The Libraries were perfect. They tried to remake Man in their image. Valijon'd been right all along. Maybe, if you dug deep enough, hellflowers didn't even hate Libraries. But they knew. Libraries and organics couldn't share.

But maybe, just maybe, in a thousand years there would be room for a Library that knew what it was to be human.